Witch in Blood

Part One: Past Imperfect

by
Lynda Panther

Published by New Generation Publishing in 2013

Copyright © Lynda Panther 2013

First Edition

The author asserts the moral right under the Copyright, Designs and Patents Act 1988 to be identified as the author of this work.

All Rights reserved. No part of this publication may be reproduced, stored in a retrieval system or transmitted, in any form or by any means without the prior consent of the author, nor be otherwise circulated in any form of binding or cover other than that which it is published and without a similar condition being imposed on the subsequent purchaser.

www.newgeneration-publishing.com

 New Generation **Publishing**

For Max.

For Dick, who believed in the dream

Best Witches

Lynda

On the surface, Ffion Harris is just like any other woman struggling to make her way in the world. Blue Moon SkinCare is preparing to make the change between a hole-in-corner business to a major player thanks to her boyfriend, Greg. It ought to sell like hot cakes because it works like... well, magic.

Ffion has other problems. Beside her family - father dead, mother in a wheelchair, two sisters to manage - there's the tiny problem of the neighbours. They're dead. Which is no real problem, if you have magic....... But when her cousin has an almost fatal accident which is not an isolated incident, and just to put the icing on the cake, one of her sisters turns up dead, she finds herself travelling a path littered with vampires, a feud from out of her own history which forces her to take the most extreme course - befriending a master vampire who has designs on her which don't include marriage, a career and children, let alone the peculiar magic in her bloodline.

How can she resolve the dilemmas facing her, and defeat the mysterious stranger from out of the past who will stop at nothing to steal her magic and see her dead...really dead....

So. It has finally come to this. The witch-child has grown sharp claws. How perverse the pleasure to watch her, the wolf in my fold. To enter my hidel, anger riding in the weave of her garments. How delicious to witness the confusion her appearance endengers amongst the lesser lights. So eager to crow in private, so meek when confronted with the opportunity. Cravens all, every last one. They scatter like rabbits, scurrying for the safety of their burrow. Oh, there are no outward signs in their demeanour. It is just that I know them so very, very well. Little safety there, for them. Now. And the reality of this bitter betrayal…... I feel the dark wings of misfortune behind my back, and will not linger here. I have lingered overlong, perhaps. Time, as they say, to downsize, redact and retreat. A wise warrior knows the moves of the game, and I am an expert. I am aware of all the nuances. They will deem me mad, of course. They are slow to catch on. We are all insane. Driven. I will not await the whim of fate in this instance. Discretion, that soft voice, decries valour.

    This will be most amusing.

Chapter One

Coming back was like rebirth. The sight of the old grey cottage, the sagging appletree which gave the place its name: the ragged exuberant philadelphus (Note to self: requires severe pruning) arcing over and sheltering a sunny bench, the roses so completely intertwined with the wooden fence that the one supported the other - inextricably linked now, generations after great-grandma had planted them, all these things meant only one thing. Home. Awash with memories, the sights and sounds of Family, a solid bedrock of inner life that supported and nourished those first tentative forays into the great beyond. It was nearly painful as remembered childbirth is painful. It changes and it doesn't.

Ffion was out of the taxi almost before it stopped. No matter how often she came back, how long or short the absence had been, Pippin Cottage was still home to her. Here she could be herself. Really herself, not some pale imitation, and the thought brought a smile to her face. She was looking forward to spending some time with her sisters. Quality time, as they said now. She felt something coiled tight in her gut unwind, relax, and send out tentative feelers, tasting the air, ready to scoot back into the safe darkness at the first sniff of…. What? Danger? Here? Perish the thought. Okay, so it wasn't a pretty-pretty black-and-white, nor one of the chocolate-box thatched Devon cottages. It was starkly functional in a kind of grey granite way, with its stone-tiled roof; quite ordinary, in fact. But she had been born here, grown up here, and the memories that it brought back were far from ordinary. Snag made a graceful leap out of the door as she opened it: he shared her enthusiasm for the ancient cottage, and was not held back by evils such as paying off taxi drivers, especially after being mauled by the vet. He sailed over the gate, a streak of furry black lightning, his leash trailing unheeded behind him. He was *home* and was impatiently pawing at the door and yowling that curiously guttural yowl that some Siamese cats have. Not that he was completely Siamese, of course. He was a mongrel. His mother, whose owner had been patiently awaiting the arrival of a stud tom, relaxed her vigilance over her little trollop. She had escaped and made an assignation with a local bruiser known casually as Bigfoot on account of his having six toes on his paws. When the little bastards arrived, it was evident that Snag had inherited his sire's genetic mutation. His paws were the size of plates. Philosophically, the thwarted owner had sold the litter at a discount and written the loss off to experience and fitted a remotely locked cat door to an enclosed outside run.

'You wanna watch that cat, Miss.'

Snag had spent the entire trip prowling the back parcel shelf, muttering. He did not approve of cat baskets, no matter how nice the purchaser thought they were. He had made that very clear, and the scars from his claws still adorned the flesh of the unwisely confident Lily who had tried to insert him into one. It made travelling with him slightly difficult. As a tiny furball, he had been trained to a leash and collar, and allowed that small infringement on his feline dignity since it permitted him, once installed in a car, to watch the scenery flow by and the faster the better. It had got on the driver's nerves, Ffion could tell that. He had also left a calling card: damp paw prints decorated the parcel shelf. His paws always sweated when he was anxious. Snag didn't care what, or who, he clawed to maintain his dignity. The favoured position was in the front seat, paws on the dash, whiskers forward at attention, commenting caustically at his chauffeur's failings. Cornering became interesting. No taxi driver would want that: he had been relegated to the back, much to his disgust, and he had let everyone know.

'Sorry about that.' Ffion paid the man, who roared off with an emphatic spray of gravel. She hoisted her overnight bag onto her shoulder. Her car had to have chosen right this moment to let her down, just when she needed the bloody thing to pick the cat up from the local vet's. Having come to terms with the death of her little Fiesta, worn out running her back and forth to the Smoke, reliable as sunset and sunrise and about as temperamental as weather, the New Car was having an identity crisis. It thought it was a bollard. Again. At this rate, it was going to find itself vehicular non grata and dumped on another unsuspecting owner.

Or, worse, handed over to Uncle Tom, who had a short way with things that didn't impress. It was adapted and Snag-ready, an amenity not generally available in vehicles. Taxi's, ugh. Snag *and* taxis, double-ugh. At the gate, her fingers wandered fondly over the carved gatepost. It looked like a Celtic cross at first glance, but the incised carvings were certainly atypical of the genre. Just as well that the weather, and lichens, has taken their toll. Sharp-eyed visitors might have complained otherwise.

She walked up the path, smiling at the nodding flowers. Time for the gardener to harden her heart. End of August and the summer bedding would soon have to be evicted. Unaware of the grim fate awaiting all annuals, the innocent little buggers were flowering their little hearts out in a magnificent, untidy jumble. Their last flowering glory was spectacular. The green paint on the door panels was peeling a bit. Oh well, another job for a fine day, to repaint the door. There was always something waiting to be done. It's the nature of things to need doing, and for people to avoid doing them. Fact of life. Ffion lifted the old-fashioned black latch and slung her bag onto the hall stand. The cat disappeared into the depths of the house, looking for whatever meal cats had at that time. Snag ate one meal a day, an all day long, a breakfast-lunch-dinner-supper gourmet gorge interrupted only by bouts of sleep and indolence on the windowsills.

'Zoe? Zoe, are you home?' she called out. Turning, she reached for the base of a bronze statue set into a wall niche by the door. She remembered the day that Uncle Tom had brought Our Shelia and her mate to the cottage, and her father had fixed them on the walls by the door. She was faintly ugly, was Our Shelia, with her lascivious grin, huge breasts and belly, her legs wide apart and her hands holding open her thighs, displaying her bits to the world. Mother had explained that they were images of the Genius Loci, the gods of the place. 'If we treat them right, they'll treat us right,' she had said, fluttering in from the kitchen drying her hands on a teatowel. Thus, Our Shelia became an institution, greeted every time a family member came home, or went out. Okay, so it was just a 'Bye, Our Shelia', or a 'Hello, Our Shelia, I'm Back!' but it seemed to be enough. She was routinely offered 'first fruits' - the first tomato from the greenhouse, the first apple off the tree, the first strawberry from the patch: the first cake from a new baking, a drop of wine from the first bottle of the latest brew. Oh, and flowers. Our Shelia always had a floral offering, from the hedgerow, definitely not the garden, even if it was berries and twigs in winter. Shiny conkers, heather, sticky buds, mayblossom, cranesbill, oxeye daises, thistles, teasels, they all appeared in their seasons to grace the niche she squatted in. Today it was grasses, their flowering heads nodding, and a faint echo of frankincense. Zoe was back, then. She was a weekly boarder at a nearby college. Well, nearby was a slight exaggeration. Carting Zoe to school was an ongoing chore shared between Ffion, Sophie, and anyone else they could rope in. Our Shelia had brought her name with her, but the Imp, all grin and knees, had not.

'He looks just like the Grinneg,' Sophie had said.

'What's a grinneg?' asked Zoe, then only about five. Sophie took Zoe away to see a DVD of the children's programme, so she knew what a grinneg was. 'No, he's not,' Zoe had declaimed after watching the programme closely. 'He's nothing like.'

Later that night, three girls had sat up with Mum, watching a rerun of Life On Mars.

'That's him, there,' Zoe had said. 'He's not a grinneg, he's a Gene Genie.' And the name had stuck.

Whereas Gene Hunt had a moral code, and stuck to it, obscure though it might be, the Grinneg had not. Or not one you would easily recognize. Zoe especially regarded him as her own personal Saint Jude.

'I've lost my dolly, Gene. Where have you put it?' and on to 'Ziggy's run away. Bring him back, Gene.' (Ziggy was Zoe's parakeet, a vicious bird with a taste for human fingers, and finally, the proud possessor of a finely tuned swearing muscle. 'I don't know where he learned that. I don't even know what those words mean. I don't use language like that.') then 'You've taken my lippy again, Gene. Put it back.'

Certainly Gene had a way with the lost and foundered. His specialist subject was car keys, which were supposed to live on hooks by the front door beneath his perch. Maybe he took a proprietary interest, them being so close. Family opinion differed as to the reason keys went missing. Was it family carelessness or Gene's mischief? It was about fifty-fifty, wavering upon the desperation of the search and the emotional state of the searchers. Anyway, an appeal to Gene meant that sooner rather than later the bloody things would turn up. Their father never appealed to Gene. Instead he would accuse everyone else of misplacing his keys, until, one day, their mother, reaching the end of her tether, had yelled, 'For pity's sake, Gene, put the bloody keys BACK!' Gene disliked swearing, but he was too wise to cross the Housemother in such a mood. With a regretful tinkle, the keys fell gently into the bowl kept by the phone - ostensibly for children and adults to pay for phone calls, but in fact held everything under the sun, from odd coins to freebies from McDonalds, single earrings and old sweeties. Father had not complained again. The Gene Genie left his keys alone. Just his. Everyone else's was fair game.

Another thing that Gene did not tolerate was casual profanity. Habitual swearers visiting the house were quite likely to wake up to a wet bed and smelling of rank flower water. Gene also had a watchful eye on the wellbeing and happiness of young Zoe. One friend of the family, who was old enough and wise enough to know better, and whose less damaging habit - though no less insane to the casual observer - was to suddenly yell 'ODIN!' at the loudest register he could produce. Fee and Sophie, being older, were inured to this habit: Zoe was not. One day - perhaps he hadn't seen Zoe, closeted in her favourite bower under the roses, or perhaps he didn't care, or worst of all, had done it on purpose: but he flung back his head in the middle of the summer garden, long red hair and beard awry and aflame in the sun, bare chest swelled with air, and let rip. 'ODIN!' echoed throughout the surrounding hills, startling Zoe out of her reverie and bower. In her panic, the roses had wrecked such havoc as roses will, and by the time she found her mother in the hall, her arms and legs were running with blood, mixing with the tears. Both mother and Gene were privy to the secret that she had been so startled she had wet herself, and was crying more out of shame and frustration than pain. After fresh knickers, a dab of Germolene for the scratches, a cool cloth for the tears and some homemade lemonade for the shock, she was right as rain. But Gene's sense of right and wrong was not satisfied. Mother's lambasting of the culprit, was, in his opinion, not enough.

Next morning, Uncle Brian could not find his trousers. He was reduced to wandering around wrapped in a towel, plaintively asking if anyone had seen his 'strides'. 'Come on, you lot, it's not funny. I'm bollock naked here.' He had a habit of going commando. It was a shame to see a strong man reduced to tears. Almost, but not quite.

Several hours later, Mother found the absent article, neatly folded under his mattress. 'Clever of you to put them there to press overnight. You must have forgotten. You were pretty wasted last night.' Everyone kept a straight face, even if Zoe had to stuff a fist in her mouth. Gene got fulsome whispered thanks and an entire currant bun for that one.

It became a family habit, in crisis and at the end of the tether, to mutter 'Trust the Gene Genie.' anyone in earshot would respond with Sam Tyler's riposte, 'Not if I can help it!' Once the chuckles had died down, Gene would come through, the crisis would be averted and family life continue as it had done in Pippin Cottage. The storms, when they came, might be fierce, but they rarely seemed to last long.

Ffion's reverie was broken by a clatter on the stairs, and she braced herself for Zoe's traditional greeting. Launching herself from the third stair, Zoe flung herself into Fee's arms. She was getting big for this display, and Fee staggered from the happy onslaught.

'Welcome home! I'll get the tea on. Or do you want a bath first?' Fee smiled. Zoe had her great grandmother's hair, so deep brown it was almost black, falling in slow waves round her face, which was rapidly losing the childish chubbiness in favour of what would be, eventually, Zoe's adult face. The eyes, however, were their father's: pale, pale blue. Strange to see those eyes in that face. Fee herself was brown-on-brown. Sophie, the bitch, had inherited the swimming violet eyes of Grandma, but had teamed them with a reddish blonde mop. Where in the genetic pool she had fished those locks out, no-one was sure. Mother Lily said it came from the Howe line. Since she didn't play away, it had to be true. Speculation had been cast on Uncle Brian as the originator of Sophie's hair. No-one in the family believed it. Lily and Robert had been fool in love, totally besotted with each other. The incandescence of the rows proved it. No-one could be that passionate about trivia and not care.

'I want to come to the ritual. Pretty please?' Zoe assumed her most appealing look. It was pretty devastating, and it usually worked.

'No, Mouse. You know the rules.'

'But it's filling up. Soon there'll be no place for me. I've been courting longer than everyone. I've been courting longer than *plankton.*'

'John's wytchen. He's not taking your place, Zoe.'

That John had the wyth there was no doubt. The first time Abby brought him to meet Fee - simply as a relative - her own wyth had jumped in recognition of his. She and Abby had shared one of *those* looks, and his fate was sealed. Unlike Abby and Fee, and indeed Zoe, John had not been born into a Fratten family, to live with the reality of wyth from day one. Oh, the wyth. Having the wyth, and from it the Gya, was like sharing your life with a schizophrenic rottweiler. On the one hand, it would protect you, cuddle up to you and keep you warm at night: but you never knew when the slobbery face-licking would turn into a terrifying maelstrom of teeth and claws. One day it was granting your wishes and smoothing your path through life, then suddenly, and without any warning it would suddenly spring on you, fight you, rip-your-face-off fight you.

It never did to take the Gya for granted. It is no servant. It is not biddable, nor tameable as a lapdog is tameable. It will always be wild and ungoverned. When it spoke to you, you could not know, listening to it, whether it was leading you into gentle pastures or tossing you off a cliff. It was not evil. It was not good. It just was. Is Mother Nature a kind, nurturing sort? No way. She raises baby birds to feed to cats. Some of her beasts are killers and others are prey. And if you are the best, the swiftest, the most cunning, then you will live. If you fail the examination of your survival skills, you die; it's as simple as that. John had a laughingly normal upbringing, with cys - magic - definitely consigned to the realms of fantasy and children's fairy tales. It would take a huge push to make this logical, rational man accept his abilities and use them. So, the Frais was going to grandstand for him. Bringing a wytchen to the Frais was very different from enfolding a Fratten. Fratten knew how to accept wyth in themselves and others. They knew that the physical laws that governed the world were not the only ones. Okay, so few of them could really defy gravity. But convincing it to lose an intense personal interest in you for a little while, that was possible. Though to venture into a place where, if gravity suddenly decided to turn it's full attention on your shenanigans might mean a fall of several feet was tacitly discouraged, by and large. After all, it wasn't the fall that hurt. It was the landing that was the real bugger.

Finding a life partner, for the Fratten, was a more complex business than for most people. Sexual compatibility: check. Convergent and divergent interests: check. That their personal little habits, like leaving their socks balled up in the wash basket, or leaving the toilet seat permanently up or down, dumping damp towels in the bathroom or using up all the loo paper or toothpaste without replacing same doesn't drive you bug nuts: check. Personal preferences for body hair or lack of it: check. Sense of humour, check. Suitable ambition levels, check. Okay so far, we're on a winner. Then you hit the wall. Do they have the wyth in their blood? And that was the poser. Although it's not exactly illegal do be able to defy what most denizens of the planet regard as the immutable laws, neither is it wise to advertise the fact. As Fee could hardly wear a t-shirt with "I'm Fratten, try me" emblazoned across her tits, it was a delicate business ascertaining if the current light o' love was hiding his talents under a bushel. Especially as it was second nature to all of the Fratten to treat possession of the wyth like a deadly virus, a secret to be kept at all costs. There were legends about famous couples who had danced the attraction fandango around each other for years, each hiding their wyth from the other. It was easier to find the wyth outside of the Families than crack the armour of a Fratten who didn't want you to learn their secret. Wytchens didn't hide the wyth, even if they were aware that they were subtly different from the vast majority. It drew them in certain ways. Some Families kept a presence in the Neopagan world, watching and waiting for the wyth to betray itself to them unwittingly. Some were even active as wiccans, being members of groups and covens, carefully hiding the very real talent of cys amongst the magical milieu. Jean and Alex had discovered Alec and Claire that way, by openly hosting a pseudo-wiccan presence in the so-called occult world, and their young Josie bid fair to become a serious farer when the time came.

Be that as it may, Abby had found John, and John had decided that Abby, for all her myriad faults, was too good a thing to let go pass in the night. So he had proposed. Abby would not need to carry on a clandestine double-life around him, making like the perfect Stepford Wife one moment, then slipping into her alter ego like Clark Kent to reveal another Abby who could and would weave wyth and Gya and change the world, whose eyes saw an alternative universe of energies and ebbs and flows that she could tap into: a tweak here, a twist there, and hey presto! Not that the Fratten were given to outrageous displays, oh no. Their lives just seemed a little smoother, a little more fruitful, more generous. The grass really did grow greener on their side of the fence, oh yes it did. And if they were a squidgin more prolific on the baby front, well, they had the resources to raise those squirming bundles of joy without having recourse to the support of the State.

'Yes, I know. But I'm good at it. You all know that. I'm better than John.'

'Rules are rules….'

'I know. "No blood, no tat, no ritual." Mum said it often enough to you. And I'm almost sixteen.'

'You're a late starter. So was I. Sophie was wyted before me, remember?'

'And you cried all night. I heard you. Then you sulked and wouldn't go to the party afterward.'

'I was gone eighteen before Mum let Uncle Tom tat me the first time.'

'That's three more years. Three! That's *forever!*'

'Mum told me that in her day you had to wait until you were twenty-one.'

Zoe looked at her, horrified. If three years was forever, what were six? Torture. Fee hugged her, and disentangled herself.

'How was it at Claire's?' Best to try to steer away from that subject. It had been a sore point for a long time.

'Way awesome. Why can't we have a swimming pool?'

'You can swim at Claire's anytime. We've got the sauna. Tom's got the hot tub. Don't be greedy.'

'Luke and Matt finished the sweat lodge.'

Zoe swung off into the kitchen. The kid would surely break hearts someday soon. She was growing into a beautiful woman, like her sisters.

Luke and Matt lived nearby in the village. Openly gay, they had been treated first with suspicion, later with guarded respect. By now, they were a fixture, the interest in their sexuality on a par with the that of the church spire. They were oddly matched as a couple. Luke was a geologist, conservationist and all-round outdoorsman, most likely to be found far and wide walking, taking copious and detailed notes about the habits of birds, small rodents, trees and flowers, and photographing grand moody land and seascapes while Matt preferred his creature comfort, reading, and mucking about with his kilns. Luke hated being indoors. Matt meanwhile despised weather, preferring his boring indoor job at the bank, poring over his sums and moving money from here to there. Apparently he had a flair for it. The strange pairing worked. Their home had been extended to accommodate their interests, and the latest project, driven by Luke, was to build a traditional sweat lodge. Matt would have preferred a Finnish sauna, but the two of them had perfected their own particular brand of give and take long ago. Matt had driven the kitchen and bathroom, adding luxury and modern taste. Luke had taken care of the living room and bedroom and garden, making them colourful and exotic. As the sweat lodge was outside, he got to define what did, and didn't, go in his garden. Matt could escape the squashy, cosy living room into his state of the art office-cum-library, or into the garden room where he had a kiln and produced the most wonderful glazed mugs, plates and bowls. He also sidelined in blown glass. If Luke was all earth and water, Matt was all air and fire. The bumps on one fit the crevices of the other so well that by now they were MattandLuke, one entity, indivisible and entire.

Zoe collected cups and plates, ferreting in cupboards and fridge. These were Matt's, no two the same, iridescent glazes set against rough ochre bases, sitting comfortably in the hand, a warm, heavy weight and substance.

'Cecile sent cakes.' Zoe was pouring boiling water into a Matt teapot. Fee kicked off her shoes in the hall, relishing the sun warmed heat of the kitchen floor. Rays of light threw multicoloured rainbows off a row of wine glasses on the window shelf. Cecile was a vampire.

Ffion's great grandmother had taught Cecile to cook, since, as she said, boredom bred mischief, and Cecile had turned out to be a born (or dead) pastrychef. ('It's the cold hands. You need cold hands for good pastry.') She had recently taken up catering as a hobby, and was becoming quite sort-after for weddings, parties and other such pivotal events. None of her clients suspected she was undead. Hell, no-one, seeing Cecile these days, would suspect.

It had been Sophie who had coached Cecile in modern dress sense. The vamp wore Prada now, and Jimmy Choos, and Agent Provocateur. When she walked down the street, heads turned, and not because she was dead. Oh no. She was a killer.

Cecile lived, or more correctly didn't live, with Theo, the vampire hegarsa. 'Vampire' wasn't their term for themselves: they called themselves the Metae. Years ago, Theo had tried to put the bite on Ffion's distaff great grandmother, and that formidable matriarch had soundly boxed his ears and according to Theo, given him blood poisoning. The familial association had continued down the generations. The Fratris had an uneasy relationship with the metae, in general. Bellicose toleration was the best you could expect. Ffion's family was quite unusual, since their link with the metae was a wary friendship. Theo had been called David back in those days, for reasons he wouldn't go into, and to some he was Dave to this day, though rarely to his face. He disliked it, and an irritated vampire is not a comfortable neighbour. Theo's last mete had been a cousin of that matriarch. The brilliant youth, destined for high honour and renown, had dived off a cliff; acceptable as a rite of passage in Acapulco but downright stupid in Devon. Whether this had been the result of a dare, or to impress the current girlfriend, was uncertain. What was certain was the broken back that had left him unable to move, or breathe without an iron lung. He had hit rock, not sea. Grandmother's cys was unavailing: no-one, not even a farer as clever as she, could cure a severed spinal column. Medical science was not so advanced then, the mechanisms of spinal paralysis not so well understood. Fred had been a quadriplegic with a short life span. Now, by whatever agreement had been reached between Theo and Grandma of the violet eyes, he was 'The Vampire Witch Simon Lake', and made his living as an illusionist. Not the children's party kind either. His illusions were dark and dangerous, promising gore and mayhem out of a flickering torchlight darkness. They were not all illusions. He was *very* popular.

The two sisters sat in the comfortable, worn chairs in the parlour, drank tea and caught up with each other's world: who was doing what, and where, the general family business that characterized a large and scattered family, some of them not even blood relations.

'Sophie will be here in about an hour,' Zoe announced.

Ffion lifted an eyebrow at this pronouncement.

'Gene told me. Oh, he's not here now. He buggers off sometimes when we're not all here.'

'So you can tell if Gene is here or not, and when Sophie will arrive, but not me or Snag?'

'Oh, I always know where Gene is. Anyway, you told me not to locksey you after that first time.'

That had been a row to remember. Ffion had met Gregory at a conference in Leeds. She had gone there prior to launching her own personal skincare range and wanted to check out the competition, and it had been inevitable that they would become a couple. Sparks had flown, electricity had been exchanged, apple trees had blossomed and bluebirds tweeted in chorus. Greg was into freelance advertising, and his first interest in Ffion was commercial. They agreed to meet for drinks the next day, and by then his interest had become personal. Very personal. Deeply personal. And right in the middle of a mutual exchange of credentials, Zoe had flipped into Ffion's mind, a recently acquired skill she was intent on honing to perfection. She could not have chosen a worse moment. Not having the expertise to gently disengage and draw back, she got tangled up in Ffion's rising sexual heat and ended up sharing the experience of the first tussles that precede a sexual encounter - an experience which shocked her and disgusted them both. Returning to Pippin Cottage, Ffion had lit into her youngest sister with venom. It was only prevented from becoming a knock-down, drag-out catfight by the timely arrival of their father, who had separated the screaming sisters and restored order.

'She's just learning, Fee. You were worse at her stage. You dumped me in the pond, remember. At least she didn't take over like you did. Clumsy wasn't the word for it. If you had been paying attention, you could have disengaged her, but you weren't thinking with your head, were you?'

They exchanged prickly apologies. 'Don't you EVER overlook me again!' 'I wouldn't want to! Spit swopping, ugh!'

'You can locksey now at least as well as anyone I know. Or you can *call* me, so I know you're there.'

'Anyway, when you're away from here, it would take a direct nuclear strike to get through your shields. You do that on purpose.'

'Not to keep just you out.'

'Oh, *sure*.' Zoe's voice dripped sarcasm.

'You have not got what I could call a light touch.'

'See! I *can* do it. You let me help with the wyth, but you won't wyte me. It's not fair.' She flounced out.

As Sophie said later, your own children are your parent's revenge on you. Mum got hers in early with Zoe…..

Zoe was a late flowering branch on the family tree. Believing that she had hit the menopause at a dead run, Lily thought to exchange her birth control pills for hormone replacement therapy until the hot flushes and night sweats abated. The diagnosis turned out to be slightly premature. Ascribing the changes in her body to The Change, she viewed increasing body mass as a lack of exercise and too much food and morning sickness as 'out of sorts' until it was too late to do anything about the advanced pregnancy but carry it through.... and the result was Zoe, so far out of sync with her sisters she was more like an only child of three mothers than the last sister of three.

Once her business meetings were over, Fee had intended to visit their mother. The car-that-thought-it-was-a-bollard put paid to that, and a visit was long overdue. The accident that, after three weeks' lingering, finally carried off their father had left their mother in a wheelchair. This had caused the entire family to rethink the future. Choosing to live and raise a family in splendid bucolic isolation, both parents actively encouraged their offspring to fly forth and taste the world in all it's myriad forms. Ffion had not been the first to leave the nest. It had been Sophie, following her star first to Bristol and then London. Ffion had joined her there, and once over the first shock had found she enjoyed the vibrant life of the capital. Her parents might have lived as rural recluses, but mentally they inhabited a much wider world. It was nigh-on impossible to walk down a street without encountering someone who knew Lily or Robert in some obscure fashion. Relatives appeared like weeds. Sometimes they were just as welcome.

Anyway, the aftermath of the accident which took Rob from their lives meant that Zoe was, in effect, home alone. Oh, there was Tom and Ellen, even Jean and Margie, real, actual relatives able to take care of her. And friends like Claire, with her daughter Josie, who cheerfully took up the slack: but they weren't any substitute for a real mother or father. Fortunately, neither sister was limited by a nine-to-five job. In any case, Zoe's needs outweighed any other consideration. Weekends and holidays saw one or both sisters back home. Upgrading Zoe from a daygirl to a boarder at her school had gone as well as could be expected. Provided that her time with her computer was not in any way restricted, Zoe was as happy as a pig in shit. The pill was further sweetened by the upgrading of her mobile phone into a state-of-the-art, all-singing, all-dancing sliver of technological wizardry that was quite capable of running the entire cosmos unaided.

Lily had left Pippin Cottage for a place where the flat landscape held few hindrances to a powered wheelchair. Some

friends wondered at that, but others who knew her better understood the sadness and frustration of seeing the hills and windy high places that she loved and would never walk again. A broken leg, hip and comprehensively shattered ankle had seen to that. No, Lily had decamped to stay with some cousins or other in Norfolk. The cottage had been left for the three sisters, even though two of them had by then fled the nest: Ffion splitting her time between the cottage and a small flat in London which she shared with two cabin crew (a fortunate find, and let's be honest, fuelled by the wyth. It took a bit of organizing, and the flight schedules were marked up on a Sasco chart by the door. They just blocked in the days they were away.) Not only was cheap air travel a distinct possibility, Ffion could not see herself having a place that was left vacant so often. Her co-lodgers rarely twinkle-toed into London at the same time, so a two-bedroomed demesne suited them all. In fact, quite a lot of the time the occupant had the flat to him/herself. It was here that she confined her assignations with Greg. Sophie had completed a stint at art school and thence to Cornwall, first staying with friends, then to her own pied-a-terre in Falmouth where she made a more than decent living selling faintly twee pictures of children on the sands, dogs running through the surf and horses galloping in fields and on beaches. She supplemented this with teaching art classes to holidaymakers at a summer camp nearby. 'Emmets in summer, art in winter,' she remarked carelessly. She was better known in certain circles for huge evocative murals. Lonely standing stones in moonlit heather, racing night skies lit by improbable moons and galaxies, wild high surf breaking on rocky shores - but most especially for her wildly, suggestively, but never openly, erotic mythical paintings. One of the best had been based on Theo and Cecile………
   Ffion, though the eldest, had been a late developer. After a few forays into several other unsuitable dead ends - one being a trainee cook in a provincial hotel, a ghastly experience - she had discovered in herself a talent for cosmetics, or rather, those lotions and potions which smoothed the skin and especially brought the bloom of youth into the cheeks of the over fifties. She had been browsing in an ancient book called 'Enquire Within',

and amongst instructions on how to refurbish clothes, cook (Recipe for steak and onions: 'Obtain some steak and onions. Cook them.') she found some 'receipts' for face cream and hair lotion. She tried these out, and on a whim, added something else very special. 'You ought to market this,' one happy recipient of a tiny pot remarked, and Ffion was on her way. Small gifts to friends became sales in local independent shops. Business became so good that it outgrew brewing the stuff up in the kitchen. ('For Ayen's sake, Fee, move that off the stove. I need to boil potatoes.') The home was busy enough with Zoe's computers and books, Sophie's artwork, Mum's bottling and cooking, never mind Dad's gardening. At show time, the house ran over with fruit, vegetables and flowers. 'Lord in heaven, Dad, It's my bedroom, not a greengrocer's shop,' was Sophie's response when an effusion of cabbages overflowed into her private quarters.

The only available extra space was Dad's shed, where he relaxed from his day job as a chemist (one of *those*. He never talked about his work. Something to do with research and the Government. Developing WMDs, with the lazer death ray on the side no doubt) by creating the most stupendous fireworks in between frenzied bouts of gardening and home improvements. Plant fertilizers jostled for place on the shelves with more exotic and brizant compounds. The inside of the door was decorated by a poster (one of Luke's finest, in the family's opinion, but that was biased on account of the subject) showing their huge bear of a father outlined against a brilliant splash of white light, a perfect semicircle arcing out from a yellow sunburst with a dark and crimson heart. It had been a new creation, and he had taken it to the field to test it. He had to stand in the pig's enclosure to watch, and Gudrun the sow had ambled up to join him, trailed by one of her piglets. They were long gone now, along with Lily's chickens and geese. Animal husbandry was not a part-time occupation. Far from being panicked by the display, the pig had simply looked up at him, as if to say 'Did you do that?' The piglet had stared at the light, then snorted and run off, not before Luke had caught the moment: The brilliant light, the man and the two pigs, their shadows streaming back towards the observer. He had called it 'The Illuminated Man'. The fireworks displays their father hosted were costly, so Pigsty Productions was born. The picture appeared on the posters, business cards and everything. The end of October became a busy time for the family.

No, Fee needed her own factory space.

While this was certainly a problem, Fee saw a more immediate drawback. The one special ingredient no-one knew about was a weave, a cys, a sprinkle of wyth. Doing wythen over the stove in the kitchen at home was one thing. Doing it in a factory with near strangers around was another.

Ffion agonized, in those early days, about the way the weave faded. Once the pot was open, it only lasted a month. It was Zoe, looking up from her maths homework, who supplied the answer.

'It's no good to you if they buy it once and it works forever. You want them to keep buying the stuff, don't you? Sell it in small pots, enough for one month. Then the weave won't have time to go off, and they'll keep buying, which is want you want. Easy money.'

Ffion had stared at her younger sister openmouthed.

'You might have made the product, but on the business front, but she's beaten you cold. Pay her a retainer: she's worth it for just that,' her father had remarked, smiling, and so it had proved.

It was Zoe who searched the Internet, found and organized suppliers of raw ingredients, bottles, pots and tubs: organized the making of packaging using Sophie's artwork, and all the other paraphernalia of a small manufacturing business that is so often forgotten in the first heat of enthusiasm. She gave away free samples. She sent finished pots as gifts to various women's and lifestyle magazines. It took off like one of Rob's rockets. The one thing she kept secret was the 'miracle ingredient'. She admitted to the careful extracts of herbs and oils, the use of royal jelly, beeswax and palm oil and cocoa butter. She allowed the addition of extract of ginger, frankincense and myrrh, the attar of roses, geranium oil, aloes, and sandalwood and jasmine. She stressed the use of fresh, natural ingredients. She totally omitted to mention the addition of fresh natural spellcraft.

Lily came up with the factory. One of the local farmers had taken an European Union grant to develop some of his old farm buildings for local small businesses. He had grandly called it

'The Hall Farm Project'. She got Fee in on the ground floor with the old milking parlour.

'It's already got power and water. A bloody good scrub and a coat of whitewash will be enough to start with. And miles cheaper than anything you'll find in London.' That much was true. All Fee had been able to find had been a garage without water or electricity, but with a ruinous rent.

Robert had bent a few ears and called in some favours from his friends and presented her with a redundant pilot plant, it having been due for replacement at the facility where they worked. He had also bespoken some old laboratory equipment and donated that too. 'Do for practicing with,' he said with a smile.

The local jack of all trades was roped in to remake the milking parlour into a cosmetics plant. Friends weighed in, and before too long Fee was the proud proprietor of Blue Moon SkinCare. She had wanted to call it Natural Magic, but had been overruled by Zoe, who had been taking internet courses in business management and advertising.

'You can't imply that it's magic. Advertising Standards wouldn't hold for it. You can't prove it scientifically. You have to have data to back up any claim you make for the stuff.' And, lo and behold, Zoe had that data. Everyone she sent samples to had filled in a questionnaire and sent it back. Testimonials were coming out of Zoe's ears.

She was Fee's first employee, and it at last healed the rift between them. Zoe had chortled over her first pay-packet, a thirty pound slice of the profits, then began to haggle like a Moroccan shopkeeper.

'No, Fee, I don't want a wage. I want a cut of the profits. I want to be a shareholder. What part of ten-percent-of-the-gross don't you understand?'

Zoe was now taking an internet course in accountancy. Great-grandfather Howe had been a shopkeeper and Zoe was channeling his spirit fiercely. She had the blood of merchant princes flowing through her veins and was thirty quid into her first million already.

Spot and acne creams followed the anti-aging potion: body washes and scrubs, soothing bath creams, foot coolers (her mother had suggested that one after a particularly long and arduous ramble,) hand lotion….. If you could smear it on your body, Ffion made it. She had few failures. The most drastic had been her first shampoo, designed to transmute frizzy locks into smooth, sleek, shiny waves. That worked. It also turned the guinea pig's hair a deep shade of green. After the initial shock had worn off, she started to appreciate the colour. No-one else had such lustrous green locks after all. Ffion still made the original, just for that one friend: the experiment never made it to commercial production. Lily had taken the recipe and turned her own hair a deep burgundy red: but Ffion decided that hair colour was too emotive a subject and left it well alone after that. Subsequent formulations confined themselves to smoothing-and-shining.

She became an employer. She had little trouble staffing her factory. At the start, she couldn't afford to pay much more than the basic minimum, but the work was fairly pleasant and the workforce was allowed to take advantage of the products. They went home smooth skinned and smelling sweetly, which was better than the pong which clung to you after mucking out a byre. The young men and women in the area were delighted to find such amenable jobs locally, as did the older. Most of Fee's people worked part-time. Wages clerks and production supervisors appeared, mostly from the older ranks: some worked from home, or shared jobs. One young girl with a need for speed suggested that if Fee put up half the money for a motorcycle to replace her old bicycle, she could deliver further afield. The idea appealed, and two more motorcycle couriers joined the expanding company. Fee's customers might have been taken aback by having face creams and body lotion delivered by hairy Hell's Angels, but they never complained. The couriers were courteous and prompt, and smelled more of geranium and jasmine than rum and Coke.

Back at the milking parlour, Fee prowled between her basic laboratory and tiny office. In the office sat a safe, ostensibly to guard the secret formulas, but in fact holding very little apart from Fee's purse and shoes and the petty cash. It was here, behind a locked door and closed blinds that Fee made those very special, final ingredients for the products.

If her employees did not comment on the instructions to leave the compounds in the mixers overnight, it was their choice. Neither did the night shift who came in after dark to complete the process and load the mix into the hoppers for tomorrow's filling runs. It was easy work, it paid fairly well, and the night shift were used to strange. Nothing they did would excite comment anyway. Some industrial espionage and pilfering went on. It amused the night shift to allow the perpetrators free range, and in some cases, forgetfulness was only a bite away.

'Hello the house! I'm home!'

The door slammed behind a radiant Sophie. Unlike Ffion, who had come direct from work in a business suit and high heels, Sophie was in bohemian mode: paint spattered jeans, sandals and a multicoloured floating blouse, the strawberry locks tied up in a fringed scarf that trailed behind her. She flung her oversized shoulder bag onto the floor.

'Fee and Zoe-ee and So-fee-fee

Are going to have a par-tee-tee!' she carolled.

'You two are. I'm not,' Zoe called down the stairs.

'What's with baby sis?'

'No blood, no tat……..'

'No ritual,' Sophie finished. 'I'll deal with this, shall I? She doesn't hear you as well as she does me. It's not your fault,' she continued, 'Zoe's just that way. She never heard Mum either. You and I heard Mum, but Zoe only ever heard Dad. Now where are the light bulbs?'

Sophie didn't try to coax Zoe out of her eyrie under the eaves. Instead, she breezed up to her den, plonked herself down on the bed and got straight down to it. Ffion could hear her over the hammer of the bathwater.

'Okay, Zoe. Now where does the wyth for a weave come from?'

'Mostly from you. You can get a bit from the things around you, but it's mostly you.' Zoe sounded sullen. Sophie ignored it.

'Why are some Fratten more powerful than others?'

'They understand the mechanics better. They've done more weaves.'

'So weaving is like exercising? Say, if you run a bit further and faster every day, you can get to beat Damon on the track one day?' Damon was a local lad who bid fair to be the county sprint champion.

'I suppose.'

'Now imagine I have to do a really powerful weave, so I need more wyth that I have on my own, how would I do that?'

'Get some other fratten to join in and add their wyth to yours.'

'But they'd have to agree with me that the weave was right, yes? Or we'd not work together, and they wouldn't put their wyth to my weave, and it wouldn't work properly.' Zoe humphfed. 'With me so far? Now I have two choices. Either dominate the wyth of my friends to add that to my weave, or get the wyth from somewhere else.'

'Ooo-kay...'

'Where else would I find that wyth?'

'From everything around you. The living things, like plants and trees and animals and stuff, and the stones and stars and.....' Zoe trailed off, beginning to see where Sophie was going.

'So I would have to be capable to take that sort of wyth. What sort of ability would you think I'd need to do that?'

'I dunno.'

'You are being unhelpful, because I know you're not stupid.'

Zoe capitulated.

'You'd have to understand yourself, and what you were, and themselves, what they were.'

'And if I didn't have that understanding?'

'I don't know.'

'Ah. And there's the rub. As Dad used to say, one demonstration's worth a thousand words. Here's two light bulbs. You are young, so you are the twenty watt bulb. Take it. I am older, I understand more who I am, so I am the hundred watt bulb. Here, gimme your bedside lamp.' The water hammered on, filling the tub.

'Now, having the ritual, being wyted, is like plugging into the National Grid. Because of what it is, it can't help what power it works at: it's up to the person who uses it to use the right bulb, fuses, whatever, to make it work. The Gya is like that: all the wyth, the lines in the land, and the sky, don't know what how much you are capable of handling, like the electricity that flows into your bedside light doesn't know what type of bulb we've plugged into it. When you weave now, you only use your natural wyth, so there's no question that you can handle that. But, when you've been wyted and you start weaving you open the switch to the Gya, and it will flow into you. Put your bulb into the lamp, and switch it on.' There was a distinct pop. 'See, the bulb's blown. It wasn't strong enough to take the power. That would be you, right now, if the Gya was to flow through you. You don't have the cys for it, yet. But you will. Now let's try mine, I'm older, stronger, more aware of who I am.'

'Now the lamp's lit. The bulb is strong enough. Now Mum and Dad, and Fee and me, we've invested too much of our time and love on you to see you blown like that light bulb. Fee and I have been to lots of rituals, we know what it's like to have the Gya flowing through us, what we need to be, and know, to be safe. You think you do, but you have never been to a ritual yet. We know, you don't. We love you too much to risk you too soon. Stop trying to teach us what we know, and you don't.'

Fee turned off the water and listened to the silence.

'Do you understand?'

'Yes. No. Not really. A bit.'

'All right. You know, and I know, that way back when….'

'When dinosaurs walked the earth and the moon we had then wasn't the moon we know now and we all wore skins like savages…'

'Don't be sarcastic, Zoe. I know where you're coming from. Would it surprise you to hear that I had the same argument with Mum years ago? We both know that once, if you were Family, you were wyted as soon as possible…..'

'Why not now?'

'I'm trying to tell you. Once, having the wyth made you an important member of society. You could heal injuries, tell where the game was, where you could get all sorts of food. Having you, and your wyth, made everyone feel better. We were special. We could talk to the gods, to the ancestors….'

'And we're not special now?'

'Well, times change. People change. They need new things to make them feel secure.'

'Ah. Christianity. The Faith Out Of The East.'

'The priests of the new faith came to the rulers of the lands and told them that if they changed their beliefs things would be better….'

'For them.'

'Yes. But it was just another solution based on fear. Fear of what would happen after you die. Okay, you're here for fifty, sixty years and then what? Once you're dead, and dead is forever, you have two, no, three choices. If you've been bad, you get the eternal fire. If you've been good, then you get a sort of misty afterlife until you are deemed worthy of entering into heaven.'

'Hogwash.'

'Yes, but did they know that? They believed in what they were told.'

'We could have told them different.'

'And we did. At first. But we couldn't stand against swords and arrows. The Gya's good, but not that good. We couldn't confront them, so we slipped away. To wait for another time, when people felt freer to listen.'

'That doesn't explain why we have to wait for puberty and not before.'

'I'm getting to that. To be safe, we had to be secret. Adults know when to keep schtum, but kids?'

'My dad's better'n yore dad, nah-nah.'

'Exactly. And not just that. You've done it too. Used wyth to settle a score. But in the past, disease was seen as the devil's work, so there had to be an agent behind it. If the agent was eliminated, so the illness went away too.'

'And did it work?'

'The church and the state said it did. Also, not to worship their deity in the proper way was evil, even if it was the same god.'

'Stupid.'

'We all do stupid sometimes. But this was mostly political. So, it was decided that the Families would only accept adults. And the best way of knowing an adult from a child, especially if you are a bit hazy about how old you were, was the evidence of puberty.'

'Only that?' Zoe sounded sceptical. She knew precisely how old she was.

'Not only that. Puberty's a bit of a crazy time.'

'Crazy, how?'

'All over crazy. All of you, your physical body, your mind, and your spirit, they change.'

'So you say.'

'You like the Jones boy, don't you.' Jonathan Jones was the school stud.

'Not.'

'So, who do you like?'

'Prof's okay. Sometimes.'

'Have you kissed him yet?'

'No! Yuk, how gross!'

'But that's the point. You know this. We've told you. Mum told you. Your….. attitude changes. You find new pastimes. You put your dollies away and move to bigger things. Like…….. Fee kisses Greg. I kiss Caleb. Mum and Dad used to kiss, and the rest of it.' Silence. 'All that sticky yukky stuff grown-ups do is part of what we are, part of our nature to want to kiss, and cuddle and….'

'You don't have to give me a full report. Too much information.'

'Trust me, the sticky yukky stuff gets interesting when you're older. Until you see that side of you, you can't know who you are, not really.'

'Like Matt and Luke?'

'Sort of. Until they met each other, they didn't know who they really were. Being together, they can see themselves more clearly. Your real self can't be appreciated unless another person can see it in you and reflect it back to you. No-one's done that for you yet, so you can't really see yourself clearly. It's part of growing up.'

'And when I bleed for the first time, it means my body's ready to do the sticky yukky stuff. But my mind might not be. So how come we're wyted when we bleed?'

'When you start bleeding, your body starts making all sorts of interesting chemicals. Those chemicals make you interested in sticky-yukky.'

'And get you moody?'

'At the start, yes. Your body is not used to them. You get pimples and all sorts of gross stuff. Your hair goes greasy overnight, and you feel like Medusa on speed. Add the Gya to that, and you've got the recipe for disaster. We could wait until you're twenty-one, like Mum.'

'No way!'

'Your day will come soon enough. Your mind and body will know when they're ready, even if you don't.'

'So it's not you and Fee stopping me being wyted?'

'No, it's you.'

'I see I'll have to give myself a talking to.'

'Then you'll come to the party? Take care the lentae and stuff? Be mysten of the court for us?'

'Okay.'

'Give us a hug. That's my Zoe. Are we all ready for Saturday?'

'Yes. Margie and Jean took all the stuff from the Roundhouse and took it home to clean it. Cecile will bake cakes, Luke mentioned two huge bunches of grapes and some figs. Lottie and Carl are bringing chicken and salad, Abby's doing potato salad *again*, John's bringing himself, Claire's got fish……'

Ffion sank gratefully into hot, scented water. Crisis averted. Trust Sophie.

The next day dawned clear and bright. Sophie, always a dawn bird, was presiding over the breakfast table. Yoghurt, chopped fruit, toasted muffins and marmalade graced the table along with a steaming pot of tea. She was nursing her second cup when Fee's phone shrilled. She grimaced.

'Expecting anyone?'

'Not right now, though Greg mentioned something…' Zoe extended her tongue over her chin. It was her particular mark of disgust.

'Hello… oh, it's you, Greg. No, I don't have number recognition on this phone…..' She stood up and walked into the hall. They could hear her side of the conversation through the door.

'No, I'm at home. I told you I was going back to Devon this week……… What? When?..... No, I couldn't possibly. I've got something on this week. I have commitments too, you know……… No, it's not something I can get out of. I could do Thursday morning, I suppose…' They could hear the reluctance in her voice. 'Can't they meet me next week? Oh. I see. A once only opportunity. If I miss this meeting, then it's Goodnight Vienna. It would have to be hit and run, if I came down Wednesday night and left Thursday lunchtime, but it's a real bother………..Okay. Okay. I can do it, this once. But next time I tell you I'm off home………..I see. All right………… Yes, that would be okay. You can brief me then.'

'See, the tycoon returns. Worlds to conquer, people to see, problems to resolve. Ah, the cut and thrust of commerce.'

'Be glad it's not part of your life.'

'So? What's so important that Greg can whisk you away? Especially with John on the front burner.'

'I can be back for that. No, Greg's been trying to put together a business package for Blue Moon. It will take serious investment to take the project to the next level, and he's arranged a consult with some money men who are interested.'

'Listen to her. 'Take the project to the next level.' You'll be talking accountantspeak anyday now. How interested?'

'Interested enough to contact him rather than the other way round.'

'They have funny money? Cool.'

Fee sat down and reclaimed her tea.

'Not that funny. We're not talking thousands, or tens of thousands. We're looking at *hundreds* of thousands.'

'Why so much?'

'I can't set off an advertisement campaign if I haven't the manufacturing capacity to fulfill my expected orders. The money is for new factory equipment. More lines, bigger batches, more margins.'

'Why you?'

'Our stuff's getting good reviews. People are asking for it.'

'Don't I know it. I get letters every day, asking for lists of stockists.'

'What do you say?'

'I say, What do you want? By the way, we're on the Internet. We take cheques, PayPal and cash at the door.'

'Why not credit cards?'

'I'm working on it. Do you know how much it costs to get that sort of thing? Up until now, it's not been an issue. Now, it is.'

'Always nice to hear that the money's coming in.'

'Not so nice to have to turn away the High Street retailers. We haven't the capacity to stock them, not if we work forty-eight hour days at the factory. Hence the need for investment.' Fee sighed. 'I loved the idea of having my own business. Now, I'm not so sure.'

'Go see the dragons. If some fool can sell them Reggae Reggae sauce, then you can sell them Blue Moon.'

'How?'

'Give them samples. Tell them to go away, try the product, and if in seven days they're not delighted, they can call it quits.'

'I can't see a bunch of male accountants going doolally over skin cream.'

'Their wives and girlfriends will. And before you play the gay card, so will their boyfriends. No-one likes a good emollient like a gay man.'

'Where did you get that gem from?'

'Matt's got friends. So's Luke. You, my sister, are fast becoming a gay icon.'

'Watch out Shirley Bassey.'

Sophie finished her tea and went to the sink to rinse out her mug. She stared out of the windows, where the sunlight was shafting knives through the fluffy white clouds.

'Lovely day, perfect for a walk. I'll take my camera. No classes until Monday, thank the lord. I'll indulge myself. Anyone else?'

'No thanks. I've promised myself some home time. I'll potter in the garden. I ought to look in on the farm too. That idea of Zoe's was a good one.'

'All my ideas are good ones. I've got some projects to do for school that I haven't finished yet. I ought to get those out of the way.'

'You'll get a fat bum sitting at that screen all day. Come on, it's a family tradition.'

'What is?'

'A hike when we get together.'

'First I've heard of it.'

'It's a new tradition, then.'

'If I must. I'll make sandwiches.'

'Oh no you won't. After I ate your last offering, I was picking bits out of my teeth for days.'

'Wholemeal bread is good for you.'

'Not if you break your teeth on it, it isn't. Fee?'

'All right. I have that breakfast meeting with Greg on Thursday now, I'll have to be back in London for that. I'm free until then. I can fit gardening in later.'

From the table came the sound of Zoe gagging.

'One day, my girl, one day……….. Exams soon, then you'll be off to Uni, I suppose.'

'Whatever for? I can get all the stuff I need from right here. Alan Sugar and Richard Branson did okay. And Einstein was no genius at school.'

'Qualifications, lass, qualifications.'

'Get them online. Open University. Business studies and accountancy.'

'You don't want a proper University degree, then?'

'What do I need one for? I'm a gen-u-wine GUK. That's Genned Up Kiddie in case you're wondering.'

'What about your writing? I thought you were going to take literature. Or was it archaeology?'

'Ancient history. Okay, I'll think about it. But NO student loan. I've saved all the dosh I got from Fee, and I can still do Blue Moon over the net.'

'Speaking of the net, how's the website coming on?'

'It's with Theo at the moment. He hates my designs.'

Theo, after Cecile took to baking in a big way, decided he, also, needed a hobby. Following a sixty hour marathon with an exhausted computer geek, he learned how to devise and design websites. Eidetic memory was a useful vampire skill: he never forgot anything. It made being with him embarrassing at times, when you remembered that he had changed your nappy. Some Fratten had frowned at that, but Lily and Rob trusted Theo absolutely around their babies. The reason behind that became clear during one of Theo's later visits. Fee had seen his face when he talked about his one and only crusade. She had never forgotten the look of horror, sadness and anger that settled on his face as he recounted the tale. It had started with a mete who, through laziness or incompetence had taken to feeding off children. That, Theo said, was a violation of principle. If he couldn't manage to feed off adults, he had no business being a vampire. Theo didn't go into detail about what had happened, only that the vampire in question was no longer meta. Then he went onto tell her that one of this creature's victims - a young mother, scarcely out of her cradle herself - had taken a baby and Changed it. When he found out, Theo had visited the two of them, fully intending to separate the vampire's head from her body, only to find an undead mother weeping over her own undead baby. She had not been able to bear parting from her baby son, and thinking that he would, once the blood had been exchanged, grow up normally, made a vampire of him. She had nursed him for twenty years, as a baby, always as a baby. He was quite, quite mad. Theo had wept tears, real tears of blood, over the finally dead corpse, and then outlawed feeding from any child, anytime, anywhere. The sentence was death. Irrevocable. He hunted down the mete who had taken the mother and had 'talked' to him about it. 'Just talked?' Ffion had asked, knowing by now from the bleak look on Theo's face what that actually meant. 'It took twelve years,' he had replied. It had taken the mete twelve years to succumb to whatever Theo had done to him. Twelve years of pain and hunger. No hope, no respite. And finally, extinction, despite the fact that the ending of any vampire existence freaked the entire crew out. No metae in Theo's ken fed from women with children now. If Theo heard about it, he would hunt that metae down and take his own revenge. And she never asked what had happened to the vampire mother. One look at Theo's face spoke volumes of a book she didn't want to read. Dangerous as he was to adults,

Theo was safer than the family dog around children. He would cheerfully slaughter the babysitter, then play with the babies while the bloodless corpse lay sprawled behind the sofa. One hoped he hadn't done exactly that at some time or other. You never knew with Theo.

He had designed Ffion's and Cecile's websites as a dry run, then gone public. Since he could, and did, work a twenty four hour day, seven days a week, he was practically a millionaire. Cecile and Ffion were doing very nicely, thank you. Just as none of Blue Moon's customers suspected that the 'miracle' cosmetics Ffion made and sold contained wythen to reduce wrinkles, and make the wearer look younger and more luscious, none of UnReal Catering's clients suspected that their Cecile was a vampire. It was only a living, after all. The path to their respective doors was trampled (figuratively speaking) by mobs, not with stakes and firebrands, but chequebooks. And the Internet worked twenty four hours a day, seven days a week, and not a stray ray of sunlight anywhere.

Now Zoe was about to join the club. She had decided that the Frais, and the Fratris, needed updating to the twentyfirst century, and sometimes mobile phones were inadequate. It needed a website with industrial security, and Theo was her first port of call. Facebook was not an option. If Zoe was going to upload any of the Fratris' secrets, it would need less of a firewall and more of an inferno. Theo had a skewed take on life. He had a standing bet, published on every website he created, that no hacker could break his firewalls. The admitted reward was ten thousand pounds: it would probably include immortality as well, but it was not wise to publish that fact. Anyway, he might not like the winner of the prize. Then, eternal oblivion might well be on the cards for the lucky, or unlucky, winner. After he spent the dosh, of course. Theo was not that tightfisted.

'I suppose you are keeping an eye on the forums and boards while you are waiting for Theo. Anything we need to know?'

While being 'other' was not exactly illegal, neither was it a thing you admitted to publicly. Zoe's brief was to watch out for those who appeared to truly have the wyth, and keep a weather eye on them. Things could go horribly wrong if you didn't know how to control the wyth properly. There were covens and witches out there, but from the websites and chat, they weren't the same as Fratten. They couldn't shatter glass by glaring at it, nor *lift*, or *reach*, or many of the hundreds of 'abilities' (sometimes called 'persuasions' by the older Fratten) that were normal for this family. They met to celebrate ritual: they made spells which appeared to work some of the time. All Sophie's and Ffion's weavings worked. Every time. And while there were wytchen in the Frais, they were never so talented as pure Family. Their weaves worked all the time because they were sharing with cyscans whose known genealogy reached back so far they had given up naming their ancestors beyond the battle of Agincourt. The only reasons non-blood relatives were admitted was because they were both partners to blood relatives, and had a smattering of wyth that set them apart. Otherwise, why would the family have chosen them as partners?

In this regard, only Ffion did not have a partner for ritual. She had to make do with Tom, or Luke. It was okay, but not perfect. Greg, attractive though he was, sexy as he was, enjoyable as he was, did not show even the slightest hint of wyth in his blood. Ffion had to reluctantly admit that, even though she revelled in his company, one day she would have to leave him. She could not be herself and live with him on a permanent basis. One day she would slip up, and the family skeleton would be out of the closet. No, eventually, Greg would have to go. But for now, with him living separately, things could continue, provided Ffion was careful. He was starting to make pointed comments about meeting Ffion's family, and about Ffion meeting his parents and siblings. Hell's bells, they'd being going out together for yonks, hadn't they? She was avoiding that, adroitly avoiding each request / opportunity as it arose, but the boy was getting more insistent by the day, and it would soon come to a head. Then, she and Greg would have to part company. Ffion felt a strange, lonely pang at the thought. The sex was brilliant. She would miss the sex.

'No, there's nothing unusual. Simon updated his website again, though. He's getting a bit near the knuckle, but everyone believes its all hype anyway. And I'm beginning to get bored with some of the stuff out there. It's all chitchat. What my cat did. I've got a new dress. Have you heard this band. Where are you going for your holidays. Oh, by the way, I'm a witch and here's my Book Of Shadows, read it, *please*. And if they do have something relevant to say, it's deeply trite. It's mostly the youngsters. Teenwitch, gah! All they burble on about is how brilliant it is to be a witch, to initiate yourself and do spells. They don't have the first idea. They complain about their teachers, their parents, their friends, the boyfriends they haven't got and want, and the ones they have and they don't want. So they want spells for everything. They complain when they work, they complain when they don't work. One little madam wove a spell to get the attention of some jock - she's American, so he's a footballer player and not a Scot, by the way, it worked and now she can't get rid of him. He's hot to get it on, and she's too immature to want to, but she can't say no because of the spell. So she wants another spell to get rid of him. Make him crash his car or something, not undo the first spell. Idiot.'

'Let me guess. Everyone's got a tried and tested spell, and they're telling her about them all.'

'Oh yes. Hexes, curses, the lot. Not one of them suggests releasing the poor bugger from the original spell.'

'You haven't been joining in the debate, have you?'

'Do me a favour. It would be a waste of breath. They wouldn't listen to what I had to say.'

'And that being?

'Grow up and stop mucking with stuff you don't understand. Spells are not the answer to everything.'

'Hmm. I know someone else like that.'

Zoe threw a book at Sophie, who dodged it, smiling.

Chapter Two

Wednesday night, Ffion was roused from the dead sleep of the just-after by the noise of her mobile murdering Handel's 'Zadok The Priest'. She groaned and rolled over in the darkness to scrabble at the blue-green light on the bedside table. Behind the blinds, the night was dead black. What the hell time was it? Beside her in the rumpled bed, a mass heaved.

'Ugnnh…. Uhnaah… waazzitt?' The mass heaved over, and an arm slid round her waist. Greg had turned up at her door moments after her arrival bearing the best Chinese Chalfont had to offer. The Blue Dragon did a glorious aromatic duck. His excuse was that he had brought her car back from the garage. Flat battery, un-huh. The bloody thing was only six months old. She would dump the lot on Carl when she went back.

They had fed each other tiny pancakes filled with duck, plum sauce, spring onions and cucumber. They shared a bottle of very nice Australian shiraz. The lemon chicken had been crisp, sweet and sharp, the Kung Po beef had enough chilli to sear your throat. They shared food, sitting on the floor round the coffee table, feeding each other with morsels in chopsticks. They had licked sauces off themselves and each other. Dribbles of sauce on clothes were an excuse to lose the garment. They had kissed, tussled and giggled, ending up in bed with their clothes decorating the light fittings. They had finally fallen asleep covered in each other's sweat. Greg had stolen most of the bedding, as usual. Ffion snagged the phone, ending Zadok's torture. She would have to change the ringtone again. Bach's 'Ode To Joy' had been bad enough, but this was pure hell. She had only chosen this because Zadok and Zoe started with the same letter. Realization made cold mice fingers run over her skin. A fleeting thought: when Zoe had been a baby, she remembered her mother crooning 'Poor little cold mice fingers' at Zoe while she breastfed her….. Zoe's baby blue eyes fixed on her mother's smiling face, one tiny paw on the milky warm breast, the other enfolded in the massive maternal hand, warming them up after a night outside the covers. Ffion shivered, and pulled a corner of the duvet over her naked body.

'Fee? Fee, are you there?' Zoe's voice was thick with tears, shaking with fear. The last dregs of slumber fuelled by good food, good wine and really great sex fell away. Fee was wide awake now, the freezer ants doing a march-past from her scalp down her spine. She felt as if the wispy hair at the nape of her neck was standing upright from the skin, and her belly was filled with a single block of ice.

'I'm here……'

'Oh, Fee, it's Luke…….. He didn't come home yesterday. By nine o'clock Matt was frantic. His mobile was out or something, Matt couldn't get him……. So he called Tom, but Luke wasn't there either. Ellen did a locksey………. Tom called out the police, fire service, ambulance, moors rescue, everything…….' Zoe trailed off into snuffles. Fee started to fumble for clothes, any clothes, in the darkness, the phone still pressed to her ear.

'Chase, Zoe,' she said, using the sisters' private shorthand. Cut to the chase: tell me what's happened……. we can fix it…. Can we? Can we? What's wrong? Where's Luke? What about Sophie? What happened? Behind her in the bed Greg, realizing that something was horribly wrong, hit the light switch. Fee squinted at the sudden brightness and scored her jeans. No time for knickers………

'They found him at the bottom of Bridlip Gorge, in the water. They said he'd fallen, but……….' Luke was part mountain goat: Zoe didn't have to say it. Luke never fell, never stumbled, never twisted his ankle.

'Where is he now?' Where is my bra? Sod it. Jumper. Socks? Boots. Bugger socks. Greg was up now, in jeans that hung unzipped round his waist, hunting for shoes. Oh, he's found his trainers......

'He's in the General. Ellen's with him. Tom's there with Matt.'

'Where are you?'

'I'm at Tom's. Babysitting. I can't get Sophie. She's not here. And she's switched her phone off. I thought she was staying here until after the weekend. Abby's holed up with John somewhere as usual. The old bats have gone to bed, they aren't answering, Claire's twittering that Josie's having kittens so she's no use… I NEED YOU.'

'Where is Soph? She ought to be there.'

'If I knew that, would I be calling you?' A knife edge of anger threaded into the panic. 'Her phone's switched off.'

That was unheard of. If Luke was hurt, what about Sophie?

'Fee….' the little-girl voice. 'I can't even *Reach* her.'

'Hold tight, Mouse, I'm on my way. Right now.' Cold little mice fingers…… the family nickname for the youngest…… Bag… Bag, where are my keys? Gene……

Greg was squatting in front of her as she sat on the bed, half dressed. He offered her a mug of coffee.

'Are you sure you're okay to drive? Do you want me to come with you? And what is going on?'

'I'll be okay. It's my cousin, Luke. He's had a bad fall. I don't know the details. I've got to go back, Greg. Sorry.'

'Don't be. Do you want me to come?'

Fee shook her head, her hair swinging round her face and sticking to her cheeks. She had been crying, and she hadn't noticed. Ought you to notice when you cry? She sipped the warm coffee gratefully. It didn't make any impact on the cold in her belly, in her mind. She still wasn't thinking straight, and she needed to. Right now. She needed to do other things too, but she couldn't with Greg there……….

'Okay.' He opened his fist, and the keys to her Golf GTi dangled from his fingers. 'If you're sure.' It wasn't her Golf, not really. It belonged to Blue Moon. Get a grip. Get a grip RIGHT NOW………. 'Ring me as soon as you know anything. I mean it. I won't be going back to sleep tonight. Today, I mean,' he concluded as he consulted his watch.

Fee stood up, placing her mug carefully on the bedside table. Her eyes looked round the room, as if to store the image. As if she weren't coming back. It had the feeling of ending……… Pale cream walls, ecru drapes and blinds shutting the world out, the world that had come crashing into her sanctuary. Rumpled bed with red and gold covers……. Pine shelves with books and CDs and DVDs…… not important now……. She collected her laptop off the table, hauled the strap over her shoulder with her bag and opened the door. Turning, she kissed Greg's concerned face and held him close, her tears smearing onto his sweatshirt. The thudding of his heart was a comfort, and she took it.

'Stay as long as you like.' She gave him her spare key. 'Lock up when you go. I'll call. Soon.'

'I'll see you again.' She looked at him, uncomprehending. He waggled the key in her face and smiled. He had a lovely smile…… 'Be safe.' He hugged her close, then released her. If only…….

She was halfway out of the door when he called her back.

'Don't you want these?' He'd found her knickers in the depths of the bed. They depended from his index finger like a guilty secret. Ffion had quite a few of those. The grin on his face was sly and suggestive, but warm at the same time.

'You keep them.'

'Actually, I don't think they'd fit.'

Ffion made good time from Chalfont to Exeter. At that time of day (night) the motorways were virtually empty, there were no roadworks to slow her down. She pushed the Golf to its very limit, her mind searching before and behind. It would not do to be caught speeding, and she was. Uberspeed. A techno-witch flying a vorsprung durch technik broomstick in the black night. With no underwear. All it needed was 'Night on Bare Mountain' blaring out of the speakers. In fact it was Ace of Spades and Born to be Wild. So what? She beat the dawn to Tom's rambling home, where the lights were blazing and Zoe was watching the windows. They fell into each other's arms, Zoe crying, holding Fee in a death grip. Ffion held her as she watched her sister's immortality crumble and fade. All kids believe they are immortal. They take risks, never thinking for a moment that they might be hurt or killed, or that anyone around them might be. Zoe was crying her childhood away, and Fee couldn't get a word out of her. All the questions like, how is Luke, where is Sophie, what the hell happened, all had to wait. Zoe didn't know anyway. Once the storm abated, they could talk. Nothing could be done right now: Tom or Ellen would call with any news but it was hard waiting all the same. Worse for them: Luke was their son. Worse, much worse, for Matt. Ellen had Tom and Tom had Ellen. Matt had only Luke. How alone he must feel. He didn't know, as the rest of the family knew, that death wouldn't part them. The Family. Dead members were still *there,* just beyond the veil of sleep, still reachable, still available, still loving. Would the wyth let Matt and Luke be together, sometimes, if the worst happened? It hadn't yet. Was Matt considering the alternative? The Path Of Fred? Ask the vamps to take him as mete - and would they refuse? And what would Luke think of that? Impossible questions, with no right answers.

Ffion had listened to Zoe's caustic comments on her lack of underwear (very obvious in the boob department,) and the possible cause of it. She had continued at length, until Fee had gone home to Pippin Cottage and made herself decent. At least it took Zoe's mind off the tragedy. A little light criticism of the elder sister was just what Zoe needed, but she did carry it a little too far. Fee let most of it go, until she realized, in the midst of her own preoccupation, that Zoe was genuinely trying to pick a fight. It was a splendid little affair. I didn't know 'breakfast' was an evening meal. I suppose you left off the smalls so you could get back to basics quicker. You're just a trollop, a nasty, low trollop. Having sex while Luke was out there in the dark and cold dying……. maybe *Sophie* as well….. You don't think about other people, not at all…… Why don't you just go back to Greg and leave us alone? Ffion held Zoe while she cried again, washing all the fear and anger and helplessness away, wishing, wishing, that Lily could be here and take away all her hurt and confusion too…… That Robert was still here, their rock, their comforter, the bedrock of reason that had underpinned the whole of their lives. Fee cried as well, until it was Zoe who comforted her in the end. And still no word from Sophie.

With the dawn came industry. The last of Tom and Ellen's brood had to be aroused, fed, watered, dressed and prepped for the holiday club. Questions about where's Mum and Dad, how is Luke, what happened, had to be fended off. It was exhausting. Holiday club was a sort of creche-cum-summer camp the community had cobbled together for working mums and dads. Of necessity, it started early: stupid-o'clock-of-the-morning early, since farmers tended to kick the cockerel awake themselves. The schoolhouse was used for all sorts when school was out. There was no village hall; the place simply wasn't big enough to merit one. It barely merited the school. There had been a lot of fuss two years ago when the DOE tried to shut the place down, but the local pressure group had prevailed. For now at least, the village still had a school. Zoe washed her face and walked with them, so she could tell Mrs Hathaway and Miss Wilkins (Please call me Dora) that Tom and Ellen were at the hospital with Luke, and that Lottie would collect Suzie and Adam after. Necessary in these sad times, even in such a close rural community where everyone knew everyone else, because maybe you didn't know them at all. Fee had to contact Zoe's team leader at Blue Moon - she worked occasional shifts there when they were shorthanded - and explain that Zoe wouldn't be in today. Yes, a horrible accident, Zoe was very upset, no, she didn't know anything beyond that. No need to fuel the gossip any further, it was hot enough as it was. Yes, yes, she would keep them informed. Rotten business. Thank you for your good wishes. Goodbye.

One good thing about an early hospital call was that parking was easy, right by A&E, next to Tom's battered Landrover. Tom met them at the door of the Accident and Emergency unit. He was untidy, uncombed, like an unmade bed. Situation fairly normal there, then. Luke had been brought in unconscious, suffering from concussion, a dislocated shoulder, a broken hip, leg, ankle and ribs and ruptured spleen. And lots of bruises and scratches and cuts, which didn't matter in the light of the rest of his injuries. Ellen was with him in theatre. The surgeons were very good, the broken bones could be set, the spleen had gone already, but it was the damage to his head that was worrying them all.

'It's bad, Fee, very bad. His skull's cracked. They're doing their best, but.......' Head injuries were the worst. What damage had been inflicted on the delicate, complex brain tissue with such massive trauma? Only time would tell.

Matt was sitting in a hard hospital chair, pale, red eyed from lack of sleep and worry. His hands dangled between his knees, his head bent over - the very picture of abject misery. A plastic cup of cold vending machine coffee stood on the table, untouched. Tom rested a hand on his shoulder, squeezing gently. Matt did not react to the comforting gesture.

When he had learned of his son's sexual preferences, Tom had taken it very well. There was no bluster, no declamations of 'No son of mine is a pansy!' Luke was what Luke was. Luke. Irreplaceable. The first time Luke had brought Matt home, Tom had been a bit distant. It was all very well acknowledging that your son was gay, quite another to have the fact thrust in your face in the person of that son's chosen life partner. Tom didn't know how to deal with a son, rather than a daughter-in-law as a companion to his much cherished oldest boy. He had sought advice from his brother. 'He's just another one of the family. Treat him like you'd treat any boy that one of your girls brought home. Just be yourself, let him be himself. Find out what it is about him that attracted Luke to him.' They had stepped around each other like a pair of tomcats for several months, each one being careful not to raise the other's hackles. Polite, not connecting. Until, one day, after a pronouncement of Tom's on the social issues of housing, brought on because the field behind his oddly and haphazardly extended home was being earmarked for development into a new housing estate with so-called 'affordable' housing for new couples. The idea of having houses backing on to his ramshackle garden, blocking his sunlight and obliterating his view did not appeal to Tom, nor to Ellen either had she been consulted. Matt had mildly remarked that new houses needed to be built, and they had to go somewhere. Tom held forth on the unsuitability of his backlot for this specific enterprise, citing the lack of amenities, shops, schools, roads and jobs in the local area. And the field in question was liable to flood, since it ran down to a rather energetic stream that Tom used quite illegally for trout fishing. It was not a meeting of minds. Matt had finally lost his temper by yelling that if Tom really didn't want the development, he ought to either a) buy the field up, or b) find some ecological reason why the field couldn't be used, like 'crested newts or something!'

'What did you say, boy?' Tom had yelled back, his red face inches from Matt's pale one, a dynamic invasion of space that had brought stronger men than Matt to their knees.

'I said crested newts, Sir!' Matt had shouted back, not giving an inch.

'Don't call me Sir, you haven't earned the right!' Tom had blasted back.

'Actually, there *are* newts in the field, Dad,' his third son had offered from the table where he was eating a cheese-and-tomato sandwich and watching the battle with relish. Tom had stared first at his son, then at Matt and back again, had roared with laughter and caught Matt in a bear hug. 'That's my boy!'

'I'm not your boy,' Matt had grumbled, then smiled, still held in the massive arms of a man who beat iron into a pulp for a living and was known for miles around for the shortness of his temper and the fearsomeness of his right hook. And that was that. As far as Tom was concerned, Matt was family now, to be gurned at and shouted at in turns, expected to grimace and shout back with equal gusto.

Matt looked up at Fee. The abject misery in his eyes was painful to see. He had been crying and it showed. So did the mismatched socks on his feet. Zoe slipped into the seat next to him, shifting Tom back with shoulder and hip to cuddle Matt with both arms and rest her cheek on his hair. Matt patted her arm, more for his comfort than hers. He was beyond speech, and the tears began falling again. Zoe searched in her pocket for a hankie, and wiped his face.

'Why don't you go home and rest? You must be whacked. And you smell *awful*.'

Fee pursed her lips at Zoe, but Zoe shook her head. He needs to go home, she mouthed at Fee, Matt still securely held in the circle of her arms, smelly or not. Matt smiled at her wanly.

'I can't go. Not yet. I need to know....' he trailed off before completing the sentence, tears coming to the surface again. Zoe stroked his hair and murmured wordlessly to him. Tom stiffened at his side, and they all looked up to see Ellen walking down the corridor towards them. Her usual determined stride was slowed by the tiredness of a sleepless night spent in surgery, watching other hands than hers cut through her son's flesh and bone. She was wearing hospital scrubs, her fine fair hair hidden by a cap speckled with incongruously perky daisies. A stethoscope dangled round her neck. She stopped some distance away.

'Luke's out of surgery. He's in ICU now.'

'How did it go?'

'It had its moments. It was quite hairy there for a while. But they pulled him through.'

'What now?'

'Now, we wait.' She moved to stand in front of Matt. 'Go home, Matt. You are no use to Luke like this. Have a shower, sleep, get something to eat. All of you, go home.' Fee knew at once what she was asking. You can't do what's needed here, in this place. Get away with you, and do what you have to do. You know very well what that is. I need you to do this for me, and Luke. Now go and do it.

She went to Tom and leaned against him, hugging his waist. His arm went automatically round her shoulders. 'Me, too. I'm so tired I can hardly think.' She looked around, curious. 'Where's Sophie? I would have thought that she would have been here.'

'Now that's the question.'

'She's not.......' injured too, lying somewhere helpless, Ellen left the words unsaid.

'I don't think so. I had a flash of her, but I couldn't *get* her. You know what I mean.'

Ellen nodded at Zoe.

'First things first. Mind you, when I do see Soph, I will have a few words to say to her. She was supposed to be here while I was away.'

'It's not like her.'

'I know. And that worries me.'

Somehow, they got Matt to his feet and into Fee's car. Ellen slipped her a fold of paper. 'Sleeping pills,' she winked. She and Tom drove off into the new day, her head on his shoulder. Zoe slipped into the back seat with Matt and held him while Fee drove them to the schizophrenic house Matt and Luke called home. He walked in like a zombie, allowed himself to be put in a chair and given tea and tuna sandwiches that Fee rustled up from somewhere. 'Didn't know we even had tuna.' He balked at being given a bath by Zoe, who had offered to wash his hair. 'Mum used to do it for me when I was upset.' Ffion oversaw running the bath while Zoe turned down the bed and drew the curtains. She put his mobile phone by the bed with a glass of water, then she and Ffion went back downstairs to make hot chocolate. Just a small cup. And it dissolved two of Ellen's pills beautifully. Matt finally made it to bed, his hair still damp, his face dark with stubble. He couldn't cope with shaving yet. The chocolate went down a treat. Once he had drifted off, Ffion and Zoe left quietly, locking the door.

Back at Pippin Cottage, Fee left Zoe to dish up Snag's breakfast. She could hear him complaining about the lack of service as she tried again to contact Sophie. She left a message on the mobile, surely one among many. It was strange. Sophie was a communication addict and it was not unusual to hear from her at least twice a day. It would require surgical intervention to remove her from her Bluetooth, Zoe had remarked, she even wore it in bed with Caleb.

    Ffion was very good at diagnostics, but the real healing hands in the family belonged to Sophie. She needed to be here. She ought to have been here. There would be *words*, sooner or later. But it was so unlike Sophie to take off and leave Zoe alone. Despite her Bohemian take on life, she loved her sister. Fee made her decision, and sank down into her favourite armchair, the cushions cuddling her back and thighs.

    'Quiet for a bit, Zoe,' she called, aware that her younger sister would not disturb her if she knew what was afoot. She closed her eyes and sank into the darkness behind the lids, slowing her breathing and drawing all her concentration inwards, sinking into the place where all things came together, the bright axis around which her being revolved, where the impossible was made possible and all the threads tangled…. The door clicked softly as Zoe shut Snag out of the front room. He was a bugger for leaping in your lap when you were entranced and scaring the living daylights out of you. Maybe he thought he was helping. He wasn't.

In the warm heartbeating darkness, Ffion conjured up the image of Sophie: violet eyed, strawberry blonde, with an impish grin on her features, her head held slightly to one side. She held the image, focussing on it, and *Reached*......

Sophie. Sophie. Sophie. Hear me. Sophie. Sophie. Hear me. Sophie. Sophie. Hear me.

She repeated this several times before she 'felt' the contact, an echo of Sophie's laugh, her presence…

Sophie. Sophie. Sophie. Come home. Come home now.
I am here.

There was an image in her head, of boats, their masts against a blue and cloudy sky. The sea. A large river. A shopping centre by the marina. Sophie was in Falmouth? What the hell was she thinking of? Surely if she needed to go back to sort something-or-other out, she could have taken Zoe along. Unless, of course, the idea was to screw Caleb senseless. Not that they didn't do that to each other anyway, anytime. Sophie had a careless air about her, ignorant of what she had gone and done, leaving Zoe to face this mess alone. To be fair, she couldn't have known that it would all go tits-up. But she had left Zoe, and hadn't even taken the time to tell the poor kid she was offski. Fee swallowed her anger, and with it all the things she wanted to say to Sophie.

Luke is hurt.

Fee sent an image of Luke falling through the sky into Bridlip Gorge, then the hospital. She felt an answering pang of shock and disbelief.

I AM COMING HOME RIGHT NOW.

Sophie broke the contact, and Ffion felt a flurry of movement, as if Sophie herself had hurried past her to the door. Well, it would take her an hour or two. Best to deal with that meeting she missed. Those astute businessmen she had been scheduled to meet would surely be pissed off with her, wasting their time like that. It didn't reflect well on Greg, either, who had arranged the meeting and wooed the asset-rich angels for her own personal Dragon's Den, the pitch that would raise Blue Moon from a local hole-and-corner mini project into a national business. Oh, well. If it all went down the pan, it wasn't for lack of trying.

She found her phone and called Greg to let him know how Luke was. He was sympathetic, assuring her that he could surely postpone the meeting. A serious accident to a close family member was reason enough to reschedule, but they would not wait forever. He repeated his offer to come down, and Ffion was in the process of refusing him, again, when a voice floated in from the kitchen. Zoe had been eavesdropping. Typical. Only on this occasion she was minded to be helpful.

'Four words, Fee. On. Line. Video. Conference. We can set it up from here. I've got the technology. Give me an hour to prepare the presentation and you're hot to trot. Tell lover boy to set it up his end. Maximum approval guaranteed. Did you leave those samples in the flat? He'll need them.'

That would certainly solve Fee's immediate problem. The expansion plans for the business required the money these industrial moguls had to invest, and they had no time or patience for family matters. They had 'people' to do that. 'Get your people to talk to our people.' The only people Fee had was herself and her by now indispensable assistant, the resourceful and redoubtable Zoe. Quickly she passed the idea on to Greg, who promised to set it up 'ASAP' and call her back. The relief in his tone was palpable. At least he couldn't leap in his car and beard her in her den now. Another crisis averted. Thank the Gene Genie.

Since it was 'practically lunchtime', Zoe had put on some vegetable casserole from the freezer to heat up. While it was doing that, she set up Fee's laptop, ready for Greg's go-ahead. When it was, she declared it 'Skype-and-go', and served brunch. The two girls picked at it, over the kitchen table, desultory. As they waited for Sophie.

'Can't we do anything while we wait? Find out what exactly happened, for instance?'

'A wraithweave, you mean? I suppose we could talk to Luke, wherever he is. We gotta have a weirding for him somewhere.'

'We must have a photo lurking about. That'll do.' Zoe forked spinach into her mouth and got up to rummage. A few seconds later she was waving a piece of paper. 'Gotcha.'

They cleared the table of the remains of the casserole. Ffion drew the blinds and Zoe brought in a candle from the front room.

'He was here the last time we used this.' She dumped it on the table, and poured some salt from the shaker into a small glass bowl. 'We need incense. I know he made us some.' She vanished again into the depths of the house and returned with a miniature brass bowl and a small squat stoppered bottle. She took down one of the brightly coloured glasses from the shelf and filled it with water at the sink. 'Now we're all set.'

Ffion struck a match and lit the candle.

'I light this candle in the name of Luke, son of Ellen and son of Tom, beloved of Matt.' She took a small round of charcoal from the tiny bowl and a pair of tongs from the kitchen drawer. Holding the charcoal over the stove, she lit the burner and held the black disc in the flame. It hissed, spluttered, and bright sparks flew like fireflies over the crumbly surface. An acrid perfume filled the air as the nitre burned off and the charcoal caught, glowing a sullen red in the watery gloom of the kitchen. Zoe sat at the table, watching intently. Wyted or not, she still had wyth and was eager to grab any opportunity to exercise it. Kitchen sink cys was nothing new. This room had seen many weaves brewed over the table, along with family meals, wine and preserves. It was a holy kitchen, the heart of the house, where the family pulse beat most strongly. Petty wythens were often done here. And in this case, Fee was minded to go the whole hog. A,B,C: Always Be Careful. Especially around children and dead people.

Fee returned to the table, carefully placing the ashy disc in the bowl. Zoe poured a few grains from the stoppered bottle, and a thick cloud of incense rose, overlaying the acrid note of the nitre with a sweet, drowsy perfume.

Standing at the table, Fee intoned the beginning of the chant to open the doors between the Midess and the Asha, where Luke's intelligence, that essential part that made Luke himself would be were it not home - which it certainly wasn't.

'I conjure thee, O wyth of ayen, to protect me. Aid me and do my bidding............'

She turned round, pointing her finger to draw a circle round herself, Zoe and the table, whispering under her breath as she did so. Her heart was thudding behind her ribs as it always did as she picked up the wyth of the four elements, and Zoe, sitting at the table.

'I conjure thee, O spaca, to be my focus and defence. Be thou a gateway between the Midess of men and the Asha of the wraithen. With the wyth of earth I bless and sanctify thee.....'

She picked up the bowl of salt and sprinkled it around them.

'With the wyth of water I bless and sanctify thee.'

She dipped her fingers in the water and scatted droplets round the table.

'With the wyth of air I bless and sanctify thee.'

Carefully, she walked round the table with the smoking bowl. It was getting quite hot from the sullenly glowing charcoal. She repeated the actions with the candle. Thankfully, Zoe had brought one with a decent holder. She always had visions of Wee Willie Winkie when the candle was stuck on a saucer.

'With the wyth of fire I bless and sanctify thee, that thou mayest contain the wythen we shall raise within thee, in the names of the Arda and the Karna.'

She replaced the candle on the table. Holding her hands in front of her waist, clasped together, she gathered her forces.

'By the wyth of this spaca here conjured and sanctified, and by the wyth of the elements here gathered, I summon thee, Luke, son of Ellen, son of Tom, to come to us now, here, in this circle, that I may hold converse with thee and enjoy thy society and aid. Luke, son of Ellen, son of Tom, I summon thee by earth, by water, by air and by fire, by sun and moon and star to be here and present in this place as I demand. Luke, son of Ellen, son of Tom, thrice called, thrice summoned, heed your oath and come to the one who calls you. Luke, Luke, Luke, I summon, stir, and call you up from whatever part of the world you may be, to come to me here and now, and answer truthfully my questions.'

She sat down at the table, and took Zoe's hands. The smoke of the incense rose up, wavered across the table, and rose up again. Zoe shivered and closed her eyes. After a few seconds, she shuddered. Her eyes opened and focussed on nothing within the room.

'I see Luke.' the voice was remote. Zoe and not-Zoe at the

same time.

'What does he say?'

'Nothing. He's just looking at me. He's sad.' She sighed, and her chin dropped down onto her chest. She drew a shuddering breath.

'Luke. Speak to Zoe. She is your friend. Speak to her.'

'Buzzards.' Zoe's voice held the faint overtones of a deeper, more masculine timbre. It might, or might not, be Luke. Wraiths were tricky that way: they would impersonate each other and lead you quite a dance unless you were wary. You had to know how to ask the right questions……

'Luke. You went to Bridlip Tor and saw the buzzards.'

'Tor. I can't hear him. Tor. Buzzards. Sophie! I see *Sophie*.'

Sophie was there? Was she there when Luke fell? How was she involved in this? And then, she went away, without so much as a word to anyone. She had questions to answer, their sister.

'Luke. You met Sophie at Bridlip Tor.'

'Sophie. Tor. Man. Man, black…….. man walking. Sophie……'

'Sophie met someone on Bridlip Tor?'

Who did Sophie meet? Did she know him? Was it arranged? Oh, Soph…….

'Man, man and Sophie. Buzzards. Picture. Camera. Rocks.'

Zoe's head came up. Her eyes were bright, dazzling, intense.

'Camera. Camera. Camera.'

'Luke, did you fall off Bridlip Tor?'

'No.'

'Did someone push you?'

'No.'

Fee sighed. The literal nature of the wraith. He would answer the questions, but not offer information. That was good, as far as it went. He wasn't trying to confuse her, anyway. But he was confusing her. He didn't fall, he wasn't pushed…..

'How did you get from Bridlip Tor to the gorge?'

'I flew.'

'You *flew*?'

'I flew, I can fly. With the buzzards.' Zoe's face was transported, amazed, wonderful. She was in a state of pure joy.

Fee began to feel the first tickles of the freezer ants skittering down her spine.

'You can fly.'

'I flew. With the buzzards. I. Can. Fly.' Vertically downwards, at least.

'Where are you now?'

'In a dark place.'

'Are you alone?'

'We are many. We belong to the master. He holds us here.' This was wrong, way wrong…….

'I have called you out of the dark place.'

'I must go back. The master holds me. I must go back.' Zoe's face was stricken now, with something more profound than fear. Fee knew she was in way, way deep, but she wasn't about to give up now.

'I can hold you here. I have that wyth. I command you.'

'You are not the master. You cannot command.'

'I can command those whose oath I hold. I hold your oath. I command *you*.'

'I must go back. The master binds me.'

'I will hold you here. I have the wyth, here, now, in this place.'

'You must not hold me. He calls me. I must go back.'

Fee stood up. She pointed her finger at Zoe.

'Luke, son of Ellen, son of Tom, bonded to me by blood and by oath, beyond life, beyond death, I command you to obey me.' Zoe flung back her head and screamed like a lost soul in torment.

'Luke, son of Ellen and Tom, bonded to me by blood and by oath, I bind you to this place, to this spaca of wyth that I have conjured. I bind you by the wyth of earth, by the wyth of water, by the wyth of air and the wyth of fire, to obey me.' Zoe screamed again, shaking her head, her hair whipping about her face and scattering the plume of incense all over the room.

'Luke, son of Ellen and son of Tom, bonded to me by ties that cannot be broken, obey me now. Return to your proper place upon this instant. This I command by the wyth instilled in me by the holy Cys of Aya. This I command by the wyth of the Fratris, linked by blood and through Time. This I command by the wyth that prohibits revolt against the proper order, by the Aya of Arda and of Karna. This I command by the Gya that I now hold. I command that you return to your proper place, without hindrance or delay. Now.' Zoe was screaming continuously now, a high, thin wail, her hands gripping the table. The candle began to shake, and the incense trailed around Fee, wreathing her in smoke. She glared directly and intently at Zoe, focussing all her strength into her will that the wraith of Luke should return to, if at least not his body, certainly somewhere else other than the place she had called him out of. Zoe's wails began to subside, and she began to pant.

'You cannot rule me, Farer.' The voice was low and grating. Zoe's talents did not include direct mediumship. At least until now.

'Here, in this place, in this spaca, I rule. And you WILL obey.' Fee knew for a fact, from deep within her bones, that this was not Luke's wraith she was facing. And she wasn't about to face any Dark Lord without the psychic equivalent of a howitzer. 'I command you, wraith, by the wyth and Gya here gathered, to depart this place. Return to your proper place, harming no one and no thing in your passing. In the name of the Aya that cannot be denied, I command you to leave this place. Now.'

Zoe was looking up at her, her head drawn in like a wary tortoise, her eyes slanting up, feral and gleaming. Spittle dripped on her chin. The look in her eye said, I am the predator. I am going for your throat. There was nothing of Zoe in her.

Ffion traced a sigum in the air in front of the face that wasn't Zoe's.

'**Ackrest**!' she shouted. Zoe slumped. 'Wraith accursed, flee this place before the wyth of my blood. Wraith accursed, flee this place before the wyth of my Cys. Wraith accursed, flee this place before the Gya which commands all, orders all and prohibits revolt. Go thou and trouble this world not again until you have counted every grain of sand on every beach, passed over every hill and dale, crossed every stream and river and enumerated very star within the night sky! By Arda and Karna, I cleanse this place of your presence and influence. So it be. Amen. Fiat. Fiat. Fiat.' At least that will keep you busy while I find out who, or what, you are. And then I'm coming after you. You don't treat my sister like a telephone exchange, you just don't. And I'll have you for that alone. I promise you.

Fee held the wyth until Zoe, slumped on the table, began to stir. Fee placed both hands on her sister's hair, which now felt like dry straw and looked like rat's tails.

'Holy Arda, bless this your daughter. Guard and protect her from all invasions and phantasms of the wraithen. Keep her, in body and mind, as your true daughter, and defend her against the toils of evil. This I invoke by your sacred name.'

Zoe coughed. 'M'throat's sore.' She took a sip of water from the glass on the table. 'That didn't go as planned, I take it.'

'You could say that.'

'I'll review the tapes later.' Zoe threw open the window. 'Sophie will be here soon. And Gene's in a right swit.' She started to clear away the evidence of the weaving as bright sunlight and a fresh breeze completed the cleansing of the room, wiping away the invasion with the last traces of incense.

'You taped us?' Fee asked, slightly outraged.

'Tape it? Hell, I videoed it. It's all on CD now. We're all wired for sound and vision, didn't you know?' Fee looked at her sister, aghast. Truly, there were no secrets in this family.

Chapter Three

When Sophie arrived, Zoe was drying her hair. She had taken one look in the mirror and decided that nothing less than a full ablution would repair the damage. Anyway, she said, I feel dirty. Used. Mucked about with. The next time you want to consort with the denizens of the nether hells, you can use materialization like anyone else. Stuff mediumship. I dread to think what's been crawling about in my brain. Yuk. Fee made her put salt in the bath and invoke a cleansing and purifying charm on the water. Just in case. And to seal the openings of her body with oil. Better be safe than sorry. Zoe agreed. In any case, the oil smelled nice.

While her sister was ridding herself of the dregs of the wraithweave, Fee powered up her laptop and sat down to business. Her contacts were pleased that she had made the meeting, although late and electronically rather than in person. She made her presentation, with a mental note to thank Zoe for the professional finish. The kid had worked hard on it, pressed all the right buttons. It went over as well as could be hoped. If these old gits were not inclined to be generous, then it was back to the drawing board. That, or get a loan from Theo and Cecile. Oh, no…….

Sophie was not impressed with getting the third degree from both sisters about her visit to Bridlip Tor and the vanishing act that followed. Nor having to explain what she had been doing in Falmouth, for heaven's sake. Good grief, she lived there, didn't she? Zoe was quite capable of looking after herself for twenty four hours at her age, surely? And there was an exhibition there she wanted to show in. And she met one of Caleb's friends. For coffee. Another artist. What is this? A murder enquiry?

She listened with thinly veiled anger to the tale her sisters related. She insisted on calling the hospital, Tom and Ellen, and Matt. This last she was vetoed on. Matt, they hoped, was still asleep. But she could watch the DVD of the séance. Armed with tea and biscuits, they settled down to learn what they could. No doubt Zoe was recording this as well. Fee made a mental note. Put it on the agenda: find out exactly what rooms Zoe had bugged, and when she recorded. And make damn sure she destroyed the copies. In the microwave would be favourite.

'Yes, I did meet someone on Bridlip Tor. And no, I don't know who he was. I'd never seen him before. I certainly didn't arrange to meet him there. I was expecting to see Luke, but no-one else. I was taking pictures of the valley. I'd had my eye on it for some time. The evening light was just right. It will make a beautiful canvas. He said, something like, Hello, nice day, that sort of thing. I said, Walking are you. You have the weather for it, or something like that. Then I asked him, where have you come from. He said, Over from Chillaton. I said, That's a fair way. He asked where I was going, where I came from. I'm local, I said: I was taking photographs for pictures. I paint. Him, You are an artist, then. Me: Yes. He said he was an artist of sorts, but he didn't paint pictures. He said goodbye and walked off down the hill, I suppose, I didn't watch him. Then Luke came up. We talked for a while, I asked him about some pictures I wanted to borrow for my art class. Then we laid on the rocks and watched the buzzards. Luke said that if he could have one wish, it would be to fly like the buzzards. I decided then and there to buy him a course of hang-gliding lessons for Yule. Which was why I went back to Falmouth early instead of staying here. I completely forgot that you were away, Zoe was alone. Everything went out of my mind, all except this brilliant idea I had for Luke's present.'

'Birdbrain.'

'Sorry.'

'So why was your phone switched off? You never switch your phone off. I swear if you could have it implanted permanently, you would.'

Sophie grinned, shamefaced.

'Sorry, Zoe. I forgot to charge it. And I left the spare battery at home. Once I got back to The Loft, I was going to call you, but then Fee caught me. I was watching the boats.'

'Technical failure, uh-huh.'

'Yes. Sorry.'

'It doesn't wash. You don't forget things like that.'

Sophie tossed her phone on the coffee table. She was starting to get really angry.

'Evidence, Mouse. Dead phone.'

Zoe picked up the phone and plugged it into her laptop.

'You're right it's dead. Dead, as in dead. You don't need a new battery, you need a new phone.'

'How did that happen? It was fine yesterday. I called Caleb from Bridlip, sent him an e-picture. He's got a thing about skies.' Zoe tutted at Caleb's need for firmament. 'I'll just whip over to Norway and ask him, shall I?' she asked sweetly. Fee stepped in before the fight moved to Defcon Two.

'Let's see what we can work out from this wraithweaving, since Zoe was so kind as to make a historical record.'

They watched in silence until the camera caught Zoe at the end. The not-Zoe voice echoed. 'You cannot rule me, Farer.'

'My gods. She looks just like Regan in the film Exorcist. Just before she started spewing green bile.'

'Pea soup, you mean. Yes, she does.'

'How do you feel now, Zoe?'

'You mean, am I about to produce mountains of pea soup and start stabbing myself with a crucifix where the sun doesn't shine? I don't *think* so.'

'No! Do you feel all yourself? No riders?'

Zoe knew what Sophie meant. In the early days, she had 'experimented' with an Ouija board and it had taken Lily and Robert some hours to set her to rights one they had discovered why their most cherished youngest daughter had suddenly turned into an uncommunicative termagant overnight. 'It's too early for *that* sort of moodiness,' commented Lily. Two daughters on, she knew the signs of impending womanhood all too well. Sophie in particular had been very, very difficult at that stage. The crop of spots hadn't helped either. All they could do was batten down the hatches until the sunny bright Sophie they knew and loved had re-emerged like a butterfly from a chrysalis. She had been a terror, arguing, smashing things, throwing stuff about, bursting into tears at the slightest provocation. When Fee started, they had moved most of the breakables out of the way, but Fee had simply withdrawn into herself and complained endlessly whenever circumstance demanded that she interact with the rest of the family. Zoe, never to be outdone, was certainly planning something extra special for her own rite of passage.

'No, nothing like that. It was *really* creepy, though. One moment I was speaking to Luke, then I wasn't. It was all dark and whispery. There was Something there, but I couldn't see what it was. Then I was back in the kitchen, feeling like a goat's bottom. There was this smell, see. Not a real smell. An aura.'

'Like a goat's bottom.'

'Yeah, musty and musky, just like Uncle Tom's billy goat. Sort of strong and earthy, not really unpleasant, but you wouldn't want to dab it behind your ears.'

'Hhmm.'

'So, what have we found out? Luke was on Bridlip Tor. He saw Sophie with another man. He said, 'black'.'

'He wasn't black. In fact, he was quite pale. Funny, I forgot that. He was really pale, like Jerry.'

'Prof, you mean.' Jerry was the school geek and was often in Zoe's company. Most of the children sported vibrant tans during the summer months, some because they had to work outdoors on farms, some because they liked being out from under the eyes of parents to get up to adolescent mischief. Others genuinely liked the outdoors. Not Jerry. He spent every available hour welded to his computers, and was the only one to sport a 'hacker tan'. The world outside his windows could end in flood and fire, and he wouldn't bat an eyelid provided the programmes kept running. He tended to wear dark glasses a lot out of doors. This did not set him apart as it might, since he was the first recourse for any student whose dog had widdled on their homework, (Really, it did happen. Not as much as was pretended, but it did. Cats as well. Zoe had actually taken the soggy, smelly mass in to school to prove it on one memorable occasion) or who got stuck, or merely needed to score some otherwise unobtainable truth. Jerry might not roam the world in fact, but he roamed it remotely, online. He had an endless knowledge of all things geographical, geological and biological at his fingertips. The nickname 'Prof.'

was a nod to his talents and knowledge of those essential, obscure but useful facts the lack of which caused endless agony to anyone who had a project due to be handed in. If there was something you needed to know, the Prof would supply same. Quickly. The bigger lads soon realized there was no profit in bullying him. He simply refused his help, politely. ('I don't think I want to do that. You hurt me, remember. Last Tuesday. No, I definitely don't want to do that. Hitting me again won't change my mind. Try it if you like.') Scorn from the rest of the students, who had recourse to this eminent resource, had completed the learning process. Jerry was left alone, and even rescued and guarded when forced by class tutors to join in field trips.

'Exactly like that. Unusual for a hiker. I wonder why that never occurred to me. And he was wearing black, come to think of it. Not dark blue, black. Black bush hat, black coat, black trousers. Even his shoes were black. And, come to think on it, they weren't proper walkers, more like heavy street ones.... Funny, he didn't have a backpack, now I think of it, but when he was there, I didn't notice. Very…... Strange.'

'Why?'

Sophie became animated, waving her hands to emphasize her point.

'Strange that I *hadn't* noticed that he wasn't a typical hiker. I took him completely at his word, and ignored the signals from his appearance. I'm an artist, remember? I *notice* things like that. *And* he borrowed my mobile. He said he couldn't get reception. That happens a lot on the moors, so much of them is in shadow, I thought nothing of it. Some networks work, and some don't. It's not unusual. But I had completely forgotten. And afterwards, my mobile didn't work. I had no suspicions, before or after, until now. And I ought to have had.'

'And he went before you met Luke.'

'Yes. Or I thought he did. Why would he stay? Then I had this idea to buy Luke the gliding lessons. I had to go do it right away. I *didn't* have to. I was planning on staying until you got back, but I hared off back to Falmouth like a homing pigeon. This is wrong, too wrong, all of it.'

'Could he have gone down the Tor and circled back?'

Sophie thought a minute.

'Yes. Luke and I were watching the buzzards. If he came back, he would have heard us. We wouldn't have seen him if he had come back up the fore slope between the rocks. We were watching the sky, not the ground.'

'So suppose this man didn't leave. Suppose he waited until you'd gone, and then tossed Luke off the Tor. Is it possible?'

'It's *possible*. But why?'

'Let's leave that for now. I'm more interested in what happened. I'll get to *why* later.'

'But Luke said he flew. He flew with the buzzards. Not I fell, not I was pushed. I flew, he said.'

'Quite right, Zoe. There is so much that's just not kosher about this. It's not natural. So, could it be supernatural?'

'How do you mean?'

'Occam's Razor. Once you have eliminated the possible, the impossible, however improbable, must be the truth. Sherlock Holmes was fond of it.'

'That's a bloody long jump, even for you.'

'And I couldn't *Reach* you. Okay, so I'm not perfect. But I can usually *get* the person, even if I can't get proper reception. Last night, it was like you were off the face of the planet.'

Sophie stared at Zoe.

'But I *always* hear you.'

'Not last night you didn't.'

'You were upset.'

'*You* were supposed to be *here*.'

Before the contention could develop into a proper row, Fee coughed.

'Meanwhile, back at the ranch…'

'Go on, Fee.'

'Just suppose that this walker, who might not have been a walker at all, was *talented*. Actually using wyth. On both of you. For whatever reason. He puts the chymer on you, then meets you. You treat him just like a normal hiker, though you can see he's all wrong. He borrows your phone and puts it out of action…….'

'Why?'

'How should I know? In his head, am I? To eliminate you

from the scene later? Maybe he didn't expect to see you there, so he simply wanted rid of you. Otherwise, it'd be you off the tor, and not Luke!'

'That must mean Luke was the target. *If* this guy wasn't out there for a random chuck-a-hiker-off-a-rock....'

'Anyway, somehow, Luke ends up at the foot of the tor. And you're nowhere to be found. If we were worrying about you, just when Luke has been so badly hurt, we might think the same of you, and rush off to find *you* and forget why Luke fell. Or think that you had something to do with Luke's fall. While we are busy doing that………..'

'What? You think *I* might be responsible? Hells bells, Fee!'

'Yes. No. Buggered if I know. All I know is this looks too….. convenient to be accidental.' Fee was letting her words run away with her. She was talking quickly, the ideas tumbling over each other: she was on the right track, she *knew* it. 'You weren't here. We wanted to know what happened. Maybe you were hurt, too. Zoe couldn't contact you. Without that, we wouldn't have done the wraithweaving………' She trailed off, the ghastly possibilities opening like a gulf beneath her feet. 'I have been stupid, so stupid. I wasn't thinking. I never imagined …… or I wouldn't….' Have risked Zoe, she didn't say.

'It's okay. We're okay. Forget the what-ifs.'

Fee drew Zoe close. Her impetuosity might have led to Zoe being hurt, or worse. They knew only too well the dangers of the game that was being played. Death was the least worry. There were worse things….. Bugger.

'So who knew you were going to Bridlip yesterday?'

'No-one. I didn't know myself when I set off to Luke's. I wanted to borrow some of his photographs for my art class, like I told you. But he wasn't home. Then I remembered that Matt told me Luke was going up Bridlip because he was studying the buzzards there. It was part of his research project for the Uni. Right then and there, I decided to follow him. I was surprised that he wasn't there already, considering the start he had on me. But you know Luke. He can be distracted by a butterfly, spend ages trying to catch a perfect moment with that camera of his. So I snapped the valley and waited.'

'I don't suppose you got any snaps of this mysterious hiker?'

'No. One moment he wasn't there, the next he was. Mind you, I was totally intent on what I was doing. If he had come over from Chillaton like he said, then he would have come up behind me. I wouldn't have seen him anyway.'

'Who else would have known that Luke was going to Bridlip, then?'

'Half of the Uni. He runs a blog as part of the study, so other people can tell him if they've seen anything interesting.'

Fee thought a while.

'Is it possible that we could find out who's been looking at Luke's blog?'

'Not unless they left a comment.'

'But the Uni servers would register a hit, even if they left nothing. Computers do that.'

'Zoe, can you read that record?'

'Not without administrative access.'

'Could you get that?'

'I suppose. If I hack into the computer and name myself as an administrator. But people get upset if you do that. They call in the cops and all sorts. You'd think that I'd raped the computer. Before I start a new career as a cybercriminal, I'd like to try other stuff first. You are leading me into bad ways. Anyway, I'm not a patch on Jerry for hacking. If I wanted to hack something badly enough, I'd ask him.'

'Let's not involve the civilians until we really need to.'

'So Luke was really a target?'

'It's possible. Of course, I may be paranoid. Luke was the one who was going to Bridlip yesterday. If Sophie had been the target, the bugger would have followed her, and he didn't. No, he came to Bridlip, where Luke was heading that day. And Sophie gets this sudden impulse to leave.'

'Just as sudden as the impulse to go meet Luke in the first place. I didn't have to see him to borrow his photos, he's let me do it before. I wonder if something was trying to tell me that Luke was in danger. That if I was with him, he would be safe, and if I had stayed there, and we went back down together, he would still be here, not in the hospital. Damn.'

'Right. Suppose our mystery hiker leaves the pair of you, but circles back and spies on you. He's got his eye on Luke, how and why we don't know. Anyhow, he plants a thought in your mind that you've got to go. Now. At once. You said it came into your mind all of a sudden. That thing about buying Luke flying lessons. That came out of left field. Perhaps he planted it there. Because of what he'd already done to you.'

'A chymer? I got caught with my pants down, right enough.' Now Sophie was starting to get really annoyed. Someone had invaded her inner space, and injured one of her best friends and her cousin to boot. As she saw it, she had failed Luke and the Gya, both. She had left him in the eye of danger. The Gya had called her to be Luke's protection, and she had botched it. Sophie was on the warpath. 'And it would take some doing to put one over on *me*.' This was not hubris. Sophie was good. *Really* good.

'So you toddle off, leaving Luke alone. This man doesn't have to physically push Luke off the Tor. He can force him to do it all on his own, by making him believe that he can fly.'

'Now *you're* reaching.'

'I don't think so. Face it, it's possible. He got rid of you, remember? And Luke's not a patch on you.'

'Aye, it can be done, if you're Fratten. But…. we don't do that to each other.'

'Not now. But we used to.'

'Back in the bad old days?'

'So you think one of *us* did this?'

'It's one of the Persuasions……'

'No-one in the Frais would want to hurt Luke, surely?'

'Fratten don't stop at this Frais, Zoe.'

'No. That's where it falls down.'

They sat in silence. No-one wanted to chase that line of thought to its logical conclusion. The repercussions were too awful to contemplate.

'Well, isn't this a bugger.'

'Could it be a talent from outside the Families?'

'I don't think so. How could a rogue do that? We're not amateurs,' Sophie scoffed.

'You had both been lying down, watching the birds. You

would have been really, really open. You both believed you were alone, and safe. You were both unguarded. That's how he got in.'

'You're right, Zoe. It could be possible, under those circumstances, to glim me, then Luke. What bothers me is how easily it was done. All very quickly, and without us suspecting a thing. So smooth... and from a rogue? I'd be insulted to think that someone outside of the Families could pull one over on me so easily. That makes him very good at what he does. *Very* good indeed. We will have to be very, very wary of this one. He's powerful. But what's he up to? And why us in particular?'

'We don't know he's targeting only us. The Families don't communicate much. It's starting to get better, but some of us are still living in the Dark Ages.'

'So, Sophie's out of the picture. Luke's injured. What do we do?'

'Call in the Gya and heal him.'

'We go weaving for Luke, we leave ourselves open, and this sod, this man in black, shadow master, rogue or whatever, is waiting for us. Just like he did to me and Fee. It's as if he was *waiting* for us to tip our hand.'

The three sisters exchanged worried glances.

'Stop them. Stop them now.'

Fee ran for the phone in the hall and started to speed dial. The Frais had a system, an information bomb. You called two people. They each called two others. Done and dusted in minutes. There was no argument. When the Mysten sent out a call, you didn't question, didn't second-guess her. You did what she told you. Then, you argued with her. Or waited for an explanation. The order was simple. No wythens, not even to cure your own headaches, until I tell you different. Now.

'We can expect the fallout later. Now, we need answers.' Fee came back in, sat down.

'We have a powerful, resourceful enemy. He's thought this one through. He's got a plan.'

'How did you work that one out?'

'Come on. You can't believe it's an accident that he was there on Bridlip Tor at the same time as you and Luke. He planned it.'

'Amazing what you can come up with on the fly, Zoe.'

'Also, I don't think he expected you to be there.'

'Hence the overwhelming desire to haul ass out of there and buy Luke gliding lessons. In Falmouth of all places? When you were supposed to be here until the weekend. How clumsy is that?'

'And how complete. I plain forgot that I was here until Sunday. No wonder Gus was so surprised to see me.'

'So Luke was the target. But was the intention to kill, or injure?'

'Why's that important?'

'If Luke had been killed outright, perhaps there was no further interest in the rest of us.'

'Or maybe it was simply that he took the opportunity. It's pretty difficult to gauge how hurt someone's going to be when you push them off a cliff.'

Something pinged in the back of Fee's mind. A piece of puzzle looking for a place to fit. Unable to find a suitable link, the idea fizzled and died before she could fully realize it.

'Opportunist, then.'

'No. Let's assume, for a moment, that the intention was to kill Luke outright. Then, when he found it hadn't worked as planned, he instituted Phase Two.'

'Whoa, whoa. Let's not take this too far. Why should he be interested in someone he thought was already dead?'

"He holds me captive. We are many."

'Shit.'

'Double shit. He knew when I pulled Luke out of…. Wherever he was.'

'Hell's bells, Fee, this is a mess.'

'Ah, no. I beg to disagree.'

'If we hadn't called Luke, he'd have buggered off and left us alone, Zoe.'

'Do you know that for sure? True, he might have vanished and we'd have no way of finding him. But now, he'll have to watch us, and what watches us we can watch back.'

'Does he know that?'

'I hope to Ayen not. He knows we are Fratris.'

'How so?'

'He called Fee 'Farer' in the wraithweave. He *was* waiting for us to do something. He overlooked us on purpose. He expected our response. He cuts Soph from the herd, then tosses Luke off the tor. Why him? What was it about Luke that made him a target?'

'Did he know something? Something this man didn't want known? So he kills Luke to prevent us from learning whatever it is?'

'Even if Luke was dead, we could still contact him. No, there's something else going on here. He captured Luke. In the 'dark place.' And he's done it before, I'm sure of it. The whole thing was too slick. I've never heard of anyone being able to do that. Dead is dead. You aren't subject to a living person's cys once you've passed that boundary. Luke said he wasn't alone. We are many, he said. If this bloke's been targeting the Fratris, why haven't we heard something? Hell, most of us have blood ties by now. The Harrises, Davies and Howe lines have been intermarrying for ages.'

'Could he be a Ross?'

'I doubt it. The Rosses have been dealing with renegades for yonks. Remember James Alexander MacArthur Ross?'

'Not personally, thank goodness. But we know the tale.'

Zoe was going to relate it anyway.

'James Ross's mother was a Howe - Agnes Howe. The Rosses and the McEirchans all claim descent from a pharcy line, so they're all a bit wythen. James was a prodigy. It was all they could do to keep him reigned in. Luckily they lived in a remote Highland castle, so they didn't have to worry about the neighbours. And if they did complain, it was an out-and-out clan feud. Anyway, James' wyth was really strong, and it was only Agnes who could keep him down. And she did. All her life, making James toe the line. Until she died. Then, James went mental. He terrorized everybody. The only one who could get close to him was his sister Elizabeth.'

'The fair Betty. Married a Harris and escaped to England. Pissed James off right and proper.'

'Well, Agnes must have known that her son would be a bugger once she died. So she made a box, which went to Elizabeth on her marriage. Everyone thought it was her dowry, and it was, in a funny sort of way. It was a Griearch.'

'A constructed ghywlli, imprinted with James' spirit.'

'Och, aye. And the old biddy keyed it to her daughter. With the pleas of the clan beating in her ears, Elizabeth released the ghywlli and sent it after James.'

'And it did what it was created to do. Ate James' wythen and left him a dribbling shadow of his former self. Mind gone, wyth gone, all gone.'

'Once the Griearch had completed its mission, it returned to the box. Elizabeth realized that the Howe-Ross line might throw up a similar problem later on, so she retuned the box to *her* daughter and left precise instructions. How to fix the Griearch onto its next victim. Legend has it all the male heirs of the Ross clan are subject to the ghywlli, but that's rubbish. Elizabeth simply put that box in another box, *with* the cys that would name the victim and set the Griearch off again. And she added a personal curse to anyone who used it unwisely. The Ross girls are shit scared of it, but they *will* use it if necessary. They all take an oath on it when they get the box.'

'How did you get to know all this?'

'I asked Aunt Effie.'

'And she told you?'

'I am the Frais archivist. We've got Ross blood in here somewhere. I wouldn't call her Aunt Effie otherwise. She's a bit gaga, but sharp as a knife on family history.'

'So how does she know all this? I knew about the curse, but not the other stuff about Betty. Only that the Rosses knew how to cope with family who've gone bad.'

'Effie's got the box. Meanwhile, back at the ranch, if it was a Ross, he'd be toast by now. Effie's got no qualms about opening it. Privately, I think she'd like to. To be the only Ross apart from Betty who opened the box.'

'So a Ross is unlikely.'

'I doubt it. Anyway, the answer's simple: Call Effie and tell her to open the dreaded Box. There are all sorts of sports springing up in the remoter reaches of the Families, especially the Davies, who are not so hot on keeping up with family genealogy.

They're Welsh, see, and feuding is a hobby with them. Some of them haven't spoken to other branches of the Family for generations because of what someone's Uncle Taffy did at Our Jean's Wedding. So it's on the cards that one Davies descendent might marry another remote Family member and produce a fratten, and they didn't even know it was in their blood. Sad, really. The poor kids have no idea, until some distant relative notices them and gives them a bit of a hand. Most of the Welsh are a bit fey anyway, so it's not an issue.'

'That leaves the Howes and the Harrises. Which is us. Do we have any cousins we don't know about?'

'Probably. I'll look into it. We're doing an ancestry project at school anyway, and this will make it way more interesting. But I think it's a dead horse, frankly.'

'Dead horse?'

'I won't be able to ride it anywhere.'

'So this……. person comes onto our turf. He chymed Sophie and injured Luke. He knew Sophie was a threat, so he sees her off and cuts her line of communication. But he doesn't know all our skills - not all the Families have the same abilities to the same degree. If Sophie hadn't been on Bridlip Tor yesterday, we would have thought that Luke had just had a nasty accident. Sad, but it happens. We would have acted as normal, and we'd have been sitting ducks.'

Zoe gasped.

'Luke's camera! Where is it? He never goes out without it. And he kept repeating, Camera, camera, at me. Did he take a picture of this 'black man'?'

'Luke's camera was smashed in the fall. I saw it at the hospital. Matt had it.'

'Didn't the police want it?'

'No. they are happy that it's an accident. Sergeant Brice is, anyhow.'

'So Matt's got Luke's stuff.'

'The camera's smashed.'

'The picture card might not be. And it will fit into Sophie's Halina. I could download it onto the computer.'

Sophie stood up.

'I'll get it. Give me Matt's keys and I'll go over there now. I'll bring Matt back with me. No-one ought to be left alone until this is sorted out. The one I'm really worried about is John…..'

'He's with Abby. Somewhere.'

'It's best if he stays away. Weren't he and Abby going up to visit Effie after the wyting? Maybe we ought to send them now. And tell her to dust off the box and see if it will work on a non-Ross. We want all the ammunition we can get. And it'd be better keep Tom and Brian out of it, you know what they're like. They'll band together and go off at half cock. If we tell them that we're already on it, they'll wait.'

'That'll be a first. And when, pray, did you take decisions about what this Frais does?'

'Since it became obvious. Would you do different?'

Fee stared hard at Sophie. She was right. She sighed.

'Okay, you're right. But don't make a habit of it. And don't go off at half cock yourself. We will deal with this, and we will deal with it together. No heroics. Your rule. No loose cannons, no suicide missions.'

Sophie pointed her two index fingers at her sisters, pretending to hold a gun.

'You got it. See you.'

'And take Gene with you!' Zoe yelled as the door opened.

'Bye.'

'Zoe. I want you to transcribe that wraithweave for me.'

'Already done.'

'So soon?'

'I've got voice recognition software. Got it off Theo. He's a lazy bugger sometimes.'

Sophie returned with the sad remains of Luke's smashed camera and Matt with an overnight bag. He still looked haggard and worn, and could barely raise a smile in greeting. Zoe picked at the broken corpse until she could extract the card with a pair of tweezers. Dusting it off with a camel hair brush, she inserted it into Sophie's Halina and plugged it into her computer. A download window opened.

'Paydirt.'

'These were the last photos he took.' Matt's voice wavered.

'Buck up, Matt, we've barely started putting Luke back together. And we will. Once we sort this mess out. Promise.' Fee hugged him. None of the Frais were stirring the wyth now. Tempting Fate was okay, but only when the odds were in your favour. Until they knew what this shadow man was up to, or who he was, no-one would risk it. The word had gone out. It had begun to trickle into the other Families, too. No-one, not even a Mysten, can stop bad news like this spreading. No matter what you said, the whispers went out. Keeping real danger to yourself was a bit unethical. Not to tell Auntie Fran (for example) that there was some sort of trouble in the air? Bite your tongue. It said, beware. We think there is a predator on our turf. His eye may be on you, so be careful. It had been a long time since the Fratris had this sort of crisis to deal with. Real enemies didn't pop up often. Oh, there were spats. Fur flew, curses sizzled the air, but it was all a flash in the pan. A visit from Uncle Tom had the habit of settling such petty disputes. Really quickly. Tom had a devastating way with squabblers. He would bash their heads together, and once they regained consciousness, would threaten to come back and break their legs if they started up again. He had an excellent track record. No less effective was his brother, Robert, their late father. He was more likely to enquire carefully into the matter and suggest a solution. Well, more like demand, really. A hint to the warring parties that Tom or Robert were on their way tended to settle differences on the spot. But Robert was dead, and Tom had put up his staff years ago. But, as he said, once a Wythwode, always a Wythwode. The only flaw in this otherwise faultless plan was the time element. Did Luke have enough time, or was it running out? They could hardly raise wyth and Gya now to find out. All they could do was plough on regardless. Dangerous, that.

Small icons began to appear on Zoe's computer. At least Luke downloaded the images regularly, unlike Sophie. The last time she had asked Zoe to process the results from her Halina, it took so long that Zoe refused to do it again. Luke had been busy. It was almost a complete record of his day. Shots of the valley and the village. Panoramas of sky and moor. Trees against the sky. Some small studies of plants. One very nice image of spider webs, shining with dew, on gorse. One bucolic cow, and a small herd of ponies drinking at a stream. A shot of Bridlip Tor against the sky.

'Here we go.' Zoe called up the images one by one. Four heads crowded round the flat screen monitor. A tumble of rocks with a peewit. Some studies of Sophie on the skyline. Wide skies, with dots that were buzzards. A few vague panoramas. Nothing.

'Another dead horse.'

'Hhhmm,' muttered Sophie. 'Funny he took all those shots of me. He must have been using the motor drive. I thought that the man left just before Luke arrived. He *must* have seen him.'

'Perhaps he saw him, but didn't take any pictures; he can be sensitive that way. Privacy and all. He knows you don't mind, and I don't mind, but Fee does. He doesn't snap Fee unless she knows he is going to.'

'But these here, they aren't his style. No framing, no emphasis, as if there's something missing.'

'Perhaps they were the buzzards and he missed them.'

'Perhaps? I don't know. Maybe it's all so strange I am reading things that aren't there.'

'And maybe this geezer can bugger up cameras as well as mobile phones. Same technology, really.'

'Great.'

Zoe shoved a memory stick into the computer and saved the pictures. She turned away from the screen.

'There is one thing we haven't considered.'

'Eh?'

'What if… what *if*…. Luke *had* taken pictures of Sophie and this geezer?'

'But he didn't.'

'Unless what he saw didn't register on the camera. What do we know that does that?'

'Come on!' Sophie scoffed. 'Are you trying to say I met a vamp in broad daylight on Bridlip Tor?'

'Well, did you?'

'Absolutely not. I'd have known. I'd have felt his sig.'

'Do *not* use gobbledegook round me.'

'Look, you know how vamps disturb the wyth?'

'There's no wyth in them. Kinda like a black hole?'

'Nah. Dad called it occultation. Don't curl your lip at me.'

'Ah. That's when you know something's there because it comes between you and the light. You don't see it, exactly, but you can see the shadow of where it is.'

'Exactly. The mete are like that. Think of stones in a stream. The water, the wyth, flows around them and makes ripples. When they flow together, the ripples either reinforce each other or cancel each other out.'

'We did that in Physics.'

'You can sort-of hear it. Thump-thump. Like there's something beating a tattoo inside your eardrums. Once heard, never forgotten. You sense that, and you know the mete are about.'

'And you draw your wyth in, and your claws come out.'

'Oh, yeah. Well, there was nothing like that. So unless some mete has learned to fill themselves up with wyth, *and* walk in the sunlight, what I met on Bridlip was *not* a vampire.'

'Bang goes the theory.'

'There's something else. This 'accident' has none of the earmarks of our life-challenged friends. You've heard Theo wax lyrical about how special we are to the mete?'

'More than once.'

'So tell me, would a mete refuse the chance to partake of our unique, special blood if the opportunity arose?'

'Suppose not.'

'There you are, then. It's not the mete.'

Zoe sighed, and slumped. Fee glanced at the clock.

'Who's making dinner? The Frais will be here soon, and we need to eat.'

Not even Sophie's pasta primaverde, her signature dish, could make them feel like eating. The four of them sat round the kitchen table, forking pasta, not tasting it. It was a miserable meal, and they did not linger.

First to arrive were Ellen and Tom. There was no question of keeping Tom out of it. Luke was his son. The hospital had called. Luke had opened his eyes, but apart from that, there was no change in his condition. He was still unresponsive. Ffion wondered about that, but said nothing. Maybe her attempts to free Luke's wraith from the 'dark place' had been the cause. If so, it might have been a monumental blunder, considering the severity of Luke's head injury. People are usually unconscious for a very good reason, and bringing them back too soon might be worse than not bringing them back at all. Still, Fee could not have lived with knowing Luke was being held as some sort of hostage in an unknown game of cat-and-mouse by an opponent who apparently had the ability to command the dead. How was that? He was probably much safer tied to the ruins of his body than to be left in the toils of the shadow man, whoever *that* was. It was far from ideal, but it was the best she was going to get. She moved on.

Jerry had cobbled together a CD of music, birdsong, wind and bubbling streams which was playing by Luke's bedside. News travels superfast in small communities, and Luke was an especial friend. No doubt the computers in Jerry's bedroom had been running on overdrive seeking out salient knowledge about the treatment of head injuries, and the CD was the first result of his researches. He had also lent a i-pod from his collection, and earphones, so the noise wouldn't annoy the hospital staff. Zoe muttered at this, since she had planned to do the same and Jerry had stolen a march on her. Still, he was one busride from the hospital, whereas she, Zoe, was far enough to deserve two buses, one of them which went only twice daily. That or wheedle someone into driving her. With Tom gone, that left Margie, and the world could end before Zoe got into a car with Margie at the wheel again. 'Once was enough.'

Claire was next, with Josie in tow. ('I'm not leaving her alone. And I'm not sending her to Alec. He wouldn't notice a contrary wythen if you hit him with it. All the sensitivity of a roast goose.') Claire and Alec had parted company by mutual agreement after they had produced Josie. Alec had eyes for a pretty young thing in Exeter. Truth to tell, he had eyes for every pretty young thing, whether in Exeter or anywhere else. He sowed his wild oats far and wide, and not even the sacred state of matrimony put the brakes on his philandering. Claire had a novel approach to the problem of her wandering spouse. She collected all his conquests, one of them pregnant, and brought them home. To do this, she had cheated. More than suspecting that Alec played away from home, she had watched him in the locksey mirror. 'Made me sick, some of it, to see him letching at some girl young enough to be his kid.' Nausea notwithstanding, she had persisted in her investigations of Alec's private sexual encounters. Then she had gone to meet each and every one of Alec's 'girls'. Belly in forefront, she had met each one and befriended them. (Cheating again: a simple weave intended to win trust, initiate friendship and be amenable to suggestion. What girl, accosted by the blatantly pregnant wife of the man she was sleeping with, usually falls in with her plans to bring the aforementioned roué to book? And meekly agrees to up stumps, go live with the cuckolded wife and handful of other girls, all of whom had been sleeping with the same man who had vowed sole and undying love to her alone? Alec was lazy in this respect: he only had one seduction technique and he used it all the time. At least, the throes of lust, he had never called one of the girls by the name of another. Miracles do happen, even if you don't deserve them,) Claire had filled the house with these nubile young females, then invited Alec to cut his travelling costs by keeping them, all of them, right under his own roof, there with her. It would never have worked. While most of the girls, under the influence of the wyth, were friendly to Claire, none of them could stand any of the others. Claire and Alec lived in a storm of squabbles and catfights for two weeks until he capitulated. The girls left. One of them promised Alec faithfully to cut off his balls if she ever saw him again. Claire was still friends with that one: they exchanged e-mails regularly, and it was Claire who went to the hospital when Pat went into labour. Asked if she were Pat's mother, she said, with the most winning smile in the world, 'No. I'm the wife of her baby's father.' The staff shook their heads and went away bemused.

 Margie and Jean arrived at the same time as Lottie and Carl. Margie and Jean were relics from the original Frais inherited from Lily's grandmother. She and Robert had ruled it in their turn, and passed it on to Fee. One a widow, one a spinster, they had set up house together, and got on like a house on fire. A real one. They argued constantly, but criticise one in front of the other and they closed ranks like a rat trap. The arguments and bickering masked the fact that, deep down, each one liked and admired the other, but neither would admit it openly. Their constant jibbing and digging at each other could set your teeth on edge. They did it to other people, too. Nothing was below their notice. They had all the local gossip: who was sleeping with whom behind whose back, who was in the family way and shouldn't be, and who wasn't who should be. All the village news came to their ears eventually, and they were not above ferreting it out if it didn't get to their door quickly enough. They had earned Zoe's early enmity by asking why she didn't wear a liberty bodice, a fact they discovered upon seeing her one bright sunny day, earning a fiver from her father by washing his car. She had stripped off to a tiny blue bikini top, regardless of the fact she had little, if anything to conceal around the upper deck, and cut-off jeans. So they sent her one for her birthday. Zoe was not impressed. Interfering old biddies, she called them, and that was the most polite epithet in her vocabulary. They had managed to mollify her slightly by suggesting 'recipts' for hair washes and skin creams, some of which made it into Blue Moon's products.

Lottie and Carl were heavily pregnant. Carl regarded Lottie's physical state as his own. 'We're pregnant,' he had announced. It was 'our bump'. Despite this affirmation of twosomeness, Lottie was still expected to keep the house spotless, the home fires burning and cater for his physical, sexual and emotional needs at home on her own in 'their' house. Carl had very old-fashioned ideas about 'Men's work' and 'Women's work'. He brought home the bacon, and he expected Lottie to give tangible evidence of her gratitude by keeping him in the manner in which he intended to become accustomed. To be fair, Lottie was as much responsible for this state of affairs as was Carl. She was a born homemaker and a competent if unimaginative cook. She ran up curtains, cushion covers and other soft furnishing on her Singer Electric. She made all her own dresses. These skills she farmed out, bringing her in a fairly decent sum of pin money, if it was sporadic. But on some things, maybe baby hormones were responsible, she rebelled. The final screaming match had been spectacular. In the front garden. Lottie had earmarked a room for the expected new arrival which was full of 'stuff' that they had no room for elsewhere. Most of it was Carl's - old bits of a motorcycle he was reconstructing in the spare bedroom. Despite repeated requests for help to remove the larger chunks, some of which were unwieldy and heavy, and quite unsuitable for pregnant woman to try to move by herself, Carl persisted in coming home, flopping down in a chair with the paper and expecting some of Lottie's cooking to appear on the table. On that fateful day, Lottie had spent most of the time trying, and failing, to manoeuvre the best part of a motorbike out of the bedroom and down the stairs. It had stuck, and Lottie, after a storm of weeping, had given up and gone back home. To Ellen and Tom. When Carl arrived home from the garage where he worked, there was an absence of Lottie. No cup of cheering tea after a hard day. No food on the table. Only the motorbike perched ominously on the stairs. Supposing that Lottie had indeed gone home for help, he went outside, where he found the returning Lottie. 'Where's my dinner?' is a bad place to start a reconciliation. So is, 'you could have asked', when the respondent had asked more than once. This Lottie told him, at length and at high volume. She had had enough, she told him. This stops now. To put the cap on it, Tom then hoved into view, a battle cruiser in full sail, all cannon locked and loaded. 'I thought better of you, son, I really did. That's my daughter and grandson there (Ellen had been at her tricks again. The ultrasound only confirmed later what everyone already knew. Lottie's bump was a boy,) and you're not doing right by them. Not doing right at all.' Tom shook his head sorrowfully and walked away. Carl, who fully expected at least a supersonic fist and a period of blessed oblivion from Lottie's screaming, submitted to the inevitable.

 After a consult with Tom, Carl built a large shed in the back garden. Some of his mates from work helped. Tom lent a hand. They raised the shed in one day while Lottie, dressed in a bikini ('I don't have a one piece bathing suit,') took her ease in a garden lounger, shaded from the sun by a vast sunhat and oversize sunglasses, sipped cool drinks and watched them. She relented sufficiently to produce cold beer and sandwiches at lunchtime. By the time evening was painting the sky, all the motorcycle parts were rehoused in the new shed, and the back bedroom was waiting for a coat of paint. Love fifteen to Lottie.

The only one missing was Abby. Mind you, since she was off with John, her phone was most likely switched off. She would call eventually. Maybe it was for the best, her staying with John…….at least he wouldn't be alone, and he, of all of the adults, was most vulnerable.

The Frais disposed themselves on the mismatched seating, and helped themselves to Old Brown Java, orange pekoe and biscuits. Cecile had been busy again, and had flitted by just after dark. All right, so the Jammie Dodgers were in the shape of bats. They were delicious all the same. She had offered halfhearted condolences. She knew the correct forms, but there was no real feeling in it. How could there be? She was meta. 'Such a sweet boy. So polite, always.' She had sort-of abducted the seven year old Luke to show him where the bats roosted. Luke had gone willingly. When Tom realized his son was in the clutches of a vampire, he had fired up the Jeep and nearly broken the suspension driving to prevent what he thought of as the inevitable. He had found Cecile and Luke by the mouth of the cave, Cecile lying against a boulder, Luke's head in her lap, her long white fingers playing with his baby blonde curls. Tom had launched his famous haymaker, only to have it caught in a delicate fist. 'Let's not be unfriends about this.' Luke was not only unharmed, he was enchanted. 'Bats, Dad. All flying about. So cool.' 'Bats get rabies, son,' was all Tom could say. Cecile would not have harmed him: not then. She preferred her pash more mature. And Theo would have punished her for it, for a while at least.

To say the Frais meeting went badly was the understatement of the decade. Ellen would not take the sister's word for it that a healing wythen, *any* wythen, might bring down unexpected consequences. As his mother, she had a driving need to use her skills to repair her son. Armageddon might stop her, little else could. Matt would support neither point of view. He still seemed to be in a state of shock. Margie and Jean refused point-blank to consider the very idea of an enemy using wyth or cys against the Frais. 'It doesn't happen. It just doesn't.'

'What about the Red Night?' Zoe asked, with venom. Being one of the only two people with any direct experience of the shadow man, she was in full battle mode. Especially as the two old biddies' first comment as they entered the room had been 'You ought to send young Zoe out. She's too immature for this. This is Frais business anyway, and she's not a farer.' 'Neither is Josie, in case you've forgotten, AND she's younger than me. You didn't ask for her to be sent out,' riposted Zoe, quite accurately. Claire would not hear of Josie being anywhere but at her side, Ffion and Sophie defended Zoe both on the basis that, firstly, no-one was to be left alone and that included being with another youngster: and secondly, that she had been intimately involved in the wraithweave and therefore had more right to be here than anyone. Margie and Jean persisted until Tom backed up Ffion.

'It's her Frais. She's our Mysten. So it's her decision. If she says Zoe stays, I'll back her.' Claire added her vote to his. That made it four against two, since Lottie and Carl had no strong feelings either way about the matter. The old biddies subsided, muttering. 'It's not right,' sotto voce.

The 'Red Night' to which Zoe referred had been a turning point in the Frais' history. In those days, Jean had been the Frais Mysten, and her husband, Andrew, the Mysta. Lily had brought Robert to the Frais and married him. Robert proved to be not only a brilliant Cyscan, but a better judge of horseflesh (as Tom put it, but then he was biased, being Rob's brother) than Andrew. Jean, riding on a Sixties wave of hedonism, free love and an upsurge in mystery and magic, was intent on expanding the Frais to include anyone, whether they had wyth or not. She rode roughshod over the objections of the Eldren in the Frais, now all dead. Especially Rina. She disapproved of Rina's association with the vampires. Only because she had wanted that for herself, but had been passed over by Theo. That really rankled. The reason Rina did not head the coven at that time was because she was too old, she said. She had 'gracefully retired in favour of a younger woman' as the skyen gently suggested - much against her better judgement. Jean wanted notoriety to rival that of the new upstarts who were all over the Sunday rags like a rash. She would have succeeded but for the resistance of her Eldren. 'Act in haste, regret at leisure,' they told her. Further, if she persisted, they would banish her. They had Lily and Robert. If it had come to a vote then, Lily and Robert would have carried the day. Jean had a haughty streak in her a mile wide, but she was full blooded Family, and she held her ground. And moderated her ambitions. Slightly.

Shortly after this, Robert began to notice that petty things were going wrong. There was an air of unease about the home he shared with Lily, Rina having moved out of Pippin Cottage by that time and living in the Orchard, now occupied by Lottie and Carl. He was woken at night by feelings of foreboding he could not place. Weird smells drifted through the rooms, some nice, some not so nice. No-one else could detect them, only Rob. A picture fell off the wall, scattering glass over the hallway. Rob was by now very suspicious, and he took his concerns to the Frais. Jean pooh-poohed the idea of wythens being responsible for the events he complained about. He went away with little more than a half-hearted appeal to the Gya. Rina had been less sure of Jean's assessment. Using the excuse of Lily's advanced pregnancy, she moved back into the cottage 'in order to help with the baby.' The very first thing she did was burn incense and candles in the fireplace. 'Wraiths of the house, take heed and live. To every room this light I give. To every corner, breath I send. Favour now my willing hand.' She then proceeded to clean the place from top to bottom, opening every door even on the cupboards and drawers in every room, and every window. As she completed each room, she closed all the doors and windows, finally ringing a bell to each corner of the finished room, and placed saucers of vinegar, each holding a freshly cut onion, on every windowsill. It took her all day. She finished in the front hall, at sunset, sweeping a pile of dust out of the front door and closing it. Only then did she allow Lily and Robert back into the place. 'I need a cup o' tea after all that. Make us one, will you, love.' All continued quietly until bedtime. Rina settled down in the room next to the master bedroom where Lily and Rob slept. Late that night, she was roused by Lily's screams. Clad in her red flannel nightgown, she had rushed into the room, grabbing the first thing to hand - a fireside poker from the companion set in the hearth. Robert, his lips an unhealthy blue and his face suffused with blood, was gasping on the pillow next to his wife, thrashing around and growling under his breath. One flailing arm had hit Lily, and she had given voice. Rina did not hesitate. Quicker than a wink, she had a wyth-spaca surrounding the bed, Lily, Robert and herself. A down-and-dirty exorcism followed. 'Sod off, you bugger. I knows the likes of you. Sod off down the pits of Hell or I'll skelp your arse, see if I don't.' It might not have been traditional, but it worked. If Rina could see off a vampire and give him stomach ache to boot, she was not about to stand any nonsense from the Asha. In the face of her determination and rage, the said wraith departed. Robert subsided, woke up and asked 'What the hell is going on?' Rina and Lily gave him chapter and verse. No-one felt like sleeping any more, so Rina, still armed with the fireside poker, went downstairs to make tea. 'Good as a wythstaff any day, a proper poker.' They sat on the bed until daybreak, the poker by Rina's hand, then went downstairs to the kitchen and ate a hearty breakfast. 'You'd better come see me later,' Rina had told Rob. 'You and I need to discuss things.' Thus, Robert became Rina's apprentice cyscan and learnt a lot of things that were not common knowledge. That night became known as 'Red Night' in honour of Rina's flannel nightie.

   Rina called a full council of the Frais. Not only had a Family member been attacked, it had been done on Jean's watch, and she had missed it. Completely. Jean tried to bluster. It was a poltergeist. Nasty but nothing a full blood family member was incapable of dealing with on their own. This slight of her husband started Lily off. If it was a mere poltergeist, why did she, Lily, not notice? She was full blood, after all. Was Jean calling her defective too? The Eldren cut that line right off. If they might have an enemy, it would not do to be bickering amongst themselves. Rina sat, saying nothing, until the various opinions had all been aired. Finally, someone asked her opinion. About time, she sniffed. She pointed at the mantelshelf, where a line of saucers, each one containing a shrivelled half of an onion, sat in a row. 'What do you call that then?' was all she said. It was enough.

This forced a chastened Jean to convene the Frais for a full wythweaving. She passed control of the spaca over to a dominant Rina. 'None of your apologetic stuff, my girl. These buggers don't understand please and thank you. All they understand is the wyth. Herbs and incense and candles and dancing with your knickers off is all very well and good, but we're at the sharp end now.' And Rina, standing in the candlelight tall and proud, a black robe swirling round her ankles as she moved, gave them a masterclass in 'the sharp end'. By the time she made an end, the group was covered with sweat and shaking with exhaustion. Rina held the spaca from sunset until well past midnight. She had done her preparations in the daylight hours, so by the time they were finished, she had been on the go for well over forty-eight hours - a considerable feat for a lady well past her eighties. A veritable tour de force. She finished towering over a triangle which gleamed darkly in the subdued light of the candles. Outlined in incense smoke, a figure seemed to cower. She held a wythstick over it. 'You're beat, son. Admit it, and we can all go home.' A whisper moved the air. It sounded like, 'I acknowledge you the victor. I submit to your Cys. Do as you will.' 'Then I pronounce you subject to the justice of the Aya. Go thou, and never trouble this place again. By my will, so shall it be.' The figure wavered and vanished with a faint 'Thank God....' There was a sort of twang, like your knicker elastic giving way, and everything went back to relatively normal. Rina handed control back to Jean with a 'Finish this off properly now, will you, m'dear. I'm going to bed. Anyone else want cocoa?' The frais collapsed into a faintly giggling, slightly hysterical heap. Jean tried hard for dignified, but failed. She did as she had been told.

That heralded the beginning of the end for Jean's mystency. It might have been the strain of the wythens, or it might not. Andrew, it appeared, was not a well man. He started to waste away. He might have been wasting already and no-one noticed.

He became weaker. A short walk round the village would leave him gasping. Jean took over the village store from him, running it with a firm hand and help from her best friend Margie. The Frais locksey'd, they called wyth and Gya, but to no avail: Andrew continued to decline. Margie used her extensive knowledge of herbs. She was the Frais' leech after all. Doctors were consulted, specialists called in. They examined Andrew's progressing weakness and loss of flesh, his breathlessness and pains in his joints. Rina talked to the vampires and eliminated them. They wove spaca of wyth around Andrew's bed and house. Whatever was ailing Andrew was purely physical. It was as if his body was giving up. Finally, Jean asked the Frais' Eldren to read Andrew's weirden, his life path, his future. No-one asks for that lightly. Knowledge of the future has its own dangers, its own prices to pay. Whatever else her faults, she truly loved Andrew. She was not alone. His illness affected all the Frais. The readings were not encouraging. Andrew was dying, and he would take a long time about it. Jean asked Rina, tearfully, if anything could be done. Fred was still walking about, wasn't he? Rina was gentle. She would not ask Theo again. Even if she did, it would spell the end of Jean and Andrew's life together, unless Jean embraced the meten-nature herself. Jean was enough of a farer to see the defects in this, and did not ask again. The Fratris embraced the precept of reincarnation, living through the eternal years by entering and leaving the Midess, to re-enter it again and again, always changing, always growing. Metae were fixed in place in the Midess, they didn't grow or change. Go the pretty way, Rina had advised. Take the blessing of forgetfulness from the hands of the Arda. Do you want to continue through life, with all your guilt, forever? Remembering everything that you did, and wishing, forever, that you could have done it differently? And knowing that you were stuck with the memories, the burning guilt, forever?

    Jean gave up pride of place in her turn to Robert and Lily. She had nursed Andrew every day for the rest of his life. It did not really soften her. Ffion had young memories of the wasted Andrew, sitting in dappled sunlight in the orchard, tiny flower petals falling like rain around him, wrapped in a soft pale blanket against the chill of the spring breeze. Andrew sitting by the fire, sipping a hot tisane. Andrew lying in bed, his hand grasping the patchwork coverlet, partly asleep from drugs at the end. Andrew, in a box, covered in flowers at the county crematorium. Andrew's ashes, scattered beneath apple trees, their petals falling once more, their white-and-pink mixing with the grey dust. 'May you return eternally….'

Jean and Margie ran the village store until old age, the great leveller, forced them to stop. Jean still made jams and chutneys, Margie distilled herbs in the old bathhouse. She distilled other things too, which were best not talked about. They moved from old age into a state of stasis, growing no older, as if they would persist for ever, kind and cantankerous by turns, a fact of life.

Mention of her nemesis chastened Jean anew.

'If you feel you must consider this option, then we will. You were there, I was not. I will accept your interpretation.'

'Big of you,' Zoe muttered, careful that it would not be heard.

'One thing's for sure. We can't risk the wyting now. If Sophie can be taken in, John'll be a pushover.'

'With that I wholeheartedly agree. We cannot risk him. Indeed, it might be a good thing if he and Abby went up to Lanark to Effie. They planned to do that after the wyting, on Sunday.'

'He'll enjoy that.'

'Sarcasm does not become you, Zoe.'

'We must help Luke. Can't you see that? We have to.' Ellen was not giving up.

'We will help him, Aunt Ellen. I never said we couldn't, or ought not to. Only that we must take precautions. I'm not sure my weave really freed him from that dark place he talked about. We will have to do that sooner or later. And to do that we will have to confront this shadow man. If we have to do that, we need to be ready.'

'What if Luke was not the real target? Perhaps he wanted Sophie. Perhaps Luke coming on them like that skewed his plans, so he kills Luke before going after Sophie again?'

'We've been through this. As far as we know, he was after

Luke. Sophie was collateral damage.'

'And he didn't. Go after me again, I mean. I went to Falmouth. Why didn't he follow me there? Did he spend so much time on Luke that I had already left Bridlip Tor to drive to Falmouth? It took me an hour at least to get back to the car. He had me like that,' Sophie snapped her fingers, 'so how long would it have taken him to deal with Luke and then come after me? And he trapped Luke in that dark place. No, he wanted Luke. Why?'

'Too many whys, girl, not enough answers.'

'I agree, Tom. Can we locksey him and be safe?'

'I'd leave him alone. Luke can't tell you what he did. Luke's camera can't tell you what he did. Where are you going to go now, for answers?'

Ffion sat, considering.

'I could ask the stones. They have different memories, though. A day is like a flicker to a troll. Something that took a hour or so would be like trying to follow a lightning flash. Hhmm.'

'What are you considering? A family fun day in the Asha?'

'Something like that. The three of us could do it. Two to raith, one to stay behind and ride shotgun. You up for it, Sophie? Mouse?'

'So long as I don't get to be the gooseberry, I'm game.'

'No, Sophie will be the best one for that. She's got the most sensitive antenna for danger. And you've got this trick of seeing things no-one else can. I think we'll need that.'

'What if someone were to create a diversion? Weave a spaca to draw the eye away from everything else? Then another group could start using wyth for Luke. No matter how good a cyscan this man is, he can only deal with one thing at a time. If there's one group of us making a loud noise, another going on a quest into the Asha and a third quietly weaving, which one would you go for? Not the quiet weavers, you'll go for the noisy ones or the questers. Anyhow, we need to help Luke now that you've already interfered. If his wraith is free, it will be no use if he has no body to call home. We'll lose him. We need to look at that head injury. If it's too bad, we must reconsider.'

Give her her due, Jean had a mind like a rat trap at times.

'We'll do that then. If you and Margie can take Claire to help you, then Ellen can start with what she does best, with Tom and Matt to help her.'

'That's not what I meant……..'

'Jean, you are brilliant at ritual. You pack a real wallop. I always know when you're weaving. If we want someone to catch the eye, you're our man. Woman.'

'I can't persuade you out of this foolishness, can I.'

'No, you can't. Whatever you meant, you suggested it. So, you do it. It's your baby.'

'What happens if I do attract any attention?'

'According to you, there is no attention to attract. If you get to feel squiffy, let go of the Gya. If anything looks like making contact, just melt away. Act squeamish, like girl surprised by a man's hand down her drawers.'

'Tom, really! Tiny ears!'

'Jean, Jean, if you don't know that I don't give a rat's arse by now, you don't know me. And you've known me long enough. Come on, Claire. Josie can come with us, her'll be safe hidden in our rath. Have you got a bag? No? I suppose we can scare up something for you to wear in bed from the tribe. And a toothbrush. An' you too, Matt. Might do you some good, old son. That'll be three and three and three. What time will you start, Jean? I wouldna want to beat the gun, like.'

Jean looked at her watch.

'My, is that the time? We have chattered on. Let's say ten o'clock. Is that all right with you girls?' She was trying for pleasant now she had no other options.

'That will suit us fine.'

'Not too late for Zoe?'

'She stays up playing with the computer all hours. You have no idea what time she calls bedtime,' Sophie chipped in, seeing Zoe's mouth open for a rude rejoinder. She turned her head close to Zoe's ear, so no-one could see her face. 'Let it go, Zoe, while Tom's got them on the back foot.' Zoe's face flicked from insult to good will like that.

'There are still some cakes left over. Do you want any? I'll get a bag.' She exited hastily into the kitchen. Fee heard a muffled explosion of laughter. She didn't think anyone else did.

Lottie had been quiet during these exchanges. Typical of her. She would look, and listen, then accept whatever had been decided without a word, like a sponge. Brooding over her enormous belly, perhaps.

'What do you want us to do?' she asked, heaving her bulk off the chair she had insisted on dragging in from the kitchen.

'Thank you, Lottie. I want you and Carl to watch. Just watch. Do it in a wythspach that nothing can cross. If you sense anything, close the wyth, close it right down. You are not, I repeat, not, to engage in anything else. All of you, call me in the morning, and we'll compare notes. Everything matters now. If an owl so much as twits, I want to know about it. And I will set the wards too. Use your faths, and do the same. I want eyes in every clump of grass by morning, and I want them to be my eyes. Let's go.'

Chapter Four

In the Roundhouse, three robed and hooded figures stood in a circle, holding hands. Rob, their father, had decided one day that the glade in the woods was too uncontrolled an environment for him to practice his cys in. Actually, when he got caught in a hailstorm he had muttered "Bugger this for a lark," and set himself to provide an alternative that he felt was an improvement on an unweatherproof woodland glade. There were too many distractions, he said. And when the place froze solid, it could be a bitch to get to. Pippin Cottage had been just big enough for the two of them. Squeezing in other one or even two or three bodies in any room in the place was well-nigh impossible. It just wasn't built for it. So he opted instead to improve matters by adding a sun room on the back of the parlour. He had drawn up the plans, talked to the local builder, Ron Hopkiss, who found a supplier for the glass and they were away. It sat in the corner where the kitchen jutted out from the back wall. Originally it had been a sad, dreary courtyard, devoid of sun and haunted by incontinent cats and moss. Not even ivy grew happily there. It was further shaded by a mature conifer, one of the detested Leylandii happily planted with gay abandon and ignorance of the consequences for hedges and then grubbed out later at great expense when the sod reached twenty feet and cut out all the light. Whoever had planted this one had been either mental or just plain daft. It was fully sixty feet high and dominated that corner of the garden. With much sweating and swearing, assisted by a Landrover winch and his brother Tom, Rob had removed it, leaving a gaping hole. He then made some fairly careful measurements, hammered a stake into the lawn and tied a string to it. A few moments later the footprint of the conservatory had been marked out in red paint, cutting through the flower borders and the lawn. It had looked, as Lily said, sodding enormous. Rob was not to be deterred. Two days later he was pouring concrete into a trench and the dread deed was done. The builder arrived and installed a low wall of local granite. There was plenty of building stone around if one cared to ask for it. Things were always falling down and being rebuilt. Lily, huge with what would turn out later to be Fee, wandered over and opined that she thought the red line delineated the inner wall, and not the outer. There was a full and frank exchange of opinions, and the wall came down. Lily assumed the role of project manager, since she was on site all the time. The wall went back up. Lily commented on the fact that it was a pity that there was no way into the new annex from the kitchen. Another wall went in. A jobbing carpenter arrived to erect the frame while Rob and Tom laid a damp proof membrane and screed on the floor inside. A couple of men arrived in a truck marked 'GreenGlow' and proceeded to install underfloor heating. This would be powered by solar energy. Heat from the top of the roof would be pumped into a vast pit in the centre of the floor - a heat sink. Alternatively, it could be run from the mains if the solar sink couldn't be charged by heat from the sun. It was intended to be a warm, cosy place. Expecting the glass to arrive the next day, Rob had borrowed a masonry saw and chopped through underneath the back window, opening a gaping maw into the parlour. Lily spat nails when on the morrow the glass failed to materialize. Rob blocked up the hole with a sheet of ply and Rina lent a large patchwork bedspread to reduce the draughts further.

Two weeks sitting in a chilly parlour had brought the relationship to a similar level of frigidity when the glass finally arrived and the hole no longer spewed freezing air into the room. Vast sheets of glass were slotted into place with much puffing and heaving and swearing. Special plastic sheets went into the roof. They had channels inside. Pumps were connected to the channels and the warm air blown down pipes set in the frame which led to the solar sink. Tom had commented acidly on the extra work involved in that part of the project. It was too complex, he sneered. Still, even he had to admit, once the project had been completed that it worked. Other people objected too. It was not in character with the village, they said. But since the erection could not be seen unless you were actually standing in the garden, *and* the man from the Council said that since that was the case it complied with planning regulations, they had to let it go. By now it had become Rob's Roundhouse and no-one thought any more of it.

Rob laid moss-green mosaic tiles on the floor. He had taken his inspiration from the floors of Roman baths. Lily had almost forgiven him for the premature destruction of the parlour wall when he suddenly shot off at a tangent, abandoned the floor and began building a shed from the inside out. Once Lily had calmed down enough to listen (had shouted herself to a standstill, actually) Rob explained that since he had run out of a certain colour of tile, he was amusing himself by erecting a sauna while he waited for them to become available. Lily was amenable to this planning deviation, once it had been explained. The sauna was shelved once more tesserae arrived, and Rob let his imagination run riot. When he had finished there was a circular design on the floor with animals and plants in the corners. It took a knowing eye to see the glyphs in the designs, but they were there. Rob had created an indoor outdoor temple.

Lily filled it with ferns, mind-your-own-business (She mentioned this deliberately to some people. They really ought to mind their own business) Kentia palms and a fig tree that covered the wall outside the kitchen. Other plants appeared until the entire place became almost a green cave.

Four small tealights in frosted glass holders marked the quarters of a double circle marked out on the tiles. Between them, bowls of water and salt, herbs and incense dotted the perimeter of the circle between words and complex siga. Ffion was leaving no i undotted, no t uncrossed. A belt and braces job, as Rina would have it. In the centre of the complex spaca, where they stood, was a five pointed star, the points of which touched the outer circle. More siga decorated that.

Zoe had rebelled against wearing the heavy black robe. She was young enough, and pretty enough, to be vain. She had wanted to wear a wispy blue nothing in floaty georgette, but had been heavily overruled.

'You will be lying, still, on the floor. You will get cold. Believe me, I know.'

They had been breathing together for several minutes, first in harmony, then in counterpoint. Breathe in. Hold. Breathe out.

Hold. The cleansing breath. The energising breath. They had started the sequence standing, holding hands, pulling the Gya up through the soles of their feet, their legs, their spine, and out through the crowns of their heads, washing down and back to the earth. They exchanged wyth. Breathe in; pull the wyth through your right hand, up your arm, across your chest, into your belly. Hold. Breathe out; circle the energy up from your belly, down your other arm and into your left hand. Hold. Breathe in, pull the wyth into your right hand……. until it was flowing like a river from sister to sister round the circle.

They sat down cross legged, knees touching, eyes closed. In the centre of the spaca, they imagined a door. A very particular door. They were going slowly, and not only for the benefit of the youngest, the lente. If something went wrong, Ayen forbid, they would need the wythen they were channelling now.

Finally, Sophie stood up. She would not be joining her sisters on this excursion, but would be the link back to the spaca, and safety, for the other two. She was the castellan, the keeper of the spaca. They linked hands, and Sophie placed a hand on each cowled head.

Ffion and Zoe moved to lie head-to-head, foot to foot, their inner hands still linked. Sophie arranged robes and inserted cushions under their heads and knees. She covered their bodies with a soft woollen blanket and tucked it in carefully. The she drew their hoods over their eyes, leaving only their noses and mouths showing. In a low voice, she started to describe the opening of the door.

'You are walking together, holding hands, across a low hill. You are surrounded by mist, grey mist. You walk further, into the mist, the grey mist.' She paused. 'From out of the mist appears a grey stone wall. The wall is higher than you can imagine, the top lost in the grey, grey mist. The wall curves away to the right and left, and there is no end to it. Before your eyes, you see a door set into the stone wall. See the door. It is square and has a pointed arch. It fits closely into the stones which surround it. It is old wood, hard wood, black wood. You can see the grain in the wood, the old, hard grain. In the centre of the door, the very centre, is a raised design. It is green, a green circle cut with a quarter-cross. As the arms of the cross cut the circle, they curve to meet it. It is beautiful. It is glowing with life in this grey, misty world. See it.' She paused again. 'You reach out your hand, your right hand, your left hand, and touch the circle. You trace it with your fingertips. You feel the designs carved into the symbol on the door. Once, your fingers trace the cross. Twice, your fingers trace the cross. Three times your fingers trace the cross. Three times is the charm, the door swings open. As the green, green cross leaves your skin, your fingertips, it draws from your skin a fine, bright cord of woven strands. Close your hand on the cord, it will lead you back to the door, the door between the worlds, back to your body, back to this spaca. Walk through the door, and may the blessings and protection of the Ayen of the Asha be with you on this, your quest.' She fell silent, and sat down by her sisters' heads to keep watch over them.

Fee felt the familiar lurch, the feeling of separation. She had made this journey, or one like it, many, many times. She opened her eyes. She saw the spaca far below her, the wyth pulsing with a bright soft glow like a heartbeat: the twinkling lights of the little candles behind glass: the figure of Sophie, sitting, with her robe drawn about her. Sophie was enveloped with a bright glowing lambency, pale gold and shot through with silver and clear pale green. Her wythlight reached over her head, steady, connected. Fee could see her own body resting down there. Her wythlight was more contracted than Sophie's, pulsing with a warm, red glow. The hue marked her out: it was the signature of the Wardens. Sophie's clear pale green revealed her as a Challiser, a healer. Fee looked at Zoe. Her wythlight was pulsing gently too, and no less bright: but the dominant colour was a clear, clear blue: a rare sign, that of an Intelligencer.

Feeling out beyond the spaca, but oh, so gently, she felt other spaca: Jean, Claire and Margie were noisily tumultuous, ragged, colourful, a fairground blaring and sparkling coloured lights to catch the attention. A softer, but more calculated beat came from Tom's house, or his rath, as he preferred to call it, echoing the ancient Celtic settlements out of the dim and distant past. Quieter still was the watchful presence of Lottie, and behind her, Carl. Fainter still were the echoes from the wards and faths and pharcy that now kept watch over the village and the Fratten within. Of John and Abby there was no trace. That would be Jean, masking their departure for the North and safety. She brought her attention back to her own spaca: it would not do to be caught wandering tonight. There was definitely Something out there: a mighty hunting cat, or some other carnivore: out on the prowl, watching, waiting, assessing the herd for weakness in order to pounce, to kill, to feed. It was enough to make your neck hair ruffle.

As Fee watched, she saw the light surrounding Zoe flicker, dimming a little, then flaring up. Zoe was not so practiced as her sisters at the art of rathing, of separating her mind from her body to range over the Asha free from the constraints of physical form. Come on, girl, she encouraged. You can do it, I know you can. As if in response to this wordless summons, a misty form started to coalesce over Zoe's body. It rose higher and began to take on more definite features, looking more like Zoe. As the wraithform rose, it swung more upright. By the time it reached Fee's level, it was standing artlessly. Fee reached out her left hand. As she touched the wraith of her sister, Zoe's eyes opened.

'Look at you. What on Earth are you wearing?' Zoe's voice was slightly thin, but it had her typical lilt and cadence. Fee looked down. No matter how many times she did this, unless she paid attention she always looked like she was part of the Valkyrie chorus in a Wagner opera. Sophie had called it her 'Brunhilda look'. Zoe was less kind. 'It looks like a tin bra. Thank the Ayen you didn't wear the hat that goes with the costume. You would look really stupid with a horned helmet.'

'Ooops. That sometimes happens. A tinge of Norse blood in here somewhere, I think. I can modify it a bit.'

'Do, do, please do. I am *so* not walking around with a sister in a couple of tin lids looking like a Madonna reject.'

Fee made some discreet adjustments. The skirt less full, hhmm, looks like I'm wearing the sheet off a double bed down there. Embroidery on the bust, a bit less......, NO, NO, never sequins......

'There. Better? And speaking of costumes, have you seen yourself? Talk about the pot calling the kettle black.'

Zoe looked down. Her face assumed a look of sheer horror.

'Ye gods, I look like Pocahontas on a bad day. Where did all these beads and feathers come from?' She felt the fabric of the tunic. 'It's buckskin. I am wearing Bambi here. Please tell me I don't have plaits.' Her hand rose to her hair, and her eyes widened in horror. 'Bugger. Those will have to go.' She closed her eyes and screwed up her face to aid concentration. The plaits unravelled, and her hair wound itself round her head in an elaborate mass of loose curls. A narrow string of pearls threaded through the tresses. Pocahontas' leather morphed into something shorter, sheerer, more blue and floaty.

'A bit less of the trailing stuff, Zoe. You look like an explosion in a ribbon factory.' Zoe made the necessary adjustments.

'That's better.'

Turning her attention away from matters sartorial, Zoe surveyed the landscape. During their exchange, the spaca with its warm, friendly glow and twinkling candles had vanished, to be replaced by a dreary, monotonous landscape of bare, scrubby low hills. The soil beneath their feet was a grey-brown fine sand, stirred by a weak breeze that soughed between the scrub. There was no blade of grass, anywhere. Every bush looked as if it was dying from lack of water. There was no horizon, only a grey mist in the near distance.

'This place always depresses me. I used to think that once you left your body, everything would be brighter, more vibrant….. Prettier, somehow. And then you get this.' She looked around disconsolately. The place didn't deserve that level of condemnation. After all, Zoe had been here before. Usually, the ability to function in these regions of the Asha was only taught under the seal of the wyte, but once Zoe had heard about the place there was literally no keeping her out. Lily had decided there and then to teach the whys and wherefores of the Asha to her youngest offspring. 'I'd feel better knowing exactly where she was and when. Then I wouldn't have to drop everything to go out and rescue her,' she reasoned. Young though she might be, Zoe was therefore a seasoned raither, otherwise Fee would never have considered letting her join this esoteric safari.

'You can make it beautiful, if you want. But no-one stays here very long, so few of the Fratris bother. It's just a way station for most of us. There are some who make realms here: this stuff is just the start, the raw material. You can visit them anytime, you know.'

'Cool. But not today.'

'No, definitely not today. This is not the place to linger. Something might find us.'

'That won't be a problem, I take it.'

'Not for you and me: but it could delay us. All sorts of creatures haunt this place. Some of them hunt. It used to be called the place of nightmares, or Purgatory. Dreams get real here.'

Everyone finds themselves here at some point in their lives. Usually, it was in dreams. If you 'woke up' to a dream where you were running through treacle to get away from something horrible you couldn't see that was chasing you, it was a fair bet that you were here. Most people escaped by waking up in their beds, shaking and covered in sweat with the fragmented memories fading away fast. Fratten knew the best thing to do was stop running, turn round and confront whatever bogyman was chasing you. Fee could recall a series of youthful dreams in which she was being chased by a pack of huge, dribbling dogs. She had run into house after house, slamming doors behind her as she sped in panic through the rooms. It was like trying to swim in mud. No matter how hard she tried, she couldn't get a decent speed, nor increase the bare lead she had on the pack. Either the doors didn't fit, or the slavering beasts were opening them with mutated paws, or they were squeezing through the keyhole or letterbox, either of which seemed unnaturally large. She had ran up and down stairs in a welter of fear, climbed trees only to find the bloody dogs roosting along with her among the branches. Attempts to escape by flying were equally useless. She couldn't get any height to speak of, but was reduced to hedge-skimming with dirty yellow teeth snapping at her ankles. Finally, she had decided it was 'only a dream' and that the dogs, even if they bit her, couldn't hurt her. She knew better now. But she had stopped running, turned and faced the lead canine, a huge, grey wolflike sort of thing. It had leapt at her, and she had rammed her fist into its jaws. It licked her. The bloody thing licked her! It covered her in slobber. She was furious. For some time thereafter, her nightly rambles were accompanied by at least one large dog, tongue lolling, drool everywhere.

One of the more exotic so-called 'ordeals' that a farer had to face as she progressed in the Cys, along with lists of herbs and stones and colours and other mystical crap, as Zoe put it, was to come here, to this place, hunt down and confront one of the 'things' that called this place home. And some of them were right buggers.

'Coo, I'm standing in Freddy Krueger's back yard.'

'Shut up, Zoe. Those things are real here. Think about a monster and it will appear.'

Zoe looked around guiltily. She ought to know better.

'We'd better find the wall, then.'

'Oh, no. It's found *us*.'

Like a rejected cut from The Matrix, a huge grey stone wall created itself out of the nothing, flowing, undulating, looming over them. It came with a sound, a rushing, like the onset of a tornado or a violent flood. Loud, but not-loud. You heard it and you didn't: you kind-of felt it instead. Maybe the wall itself was silent, and your mind supplied the sound because something that big couldn't just *appear*, in ghostlike silence like that. It was a threatening presence in the dreary landscape. It surged interminably from mist to mist, following the landscape, filling the sky, filling everything with a menacing reality. This must be how a Dark Ages foot soldier saw the walls of a Norman castle after the battle commander yelled 'Attack!' It was just, simply, impossible. You knew that it surrounded you, that you could walk forever round the foundations of that wall and never find the end, until you were right back where you started. It was wall, wall, wall, until the ends of the earth. Hadrian would have been proud of a wall like this. Hell, he'd built one. Clear across Britain, to keep out the Picts. This wall was for keeping out the boogie-man, the monster, the dragon. And to keep out *you,* if you didn't belong.

'Think of the door, Zoe.'

'I am *sooo* thinking of the door. Nice Door. Friendly Door. Door out of here.' Before Freddy finds me……..cut that thought out RIGHT NOW.

99

'There are hundreds, thousands, *millions* of doors in this wall. We want the right one. The one that will take up where we need to go.'

Another ordeal, or set of trials, was to find this wall, this door. Further expeditions took you through other doors. You had to be able to get through them and describe what you found on the other side. Later, you would have to find someone, or something else by locating a particular door, and then, finally, making your own door in the wall, and your own private Paradise behind it. Some doors, like this one, led to a collective Paradise shared by a frais who used it as a hangout, to meet, find information and build wyth. Some doors led to your past lives. Some doors might even lead to future lives, if only you could find the buggers…….. Some were harder to find than others. This door, with it's green circle, was very familiar to this Frais. It was 'their' door.

'I *am* thinking.'

'Ah.'

Right in front of the sisters, the door appeared in the stones. No, it didn't appear: it had always been there. Set in a pointed arch of stone was a door, the wood black with age, featureless apart from a bright green disc quadrisected by a cross, the arms flaring out as they met the circumference. The vibrancy of the colour glowed in the dreary world, a precious gem, a carved emerald, now a snake biting its tail, now a leafy head, now a leaping fish, the carving changing as they watched.

'Now, Zoe.'

They each reached out a hand. As they touched the carving, it seemed to flow under their fingers, the stone, surely it was stone and not wood, warm to the touch, alive. Their fingers trailed over the surface once, twice, three times. The carvings began to solidify beneath their skin, writhing, setting, twining.

The door swung away. Another not-sound, like bell tolling, felt not heard, announced to whatever was interested that the door had been opened. The carving on the emerald was now a generous Celtic design of interwoven dragons, two of them, their heads meeting in the centre, their front legs the arms of the cross, their bodies like snakes arcing away to make the outer ring. From their jaws came two lines of light, reaching back to the sisters' fingertips, stretching as the door swung wide, then becoming less like light and more like a woven string which coiled around each wrist, anchoring them to the door. They stepped through, and the door swung shut behind them and vanished. Along with the wall. They might as well never have existed. It was unsettling to put it mildly, the first time it happened to you.

'Now this is more like it.' Zoe looked around in approval. From their feet, a grassy meadow ran down to a calm lake. Dotted on the landscape were huge trees, each head starting at the same height. The first thought that came to mind involved the exploits of a demented topiarist with OCD. Wrong. These trees were natural. Deer stood in the parkland, beneath those trees, occasionally reaching up to crop the leaves. It was peaceful, beautiful, serene. The grassland flowed round the lake, round the trees, to the feet of a dark wood. There might have been mountains in the far, far distance. It felt untouched, as if they were the only people ever to have been here. Elegant swans cruised over the lake, their reflections immaculate in the still water. The green of the grass was like a fine lawn. The blue of the lake reflected a tranquil sky. The darkness of the wood held silence and mystery. The deer would eat from your hand, fearlessly. Skylarks would fill the sky with song, and nightingales would sing in the woods. Water flowed out of the lake, bubbled over stones, sang down into a cheerful stream. Hazel trees dipped their branches in the pools, and salmon would rise to catch mayflies, forever. Willows, graceful as a giantess's hair, drooped into the lake. It was perfect, perfect, *perfect*.

'Let's go talk to the troll.'

Impelled by Fee's deliberate thought, the landscape shivered like the coat of a horse dislodging troublesome flies. They were standing, not on Bridlip Tor, but on its absolute equivalent in the Asha. The dry bracken was the brilliant hue of Victorian old gold, more red than yellow. The gorse was blue-green with vivid saffron yellow flowers. The heather was white, pink, mauve, alive with bees, the sedges dark, sharp and full of sap. The stones reared into the sky, sparking with quartz and mica, the soft grey rocks spotted with lichens in green, grey, yellow and orange. The water in the dewponds was black with peat, the sunlight hard-edged and the shadows cool. A soft wind scurried between the rocks, setting scarlet berries on the rowan tree anchored by strong, deep questing roots dancing against a blue sky fretted with white and grey clouds. The only thing missing was the ponies, sheep and cows that grazed it. There were no animals here, only soil, and rocks, and plants, insects and spiders, whose webs graced the gorse, the dew on the strands catching the light and refracting it into rainbows. There was a sleepy, watchful presence here, an awareness of the place, a deep cherishing of each blade and stem, each rock and hollow and pool.

Gently, oh, so gently, a face rose out of the rock face like bather surfacing from deep water. A nose, a brow, a lip, cheeks and chin formed beneath the grainy surface. They had found the troll. The lips moved.

'What do you want of me? Why disturb my reverie? What use am I to you, or you to me?'

The voice was old, slow, deep, considering. Rocks don't scurry about much. They sit, and think their own deep thoughts.

'I offer you my respect, King of the bones of this place. You are possessor of a knowledge that I would win, if it would please you to converse with me and share your thoughts.' Fee spoke slowly.

'Events in your world do not concern me.' The face turned, as if to sink back into the stones away from sight.

'You, too, are part of our world. We share your world with you. The doings of men have much to do with you,' Zoe said formally. The face stopped sinking.

'Men only come to break my bones and steal my bloods. They do not offer me respect or sacrifice. I have nothing to do with men.'

'You have much to do with men.' Zoe continued, 'You shelter them in your stones, you assist their passage from place to place. Each and every day, men bless you and those like you, the sacrifice you make. Without you, we would be less than we are, and we bless you for it.'

The troll sighed, a sound like rocks grinding together.

'They steal my bones and then forget me. They drown my valleys in water, break my bones and raise shelters. They drive

their paths through me, through my body, hack me and hew me, grind me and pound me, and give me no thanks.'

'Before men, you were there. But you did not know yourself. When men became aware, and walked the land, they named you, and woke you. The wyths in the land awoke, and flowed from place to place, because men felt them. You have much to do with men,' Zoe repeated firmly.

Fee left it to her. Hell, she would never have thought to *persuade* a troll. No, if Zoe hadn't chipped in, it would have been threats all the way. She was learning from her youngest sister.

'You are the sustainers, the earth from which we grow. You are the rainmakers, without whom we would starve. You are our fathers. How can you say you have nothing to do with men?'

'I will consider your words.' The rumbling voice fell silent. Fee waited in an agitation of impatience. You just couldn't hurry trolls. Being in the presence of a troll slowed you down. Fee was a creature of fire, swift and flickering. Blasting over the landscape of life and changing it as she passed, sometimes leaving ashes and chaos in her wake. Sophie, on the other hand, was like deep water, slowly laying down sediments, changing by increments. Zoe was restless, like the winds, questing everything, seeking to know each cranny and crevice, each nook and hollow that made up her life. Strange that the windchild could have such an influence on the earth creature. But it's head was in the sky, true. Fire would scorch it, water wash it, but air was the friend of the high places where the rocks met the sky. Wind whispered through the rocks, talking to them, falling on them from the sky as rain, running down into the deep places, gracing the rocks with grasses, lichens and small starry flowers, keeping the tors company on a starlit night, whispering, howling, moving the trees and grasses in an elegant dance. Making them live. Fee was swallowing her impatience for the gazillionth time. Her foot would start tapping next. Before this irreversible level of exasperation was reached, the Bridlip troll completed its deliberations.

'I have weighted your words, and found something of merit in them. If I assist you, what can you give to me that I will value?'

'I will speak to you of far places, where the mountains rush up to the sky like giants. I will tell you of places where the ice never melts, and storm clouds wreathe the crowns of the high hills. Shall I speak to you of secret worlds from the inside of volcanoes, where the rocks run hot and liquid as in the days of your youth? Shall I speak to you of those memories of lives past and lost forever which you hold in your substance, how we have learned them from the study of you, of the creatures long dead you hold in your close embrace? How we learn the movements of you, how we learn to cherish you as our teacher? How we learn from you the history of our lives? Is this a thing of value?'

'If your words be true, and not lies, then they are of value.'

'I am here, with you now, in this place. Here in the Asha, I cannot lie.'

'Then you have won my aid. We will hold converse, you and I. You will tell me of the things you have found, and I will tell you of the things I know. What do you will of me?'

Fee let out a breath she didn't know she had been holding.

'What can you show us of the doings on your rocks, the comings and goings of the creatures who have visited your fastnesses?'

The troll chuckled. It was a comforting sound, even if it did have grit in it.

'I have memories of all who come to my fastness. I keep them all, and forget none. Would you see the elder tribes who first came, wrapped in skins, who cut down the trees and raised crops here? Or would you seek knowledge of the makers of metals who delved me? Or is your thirst for my memories of times less remote?'

Zoe sat down, comfortably, in front of the rock face. It smiled down on her as she tucked her skirts in.

'The day before yesterday would be nice.'

The troll let out a deep, rumbling laugh.

'Very recent history, then. Come and see.'

Fee settled down next to her sister, who was grinning broadly.

'See? Easy money.'

Fee wondered if Zoe realized exactly what she was going to have to do to pay the troll back for this, then realized that she probably did. She knew more than you thought she did, her sister.

The first thing that happened was a tuneful whistling on the wind. ('Bring Me Sunshine, In your smile'.' I wish she wouldn't do that.') It was Sophie, hoving into view along the skyline, taking the easy way up the back of the tor, along the long backward slope, her camera swinging at her neck. She still wore the paint-spattered jeans, but had exchanged the floaty blouse for a sky-blue t-shirt, and the sandals for stout hiking boots. The satchel that depended from her shoulder was the same. She called it her Tardis, and it did seem to contain more stuff that it had a right to. Notebooks, chalks, charcoal, pencils, artist's paper, watercolours, hankies, chocolate, spare cash, cameras, mobile phone, half the local pharmacy….. Sophie could never find anything on the first try. Her coat was tied round her waist by the sleeves, and her hair shoved under a bush hat that was faded from wear and sun. She won to the top and stood looking around, breathing deeply. It was quite a steep climb, and she had taken it at a reasonable clip. Once she had got her breath back, she hefted the Halina and started to take pictures in her typical way. Snap, snap, snap. A pattern of shadows on the rocks. A particularly vibrant rowan twig. Spiderwebs in gorse.

'She'd be spending a fortune if she were using film in that camera. No wonder she always has spare cards,' Zoe commented.

From their seat high up in the rocks, they had a very good view of the surrounding countryside. While Zoe watched Sophie, Ffion tried to see which direction the shadow man was coming from. Then, she saw him, picking his way through a tumble of rocks. Reflexly, she ducked down, even though she couldn't be seen. She wasn't even here. There. Wherever.

'Here he comes, Zoe.'

Zoe stood up, craning her neck.

The man was tall, almost spindly, like a scarecrow. A good breeze would crack him, as Tom might say. He wore a black leather slouch hat, black jeans tucked into black boots - ordinary black boots, not hiking boots like Sophie's. Street shoes. His t-shirt was black under a black bomber jacket, even his gloves were black: a monochrome man down to the black aviator shades covering his eyes. The hat brim further shadowed his face. It looked - well, odd, shiny, as if he was sweating: but the day although sunny, was not that warm. There was a brisk breeze, you could see it in the movement of the sedges and the wandering tendrils of Sophie's hair.

He was approaching from behind Sophie's back, and she hadn't seen him yet. Fee watched him intently. He stopped, a few yards from Sophie's back, watching her click, click, click with the camera. Zoe walked round fearlessly, and was peering intently into his face below the hat brim. She backed off as he stepped forward.

'I think he's wearing a mask. You know, like they put on really bad burns. His face is all smooth and shiny. His features are, like, melted……. He's certainly wearing dark glasses, the wrap-round kind like blind folks wear. I wonder if he has been burned? And those gloves. He was fiddling with his fingers. Sophie didn't mention anything like that.'

As the man approached Sophie, she turned. Seeing him, she smiled and her lips moved.

'Good afternoon, lovely day, blah-blah……' Zoe filled in.

'Can you hear them or are you guessing?' Fee narrowed her concentration until she could hear the natural sounds of the scene. She didn't interrupt Zoe's voice-over, why she was not sure.

'I can hear Soph, but I can't hear him. Hang on.' She paused, concentrating. 'Got him now. He's saying yes, he has walked a long way, over from Chillaton…..' she followed the gesture. 'Photography, yeah… now he's asking if she has a mobile phone. He'll be late meeting his friend, doesn't want him to worry…….His phone hasn't got good reception…….'

They saw Sophie proffer her phone, and the man stepped away slightly, turning so his hands were in shadow. He was doing more than dialling a number……… He lifted the phone to his ear and listened.

'He's just saying he'll be late, and not to wait but go on…….. Meet you in Merrivale……. Bloody hell, that's a long way…….'

He returned the phone to Sophie, then stood by her shoulder, pointing down the far slope of the tor.

'He's asking the way to Longridge Hill. Wow, he's going the pretty way. This stinks. No way can he get from here to Longridge and then over to Merrivale before dark.'

The scarecrow man started to walk down the tor, leaving Sophie behind. She climbed higher, onto the rocks, and started snapping again.

'Single-minded, our sib. I'll give her that. You follow him, and I'll stay here.'

'No. We'll stay together.'

Fee grabbed her sister's hand. Together, they rose into the air until they had a bird's eye view of the scene. The first thing they saw was Luke. He was closer than they expected, and he was taking pictures too. He had definitely seen the man, and from where he and Sophie had been, the man could not have missed seeing Luke. So why were there no pictures of him from Luke's camera? He had a physical presence, Sophie had reacted normally to that…… Were those vague shots with Sophie on the skyline supposed to show *two* figures, not just the one? What sort of being doesn't affect digital cameras? Well, vampires don't photograph that well, but out in broad daylight? Not if they could help it. And can they screw up mobile phones? That was a poser. They could see him striding purposefully away as Luke climbed up the tor to greet Sophie. Once he had lost their attention, he doubled back, keeping the rocks between himself and them. He found a gully between two rocks close to the summit. From there, he could see Luke and Sophie. His attention on them was complete. His hands flexed on the rocks like black spiders, but what they could see of his face showed no emotion whatever. His face actually looked unfinished, a wax model that had the details yet to be impressed on it….. Luke and Sophie were lying side by side, looking up at the sky, pointing, laughing, commenting as the buzzards circled, circled, circled lazily above them and the unfinished man listened, his fingers flexing on the rock.

Below, Sophie rolled over on her stomach and touched Luke's hair. It was her way to touch, it meant nothing other than it was. She crawled over Luke and retrieved her backpack, slinging it over one shoulder. She blew Luke a kiss, a careless gesture, and started off down the hill, almost running, jumping from boulder to boulder.

'Quick, Zoe, zoom in.' They fell like stones. There was nothing they could do, no way they could interfere in what was going to happen, but Fee didn't want to miss a second of it.

Luke was still lying on his back, watching the sky. In his eyrie, the man was gesturing at Luke, flipping his hand… get up, get up. Luke's body jerked. His hand shot out. The man emerged slowly, out of Luke's sight. He crept closer, his body low. Fee, concentrating, could hear his voice very clearly now.

'They are so beautiful, the kings of the sky,' he said. His voice was low, hypnotic. 'You want to join them, don't you. Don't you?'

Luke lay there, half sitting, half reclining. Zoe muffled a sob. All she could do was watch. Fee squeezed her hand in mute comfort. She was finding it difficult too. Every instinct in her wanted to throw herself at the crouching figure, but such an action would be futile. She wasn't really there. This was over and done.

'They float on the air, circling, watching, as I have been watching you. I feel you reaching out to them. Reaching out,' he repeated. Luke's hand rose towards the buzzards. One let out a lonely cry.

'They are calling to you, those kings of the air. They are summoning you. You can feel them calling. You want to go to them, don't you.' It was not a question. Luke's still face watched the sky, only the sky.

'You can feel the power of their flight, the rush of air through their pinions. You can feel that fierce joy, riding on the wings of the wind, riding to a kill. You want to be part of it.'

Luke was transfixed. He was under the claws of the predator, and he didn't know it. He didn't know it at all.

'Feel the wind on your face. It is the wind in the pinions of the buzzards. It is the same wind, in your face, in your pinions.'

'Yesssss…..'

'You feel the wind in your feathers, you want to fly. The air will lift you up, up, high into the sky.'

'Yess… yes…'

Luke, helpless against the insidious voice, was coming slowly to his feet. The man straightened, and reached out his hand.

'Come with me. We will go together. We will lift our wings to the air. It will bear us up, and we will fly, fly…..'

He urged Luke up the tumble of rock until they were standing on the high, flat summit.

'Reach out your wings. Feel the air lifting you, lifting you...' He was hissing in Luke's ear now, the strangely taut pale face close to Luke's tanned skin. Luke held his arms aloft, threw his head back. His mouth opened as if for a lover's kiss, but there would be no kiss here.......

'You are flying now. Flying up to meet them. Can you hear them calling to you, calling across the skies for you to join them? Such a little thing, a little step. Nothing at all. It's so easy. So simple. No cares. No pain. Just the freedom of the wide skies, just a step away.....'

Luke was on his toes now, on his toes in his hiking boots. Boots meant to keep you safe, safe on the earth, not in the sky. Oh, Luke........

'You can feel your wings beating, your heart beating, the beating of wings in your heart for the freedom of the skies. The buzzards are waiting, Luke.' The soft, seductive hiss had become sharper, more like a command.

'Yessss....' Luke took a small step, a tiny step, closer to the edge. Zoe stifled a sob. Tears were running down her cheeks. Fee was watching impassively.

'Yess...'

Closer to the edge now. Too close. The man stood behind Luke, his arms folded, one leg slightly bent, forwards.

'They are waiting for you, Luke.' The last words dripped with contempt.

'Yes.'

Luke spread his arms wider and pitched forwards, spreadeagled against the sky, and fell away. The man didn't even spare him a second glance, just clenched one fist, raised it and looked at it. When he heard the distant thud of a body hitting the ground, the Unfinished Man turned and walked away.

Zoe streaked after him, Fee in her wake. He walked calmly down the rough slope away from the valley. Zoe was almost upon him when he turned to face her. He slapped her away. The impact winded her, threw her to the ground, her short sheer skirt riding up over the swell of her hips.

'Well, Farer?'

A wash of adrenalin flooded through Fee. This couldn't happen! This was the past...... Oh no. He'd sneaked in, and overlaid his own wraith on his ghostly self. This was bad......

She held out her hand, and snapped a command. Out of her palm, extending in both directions, a line of intense white light painted itself and solidified into a long staff. Fee banged the rounded end of the wythstaff into the ground at her feet. There was a Crack! like thunder, an instant of darkness, and the ground itself shook. Bloody hell, she was *furious*. Blindsided *again*. Time for a little *payback*.

From out of the clumps of grass by her feet, small figures moved. Suddenly, the ground was alive with little, running figures. Agile, malevolent, they swarmed over the boulders, jostling for position, their eyes alight, bodies quivering with restrained bloodlust. From the sky above came the mournful howl of a wolf. It was answered, and answered, again and again. Some of the little men hissed, showing sharp pointed teeth and an absolute willingness to use them on the first thing that so much as blinked. They surrounded Zoe, touching her, stroking her, crooning at her and hissing at the black clad figure who had hit her. She had the good sense for once to lie low. The sky lowered, darkened. Sheet lightning flickered behind the massing cloud. Thunder muttered an ominous counterpoint. The wind freshened, blowing Fee's hair about. This was her Asha, and by now she was mistress of it. Oh yes, he had tricked her. But he was in her domain now, as she knew very well how to use it. A huge flock of dark birds took to the air, wheeling and cawing. Gorcrows. Something snarled in the undergrowth. Lightning flickered again. The man folded his arms over his chest and looked at her.

'Is this meant to intimidate me, farer?'

'Oh no.'

Fee continued to watch. This was an old game.

'You are wasting your time, and mine.'

'Wrong again.'

The first flicker of uncertainty. Good. He's not played this game before.

'It is meant to instruct you.'

'Instruct me? In what?'

'In the exercise of futility.'

Fee raised her staff, and brought it down hard, striking it on the earth below her feet. The ground rocked, tore, and opened up. Thunderbolts crashed to the ground where the staff met the earth, filling the world with white, white light, the reek of ozone and a sizzling crash of thunder. The army of little men blasted forwards, the birds fell out of the sky, huge wolves streaked into the fray, the ground itself rose up like a tsunami and crashed down on the lot of them........

Sophie was standing over Fee and Zoe in the spaca. In the guttering light of the candles, a blade flashed in her hand.

'You're back, then.'

Fee groaned and rolled to her feet.

'Bastard was waiting for us. Just as well we were prepared.'

'I saw what he did to Luke. Damn, he's good. But Fee's better. He caught me a right whack.'

On the floor, Zoe was examining her leg. A dark bruise was starting to purple her thigh. Sophie knelt down to look.

'First time, eh. You let your enthusiasm get away with your pragmatism. Expect the unexpected.'

'Stop trying to teach me a lesson and help me up,' Zoe grumbled. 'I know I was wrong to go after him, but damn! I was that angry. I just wanted a piece of him, I wanted to smack him, I wanted to hit him, hurt him for what he'd done to Luke. I forgot we were spying on the past, I forgot *everything*. I'm sorry.'

Sophie hugged her. Fee joined them.

'Group hug, group hug.'

They held each other tightly.

'I don't want to sleep alone tonight. Can I crawl in with one of you guys?'

Fee smiled.

'Tell you what. We'll close this spaca, and reset the wards. Then we'll have hot chocolate and pile into Mum's bed.' Robert, a large man, had spent the virgin nights of his youth in a single bed sleeping corner to corner. He continued to sleep so in the first double bed he shared with Lily, who was forced to sleep curled up in one end. To add insult to injury, Robert stole all the covers. Fed up with being cramped and cold at night, Lily had installed a superking size bed in the master bedroom. It had been brought in piece by piece, and was too large to be removed. So it was still there, and still kept made and aired. Often, one or more sister would crawl under the duvet and wake up there, safe in the echoes of parental warmth. It was the ultimate haven.

'Can we take the poker?'

Chapter Five

The next morning dawned with the snap of autumn in the air. Fee was sitting at the kitchen table, huddled round a cup of tea while Sophie made toast and scrambled eggs. Zoe was upstairs with her computer, scaring up some arcane knowledge out of the Internet.

'I worry about Zoe,' Ffion started. This was going to be a difficult conversation.

'How so?' Sophie was adding chopped herbs and scallions to the fluffy mass in the pan.

'I don't trust her to stay out of this.'

'Neither do I. We both know our Zoe.' Sophie rummaged in the fridge, found yoghurt, and slopped it into bowls. 'I can see where this is going. You want to either send her away, which she will hate, and incidentally won't work. She'll just barge in anyway, and we won't know what she's up to until the brown smelly stuff hits the revolving circular item. Or you want to involve her properly, which means you are considering wyting her.' She added chopped fruit and seeds to the bowls. She was on one of her health kicks. 'And how far would we have to send her to stop her from coming right back? The moon wouldn't be far enough and you know it. You know Zoe. She's got her teeth into this. No matter where you send her, she'll still involve herself one way or another.'

'I could park her on Lily.'

'I can see that happening. Anyway, would Lily stay out of it? And if she's involved, Zoe would be right there. No, that wouldn't work.'

'There is the other way.'

'Oh, yes.' Sophie went back to the pan and stirred it.

'We didn't always use the onset of puberty as a sign. In Mum's day, it was the legal age of majority, which was eighteen. Who's to say another change is in order?'

'How so?'

'Wyte them when we think they are ready, regardless of age.'

'In that case, some won't be wyted at all. Look at Lottie. Lovely girl, but all the nous of a turnip when it comes to matters esoteric and mystical. Even Tom admits that, and she's his daughter.'

'And others were born ready. You start to tell Zoe something, then you realize she understands more about it than you do. I wonder about her, I really do.'

'Thinking about early retirement, are you?' Sophie grinned. 'Don't bother. When Zoe wants the Frais, she'll take it off you. She might even say please.'

'Days like today, she can have it and welcome.'

Sophie started to dish up breakfast.

'Er, guys……what you were talking about……'

'Listening at doors is a *really* bad habit, Zoe. One day you'll hear something you'll regret. It is not an endearing trait.'

'That's not the point. The point is, it's all academic now. You don't need to go changing the rules for me.'

'Zoe?'

'I'm bleeding.'

Fee stood up and hugged her. Sophie smiled over a plate of toast she was putting on the table.

'Busy day ahead then, sibs.'

'You'll do it today? *Today*?'

'No, in a few days' time. There are things we need to do, first. Come and get these eggs before they turn into rubber.'

It is difficult to grin and eat scrambled eggs on toast at the same time, but Zoe managed it. Then there was Tom to call, and all the others. They might not be needed, but all hell would be let loose if they weren't kept informed.

Margie and Jean twittered, and came round post-haste with a herbal mixture supposed to 'help with the pain'. Zoe had thanked them politely, and took the small bottle. They kissed her, congratulated her, and wrung their hands in a show of shared sympathy for the 'agony' they promised she would be subject to now she was 'a real woman at last'. While they were distracted with describing their own passage into womanhood ('the cramps were bad, so bad, I took to my bed for three days. I was in agony,') Zoe sniffed the bottle, grimaced and set it aside. She agreed that it was 'agony' but that she would 'bear up' and endure the process with fortitude. And aspirin, though she did not mention that. She would let them know how helpful the concoction was. It could be 'tweaked' Margie said, to suit her better. Privately, Zoe resolved never to even look at the vile stuff again. Later that day, she did try it, and poured the lot down the sink.

Claire appeared, with Josie in tow, looking furtive. She congratulated Zoe in passing, then got down to her own business. That was usually the case with Claire. She was moving on. This was old news to Fee. Something like it, anyway. After she had evicted Alec, Claire had developed wandering feet. It was nothing to her to pack up and move away for a month or two. Her Avon business had a substantial client base, but provided she had her mobile and an internet connection, she could operate from anywhere, and did. Last time she left, it had been embracing self-sufficiency up in the Hebrides with the latest soul-mate. It hadn't lasted out the year. Claire came back, declaring that although she had loved it, Josie had come down so many colds and coughs that she, Claire, feared for her health. A convenient get-out from a situation she found less than perfect. Reluctantly, she had quit Paradise for the milder climes. Bitterly disappointed, they had slunk back. Today, Claire was not a happy bunny. She seemed to blow hot and cold by turns anyway, so this was nothing Fee hadn't seen before. Claire was a sort of on-off-on person. If something caught her imagination, it became a passion, at least until the going got tough. The lass lacked tenacity, or persistence, or something, which was strange. Otherwise, she was a bloody-minded obsessive. She had bulled (it wasn't bullying. Not quite) her way into becoming a very successful Avon rep, descending like a Biblical plague on the rural farming community and beleaguered wives and mothers stuck out here in the arse of beyond, deprived of retail therapy in the cosmetics department. This being so, her business could have been in direct opposition to Fee's. At first, Fee had tried to woo Claire into Blue Moon, but Claire wasn't having any of it. The benefits of Avon, if you consistently hit your targets (holidays in France, Kenya and Hong Kong, for example,) were beyond Fee's slender means.

Eventually they reached a compromise. Fee wasn't interested in what Claire called the topcoat cosmetics - lipsticks, eyeshadows, liners, perfume, jingly bangles and floaty scarves. She dealt in skin condition, not adornment. So, they came to an agreement. Fee would offer skin treatments, and Claire would concentrate on finish. So far, it had been working. You might think that farmer's wives had no time for painting their faces between birthing lambs and milking cows, making cheese and baking cakes, but no. One farmer's wife never exited her rural kitchen without warpaint. She mucked out the stables in full slap and a touch of Givenchy behind the ears. Claire did very well out of it, and often was the most prolific saleswoman-of-the-season.

It was not her business life that concerned Claire now. Something about last night had sent her into a funk, and Claire in a funk was not to be reasoned with. She had made up her mind, and she went at it full tilt. The point of the matter, said Claire, was that Josie was in danger. She, Claire, knew all too well that, as a frater, she was not in the same league as Fee, and Sophie, or even Jean. It was her own stop-go personality which was the problem. Claire wasn't interested in 'bloody meditation' to strengthen her wyth. No matter how often she was told, no matter what simile was used to illustrate the point (babies roll, crawl, fall down, toddle and walk before they can run, for example) she expected to be able to weave wyth like a pro from the get-go, despite having been brought into the Frais as an adult. The disadvantage of not having ten, twelve, sixteen years of preparation before getting her eager fingers onto the Gya was so much hot air. Several times, she had buckled down to serious study, and the early results were promising. Then as suddenly as it had started, the interest waned, the study was set aside 'for a bit' and then shelved. Only as a frater alone was this a problem. Once in a spaca with someone - anyone - else, she was wholeheartedly in. Her grasp of the physicality of ritual was superb. It was her strength in the Gya that let her down. This latest move was one that she had been considering for some time, she said. It was obvious that she wanted to bail out. It was all right for Zoe, now she would have the Ritual, but she, Claire, had Josie to consider. 'She's much too young. I can't risk it.' Last night's events had caused some psychic feedback, which had been felt by the trio of ladies. Margie and Jean's wittering had made Claire even more determined to put some serious geography between herself and ground zero. From where she was standing, France looked a good bet. She had taken the dire warnings of the two old trouts at face value, and was intent on heading for the hills as a safer option than staying put. Claire, the drama queen. She liked the feeling of importance that being Family gave her, but she was starting to have second thoughts now, when the going got tough. When the going gets tough and the tough go shopping, Claire would scuttle for the doomsday bunker. She was, not to put too fine a point on it, a scaredy-cat. And she was not above using concern for her daughter as an excuse for lamming out of the danger zone. But just as this man had cut Luke from the herd, she was concerned that she would be targeted. What would Ffion do? Ffion was staying put. Ffion was going to fight, to resist, but with Claire in this mood it was useless to protest. Claire knew the warding weaves, and she was not in the front line, was she? Sophie, angered by what she saw as Claire's dereliction, stalked into the kitchen and refused to say anything further. Not because she would regret it, but that she wouldn't. Ffion considered the problem. She had instructed Abby to keep John safe in Lanark with Effie. Could she do less by Claire? Was this an attempt to isolate Claire, or was this adversary trying to strip Ffion of her protection? She had lost three already if you counted John. Claire in this mood would be little use. All she could do at the moment was witter. Why stand in the way? Claire had never really taken to the more advanced uses that wyth could be put to. She was an engaging companion, friendly, witty, inventive and full of fun when the mood took her. In the Frais, she would provide solid backup for whatever was on the go, but that was as far as it went. Fee instinctively felt that there was steel in Claire, somewhere. Unplumbed depths. That the Claire she knew was sitting on top of her real self, and the Claire that everyone saw was an oil-slick over water, concealing something. Hidden drives and ambitions. Secrets. She could do without the additional hassle of managing something like that right now.

Claire was intent on going whatever Fee said.

Be that as it may, her concern for Josie was real. Fee, thinking about Zoe, could do no less than listen and concur. They had sent John away with Abby, hadn't they? If it was only herself, Claire would, naturally, stay and face whatever was coming with the rest of her sisters and brothers. They had taken her in. As outsiders, she and Alec had been welcomed by the Frais, enfolded by them, befriended by them - more, even, since individuals had told her more than once that she was 'like a sister' to them. This was important to Claire. She needed to belong, but that 'sister' tag was too much like cant. They settled on 'cousin' instead - 'kissin' cousins' Alec grinned before trying to bring the idiom to life, sod that he was. But Alec was gone now, and it had been Alec that had tamed Claire's upsy-downsy ways. Letch he might be, a plodder he might be, but even plod has something to recommend it. Keeping on keeping on is a strong cys. In terms of the Frais, Alec was no freeloader on Claire's talent. He focussed it, held it steady, but in his absence Claire had reverted. Fee needed strong, dependable fratten around her now. She weighed the pros and cons carefully. Which would be best - keep Claire close by and hope that the danger to Josie wouldn't distract her at a critical moment, or their hidden adversary wouldn't use Josie to hurt Claire... or send the two of them away, far enough to be safe, and so lose Claire's support? And what about Josie? Lacking the links to the Gya, she would also be vulnerable. Fee came to a decision.

'Where would you go?' she asked.

'There's a guy I knew, back when I was with Alec, before I came here. (Of course there was.) We kept in touch. (Of course you did.) Well, he's moved to France. He's renovating this farm, and he's invited me to visit him more than once. (I see.) We could go and stay with him. Josie would love it there.'

Fee sighed.

'We would come back once it's all over.'

Or maybe you won't. I know, and I suspect you know, that this isn't the right place for you, not the right time. But you won't give it up until something better comes along. Perhaps you will be happier on your own, weaving your wyth without us as yardsticks of how good you are. We wouldn't give up on you, but you can give up on us. It's for the best. Ah, here we go, down the steps to hell, each step a good intention. However, I suspect, more than suspect, that you'll go with or without my consent. So, I won't lay that burden on either of us, which will leave you with a way back at least.

'Then you must go. Take Josie, go to your friend in France. But, Claire, I can't guarantee that it won't follow you. Or that it will be waiting for you when you get there, even. So it would be best if you kept away from the wyth, at least for the time being.'

Claire considered this.

'I hadn't thought about that.'

'You must think about it. For Josie's sake.' Fee wasn't above a bit of guilt-tripping herself. 'When will you go?'

'No time like the present.'

'Do be careful. Take some time to plan ahead. Don't just toss your life into a suitcase and bolt. Being caught in the carpark at Southampton ferry could be worse than being caught here.'

'I see what you mean. And I'll start right now. If I don't tell anyone where I'm going, or when, I'll be safe.'

'Safe-*er*.'

Claire got up from the chair and collected her bag.

'Can't tempt you into a new lippy before I go, can I?'

'Oh, go on. I rather liked that one you had on the other night.'

'Ah. Cherry Delight. Nice. But a smidge too pink for you, I think. Try this one. Very Berry. It'll go better with your colouring.'

Say what you wanted, but Claire knew her colourings.

She left, probably to finish the packing she started last night. There might be the piper to pay when she came back, if she did: but that was for another day. Sophie was incandescent with rage.

'You let her go? Are you mad, Fee?'

'She'd have gone anyway.'

Sophie slammed a cup down on the table. Tea slopped out. Sophie turned to the sink and grabbed a cloth, mopping up the spill. She tossed the wet rag back into the sink, turned and faced Fee, her hands on the tabletop, her arms braced. Her face was set, her mouth a thin line.

'She could have been a liability.'

'She was an asset! We might need the help!'

'And I can do without the hassle. Anyway, it's a moot point.'

'What is the point, then?' Sophie was being truculent. She did it very well.

'The point is that we've sent John away with Abby. Claire's taking Josie away. Maybe we needed Claire, maybe we didn't. But Josie? She couldn't have defended herself any more than John could have. I can't use one argument to ship someone off and then turn round and contradict myself over Josie.'

'Perhaps.' It was the closest Fee would get to an apology.

Sophie might have likened Lottie to a turnip, but she had more backbone than Claire. She hugged Zoe over her belly, and asked what they were going to do next about the 'bloody bastard' who was the cause of 'all this fuss'. She wanted things back to normal, as soon as possible, and was ready, she said, to do anything to get it. It more than made up for Claire's dereliction. There was a warmth in Lottie that Claire, for all her sophistication, could not compete with. 'My little Sunny,' Tom had called her. Still did, in fact. Carl, too, would be right there behind them, Lottie said. He was at work right now, but could be available anytime. She, Lottie, would see to it. The glint in her eye said that Carl would comply or suffer the consequences.

Tom rolled in with Matt. He put a large black box on the floor by the sofa, which Zoe eyed hungrily. A tat, finally! What exotic design would she opt for? Something unusual, no doubt. Tom hugged everyone. Ellen was at the hospital, it was her shift. She sent her congratulations, but there was no change in Luke. Matt collapsed into a chair and accepted tea.

'I refuse to keep calling this ….. person……. a Black Man, Shadow, Master, or whatever. Gives the bugger too much importance, makes him loom too large in the mind. Sets up echoes. If we start believing that he's strong and dangerous, we'll get afeared. That's not good.'

'He is strong and dangerous, Tom.'

'Aye, lass. But any enemy who's got you thinking he's better'n you's got you beat already. Call him Master once too often and he will be. He may even be able to hear himself named. If he can do that, we give ourselves away every time we name him, if he listens in.'

'Shades of Harry Potter. Lord Voldemort, here we come. Okay, let's call him…..'

'He's the Unfinished Man.' Everyone listened. Zoe had a talent for naming.

'Why the Unfinished Man?'

'Because of his face…….' Zoe trailed off as she mused. 'That's too long. How about Tunfen?'

'Sounds like a favourite uncle. Or an unfavourite one. Slightly slimy, and you don't want to sit on his knees too often.'

'Then Tunfen it is. You can't be scared of a Tunfen.'

'But you can dislike him, and be wary of him. Perfect.'

'Let's get to know Tunfen better, then.'

'He likes wearing black.'

'He might be badly burned.'

'He's a good hypnotist.'

'He can affect electronic equipment, note, mobiles and possibly digital cameras. Hey, Zoe, could he interfere with your computer? Like he did my mobile?'

'I hope not, but expert advice is on the way. So, I hope, is a new mobile for you, Soph. I managed to download your memory card, so you'll still have your contacts.'

'Thanks, but I've got them on a memory stick anyway.'

'Wow, you are really getting the hang of this twentyfirst century technology. You'll make a cyber-babe yet. Anyway, Tunfen knows about the Fratris, and us in particular. I have sent out the word, asking if any other Family has had a tragedy lately.'

'How lately?'

'Didn't put an exact time limit on it, but suggested anywhere in the last ten years or thereabouts.. What I said was, unusual accidents. I'm including Dad and Mum in the list. No-one knows why the car went off the road like it did.'

'What about Jane?'

Jane had been Rina's daughter, and Lily's mother. That was a family scandal right there. No-one knew who Lily's father had been. Jane had just turned up pregnant one day, out of the blue. Entreaties and threats had failed to make her name the boy responsible for her condition. It certainly hadn't been her long-term lover. He had heard the call of the sea and joined the Navy, and the dates didn't add up.

It was suspected that Rina knew more about the affair than she was letting on, but she took Jane back into her home and saw her through pregnancy and childbed. Outwardly she had been supportive, but who could know what went on behind the closed doors when they had been alone? The fact was that shortly after Lily had been weaned, Jane went off and killed herself. She had stepped in front of an express train, and there hadn't been much left to put in a coffin. Dry eyed, Rina had buried her daughter and got on with the business of raising Lily. Whispers behind her back spoke of mental cruelty to the poor unfortunate dead girl. Perhaps Jane couldn't stand to live with her mother's disapproval of an unplanned pregnancy. Whatever the reason, Rina had kept her own counsel. The gossip eventually died out. Rina had brought up Lily with tact and gentleness, liberally sprinkled with stern discipline when needed. When she had died, quietly in the night, the last thing Lily remembered her saying was, 'I am so tired.' At least she got to hold two of her great granddaughters first.

'How long has this been in coming? He could have been picking us off for years, and we never noticed, never suspected. Like with most serial killers, until you suspect the crime, you don't see the pattern.'

'You've been reading too much Val MacDermid.'

'Have I? We'll see. When this is over, you'll thank me, I bet.'

'You just like watching Robson Greene on the telly.' Re-runs of Wire in the Blood had been on recently, and Zoe had been a religious watcher.

'I watched Cracker too, but you don't accuse me of fancying Robbie Coltraine, even though he is a love god.'

'So, Detective Harris, how many corpses have we?'

'Twenty, so far.'

'WHAT!!!!'

'I haven't got to the best bit, yet. The body count is twenty, and that's without looking too hard. I've been looking for lost cousins. We're a big Family, but we tend to keep to close family groups. A tragedy in one barely gets a ripple in another. No-one's looked at the big picture. When you trace the family tree, most of the branches have at least one 'accident'. But accidents happen, right?' Zoe flipped the screen round, so they could all see. 'This is the Harris line. I haven't started on the Howes and Davies and Rosses yet. The names in red died recently, in 'accidents'. As you can see, there are too many for pure chance. Someone is picking us off, and it goes back years, if I'm right.'

'Ought we to involve the police?'

'Only if they've got Tony Hill. Or Morse. Otherwise, they wouldn't believe us. They'd certainly not believe me. I'm only sixteen, what do I know of serial killers? Add the suggestion that it's because we are a "magic" family, and the cops will be screaming for the white coat brigade. Hello, funny farm. Can you picture me strolling up to Sergeant Brice and telling him he's got a serial killer on his patch? He'll laugh me off the station. Tell me to go away and play.'

Fee collapsed into a chair. This was bigger than she had thought. If Zoe was right, and she'd bet good money on that, Tunfen had been gleaning at the Families for a decade at least. What the hell was going on? This was too much for one person, one girl, alone, to deal with. She needed to share the load, but there was no-one to share with. Tell Greg that her family was being targeted by a serial killer? Right. How To Lose A Lover In One Easy Lesson. Claire was jittery enough already. Tell her this, and she'd head for the hills in Australia. Margie and Jean…… She could hear them telling her 'This just doesn't happen' already. Ellen had enough on her plate with Luke. Matt's stuffing had been knocked out of him completely. Lottie was a turnip, Carl was only interested if it had an engine. Lottie used to joke that if she wanted more of Carl's attention, she would have to get a boob job and have her hooters replaced with headlamps……. Tom was, well, Tom. Strong, dependable, but not exactly bulging in the brains department. Sophie was dependable, sure…… and Zoe? Fee's brain was grinding to a halt. She needed a shoulder to cry on, but she was the Mysten of the Frais, everyone cried on her shoulder. It was her privilege and burden to take this weight, and no-one to share it with. How right it was that the Family preferred to be headed by a couple! Then they had each other. Oh, Mum, I wish……..

Then it hit her. She *did* have a shoulder to cry on. In Norfolk. Zoe ought to see her mother before the Ritual. Lily ought to be the one who brought her daughter to the Gya. It was a legitimate excuse. And Fee had been going to see Lily a few days ago before her car let her down, but Zoe hadn't seen her mother for a month or two. Perfect. She sat up with renewed vigour.

'What else do we know?'

'He can invade our Asha.'

'So, he must have links with the Family.'

'Or he can get round the Doors.'

'I'd prefer if he were Family. The alternative is far worse. The only one I knew who could ever bypass the Doors was Rina. And she never did it without good reason.'

'Can you bypass the doors, Tom?'

He shook his head, sadly.

'No, it was Rina's gift. She might have taught it to Robbie, but never to anyone else. Too dangerous, see.'

'Can you do it, Fee?'

'I never tried. I never needed to. I suppose you could go from one realm to another, once you were past the Wall, but the Asha is huge. You could spend forever searching. If a thing doesn't want to be found, it won't be. Unless you have a link, and can call them to you. Hey, I'm liking this better already. If Tunfen's got a link to us, then we have a link to him. It works both ways. And he's used it on us. So we can use it on him.'

'I like this, and I don't like it. Yes, we have the link. But it will be like walking into a cage full of hungry tigers. I know you can use your realm, Fee, but if he can use his, and I suppose he can, you will be in the crosshairs. He sneaked up on you, remember.'

'I can be sneaky too. I have no intention of walking onto his turf and yelling 'Come on if you think you're hard enough!''

'What, then?'

'I need to consult with my Eldren.'

'Which ones?'

'Lily, Robert and Rina.'

'Two of those are dead. They may not be able to help.'

'Never try, never know. It's asking the right questions that rows the boat. How do you fancy a trip to Norfolk, Mouse?'

'I suppose you'll want to stop off and see Greg on the way.'
'Is that a problem?'
'Only if you expect me to watch.'

Chapter Six

The next day, they set off early. Sophie was going to keep Matt with her. The constant reminders of Luke in Tom and Ellen's place was too upsetting, and he said, quite sharply for him, 'I'm not staying with Jean and Margie. They'd drive me bonkers in a minute.' He and Sophie could help with the children if Tom wanted to get away, and she could still keep up her painting. She called a friend to take over the teaching course. No-one could expect her to teach art with close family at death's door. Tom was secure in his house.

'I've been wything and warding that ground with Ellen since before you were born. Any bugger gets in there, they're in for a shock. Rina taught me a few tricks.'

Claire was off to France with Josie, in most indecent haste, taking advantage of the school holidays as her excuse. Thank God for small mercies. Fee half-expected to run into Claire on the village road. Not literally, of course.

Jean had finally come to realize that there was a real threat. But the change in her attitude almost stunned Ffion. Expecting denials, or witter, or even some stunt like Claire's, Jean and Margie flatly refusing to back the Frais and deciding to go visit far flung friends for a week or two, she was both surprised and gratified to meet a strangely serene Jean.

'I'm an old woman, Ffion. I know how to protect myself. We have lived in this village all our lives. There isn't a bush or tree I'm not familiar with. There isn't a corner without a ward. There isn't a person or child or cat or dog living here that I don't know. Why do you think all this progress has passed us by? Because you can't get mobile phone reception here? We can. Incomers can't. So they don't stay, the roads don't come, and we are left in peace. That's all I ever wanted, to be left in peace, after Andrew passed on.'

'I wish I could promise you that. But I don't think I can. We didn't go out and look for this, it came looking for us.'

'And we must deal with it. I'm sorry, Ffion, most of my wythen is the quiet kind. I am not like Robert, or Rina. I am not like you. I will not be much help, I'm afraid.'

'At least you are staying put.'

'Poor Claire. She was one of mine, you know, and so young then. She came to terms with her wyth, but never properly understood the Gya. Lily was very patient with her. But then she never saw Rina riding the Gya. If she had, she would not have been so fretful. But most of her concern is for Josie. She loves that child, maybe too much, I think.'

'We may need a bit of your peace, at the end.'

Jean had patted her hand.

'You can have it and welcome. You are Rina's gift to us. We will keep watch while you are gone. We will always keep watch. It's what we do, watching. While the world passes by.'

The journey was long, but uneventful. If you don't count the roadworks. They listened to music. Zoe was trying to wean Fee off heavy metal. She had an astonishing arsenal. The Zutons, Red Hot Chilli Peppers, Kaiser Chiefs, Artic Monkeys, Foo Fighters and Muse. She had even discovered Leonard Cohen. To Fee, this last was just too depressing. Music To Slit Your Wrists By. 'Democracy' had something to recommend it, especially the bit about it happening to the USA. They made good time up the M5 and M4, picking up the A34 and A43 to the M1, then the A14. By the time they rolled into the little village between Thetford and Diss it was late afternoon. Zoe, studying the map, commented that it was easier to drive up and down England than across it. It might have been shorter to go via London, but the thought of the M25 horrified Ffion. At Chalfont, it was easy to sneak out to the West Country, but getting from there out to Norfolk and back was a trial. Some days, she thought, it would be quicker to walk than drive round London.

Lily's carer, Dilys, was waiting for them at the door. 'So pleased to see you. I know Lily will be delighted. So grown up, her little ones.' She smiled at Zoe, patted her face. 'Come in and have a cup of tea, and tell me the news. How is everyone? Is Luke still the same? Poor boy.'

She ushered them through the house to the back room, where Lily was watching the world outside the large windows from her wheelchair. She reached out to them, held them close against her. A faint waft of Dior, pure Lily, and everything was all right again. A comforting illusion. Lily disentangled herself, waved them to sit down. Fee dropped into a wicker chair and rearranged the cushions. Zoe perched on the arm of the wheelchair, her arm round her mother's shoulders. Lily got right down to it. Her speech was slow and deliberate. More than her body had been injured in the crash.

'So tell me.'

'It wasn't an accident, Mum.'

'I know, Zoe, I know. Tom's been on the phone. Every day. Tell me what you need. Don't look at me like that, Fee, I'm still your mother.'

'It's bigger than just Luke, Mum. Tell her, Zoe.'

Lily listened quietly to what they knew, and what they supposed.

'You have a battle on your hands. You know that, don't you?'

'Yes.'

'So I will arm you both for that battle as best I can. And the best way I can arm you is with information. We must assume that this Tunfen, as you call him, knows a lot about the Family. But he does not know everything. I hope he thinks he does. Still, we will deal with that later. How is Greg?' Ffion blushed. 'Oh ho, my girl. True love at last? Whatever will poor Michael think of that? He carried a torch for you, back when you were eighteen.'

'I haven't seen Michael for ages. Last I heard he was in America.'

'He's getting married next week. Facebook,' Zoe explained.

'To some blonde surf bimbo, I expect.'

'She's a doctor, actually.'

'Tea will be ready soon. We will consider this problem after. I am afraid that Dilys has invited any family she can lay her hands on to tea this evening. Well, you may be able to hear some rumour, or at least ask questions. Someone may know some little fact, unimportant in itself, that may help you solve this riddle. I advise you to listen carefully, no matter how trivial the chatter is.

You know how young people like to talk. And there is little privacy in this house. I am grateful to Dilys, but she can be a trial all the same. Still, we each have burdens to bear, and some are heavier than others.'

At that point, Dilys appeared to announce that the tribe had gathered and tea was ready. Fee steered the wheelchair through to the parlour. The bungalow had been built specially for wheelchair users, the halls and doorways wide, no whatnots or knickknacks to bump into, and most of the fixtures set conveniently for a seated person to manage.

They were crowded in the parlour. Lily refused to be shunted into a corner, and held court from the table, pouring tea and offering round plates. There were tiny cucumber and salmon sandwiches with the crusts cut off, little cakes, bread and butter, a Victoria sponge oozing cream and raspberry conserve: there was ham and salad, canned peaches and a trifle. There was potted meat, sliced boiled eggs and pickles. A real, old-fashioned High Tea. It was a merry meal. It was interrupted several times by new arrivals, all come to see Lily's girls and share news. Everyone was invited to stay, sit down, have a cup of tea. They asked about the health and doings of the West Country cousins, and shared local gossip back.

'Tom, Tom, how's he coping? Poor Luke, so sad, such a tragedy…'

Poor Luke, indeed.

'Jean and Margie! Haven't seen them in years. Still the same?'

Some things never change. Margie sent cowslip wine. Watch for the kick…..

'I can remember when Rina had the corner cottage. Are the apple trees still there?'

They've got pear and cherry trees now, as well…..

'And how's Lottie? When's she due?'

Big as a full moon, and in her last weeks, thank you……

'Gracious, Zoe, all grown up now! Are you excited, dear?'

I am sitting here wetting myself…

'Got any boyfriends, Zoe?'

Humph.

'How's Jerry? I was skyping him last week. If I come to stay, will you introduce me?'

As if. Stay off my turf, bitch. Wow! Did I think that? Me and Prof? No way.

'Here's my Suzie. Six months now! Isn't she a beauty?'

In the eye of the beholder. At least she doesn't resemble a bald gorilla…

'My David brought his latest girlfriend home last week. Hardly said a word. A bit of a trollop, if you ask me. All that plaited hair and ribbons and black fingernails….'

Poor you. I thought the Goth look was passé by now. Better luck next time…

'It was a pity about Jack….'

Fee's ears perked up.

'…. losing that job in Thetford.'

That's all right then. Thought he might have met a man dressed in black….

'Hilary's pregnant again. She's thrilled. I do hope it's a girl this time, or Mike will have three boys and Hilary will go for it again as soon a she can manage it…'

Hilary wants a girly doll to dress up, not a troupe of unruly boys. Poor Mike…..

Zoe, meanwhile, was over in the corner with a group of the younger cousins.

'Do you really know the vampires?'

'We haven't got any here.'

'Not that we know about, anyway.'

'I went to see a Simon Lake show last month.'

'Wow, you rate, boy. Getting tickets for a Simon Lake show is harder than scoring tickets for Reading.'

'The Dark Desires tour. Was it good, or what?'

'Better than good. Stupendous.'

'I wish he'd go on the telly.'

'He can't, you goose. He's a vampire. They don't *do* film.'

'They don't photograph well.'

'They don't photograph *at all*.'

'What about the posters?'

'What century are you living in? Never heard of Photoshop?'

'I heard that when he does a show, all the regular staff have to leave. Then he sends his own people in to set up the show, do the staffing and everything.'

'Must cost a bomb.'

'But he rakes it in. Every show a sellout. And the cost of tickets, it's unreal.'

'But worth it. The special effects are awesome.'

'If they are special effects.'

'They say all his staff are vampires.'

'That's hype. The ushers are all warm-blooded, at least. They just wear slap and fangs. I brought a set for Halloween. They sell cloaks, fangs, makeup, the whole shebang. Instant vampire kit. I swore I saw one of them having a crafty fag while I was queuing. She was wearing this long white thing, and had pale stuff on her face. It was all shiny.'

'If *he* finds out, she'll get the sack.'

'For sure. He really lives up to the vampire hype. Travels with a coffin, won't be seen in daylight. Anyone with a camera anywhere near him gets rousted by the bouncers. You get a body search on the way in. They even took my MP3. Let me have it back when I left, though. Checked it in with my coat.'

'There was one photo, supposed to be of him, published on the Internet. *Very* unsavoury. There one day, gone the next.'

'Was it him?'

'Hard to tell. The girl was having a good time, though.'

'They have this after show party. I saw a girl handing out little golden tickets. She was got up like a French maid, all ruffles and ribbons. Very short skirt.'

'Wow! Did you score one?'

'No, bummer. But the lass next to me did. I tried to get her to show me, but she wouldn't.'

'Probably thought you were going to steal it off her.'

'I would have, if I'd've thought of it. They say the party is really way out there.'

'And those that go are…..never…seen…again….' chipped in one boy, trying for sepulchral. It might have worked, but his voice broke. The girls giggled.

'Don't be daft. He'd be a fool to chow down on the general public. He's got these groupies, that follow him everywhere.

Some of them get to go to the party. I saw a couple, all got up, pretending to be like, so cool, so unimpressed. One was wearing suspenders and a basque, looked like a Rocky Horror reject.'

'They're doing the Rocky Horror in Norwich at the end of the month. Wanna come with me?'

'As what?'

'You be Brad and I'll be Janet.'

'No way. Riff Raff, or nothing. You can be Magenta.'

'Before or after?'

'Before. If you want to see me in suspenders, you gotta pay.'

By now, the teapot was empty, the sandwiches long gone and the cakes and trifle devoured. A few shreds of limp lettuce and an odd slice of unwanted bread and butter curling morosely on the plate was all that remained on the table. Dilys started to clear plates away. This was the signal to leave. Otherwise, you might get roped in for the washing up. E-mail addresses and mobile numbers were exchanged. Zoe upped her street cred with a voice activated memory stick. Lily gathered the girls with a look. Fee maneuvered her back into the garden room. Evening was falling over the garden.

Lily looked at Zoe.

'Be a good girl and fetch my blanket. It gets quite chilly at night now. And since I am losing feeling in my feet, it's better to be safe than sorry.'

'If you want to chat to Fee on your own, all you have to do is ask.'

Lily smiled.

'Smart girls, I like. Smart mouths, I so do not. Fetch the blanket, please.' She watched Zoe out the door, then turned to Fee.

'I know that you must be confused by all this. It is not every day that such things happen. But it is the way of the world, the way of the Gya, to test us all from time to time. Those of us at the top of the chain, we sleep in the sun like well-fed lions, never suspecting that there is a predator hiding in the grasses around us. We see ourselves as predators and not prey, and so shape the world we live in. But there are predators.

'It is the nature of man to want more than he has. Imagine the terror, the horror, that we could visit on this world should we decide to reach out our hands and take power over other beings. Look at the mess that politicians have made of their world, only thinking to do good, imposing their own views on a world that, when you get down to it, does not share their values. Life preys on life: you are smart, or swift, or you are prey.

'Like lions, we have slept lazily, and so this predator is upon us. But we have seen him now, and will defend what is ours. Make no mistake, even in the Fratris there are those who will reach out their hands for power here in this world, who seek to impose their rule on us whether we want it or not. The law of Nature is red in tooth and claw, we know that. Every day we learn how conflict challenges us to change or die. Darwin saw it first, but we never realized how ruthless our world really was. Now, we are coming to realize it. Nature is not gentle. Every nook and cranny of this world is shaped by conflict, by warring desires. Even trees challenge each other. The smallest of plants will compete against its neighbours for food, for water, and the strongest will survive. Never believe that there are no predators out there waiting for you. The Gya itself will test you. The world will test you. This world does not need the creatures in it to kill you, maim you. Earthquakes, tidal waves, snow, hurricanes, all these can and will kill you. Catastrophe brings out the best, and the worst, in all of us. And so we are tested.'

'How do we know when we've won?'

'If we live through the catastrophe, then we have won. Until the next test, and that will come. Always, the next test will come. And the testing is never over.'

'What must I do?'

'I shall arrange for you to visit Rina. After that, I have my own tasks. Think carefully what you will ask of her.' She shifted restlessly in her wheelchair. 'She will not be able to tell you all she knows, but she will tell you what you need to know. She told me that, once, that there were some things I did not need to know. I accepted that. You must do the same.'

'What about Dad?'

'I was never able to reach my Robbie after he passed on. I wondered about that at the time. But life is for the living, and I had other concerns. I will look into that now, you can be sure. Leave Robert to me.'

'Do you have any idea who might be behind this?'

'None that will help you. You must start talking to the Families. Get them to confide in you. They will be very happy to leave you to deal with this, believe me. The traces of what this enemy is doing to us will be there. Collect your evidence carefully, ignore nothing.'

'Zoe would be better at that than me.'

'Very well, you know her best. A sad thing to say, a mother not knowing her daughter as well as her sisters do, at that age. It has been hard on her, losing her mother and father. But I had to leave. I think that you and Sophie have done very well without me. And Zoe calls me often.'

'Mum, I'm scared.'

'So you ought to be. I would worry more if you had breezed in here and told me it was a piece of cake. You will take this seriously because it scares you. But you will not run away from it either. You will be capable of this task. You must be. You are the only one who can end it. Do not ask me how I know this: I don't know myself.'

'Is there anything you can do to help me, Mum? Anything you can tell me?'

'Don't be overwhelmed by the size of the task in front of you. Remember the elephant.' Fee looked at her, questioning. 'You can't eat it all at one sitting. Split the task into smaller pieces. Use your friends to help you. You don't have to do this alone. I will do what I can. Believe me, if I could go with you back to Pippin Cottage, I would. But I cannot.' She gazed out of the window at the darkening garden. 'I will do what I can. Rina will help you, I am sure. And do not assume that Jean is the feckless twittering crone she pretends to be. There is a strength in her, an endurance, that is rare in these times of instant gratification.'

There was a tap at the door, or rather on the wall by where the door ought to be.

'Have you heard enough, my girl? That's a nasty habit, listening at doors.'

'So they tell me.'

Zoe arranged the blanket over her mother's lap, tucking it round her legs.

'So stop it.'

'No.'

'A true Intelligencer, then. Even if you heard things that you did not like, you would rather know that remain in ignorance, eh?'

'Yes.'

'I can only hope that you will be gentle with what you find out. If you are not, then you will have an unhappy life, which is not what I would wish for in a daughter. It has been a long time since I found a real Intelligencer, and it raises my hopes. You saw what no-one else had noticed. You looked, and you understood what you saw. But not what to do with it.'

'I've got Fee for that.'

'Still, you will want to act. You will see no danger in it. Before you know where you are, the trap will close on you. I am glad, really glad, that you will have the Ritual before this situation comes to a head. You must promise me that you will concentrate on your job, and leave Fee to do hers.'

'Once was enough.'

'Once will never be enough, not for you. Not this time, my girl. There will be risks enough without trying for honour and glory as well.'

She looked directly at Fee.

'Leave us now. Zoe and I need to talk. Alone.'

'What? Oh, yes.'

Fee trailed back to the parlour. In the kitchen, Dilys was bossing some Darwinian rejects who had not been so sharp as their friends, who had left, scenting that once the social event was over they would be roped in to the clearing up. Or maybe they were lingering in the hopes that they would learn something tasty to share later. Even domestic chores have an advantage, if what you overhear increases your street cred. Everyone's a vulture.

She joined them in the kitchen. The teatowel was wet, so she hung it over the stove to dry out, and fished a clean one from a drawer. This lot were mostly younger teens, more easily bossed about than their elders.

'Wash up? Me? No way.' Exit, stage left, sneering. Common household toil is below me. I am meant for better things. Like skateboarding, and hanging out on street corners with my mates. Or was it 'crew'? Did nice Anglo-Saxon boys in Norfolk have crews? 'Yo, ma maa-aan!' Nah, didn't fit. Crews didn't dress up and watch the Rocky Horror show. Or did they? Do baggy pants go with suspenders? No.

Dilys announced the task completed, and chased them out while she prepared supper. One kitchen one cook, she said, then ignored her own pronouncement, snagging one girl to chop carrots, another to peel potatoes and a third to chop garlic and herbs. Oh, two of them were boys.

'You need to learn to cook. You may find it useful one day. Remember Issy? Failed his degree, and now he's a chef in Yarmouth.'

Oh, yeah, Issy. Doomed from the start, his fool mother saddling him with a name like Ishmael. What was the daft carlin thinking of? Fee's experience of name-calling had been bad enough. School had been all right for the first two years. Then, she was Ffion. But when Sophie started it all went tits up. The first break, the very first, she sought out her elder sister, running though the playground yelling 'Fee-Fee! Fee-Fee!' at the top of her lungs. Everyone heard her. *Everyone*. Fee had wanted to run away and hide. By the ayen, she had tried. They had run her to ground, and finally cornering her in the outdoor toilets. With the finely tuned instincts of hunters scenting prey, the pack had gathered like hyenas round a wounded gazelle. Blood was in the air. The feeding frenzy followed.

'Fee-Fee? *Fee-Fee*?'

'Nah, nah, Fifi, *Fifi*! She's a poodle! Fifi's a poodle! Poodle, poodle! Fifi's a poodle!'

Ffion's hair, at that stage, had been, well, frizzy. Little girls didn't use conditioner. They used plaits. The fortunate ones with straight, shiny tresses, those bitches with a bit of wave to ornament their juvenile beauty, the boys, Oh, the boys, they all took up the cry.

'Fifi's a poodle! Fifi's a poodle!' She could hear the jeering cadence right now. She had turned her back to them, trying to hide the tears of frustration and rage. She had no strategies for coping with this. They had been her friends, hadn't they? How could they do this to her? They had shared secrets. They had shared sweeties. They had put their heads together, laughed together, cried together. She wanted to lash out, to hurt them back, but she couldn't. Girls didn't fight. But they surrounded her, repeating, repeating, the hurtful lines.

Sticks and stones may break my bones, but words, words.... Hurt. They don't draw blood, but they hurt, and the wound goes deep, deep. You can't see the scar, but its there, down in the darkness. Peel away the veneer, and underneath the finely honed and polished exterior of Ffion, skin care magnate and Mysten of a Frais of the Fratris, was little Fifi, crying because her friends were hurting her and she didn't know why. The casual, unthinking cruelty of children was the law of the African plains, hunter and hunted. Bloody scenes played out every day, where you learned the laws of survival quickly, or you were a lion's dinner. Children don't have strength, or claws, or fangs. They have words. They have shunning. Adults might smile indulgently at the uncivilized conflicts of brats growing up, but it was a bloodless battle, to remain with the herd, not to appear weak, or vulnerable, but a battle none-the-less.

Two things rescued her from her torment. First was the advent of Sophie. Attracted to the bait ball by the repeating cry, she screamed and went on the offensive: a five-year old fighting ball of fury, all striking fists and kicking feet (and, let's be honest here, biting teeth,) unconcerned about damage done and damage taken.

'That's my sister! You leave my sister alone, you bullies!'

Ah, that was the word, the clarion call, that brought the second wave of relief troops. The playground supervisor, that unfortunate teacher who was not barricaded in the staff room enjoying a short respite from the war against ignorance and the natural desires of feral children and sipping too-hot coffee, but condemned to walk the mean streets with the predators and prey. For twenty minutes at least, until the magic handbell rang and the wild pack were transformed, almost immediately, (apart from some residual shoving and hissing,) into two lines of silent, polite individuals with a 'Yes, Miss,' and 'No Miss,' servility drummed into them by the threat of seeing the Headmistress, a veritable dragon whose lair, where she prowled and blew smoke and flames at the slightest infringement of her Rules, looked out at the peaceful rose garden at the front of the school, not the unruly back where the monsters on whom she fed prowled and fought, made alliances and broke up and made friends again.

When Ffion had revisited her infant school in that convenient hiatus between final exams and end of term when those select few escaped the hallowed halls for real life beyond the confines of the houses of learning - even if it was to transfer to a more rarefied and select establishment, the august institution of debauch and licentiousness, namely, University, she had found the Dragon, a woman who had loomed large in her infant mind and beyond as a stern termagant, a draconian embodiment of Truth, Justice, and having to explain just why you were scoffing sherbet lemons in class instead of concentrating on Arithmetic was a genial, dumpy, five-foot-two scrap with an infectious laugh (Why she had never used in on those tiny terrors was a bit of a mystery. Maybe she was mellowed by age, but one had one's doubts) and a zest for life that made you smile. She always had turned a stern countenance on her wee charges, hauled up before her for unmentionable and unpardonable sins. The only smiles she saw from them were those nervous tics that plaster themselves on your face when you wanted to evince remorse but it wouldn't come. Just this silly, ridiculous simper. How she kept that mask in place was a thing of mystery. Maybe she had a secret stash of lemons that she sucked before those knicker-wetting interviews.

Meanwhile, in that years distant playground, the furious blowing of a whistle silenced the taunts. A bruised Sophie was hauled off her more damaged opponents, and a tear-stained Ffion rescued from the damp and smelly corner by the wash hand basins where she had taken inadequate refuge. Sharp reprimands were issued, dire warnings given. You *will* stand quietly in two straight lines. Joseph (an older boy who had wandered over to see what the fuss was about and was now irrevocably implicated in the scandal,) go to the staff room and fetch Miss Williams. Stand *still*. I will not *tolerate* this behaviour in my Playground. You will walk into the school. Now. You *will* go to the hall and sit on the floor. You *will* be silent. Torquemada could have taken lessons from Miss Harcourt. She was ancient. She was a force of nature. She could see through walls, and possibly move faster than a speeding bullet. She could hear you whisper to the girl in the next desk *with her back turned*. She knew what you were thinking. She was twenty-two.

Miss Williams, on the other hand, was thirty, and embodied the power of the Almighty Himself. She sectioned the main culprits and sent them to sit outside the Headmistress's study, a fate worse than death itself. To the rest, she issued a sharp lecture. Bullying was a sin, the worst of sins. They were all wretches. They ought to be ashamed of themselves. They giggled nervously, even the boys, behind their hands. She called them to task. She called them by *name*. The giggling stopped. Nearly every face held that nervous simper. The boys as well. Letters would be written, letters home. Now they were in for it. The wrath of doom hung over them. They could not escape. Chastened, they were sent back to class. Quietly, they went. 'I'm disappointed in you. Very disappointed indeed.' Oh, hell.

Meanwhile, Ffion was having her face washed. Gently. By Miss Harcourt. She held herself in a welter of fear. It was her fault. She had caused a near riot in the playground. She could not conceive of a worse infraction of the Rules governing the etiquette of the playground. You could run, and play catch. You could skip alone or with friends. You could do handstands against the wall, where the boys looked at your knickers. You could play tag, or Blind Man's Buff, Farmer Wants a Wife, Wallflowers or anything. But not this. What would Mummy say? Or Daddy, when he came home? Because of her, the iron routine of the school had been disturbed. Sophie had been hurt. Surely they could not love her any more, not after this. The punishment would be.... would be....... She couldn't stop crying. The tears kept coming, falling down her cheeks. 'Shush, shush,' Miss Harcourt urged. But she couldn't shush. It wasn't possible.

Another teacher was dabbing lotion on Sophie's bruises, tutting. 'And on your first day, too.'

Lily turned up. As a further punishment for curiosity, Joseph had been sent running across the green to Pippin Cottage. He had started out with a carefully worded message to deliver. Which he forgot in its entirety. What he actually said was, as Ffion found out later, 'Miss Harcourt says you gotta come t'school, Missus,' as if she were a naughty pupil summoned into The Presence rather than a mother whose cherished offspring had been subject to mob violence. Lily had torn off her apron, abandoned her cooking, and outpaced Joseph back to school appearing with her hair tied up in a haphazard turban and flour on her hands. No sight had been more welcome to Sophie, who threw herself at the maternal presence and announced that 'they were being nasty to Fee,' which just about summed up the whole affair.

Assuring herself that her girls had sustained no mortal wounds, Lily had gone into a huddle with Miss Harcourt. There was much nodding of heads and hum-ing. Sophie had plonked herself down on the chair next to Ffion and awaited developments. She was completely unaware of the depth of her perfidy that Ffion saw all too clearly. Then, the Headmistress appeared. Now, they were going to die. It was sure.

Mrs Carmody came over to the two girls, hauled a chair over, sat down and looked them in the eye. Behind her, Miss Harcourt and Lily loomed large, avenging giants waiting for permission to devour their hapless victims.

'So tell me,' she asked, the very quietness of her voice indicating the depth of the morass of trouble they were in, 'exactly what happened in the playground?'

Fee saw an out. It had not happened in the playground. It happened in the toilets. She did not need to lie. She could keep the honour of the playground intact. You. Did. Not. Tell. On. Anyone.

'Nothing,' she mumbled.

Mrs Carmody glanced at the battered Sophie, her new school frock torn and dirtied, the bruises and scrapes starting to colour up magnificently.

'Looks like more than nothing to me.'

She turned to Sophie.

'You are Sophie, aren't you? This is your first day, and I don't know you so well as I know your sister. Will you tell me what happened today?'

Sophie did not know the Rules. She would tell. They were going to die. No-one would ever speak to her again. Her friends would turn their backs on her and stick their noses in the air. 'Tattle tale tit.'

'They were calling Fee names. They called her a poodle. Fee's not a poodle. She's my sister. They called her Fifi. That's not her name. She's Ffion.'

'I see.'

'So I hit them. They're nasty. They were nasty to my sister. That's not right,' Sophie had insisted, plain on her rights to create mayhem when something was wrong with the world as she expected it to be.

'And is it right to hurt someone because they're being nasty?'

'Yes.'

'Well, things are a little different here. I can't have my girls and boys fighting with each other all the time. In future, if someone is doing something you don't like, you will not hit them yourself. They may hit you back. Neither you nor I would like that to happen. You will, in future, tell a teacher, and they will deal with it. Is that clear?'

'Yes.' From the defiance of the tone, it was clear that Sophie did not agree that foisting your personal battles on someone else was an acceptable alternative to hammering seven bells out of them yourself.

'Is that clear?' repeated Mrs Carmody more forcefully, sensing the dissent in her most recent pupil.

'Yes.'

'That's better.' She turned to Fee. 'I think it would be best if your mother takes you both home. You are excused school for the rest of today.' She stood up, and turned to Miss Harcourt and Lily. 'Take them home, Mrs Harris. I will come and speak to you later. Miss Harcourt, my study, if you please.' She was sending Miss Harcourt to her study. *She was sending Miss Harcourt to her study!* A *teacher!* What naughty thing had Miss Harcourt done to warrant such punishment? And she would speak to Mummy later! The world was about to end. Apocalypse was due and ordained. Oh god, they were in trouble now……….

Lily smiled and thanked Mrs Carmody. She said she was sure Mrs Carmody would deal with it. Properly. There was a bite, a sting, to that statement. Mummy? Rebuking Mrs Carmody? Mrs Carmody's lips got tight. Oh, indeed she would deal with it. She took a *very* dim view of this sort of thing. She would not have it in her school. It would be, she said, nipped in the bud.

Lily collected their coats and plimsoll bags. They changed their shoes and walked home in silence, Sophie because she saw nothing wrong in what had happened, and Ffion because she was deadly afraid of the wrath shortly to descend. They were sent to change their school clothes 'and hang them up nicely for tomorrow' except that Sophie's dress would need cleaning and mending. She would wear her spare dress tomorrow. Lily's cooking had not survived. She threw the charred remains into the bin. Something else to be blamed for……..

They were given milk and biscuits and sent outside to play. While Sophie chattered and chased butterflies, Ffion sat on the garden swing, morosely kicking the dry earth with her pumps. Waiting.

When Robbie came home, after the first greeting, Lily swept him into the sitting room and closed the door. Murmured phrases, too low to hear, filtered into the kitchen where Ffion sat at the table, head in hands, trying to shut out Sophie's babbling to her dolls. She felt utterly wretched. Then she heard her father laughing. Laughing! The door swung open.

'…. and it was all I could do to keep a straight face. I suppose Barry or Mary will be along later to complain about the abuse. Sophie copped their Graham a right wallop.'

'Serve the little bugger right. And I'll tell Barry so. Where's my little bruiser, then?' Robert swung Sophie up from off the floor. 'Fighting with boys? Whatever next!' He dumped her back with her dolls. 'C'mere, Fee.' He sat down and patted his knee. When she was slow to move, he lifted her up. 'You are getting too heavy for this, my girl. What are we going to do with you?' What indeed….. 'I know you're hurting, little one. They called me Fat Owl at school, did you know that?'

'Really? What did you do?'

'I hit them. Hit them till they stopped. Hit them till they bled. And they hit me back. Tore my jacket, gave me a black eye, the lot. Me Mam was furious. Hared down to the school and raised merry heck. Embarrassed the hell out of me, I can tell you.' He paused. 'I learned the real trick later. Got to be a bit of a bully myself, sad to say. But there was this one guy, John, his name was, we called him Little Weed. His mum always used to send him with notes to excuse him from PE. He wouldn't play the game. He'd just walk away. And we'd run after. We'd catch him, and hit him, and taunt him. We bled him, but he never said a word. Never shed a tear. Then, one day, I found him behind the bike sheds. He was hiding there, reading a book, and crying. No sound, just tears. There was just the two of us. He looked up at me, the tears on his face, and said, 'Why?' I said, 'I dunno,' and then I sat down next to him. I saw the fear on his face, like he expected me to hit him, and I looked at myself, and I didn't like what I saw. I'd been a victim, and grew into a bully to escape it. But I hadn't. I'd made it continue. I'd done to this boy what others had done to me, and I didn't like it. So I said to him, 'Do you want me to hit them for you?' and he said 'No, they're not worth it.' And I saw, in an instant, that that included me. I was not worth it either. He was right, I was wrong. The next time they started on him, and I was with them, he turned away, and I turned with him. We both walked off together. They followed us, and when they surrounded us, I was right scared. I was in for a whupping. Cruising for a bruising. John just looked at them and said 'Yes?', and kept right on looking. He would look at them while they hit him. God, how I admired his courage right then. He looked them in the eye, this weed, against all that muscle, and just said, yes. You can hit me. And I don't care. Or, if I do care, I won't show you that I care. Hit me all you want, nothing will change. And there was I, balling my fists, mouth dry, ready to run or fight, and he was better than me. So I stood up, let my hands open, and waited for the pain. It didn't come. They walked away. There was no fun in it. That wasn't the end of it, no. There were times when we did get hurt. But they got less and less.

'By the time we left school, John and I were mates for life. We got into more than a few scrapes together, I can tell you. But John taught me the only lesson that really works against bullies, that ends the bully-victim-bully merry-go-round. YOU CHOOSE TO BE NEITHER. That goes for you too, Sophie,' he said, collecting her onto his vacant knee. 'I'm proud that you are courageous enough to defend your sister, really proud. But don't make a habit of hitting people. It's not nice. Now give me a kiss, both of you, and let your Mum serve up dinner.'

And that was that. Ffion heard later that the main ringleaders had been made to stand up in class (stand up in class! The ultimate sanction! The humiliation!) and admit before all their classmates that they were bullies. That it was not acceptable behaviour. That they would not do it again, ever.

Ffion took her father's words to heart, and told her friends that her new nickname was Poodle. And what had been a source of humiliation and pain became a mark of honour and esteem. Only her really bestest friends were allowed to call her Poodle. One or two still did. Oh, and she started to use conditioner.

Fee shook herself out of her past and into the present. Dilys had finished whatever preparations she needed in the kitchen and had released her sous-chefs back into the parlour with tea. Always the tea. Fee was beginning to crave the touch of a little wine. And still Lily held conference with Zoe. Fee slipped back into the past again, back into her mother's bedroom, Lily reclining between the cushions, patting the bed next to her. 'Sit down, Fee, we need to talk. This is for you, and you alone. Some you may share with others, some not. It is up to you…..'

All the girls in the Family got this 'talk' at some point in their lives. Boys got it from their fathers. The birds and the bees it wasn't. It was about the Family, and the wyth. A rare few decided it wasn't for them, but the ability was still there, it could still be passed on. You could ignore it, turn your back on it and never use it, but never lose it completely. Your sons and daughters could well inherit it from you, and decide to bring their blood back to the Frais, have the Ritual and go on from there. You had to be able to tell them that seeing things others didn't see, feeling things they couldn't, and doing things they were not capable of was not a curse, it was almost a sacred trust. But it was never spoken of it that way. It was just there, like curly hair or blue eyes. You just didn't talk about it, except to the Family.

Meanwhile, the natives were getting restless. They had been hoping to see Zoe again before they left, but they had clearly outstayed their welcome. Dilys chivvied them out the door: have you no home to go to? They went, proffering kisses and eternal friendship, into the night. Dilys collapsed into a chair.
'Well, my.'
'What have you heard, Dilys?'
'Not much. One of the Duke boys crashed his motorcycle into a shop window. Got cut about, lost a lot of blood, but survived. Said there was something in the road, like a dog or something, but it ran off. Oh, there was the Madison girls. Twins, they were. Quite forgot about them. Went off on a surf safari to Porth, down your way. Deirdre and Edain. Jackie was really fond of the Irish myths, see. Swept out to sea, the bodies were never found. Strange to think on it, now. There were so many of them there, surfing on that beach, but only two got caught in the rip. Deirdre and Edain.'
'Did the police investigate?'
'Went to the Coroner's court. He gave a verdict of death by misadventure. An accident, in other words. There were loads of witnesses. Come to think of it…. Well, well.'
'Give, Dilys.'
'Naturally, after the girls didn't come back, the police were called, and they asked for witnesses. Most came forward with nothing to tell. But we kept up with the case yere, being so close and all. One of the lifeguards - there were lifeguards on the beach - said he noticed one bloke on the beach, noticed him particularly, since he wasn't wearing the usual beach clothes. Stood out, he said. Like a sore thumb. All the rest were in summer dress - you know, bright clothes, swimming cozzies, sarongs, sun hats, wetsuits, that sort of stuff: but this bloke, he stood out. Coz he was wearing black. At first, the guard thought it was a wetsuit, but then, he said, he saw the trouser legs flapping. So he had a dekko. The bloke, he said, was all in black. Black fedora, black shirt, black trews, even black gloves. He was just standing there,

shading his eyes with one hand, looking out to sea. Stood there for a while, then walked off. This lifeguard said, when he was questioned, that he was paid to notice stuff. He noticed this guy. He said, that if anyone saw what happened, he would have, because he was standing there, looking out to sea, for some time. Oh, it was in the newspapers. 'Were you the man wearing black who was on Porth beach on May 23rd. You may have seen something to help with our investigation, blah, blah.' But no-one came forward. Ever. And since there was no hint of foul play, the coroner closed the case. Was a nine week wonder round yere. Big memorial service. Even the lifeguard came. No funeral, of course, since there were no bodies. Poor Jackie.'

'Madison? I don't recognize the name.'

'You wouldn't. Jackie Madison was a Harris on her mother's side, but her father was a Smith. Not Family. But the blood bred true in Deirdre and Edain. Lovely girls. Tragic loss. Dave Madison wasn't Family either, but he got the wyth from somewhere. After the girls died, he and Jackie moved to Ireland. He got a transfer from his firm, I think. I've got their address somewhere, I'll let you have it. Talk to Dave: Jackie can't talk about the girls.'

'And the Duke boy?'

'Michael's still here. Manages one of they big stores out by Diss. I'll tell him to get in touch. He'll be sorry he missed you. No-one believed him about the dog. His mam wouldn't let him have another motorbike after that, not while he was living under her roof, she said. So he moved out over to Diss way and brought one anyway.'

Fee rummaged in her bag, found a pen and made notes in her diary. Dilys went over to the bureau by the window, opened a drawer and sorted through the contents.

'There you are, Jackie and Dave Madison, County Mayo, Ireland.'

Fee copied from the foxy scrap of paper.

'I suggest you set the wards and send out the faths.'

'Yes, Mysten.' The formal use of her title was a bit of a shock. Hearing it in the Frais was one thing, but hearing the same from Lily's carer was another. 'I'll pass it on. We've got all sorts round yere. We're not like you in the West: there's a bit of the mongrel in most of us. Leave me awhile, midear. By tomorrow morning, most of the Family will know that we've got real trouble.'

'Tell them to contact Zoe with any information.' Fee scribbled Zoe's e-mail on a sheet and tore it out of her diary. Dilys took it.

'Prefer the phone meself, I do. But there, times do move on. Lily's got one of them newfangled computer things, keeps on at me to update meself. But I've got her to look after, bless her.'

Fee took their bags up to the guestroom to unpack and wait for Dilys to finish her telephone marathon and Lily to complete her talk with Zoe. She quashed her impatience: tonight she would see Rina, Scourge Of The Vampires. That'd make a good film.

As they sat down to dinner, Fee wondered how she would manage to eat anything. Not only were the cucumber sandwiches and trifle from teatime still weighing in her stomach, but there was a curious subsonic whine about the place. It felt like there was a vibration, too low to be really felt, but there nonetheless. When Dilys set wards, she didn't muck about. The air felt - empty. Vacant. Void. No sense, no smell, no…. presence. She felt she was swaddled in cotton wool. Zoe was preoccupied. That made sense. There had been more to her 'talk' than Lily had said to Fee, obviously. Well, when Fee came to the Gya the first time, things had been different. Calmer. No sense that World War Three might break out at any moment and they might have to run to the old Anderson shelter that still haunted the depths of the garden at the cottage. Some old fool had built it ages ago. It made a great den. Both she and Sophie had experienced the first furtive adolescent sexual fumblings in its musty darkness.

Dilys had kept it simple. Lamb chops, peas and carrots, mashed potato, gravy and mint sauce. She had produced a bottle of wine from somewhere. Thank the ayen it wasn't Margie's cowslip. That had a reputation on a par with poteen. One glass and you were on the floor. Two, under the table and unconscious for the rest of the evening. Dilys' offering was clean and lemony, with a faint hint of cut grass. When she'd asked, Fee was surprised to find that it was dandelion wine.

They helped Dilys clear away, folding the Pembroke table and shoving it up against the wall to get more room, then sat for an hour to watch 'a bit of telly'. David Attenborough at his finest, showcasing the beauty and tragedy of the natural world. Best to stay away from horror movies when you appear to be living in one.

The clock ticked round, until Dilys took Lily away to help her get ready for bed. Fee and Zoe shared the shower and bathroom. The oppression was starting to get on Ffion's nerves. She cleansed her face and scrubbed her teeth, then piled her hair up and exchanged places with Zoe in the shower. She could feel Zoe's gaze, freshly appraising the tattoos on her body, and considering their merit and suitability to decorate her own.

'What does Greg think of the tats?'

'He's never mentioned them.'

'Huh.' Zoe was going to add to that, but reconsidered and started to clean her teeth instead.

A pang of regret, bitter as aloes, flooded Fee's mouth. She had cherished a hope that, once Greg saw her tattoos he would realize what they were. If he had the wyth, surely something in him would have responded to the exotic designs that adorned her skin. He had not ignored them. Instead, he had gently traced the designs with his fingers and his lips. Fee had been forced to grit her teeth to swallow the surge of wyth which was threatening to overwhelm her. He had glanced at her face then. Afterwards, he left the tats alone and never mentioned them. Maybe he thought they were a legacy from some other involvement too painful to be discussed at that time. In any case, his lack of reaction had caused a deep sorrow in Fee. Surely, surely, if he had the wyth, it would have responded? If he were Family, he would have seen them for what they were? But his body was unmarked, innocent of any designs that might have betrayed his affiliations. The affair was doomed in the long run. He was a distraction and nothing more. A pleasant distraction, true, but a distraction only. For her life partner she would have to look elsewhere, or accept that there would be a part of her life she could never share with him. The realization burned. Whichever way it turned out, it would hurt them both. Better to end it now than continue with impossible hope.

Finally, swathed in bathrobes, they went to say goodnight to Lily. She was in bed, her greying hair in two long loose plaits on the pillow. Above her bed, the 'apparatus' as Dilys called it, swayed gently. Lily could use the hanging straps and grips to help her get up. Her legs had never mended that well, and if she could move about on crutches, it hurt so much she kept to her wheelchair most of the time.

Accepting mugs of cocoa from Dilys, though Fee would have preferred a stiff brandy, they went up the stairs to the attic bedroom that was set aside for visitors. All it had was two twin beds with cream sheets and comforters, a bedside table with a lamp and clock, a small set of drawers and a tiny wardrobe. The walls were decorated with a tiny floral pattern which matched the curtains. They edged round the beds and sat there, sipping the cocoa. Zoe didn't seem interested in drawing Fee out on what the cousins had told her. Unusual for Zoe, but Fee let it slide. The kid had more on her plate tonight.

'You okay, Mouse?'

'I expect.'

'Anything you want to tell me, to ask me?'

'No. Yes. I want to, and I don't. You know?'

'Yes, actually, I do. I remember what Sophie was like back then.'

'Oh, how?'

'She was sort of - well, remote. Changed. I felt really angry at that. Mum had taken my Sophie away from me. I wanted the old Sophie back. I didn't understand then. She'd grown up, grown away and in some place I couldn't follow. She wasn't the Sophie I had known. She was off in this other place, away from me. She was this other person, someone I didn't know. It went on for about, oh, about a week or so, then, one morning, the old Sophie was back, as if she'd never gone away. Oh, there were flashes of the new Sophie from time to time, and just as I was getting used to it, it was my time. Then, I understood. Just as I understand now, what is happening, has happened, to you.'

'I forgot you'd been through this before.'

'But this time, you're not growing away from me. You're growing closer. I can feel it.'

'That might be a problem.'

'How so?'

'I might fancy Greg. I might take him away from you.'

'Some chance. Drink your cocoa, and let's get some sleep.'

'Before we have to go back, you mean.' Zoe's voice had started to drag with the edges of sleep. That crafty Dilys had spiked the evening cocoa, like as not. And no doubt Lily was behind it.

They snuggled down between the sheets. Fee reached over and switched off the light. Darkness claimed the room. It was that deep dark that you only get in the depths of the country, or have really good blackout blinds. You can't see your hand in front of your face darkness. Fee remembered going with Luke (none of your country affairs stuff, please. Luke was only eight, for heaven's sake) into the caves on Pike's Head. They had paid out a spool of string, and taken a torch. Once they had threaded their way deep into the bowels of the cave (or, more properly, the string gave out. There was probably plenty of cave left over) Luke had switched off the torch and they had sat in complete and utter darkness. Okay, so it had been a dare. Eyes open, eyes shut, there was no difference. You really couldn't see a hand in front of your face. They sat there and completed the dare. They each ate a Mars bar, there in the darkness. It would have been fine if Luke hadn't lost the torch and Fee the end of the spool of string. They had been more annoyed than panicked. Luckily they were saved from the ignominy of rescue when Luke found the torch. Fee was quite sure he had done it on purpose, to see her freak out. When she didn't, and just called him a 'Stupid, *stupid* baby. Now I suppose we have to wait here until someone finds us,' and just sat there, fuming, Luke had lost his appetite for the joke and 'discovered' the torch in the crevice where he had left it. Fee never told him that she had not lost the string, either. Oh, the joys of childhood. A soft snore indicated that Zoe was asleep. Fee closed her eyes. There was no difference.

She slowly became aware that she was dreaming. There was a soft focus to her perception, like she was looking down a plastic tube. What was in front of her eyes was clear, bright, and detailed, but her peripheral vision was cloudy and distorted. Everything she saw was, well, brighter, more alive, more vibrant. She was walking down a dusty path, a small road really. On either side were high green hedges. Had she looked at them, she would have seen every leaf, and every vein in every leaf on every twig. It was like that, dreaming. But the littlest things distracted, drew you away from the purpose of the dream. Behind the hedges she knew there were trees, though she could not see them at all. She just knew they were there. They were not important. She had been walking down this road for some time. Forever. Her sleeping self had joined her dreaming self on this road. It had destination. Fee felt that. She also felt she was not alone on this road. Something or someone was following her. Not that she could hear a footfall or anything like that, but the tiny hairs bristling at the nape of her neck said, you are being watched. She could not, dare not, look round. If she did, she would lose this road, this purpose. She would just have to put up with it and carry on. She concentrated on the road, walking the path, going forward, approaching. It would come when she was there. Wherever there was. The road started a gentle bend. It curved between the hedges. Grasses nodded at the foot of the hedge. Ragged robin bloomed in the grass. Cow parsley, hemlock and sweet cicely lifted lacy heads into the air. Scarlet pimpernel and blue-bird-peck-your-eye-out dotted the grass below white and yellow oxeye daises. The dreamscape was becoming more detailed. A gentle wind blew the grasses and flowers about, but Fee could not feel it. She was neither hot nor cold, fresh nor weary - she just was. It was totally silent. No rustle from the hedge or grasses. No sound of her feet stepping, stepping, on the path. No scent, not of flowers, not of grass, not of anything. Fee's world was totally, and only, visual. And still, she was aware of another consciousness, as clear to her as her own, was there with her. Neither amicable nor inimical, just…. Watchful. Without interest. How strange…..

Then, the hedge was gone. In its place was a white picket fence. Fee could see the fence, knew there was a garden beyond, but could not see details of the planting. A gate was in the picket fence. Five stiles and a Z-shaped crosspiece. There was no latch.

Fee touched the gate, and it swung open. Now, she could see the garden. It was a rose garden. Roses, roses, roses everywhere. White, cream, all shades of pink from the most delicate blush to almost scarlet. And the fragrance! You could taste it. A crazy paving path wandered through the massed blooms to a door which stood slightly ajar. Moss grew between the stones on the path. It was vivid, vivid green. Mind-your-own business scrambled along the edges and under the roses. Fee followed the winding trail, drowning in the heady scent of roses. Then she was at the door. It was very like the gate: five broad planks of wood held in place by a Z-shaped tie. Fixed on the door and hanging from a hook by its mouth was a fish. No. The fish was gripping a ring in its mouth, and that hung on the hook. The fish was black, shiny, and Fee could see every scale on its body, every gill. Its fins were laid back close against its body, its eyes open and aware. Fee felt that if she touched it, it would jump off the hook, alive as can be. How can a live fish hang from a hook and pretend to be a doorknocker?

She touched the door. It remained as it was, the gap too narrow for Fee to pass through. The gate had opened at her touch, but this door had other ideas. She lifted the fish, and let it fall back, knocking the door. The striker was a intricately detailed scallop shell. As the fish fell back, it was not so much like a knock, more like a gong. Not one of those silly little ones, either. More like the gong at the start of a Rank movie. It vibrated. It had substance. The door swung open.

Then she was standing in a kitchen. She could see an old grate, the fire twinkling behind black bars. A poker leant against the hearth. Over the fire hung a blackened pot. On the floor was a rag rug. She could not make out what the pattern was. Now there was a wingback chair by the fire, with an old lady sitting in it. One moment she wasn't there, the next she was. She leant forward, and stirred the contents of the pot. The fragrance of herbs, and good stew, and new-baked bread wafted from the pot. The old lady had white, white hair, masses of it, piled into a bun. Not thin like real old hair, but thick and as springing as that of a young girl. Her face, her face ought to be a mass of lines, in common with the sense of age that was pouring off her, but it was smooth.

There was a slight serene smile on that face. She was wearing a long dress which fell in full and ample folds to the floor, hiding her legs and feet completely. It was high-necked, ending in a ruffle, and had a row of tiny buttons on the bodice. The fabric had a dainty sprigged design which, again, Fee could not quite see properly.

'*Come in, child. Sit you down.*' At first, Fee could not hear the voice, only know that the old lady had spoken. Another chair was on the other side of the fire, facing the old lady. Fee sat down, then suddenly they were in the garden surrounded by roses. The old lady had one perfect creamy blossom in her hand, an old-fashioned cabbage rose.

'*My roses never fade.*'

They were back in the kitchen, sitting in the chairs by the fire, and Fee had the rose in her lap.

'Rina.'

'*You have found your way to me, child, and you are welcome. Ask me your questions, and I will answer as I am permitted.*'

'How can I stop what is happening to the Families?'

'*You cannot stop it. It must run its course. The seed of this tragedy was sown long ago. The time to stop it has long past. It has been long in the making, sown of good intentions as many evil things are.*'

'I cannot stand by and watch while those who are in my care are harmed.'

'*You cannot prevent this axe from falling, child.*'

'You do not have to sit meekly under the axe and watch it fall. You can move out from under the strike, or deflect the blow.'

'*Only if you know where the axe is falling.*'

'I will not stand by and allow this senseless slaughter.'

'*And if the victim deserved his fate, what then?*'

You do not deserve to be talked to death, nor persuaded to commit suicide.

'What did Luke do to deserve that fate?'

'*I did not say Luke deserved his fate. I ask what if he deserved his fate. Tell me, does it hurt more to be hurt yourself, or to watch another suffer senselessly?*'

'To watch another suffer.'

'This is a vengeance, visited upon another, to cause pain. To cause despair. And since the object of that vengeance is to cause suffering, what better way than to visit it upon the innocent?'

'Why Luke?'

'Why not Luke? The object has been achieved. This is a long, cold vengeance. This is reparation for what has been done and cannot be undone. It has been brooded over and nurtured these long years, and now we see the flowering. It is a means to an end, child, and the end is a deadly fruit.'

Fee opened her mouth to speak, but Rina raised a hand to silence her.

'Yes, I know who is behind it. But if you ask me that question, then you forfeit my aid. And you will need it again, before the end.'

'Then what must I do?'

'You must wait. I fear there will be much pain and heartbreak before events reach a climax. You must not act before this nexus is reached, or your enemy will simply crawl back into his lair and hide, only to re-emerge later and visit the whole trouble on you again and again, until either he succeeds in his endeavours, or you succeed in destroying him. You are both joined in battle, a contest of wills. You will have one chance, and one chance only, to end this. Be very sure, that when you act, that you are righteous.'

'How can I do this?'

'You must keep your heart pure and your intentions clean. Steel your soul, child, for a storm of trouble is come upon you. Seek strength in those you love, and share your strength with them. Do not act rashly or without good cause. Remember, your task is to end this threat, end it once and for all. You are the only person who can bring this about. You form a crucial focus in these events. Do not be distracted by anything less important than this.'

Her voice, her kitchen, started to fade. Fee strained to keep hearing, to stay longer.....

'Fix your mind on the prize. All else, all sorrow and pain that this storm brings, are merely trifles. Make yourself the hunter, not the prey: remember, a true hunter knows his quarry. He sits

and waits for the quarry to come to him. He does not wear himself out chasing shadows on the wall. Weave your web like a spider, entice him to you, trap him in your web and then consume him.'

Fee remembered no more.

She awoke to birdsong and predawn twilight. Zoe was sitting up in the other bed, a notepad and pencil on her lap. She had moved the bedside light from off the table onto the floor by her bed, so she had all the light and Fee was left in the cosy half-dark. Zoe's phone sat on the table, set to record. They both knew only too well how the gossamer memories of night vanished in the reality of a new day.

'Give, Fee.' She spoke softly, so as not to disturb Fee's dream memory.

'I was walking down a dusty path.......' she started, eyes closed, recalling. Zoe insisted she relate every detail, no matter how tiny.

'What colour was her dress?'

'Did you sense anything else in the kitchen?'

'Did you see the house at all?'

'What did Rina look like when she said that?'

Once the first recollection was done, she started off again.

'Describe the knocker, as much detail as you can remember.'

'Try to see the house. Describe it.'

'Focus on the path. What was following you? What did you sense about them?'

'What were you wearing?'

With a shock, Fee considered that she might have been wearing sod all. Finally, she caught a detail: she had looked at her feet and seen the hem of a pale skirt.

Zoe was good. She forced details that Fee hadn't noticed. The trick was not to strain, not to reach, not to invent. If you hadn't brought it back, it either didn't matter, or you would regret it later. Fee hoped for the former and suspected the latter. She submitted to the inquisition with good grace.

At last, Zoe expressed herself satisfied. 'For now. I wonder what we get for breakfast round here?'

'I heard Dilys clattering about. Let's get this day started.' She threw back the covers.

'I've decided what music I want.'

'Huh?' Fee muttered through the t-shirt she was pulling over her head. Zoe was messing with the bedclothes.

'My music. For the Ritual. Mum said. I've decided.'

'What is it?'

'It's a secret.'

'Oh, okay. Get your kecks on, girl, or we'll have to skip breakfast. We've a lot to do today.'

Lily sat in her wheelchair, pale and lethargic at the breakfast table.

'It's nothing, my dear. Just had a bad night, is all.'

She hugged them both. She seemed to revive a bit over breakfast. Cornflakes, toast and soft boiled eggs. And more tea. Zoe rebelled and went to make coffee.

'I think, Dilys my dear, you can tone down the wards a notch or two. I don't think the denizens of the Nether Hells are about to make an immediate assault on us here,' she commented with something like her usual asperity. 'I could hardly get to sleep last night for the whine.'

'We slept all right,' commented Zoe, coming in from the kitchen with two steaming mugs of coffee.

'You,' Lily said, 'Slept in the attic. I slept on the ground floor with the ward right outside my window. Thank you dear, I think I'll have a coffee myself.'

Zoe motioned Fee into the kitchen.

'I think she's been got at.'

'I think you may be right.'

Zoe dumped a pinch of salt in the coffee.

'For the health of the body and the mind, the soul and the spirit, I invoke you, wyth of earth, into this body of water.'

She handed it to Fee.

'Avaunt, ye creatures of the night, assail ye not the children of the light.'

It was an old cantrip. Maybe you were simply 'out of sorts', or maybe you had brought back a rider. Lily was definitely acting unLilyish this morning. Fee took the mug to the table.

Lily took a sip.

'Been putting salt in your old mother's coffee, have you?' She cocked an eyebrow over the mug. Fee had the decency to look ashamed. 'Tastes all right, anyway. Thought your old Mum brought back a rider?' Fee nodded. 'I'm not the same as I was. And Dilys is a tightwad with the morphine.'

'Too much is bad for you. I'll speak to Doctor Russell later today. Or I could call young Mark, get you some wacky baccy. But the ward stays. Mysten says so.' She flounced out. Fee followed her.

'You can turn it down a wee bit. It was even setting my teeth on edge last night.'

'Don't you worry none. Old Dilys knows what she's about. I like to give 'er a bit o'summat to complain about, now and then. Keeps her interested. Doc Russell'll have summat, I don't wonder. An' I don' need the service of young Mark to get wacky baccy neither.' She touched her nose. 'Grow the bugger myself, I do.'

Fee laughed. Dilys certainly had Lily's number.

All too soon, they were ready to leave. Kisses were exchanged, hugs given and received. Lily was a bit tearful. Her bad night must have been worse than she was letting on. But Fee was comfortable leaving her with Dilys, more so now than before. She had always known Dilys was Family, but some you liked, some you didn't. Dilys was growing on her.

'I've called Lucy, she'll be expecting you. Don't shove the boat out too much, Zoe, I'm not made of money.'

Chapter Seven

Lucy lived in Wandsworth with her long-time boyfriend. Zaphriam was otherwise known as 'Doc Zedd, The Soundmeister' and ran 'events' all round London. Juicy Lucy, as she had been known in her singing days before the brood of coffee-coloured kids interrupted it, made what she called 'Pagan Couture' and was the Family's designer of choice when it came to robes. Zoe would need her own now, and Lily was paying. There was another reason Fee wanted to see Lucy. Most of her Family were bucolic. Lucy was an urban chick and listened to a different drumbeat. If she could pump Zaph as well, she might get to hear other, weirder things. Oh, no, the Family wasn't all white, nor confined to the UK. The Gya was everywhere, so the wyth was everywhere too. It just surfaced in different forms, but at heart it was the same. The Blood surfaced and the flesh gave it form. Zaph's Voudun might be closer to the darker heart. It would not hurt to ask.

As they drove off, Fee announced that she intended to drive to Chalfont and leave the car there, and 'bus it' over London. Zoe commented that Wandsworth was closer to Norfolk than Chalfont, but Fee cited the congestion charge, and the M25, and probable gridlock, and Zoe subsided. The tube came as far as Chalfont anyway. That was the plan.

Lucy lived in one of those tall houses that are typical of some parts of London. The singing career must have been more successful than anyone had supposed, to be able to afford such a pile in London. That or Zaph was on the take. Or 'eventing' paid very, very well. The house wasn't too far from Wandsworth Common.

Lucy met them at the door. Muted music with a West African beat was coming up from the cellar where Zaph had his studio, mixing music for his 'events'.

'He'll be up later. I like to leave him alone when his creative muse gets going. Glass of wine?'

'Please.' What a relief. Fee couldn't stand the thought of more tea at the moment, and she wasn't driving tonight.

Juicy Lucy was wearing cornrow plaits. And beads and ribbons. A baggy white t-shirt with 'Doc Zedd's Stupendous Sound Machine' blazoned across her tits was only slightly hidden by a multicoloured velvet waistcoat. Her lower limbs sported leopard print tights. Even after four kids, her belly was as flat and her thighs as firm as a virgin's. Bitch. She handed round oversize glasses of chilled white wine. They arranged themselves on soft sofas swathed in coloured throws and watched the baby crawl across the rugs.

'Paco will be standing soon. Bebe's upstairs having a nap. The other two are at playgroup.' With the nanny. 'Some French bird Zaph picked up at a gig somewhere.' They were a Bohemian couple. Lucy didn't have much to add to the mix. She had heard about Luke, and admitted to feeling 'a real down vibe' about it. 'Don't do much Family stuff no more.' But she was genuinely pleased to know that Zoe was 'fronting up at last.'

'I'll do you a good deal. Always do a good deal for Lily's lot. None o'you done hitched their fanny at me.' She was regarded as a bit of a rebel. 'Difficult' had been the mildest term used of her. 'Toffee-nosed wankers' was the politest she had been about her family when she had run off to join a pop group. Anyway, Lucy had done good, had not been found dead of substance abuse in a gutter nor gone on the game to support a drug habit or pimp. 'They gotta catch me first. And when they do, I'll give 'em what for.' More than a touch of Rina in there.

'I got some really nice West Indian fabric. You oughter go blue, Zoe.' Like it or not, Juicy Lucy could sum up a person in a glance. She had never admitted to a talent for seeing auras, but she was right….every time. 'It's got a light heft and will sit well. Ah, no hips yet to speak of, so's I'd better not fit it too close. No, something loose, but not too loose. This one's got a hint of gold, really nice, you go with that. I've already got the cloak made, Lily told me your height. I thought a snake clasp, okay?' She vanished into the back, leaving them with Paco who dribbled on the rug, looking at them, his round baby face intent.

Lucy returned with a swathe of black over one arm and several swatches over the other, all various shades of blue.

'Try it on. There's plenty of hem, so you can let it down. Can't stand these cheapskates who leave no hem. Never hangs right. You need the weight. Perfect!'

She spread the materials over the opposite sofa. One swatch of deep blue, with lighter tones in a swirly pattern, caught Zoe's eye. When she lifted it up, it glinted gold in the sunlight.

'That's the one. Gimme an hour or so. Don't take no mor'an that to do one o' dese.' Zaph was rubbing off on her.

'You getting awful West Indian in your twang.'

'Comes from cohabitin' wiv de black boys. Ah lord.'

She swanned off, leaving the cloak on the sofa. Zoe lifted it out of the way before Paco dribbled on it. There was a change in atmosphere. It puzzled Fee for a moment, until she realized that the sounds from the basement had ceased. A few moments later, a tall, very black man entered the room. He was dressed in black from head to foot: tight black t-shirt with cutaway shoulders, cargo pants with more pockets than pants, black trainers and a black bandanna on his head. Fee felt Zoe start beside her on the sofa.

'Well, hello dere. Where you two honeys be comin' fo'?' The voice dripped honey and West Indian sun. The teeth flashed very white in the black face. He draped himself over the sofa, too close for comfort. Before Fee could frame a reply, Lucy's voice came from the back room.

'Zaphraim Ababita, you leave those two ladies alone, or your black ass is grass. They're *Family*.'

He lifted himself off the sofa.

'I do beg your pardon.' The patois and accent were gone. It was pure Received BBC English, straight from Eton and Harrow. He bent down and retrieved Paco from the floor. 'How's my little man, then?' He swung the child high over his head. Paco grinned, chucked, and dribbled on his head. 'Messy boy.'

There was a wail from overhead.

'Hello, Bebe. I'll get it,' he raised his voice over the whine of an electric sewing machine. 'Where's Jaqueline?'

'Playgroup, then park. Should be back soon,' Lucy called from the back.

'Excuse the chaos. We're not usually this disorganized. Back in a moment.' He hefted Paco under one arm and exited in the direction of the increasingly furious wail. The door slammed. Jaqueline was back with the remains of the brood. Two coffee-skinned children ran into the room and stopped dead, seeing two strangers there. Twins. One boy, one girl. Lucy came back.

'Hello Asia, Angel. Say hello to Ffion and Zoe. They are your Aunties.' Asia shoved her fingers into her mouth, and Angel hid his face against his mother's leg. 'You'll have to forgive them, all their other Aunties are black. Gotta love this multiculturalism. Jaqueline, take them out back and we'll give them their tea. Zaph's bringing Bebe and Paco.' From the back came excited squeals. Zaph was entertaining Bebe and Paco. Jaqueline collected Angel and Asia. With a slight smile and a very French 'Adieu' she swept them away.

Lucy held up the finished garment for them to see. The material was gathered at each shoulder, sweeping down in a deep vee front and back to the waist, which was caught with a twist on one hip.

'Isn't it a bit, well, low? In the neck, I mean.'

'Scared you'll fall out? Never. The way I've done it, this'll take a double-f. Not that you'll get that big,' she grinned. 'I've set the hem to just above your knees, so as you grow it'll rise to mid-thigh. You don't want it shorter. Now, for the cloak and robe I could bet on getting about five hundred if I sold it to a shop, and between seven hundred and a thousand if I sold privately depending on the client. I'll let you have both for two-fifty.'

Zoe opened her mouth to haggle, but Fee cut her off. It was a good deal. A very good deal. Lucy's creations were quite sort after.

'Done. If you can give us a little help.'

'What sort of help?'

'Black help.'

'Now there's a thing I never thought to hear.'

'We've got trouble, Luze.'

'I've been hearing some stuff.'

'Ah.'

'I heard there's more to Luke's tumble than just bad luck. Nasty.'

'It's bigger than that.'

'Not an accident?'

'No way. Some arse talked him into taking flying lessons.'

'And that's not all,' Zoe chipped in. 'Looks like something else is happening. Strange accidents. Unexpected deaths. And if Luke's 'accident' isn't connected with them, then I'm a monkey's uncle.'

Lucy considered.

'I'll speak to Zaph. He still owes me, big-time. But they can get strange about this sort of stuff, the West Indian community. I wouldn't want to alienate them.'

'All I want is information. At the moment.'

'Okay. But these people, they can run scared. There're very superstitious. I wouldn't want to lose Zaph. He's very good with the kids, considering.'

Fee looked at her.

'I'll tell you later. It's a good story, believe me.'

She picked up the two garments.

'I'll just get these packed and then start on dinner. You will stay for dinner? Do you like West Indian?'

'We can't be too late. Got a run back down West tomorrow morning.'

'Neither can we. Zaph's got a gig tonight. Gimme twenty.'

Zaph reappeared, minus offspring.

'Ah, ma woman. Couldn't cook until she met me.' He slid both hands round her waist and nuzzled her neck.

'You liar! I so could cook.'

'Not real food, not soul food.'

'If you want feeding, you'll have to let me go.'

'The hell of compromise. Off with you then, woman, and cook mah food. An' it better be goo-ood.' his accent slipped south. Way, way south. Lucy laughed and slipped out of his grasp.

'No letting de cat out o' de bag until Ah comes agin.' He patted her bum as she hurried off.

'Ah, wine.' He poured himself a generous helping. 'Ladies?' Zoe shook her head: Fee held out her glass. He poured for her.

'Luze!' he shouted. 'Do you want wine?' a muted 'No thanks,' issued from whatever depths of the house she was occupying at that moment. He flopped onto the other sofa and arranged himself comfortably.

'You like black music?' he aimed a remote at the sound system in the corner. A reggae beat filled the room, and a sultry female voice slipped into the beat, bewailing her lot.

'That's Lucy?'

'Yes. First time I heard her, it was like *that*.' He snapped his fingers. 'Knew she'd be a player. Wandered up and introduced myself. I was just starting out as a DJ, and she blew me off. Told me to take a hike. She had attitude then. The band she was fronting, Visor, was second-rate. Wasn't going anywhere. Eventually, I persuaded her to record for a mate of mine, had a studio in Hammersmith. In his dad's garage, would you believe? Hustled it round the local radio stations, got some air time, and we were on the way. Once she saw that I wasn't some bloke on the make, she unwound a bit. Gave me less attitude. We cut some tracks and I started to play them at my gigs. It was quite small time then. It was her idea to come up with the Doctor Zedd persona, the Wild Man of Reggae. I'd have this bottle of rum I'd swig from during the gig, then she'd come on, do a set to backing tracks and share it with me. Didn't have rum in it though, it was my Grannie's kombucha tea. We added the Voodoo vibe later. Got some sessions guys in, hired a good producer, found a studio, cut her first album. When the twins were on the way, she bowed out. I kept up the Sound Machine, kept her music rolling.' He sipped his wine. 'Mother hated the patois. She'd tell me she'd paid good money, worked nights, to give me a good education, and here I was, wasting her money. I told her that I had to talk the talk, but that didn't make me a street kid. We're tight now, but it was bad for a while. Especially when I moved in with Lucy, but that's another story.'

There was a hail from the kitchens. He ushered them into the dining room, where Jaqueline was sitting with the four children. He chucked the nearest under the chin, and she giggled. Lucy appeared with a dish of dirty rice and a bowl of salad.

'Get the cornbread, Zaph.' She vanished again, to reappear

with a huge bowl of chicken legs. Zaph added salad and cornbread, and then there was a dish of pork, pineapple and mango that had made friends with shredded ginger and a whole lot of chilli. Lucy ladled rice, pork and chicken onto plates and bowls, Zaph passed bread and salad and poured wine. Bebe started stuffing her face with rice while Lucy mashed cornbread in gravy for Paco. Jaqueline didn't appear to like the food, or maybe she had enough to do overseeing Angel and Asia, who were trying to start a food fight.

It was a generous meal, and there was plenty left over when they had all had enough, or thrown enough at the walls in the case of Angel and Asia.

'Bath, Jaqueline, I think. Or would you rather clear up dinner while Zaph and I do the honours?'

For answer, Jaqueline hoisted Paco from his seat.

'Come, Bebe, Angel, Asia. It is time for your bath.' As the twins scrambled from their seats, she took Bebe's hand and shoo'd them out.

'Zaph, you go help Jaqueline. Fee and Zoe will help here.'

At last, time to talk. Zoe had been strangely silent, for her. As Lucy rinsed glasses and plates, Fee loaded the dishwasher while Zoe made coffee.

'I suppose you've heard tales about me and Zaph, how he voodoo-ed me away from the family, seduced me and turned me into a sex slave?'

Such stories had been circulating. Some were quite detailed. Fee nodded.

'Well, here's the truth of it. The band was struggling. We thought we were good, but actually, we had no idea. We thought all we had to do was get a few gigs and everyone would be blown away by our sound. But there were too many bands, and we were, frankly, no more than competent. Oh, the boys could play. Even write songs. But we hadn't got the edge, the contacts.

'When Zaph first spoke to me, I thought he was coming on to me, so many boys did. So I told him to get lost, and it might have ended there. But he kept on coming to the gigs, and eventually I let him have his say. He convinced me to go solo. The band were all for packing it in anyway, so it was no big deal. The first time I heard myself on the local radio, it was like, Wow! That's me! Zaph and I got tight.

'But there was this girl, thought she had him, and then I came along and she's sliding out of the picture. Zaph and I weren't getting it on then, but she decides she's going to picture me out of Zaph's scene. Anyway, she turned to voodoo. She was a hounsi, and she did this ouanga. Decided that if she couldn't have him, no-one would.'

She paused and set the dishwasher running, then led them back into the lounge.

'It was weird. I was shacking up with Zaph in his pad. It was someone's basement, one room, share a bathroom, but I had nowhere else to stay. We'd vowed to move out as soon as we got some cash. Anyway, one day we came back, and there were these ashes on the step and a little black bag tied to the door. Zaph pretended that it was all so cool, but I could see he was scared. There was a set to his eyes, and his lips were, like, white. That night, I knew something was up. He was tossing in his sleep - I was dossing on the sofa - and muttering. Like, 'No, no....go away, I don't want.....' sort of stuff. So I did the onion thing, and sprinkled salt on his pillow, which seemed to do the trick. But he was freaked out. Wouldn't talk to me. Just went out. When he came back, he was like, so freaked he could hardly talk. All he said was, you gotta go, baby, I can't have you here no more. I got it out of him eventually. What this bitch had done, she'd sicced one of the Voodoo loa on him. Erzulie. In short, she's a succubus. A voodoo goddess, but a succubus. She comes, at night, to the men she selects, and has sex with them. She won't tolerate her lovers having any other females about, they have to live in seclusion and every Friday night, do this ritual to please Erzulie. And she comes and has sex with them.

'He'd been to see his mamaloa, that's the priestess at his hounfort, his temple. She'd told him that now he belonged to Erzulie, and there was bugger all he could do about it. He was shitting himself. He'd done all this for me, got my career started, and this ex-tart of his had given him to this bitch goddess on account of me!! I got so mad. I said, that if this Erzulie wanted him, she'd have to get through me first. He says, she'd do that anyway. So, I'm damned if I do and damned if I don't, nothing to lose. It was Friday, and the bitch was coming tonight to get her ashes hauled, and I was damned if I'd let her. So I told him. Not everything, but I said I'd see him outter there, whatever. We cleaned the room, put clean sheets on the bed, lit candles and incense. But it wasn't for Erzulie, oh no. He gets on the bed, all bathed and dressed in white, like he's accepting, just like the Mamaloa told him. But I was there. I put a spaca round the bed, then stood at the foot, just looking at him. And I felt all this great love for him rising in me, him lying there all afraid, and I knew what I had to do.

'Well, I felt this presence. Erzulie had come. I told her, this is my man, not yours. You cannot have him. And I started to undress him. I kept talking to Erzulie, like, see how beautiful he is, and you can't have him. See how perfect he is, but he's not yours, he's mine. I touched him and stroked him, kissed him, and he's lying on the bed, doing nothing. I say, Look, Erzulie, what I have that you do not. What I can do and you cannot. And I can feel this rage building outside of the spaca. Then I get on him, like, you know? I dropped my pants for him that night. Sitting on him, facing the wall with the picture of Erzulie over the bed, and I look at her while I'm doing up and down. Then I tell her that I will have this man, and she never will. Nor will the bitch that sent her. I told her to watch as I possessed the man she had been promised. I told her to go back to the one who had summoned her.

'By now, I've got Zaph going, and he's getting there, and so am I. Just before I came, I heard this voice saying, You have him now, but when you are gone, I will come back. Found out later that Zaph's heard it too. Anyway, we slept.

'In the morning, there's this huge banging on the door, see? It's the ex. Zaph answers the door, and she like, marches in. I'm on the bed. I don't bother with the sheet. She looks at me, buck naked as I am, then back to Zaph. I tell her, don't bother offering to call Erzulie off. If I were you, I'd run. I might be able to run fast enough and far enough to get away from her if I start right now. She just like, looks at me, and her face just like, crumbles.

There's these huge tears rolling down her face. Turns out that there's no escape from Erzulie. Now she's the one that's shit scared. The three of us go to the hounfort, only it's hers, not Zaph's. And the houngan there tells her there's nothing he can do. She's brought it on herself. Erzulie's a vicious bitch, and when she don't get what she's been promised, then watch out! And here's this daft girl that's promised her a man, only to find she's been denied? She's in deep deep shit.

'Who comes up with the solution? The white girl. Send her away, I say. Give her a new identity. Rebaptise her as someone else, give her a new father and mother. Basic wythen stuff, right? The houngan agrees that it all might work: anyway, it's better than nothing. So it's all arranged. She's to be shipped off to Birmingham with a new name, a new mother and father. The houngan like, sniffs at me, and says I'm a powerful conjure woman, and very wise and forgiving. He further tells us that to complete the exorcism of Erzulie, we ought to get wed. She's got less interest in used goods, apparently. And Zaph ought to consider studying Voudun. He says no, yes, maybe. But later he goes to his own mamaloa and she agrees. So he gets to be a Voodoo priest and I get to be his legal wife. So now you know why he owes me bigtime. But since he started to do the voodoo thing, he's got more superstitious, he's more scared of the Ayens than we are, he sees them as more vengeful, more malign, than we do.'

Zaph came back.

'They're in bed now, baby, waiting for you. Go kiss them goodnight and get ready.'

He sat down.

'So now you know what's going on between me and Lucy. Never thought I'd end up married, let alone to a white girl. She tells me you got some trouble.' When there was no reply, he laughed outright. 'I ought to be ashamed of myself. Here I am forgetting.' He fished down his shirt and hauled out a small green bag. 'Bless mah mojo.' He offered the bag to them. 'Just touch it. It's a leave-me-be ouanga. Me Mama gave it to me, stop folks badgering me. I gotta stop wearing it. But it gives me a peaceful life.'

He gave the bag to Fee, who passed it to Zoe. There was a faint tingling in her fingertips. She swallowed, and a bit of her mind cleared. It was a docility weave of sorts, Lily used to use one occasionally when the 'why why whys' of childhood got a bit much for her and she wanted some peace and quiet. It was a benign weave, but she didn't appreciate the casual use of wythen, especially on herself. She decided to be polite. At least until it was time to get nasty. Zoe dumped the mojo bag on a side table and wiped her hands together.

'That's useful. Though I don't appreciate having a wythweave on me. It's not the sort of things friends do to each other.'

'I stand rebuked. Truthfully I was only wearing it to get the tracks laid down. Important gig tonight. I finally persuaded Lucy that it was time for her to get back on stage.'

'Pity we don't have time to come and listen.'

'I'll send you tapes. Soul Wagon, Walk me out in the Morning Dew, Superstitious, Badlands, Hallelujah and Wide Open Skies. We're working on a covers album of old classics, sixties stuff. Frankly, there's too much to choose from.'

'Give some away free on the Internet. Hell, give them a whole album. Then do another, and make them buy it.'

'It's an idea. Never thought of that.'

'Wait till you see the bill. Zoe doesn't come cheap.'

Lucy came back. Now she was really Juicy Lucy, a rock chick with huge smoky eyes and dark red lipstick. She had changed into a tight black t-shirt and exchanged the tights for skinny jeans with a huge silver studded leather belt. The waistcoat was now a fringed sleeveless jacket in bright green.

'The car will be here in ten. You'd better get changed.' She kissed Zaph. 'We'll give you a lift. We kept you too late. The gig's in Wembley, at the old picture house. I'll tell the driver to take you to Chalfont and charge it to Stupendous Productions. Otherwise you won't be back before midnight.'

'Be careful, Lucy. Perhaps you'd better dust off the Family stuff. I don't know where this creep will strike next.'

'Okay. But this place is bristling with Voudun. Maybe he can't psych that out. Perhaps I'd better ask Zaph to make you some mojo bags. Never hurt to have too much protection, as his folks say. Next time you're in town, I'll see if I can't get you to meet one of the Mamas. There's Mama Africa, Mama Ababita and Mama Sunshine. The Papas are a bit more of a problem. Papa David might oblige, since it was his sister's girl that did the Erzulie thing and I got her out of it. But, like I said, they can be strange. Ah, here's Zaph. Or rather, Doctor Zedd.'

'You look like Adam Ant.'

Zaph had kept the tight black t-shirt and black pants, but had added a tailcoat and painted red and white horizontal stripes on his face.

'Hush yo' mouth, pussee girl, Dese here am me tribal markin's. Dese do invite mah loa.' He was talking the talk again. His voice slid back into Received English. 'Or that's what I tell the punters. Let's go.'

They piled into a black taxicab. The driver was evidently a regular and took the foursome in his stride, even helping to load Zaph's boxes in the trunk. You don't get that often from London cabbies, except on the airport runs. Zaph and Lucy bickered amicably through the journey, mostly about Lucy's comeback. Some of the dialogue was on the subject of whether it was fair on the tribe to drag them round the country on a tour, or if Zaph should decamp with his household to Ibiza for a summer season next year.

Outside the picture house, a crowd was already beginning to gather. Zaph was greeted noisily. He high-fived and 'Yo, mah man'-ed and signed autographs until several huge minders appeared to thin out the crowd around him. He turned to the cab and handed Lucy out. The shouting and yelling reached an even higher pitch, if that was possible. Mobile phones and cameras flashed. Zaph and Lucy posed, allowed pictures to be taken with fans, and generally worked the crowd. No celebrity posturing. Local celebs, huh. Looked like nothing could stop them going stellar. A few curious faces peeked into the cab, tapped on the windows which remained resolutely shut. Lights flashed on the offchance of getting an early snap of the next upcoming Big Thing that Doctor Zedd had under his wing. Eventually, the crowd began to drift from the cab, which moved smoothly away.

'Is it always like that?' Zoe asked the cabbie.

'Almost always. Smaller crowd when he does studio work. Why they don't mob iz home is a mystery.'

Perhaps there was something in the Voudun mojo after all.

The cab moved through the darkening streets. Neither sister wanted to start a conversation in the hearing of the cabbie, but he filled the silence with tales of the people he had shifted from place to place. It was going over Fee's head until he mentioned a name she recognized.

'You drove Simon Lake?'

'Ah. Someone scored an interview. On the radio. I had the contract then, from the radio station, I mean. Up all hours I was. Early morning pickups, late night home runs, I did the lot. One sassy gel on the late night shift went along to try to get a few words, but it went a bit Pete Tong, ya know? No-one got the full gist of what happened, suppose that was part of the deal. Lake agreed to do an interview, live, on the graveyard shift for Halloween. Provided she shut up, of course. He's only ever given a few live one-on-ones, so it was a great coup for her. I had to pick her up from the theatre, see, so he comes along in the cab to prep the interview. What she can ask, what she can't. Drew the privacy screen over, but silly bugger forgot to switch the intercom off. Heard the lot, I did.'

'Oh?'

'Wasn't much. She was clearly taken with him. Creepy bugger to my mind. But very polite. Anyway, he's got two gorillas in the back with them so there was no hanky panky.'

As much as you know. Those gorillas were his. If he'd wanted to drain her dry in the back of your cab, you'd have been none the wiser.

'Here we are, Chalfont. What street you want?'

Fee gave him the address. As the cab slowed, she noticed a figure lounging by her apartment block door.

'What the hell's he doing here?' she muttered.

'Is everything okay, miss? I can get the po-lice here in a jiffy.'

He drove the mean streets, and wasn't about to have his copybook blotted by leaving a young lady, no, a *pair* of young ladies, in a dark street with a possible attacker.

'No, it's okay. I know him.'

'If you're sure. Ababita'd give me hell, if anything happened to you.'

Fee shook her head and opened the cab door.

'It's my boyfriend. I just didn't expect him tonight, that's all.'

Greg sauntered over. Oh, well.......

'Hello, Greg. Meet my sister, Zoe,' she said, forestalling the inevitable kiss and close embrace that usually marked one of their meetings.

'Hello, Zoe.' He held out a hand to help her from the cab. She dumped her parcels on him and exited unassisted. 'Delighted to meet some of Fee's family at last.'

'What are you doing here?' Fee asked him. She had expected to have the flat to herself tonight. Tussling with Greg, though thoroughly enjoyable, was not on her menu tonight. Not with Zoe there, and definitely not in a bijou apartment where everyone can hear everything.

'Waiting for you.'

'How did you know I was in London?'

'Saw your car in the parking space.'

'Go past here every night, do you?'

He ignored this. She was being rude, she didn't want to, but it was happening. She was aware of Zoe's scrutiny as she trailed behind.

'How did you know I was coming back now?' he smiled, that lazy, knowing smile that usually made her pulse race, but tonight it merely increased her annoyance with him. 'You haven't been waiting here all evening, have you?'

If he had, the local busybodies would have been on the phone to the police like that. 'Officer, there's a stalker in the street......' Oh yes. Just what she wanted about now. To explain to a serious young man in a uniform and utility belt that the 'stalker' was her idiot boyfriend, hanging about in the hopes of a shag.

'No, just came by on the offchance.' Of a shag. As if. She had more important things on her mind than satisfying Greg's libido. Or her own, for that matter.

They were standing at the door. Fee entered the security code. Greg might have the key to the flat, but it was a hanging offence to tell non-residents the keycode for the front door. And the security guard would take dim view of any non-resident walking in off the street. She suspected he was ex-Army and probably had files on all the residents. If there was a murder here, he would have a full dossier of everyone who had visited, ever. While she appreciated the security, she hated the lack of privacy. The fact that she left the flat at two in the morning looking like the wreck of the Hesperus, leaving the boyfriend in occupation, probably merited a court martial at least.

Fee didn't want to air her private affairs in the street, so she made no complaint as Greg followed them into the 'vestibule'. Other places might call it a hall, but this place was supposed to be upmarket. The prices were, anyway. If they went up again, she'd have to look for another place, and that would be a shame.

The lift took them to the fourth floor. A silent transition, but questions were buzzing like flies, unspoken. They all stared forward, eyes front, at parade attention. Each one ignoring the others. When she reached the door, Fee held out her hand.

'Keys.' It came out sharper than she intended and she winced inwardly. She still had hopes of being with Greg for a while longer, but the way it was going tonight, it was on the cards that the sweet sorrow of parting would come sooner rather than later.

'Keys.' He slapped them in her hand. Ah. He thought she was playing at surgeons. 'Scalpel.' 'Scalpel.' 'Retractors.' 'Retractors.' 'Knickers, stat.' ……. Perhaps this was salvageable. But they couldn't continue this game, not tonight, not with an audience.

The low indirect lighting made the room cosy. Greg had tidied up and made the bed. She must thank him for that. He had moved to the kitchen.

'Coffee? Or something stronger?'

'Coffee, please.' She would have preferred something stronger, but... Hey, wait a minute! Wasn't this her flat? What was Greg doing making coffee for them in her flat?

Zoe had claimed the reclining chair over by the bookcase and was pointedly engaged in reading the titles. She had dumped her packages by the door as if they meant less to her than they really did. What she had really wanted to do was rip open the brown paper and gloat over the contents, and what they meant. She ought to have been able to. She was sulking, a little, and Fee could understand that. She walked over to the counter where Greg was doling out coffee into the filter.

'Greg…' she began in a low voice, but he cut her off.

'I understand that I'm about as welcome as a dose of the clap in a nunnery at the moment, but I wanted to see you. Even for a few seconds. I was prepared to wait all night if I had to.' He looked over at Zoe. 'And getting to meet even one of your relations is a bonus. One cup of coffee, and I'm history, okay? I promise.'

How could she refuse? Tell the truth, what she really wanted was to fall in his arms, cry, and tell him that she needed his shoulder, his strong shoulder, to lean on. To have him kiss it better. All over. To take her back into the safe places where physical delight banished the darkness. Have him take away some of the fear, yes, we are being honest here, fear, that she was starting to feel about all of this. But it would not be fair to involve him, not fair at all. She couldn't put him in the shooting gallery that her life was promising to become, he didn't deserve that.

'Okay.'

She wandered over to the sofa and kicked off her shoes, threw her jacket over the back of the sofa. She leant back her head, resting her neck on the back, feeling the tension in her muscles. If they were alone, she could have asked him to massage her neck. He would kiss her in that ticklish spot behind the ear, and she would giggle…….. Instead, she would have to settle for coffee. Just coffee. No more alcohol now, since she had a long way to drive in the morning, even though the brandy bottle called beguilingly.

Greg offered Zoe a mug which she took with a muted 'Thanks.' She was eyeing Greg intently, her eyes narrowed. She was seeing something….. Fee could ask later. He sat in the other corner of the sofa, leaving a polite distance between them.

'That was a sterling presentation you made. It impressed the accountant, and that's a feat in itself. I think he's going to make you an offer.'

'I didn't do the presentation. Zoe did. She's my partner.'

Greg looked over at the girl in the corner. There was a slight smile on his face, a twinkle in the depths of his eyes.

'If you ever get tired of working for Fee, I can always find a use for you. I was well impressed.'

'Is it time to discuss a raise now, Fee?'

'What do you want now? Forty percent?'

'Preferred shares when you float the company.'

'Where have you been hiding this genius?'

'She's just a hustler.'

'Branson better watch out, there's a new kid in town. No, I mean that, I'm not teasing. Is it something in the water, or what? First there's you, a hick from the sticks, hitting the City like a tiger. Then I find another one of you. You've both got 'It'. My palms are itching. I wouldn't like to see what happens to anyone who gets in your way.'

Please, please, let it be so...... And no, you don't want to see the result of crossing us. You wouldn't believe it anyway.

'I hate to break up the party, but I'm tired. I want to go to bed.'

'I can see I've worn out my welcome, what welcome there was.' His smile took the sting out of his words. 'I'll go seek my cold, lonely bed. Any chance of a goodnight kiss?'

'Now you're stretching it.' Fee smiled.

'I'll go clean my teeth. Don't be too long. There's only so much one can do in a bathroom.'

Fee blushed. There was a hell of a lot you could do in a bathroom. She and Greg had done it, well, most of it. She was hoping her hair was hiding her red cheeks.

'You're blushing. Blushing!'

'Shut up.'

'I mean it, you know, about Zoe. And you. And I get this feeling there's something going on that you're not telling me about.'

'There's nothing, Greg, really.' She kissed the tip of his nose.

'Why don't I believe you?' His arms slid round her.

'You don't tell me everything.'

'I suppose I don't, at that. Okay, keep your secrets, if it makes you happy. I hope one day you'll trust me enough to tell me.'

'It's not you I don't trust, Greg. It's me.'

Then, they kissed. Gently. Then again, not so gently. Greg drew back.

'Any more of that, and you won't get rid of me. Are you staying?'

'Back to the sticks tomorrow.'

'Too bad. Call me when you are in town again. Save me from loitering on street corners. The harpy in Flat Ten had her eye on me. I was fairly sure she'd call the police if you hadn't arrived when you did.'

'You could have dropped the keys off at reception.'

'And get you in trouble with Pete? You know what he'd say.'

'If he had his way I'd be living as a Vestal. How do you know he's called Pete? I never knew that.'

'I asked. If you want to have it easy in life, it does to have friends in low places. Like I said, I didn't want to have to explain to the boys in blue why I spent so much time hanging about your front door. If Pete knows I'm your friend, he won't jump to the conclusion that I'm some pervert when he sees me around, like the Harpy In Flat Ten. By the way, the other three are Barry, Mike and Sue.'

'Sue?'

'He's a Singh and I can't pronounce his name. Neither can anyone else, so he sticks to Sue to save time. I think he gave up with being annoyed about it some time ago. You really ought to pay more attention to the little things.'

From the bathroom came an impatient voice.

'Good god, are you two not finished yet? How long does a kiss take?'

'Bossy Boots. You'd better go before she does something I'll regret later. I'll see you next time I'm in town, I promise.'

'Only if you have dinner with me.'

Zoe started hammering on the bathroom door.

'Okay, okay, if only to get you out of here before I need a new door.'

Greg blew her a kiss as the flat door closed. Zoe joined Fee as she watched from the window.

'Can't get enough of the sight of him?'

'No, making sure he's gone and not lurking in the bushes.

There he goes. Now, parcels or bed?'

'I shall have great fortitude and save them for when we get home. What time are we leaving?'

'Early. Crack of sparrowfart early. I want breakfast at Exeter. You ought to spend as much time at home as you can tomorrow. Mum's told you what you need to do. Concentrate on that, for one day at least. We'll stop at dawn and find somewhere rural for your first devotion.'

'Does it have to be at actual sunrise?'

'Why?'

'I fancy doing it at Uffington Castle. At the White Horse.'

'We can do that. Don't forget to pray before you go to bed.'

'I'll do that while you wash.'

When Fee came out of the bathroom, all the lights were out. Zoe had lit the mass of candles in the hearth, and a dreamy scent filled the room. Zoe's next twenty-four hours would be punctuated by observances, prayers and meditations. It was a pity that all of this should be hanging over a day she had looked forward to ever since she had realized what it meant to be Family.

Chapter Eight

When Fee awoke, it was still dark. The feeling of the room had changed. An emptiness in the bed they had shared that night meant that Zoe was already up. Moving quietly, Fee rolled over. Zoe was sitting cross-legged in front of the hearth. Only one candle was lit, and a single trail of incense curled up toward the ceiling. The light outlined Zoe's naked form, her hair tumbling down her back. Her eyes were closed, and her lips moving silently. The backs of her hands rested on her knees, the fingers curling in loosely, painted in light and shadow. Sophie would have loved to paint that picture! How would she have shown what was going on behind the eyelids? It would have been too crass to whip out the mobile and catch the moment. It was too private to be invaded. Fee watched, her head propped up on one bent arm. That was okay. Zoe had spied on her, just as she herself had spied on Sophie, as they had all spied on Lily. 'Bugger off, you hoydens,' Lily had said, eyes closed. Robert had been more circumspect. They had rarely caught him meditating in the buff. He'd realized he was a target and foiled all attempts by wearing a long black robe. The 'bugger off' had been the same.

Zoe brought her hands up, palms together, and touched her lips to the tips of her fingers. Her eyes opened.

'I hope you are not considering doing the dawn meditation naked as well,' Fee commented, her voice quiet.

'So you are awake. I thought so.' Zoe stood up and walked over. She kissed Fee gently on the lips. Fee returned the pressure in a sisterly way.

'Coffee?'

'Strong, black, instant.' Fee rolled out of the bed and smoothed the covers. The lights came on in the kitchen as Zoe, still naked, poured water into the kettle and set it to boil. She found two cups, heaped coffee granules and sugar into them and waited for the pot to boil. Once the coffee was steaming in the mugs, she joined Fee in getting dressed. It did not take long. They rinsed out the mugs and left them to drain, checked that they had everything. Fee locked the door and they went downstairs to the vestibule. Fee left her key with Pete, and surprised him by greeting him by name.

'I'll be back in a week or two. The concierge service can come in and clean. I'll call you before I come back.' He smiled, and tipped his hat at her. Four o'clock in the morning and he was wearing a peaked cap. It was most likely in his contract. 'Yes, Miss Harris.'

It was bloody cold on Uffington Castle. The lazy wind was blowing, the one that goes through you without bothering to go round. Fee's fingers were frozen by the time they had climbed from the tiny carpark to the summit. Fee let Zoe stand more or less alone on the ramparts, facing the place in the sky where the sun would first appear if the clouds weren't in the way. It was dull and overcast, and a thick mist obscured the details down in the Vale of the White Horse. While it might have been nice to stand there and see a glorious sunrise, the mist made the scene otherworldly. From the trees, the rooks called to one another. The only other sound was the wind in the grass. Zoe was standing, chin raised, letting the wind play over her as if she wasn't cold. At least they had hot coffee in the car. Fee thought she'd better switch to herbal tea before she got caffeine overload, then killed the thought. This was Zoe's day, and, she, Fee, was the companion and supporter of her candidacy. Zoe lifted her arms to embrace the wind and for one horrible moment Fee saw the similarity in the pose her sister had adopted and the one Luke had assumed just before he fell. Her heart was in her mouth. The mist could be hiding anyone. But Zoe remained unmolested. A tendril of mist seeped between them. Fee was torn between joining her sister, telling her to hurry so they could leave, and held by the wyth of the moment: Zoe at one with the mists and the winds, communing with the cycles of Gya she would later assume in the Ritual that night.

Before she could act on her impulse, Zoe lowered her arms and turned to her. She shoved her hands in her pockets and came down to join her sister.

'Brrr. Why couldn't I have chosen a warmer time of year?'

'Feel grateful it's not January. I did my salutations in the orchard. It rained on me and I got soaked. Mum tried to persuade me that I could do it indoors, but I wouldn't listen. None of us do. Lily did hers on the seashore, she told me, then went for a swim. She was blue when she came out. I suppose that deep down we feel it's some sort of sacrifice, but it's not meant to be a feat of endurance. We do that to ourselves. We must be daft.'

They were walking back to the car.

'What did Sophie do?'

'She climbed to the top of Pike's Head, only to find some hikers camped there, the daft buggers. So she edged round the rock face and wedged herself between the rocks and watched the sun come up. She had a devil of a job getting back down. But she came back wreathed in smiles, anyone would have thought she'd climbed Everest.'

They warmed their frozen hands round steaming cups and waited for feeling to return before setting off again. Exeter Services were not open for breakfast, but there was a lorry drivers' rest stop a few miles off the motorway that Fee had found one evil rainy day when the motorway had been closed by a jacknifed monster and she'd taken to the back roads. They sat in the steamy warmth with eggs, bacon, sausages, fried bread and tea, sharing the place with the drivers who conducted the megatrucks of commerce here and there. In the background, a local radio presenter imposed a cheerful banter on the air. At least it wasn't Country and Western, and they were nearly home. Zoe was pensive and garrulous by turns. She picked at her food, then shovelled mouthfuls as if she wasn't sure she was hungry or not. They didn't dawdle. It was spattering with rain as they drove off.

The rain worsened as they skirted Dartmoor. Then the clouds parted and the sun came out, painting the waterlogged moors in more cheerful colours. They left the main arterial routes for the winding back lanes of Devon, until the road brought then back into their own backyard. It was a relief to be back home.

Sophie was waiting in the kitchen with Snag. That ungrateful beast ignored them completely, saving his attention for a through clean of his departed boy bits which was obviously more important than the return of the spare meal tickets. Sophie was more gracious. She kissed and hugged them both. She had made chicken soup which stood steaming in bowls on the kitchen table along with fresh baked bread. She was making every effort to counteract the depression that had fallen since Luke had taken impromptu flying lessons. She still blamed herself for leaving him on Bridlip Tor, even though it was not her fault. 'Blame him (meaning Tunfen) not yourself' was something she was finding it hard to accept.

'Who's on for tonight?'

'Ellen's not, she's glued to Luke's bedside. Tom will be here. Lottie and Carl are staying at Tom's with the tribe. Matt's a will-he-won't-he right now. He's at the hospital with Ellen. Jean will be here, but Margie's had a recurrence of the old trouble. Claire's over in France, and Abby and John are in Lanark with Effie.'

'That's okay,' Zoe commented, blowing on a spoonful of chicken soup. 'How is Margie? Good soup, by the way.'

'Thanks. Doc Rowbottom seems to think its old age taking it's toll, but I think she's working herself up from a bit nervous to really full-on panic. She was having palpitations, then she collapsed over the still. Since she was distilling lavender oil, I think we can discount inebriation. And she's been a right Cassandra, prophesying doom and gloom all over.'

'You mean a right Senna, like on Up Pompeii. 'Woe, woe and thrice woe! The time has come, the end is nigh!''

'Yes, I probably do. I must say, I am inclined to agree that things aren't perfect around here.'

'They never were.'

'They were never this bad, though.'

'You're right there. Now, Mouse, anything I can do for you today?'

Sophie was looking for distractions.

'No. Oh, have you got any of those bath bombs you made? The ones with rose petals and stuff?'

'Yes. What flavour?'

'Clary sage? Geranium? Ylang-ylang?'

'Not all in one bomb. I have got one of those vanilla spice

ones you liked so much. And I can make you an oil as well.'

'I'd like that. Thanks.'

'If you've both finished your soup, you'd oblige me by vacating this kitchen. I've got work to do.'

Fee stood.

'Do you want any help?'

'If you've nothing better to do. The rest of the house is yours, Zoe. We'll be in here. But if you want to go out, one of us goes with you.'

'You were alone here when we arrived.'

'I was not. Lottie'd just left.'

'Oh, okay.'

Sophie had procured a whole salmon and intended to poach it with spices and cover it in cucumber scales as the centrepiece of Zoe's feast. 'The Salmon of Knowledge', as she put it. Very appropriate. It was to be served on one of the large platters in a watercress ocean, dotted with tomato and egg flowers. She was also making spicy chicken strips, chilli prawns and curried potato dumplings. There was going to be salad and crudities and dips. Fee surveyed the mass of food doubtfully.

'Are you sure this isn't too much?'

'Tom's coming. You know what he's like. Has she decided on her music yet?'

'Yes, but she won't tell me what.'

'You wouldn't tell me.'

'You didn't tell me either.'

They laughed.

'That's better.'

They chopped and spiced companionably in the warmth of the kitchen. Sunlight started streaming in through the window. The back door closed and Fee saw Zoe walking in the garden. Before she could open the window and yell at her to wait, Zoe turned and waved, and pointed to the covered seat by the rose bed. Fee dried dishes as she watched Zoe light a candle and stick a handful of joss sticks in the ground. Then she composed herself on the seat. Sophie joined Fee at the window.

'At least it's not raining. Why do we put ourselves to all this trouble?'

'We need to, I think. After, we can plonk down anywhere, but it seems that we all have this drive to seek somewhere special for these meditations, on this day.'

They regarded their sister fondly. The sun shone on her. Hopefully, it would continue to shine. They made a tacit decision not to discuss The Accidents that day. It was like inviting bad luck. Zoe's wyting was more important. Instead they discussed Zaph and Lucy.

'Voodoo? He's a voodoo priest? And Lucy's married to him? Fancy.'

'Do you think that it could help us?'

'Really, I don't know. I've never had any call to deal with voodoo. But I'd not discount it. Let's not go there yet.'

Another item on the to-do list. It was getting longer.

The afternoon wore away as afternoons will. There was an ache of waiting in the cottage. Even Snag came wailing round, and he tended to disregard anything that wasn't food. They tried to listen to music. They tried to read. They tried staring out of the windows. Restless, not wanting to do anything. It was coming on to evening when Zoe suggested they walk down to the Nearly Spring. Everyone called it the Nearly Spring around here. It probably had another name, once when it had been a little more than a bright green patch of moss, not nearly...... Yes, that's why it was the Nearly Spring. It was only a wetter patch where water seeped up through the peat, but the walk down through the woods was pleasant, if a bit soft underfoot.

They collected coats and boots and started down the lane in the late afternoon sunshine. They saw Jean coming out of the Post Office, and waved. She waved back, but continued on her way back to Station House. Why it was called Station House, no-one really knew: there had never been a train station in the village. Or anything else they could think of that might require a station of some sort. They turned off the road over a stile and onto the bridleway that led down to the brook that ran behind Tom's house, over the field and the stepping stones that peeked up over the tumbling waters. The sun shone fitfully on small trees with lichen encrusted branches, highlighting the drystone wall that ran beside the path. A trickle of water tried to share the path with them, painting the ground with hues of umber and rusty red. Above them, bunches of rowan berries contrasted the blue of the sky with their brilliant scarlet. As she walked, Zoe collected rowan twigs, grasses, a few late knapweed flowers and other bits and pieces into a bouquet. As they approached closer to the Nearly Spring, the ground got softer until they were sinking into it at every step. Zoe was undeterred and kept going. Sedges and bulrushes, their dark brown heads bursting to release creamy masses of cottony seeds began to crowd them until the path petered out.

By the Nearly Spring a hawthorn bush, smothered in lichen and ruddy berries, stood on its own. Tortuous and twisted, how it managed to survive in the waterlogged ground was a mystery, but survive it did. On the ground where its roots writhed into the moss were scores of tiny clay models: some little discs with designs crudely scratched or more artistically embossed, others petite models of animals, flowers and miniscule people. Hundreds had been placed here to weather away, the rains dissolving the clay or the peaty water seeping it back into the earth's embrace. Some bunches of wilting flowers, tied with grass or hay or coloured twine rested among the figurines.

On the branches of the tree, bleached rags vied with more recent colourful offerings. Someone had left a tiny bracelet on one branch to tarnish and sparkle in the sun. A concoction of twigs bound together with bright wool here, a collection of foil caps there, one particularly gaudy bunch of what used to be coloured plastic bags waving artistically in the wind, each one an offering to the spring, a prayer, whatever. Wherever you find a seep of water these days, you will find votive offerings. If there's a handy tree, so much the better. Fee could recall a trip to Madron's Well. It had looked like every bush in the vicinity had sprouted ribbons. There was even one with the name of a school.

Zoe squelched up to the tree and put her bouquet on the ground. She selected a branch, and tied a gauzy scrap carefully onto it, so as not to break off the lichens. It was an offcut of her new robe she had wheedled off Lucy. She stood back to admire her handiwork.

It was getting late now, the sun lying low on the hills. Soon it would be dark in the valley. Sunlight slanted on the gaudy tree and threw long shadows on the ground. The blue scrap fluttered in the evening breeze. Birds cheeped from the hedgerow and sedges.

The thought came to Fee that they ought to be getting back to Pippin Cottage. But it was Zoe's day, and if she wanted to stay here until full dark, then Fee would wait with her, as would Sophie. Zoe seemed quite content to stay, up to her ankles in mossy water.

The shadows lengthened. Sophie shifted restlessly from foot to foot, and still Zoe stood there. The kid was drawing this out. At long last she sighed, and turned away.

'Let's go home.'

They trudged up the path, splashing through the rill of water, over the stream and back to the stile. In the lane, long shadows wove across their path.

'I don't see why I have to have a shower *and* a bath.'

'You like lying in dirty bathwater?'

'You have to wash too. There's only so much water.'

'We'll bathe now. If you wait an hour, the water will be hot again.'

Sophie was in the shower and Zoe was arguing with Fee. It wasn't real arguing, just sisterly bicker to pass the time. Everything was ready. Fee and Sophie had refused Zoe's offers of help. Tonight was her night, and all their efforts were for her. It wasn't right that she helped. She sat in the front room drinking some herbal concoction. She had stripped off her jumper, jeans and boots and was swathed in a deep pink kaftan. The bickering was nerves. They all got it. The plan was to have Sophie and Fee ready, downstairs, when Tom and Jean arrived, with Zoe upstairs either in the bath or sitting in her bedroom. Matt was in a not-coming mood at the moment. Fee felt like going over there and giving him a piece of her mind to chew on. Fortunately, she was summoned to the shower before she could act. She soaped and scrubbed, rinsed and conditioned, and was drying her hair when she heard the phone warbling. She switched off the drier, but could only hear Sophie's soft murmuring, so she went back to drying her hair. Then she piled it up on her head and went back downstairs.

Sophie was alone in the front room. From overhead came a pounding beat.

''Knights of Sidonia.' Kid's a bit wound. That was Matt on the phone. He's changed his mind. Again. I told him to come over right now, before he changes it back.'

Fee wandered into the Roundhouse. The room was warm. Candles sat in holders, tealights in their little glass bowls. Everything was ready: there was nothing left to do. Fee went into the kitchen and chewed on a piece of celery from one of the bowls that stood on the table. Upstairs, the music changed to 'Supermassive Black Hole'. Waiting, waiting….

Matt arrived. He had made a superhuman effort, considering the state he had been in. Shaved and clean, he had a bottle in one hand and a wrapped parcel in the other. Fee kissed him.

'Changed your mind,' she asked, gently.

'I can't stay at Tom's. Frankly, the kids get on my nerves. And home isn't home without Luke.'

'You're very welcome here, you know that. We'll sort something out.' She kissed him and drew him inside. As she closed the door, she saw a movement in the garden by the hedge. 'Go on in.'

Keenly aware that she was wearing little more than a kaftan - they had been the chosen relaxed evening wear for the family as long as she could remember: even Robbie had worn a kaftan of an evening, though his had been, at the start, terry bathrobes made by Lily, then his prize possession, a real Egyptian djelabeyah - she closed the door behind her and stepped, barefoot, into the gathering darkness. It was completely still. Too still. Hackles rising, she centred herself. Where was a poker when she needed one?

'I know you're there. Show yourself.'

She waited.

'Don't make me come and find you.'

Out of the corner of her eye, she saw the curtain twitch. Sophie was looking out. Her hand was on the window latch.

There was a faint movement in the deep shadows. A sombre shape detached itself from the umbra of the bushes.

'Hello, kitten.'

The vamp had come calling. From upstairs, the music stopped, and a ray of light from Zoe's window penetrated the gloom.

Fee could see the shape more clearly now. He was dressed in catburglar chic, a black silk shirt tucked into tight black trousers, dark blond hair falling over one eye. His hands and face floated disembodied in the darkness.

'Hello, Theo.' Her voice was flat. She couldn't make it otherwise.

'Not pleased to see me?' His lips smiled, showing perfect, even white teeth. Fee gritted hers.

'And to what do we owe the honour of your presence?'

Suddenly, he was right in front of her.

'Sarcasm does not become you, kitten. I come because blood calls to blood. As I always come.' He was walking around her, slowly. His eyes were drinking her in, possessing her… she slammed her mental gates shut.

'You always have to try it on, don't you.'

'Of course. It is my nature. It is a game, little kitten, only a game. I offer you no threat. Not….. now.'

She remembered. Sophie's Night, he had come. And she had gone into the garden with him. Fee had tried to watch, but they had vanished into the deep shadows. Sophie had returned, untouched. Seemingly. Robert and Lily had waited, tense, until she returned. Then, on her Night, Theo had come again. For her. And she had walked into the darkness with him. Now he had come for Zoe. 'The darkness will come, and you will have to walk into it…' That's what Lily had told her.

'I will call her for you.'

'No need.'

He looked up at the lighted window. What he saw was invisible to Fee, standing on the porch. He smiled, and reached up a hand. Then he turned to Fee, his hand falling back down, an elegant gesture. Well, he'd had several centuries to practice.

'This is for her, and me, alone.' He looked directly into her eyes. She made herself look back. She had gone with him, into the darkness, hadn't she? And come back. It was a test, of sorts. He took a short step back. No, he was simply a mite father away. She reached back, her fingers finding the door latch. He smiled at her again, his face half hidden in the autumn night.

'Afraid of me, kitten?'

He liked that.

'And wary. You do not turn your back on a predator. Not if you wish to survive.'

He sighed.

'It is not so easy, living next to Fratten.'

'It is not so easy living near to metae.'

Behind her, the door opened. Light spilled into the garden, illuminating Theo's legs from the knees downwards. Fee stepped back into the light.

'You ready to do this?'

Zoe swallowed. Her eyes were a little wide, her face pale. She nodded, not trusting her voice.

'Then go forth into the darkness, and confront your own darkness. And if you are strong, and honest, and true, return to the light.'

Zoe stepped outside. Fee closed the door. She was fairly certain that Theo wouldn't do anything unnatural. He wasn't unnatural, he was….. different. But there was always the risk. If there was no danger in an ordeal, what was the point? She had a sudden flash of insight. She had been so worried about Tunfen, and what was happening to the Frais, that she had lost the plot. Of course it was dangerous. Of course it was difficult. What was the use of living if all you did was coast through it day by day, with no challenges? Nothing to pit your wits and intellect and strength against? Nothing to measure yourself by? Huh. She'd walked into the dark with a vampire. Willingly. He had taken her hand, her warm hand, in his night-chill one. They had walked round by the side of the house into the orchard. Her warmth had chased away the ice in his flesh. He had sat down on the wet grass, reclined, ignoring the cold, the damp, and had watched her from there, standing, looking down at him. He had wanted her to sit, to lie next to him. She had stood, her hair hanging round her face. 'No.'

'Then sit by me, by choice, because I ask it.'

She had lowered herself to the wet grass, shivering at the cold. He had smiled.

'Lie with me.'

He had lain right down, face up, looking at the stars. She had laid herself down, on the wet grass, in the orchard, next to him. The stars glinted coldly in the night sky, netted by naked branches. A few rags of cloud had drifted over, obscuring some of them.

'Look at them, the eyes in the sky. They see everything. Look at them and you are looking at Time.'

She had never thought of him as an astrophysicist Or a philosopher.

'They are so far away, yet so near. Every night, they watch over me, as I walk, I prowl, I hunt. I kill.'

He had rolled over suddenly, looming over her, blotting out the stars. She had swallowed, trying to return her vital organs back where they belonged, in her chest, her belly. She was shivering, with cold and with fear. Well, it was January. Frost was starting to whiten the ground they lay on. If he didn't kill her, the cold might well do so instead. There was no warmth in his body, pressed close on hers.

'That is the law of life, little kitten. The stars know. They watch, and they don't care. Or if they do, they do little about it. It is for the creatures who walk the earth to show love, and compassion, and caring, because the stars do not. I do not. I lust, but I do not love. I hunger, I feed, I am not sated. I am the stars, the night, the inevitability of death. The other side of life. This, you learn from me.'

She stared up into the blackness of his eyes. Into the coldness in them. And she knew him for what he was. That he would always be there. She had encountered Death in the orchard, beneath the trees and stars, at the age of seventeen. Had lain there with him, in the dark and cold, and known that she could not stop him.

'You could come with me, into my world, right now, this very night. You could taste the power of immortality, walk the night in beauty and strength and none to say you nay. You could have all that if you accept my loving.'

He had lowered his face to hers. Their lips had met in a cold, breathless kiss. Her breath fogged on the air, but his had not. How could it? He didn't breathe. His face had slid down, and she felt his lips on her neck, his teeth graze her skin. Her heart was hammering in her mouth. All she could hear was her own heartbeat. She was going to die here, in the cold and dark beneath the trees. And she had gone willingly.

'No.'

She heard her own voice. Her body was saying yes, but her mind was saying no. Something deep inside, some instinct was awake now, making her resist.

'I say you, *NO*.' The voice was stronger now. His face was still buried in her neck, but there was no riffle of breath to excite the skin, no warmth to bring her body to life. It was a cold weight on her, skin to skin. He had somehow removed her clothes while she had been entranced by his voice. And his own. His chest pressed to hers, his legs and her legs lying together with no clothing between. She closed her eyes, then watched the fog of her breath form in the air above their bodies.

'I will not submit willingly to you, Theo. I will not be your victim. If you want my life, you must take it from me, for I'll not yield it to you.'

He had risen up off her body then, his legs straddling hers as she lay on the grass, under the stars that didn't care. Overhead she saw one fall, then another. Surely it was too late for the Quadrantid meteor shower? Didn't that finish on the sixth?

She felt a small trickle of blood slide down her neck. As she watched, Theo drew his fingernail over his naked chest. Blood, dark blood, welled in the skin and slowly ran down his skin.

'A pact between us, then. I will not steal from you what you will not freely offer. But this is between you and me alone. I cannot stop another of my kind doing to you what I promise I will not do. But if I claim you as mine, then they cannot touch you. One vampire will not steal from another that one has marked as theirs. This is my pact with Rina and with Rina's blood. That I will not take from them, by force or by guile, that they do not offer freely to me. This pact I offer you now. Share blood with me, and I will give you my protection from the others of my kind, and you in your turn will grant me the freedom to live after my manner, here, in your world.'

'This won't make me like you, will it?'

'No. That takes an act of will and acceptance. I will not promise never to try to persuade you. But what I offer you here will not make you a vampire, nor will it oblige you to further sharings between us.'

'And if I choose not to accept?'

'Then you are free to go from here. But you will be prey to any others of my kind who see and desire you, and I will do nothing to prevent it. And, my kitten, they will come, drawn to you, your life, as I am. You cannot prevent that.'

Curiosity is a trait shared by cats and humans. Fee knew that if she walked away now, she would always wonder what it would have been like, to share blood with the mete. 'It's not what you have done that you regret most. It is what you have not done, that you could have.' Lily's words echoed in her mind.

She moved to sit up. Theo cradled her head on his hand and lifted her close to his chest.

'Tell me that you want this. Or I will not do it.'

'Yes. Yes, I want this. Just this. No more.'

He drew her face to rest by his shoulder, where the blood was running down his chest. His face nestled in between her neck and shoulder. The tone of his voice was no longer smooth and light, but tinged with a darker need.

'Then drink, little one.' He buried his face in her neck. Her stomach tightened as she felt his mouth move on her skin.

It was a small movement to touch her lips to the blood on his chest. It was not as cold as she expected it to be. Why did she expect it to be cold? Because he was cold? Hell, they were lying on wet grass on a January night with frost forming round their ankles. His arm convulsed, pushing her face into the wound on his chest. The blood was metallic, salty, heavy on her tongue. She licked the wound, and he shuddered. How long they spent, underneath the trees, sharing that blood, Fee never knew. It felt like forever, it felt like no time at all.

Theo drew away from her. She looked up at him, his eyes closed and his head thrown back, blood on his lips and fangs. Her blood. He was not holding her so tight now, but there was a strange reluctance to relinquish feeding at the wound in his chest. Her hand slid over the smooth skin, feeling the sleek muscle beneath. His head came down, and their lips met, mingling the blood, mortal and metae, in their mouths, on their faces. She could feel the slickness sliding between them as the wounds continued to ooze blood. He smiled down on her. Possessive. I have you now. You are mine. Well, as far as the other vampires were concerned, he did own her. One look, and they would know it. She might as well wear a collar and dogtag. 'My name is Ffion. I belong to Theo. Please call this number........'

He placed a finger in his mouth and drew it out, wet with blood and saliva. He drew his wet finger over the wound in his chest, and it was gone. He smiled again, then bent quickly, too quickly for her to react, and licked her neck. From the vantage point of her shoulder, he looked down at the blood smeared on both of them.

'This will never do. If I send you back like this, Lily will accuse me of being uncivilized.'

He started to lick the blood off. Slowly. Fee had engaged in some romping, but it had never been like this: slow, sensuous, assured. His head went lower. Her hand clenched on his shoulders.

'Theo......' she was going to say stop it, but the words wouldn't come. He continued his careful cat-bath of her until all the blood was gone.

'You are too delicious.'

Two can play at that game. Fee leant forward, and started to lick the blood still smearing his chest. Again, he threw his head back and showed his fangs to the sky. Her meaning was clear. Tease me and I will tease back. But he was enjoying it. He was enjoying it far too much. He wasn't going to stop her, not now. She took as much care as he had, sinking lower. Oops. It was a lie that vampires couldn't get it up, then. That was way beyond teasing.

'You don't need to stop there.' was that a rough edge in the silk voice?

'Oh, I think I do.'

His fingers lifted her chin.

'You still have blood on your face.' Her hand went to the wet grass. It crackled faintly. Frost. He held her arm still, and licked across her face. There seemed to be a lot of blood. No, he was just licking her for the fun of it. She braced her arm on his chest and pushed.

'Enough, Theo.'

He drew back, grimacing slightly.

'You are no fun.'

'I am seventeen, and still a virgin. You are several hundred and so not a virgin. Stop cradle snatching.'

'I do prefer my women more mature.'

He stood up, and offered her his hand. She took it, and there was a moment's vertigo and she was standing beside him, she in the garish kaftan and he clad from sole to neck in black. Huh?

'Those colours do not suit you. There are too many of them. I fund such a clashing of hues offensive. I will find something that will suit you better.'

He offered his arm and conducted her back to her front door. Funny, she did not feel the cold now. Lily had opened the door and Fee had walked in and just stood there. Theo had inclined his head to her, once, and was gone. In the morning, there was a parcel on the doorstep. In it there was a new kaftan all the colours of fire: reds and oranges and dusky yellows, all sweeping and swirling and blended together so you couldn't see when one ended and another began. And she found, much later, a few specks of blood on the old kaftan, by the neck. She never wore it again, but kept it, folded, as it was, in a drawer.

In the parlour, Matt and Sophie were sitting, not speaking. A bottle of red wine sat on the table, with two empty glasses beside it. Fee poured a small amount into one glass and sat down. Matt cleared his throat.

'The vampire never came for me.'

'He only comes for Rina's descendants. The pact with Theo is that we leave each other alone, and he protects us from the rest of them in exchange for a…… our blood.'

'There's a bit more to it than that, Soph.'

'How much more?'

Sophie coloured up. Ah-ah.

'How long are they likely to be?'

'Lily said about a half, three-quarters of an hour.'

'They're taking their time, then.'

Eventually Theo brought Zoe back. He inclined his head to her, once, and was gone. Zoe stood there in the pink kaftan as if she didn't believe the world was real.

'I can see why I need a bath *and* a shower now,' she commented. 'I'm all covered in vampire spit.'

Fee laughed and took her upstairs.

Chapter Nine

A couple of hours and a bottle of wine later, and they were all ready. Tom had arrived with Jean, so Fee and Sophie took her up to Fee's room to get ready, while Tom and Matt used Sophie's. Zoe, now washed clean of Theo's slobber was in her room with Snag, waiting. Once they were all ready, dressed in their long black cloaks with the hoods drawn up, Fee knocked on the door.

'Lente, are you prepared to join with us? For the time is now, or never.'

Zoe opened the door. Snag was on the bed, licking where his balls used to be. She was wearing a pale yellow robe with a faint design that looked like old lace. It had tiny pearl buttons all up the front. She held in one hand a black braided cord. She extended her other hand, palm up. From it sprang a pillar of wythlight, eerily green in the dim hallway.

'I am prepared. Let it begin.'

Fee, in her turn, extended her palm and summoned the wythlight to answer Zoe's.

'Then, by your word, it begins.'

Throughout this day, Zoe had been the one to choose where, and how, and when. That was being taken away from her. Theo had taken her, and done what he wished, which she may or may not have liked, or wanted. Now she had to give control over events into other hands, and she really didn't know what would happen.

Fee took the cord and looped it round her neck. Taking the free ends, she turned and started down the stairs, holding Zoe close beside her. The other followed, careful not to tread on the hem of the long cloak she wore. As she passed, the candles guttered and went out until the house was in complete darkness.

They stood in Rob's Roundhouse. The few stars and new moon made little impact on the deep shadows. A few glimmers sparked in the darkness. A haze of incense laid over the room, musky, fruity, sweet.

Fee raised her staff.

'Licitus lumen exisisto ab vox devii!'

She brought the staff banging down on the floor. The candles spluttered and burst into flame, filling the room with light. It was more usual to use flowery language and longer forms, but Fee had decided long ago that quicker was better. The words she was using were a shorthand version of a much longer weaving, but did the same thing in a fraction of the time. Using dog-Latin was a personal affectation, but it ensured that she didn't accidentally set stuff off.

'Licitus suavis hedychrum consurgo!'

Clouds of incense erupted from the bowl on the ayet.

'Licitus nobis ara adire: adire dominus atque esse praesto.'

She turned to Zoe, and pressed down on her shoulders until she knelt. Still holding the cords round her neck, Fee lifted her staff.

'Circus exsisto nunc.

'Turris oriens nunc.

'Turris notus nunc

'Turris zephyrus nunc

'Turris aquilo nunc.'

She laid the staff on the floor between them.

'In nomine magnate matris telluris ego benedictio.

'In nomine magisteris cornigris ego benedictio.

'In nomine aeternus fratricius ego benedictio.

'Beautus, beautus, beautus ea iam at aeternus.'

She stood there, holding the cords in one hand, the other extended over Zoe's head. She could feel the wyth building like a whine inside her bones.

'Exsistio nobis potentia.'

She pulled on the cords, and Zoe rose to her feet. Leaving the cords to dangle, Fee started to undo the buttons on the gown.

'Exsistio nobis potentia,' the other four started to chant, moving round the room. 'Exsistio nobis potentia.'

Fee stroked the gown off Zoe's shoulders. Taking in in her hands, she turned and raised it over the ayet.

'Auspice nostra beneficium.' She draped the gown on the ayet, and raised her arms high. 'We bring before you one who is yours from birth and from before her birth. Be pleased to receive her into your communion.'

She turned back to Zoe. Her knife was in her hand.

'Is it your wish to make the unreserved dedication?'

'It is.'

'Child with no name, kneel and be received.'

Zoe knelt. Fee touched the knife blade to her right shoulder, lips, left shoulder, lips and right shoulder again.

'By the power vested in me by the Fratris, and by my blood, I receive you into this communion.'

She turned to face Tom. He stepped forward. Fee replaced the knife and picked up a copper chalice. She knelt before Tom, and lifted the chalice between them. He drew out a knife from a sheath by his side and held it up.

'Let those who know draw close. Let those who lie in ignorance draw apart. Behold the true communion,' he growled in his deep voice, 'and the secret of the old ones.' He dipped the blade in the chalice. Behind Zoe, Matt stood, flanked by Sophie and Jean. Resheathing the knife, Tom took the chalice from Fee, and sipped. He dipped a finger in the red wine, and placed it on Zoe's forehead.

'The blessing of the Great Master be on you.'

He gave the chalice to Fee, who stood up. She also sipped the wine and anointed Zoe.

'The blessing of Mother Earth be on you.'

Sophie placed a hand on Zoe's right shoulder.

'Wythen of the East wind and of the ayen of air be upon you.'

Matt paced his hand on Zoe's head.

'Wythen of the South wind and the ayen of fire be upon you.'

Jean placed her hand on Zoe's left shoulder.

'Wythen of the West wind and the ayen of water be upon you.'

Tom placed his hand over Matt's.

'Wythen of the North wind and the ayen of earth be upon you.'

Fee placed her free hand over theirs.

'Wythen of the Asha of wraithen and the freedom of the ayen of aether be upon you.'

They pressed down until Zoe was huddled on the floor, a

puddle of bone, muscle and sinew, then began to walk round her slowly, their fingers trailing over her naked back

'Be born again, be born in the Gya, be born anew, child of the Gya.'

As they circled, Zoe started to rouse, to stand up. As she came upright, their fingers trailed over the skin of her rising body. As her height increased, they sank down until their hands were at her feet: then they changed directions and brought their hands trailing up her skin in spirals. As they came up, Zoe lifted her arms high above her head. Their hands traced the spirals up her arms until they were all standing, a tight huddle, arms upraised, reaching up, higher, higher.

The tingle started in their fingers, bubbles bursting against their fingerrtips. It spiralled down, following the lines traced on Zoe's flesh. The feeling of bubbles bursting, feathers sweeping, with the bite of electricity, crawled over skin. Down, down it went, into their feet, then shot back up through their spines, a rushing tide, and out through their fingertips again to cascade around the group, a tsunami of wythen and Gya that rushed out beneath their feet only to meet the barrier of the spaca Fee had woven, to break and boil against that barrier and sweep back towards them. The rebound was forceful, crashing. They were bathed in blue light, flashes, sparkles in their eyes, their hair, over their skin. It melted against them, and they painted the light down Zoe's body with their hands. It was hot in the spaca now. The chalice Fee held almost glowed, the wine inside sparkling like rubies. She held it to Zoe's lips, and she drank, her hands over Fee's. They were panting, as if they had run the hundred metres sprint. Tom, Sophie, Matt and Jean let their cloaks fall to the floor. Jean and Tom unclasped Fee's cloak and it dropped, a dark puddle of cloth by her feet.

Fee placed the chalice back on the altar, and turned to Zoe. She embraced her, kissed her, and whispered in her ear.

'This is your name. Remember it, learn it, be it.'

Tom was there, holding the book open to a blank page. Bubo's feather sat ready. Bubo, an owl, had been rescued by Luke when a chick. True to form, the ungrateful hoyden had buggered off one night answering the call of the wild. It doesn't take much to woo a twit.

Fee leant forward, the bodkin in her hand, and jabbed it sharply against Zoe's left shoulder, just above the swell of a nascent breast that had just begun to blossom. A tiny prick of blood welled up. The blood, always the blood. She took the feather and dipped it in the redness. She handed it to Zoe. The girl stood there for a moment, as if listening to an inner voice. Then, she wrote 'Zoe' on the page.

'Welcome, Zoe, to the communion of the Fratris.'

Tom retrieved the feather from Zoe's fingers and replaced it in the book. As he turned to place it back on the altar, Sophie came forward. Over her arms draped the beautiful blue dress that Juicy Lucy had made for her. She was smiling broadly.

'Welcome, Zoe.' She slipped the mass of blue over Zoe's head and fussed with it. The deep vee of the neck that had troubled Zoe looked perfect on the slim figure. Below the breast, the fabric was caught to hug closely, then flared loose, one side of the hem reaching to mid calf, the other skimming over her knee. She tried not to preen. The garment was beautiful, showing her trim waist and long legs. Fee slipped a simple silver pendant round her neck: it was shaped like a new moon and hung gracefully at the hollow of her throat. Sophie gave her a plain band of silver which sat across her forehead and held back the mass of dark wavy hair. Matt gave her a ring with a beryl cabochon, and Jean offered a tiny vial of heavily scented oil which she dabbed on her forehead.

'Now, you must greet your fratten.'

The music rose up and filled the room, a plaintive series of notes in a slow waltz, sounding a bit like an accordion, and very French. A deep, gravely voice began the refrain.

'Dance me to your beauty with burning violin…..'

Zoe began a slow, stately waltz, but the way she wound her body and arms around Tom was anything but stately.

'Dance me… to the end of love…..' Leonard Cohen continued.

She held Tom's face between her hands and kissed him soundly, then drifted with the music to Matt. Sinuous and seductive, she wound her body and arms round him and kissed him as thoroughly as she had kissed Tom. Sophie was next, and she joined Zoe in the dance, turning with her as their lips met. This was very different from the Ravel's Bolero that had been the music-of-choice for this ritual, the default if you didn't insist on a different. Zoe continued her rhythmic progress to Jean. After a stiff moment, she melted to the music and Zoe's wyth. Finally, as Leonard Cohen started to sing about olive trees and doves again, Zoe was in front of Fee, trailing her arms round her shoulders, her face approaching, lips meeting in a soft, assured kiss. As the music died away, Zoe turned again and again on herself, one arm lifted to the sky, one arm trailing to the floor, head inclined to the raised arm like a lazy dervish and stopped.

Fee took her hand, and led her to stand in front of the ayet. She stepped back. If the Gya had taken root in her sister, and Fee had little doubt about that, what the girl did next would be the keynote of the rest of her wythen. You either had it or you didn't at this point, true. But what you did with what you had was just as important. Zoe spoke with a clear light voice.

'Wythen that lies behind all life, I offer you salt, and oil, and incense. Oil, salt and incense I offer you.' She placed a pinch of salt, a drop of oil and a hefty spoonful of incense on the glowing charcoal in the brazier. Gouts of smoke billowed upward. 'My maiden's blood I offer you. Grant me the wyth to see, and know, and act. Grant me the courage to act where I must, and the wisdom to hold my hand where I must not act. Grant me the wyth to avert evil, and overcome those who would stand in malice against me and that which I value. Grant me wisdom and understanding, cys, skyen and wyth. Open for me the lordly gateways that I may achieve my desires. Let me have dominion over those ashas I must pass through, give me wyth and peace.'

The kid didn't want much, then. Should Fee relinquish the Mysten's place now, and save herself future grief?

The wyth in the spaca was much less now. Zoe, in her name of the pure and holy one, had absorbed it like a sponge. She stood a moment more, her hands resting on the cloth. Then she turned a brilliant smile on Fee.

'I greet you, Zoe. Welcome to the Ayet and the Gya of this Frais.'

'Welcome, Zoe,' Sophie smiled, hugging her sister close.

'Zoe.' Matt held her close.

'At last.' Jean squeezed her arm.

'I am ready,' intoned Tom's gravelly voice. 'Shall I mark you now or later?'

'Now, please.'

Tom slipped his shoulder out of his tunic. There on the skin was a pair of crossed lightning bolts. Hiding in the jagged lines was a tiny star. Fee slipped her shoulder out to display a rampant dragon with sparks issuing from it's mouth. Sophie displayed a red rose, complete with green thorns. At its heart was a teeny star hidden in the petals. Matt showed her a mass of falling stars, from large and detailed to so wee they were barely specks. Jean had a fylfot, a triple circle with a miniature star in each quadrant. Sophie undid a ribbon at the back of Zoe's gown, and bared her shoulder.

'I want a serpent. A green serpent. All over my shoulder. Can you see it?'

'Aye, lass.'

While the others made Zoe comfortable, Tom slipped on a pair of latex gloves and readied his inks and needles. Zoe was almost wriggling with anticipation. A tat, at last! She would be so proud of it.

'Now you keep still. Do you want a little something?'

'Get on with it, get on with it. Give me my serpent.'

A faint whine started as Tom began painting Zoe's skin, the fine needle drawing the ink below the surface. Zoe smiled up at the surrounding faces, not even wincing when Tom went over the point of her shoulder. Soon, the outline of a sinuous body draped over her shoulder, the head hanging down to the swell of her breast. Each tiny green scale was carefully traced, the body shaded so it appeared that Zoe had a real, solid snake coiling over her shoulder.

'Mouth open or shut? Make your mind up, lass.'

Tom was following Zoe's thought. As she imagined the 'serpent', so he saw it too, or so he said. Fee believed him. Her dragon had been just what she thought it ought to be. The snake grew on Zoe's skin, from emerald to a pellucid peridot, the head showing one bright eye, a vermilion forked tongue curving out of the mouth. In the very centre of that bright yellow-and-black eye was a tiny star. Finally, Tom gave the shoulder a last wipe and smeared the skin with Vaseline.

'Leave it be for three days or so. Give it a week, then come and see me, and we'll fill in any missed bits.'

As if! Tom never had 'missed bits'. Zoe craned over her shoulder, trying to see. Jean found a mirror and held it so Zoe could see the artwork.

'It's beautiful. Thank you, Uncle Tom.'

'Of course.' he smiled, putting away his needles and inks.

Sophie ambled up with a bottle of wine and a handful of glasses. She handed out glasses, and poured the first for Zoe.

'Thanks, Sophie.'

'You're welcome. But we said that already, didn't we?' She poured wine for the others and went back for food.

'Someone hit the noise button.'

'You'd better not have too much Cohen on that disc.'

'Only a bit. It's very eclectic. I am educating you.'

'Thank you, Zoe.'

'Don't be sarcastic.'

The food was good. Better than good, in fact. They ate, they danced. But an undercurrent of anxiety was in the air. Tom left with Jean, who was wanting to get back to Margie. Lottie and Carl called in on the way home: Lottie was beginning to waddle and nurse her stomach, and whittle on about dusting. There would be a new arrival very soon. Carl insisted on dancing with Zoe despite Lottie's eagerness to be home. Once they were gone, Matt fell asleep on the sofa, leaving Fee, Sophie and Zoe alone in the Roundhouse. They lay back on the cushions, watching the candlelight flicker on the glass roof, Fee leaning on Sophie's shoulder, Zoe's head in her lap.

'I say, Soph,' started Zoe, her voice lazy slow, 'What did you and Theo talk about?'

'Why ask me? Why not Fee?'

'I'm asking her next.'

Sophie stroked Zoe's hair.

'I don't think she ever asked me that.'

'I was annoyed with you, was why. Go on. I'll tell if you do.'

Sophie stared at the flickering light.

'It was strange. He walked me across the field, and we lay down in the long grass by the brook, listening to it. He told me that the night was a different world. His world, not mine. He said, I could cross over into his world if I wanted, all I had to do was agree. He stroked my hair, said I was beautiful. Now. But I would grow old, and my beauty fade if I stayed in my world. If I went to his, I would never grow old, always be lovely. Lovely enough to break a heart, he said. And all the time, the brook was chuckling, as if it was laughing at him. Putting the lie to him. Saying that beauty waxed and waned in the world and was more lovely for that, because it changed and didn't stay the same forever. I said that to him. 'Nothing lasts forever.' So he offered me a promise. That he would keep me safe from all the other vampires, and he would keep trying to get me to agree to letting him………..'

'Do it to you.'

'Make me a vampire, yes.'

'And has he?'

'Every time I see him.'

'Fee?'

'Me he took to the orchard. It was bloody freezing. Told me about the stars and how they didn't care.'

'He took me to the top of the hill behind the house. We stood there, in the wind, and he said the wind knew everything, because it went everywhere and never forgot what it had seen. He called it the memory of the world. He's a strange git when the mood takes him. He said I could become the wind. I could ride the night with him and be part of the wind and the night and the stars. I told him I already was. Then he offered me the Pact and I agreed. Suddenly we were on the grass, and……..

'He bit you?'

'Yes.'

'That's all he did? Bit you?'

Zoe coloured up, embarrassed.

'There was a bit more to it than that.'

'He got naked. Didn't he?'

'Yes. How did he do that?'

'Buggered if I know, kid. After, he pulled me up and it was as if we'd never been undressed. I wondered if it had happened at all. Then I found blood on my robe.'

'Ah.' Zoe was silent for a while. 'Is it my innocence, or does he really have a big……'

The last word was lost in sisterly guffaws.

'He's a big lad, all right.'

Zoe decided to let discretion win the day. Matt had just woken up, and you just didn't compare men's bits in front of other men. Not if you wanted to stay friends.

Chapter Ten

Next day dawned in a buttermilk sky and it was back to business. Zoe's inbox was overflowing: Greg had left six voice messages on Fee's phone and Caleb was due back from Norway. For some obscure reason, he was flying in to Birmingham, so Sophie had arm-wrestled Fee for the Golf and was driving to meet him. Matt had returned to his vigil beside Luke's bed. If death threats couldn't keep him away, nursey disapproval hardly registered. There was a quiet, watchful air about the place. Fee sorted her e-mail and went to the door with a sheaf of orders for Blue Moon. She was restless, and couldn't settle. She decided some action was in order.

'Hey, Mouse? Want to come to the gym with me?' she called up the stairs.

'Oh, okay.'

They collected their gym bags and hiked down the lane to borrow Tom's car. He had several. They followed the ringing sound of hammering, and found him out back, stripped to the waist in his home forge. It was dark inside, and ruddy from firelight. Sparks were flying off the anvil as he beat the bar of cherry red iron. They waited while he held up the piece, inspected it and then dipped it into half-barrel of rusty water. It hissed, and clouds of steam welled up.

'Can we nick a car for the morning? We're off to the gym. How's Luke?'

'Still the same. Ellen's wearing herself thin at his bedside, I hardly see her these days. Kids'll forget what she looks like, I keep telling her.'

His body was slick with sweat and gleamed in the halflight of the forge.

'What are you making?'

'You have to ask? You need a blade, lass.' He held up the metal, dark now, and still steaming. Zoe looked at it appreciatively. Tom shoved it back in the coals. 'Thrice forged, as is proper.' He drew himself up to his full height, his sweaty body gleaming in the sullen forge light. 'Tell, me, child, why a Fratten needs a blade?'

'It is the outward embodiment of our will. As fire calls to fire, so does the blade, forged in fire, call to the wyth in our blood and manifest it. The hilts are dark, to remind us of our dark nature, our shadow: the blade is bright, to remind us of the light we invoke. It is two edged, because cys is two edged: it can work weal and woe, yet bring power and peace. It is a blade, to be used as all blades are. To wound and to heal: to give and deprive. To strengthen or weaken.'

'Very good, lass. Rina would be proud of you. Take the Fiesta. Keys are in the kitchen. Help yourselves.' He turned back to his work.

They collected the keys and threw the bags in the back. As Fee backed the car out, Zoe started.

'You know, I can't settle today.'

'Me neither. A bit of controlled violence, that's what's required. Get rid of excess energy.'

'Fee.....' Zoe wanted to say something, but seemed unable to find the words to express it properly.

'Just dive in.'

'It's worse than we thought.'

'How much worse?'

'You know I said there were twenty possible accidental deaths?'

Fee's internal iceblock was back. With a vengeance.

'There's more than that? How many? Exactly?'

'One hundred and thirty five. So far.'

Fee abruptly stopped the car, and they lurched forward. From behind came the sound of an angry horn. She ignored the irate noise and turned to her sister.

'*One hundred and thirty five?* Are you sure?'

'As sure as I can be. All unexplained accidents, unexpected deaths. You'd better move the car before that twit behind gets out.'

Fee drove to the nearest passing place and stopped there. A flash of red shot by, horn blaring. The driver shot her the finger.

Fee restrained a sudden impulse to up the body count.

'I decided to look at every death in all the Families of anyone over sixteen……. I clipped it back further, until I couldn't see any more unexplained events. It started nearly forty years ago. The first death was Mary Harris. In perfect health, and keeled over at the age of fifty three from a massive heart attack. In her garden. The next one was eighteen months later. John Howe. Fell off Beachy Head. They recorded death by suicide, but John had no reason to kill himself. No-one knew why he'd gone to Beachy Head. Three months later, his daughter followed him. She had always maintained that her father's death was never suicide. She made a fuss over it, was always looking into why he'd done what he did. Then she follows him. Suicide while the state of mind was disturbed verdict.

'Then it goes quiet for a bit, and we get another cluster. Four incidents this time. I won't bother you with the details, but each on its own looks like an ordinary if unexpected death or simply an accident. One of those things. Regrettable, true, but nothing more…. Then it goes quiet again. You can see why we've never suspected. But over the last few years, it's got worse. I've looked at the dates, and I can't see any pattern. Not unless the killer's following a personal agenda I don't know about. Dates that are important to him and only him. Unless it's a her, of course. But it doesn't follow any real pattern: the dates aren't the same, year by year. And the body count isn't the same each year. Some years it's only a couple, then there'll be a rash of them. All over the place, seldom in clusters that would make you think. Next step is to see if the pattern's got an astronomical basis, because some of the sidereal clocks don't run exactly to our years. If I can find the frequency pattern, I might be able predict when he'll have another go at us. But until then we're driving blind.'

'You did all this today?'

'No. I got Jerry and a couple of his nerd friends to root out the family trees. I gave them six names each, told them to go look.'

'And exactly why did you involve them? Without asking anyone?'

'The job was too big for one person. It would have taken too long. Anyway, we're all doing family history for a class project.

And they owe me. All they did was search the records. There was another reason for outsourcing the grunt work. I supposed that if I did it all, this creep would find out and come after *me*.'

'How did you come to that conclusion?'

'The only way he'd have known Luke was going up to Bridlip Tor was if he'd met Luke beforehand and set it up, and the only people who've been round here have been villagers who live here, and the hikers who just pass through. If Luke had met anyone within ten miles of the village, we'd've known about it. We live in a small world of nosey buggers, Fee. So it had to be someone else, someone not local. And the only place where someone could have found out about where Luke was going that day was to read his blog, which is only on the Uni's server. If you discount the students, who are all too young, and the staff, which I doubt, then we're facing a computer wiz. One who can get into the Uni and log on to the computer without leaving any traces. Without knowing the passwords. Then I have to consider that this one person has actively killing for over forty years. So I've got to think about a group of people. Two generations of them at least. Where's your Occam's Razor now?'

'Rina said it was one person. She said he, not them.'

'He found the elixir of life then.'

Fee sat, musing.

'Rina also said that the seeds of this had been sown long ago, and we couldn't undo what had been done. But she didn't tell me what that was.'

'Then we'd better eliminate the obvious suspect.'

'Who's that?'

'Simon Lake.'

The air went *very* still in the car. Fee looked at Zoe, who looked back at her. It was obvious. Simon *was* meta. But before that, he had been frata. He knew all the family secrets. He had been odds-on to be a brilliant cyscan. The Metargh had taken that from him, given him a life, but not the one he had been expecting up until then. The Family occasionally had contact with him, when his show came to town. Other than that, they kept apart. There was no question of asking him directly about the matter. Whichever way it split, it would be a bad idea. If he wasn't the perpetrator, he might take the enquiry amiss. No knowing how he might react. Badly was a good guess, vampire as he was. And if he were their man, it would surely be suicide.

'It answers a lot of questions. But Simon's never been anything else than discreet. He's had ten names, for the lord's sake. He even worked as a night watchman for several years.'

'Something about this whole thing still bothers me. Okay, Simon's been around forever. But our opponent can use wyth, Fee, we've seen it. And vamps can't use wyth.'

'So we're solid with the idea that it's one of the Fratten.'

'Or a rogue.'

'Who's been at it for more than forty years. He'd have to be - what? Sixty by now?'

'No way that guy on Bridlip was older than thirty.'

They sat in silence, looking through the windscreen, not seeing.

'Why can't a vamp use wyth?'

'All their wyth is bound up with maintaining their existence. There's none left over. Anyway, Fratten don't choose to become metae.'

'Simon did. What if he found a way? After all, he used the wyth before. He knew how it worked.'

'So does Theo. Don't you think that, if there was some way he could get the wyth to work for him, he'd have done it by now?'

'I didn't know that.'

'He and Rina were close. She never hid her wyth from him.'

'Did he ever try?'

Fee shook her head. 'I don't know.'

'We could ask him.'

'And piss him off.'

'We're dying, Fee. We could be next. And Theo's got an obligation. He promised to keep us safe from the metae. And if a mete is involved in this, he needs to know.'

'We don't know a mete is involved.'

'But if some meten has worked out how to use the wyth, he'd want to know that. He'd want to know even if we only suspect.'

'You're right there. The thought that some other of his kind would be able to do what he couldn't, he'd be on it like wasps on jam.'

'Face it, if we kept this from him, it would annoy him. So he's annoyed anyway. I say we go ask him if he can find out about any mete mucking around with cys.'

'If he doesn't know already. If we barge in there and start asking awkward questions, he might turn nasty. We leave him alone, and he leaves us alone.'

'We could ask Cecile.'

'That would piss him off even more. He's the Hegarsa of that Blyd, and if we start digging in his backyard behind his back, he will get beyond annoyed. No, if we ask the metae, we go through Theo.' Fee thought a moment. 'He'll want a quid pro quo. We'll have to offer him something he wants.'

'We know what he wants.'

'I need to think.' Fee put the car in gear and drove off.

The gym was virtually empty when they arrived. One of the instructors was taking advantage of a slack period to buff up his biceps and another patron was dripping sweat on a treadmill. Why the heck does anyone bother with a treadmill when they live in the middle of what Fee thought of as the best bit of countryside ever created? They stripped down and started stretching. Fee heaved free weights about, but it wasn't helping. Her mind was still racing, tumbling over and over. Finally, she pulled on padded gloves and gaiters and wandered over to the punch bag in the corner. On the mats, Zoe was going through an aikido kata. Fee started jabbing at the bag.

Shortly after the 'poodle incident' Robbie had decided that his daughters needed to be taught self-defence and confidence. He had taken them to the judo club where he and some friends had classes. Robbie's discipline had been karate. Sophie and Fee had joined the junior judo class, and after the first bruises healed, took to the philosophy and physical discipline like ducks to water. While Sophie and Zoe found their metier in aikido, Fee found no perfect outlet for her energies until she discovered kickboxing. 'Learn to fight, and you won't have to,' Robbie had explained. 'Resist by giving way, by using your opponent's strength against him. It's better, when your opponent throws a punch, to not be where the punch lands rather than block the punch.' They had dodged most of the blows, but a few black eyes went home for Lily to tend.

'What were you doing, standing there and letting her hit you?'

'I didn't see it coming.'

'That's obvious,' Lily remarked with some asperity, laying a hot poultice on her daughter's swollen cheekbone. 'Pay more attention next time.' So much for sympathy.

Fee kicked and punched until she was breathless and the sweat darkened the neck and back of her t-shirt.

'Fancy a bit of one-on-one?'

A new arrival had entered the gym and was watching Fee avidly. Oh, no, not another come-on. He thinks I'm going to be impressed when he knocks me off my feet. All right, sucker, here comes Lesson One.

'Okay, let's see your moves, big boy.' Bugger, where did that come from? You want to watch your mouth, Grasshopper.

He had stowed his kit, and was now bouncing round the mat, loosening up, throwing a few punches, ignoring the fact that Zoe was still trying to complete her kata. She left the mat, disgusted. She padded over to where Fee crouched, hands on her knees, catching her breath.

'I'll go play with the Nautilus. Unless you think he's too much for you?'

'In his dreams.'

Running man and the bicep buffer had stopped to watch. Great. Now we get an audience. She strolled onto the mat. Zoe was sitting on the machine that had the best view.

'Ready?'

'Ready.'

Up came her fists into a defensive stance. One leg back, one leg forward. He selected a more open position and started to weave his hands in front of her face. Oh, really. He was grinning. Fee avoided the first few blows, assessing his style. Good punches, weaker on the leg-work. He bounced back, then made the first proper attack. Fee spun out of his way and let him catch himself.

'Defensive, eh? All girls fight that way.'

All girls fight that way? Girls? *Girls?*

On his next attack, Fee turned, grabbed the passing wrist at eye height, pulled, and stuck out her leg. As he fell, she stepped over him, twisting his arm against the socket and forced him onto the mat. Then she let go and danced away. He got up.

'Not so defensive, then.'

His next attack was more considered, trying to get her measure. She flicked from aikido to judo to kickboxing, never letting any style dominate, never getting close. Dance in, attack, dance back. He caught her once, but she rolled out of it, spun, and was back on the attack. She was right. He depended too heavily on his hands. She kept them busy with fast repeated jabs until she saw another opening. She hooked a foot round his calf and pulled it out from under him, pressing her attack, and he fell over heavily backwards. She offered a hand as if to help him up. He took it, and tried to pull her down, but she rolled over him, taking the arm with her, twisting it, wrapping her legs round his arm and shoulder. She pulled and twisted his arm against her legs, holding him down. He was not grinning now. He slapped the mat, and Fee released him. Immediately, he was on her. The face was angry now. She shoved both knees in his stomach and heaved, rolling. Coming to her feet. She had one wrist in a singlehanded grip, twisting it against the bone, forcing it to where it was never meant to go. He was trying to get up, but the pressure on his arm prevented it.

'She's got you, Clive. Give it up.' Buff Biceps was grinning widely.

Fee released her hold slightly, ready to re-impose control at the first sign of further perfidy. But Lesson One had gone across.

'Lemme up. Please.'

She let him go, stepping hack out of reach. He came to his feet, shaking out the arm.

'Good fight. Thanks.' He was trying to recoup lost face. He wiped a towel over his face and draped it over his shoulders. He was breathing heavily, whether from exertion or pain was unclear. 'Maybe we could go for a drink later, you and me?'

Fee smiled and shook her head. She stripped off her gloves. She turned to Zoe.

'Had enough, sis?'

'Yeah. Let's go grab a coffee somewhere. My treat.'

They retreated into the changing rooms. Fee stood under the shower letting the hot spray needle her scalp.

'We going to see Theo tonight, then?'

'I am.'

'What about me? Soph's not back yet. I suppose she and Caleb have found a room somewhere. Taken time out for bit of afternoon delight.'

'They'll be back before dark.'

'May I remind you that Luke was caught in broad daylight.'

'And may I remind *you* that the wards are set?'

'And a fat lot of good that will that do me if you're with Theo. No, I want to come with you. I *need* to come with you. Then Sophie and Caleb can get it out of their systems in peace, without me acting the gooseberry. Perhaps then we'll get some sense out of her at last.'

'So you'd rather act the gooseberry for a bunch of vamps?'

At that point, someone else came into the changing rooms, and the conversation stopped. They finished their showers in silence, and dressed in street clothes again. Once they were back in the car, Zoe started wheedling again.

'You are getting to be boring, Zoe.'

'If you don't agree to take me with you tonight, I'll tell Tom you've gone. You know how he feels about this armistice with Theo and his crowd. Any excuse and he'll be in there.'

'You wouldn't.'

'Watch me and see. I know I need to talk to Theo. Me, not you. I've got questions.'

'Tell me them, and I'll get answers.'

'No.'

Fee sighed.

'I see you're determined. Nothing I can say will put you off. Sooner or later, you'll be down there, on your own.'

'Sooner.'

'All right. Against my better judgement, though.'

'You can feel free to say 'I told you so' if it goes tits up.'

'I will.'

'I believe you.'

Chapter Eleven

Fee dropped off the orders for Blue Moon on the way back. Very little there needed her personal attention. Orders came in, orders went out. Deliveries came in on time, mostly, and batches were made. The senior staff knew where she kept the final ingredients, in carefully labelled bottles in the laboratory. Some were running a bit low. She roped Zoe in, locked the doors and drew the blinds. An hour later, all the shelves were fully loaded. She picked up a bundle of letters from her desk, locked up and went back to the car. Apart from Pauline and one or two others off sick (again! She must remember to have words with Pauline the next time their paths crossed. The girl was laying it on a bit thick) business was going well. She was having second thoughts about the planned expansion. Maybe she had been too eager to take up with Greg's suggestions. All she had ever meant it to be was a small local concern. How would she handle it if it went national, or even international? Had to have a fully-fledged HR department? Compliance? Could she hand over parts of the business to managers she barely knew? Handle a research team? What would be her position? Did she want to be a CEO, sitting on board meetings? Now it looked like it would have to expand, she would either lose control or find herself tied to the business, weaving cys day and night. Did she want that? Could she deal properly with the expansion plans with this other on her plate? Perhaps she'd better tell Greg to cool it. After all, no-one else could do what Blue Moon did. Unless they were Family, in which case a few sharp words in the right place would solve the matter.

Having got her way over the question of visiting the metae, Zoe was content to let her drive in peace. They dropped the car back at Tom's and posted the keys through the letterbox. No-one was home: the kids were in the school club and Tom was most likely visiting Luke. As they walked back, she saw there were no lights on at Matt's: he was back at work, trying to find a bit of forgetfulness there amongst his sums.

Home, and Zoe fixed a swift sandwich and cantered upstairs to her computer. Fee asked her to print out the times and dates of the 'accidents' she had identified over the last ten years. Zoe loaded it onto a spare disc, instructing Fee to upload what she found onto it as well. Holding her prize in her fist, she went down to the parlour to do some research of her own. Booting up her laptop, she Googled "Simon Lake" and waited for the search engine to respond. It threw up over two hundred hits, and Fee scrolled down until she found one promising to list his 'personal appearances' during his career as a magician. Not that eliminating Simon as the prime suspect would stop Zoe wanting to give Theo the third degree.

Fee found an impressive list of dates. The boy had been touring for years, first as a supporting act, then as a major artist. Once he was well-known enough as a magician to craft his own shows and peddle them, he became a bigtime draw. Fee compared the listings. On three occasions, he had been showing near the supposed crime scene. When Deirdre and her sister had been swept out to sea, he had been in Newquay. And up till yesterday he had been in Portsmouth. That didn't explain why the accidents had happened in broad daylight. Even Theo, who could tolerate the odd cloudy day, preferred to stay behind closed doors during daylight hours, and he was centuries older than Simon. Cecile sometimes ventured out before sunset covered in panstick and gloves, but she was never happy doing it. 'Darkness is our natural habitat. We are not comfortable in the sunlight.' One occasion, he was in Glasgow when the accident happened in Dorset. Even a vamp can't travel that fast. Or can they? Another question to ask Theo. Simon was drifting out of the frame. Another dead end. Didn't mean it wasn't another vamp, though. And the recurring thought that it might well be one of her own kind sat sourly in her thoughts.

Fee was starting to feel angry. And the anger built. It looked around for a focus. Sophie was still collecting Caleb. Greg off somewhere, doing something or other. Zoe was upstairs. Thoughts zoomed round and round in Fee's head. Blue Moon. Vamps. Cecile. Sophie. Luke. Dave. Deirdre and Edain. Lily and Robert. Rina. Theo. A man dressed in black with a slouch hat on.

Clive. Claire. She was getting really angry now. She started to pace the room, balling her fists, whipping her hair as she turned to pace back. Forward. Back. Across. Back. She was breathing heavily. In, out. In, out. The anger was building. Then it exploded. She screamed.

'Damn, damn, damn, damn!' She kicked the coffee table and sent the laptop flying. It clattered into the grate. She started to hurl cushions, but it wasn't enough. She wanted to smash, break, hear the sound of glass and china shattering. She wanted to hit someone. Anyone. Everyone. A pane of glass in the window cracked loudly. She threw a metal bowl at the mirror over the fireplace, but missed and left a dent in the wall. She screamed a scream of pure frustration and fury. There was a clatter on the stairs. Zoe yanked the door open and stared in amazement at her sister, who stood in the middle of the room, red in the face from exertion and rage, panting. Fee wheeled on Zoe, who stood open-mouthed in the doorway, her hand frozen on the doorknob.

'What the hell are you staring at?' Fee screamed, chest heaving. 'Leave it all to me, why don't you! Why am I the only one left carrying the can? Why is it always me that has to sort things out round here? What do the rest of you do to help? Nothing! Nothing! Claire buggers off to France. Margie throws a fit. Ellen won't shift from Luke's bedside and Tom's always there with her! Sophie buggers off to collect Caleb and stays there fucking him instead of coming back here to support me! Carl does nothing but piss about with engines, Matt sods off, you piss off into Wonderland with your computers and leave me to sort it out! Abby and John are useless! Margie's worse! What the hell am I doing mixed up with you losers? Lucy shacks up with a jungle-bunny Voodoo priest, Lily stays on her arse in Norfolk with that waste-of-space Dilys and expects me to sort everything out! Why don't I bugger off back to London? Stay in my flat and fuck Greg and leave you bastards alone to sort yourselves out? Why don't you go and fuck with Theo, that's what you want to do, isn't it? Why don't I drag you down there, throw you on the floor and tell Theo he can have you and be buggered? The lot of you are bastards, bastard, bastards!'

She snatched up a fruit bowl, scattering grapes and oranges

and bananas over the floor and sofa. She wound her arm back, ready to hurl the inoffensive bowl at the laptop lying forlornly in the grate. All she wanted to hear was the glass shatter, the plastic crack and break. The candlesticks on the mantel shook and juddered towards the edge. Fee was on the verge of totalling the room. She would unleash a fury that would leave no two sticks joined together, and that included her sister in the doorway. No, it *particularly* included her sister in the doorway.

'And you! What about you? All you ever wanted was the Ritual. All I heard was ritual this, ritual that, over and over and over! So now you've got it. Bully for you. So why don't you bugger off and leave me in peace? You've got what you wanted. You never loved me, never once thought of me. I was the means to an end. Your end! Well, you got your way. Much good may it do you. You and Sophie, the pair of you! Sophie the bitch! Stealing my place in the frais! How dare she! How dare she! But I'll pay her back, you see if I don't! I'll pay you all back, you'll see! You'll see! Bitches, the pair of you!'

She was drawing another breath when Zoe crossed the room, quick as a thought, and smacked her sister smartly across the mouth.

'Pax. In. Aeternis. Vobis. Dominum.' Zoe spoke each word clearly. Forcefully.

Fee tasted blood in her mouth. She realized she was holding the bowl above her head. She lowered it and dropped it on the sofa, sinking down to join it, looking at the wreck of her laptop in the fireplace.

'You,' her sister informed her with some asperity, 'are sitting on a bunch of bananas. Just thought you ought to know.' She stepped up to the fireplace and picked up the laptop. 'Looks like it's survived.' She righted the coffee table and replaced the laptop. 'Now, what *exactly* were you doing before you went mental?'

'Looking at Simon Lake's touring calendar.' She fished out a mass of squashed bananas from beneath her left buttock. 'Looks like these will have to go onto the compost heap.' She threw them in the bowl and started to pick up scattered grapes. 'He was in Newquay when Edain and Deirdre were drowned. He was in

Portsmouth when Dad crashed the car, and he was in Great Yarmouth when Mike ran through the shop window. Apart from that, no connection.'

'You've written him off, then?'

'Yes. It's a bust. I don't think Simon's our killer.'

'So you went mental instead. Nice.'

'It's just so bloody frustrating. Tonight I'm planning on pissing Theo off over nothing.'

'There really doesn't seem to be anything here?'

Fee joined her.

'Just those few dates. How the hell someone can get from Edinburgh to Dorset in that time… it's not physically possible. No, he's out.'

'Can't hurt to look a little further. Still, I can't see I've got time to do it myself. Not when I'm trying to find out if one of us is doing it. And without tipping whoever it is off that I'm on his trail.'

'Couldn't one of your nerds look at it for you? You could try showing it to them….. Tell them you're……. inventing a code you want to use in a firewall. Tell them you've embedded correlations in the text and you want to find out if it's searchable. They'll love that.'

'That, sister mine, is a plan worthy of my own genius. I'm rubbing off on you. I'll make copies. I'll just use the dates and places, and send it to the gang pronto.' She gave Fee a hard look. 'Are you sure you're all right now? That charm was one of Mum's, she used to use it on me when she reckoned I was getting antsy. It's not like you to fly off the hook like that. Have you been got at, do you think?'

'What the hell do you mean?'

'Don't you glare at me like that. I know you. When you get antsy, you go all cold. And you don't waste your energy on collateral damage, either.' She gestured round the wreckage that was the parlour. 'This is over the top, even for us.'

'What are you suggesting?'

'I'm not entirely sure. Are you okay now? No lingering desires to rip me limb from limb?'

'Don't think so.'

'Okay. You were looking at Simon's…. what, exactly?'

'Tour schedule.'

Zoe sat carefully on the sofa and set the laptop up in front of them both.

'Do it again.'

'Why?'

'Because I asked. Please.'

Fee wilted in the face of reasonableness. As she scrolled down the list of Simon's shows, the itch started again.

'Oh, *bugger*.'

'Deep breaths. Deep, deep breaths.'

'Now that's plain weird.' Fee looked at the list again. 'Now I've got it in my eye, I can see what's happening. There's something here that doesn't want me to be too curious.'

'So why the tantrum?'

'Tantrum is too little a word. I was being gently discouraged to be suspicious of… I'm not going there again. And you know how I react to being stonewalled.'

'Typically? You go off on one.'

'It might be just that, being a meta as he is, he's asked someone in the Family to place a weirding on his publicity, but……..'

'Know what you mean. And who would he ask? It'd have to be someone who knows his history.'

'That's a pretty short list.'

'We can ask about that, at least. Most of the prime suspects are our family.'

'Are you going to look at Simon any more?'

'No. Maybe. Why?'

'If every time you go looking at Simon it ends in you trying to take stuff apart, someone's going to get hurt.'

'What are you saying? That we need protecting from a weirding? Something a bit stronger than the usual?'

'Can't hurt. We don't know exactly what we're up against. That was certainly not you back there. I know you've got a temper, but that was just…….' Zoe gave up as words failed her. 'What about one of the sigas? I'm thinking of that one that's got 'Your shafts shall enter your own hearts and your spears shall be broken'.'

'Very appropriate. Shouldn't take too long to do. I'll just check the time, as do some as soon as poss.'

'It would be a better use of your excess energies than going off on one, to be sure. What's that?'

'Oh, bugger, that's my phone! Where the hell did I chuck it?'

They hunted down the warble and found the phone under the sofa. It was Greg again. She was torn between wanting to see him and telling him she never wanted to see him again. But he persuaded her that she needed to come to the city again, that was if she still wanted to expand Blue Moon. Was she getting cold feet?

'I really don't know, Greg. I've been happy the way it's going right now. All I can see in the future is problems.'

'It can get like that. Taking on more people, professionals, more staff, more manufacturing sites, you tend to lose the plot. I'm glad you've got reservations, it means you're thinking along the right lines to make this work. And you've been doing a bit of everything, right? Research and development, HR, sales, procurement, delivery, customer satisfaction, promotion…… and once you get bodies in to do that for you, you think it's going to get away from you. That you'll be sitting at the top of a heap with two layers of management between you and what you are doing now. It doesn't have to be like that. You can still be hands-on. Say the bit you really like is making new products. So you lead the R-and-D team, day to day. But you also call the shots from the Board. The rest of the bodies are there to take away the grunt work and advise you. You don't have to take that advice if you don't want.'

'And where do you fit in?'

'Me? I'll be your advertising and PR consultant. I'll suggest a course of action. If you agree, that's all you will have to do. I'll do the rest. Likewise your production team. Your production manager will deal with the petty day-to-day issues, leaving you a clear field to do what you do best. Staff worries? Dump it on your HR manager. Supplies not coming in on time? You'll have a procurement department for that. If you don't like what they are doing to your company, you say so, and it sticks. If it doesn't, you find someone else who will listen to you.'

'When you say it like that, it seems all so reasonable.'

'It is. I've been promoting small concerns like yours for a long time. Now will you come up and talk to me, at least? I'll listen to your worries, and see what I can do to minimise them.'

'Okay, you've persuaded me. How about early next week?'

'Say Tuesday.'

'What time?'

'How about all day?'

'I'll meet you for brunch. Provided nothing else comes up here.'

He rang off. Wait until I tell you that all the products have to have a wythenweave in them. I want to see your face when I tell you that. And listen to how you propose to solve it if we go for manufacture in Bogotá. Coz I'm not about to move away.

She fished in the freezer and found lasagne. As it was heating, she looked at the sky. Time enough for a little cys………

Slightly less than an hour later, three small red packets sat on the table. She was putting away the coloured inks and parchment when Zoe clattered downstairs after beating a hasty retreat to her eyrie while Fee was distracted.

'Ah, lasagne! Those the sigas, then?'

'Yup. One for me, one for you and one for Sophie. I've suggested that the others do likewise. I swear I could hear Jean getting the ink out as I was speaking. She even told me it was a very good idea, and that she'd do them for all the frais. Give her something else to think about, she said.'

Zoe fished the lasagne out of the oven.

'And how is Margie?'

'Improving. Jean's been weirding. She's told Margie that there's several years left in her yet, and to stop milking it. Lottie, she says, will produce at the end of next week, which will be a relief for her, I guess, with all that extra weight to hump around.'

'Remind me never to reproduce. Did Jean say anything else?'

'She said she'd weirded for Luke, but it was unclear. She was very cagey about it over the phone. I think there's something she's not saying.'

"To speak of bad news is to invite it to happen.' Sounds a bit heads-in-the-sand to me.'

'It's her way. She could see that I'd be run down by a bus tomorrow and she wouldn't tell me in case it happened. Then she'll be telling everyone she foresaw it. Cassandra.'

'You mean Senna. 'A little goes a long, long way.'' Zoe was serving up the lasagne. 'I hope there's plenty of garlic in this.' She took one of the packets and fiddled with it, secreting it in her bra. 'There. All ready to face what the world throws at me. I feel heaps better.'

Fee laughed and accepted a plate of lasagne.

'Sun's going down. I'd better forewarn Theo that we'll be coming. Did he leave you something?'

'Yes.'

Zoe held out her arm. Around her wrist spiralled a tiny snake, its head resting close to her hand.

'When you want Theo, you have to put a drop of your blood on the snake. Think to him what you want.'

'Like, meet me in the churchyard at midnight and I'll bring steaks?'

'A bit like that. But use visuals. English isn't his first language and he tends to think in Ancient.'

'Ancient what? Hebrew? Greek? Babylonian?'

'Ancient whatever. He never says. So it's best to use images.'

'Got it. So, 'meet me in the churchyard at midnight' would be a picture of the church door, me standing there and him walking up, and a clock at midnight.'

'Right. So we'll send him the sun setting, a clock with the hour hand going round once, us walking down the lane towards him, sitting in his house.'

'I've never been to his house. I don't know what it looks like.'

'Then send him an at-home feeling, that he's sitting inside, waiting for us to come to him.'

'Why don't you send it to him?'

'I will be. I want him to know that we are coming together, but that we are *both* coming. I am not bringing you, and you are not bringing me. It's the sort of difference that means more to him that it does to us.'

'Weird city.'
'Weird person.'
'Seriously weird person.'

Chapter Twelve

Just before they were setting out, there was a light rap at the door. Standing on the doorstep was Cecile. She declined to come in.

'Now is not a good time to be inviting any metae into your home. Theo sent me. We have guests.'

'Is that a problem?'

'Theo wishes to make it very clear that you are his, and his alone. Were you to arrive unescorted, those guests would make free with you. Then Theo would be compelled to defend you. They are not altogether welcome, but to dismiss them would be unwise. By sending me to escort you, he avoids this confrontation. No offence can be taken where none is offered. This way, we keep the peace between the Blyds.'

'Then we will welcome your escort. Is there anything we should know about your guests?'

'Only that you stay away from them, do not engage them. If they can find some excuse to confront us, they will.'

'Come to pick a fight, eh?'

'If you wish to see it so, yes. It is our way. They only know Theo by reputation, and they come to test him. If they see him as weak, there will be war.'

'Then we'd better front up for him. Hang on a sec, and we'll go dress the part.'

'You do not need to do this.'

'What I don't need is a blyd war on my turf. Not now. Not ever. We're not doing this for Theo as much as for ourselves. Every little helps, as they say.'

'Then Theo will welcome your support. Even these will think again if they have witch-women to consider.'

Fee shoved Zoe back upstairs.

'Gladrags, kid. Front it up good. And wear your cloak.'

'Do I need clean knickers?'

'Always with the knickers. Good underwear, Zoe. It might get seen. You are playing the part of a powerful farer coming to consult with an equally powerful Hegarsa with whom you have a mutual pact. Put on a show. You'll enjoy it. It's not often we get to play one of Theo's games with him.'

When Fee came back downstairs, she was wearing a low-cut red velvet dress which swung round her calves. High-heeled red boots completed the ensemble, and over it all was the long black cloak. Zoe had gone for an all-black look in silk, a wrap-round dress that came to mid-thigh over opaque black tights, showing off her slender form and long coltish legs. For her feet, she had chosen ankle boots with spike heels and lots of straps and buckles. Cecile was regarding her, especially the boots, with an approving look on her face.

'Hood up, Zoe. And look regal. You are far more important than any overnight visitor. We outrank them. And if it comes to it, leave the rough stuff to me.'

'I shall watch and learn, O mighty one.'

Cecile walked with them through the village and out into the country. She led them to an isolated group of buildings that had once been a farm. The farmhouse itself was still more or less intact, though some of the buildings were looking a bit worse for wear. Theo had chosen to live in one of the larger barns, mostly because it had a root cellar. Mind you, he'd been at it since then. The cellar was now a veritable warren of rooms. Above, it looked like a high-class conversion, all exposed beams and glass doors.

Cecile led them to a door by the back wall. Its gothic arch looked out of place amongst the more modern design of the barn. They went through the door and down a spiral stone staircase. Flickering light came from the lower arch where the stairs opened out into a broad passage. They passed more gothic arches in which doors stood closed, the rooms behind them hidden and private, until they came to the end of the passage. Here, their way was barred by two massive oak doors. Theo really appreciated gothic architecture, though he shied away from the brilliant Puginistic colours that were typical of the genre. Black oak and grey stone dominated. The floor was slate, marked in places with natural streaks of green and ochre. Cecile did not bother to knock. She opened both doors with ease. Being a vamp had its advantages. She could probably lift a double decker bus without too much trouble. Fee and Zoe followed her in.

It was a large room. Too large. The roof soared above them. Truth be told, that roof was actually one of the other barns. From the outside, it looked like a wreck: hardly any floor to speak of, and no way inside. Occasional forays by the local youngsters found.... Nothing. A couple of Theo's akelytes camped out in the farmhouse on the pretense of converting the barns, although it had been completed to Theo's satisfaction years ago. This subterfuge kept most of the interested parties at a safe distance. If anyone did chance to see anything peculiar, twenty-four hours later they had forgotten about it. Theo's hidel was a safe as meten-craft could make it. One or two wythweavings had made it even more secure. Theo had left the clerestory windows in, and a few rays of ghostly moonlight painted the walls high above. Beneath, it was lit with the warmth of candles. Not very many of them, and nowhere near enough to chase the gloom from the corners. At the end of the room was a raised dais, and on the dais was a heavy refectory table with a candelabra glowing softly. At the end of the table, on a high-backed seat, sat Theo. Tonight he was dressed in pale grey, with a long wine-red waistcoat. Juicy Lucy would have loved it. The stone wall behind him was hidden by a tapestry, too old and faded now to make out the details. Along one side of the room were an assortment of occasional tables, divans, chairs and cushions. Lounging on these were the members of Theo's blyd. Not all of these were metac. Amongst the pale faces were one or two, no, three or four or more, living souls. Pash. Fee didn't bother counting. They had all made their choices in life, and the repercussions of those choices were not her affair. They were got up in several styles, gothic to the fore. Most of the rest chose evening dress of one sort or another. Leather and chains were well represented by both sides. One or two even sported Lycra.

Closer to the dais were a group of three meten who didn't really fit in, like Hell's Angels at a bicycle rally. Hard to tell how, because their clothing was much like the rest. It was attitude, perhaps. This was not their home. And they didn't appear to have brought their own nibbles either. Cecile's entrance had interrupted something. She walked up to Theo and bent her face down to his. He reached up a languid arm and drew her down. They kissed, chastely, and she stood at his back, apparently completely at ease.

'These are not akelytes!' one of the group growled, glaring at Fee. She faced him down.

'And you are not polite.' She turned to Theo. 'Hegarsa, I expect a better welcome in your halls than this.'

'Forgive my guests. They have little opportunity for the nuances of polite society.'

That was a deadly jibe. He was implying that they were too callow to be allowed out.

'Since you ask it of me, I will overlook it. This time.'

'Then to what do I owe the pleasure of this visit? You are not a common sight in this place.'

'I have matters to discuss that may concern you. As does she who stands with me.'

Never give a mete any extra information about yourself was the rule. Especially ones you don't know very well. Or at all. They are all psychopaths, the lot of them. Regard them in the same light as you would Hannibal Lecter, if he appeared in your life. Be polite, be civilized, until the time comes when you have to be impolite and uncivilized. If your attitude amuses them, and you are lucky, they may walk away.

'These matters. Do they need to be discussed in private, or are they of general interest?' He sounded uninterested.

'That is for you to decide. You rule here. I will tell you that it concerns the pact made between your blood and mine.'

'Then it is between you and me alone, as I told you. Cecile, take them to my chamber.'

'No! We will all hear what these…….. humans….. have to say.' This from one of the visitors. He made the word 'human' sound like 'scum'.

Theo stood. It was a lazy, elegant move. It said better than words that here his word was law. Or there would be violence and worse than violence.

'Will you dictate to me, here in my hall?' The voice was soft. Be careful how you answer. Your health may depend on how I take your words. And I don't care a whit for your health, good or bad.

'Mavron will hear of this,' the apparent leader of the group snarled. Wrong answer.

Theo smiled. Lazily.

'Mavron will hear of it, you may be sure.'

The other flushed. He was in deep shit now and he knew it. He would not be the one complaining of Theo to Mavron, whoever Mavron happed to be. Theo would be complaining to Mavron of *him*. Theo flipped a hand at Cecile: she turned and lifted the ancient tapestry. Fee walked over to her, followed, at some distance, by Zoe. The girl was playing the game well. No matter how insecure she felt, she would not show it. Her body language said, I am not afraid of you. I may look like a fluffy bunny, but I have the black heart and soul of a raptor.

Cecile led them through a short, narrow corridor into windowless room. Over on one side, indistinct among the shadows, was a huge four-poster bed. Fee decided not to even think of what had been done in that bed, nor what would be done. One thing was certain: Theo rarely slept there. He certainly wouldn't today, not with his inconvenient visitors. Maybe they could walk by day, or maybe not. He didn't get to be as old as he was by taking things for granted. Neither would his secret resting place be easily accessed from his private chambers. Metae didn't survive as long as he had unless they were very, very smart. Over by a dark fireplace that could have taken half a tree with little trouble were three wingbacked chairs and a table. A fur rug lay on the floor in front of the cold hearth. An iron sconce stood behind the chairs and fat creamy candles wove a puddle of warm light. Why did vamps always do things on such a scale? Did they all live mentally in vast edifices with not enough furniture? Everything was too large, even in the spaces they chose to inhabit. The bed would be soft, the chairs comfortable, the rug luxurious, but the overall feeling was that they were camping out, or in stage sets for a drama of the less comfortable kind. At least the candles didn't look as if they came from a Seventies Corman movie.

Here Cecile left them. Fee brushed the hood off her head and shook out her hair.

'Sit down, Zoe. We might as well be comfortable while we wait.' Zoe was poking about the room, peering into the corners. Apart from the bed and chairs, the only other furniture was a large coffer, black with age, over by the bed, and a glass-fronted cabinet by the door.

'I wonder what….'

'Don't even *think* about it.'

Zoe selected a chair and arranged her cloak carefully to frame her body. She leant back and crossed her legs.

'Don't get too comfortable. We are in the eye of the hurricane here.'

'Theo won't do anything…. Will he?'

'No, but there are others here who might.'

'Theo wouldn't let them. Surely?'

'Not without a fight. And that you don't want to see. Neither do I. Let's not take any chances.'

They sat in silence, waiting for Theo. He would not come immediately, or do anything to make it look as if he was at their beck and call. He would speak with them when it was convenient for him. Keeping them waiting was a power play, but it was not directed at them. It was for the rest of his kind. His blyd knew very well that he regarded anyone in Rina's bloodline as his own personal property. It was not so well-known beyond his own blyd. What need had he to explain his doings and the reasons for them to the other blyds? That was not their affair, just as what they did, and why, was of no concern to him. Except when what they did impinged on his existence. Then, it was not a matter of explanation. It was simply because he willed it so, and had the capability of enforcing that will. No-one who had gambled their soul for immortal life wants it ripped away from them by an irritated Hegarsa. Once he had dealt with his own concerns, he would come to them.

A movement at the door caught their attention. Standing there was what looked like a fifteen year old girl. She was got up like a Goth in a purple velvet dress with lilac ruffles, carefully laced about the bodice to show off a trim waist and an impressive cleavage. She was wearing black lipstick and purple eyeshadow to match the dress. Heavy black eyeliner and mascara made the pale makeup even paler. Dense black hair was piled up on her head, a do carefully arranged to look fashionably untidy. A few artful tendrils hung down to tickle her shoulders. On one hand she balanced a tray with a bottle and three glasses.

'Theo sent me.' Her walk across the room showed that she was still mostly human. She had none of the grace which spoke of an ability to move so fast it looked like translocation. It was clumsy in comparison. Graceful for a human, but downright graceless for an undead. It lacked their style.

Fee could see that Zoe was bursting with questions. Uh-oh.

'Is it okay if we talk?' Zoe asked.

The girl smiled. Her teeth looked a bit like old parchment against the black lipstick. Her nails were painted iridescent purple and sparkled in the candlelight as she poured wine into two of the glasses.

'Sure. Call me Morgana.'

'Is that your name, then?'

'No. But whoever heard of a mete called Brenda?'

'You're not a mete though, are you.' Not a question.

'Not yet.' She ignored the remaining chair and sat down on the rug, fussing with her skirts. There was a lot to fuss with. 'But I will be.' She fussed a bit more. 'Go on, ask me. You can.'

'Why do you want to be a vampire?'

'Why not? Ordinary life doesn't hold much for me. I don't like who I am. I don't like the way I'd have to live to survive. So why not change? It's either that or suicide.'

'Why is your life so horrible that becoming undead is a better option?'

She looked at Fee.

'You've got a good life, you don't know what it was like to be me. My dad raped me when I was six. My mother hit me when I told her. She called me a disgusting little guttersnipe. My teachers at school made me feel I was thick. All the boys only wanted one thing, to poke me. All I could see ahead of me was a life at the bottom of the heap, an unmarried mum with as many kids as possible to live off the State in a grubby little house. That or be off my head with drugs and tomming it to pay for them. Thick I might be, but not that thick. I ran away from home, to

Manchester, found a squat, and it was same shit, different day. Every day. I got a job washing the floor in a pizza joint to get by. The lavvies stank. The kitchens were greasy. They let me have some pizza the customers left and the salad they couldn't sell. And chips. I'd go to the market at the end of the day and pick stuff up to eat. Sometimes I'd sleep rough to stay away from the guys in the squat. I was always looking for work, to earn money, to get out of there, to find something better for myself.

'Then, I found this bar. I was wandering around, late at night, not wanting to go back to the squat and fight off the lads, waiting while they got stoned or unconscious, then I saw these people going into a door. There was music, and voices. I went up to the door and knocked. This huge guy opens the door, and I think, Bugger. But I've nothing to lose. So I asks him, is there any work there? He looks me up and down. I look a right mess. I say, I scrub up good, mate. I'll do anything. Anything but fuck you. And he laughs, soft, like. 'Anything?' he says back. Then this woman turns up. She's tall. Long pale hair done in a French plait. Very stylish. Red satin dress that must've cost a bomb. I thought then she must be a model or something, she was so thin, and her makeup was perfect. Way out of my class. 'Rollo, she says to the gorilla, 'Let the lady in.' Lady? Me? But he opens the door. She gives me the once-over. I stare back at her. 'Can you serve behind a bar?' she asks. I say, I can learn. My customers are very..... particular, she says, and there's something else behind her words. I didn't get it then but I did pretty soon after.

'She takes me down a passage and into an office. I sit in there while she has word with this Rollo. Then she comes in and sits down. One of her barmen has left, she don't say why. The hours will be from nine o'clock at night until seven in the morning. Setting up, serving drinks behind the bar, then helping to clean up after closing. I will not leave the bar to go into the club, nor go outside for a break while the club is open. When I get a break, I will go into the staff room, where the customers can't come. If I don't obey the rules, then I will have to leave. She never says why, and I don't ask. The wages are pretty good, I'm not about to lose the chance to escape from the squat and the grubby boys there. Do I have anywhere to stay, she asks. Not really, I say.

There is a room available, she says. This is getting better and better. Right then I'd decided to take the job. You will have to wear a uniform, she tells me. Since I'd've done it starkers to get away from the squat, I accepted right away. Tonight, she says, you will watch behind the bar. Maybe serve a drink or two. See how you get on. But you cannot go into the bar looking like that, she laughs. Rollo comes back, and takes me upstairs. There are lots of rooms on the second floor, and I can hear people behind them. I asks Rollo if I've found myself in a knocking shop, 'cos if it is, I won't stay. Nothing like that, he says. Just the customers having…. fun. He takes me up to the next floor. There's a bedroom there, and a bathroom, just like a little flat. If you stay, this will be your room, he says. The door has a lock, use it. Do things get nicked here then? I ask. No, he says. We value our privacy. He's a bit weird, you know?

'Anyway, I dump my stuff and get in the shower. I scrub off all the grease and grime. There's shampoo, and conditioner, and all sorts. I even shave my legs and stuff. I'm feeling really clean for the first time in ages. Even if I don't get the job, it's worth it just for this. There's even a bathrobe hanging behind the door, and not one of your cheap ones neither.

'I'm combing my hair when the woman comes back. She taps on the door, ever so polite. She's brung my uniform. I'm Julia, she says. Pop this on, and we'll have a look at you. It's a white silk vee-neck with no sleeves and a black weskit over. Shows off my arms and tits. Black trousers and spike heels. My feet are going to be killing me later, I tell her. She changes the shoes for black pumps and turns up the pants, then sits me down and twists my hair up into a bun. Then she makes up my face. It's a bit more than I'm used to but she says I'll need it for the lighting, like on the stage. Then we go downstairs, into the bar.

'When we go in, it's like every eye swivels to look at us. She puts me behind the bar, and there's another girl, only older'n me, and two men. One's very old, got white hair, the other's much younger, like my age. He's shaking cocktails. This is Brenda, the woman says, and I wince. She laughs. The old guy's Charles, the girl's Katie, and the young man's Virgil. You look sweet, he says. We'll call you Candy. Stand over there, and watch. It's busy. Most of the people are drinking red wine. Well, I thought it was red wine. Some had spirits, and some had cocktails. They were all dressed, well, strange. I thought it might have been a gay bar, only there were women and men. Part of the place was a disco, all coloured lights and trance music. I found out later they had floor shows. Weird floor shows. And that it was a vampire bar. Oh, they let normal people in. Humans, I mean. The vamps brought them or they brought themselves. Charles told me that the ones that came in on their own were weary of life and wanted to die. And he knew I was one them. That was later, of course. Once they got used to me being there, they started showing their fangs and making offers. I found it funny that no meant no there. Sort of thought they'd have me the moment I turned my back on them. If I'd said no to the boys in the squat, they'd've had me anyway, and here were guys that could kick out a steel security door and they just took my 'no' like that. Weird. Katie said that they didn't need to steal, there were enough of us willing to go with the vamps anyway. It was a whole new world. One in which I didn't have to be a loser. Provided I obeyed the rules. Julia wouldn't have any rough stuff, and Rollo and his mates were there to enforce that.

'I was there, oh, a year before Bevan found me. Being round vamps became normal. Bevan got this thing for me. Asked me to come with him when he left Manchester and came back here. And I said yes. I'm his Pash, his eyes and ears in the sunlight, he says. We went on a cruise last year. It was great, I'd never been on a ship before. The only bummer was the inside cabin. Bevan stayed in there all day and only came out at night. He pretended to be an author, he was working on a book, see. I spent the days lounging around and napping on deck. Being with Bevan, I didn't need much sleep. So you see, being with the vamps is a better life for me than I would have had otherwise.'

'Don't you ever feel you want to get out? Be human again?'

'What for? Okay, there's a downside. I'm going to die. But we all die sooner or later. I don't believe there is a God, and if there is, he's given me such a shitty life that I don't care about any immortal soul I might have. I certainly don't want to spend eternity in the same place as a God that thinks its okay to let a six year old girl be raped by her father. Anyway, I believe that this life is the only thing you have, there's nothing there after you die. So if I get to die and stay here, I'm ahead of the game.'

'What if I could show you that there is something there after you died?'

Brenda, or rather, Morgana, sighed.

'It's too late now. I've made my choice. I enjoy the good bits, and if there's bad bits, well, that's the price. Do you know, that since I met Bevan, I found out that I'm not thick at all? I graduated from college last September. Got a BA in English literature. Okay, so it's only a one-two. It's better than my father or mother or brother managed to do. I'm going back this year to study art. Now I'm a Pash, I feel that I've all the time in the world to learn about things that were a waste of time before. I've discovered a new me. And do you know what? I like her.'

'It's never too late, Brenda.'

Brenda stared at Zoe.

'I am what I am. I dare say your father loved you. Your mother had time for you. You had sisters that didn't tell you that you were scum. I did. Brenda did. Brenda's dad raped her, her mother despised her, her sister ignored her and her brother hurt her when he could get away with it. So now she's dead. I went back to see them, you know? I wanted to see my dad dying with cancer, my mother zonked out on zombie pills, my sister a fat slob and my brother in prison. You know what I saw? My bitch of a mother living in a nice house on the edge of town with my dad. Bastard got made redundant, and invested the money. My granddad died and left them another wodge of cash. They're on easy street. So's my sister. Shacked up with some dyke with a cushy number in the local radio station. She gets to meet all the celebs, you know? Me brother's found himself a bitch to keep him, and he's going to be an accountant. He's evil enough to make it good. And did they look for me, when things got better for them? Spare a thought for me and what I was going through? No. Did they care about what happened to me? No. I want to be able to go back there, and destroy them. Take away all the niceness, the comfort, the contentment, the bloody self-satisfiedness of their lives, for what they did to me. Oh, I won't kill them. I want them to feel the same hopelessness, the same wretchedness, that I felt. Then I'll tell them. I'll stand there, in the wreck of their lives, and tell them that their chicken's come home to roost. I'll strip them of everything they value. If one of them had loved me, believed me, comforted me, I wouldn't be here now. But they didn't. And I *am* here.'

Oh, she was meten all right. She had venom. You could see why. Brenda had been buried with her hurt and sorrow in revenge and destruction. She would go down into the dark with Bevan and not return. What would return would be Morgana, a virago hell-bent on revenge. And what would she find, once she had accomplished her mission? What else could she do to fend of the weight of long years? She could trawl through the universities, getting degrees whilst feeding off the students who fell by the wayside, ground down by the wheels of the monster Education. She could travel the world. See the Pyramids at night, the Taj Mahal in the glow of the moon, the starlit peaks of the Andes. Did she know that Bevan would not be the same after her Metargh? That he would inevitably find other interests, and expect her to do likewise?

Fee shrugged inwardly. Not my problem. As if I didn't have enough, anyway.

The wine was still on the table, untouched.

'Shocked you, have I? Thought I was a *nice* person. Well, I never was. I never had the chance to be. Everyone wrote me off, except the metae. Some of the people here, the live ones, there just here for the thrill of it, like they'd do drugs or screw around to piss their folks off. Most of them even have homes to go back to. I have nowhere to go back to. All my friends are metae, or they move in meten circles. And you know what? It's not a bad life, being a Pash. I can leave here if I want. I can go away, travel anywhere. Do anything. And when I want to come back, they'll even fetch me. Welcome me back. Sometimes I even go to someplace Bevan wants to see and see it for him. He uses my eyes to see it with. He sees the world through me. We talk about it, where I've been, what I've seen. What I'm studying. My mum never did that. These dead guys are more than family to me.'

Even if she could see a way back, she wouldn't take it.

'Has Morgana been entertaining you with her stories?' Theo was, suddenly, there. He smiled down at Morgana. She flinched, slightly. 'Return now. I will speak to my guests alone.' He waited while she left, her heels clicking on the stone. 'She sometimes tries to listen. Not this day. I know the difference between the sound of retreating footsteps and someone stamping on the floor to simulate retreat.' There was a flurry from behind the curtains. 'Impossible child, I do not know what Bevan sees in her. She is an awful liar too.'

'Sounded like a pretty good lie to me.'

'Wait until you have heard it for the third time. It becomes tiresome, listening to her justify her interest in Bevan. Yes, she met him at the Shades in Manchester. Yes, she had an unhappy home life, but mostly because she was a difficult child.'

'Electra complex?'

'One suspects so. One also suspects that the brother was a more intelligent youth than she pretends. But she means it when she speaks of the revenge she wishes to visit on her family, and she will do that, oh yes, if I allow Bevan to give her the Metargh. I hope she will grow bored with it in time. But enough of Morgana. She is a petty concern, nothing more. What is this matter that concerns me and the pact with Rina?'

'You know what happened to Luke?'

'Yes. Cecile told me. She is fond of the boy, She visited him in hospital, so I believe.'

'I hope Tom didn't find out.'

'She was discreet. But it affected her, to see the damage done to him. I trust you are doing all you can to repair that damage. Or she will take matters into her own hands.'

'She mustn't do that, Theo.'

'There is more to your words than blind aversion to the Metargh. So tell me.'

'You know that we can speak to our dead relatives?'

'I know you believe so.'

'I know so. I've spoken to Luke. That fall was no accident. And his wraith isn't where it ought to be. If Cecile tries to change him, she may find she's bitten off more than she can chew.'

Theo laughed, a delighted sound.

'That's rich. Cecile biting off more than she can chew. Oh, my.' He looked at Zoe like an older, wiser uncle indulging a favourite niece.

'I mean it, Theo. Luke's been hexed in some way. And his wraith had been trapped, and he's not the only one.'

'I still do not see why this should concern me.'

'What if I told you that someone, or something, has been carrying out a concerted campaign on our Families: that it has been going on for forty years, with over a hundred fatalities? And that we might be next on the list?'

'Could one human be doing this alone? Forty years, Theo. Forty years, to plan it and accomplish it, so secretly that no-one up until now even got a sniff of what was going on. The incidents happened all over the country, sporadically, to no calendar that we recognize. Does this sound like human behaviour to you?'

'So you suspect a mete.' Theo's face was carefully blank. It was smooth anyway, but it was as if he didn't trust his features, and had suppressed all signs. This was bad: he was getting angry. This was a dangerous place to be.

'This killer does not leave an image in a digital camera. He is also computer savvy.' Oh hell, Zoe, did you have to mention that? It puts him right in the frame.

'I can see why you came to me.' That was two-edged.

'Theo, do you really think that we are stupid enough to come here and accuse you to your face? That we would walk in here and ask you point-blank if you'd been slaughtering our Family? Or that you knew that someone was?'

'So you came to me first because it was…….. proper.'

'You are the only Hegarsa we know that we can talk to.'

'The thought of my complicity never crossed your mind, then.'

'Crossed it and went right on going.'

His face was still a careful blank. He sat musing in the chair.

'Theo, whoever is doing this….. they can use the wyth.'

'So why are you seeking them here? Our kind cannot do as you do. You would be better employed searching your own houses, before you come to mine.'

'As we are. But our concern is one that could affect you. Severely. We cannot rule out the possibility that one of your kind has discovered a way to employ wyth.'

'And you have come to this conclusion how?'

'There are clues here that implicate one of your kind. The ability avoid being caught on camera. The longevity.'

'And things that fit us. The ability to use wyth, knowledge of our family lines.'

'So a sport - a cross between a mete and a Fratten would answer all the questions you are asking.'

'Yes.'

'Even though you know it is impossible.'

'Once you have eliminated everything else, whatever's left, no matter how improbable, is the answer.'

'There is one meten who has Family connections. We'd be daft not to eliminate him. That's all we want to do.'

'We have to look into it, Theo.'

'I should like to see the basis of this ….. suspicion.'

Zoe tossed him a memory stick. He let it fall into his lap. He let it lie there.

'This is……most unwelcome.'

'We're not overjoyed about it ourselves.'

'What do you want to know? That the being Simon Lake is your killer? Or that he is not?'

'Yes.'

'I can be of little help to you, then. Simon does not seek out our company. That he maintains metaae in his troupe of actors, yes. That I know them, no. That any one of them is capable of murder? Yes. Of these that you claim to be murders, no. I know that Rina had other motives than saving his life to ask of me what she did. But what those were, I did not ask, nor she tell.'

'She was like that.'

'Indeed she was. When Simon asked me to……. change him, he was full of rage. But when he left me to follow his own desires, there was little of that rage left that I could detect. Or I would not have let him go as I did. He did not seek out the Metargh of his own accord, but accepted what it could give him as the alternative was abhorrent to him - a short life of pain, wholly dependant on other people and machines to keep him alive. He did not want that. What he wanted, no-one could give:

his old life back. He embraced his meta-nature, as he had to. He shared the ophosis with us, but unwillingly. He told me that it reminded him of what he had lost, that he could not rest in our company. So I allowed him to depart. He was as careful as he could be in his new incarnation. There was no hint that he would fall victim to the madness that our kind can become subject to. He was always controlled. I let him go, and since then, he has….. avoided our blyd.'

'So you don't think he is involved with our killer.'

'I would look elsewhere. Simon is of my blyd, after all, and all my blyd is bonded to your line through me. Any of my metae who seek to harm you knowingly risk my anger, even if they do not apprehend the roots of it. But I would regard Simon Lake with a degree of…… caution.'

'Are there any other metae who might know him better?'

'There may be. But he appears to keep his interests in his troupe. I wonder if I could send Morgana to see one of his… shows. It is the sort of thing she would do. He might seek her out. She has a certain air about her that attracts us. I shall see what is possible, but I make no promises. Certainly I should be foresworn if damage should come to you from my kind. Rina was most specific. She went into exquisite detail over what would happen to me should I be derelict in my part of the pact. She wanted there to be no misunderstandings between us. And if what you have told me is true, then I am dangerously close to learning exactly what influence Rina has exerted over me. And that,' he concluded 'I most definitely want to avoid.'

'If you don't mind my asking….. What did Rina threaten you with? You can't die. You can heal almost any injury. What is it you fear that she can do to you?'

'She promised to invade my dreams. That she can carry out this threat, and from beyond her grave, I know, because she has proved it to me. I have ample proof, believe me. Now, I must get you away from here. My guests are most interested in you, and our relationship. They will try to learn what they can. It may be they think they can use that knowledge against me. And that would leave you in danger of their further attentions.'

'That's why Cecile told us not to invite her in the house. But invitations are specific, aren't they?'

'I find it so. But it would be foolish to make assumptions. If these believe that the invitation to one meten in a blyd is an invitation to all the blyd - and some do believe this - they may try to seek admittance on that assumption. Or they may come to you without my knowledge, pretending some message from me. Safer for you, and me, if you do not invite any attentions from any of my kind that you do not know as well as Cecile and myself, not admit them into your home, for now at least.'

'Thank you, Theo.'

'Do not thank me. I am constrained by Rina's influence. Know that I would have you all if I had my way.' He stood, and offered his hand to Fee. As she took it, he pulled her to her feet and brought her hand to his lips. 'Kitten.' He released her hand, and made the same offer to Zoe. When she hesitated, he smiled. 'Just the taste of skin, little one, no more. Unless you consent, of course.'

'No way. Once was enough.'

'Once is never enough. Come now, we will bid our guests your farewell. Cecile will accompany you back. I will keep them here, though they will be reluctant. They will wish to follow you.'

He swept his arm forward, indicating that they should precede him back into the main hall. There was some shifting of bodies as they re-entered. The candles picked up a hint of blood on a mouth here, a jugular there. They had been snacking. Or necking. To a meten, it's very nearly the same thing.

'My guests are leaving now.'

'Surely not so soon. May we not introduce ourselves, come to know them better?'

This was from another of the visiting blyd. This one preferred leather, and chains. A tight black vest emphasised the swell of lithe muscles. Not the bulging bodybuilder constitution, but a cleaner, sleeker line. More like a runner than a weightlifter. He was wearing a pleasant smile on his face, framed by long, dark, curling hair. The fake 'I am not dangerous, now, am I' look. They didn't believe it for a second. He stood up, and walked over. Slowly. Theo stood impassive. The vamp squared up in front of Zoe.

'Such a young one. I am Michael, pretty lady. And you are?'

'Going,' Zoe said flatly.

He backed half a pace, raising his hand to his chest and assuming a look of mock horror.

'The night is but young, my darling.' Oh, *please*. Not that old chestnut. Can't these bloodsuckers find some new lines?

'Sorry, no time.' Zoe was making no attempt to pass him. Her entire being radiated boredom in the way that only teenagers can. When you pass twenty, you seem to lose the ability. Maybe you realize that being flat rude was not viable if you aren't also young enough to be cute doing it.

'Surely you can find a moment or two in your busy life to share with me some of the joy that sustains you?'

Zoe favoured him with a blank stare.

'What is this life, if full of care, we have no time to stand and stare…

'No *time*…………'

As Zoe spoke, the moonlight high on the walls began to fade, the candles gutter. Her voice had been light and pleasant, but underneath her words there was a beat of wyth.

Along the walls, there was a faint rustle as bodies dead and undead moved, craning their necks to look about the darkening room. From outside came a faint and very definite mutter of thunder. The air of unease in the hall grew. Zoe completed her recitation.

'A poor life this, if full of care we have no time to stand and stare.' The thunder grumbled again. Louder, longer and more ominously. For a beat or two, Michael stood before Zoe, his gaze light, interested. Zoe looked back out of a calm, serene face. Then he smiled, took a step back and bowed floridly, one arm circling the air, a medieval style flourish. How old was he?

'Then I will not seek to detain you, pretty lady.'

'Thank you. Michael.' She had won the exchange. She knew Michael's name, and he had not found hers. Fifteen - love, then.

'Cecile will escort you.' Theo exchanged a look with Cecile, who was suddenly at his side. Meten speed took a lot of getting used to, even if you'd been round them forever.

'As you wish, Theo.' All this light disinterest was getting on

Fee's nerves.

'Thank you, Hegarsa, for your time and interest.'

'I shall see you again. Soon. Take them away, Cecile.'

They followed Cecile to the door. As it closed, they could hear Theo's voice.

'A word with you, Clarke. Now.'

They walked back in silence, under a lowering sky. In the distance, sheet lightning flickered among the clouds, and thunder moaned. Cecile watched from the garden gate until the door shut behind them. Then she was gone.

'Speak to me, little sis.' Fee unhitched her cloak and leaned her staff against the back of a chair in the parlour. 'I thought I told you to leave the Durm Und Strang to me.'

'I didn't do nothing.'

Fee cocked an eye.

'Didn't look like nothing from where I was.'

'Okay. I checked the local weather forecast before we went out. It said a storm front was building. It was pretty still when we walked over with Cecile, so I knew it was on the way. When we got back to the hall, I saw the lightning flicker on the wall. So I stalled them with the W H Davies thing. We had to learn it last year, remember? And the clouds blotted out the moon while I was quoting. The thunder was a bonus, though. And with the storm, there came the wind, 'cos Cecile left the doors open. Ergo, guttering candles. Mystery solved. There you go.'

'Very clever.'

'I'd've preferred an eclipse really, but there wasn't one available.'

Chapter Thirteen

The morning came. They do that, and Sophie was still not back with Fee's car. Zoe was out visiting 'the nerds' for an update, and Fee was restocking the freezer. The kitchen surfaces were full of chopped vegetables, pastry and assorted herbs and spices. Steam wafted up from pans on the stove, filling the room with the fragrance of cooking meat. When the phone warbled, Fee wiped her floury hands off on a towel and grabbed it.

'Hi there, big sis.'

'Sophie? Where the hell are you?'

'Bristol. Turns out Caleb's got an exhibition on, he needed to drop some stuff off.'

'You could have told us. I was worried sick.'

'Sorree. I'm sure you found something to pass the time.'

'Family fun day at Theo's.'

'Lucky you. You can tell me when we get home. Should be there about four. Then Caleb and I will be off back to Falmouth.'

'In my car? I don't think so.'

'Carl should have finished with my wheels by then. I'll get him to drop it off at ours later.'

'Isn't it time you exchanged that heap for something that actually goes?'

'We're not all commercial giants, Fee.'

'You are not short of a few bob yourself, my girl.'

'I'm saving for my bottom drawer.'

'He's asked you?'

'Brought the ring back from Norway. Hunted down a genuine antique and all. Gotterdammerung and all that. His idea of romance.'

'I trust he knows the story.'

'He's no Sigfried.'

'And you're no Brunhilda. See you soon.'

Sophie and Caleb were getting married! Talk about sudden. Fee could have sworn that they would have carried on the relationship at the cohabiting stage until they died. Sophie was flighty, Caleb unpredictable - witness the sudden trip to Norway. Anyone else would spend weeks planning, he just upped sticks and went. Because it was there and he wanted to see it. Sophie took this in her stride and treated his absence as an excuse to do things she wanted, like come and visit, paint, walk...... Maybe it would work. They certainly seemed joined at the hip when they were together. Fee dialled another number, delighted at being able to surprise Jean. Time enough to go back and finish the cooking later. For once, she, Fee, was first with the news! She almost skipped through the rest of the chores. Where would Sophie want to get married? In the village church? In Falmouth? Where in Falmouth? Had she told Lily? Would she want to trek up a tor in a wedding dress? What sort of dress did she have in mind? Lovely, lovely, to have something other than death and destruction to think about.

She had the phone glued to her ear when Zoe came back. Jean was twittering on the other end, forgetting that it had been Fee who had first given her the news about Sophie, about how it rained on her wedding day, and her veil flew off into the windy wet sky, which was an omen, wasn't it? She'd had nearly three decades with Andrew before he got ill....

Fee extricated herself from the conversation, promising to talk again once Sophie was back.

Zoe took the news quietly. Too quietly. Maybe you don't get so excited at your elder sister's wedding when you're sixteen going on eighty.

'What is it, Zoe? Something upsetting you?'

'Jerry's sick.' She collapsed into a chair and curled up into the smallest ball that her long legs would permit. So that's why the kid was so down.

'What's wrong?'

'They say hepatitis.'

'Can't be. How could he get that? He's never had a blood transfusion in his life, and he doesn't do drugs.'

'I know. But I'm worried that something I asked him to do made him sick.'

'Look, Hep B and C aren't that serious. You can recover on

your own. And there's antivirals and Interferon too.'

'He could get liver cancer.'

'Rare cases only. Don't buy trouble.'

'I still feel responsible.'

'You aren't, okay? Did you curse him with hepatitis? Did you wish it on him? Have you been playing with dollies again behind my back?'

In the past, a very much younger and entirely pissed off Zoe had wished a case of measles on her so-called best friend. She had taken a doll, one that most resembled the blue-eyed blonde haired minx who had dumped her into trouble in school. She had painted the face with red spots and wished fiercely and too well. Valerie had gone down with measles despite being vaccinated as most children were. The eruption had been fierce and itchy, and Valerie had been miserable and uncomfortable, but not in any sort of mortal danger. Two weeks later she had been back in school, her face still slightly pimpled with the remains of the rash. Zoe had ambled round with a satisfied smirk until Lily found the remains of the weaving in a box in the wardrobe.

She had been looking for old shoes and clothes to send for an appeal in Africa. Zoe's school had twinned with a bush school and sent regular parcels of cast-off uniforms, books and the like for the little establishment. They wrote letters too. After the third time of asking, when Zoe had not sorted out the stuff herself, Lily had gone rummaging, so what happened after was squarely Zoe's fault. When Zoe came home, she found a quiet Lily, who showed her the shoebox and asked for an explanation. She was wise enough not to dissemble.

When Robbie came home, there was another interview. What he had told her at the time, as Fee and Sophie found out later from Zoe herself, was that Robbie had told his youngest offspring point blank that if she continued to be that irresponsible, there would be no Ritual. Ever. A suitably chastened Zoe had carefully washed the ink spots off the doll's face and put it back on the shelf once she had renamed it. If she had ever re-offended, she had taken more care and not been found out.

'No. And I don't have any boy dolls anyway.'

'There's Rob's Tommy Gunn.'

'They've all got black hair.'

'So you didn't do it. You are not responsible. Tunfen is responsible. Tunfen did it.'

'Gggrrr.'

'Go peel potatoes for dinner while I ring Mum. And Tom. That's if Jean didn't get to them first.'

'Should have told her last,' Zoe commented from the kitchen.

'They weren't answering. I did try. First time I steal a march on Jean, and the buggers aren't there to tell.'

Sophie and Caleb arrived in the blaze of an extravagant autumn sunset. Carl had dropped off Sophie's heap earlier and had been given a secret mission to find a new Range Rover as a wedding present. Not a new, new one, but a good used model. There were plenty around, as the more affluent denizens of the county tended to trade in regularly for newer models. He would, he said, keep his eyes peeled. Something would turn up, it always did. Lottie was getting impatient to cuddle her lump properly, and the cottage was so clean Carl felt unwelcome in his greasy overalls and grubby boots. He had taken to leaving a clean set of gear in the outhouse and changing there. He hoped the delivery would happen soon. To this end he had 'borrowed' a reliable car from a client who had dropped it off for a tune up and MOT before going on three weeks holiday. Lottie would be travelling in style to her lying-in, in a Merc if you please.

There were hugs and kisses all round. Caleb had brought champagne to celebrate Sophie's final weakening in the face of his insistence that they make it legal. Why? Sophie was pregnant. He had always felt that a baby needed a proper start in life, with two parents and a legal bit of paper. Sophie regarded the bit of paper as superfluous. Fee chided her sister for the dereliction of omitting to mention that. Zoe had declared she was too young to be an Auntie. They had all laughed and Caleb had popped the champagne.

Fee's chicken pie dinner, complimented by Zoe's naturally perfectly fluffy mashed potatoes, buttered parsnips and Kenya beans was a triumph. Sophie wanted to know when Fee and Greg were going to tie the knot as well.

'Look, you're running daft over the man. I've seen your face when you answer his calls. Why not front up and admit it?'

Fee smiled and shook her head. Sophie let it drop.

'Hey, Soph, come and look at this!' From upstairs came the sound of Zoe calling.

'Okay, but I've not got long. Gotta get back to the pad tonight.' Sophie clumped upstairs leaving Fee to entertain Caleb.

Truth be told, Fee was not too comfortable in his presence. Since Sophie had started the relationship, she hadn't seen him more than three or four times. They hadn't exchanged more than a dozen words on any of those occasions. She knew that Caleb was aware of the Family, but how much did he really know? Where did she start? 'Hey, Caleb, wanna join our Frais? We have a lot of fun. There's someone trying to kill us right now!' Enticing, or what?

'Sophie tells me you've got a stalker.' He had pre-empted her.

'Sort of. How much has she told you?' And how much do you believe of that?

'Just broad details. Enough for me to know that she's not happy.'

'We've got that in common.'

'I can see why. The thought that some killer might be after me would send me running for the hills.'

Like Claire.

'Don't think I haven't considered it. But I think this is something you run from at your peril.'

'Since, turning, you will only find it in front of you.' Where did that come from?

'Tell me, Caleb. Are you.......' How do you put this?

'From a Family? Distantly, yes. I never paid much heed to the stories until I met Sophie. Even then I didn't really believe it. It took months of covert operations before I caught her at it.'

'Bet she was mad.'

'For a while, yes. Until she quieted down enough for me to explain. Then, I'm afraid, it got messy. I got covered in burnt umber, was finding it in my gear for weeks.' He blushed. Men did that? 'We ended up in her studio and knocked the paints off the desk onto the floor. Enough, already.'

'You're going to hate what I'm going to suggest next.'

'Do it and I'll see.'

'I think you ought to arrange to go away. Far away. You've got the perfect excuse with the honeymoon. This creep seems to delight in killing those whose deaths hurt us most. And your death will hurt Sophie more that I care to imagine, especially now.'

'I can't leave her. I won't. And I don't think she'd go away with me. She wouldn't leave you in the lurch, not Sophie.'

'Hush now, she's coming back.'

Sophie returned, with Zoe. She collected Caleb and they departed in a flurry of hugs and kisses. True to form, Sophie's car took four attempts to get it started, and they drove away in a cloud of blue smoke. Fee and Zoe retreated to the parlour.

'I had a dream last night.'

'Go on.' Dreams were important. During her postulancy, Fee had been required to record all her dreams. She still did, at least those that had some impact on her when she awoke in the morning. Zoe had been doing the same for some time. It had been a battle of wills for Sophie and Fee to keep their dream dairies away from Zoe's eyes. Now she kept her own, she wasn't so nosey.

'It was one of those when you realize you are dreaming, right? I was walking down this lane. I met this white-haired lady. No, actually. She'd been talking to me for some time. She said, you must tell the eldest daughter you must go through the gate of water and fire to the house of shadows behind the north wind. There she will find what she seeks.'

'You could have told me this earlier. Is that exactly what she said?'

'As exactly as I recall. It made an impression on me. She said other things too, but they're hazier.'

'What other things? It's important.'

'I know that. I was going to ask you to help me remember.'

'Okay. Sit back and relax.'

Fee got up and switched off the overhead lights. One wall sconce stayed on. She had broken the other and forgotten to replace it. It didn't matter now. She lit a candle and placed it on the coffee table between them.

'Look at the flame, Zoe. Concentrate on the flame and nothing else. Listen to the sound of my voice. You are becoming very relaxed. You are sinking, deeply, into your safe place. You feel completely warm, relaxed and safe. You can remember everything. All is clear to you. You are moving back in time, back through the day. You can see it behind your eyes. You can see and recall everything perfectly.' She paused. 'Now you are asleep. You are dreaming. You are with the white-haired lady, and she is talking to you. You remember every word she is saying to you, clearly and without question. You can repeat every word of the conversation. You will repeat every word of the conversation when I tell you to do that. Remember what she is saying to you.' Fee placed her phone, set to record, on the chair next to Zoe's head. 'You will now repeat every word she said to you, clearly and without missing any detail.'

Zoe was staring at the candle, but she wasn't seeing it.

'I see you, windchild. You have found your way here to me. You have hard times ahead of you. It will take all your skill and resolve to come through this test. Now you have found your way here, I can tell you where to find the devices that you will need. The way will not be easy. You must tell the eldest daughter you must go through the gate of water and fire to the house of shadows behind the north wind. There she will find what she seeks.

'Remember my words, child. Together you will win through, though I fear that before that comes to pass events in your world will sear your heart. Steel your resolve, and be not distracted by events that have little importance to this nexus.

'A great plan will come to fruition or ruin through you and what you do in this. Be not hasty. Seek not to confront, but compose yourself in patience until the quarry comes hunting for you. Remember this child, for it will help you solve many things. Actuality cannot exist in the realms of potential, and the prevention of potential can have great force for good or evil. I give you one direction, windchild, for you and you alone, your part of this great quest. You must seek out the ancient one of blood. Offer him a part of what he desires in exchange for the tales of amagus.'

She fell silent. Fee grabbed the phone and sent the recording to Zoe's inbox before the gremlins of the electronic world could interfere.

'Hear my voice, Zoe. Leave the memory of the lady and her words. You will remember them, completely. You are coming back, back in time through the morning and the day. You can see everything, it rests gently in your memory. You are coming forward, forward to the now, when you are sitting in the chair, looking into the candle flame. See the flame, Zoe. See it clearly, and come back. Float up, gently, through your mind, into the here and now. Come back, Zoe.'

Zoe sighed faintly, and moved slightly in the chair.

'You got it?'

'And sent it to your inbox. But you can remember, can't you.'

'Yes. What, or who, the hell is amagus?'

'I have no idea. I suspect you will be asking Theo.'

'And we are going adventuring again.'

'What's this we? You have your task, I have mine.'

'She said, *you* must go through the gate, and *she* will find what *she* seeks. If she'd meant you to go alone, she'd've said *she* must go through the gate. I take it that means we must go together for you to get ... whatever it is you need.'

'The devices. Whatever they may be. It covers a lot of ground, "devices".' She sighed. 'Whatever.'

'What do you know about the house of shadows behind the north wind, then? Apart from it being the castle of Arianrhod?'

'It's where Arthur was supposed to have gone after the battle of Camlann. The magic castle in old Avalon. But I think she means the Asha, not in Glastonbury.'

'Oh, the gate of water and fire. To the citadel of air behind the earth wind. The place of skyen. Ever been there?'

'Seen it. But not through that gate.'

'Meet you in the spaca, then.'

An hour later, they were lying side by side on the Roundhouse floor surrounded by candles. There was no Sophie to talk them through it, but they breathed in unison, each imagining their separation. The first thing Fee saw was Zoe. This time she was dressed in desert boots, tan trousers, a khaki shirt under a battered waistcoat and a bush hat. On a leather belt round her waist hung a whip and a gun. Over one shoulder was a rucksack that had seen better days. Her hair hung over her other shoulder in a loose plait.

'Tonight, Matthew, I'm going to be …… Indiana Jones.' She touched her hat, setting it at a jaunty angle. 'Suits me, don't you think?'

'So I see. Why him?'

'Because Indie always finds what he's looking for.'

'He didn't get the Ark. Or the Holy Grail.'

'Shut up. You are ruining my fantasy. All the Indiana Jones films end in triumph. The bad guys lose, Indie ends up smelling of roses whether he got the gubbins he was after or not.'

'Okay, okay. It's a *good* persona for a relic hunt. In other words, good choice, wrong stimulus. And I am?'

'How about Xenia? Red Sonja? Tank Girl?'

'No thanks. No fear.'

'I see you've lost the tin bra. Thank god.'

This time, the Asha had co-operated with a grey dress and darker grey cloak. Travelling in mufti, then.

The Wall loomed up before them. A door appeared. On it there was a green crescent, and on that was a bright red triangle, point up.

'The gate of water and fire. Let's go.'

They touched the door, and it swung open. They were standing on a beach before a mighty rolling ocean. Waves queued up in line, each waiting patiently for its turn at the sand. The wind blew spume back as the billows thundered and broke, painting a white filigree of foam over the beach. Low in the sky, a red sun was sinking in fiery glory. Fee turned to her right and faced along the beach.

'Ayen that is in the north wind, blow, blow, blow on me.'

At once, a brisk wind belled her skirts, plastering them against her thighs and scattering her hair behind her. In the ruddy light of the setting sun, a great tower rose between the land and the water. The dying light painted it in hues of sullen amber and scarlet; indigo and cobalt shadows threw it into stark relief. It flashed, reflecting the sun, dazzling their eyes. Towers of reflecting light reached jagged fingers up to the darkening sky, a backdrop of dusky purple and shadowy maroon shot with blood red. A thought, and the far distant edifice loomed above them, eclipsing the sky. It was higher than the Petronas towers, Taipei One-O-One, anything.

The entrance gaped before them, a pointed void filled with blue and black palls. Gleaming, icy steps led up to the portal. Fee led the way. At the threshold, she knocked three times with her staff.

'Portal, I conjure thee to open for me the way to those designs and devices for which I am sent. I adjure thee, place of wyth, not to prevent me from accomplishing that mission on which I am bound. Guardians of the Gya, protect my steps upon my ways in this your realm, and assist me to achieve that which I desire.'

'I think that about covers it.'

They entered the gloomy portal side by side. Once they were over the threshold, the opening vanished. They were standing in a bewildering maze, their reflections staring back at them from the walls and floor.

'So this is it. The House At The End Of Time. Weird.'

'You have no idea.'

'So, what's it like, inside?'

Endless tunnels, going nowhere.......

'You remember that Nautilus shell Dad gave Mum all those years ago? The one cut in half so you can see the chambers?'

'Like that, huh.'

'Not quite. Think Mobius handkerchief.'

That had been one of Rob's conundrums. A Mobius strip , a loop with a twist in it, had *only one side*. Rob asked them to imagine a three dimensional Mobius container - 'Like folding the handkerchief in your pocket. Since it's only got one side, there's no inside, no outside. So all of the universe is contained in that handkerchief. Now put it back in your pocket. Are you inside the universe, in your hankie, or not?'

'The biggest chambers are nearer to the inside end?'

'That's it. The entrance is in the middle, and the innermost, most secret chambers are on the outside edge. Which is still the inside. And that's not the half of it. It's not a simple Pythagorean spiral. It's a maze.'

'Not a simple one, I take it.'

'It's the maze on our gatepost. In n-dimensional space.'

'Nice. So this place is a sort of Tardis, yes? The inside's bigger than the outside. The question is, when does the Doctor appear?'

'Will you stop that? I am in no mood to chase cybermen, darleks and crying angels through this funhouse.'

'That's okay. The Doctor can't come here, 'cos we're outside of Time.'

'Your certainty brightens my day.'

'Can't have Time Lords where there's no Time.'

They gazed at the reflecting coridors, considering.

'You got a map?'

'No such luck. There ought to be a guide....'

'The House doesn't want you poking around freely in its attics and cellars? What might we find?'

It's not about what you might find, not in here. It's what you might lose. Fee didn't say it. There was no sense in spooking Zoe. This place was damn eldritch enough to give the most well-balanced individual the willies. Leave alone what might find you. Let's not go there.

'The guides are nothing to do with the house. It used to be simpler, they say...'

'The famous *they*. Again.'

'Do you want to hear this or not? The original Spiral Castle had four chambers, or towers. That was it, basically. Then some bugger invented fractals and all hell was let loose.'

'Bloody progress.'

'So the guides came into being. Some say.... A benevolent deity created them after a favourite human playmate got lost in the maze. Some say.... It was a group of pissed-off cyscans who said 'bugger this for a lark' when they tried to map the place. Some say..... They are part of the house. All we know is...'

'They're called The Guides!'

'Thank you, Jeremy Clarkson.'

'So how do we get one?'

'Follow the first thing you see on the threshold.'

'How do you know it's the right one?'

'Don't you start.'

The shadows swirled for a moment. Maybe they were deciding what form to take, or what today's theme was. Eventually they coalesced into a blob, which shivered itself. What was left was a sort of amphibian. It had toad somewhere in the ancestry, possibly one that had taken a wrong evolutionary step and mated with a small lumpy dinosaur with dyspepsia and an excess of bilirubin. Not a terrible lizard, more a comic washout…….

'That needs a personal stylist. Really.'

A long tongue snaked out. The thing licked its eyeballs. Fee shivered. Not from fear. More some anthropological recessed memory about things with sticky tongues, and eyeballs, and the joke about the ugly man in a bar who got all the really hot chicks….

'Okay. Follow the yellow sick toad, what?'

'For want of a completely wizard riposte, yes.'

'You disappoint me, sister of mine.'

'Words fail even me sometimes.'

'It was the tongue, right.'

'Got you too, did it?'

'Yes, but I've got less of a live reference for it to jag me that much.'

The toad-thing blinked its eyes, slowly. Then it waddled round and hopped away, the sisters in warm pursuit. The squelchy thing wasn't fast enough for a hot one…..

The curving walls followed them, their reflections splintering and reforming as they walked. When they saw their reflections walking towards them, the guide turned right. And right. And right again. At the next junction, it turned left, and the next, and the next. The guide toad made a last left turn and came to a halt at a dead end. It sat there, wobbling gently, completely disinterested.

'Whatever we were sent for, it's somewhere here.'

'Could it be inside the walls, do you suppose? Do they open? Do you know how to get inside them?'

'No. Never been this…. deep? inside before.'

'So now, you need me?'

'Yes. Please.'

'What did she say? 'Remember this child, for it will help you solve many things. Actuality cannot exist in the realms of potential, and the prevention of potential can have great force……..'

'And this means?'

'You are dense at times. Since we want a way through, there is none. If we didn't want one, it would be a piece of piss.'

'So I've got to want to not-want a door.'

'Sort of. Turn round.'

'Go back?'

'No, turn round and go *forwards*.'

'The door's not there.'

'Exactly.'

They both turned deliberately at the same time. There was an opening behind them that they had not come through. It had, simply, not been there before. They stepped in to the room. Over the walls icy panels were framed with pale yellow silk hangings. They watched themselves enter the room from each mirror. The place was perfectly empty. The floor, the walls, the ceiling, each reflected the other in a dizzying dance. Each slight unevenness caught the light and sparkled, sending shards racing off into infinity. The slightest movement was sufficient to send a surge of images racing round the walls. It was enough to make you sick. Then, the mirrors seemed to shimmer, and in each one was a seated figure dressed in a blue-green hooded robe. The shadows in the hood covered the face completely, masking the features. The light started to fade, electric blue turning to royal and then midnight ink. Imperfections in the walls and floor caught edges of light. They might have been standing in a midnight sky. A soft, echoing voice came out of the void.

'What seek you here?'

'The designs and devices that will aid us in our quest.'

'Nothing can help you. Therefore you will find nothing here.'

'Then, nothing we look for here can be found.' Zoe chipped in.

'That is the nature of this place.'

'And nothing will help us in our quest.'

'As I have told you.'

'Then, if we come here looking for the devices and designs that will aid us, we have come here looking for nothing, as nothing can aid us, by your words. So, we come here looking for nothing. And we have found… nothing.' Zoe paused. 'But if what you say is true, we can find nothing here to help us, and nothing will help us, so if we have found nothing, we have found that which will aid us. By your words, this cannot be, since we have found what we came here to find.'

The convoluted logic of this statement left Fee gobsmacked. She turned it over in her head to see if she could make sense of it. Before she could corkscrew her way through her sister's logic, she was interrupted.

'Then if you can solve the second riddle of the Tower Adamant, it behoves us to reveal that which you seek, since by *your* words, you have found it. But first, tell me, which of these appearances is real?'

Zoe didn't hesitate.

'This one I am facing. Each reflection is as real as the others, and as unreal. All are reflections of the true reality, and since that is hidden, any reflection may serve. In the place of no place, outside of Time, we are everywhere and nowhere, now, in the past and in future times to come. But, if you want the truer answer, *you are standing behind me.*'

'Since the word of truth is spoken in the place of deceit, that which is hidden is revealed. But your quest is not over. First comes the sight, then comes the possessing.'

The darkness drained away like water running out of a clear glass bowl. In the centre of the room which had been completely empty before, stood a massive block of what could only be described as ice. It held in its depths reflections of green and blue. Embedded into that immense block was a sword. The hilt was black and the cross-guard swept up like the curve of a new moon.

'This is the device that will help you. It will not cleave anything for you, nor destroy anything for you, should you be the one chosen to wield it. It will not come to you unless you need it. You will not grasp it unless you deserve it. And you cannot keep it. Do you have the power to wield it? You will not know until you try, and then it will be too late.'

They both turned. Behind them was standing the figure that had been seated in the mirrors. Colours ran molten down the robe, liquid and moving. She might have been wearing some liquescent drapery that resembled fabric only in its application. It melted into the floor, or the floor flowed up to clothe the figure: Fee was not sure which it was. The figure raised both hands to the hood and drew it back.

'Rina.'

'Welcome, child, to the Palace of Glass. Here where things are not as they seem, and seem to be what they are not. Had you been able to solve the riddle, the sword would be yours already. But you did not solve it. You led the way for the one who could.'

She turned to Zoe.

'I see clearly what is in your mind, and it cannot be. Since you lust for the possession of the sword, it cannot be yours until you learn *not* to lust for it. The very wanting of a thing in this place decrees that you cannot have it.'

'Sorry.'

'Do not apologise to me for what must be. Had you entered here, and recalled what you knew about the door, the sword would be yours already, thus denying its use to the one who will need it most. And by doing that, you would fail in this quest. No, child, your nature has served you well, here. But remember that cleverness is no substitute for wisdom.'

She turned back to Fee.

'Child of fire, speak your name in this place when I am gone. Then the sword will remember you. And take my love to Sunlight on the Waters. My love is with you also, Questing Winds. And with all of you. Do not linger in this place when I am gone, for the wythen that protects this place will try to prevent your leaving.' Then, she was gone.

At her sister's urging, Zoe also left the room, leaving Fee alone with the sword. She stepped up to the block.

'This is my name, given to me before my birth and after my death. I am the tamer of spirits, the powers of gods made flesh. I am the holy fire which purifies all and transforms all. I am Hekubara. Know me and remember me.' She turned and left the thing she had come for. At least she knew where it was, and what it was. What it actually did was another matter.

Zoe was waiting in the outer corridor. Their guide was nowhere to be seen.

'Typical. You leave the hired help alone for a moment, and they vamoose.'

'And you didn't clock the trajectory?'

'You *are* mental. My spatial memory is one of my best features. Did you?'

'I, keen reader of fairytales that I am, left a trail of wyth.'

'Let's hope the birds in here don't gobble wyth, then. Lead on, my dear, time's a-wasting.'

'So. Time to unwind the spiral.'

'Okay. Four times right and four times left each way. Don't let's get separated. This place feels different now. Which way's left?'

'We're facing the wrong way. You made us turn round, remember.'

They turned back, and the doorway to the chamber had gone. In its place was the dizzying passage with its annoyingly perplexing reflections.

'Look straight ahead. Watch until you see yourself walking towards yourself. Then you know it's time to make a turn.'

They had made two turns before they heard the first sounds.

'What's that?'

'Keep going. If you lose your sense of direction, we'll have to take the other way out.'

'And that would be?'

'Up one.'

Fee was alluding to the so-called 'levels' of the Asha, which went from One, the physical world, to Seven, which was best left undescribed. Suffice to say that if you could get to it, then you had reached the stage where the physical world had no more to teach you. Living would be a waste of effort, not worth the trouble of bothering with. You would know everything. As if. The big drawback being that at the moment they were on Two. So far, so good. But Three was a right arse to get to, let alone stay on. Fee didn't know if Zoe had ever extended her wanderings that far. If not, then while Fee could use it as an escape route, she would be leaving Zoe behind to face gods-knew-what all on her lonesome. Which meant, in real terms, that they were bollixed.

'Bugger.'

They started walking faster.

'Is that behind us or ahead of us?'

'Makes no difference in here. We have to walk between the walls. *They* can walk through them.'

'Double bugger.'

'Don't run. Whatever you do, don't run.'

The light was different now. Before it had been pellucid green and blue. Now it was tinged with a sickly yellow. The shadows looked like great bruises, crawling over the walls and floors and ceilings.

'Here they come.'

Fee didn't stop. Unless the wythen placed things actually in their way, it was a bad idea to stop.

'Last right. Next turn is left.'

'Oh my god. Critters.'

'Call the light, Zoe. Blue light. Bright blue light.'

Fee steadied her pace, conjuring up the image and feeling of her wythstaff in her hand casting brilliant azure light on the reflecting walls. Her imagination was spot on. Light flashed out from her hand, intense enough to make her wince.

'For pity's *sake*! Turn it *down*!' Zoe screeched, throwing an arm over her eyes. 'I can't see a bloody thing!'

Fee was already on it. Useful as a wythstaff was, it was sod-all use if you couldn't see what you were aiming it at. In this instance, it didn't matter. The explosion of several thousand lumens had swept the corridor clear…. But not for long. Once the thundering illumination faded, *They* were back. Fee lifted the staff, and the light flared anew. Before her, a mass of furballs with teeth, lots of teeth, fell back, chittering. They started to walk between the creatures. Carefully

'Don't look back.'

'I absolutely will not look back.'

They were on the ceiling now. The girls were surrounded. It stood to reason that the furballs would gang up behind them. It was way past uncomfortable. The chittering grew louder. They turned the next corner.

'Which roof did that escape off?'

It was a gargoyle. It stretched its wings and growled at them.

'Now what?'

'Gargoyles are meant to scare evil wraithen. We're not evil wraithen. It will only attack us if we attack it. Keep going.'

As they walked towards the massive brute, it started to turn to stone. They ducked under a wing and kept going. Behind them, the chittering continued.

'This is getting on my nerves.'

Round the next bend stood a man. He was dressed in baggy yellow pants tucked into black boots. The tips of the toes curled up over his instep. Over a similarly baggy yellow shirt, two red bandoliers crossed on his chest. A black turban covered his head. In his hand he held a scimitar. He started to weave the sword in the air between himself and the girls.

'Back off, Fee. I know this one.'

Zoe stood in front of the swordsman. An evil leer filled his sun-browned face. Zoe waited patiently. Then she drew out her gun and shot him. He fell over backwards, the leer changing to amazement.

'Raiders of the Lost Ark.'

'Oh, joy. Snakes next?'

'Now you've said it, yes.' Zoe unslung her whip. 'Pity there's no torches in this place.'

The House of Shadows would use their imaginations against them. It would reflect back to them cameos out of memory, things that frightened them. It sought for that wisp of fear and amplified it. Since cyscans spent quite a lot of time coming to grips with their personal demons, it was having to reach a goodly way back. As a child, Fee might have hidden behind the sofa (in fact, an early episode of Doctor Who had given her the heebies for years until she found out that those eerily glowing eyes were in reality (?????) attached to a teddy bear, of all things) it was having some trouble creeping her out. Zoe was likewise unimpressed. They rounded the last corner.

'There they are.'

The entire passage was filled with serpents. They packed the floor and draped over the walls. Torchlight flickered over scales. They were hissing, and the susurrus of scales filled the hall. Beyond them the portal opened welcomingly.

'Welcome to the Glass Palace. Easy to get into. Hard to escape from.'

'No shit, Sherlock.'

Zoe uncoiled her whip. It glowed with the same lambent light as Fee's staff. She sent it cracking across the floor, again and again. Behind them the chittering was getting louder.

'Zoe, think. What likes snakes?'

'Apart from other snakes, you mean? Mongooses. Or is that mongeese? Remember Rikki-Tikki-Tavi? Oh, and storks. Storks eat snakes. So do some raptors.'

The Glass Palace responded instantly to her thought. A sudden flood of furry mammals careered through the portal, their claws ticking on the adamantine floor. Sharp teeth started to bite into the reptilian horde.

That was something worth knowing. This place responded to more than primal fears. If things got rough (rougher) they might, just might, be able to summon some counterforce to their aid. The SAS would be favourite.

'It's going to take too long. Those furry buggers with teeth are coming.'

The furry tidal wave had almost got through. It was agonizing, not looking round. You knew that behind you was a mass of furry teeth. Ready to break across you like a tsunami over a low lying continent.

'Do not look away from the door. Whatever.' Surely that was movement behind them?

Fur was winning over scale. They started forwards. Behind them came a shriek. Fee grabbed Zoe's arm in a death grip. It took all their resolve not to look back. Cyscans have one glaring foible. They are curious, to the nth degree. But if they looked back, the door would, simply, cease to exist, and it would be that much harder getting out. And what you can't see can sometimes be more scary than something you face squarely. Where did that spider go, the one that scuttled under the sofa? Making a foray up your leg? The weight of fang and fur behind her back made Fee's skin crawl. One foot in front of the other, back cringing, waiting for the teeth to sink in the back of your neck. Or fangs in your ankle. Fee could feel sweat creeping down her spine. Oh, she'd been here before, but that didn't make it that much easier. You could always be wrong.

Outside the door, a wild wind was chasing ragged clouds across an evening sky. No breath of that wind penetrated. Slowly, step by step, they went down the passage, but the door never drew closer.

'It's another one of them conundrums. Fee, stop.'

The door drew away, until it was tiny. Miniscule. Far, far away. Round their feet, scales scratched on glass, claws scrabbled. Things hissed and things chattered. Something very large was dragging itself over the floor, drag, thump. Drag, thump. There was only one thing to do. Surrender.

'Pity we couldn't copy Rina's trick and leave that way.'

'She can do it that way because she's dead already. Since we're still alive, and we came through the door, unless we leave the same way the whole place will fight us.'

'Unless we cheat.'

'That might cost us a price we can't afford to pay.'

The light in Fee's staff flickered and went out. Zoe stared at her sister in disbelief.

'Surrender, kid. Stop resisting and, accept.'

'In a pig's ear I will.' Zoe's face was set in stubborn lines, just like a sheep faced with the dipping trough.

'Listen to me. We want out. The House wants us gone.'

'So where's the problem?'

'That would be us.' Their eyes met.

Zoe threw the pistol onto the floor with a clatter. For long seconds, nothing happened. Under the hat brim, her face was haunted by a mild fury. It wasn't in her nature to lie back and think of England. Fee took her hand.

'Trust me, Zoe, Let it go. Let it all go. Let the House do what it wants to you.'

Zoe's head inclined once, sharply. Then her features softened into a calm, serene mask. It was no mere façade. Through her fingers, Fee felt the seep of utter tranquility. She closed her eyes and let the peace settle deep into her bones. What will be, will be. I accept it all. I invite it all. Then from far, far off, something started to rumble.

'What's that?' Calm, dreamlike.

'You saw Raiders. You know what that is.'

'Oh. Hell.'

'Stay still.'

'We can die here, you know.'

Reach for the calm, still place………

The rumbling swelled, underpinned with a grinding. There was no escape. A wind started to blow at their backs. Something was pushing the air in front of it as it came down on them. Just before it hit, there was an impression of a pitted surface and incredible weight. Then with a vast rush, it went past them. Through them. And they were standing on the threshold in an empty hall.

'You sure know how to have a good time, girl.'

And with a jolting thump, they were back in the Roundhouse.

Chapter Fourteen

Fee was in the middle of sorting out her snail mail and worrying about the bit where Zoe was going to offer something Theo wanted in exchange for information about amagus when the phone rang. She recognized the plummy British tones at once. She winced at the memory of calling him a jungle-bunny. Talk about PC! The lad had been born slightly west of Neasden.

'Hi Zaph, how's tricks?' she tucked the phone under her ear and continued sorting through envelopes and paper. The next words she heard stopped her dead.

'Lucy's been attacked. On Wandsworth Common. Went out for a run, she usually does.'

'Is she okay?'

'Bit shaken up. As you'd expect. She was running past the tennis courts, and stopped to stretch. There was this guy, sitting on a bench. He asks her, Does she know what time it is? He was meant to be meeting someone, and they're late, he thinks. After what you said, she's a bit wary, because he's all in black, see? With a broad brimmed hat over his eyes. So she steps back and tells him, it's four o'clock. So he gets up and steps over to her. She sees this pale face under the hat, kind of smooth, yes? And glittering eyes. She steps back again, she says the whole thing feels really bad. She's getting this negative vibe from him? Gotta be getting on, she says, goodbye. Don't go yet awhile, he says. And you know what? She knows she ought to get away, but she stops. She can't not stop. And she can hear his voice saying things, things she can't remember now.'

'Oh, hell.'

'He starts touching her, her arm, her face. She's like, she says, lost. Then she hears this voice in her head. It's saying, run, girl, run like you've never run before. And she just turns and runs off. She can hear him, come back, come back, he's saying. There's force in his words, but something's between them, the voice in her head saying, run. She doesn't know where she's going. She don't care. Like she's in a bubble, she's gotta run or…. Well, she don't know what, except to get away, as far and as fast as she can.

'When she comes to, she's hard over by Mama Sunshine's place, and the old lady's outside waiting for her. Come in chile, she says, come in, for I see you've got big trouble. And Lucy tells her. That your man, alright, the Mama says. But you got you're ouanga what I gave you. An' I heard your soul cryin' out in pain. You saved my boy from Erzulie, I save you from the darkness. He won't come again, because you'se protected by a magic he don't know. The loas is over you, and he can't fight the loas. They're a black man's magic, not a white man's.

'And sure, she's wearing Mama's ouanga. And she says when she touches it, it's hot. She's seen him, Fee.'

'What are you going to do?'

'It's not what I'm going to do, it's what you're going to do. Mama Sunshine says you've got to come and see her, right away. She can see the clouds gathering, she says, gathering over you. Hungry clouds. Now she don't go inviting white folk to her place, not ever. But she's invited you.'

'I'm due in Town on Tuesday.'

'No, it's gotta be right away.'

'What, now?'

'Come on, you can do the trip and be here in a couple of hours.'

'I can't just drop everything and coming bombing to town just like that.'

'You can't afford not to, if what Mama Ababita told me is half true.'

'Okay. I'll drive in as far as Chiswick and get the tube to Wandsworth. Can you meet me there?'

'Call me when you get to Chiswick.'

Zoe was not thrilled by the suggestion that she go over to Jean's while Fee went to pay court to a vodun priestess, but there it was. Fee was invited, Zoe was not. Eventually she gave in, and went off, grumbling. With some misgivings, Fee pointed the car towards Exeter. Rina's words about not needing to hunt down the predator were coming true. He had found them. Again. Two escapees out of over a hundred. The biker in Norfolk - what was his name again? - had been no help. Maybe Juicy Lucy would have something more useful.

Thoughts crowded in Fee's head as she drove. Snippets of past conversation, juggling and jostling for place.

'Imagine the terror if one of us should reach out our hand and seize power....'

Yes. But the rest of us would jump on them like a ton of bricks. Wouldn't we? Come on, this freak's been picking at the fabric for forty years. And before that? Plotting, planning? And none of us noticed. Have we lost that cohesiveness? Lost power? The power to be what we are? All this going on, behind our backs, unnoticed. Too stuck up our own backsides, thinking that we were worthy of being what we were, couldn't conceive of one of us going to the bad? Everything's been all right in our backyard, so we haven't been watching our neighbours. Too full of our own self-righteousness: if everything's all right here, then it's just got to be all right everywhere, yes? No. While we were proudly looking inward and congratulating ourselves on how well we were handling our lives, other lives around us were being disrupted, broken, and we didn't let even a ripple disturb our calm, like a pool on the beach, isolated from the ocean by grains of sand. Now that's swept away, and the seawater is pouring into our pool, drowning our peaceful lives and scattering our smug calm. Serves us right for being so bloody self-centred. What the hell do I know about what is going on in the other Frais? Bugger all. There's this idea I don't poke at, that they are all well-ordered, gently bobbing along, just like us. What if that's not the case? What if one group, or a part of one group, have reached out their hands to take whatever they want? Do whatever they want? And are these deaths part of that? Are they a price to be paid in order to achieve the unthinkable? Well, someone's thought it, so it can't be unthinkable. But who? And how can I find out? The moment I start asking questions, someone will know that I'm a threat to their aspirations - whatever they are. That'll put me in the crosshairs, all right. And my Frais with me.

But then what right do I have to enquire into, or interfere in, the business of another Frais? None whatever. If another bugger came from Outside and started to criticise the way I handled my Frais, I'd be peeved. Okay, the mystens haven't had a convocation for ages, not since Lily was mysten. Why? Did I care? I didn't. What had they got to teach me that I wanted to learn? Did it ever occur to me that they just might like to be friends? Get together over a bottle of vino collapso and chew the fat? If we'd been doing that instead of pretending that each of us were the most important person on Earth, would we have come to grips with this sooner? Tell you one thing. When this is all over, I'm going to make the effort to contact every mysten I can track down…….

As usual, the traffic around Heathrow was vile. Fee persisted until, at the end of the motorway, she saw the sign for the rail network carpark. Locking the Golf, she grabbed her bag and brought a ticket to Wandsworth.

The train pulled smoothly out of the station, and she was left to her own thoughts. She was met by Zaph and a taxi. 'I don't know. I'm sayin' nothin. The Mamas will do that when we get there,' he said tersely. He was even mixing patois and RE, so frazzled he was by this.

Mama Ababita turned out to be a slim but curvy woman in her fifties or sixties, it was hard to tell. Fee had been expecting a large, heavy, older woman somehow. She wore a form-fitting dark blue dress with élan, and her tightly curled black hair was cut close to her head. Gold earrings dangled from her ears, and diamond and sapphire rings on her fingers.

'Come in, come in. Don't stand there on the doorstep. Zaffie, you go upstairs to Lucy. The chile's still upset. Now you come in here, and we'll talk.'

She led the way to what had once been the posh parlour. A three-piece suite took up nearly all the room. Sitting in a chair over between the window and the grate was fairly the oldest woman Fee had ever seen. Her brown face was a mass of wrinkles, and her corkscrew hair was completely white. Large ebony eyes watched her closely as she sat on the sofa with Mama Ababita. In the chair opposite sat another woman. She would easily have outweighed both of the others, dressed in a mass of colours and wearing a turban. She was pouring tea.

'You'll take a cup with us. That's Mama Sunshine,' she said, nodding at the oldest who nodded back, 'And I'm Mama Africa.' She handed Fee a cup of sweet milky tea. She tried not to grimace as she sipped it. She preferred her tea unsweetened and almost black. This sweet milky brew was not to her taste at all. And there was a weird aftertaste that she couldn't quite place.......

'Suppose you tell us, chile, what's going on? Whatever it is, its brung trouble on us.'

Fee explained in broad detail. About the Families, and how Zoe had found out the trail which led to the man they called Tunfen. She glossed over much of it, but shrewd minds behind watching eyes were listening to the silences between her words.

'Now, that Lucy's got a powerful mojo in her, but she don't talk with the spirits. Not that she couldn't if she wanted to, mind. But you got the ways in you to see them spirits an' converse with them. That's powerful mojo, all right. But this here man, now he's done come after one of ours.'

'No, Mama, he's come after one of mine.'

'I'll not split hairs with you. She's the mother of Zaffie's chillen. She saved the boy from becomin' one of Erzulie's servants. Dat give us concern wit' her. De gel could've turn her back an' walk away. No, she place hersel atwixt Lady Erzulie an' her man.'

'If I knew how to prevent this, I would.'

'I feel that, chile. The good is comin' off you like sweet perfume. Now, the loas saved our Lucy, and I see there's no loa on you. You got a powerful spirit, right enough. De loas do protect theirs, and if you're bound to protect them too, you deserve the help of de loas. The Lord of the Cemetery, the Lord of the Crossroads, dey don' look kindly on you. That's because you never done gone and given dem no devotion.'

'I wouldn't have. I'm not a devotee of Voudun.'

'An' your enemy, he never offended agin' the Voodoo gods neither, until now. But now you've both come to their notice, chile. Pay a little court to them, let them enfold you.'

'But I'm a native farer.....'

'And we're not native? Shame on you, chile.'

'What I mean is, I'm a farer, not a druid or a shaman. We all have our ways. And the ways I've been taught are not their ways, or yours.'

'De gods is de gods, and de loas are de loas. They don' give no account to that, only what's in your heart.'

'We're offerin' you protection whilst you go about your bidness. After what happen to Lucy, Mama Ababita come to me, Mama Sunshine, an' I talk with my good frien' Mama Africa. We don' ask our loas abou' tit. They do say that you the only one can do what's got to be done, an' it's powerful risky for such a young chile as yourself to be doin' of it. So we offer what help we have. There's darkness and death about you, chile. Darkness and death.'

'We is askin' you to come wid us to the hounfour. There, we do ask de loas to protect you, watch over you, come between you and yo' enemy. We don' expect more. It's de loas that ask it. Dey tell us, bring the chile to us. An' we call, an' you is comin'. Dat's the loa's doin', that is. You come wid us now.'

Mama Africa heaved her bulk out of the chair. Mama Sunshine stood and smoothed her black dress down over her thighs. Mama Ababita left the room. Fee was ushered out before the bulk of Mama Africa. There was no going round her, really, not in that crowded room or in the hallway. Mama Ababita was calling up the stairs, telling Lucy and Zaph to stay there while she went out.

A car was waiting for them at the curb. The driver was a young man, and they drove in silence, a dizzying set of turns here, there and everywhere. Perhaps they were trying to confuse her, but London had streets like that, all one way, the wrong way. Fee was sandwiched in the back between Mama Africa and Mama Ababita. Mama Sunshine got the front seat. It was only a short time before the car stopped in front of a large townhouse, the red brick grimy with age. Curtains were drawn in the front windows from ground to attics.

Mama Sunshine walked up the steps and unlocked the door. Once inside, she picked up a bunch of drying herbs standing next to a bowl on a table. She dipped the wilting greenery into the bowl, and liberally sprinkled everyone in the group. She opened a door.

'You go sit in there, chile. I'll send someone to sit wid you.'

The little room was dusky with shadows, and slightly cool. An empty hearth was flanked by two chairs done in blue floral velour, covered lavishly with garish cushions and antimacassars. The mantelshelf, the table in the window bay, the upright piano standing against the inner wall, all were covered with family photographs and mementoes. On a whatnot in the corner, an arrangement of dried palm fronds and pampas grass drooped. On the walls were brilliantly coloured pictures. They appeared to be religious, as the central character was haloed. Fee perched on one of the chairs and waited.

The door opened to reveal a girl, older than Zoe but not by very much. She was wearing a full, flounced white skirt that fell to just below mid-calf and a white gipsy-style blouse with a drawstring neckline, the only colour a belt - a brilliant fringed scarf matching the one wound round her head. She was carrying a plastic bowl of hot water, and a fluffy towel draped over her arm.

'I'm come to prepare you. You must wash your hands, face and feet before entering the hounfour.' She placed the bowl on the floor in front of Fee, then knelt in front of it. 'I'm Perianne, and I'm Mama Sunshine's hounsi.' She wrung out a cloth and passed it to Fee who wiped her face. The warmth was comforting, and there was a light, spicy smell. Perianne took back the cloth, dipped it again, and wiped Fee's hands gently, and dried them on the towel. Then she took off Fee's boots and socks and wiped her feet. When they were dry, she slipped on a pair of light fabric slippers. She picked up the bowl and left as silently as she had come. Fee's mind was racing. What on earth was she doing in a hounfour? And what the hell had been in that tea?

Perianne returned, and took her by the hand. 'Come.' She guided Fee back into the hall and up the stairs. The hounfour was a large room - perhaps they had knocked through the upstairs walls to make it that big - and was full of people, the standing ones mostly dressed in white. Over in one corner sat three bare-chested men, all in front of a range of drums: but what caught the eye was a huge table covered in a snowy white cloth. Candles in saucers, scent bottles, pictures, bottles of rum, flowers, cigars, the table was overflowing. By one side of the door was a post, brightly painted in red and green spirals. Just in front of the post was an empty chair. Ranged out in chairs to both sides of the table were older men and women, all dressed in their Sunday best: behind them stood all ages, from babies in their mother's arms to men and women in the pride of their youth, all shades of brown from milky coffee to darkest ebony. The air was heavy with incense and the staccato beat of the drum. Perianne joined the standing people over by the drummers. Their bare chests gleamed with sweat. Mama Sunshine, now dressed in white, stood to greet her. Coming over, she took both of Fee's hands in her own gnarled ones.

'Welcome, chile.' She sat her in the vacant chair and sprinkled her liberally with perfume from a bowl, brought from the table by one of the attendants. She turned, and took a handful of white powder from another attendant, started with intense concentration to draw a complex design on the floor. She placed flowers, and grains, and coloured powders on the design, taking these from various of her attendants, then took a great mouthful of rum from a bottle and blew it out all over the design. She had drawn what Fee recognized as a veve, the signature of the spirit the Mama was calling. The drums were beating now in earnest. Mama Sunshine blew mouthfuls of rum over the painted post, Fee and the attendants, who were now swaying and chanting, and clapping their hands. One brought a black chicken - no, it had to be a cockerel from the feathers - to Mama Sunshine, who sawed off the head with a knife and sprinkled the blood over the veve and her assistants, then dropped the rest in a bowl. Someone took the bird and hung it on the pole. Mama Sunshine now started to dance, shaking a huge rattle - the assoun, Fee guessed, and singing. She shook the assoun at the post, at the table, at her attendants and over Fee. She sipped the blood out of the bowl, then poured a little on Fee's head. The rest of the assistants took the bowl, sipping from it, then placing it in front of the post. They were dancing now, shuffling round the veve, chanting and clapping. The blood in Fee's hair started to slide down her cheek. First metae, now this. The drumbeat was increasing in tempo, and the hounsis were beginning to shake their shoulders. Mama

Sunshine was dancing herself, shuffling round the veve, turning on her own axis, rattling her assoun and chanting. One of the young men started to shake, and fell to his knees. Mama flitted over to him, and blew a mouthful of rum in his face. It ran down over his skin, shining. It was getting very hot in here, and very fragrant. The press of bodies was swaying, chanting and clapping. The drums were pulsing. The young man was writhing on the floor, a look of agony on his sweating, rum streaked face. Mama Sunshine continued to shake her assoun over him. He was rolling over the veve, then, he stopped. He got up and strutted to the side of the table. There, he took an old frock coat and a top hat. He was helped into the clothes, and white paste smeared on his face. Perfume was poured on his bare chest, and from somewhere on the table he found a cigar and stuck it in his mouth. One of the hounsis lit it for him. Puffing out clouds of smoke, he started to dance, arms spread wide, turning, dipping. Some of the hounsis came up to him and danced with him, shaking their breasts at him under the thin cotton. He smiled hugely at them, showing all his teeth, an impressive set.

He gyrated towards Fee, and danced round the chair, blowing smoke into her face and chattering at her in a language she didn't understand. He placed a hand on her rum-spattered, blood encrusted hair. One of the hounsis brought him a bottle of perfume, and he drenched her in it. He pulled her up and dragged her to the centre of the veve. Mama Sunshine shook the assoun in her face again. Things were starting to become unreal: the stink of the tobacco and rum, the heat and closeness of the bodies surrounding her. Her feet started to dance, her hands to clap. Smiling, everyone urged her to carry on, go faster. The frock-tailed coat whirled past her. Another hounsi had fallen down and was being bathed in rum. The heat, the noise, the stink, all seemed suddenly far away. There was a moment of awful clarity and stillness. Fee stopped.

'My sister's in danger!' She yelled loudly. The drums and chanting stopped, like switching off a radio set. Everything was, suddenly, still. Mama Sunshine shook the assoun round Fee's head.

'De chile has spoken! Damdallah-Wedo, Baron Samedi,

Mawu-Lisa, Ayza, you hear me now! Protect this chile and her blood. You do it now! You do as I say!' She seized Fee's arm. 'You go to your blood now. Take the loas wit' you, chile.' She thrust a small packet in Fee's hand. 'You place it next yore heart. Let it taste th' warmth off yore body.'

First, I need a bath.

'Baron Samedi, he say the dead are after you. The ones without souls, who walk.'

'Zombies?' that's all I need.......'

'No, not the summoned dead. The dead who walk by themselves. The loupgarou. You go now, chile. Dem loas is on you now, and the black clouds is over you. You done yo' duty by de loas, an' they will watch for you.' Mama Sunshine pointed at the small bag in Fee's hand. 'This is the ouanga, the mojo of protection.' Behind her, the drums started up a staccato beat. 'It saved Lucy. Perhaps it save you, too.'

She was outside the door now, her boots and socks in her hands. Mama Ababita, in a flounced white skirt and blouse, was with her. Silently they went back down the stairs. Outside, the car was waiting, with the same young man behind the wheel. Fee slipped into the back seat, very aware of the aroma of cigar smoke, rum and perfume that she brought with her. The orange top and blue jeans were liberally spattered, and her hair felt sticky. *And I've got to go on the tube like this. There's no way the first cop I see won't haul me in for questioning.* She struggled into her boots and coat in the back of the car as it drew away.

'You left yo' wheels in Chisik, right?' The driver was speaking to her, the first words she had heard from him. Not trusting her voice, she nodded. 'Dem loas can do that to you. Yo' be alrig' by th' time I get you Chisik.' he turned round and set his attention to the traffic. Fee's whole being was screaming for hot water, but she gritted her teeth. Her sister was in danger, and she had to get back. *What the hell was Zoe up to now?*

The car let her out at the Chiswick car park. It was starting to drizzle, and she stood gratefully in the thin rain. Zoe was not answering her mobile. Sophie was. Sophie was slightly drunk. It didn't happen often, but when it did, she got giggly. Tom and Ellen would be at the hospital, and she had no intention of calling

Matt. That left Jean. Zoe ought to be with Jean. She stood in the rain, listening to the ringtone buzz in her ear. At last, a voice answered.

'Jean here. Sorry, but I've got the doctor here at the moment.'

'Hi, Jean. Is Zoe there? Can I speak to her, please. It's Fee.'

'I'll get her for you. She should be in the kitchen. I asked her to cook, since Margie took a turn for the worse, again.' Fee could hear Jean calling. 'I'm sorry, Fee, she doesn't seem to be here. Stupid child must have gone out somewhere.'

'I can guess where.' Stupid child, indeed. She's gone to see Theo……. 'Okay, Jean. You see to Margie. I'll be back soon.' Covered in rum and stinking like a Turkish whore. Oh, dear……

Chapter Fifteen

Fee gunned the Golf back along the motorway. Details of the drive blurred. She was aware of stares when she stopped to fuel the car and pick up coffee. She must look a fright from the expressions on people's faces. Better say something, or I'll be seeing blue lights in my mirror before long. She hoped the stink of perfume would mask the stench of the rum. How do I get myself into these situations? It's a nightmare gone real. She smiled at the cashier and paid for her petrol and caffeine. She'd hit her head on the car door, she explained. And broken a bottle of perfume getting into the car. Sorry. The cashier suggested that there were some quite nice toilets attached to the garage, and that she had a key. Fee feigned relief. She had to get home, she said. But it would be nice not to have sticky hair. The cashier further offered a t-shirt from under the counter, an old promotional one that had been left over. And a plastic carrier bag. Fee took them gratefully, declining the offer of plasters from an elderly gent behind her in the queue. Plasters don't stick on hair, see? He smiled apologetically, smoothing his own bald pate. She moved the car from the pumps and retreated to the toilets, which were better than she expected. She ran lukewarm water over her hair until it no longer ran pink, and combed some of the tangles out with her fingers as best she could. When she exited, the BP logo blazed across her chest in yellow and green, the smelly orange top was tied up in the plastic carrier, and her hair no longer looked like an accident in a butcher's shop. Meanwhile, Zoe was getting close up and personal with a meta…….

Home was dark and deserted. Fee had no intention of letting anyone see, or smell, her until she changed and threw in a fast shower. Damp and smelling sweeter, she set out for Theo's lair, only to encounter Zoe on her way back.

   She hustled her sister back into Pippin Cottage. No sense in airing this in public: there was likely to be screeching.

'Get on with it, Fee.' Zoe was listless as she dropped her cloak on a chair. She looked pale. Pale and determined. This was no time to be arguing the toss. Fee had expected worse.

'Okay. Tell me.'

'What? No 'Where have you been? What have you been doing?'

'I know where you've been, and I can guess what you've been doing. Or rather, what Theo's been doing.'

'I'll swap you. Your adventure for mine.'

'I got covered with rum and chicken blood. You.'

'I talked to Theo.'

'I don't believe that all you did was talk.'

'Well, no……'

'Sit, before you fall down. How much blood did you let Theo have?'

'Not that much.'

'Not that much? Look at you! You look like death warmed over. Badly.'

'I *feel* like death warmed over. Honestly, Fee. He didn't take much.'

Fee's eyes narrowed.

'Then how much did he give you?'

'Enough. Not enough to make me likely to jump up from my grave and bite you, though. Enough to let him see what I see, hear what I hear, and know some of what I'm thinking.'

Fee collapsed into a chair.

'You let him do that.' Her voice was flat. 'So he owns you now.'

'That's not what he wanted. Oh, he *wants* to drain me. He *wants* to make me metae. He *didn't* want to tell me about Amagus. I asked him what it would take for him to tell me. And he says right off, We don't talk about Amagus. That I know about it is more than enough. So I used the magic word. Rina. And he went all close and quiet, you know? She surely would not want what this would entail, he tells me. So I told him, she sent me to you, and you must reveal to me the tales of Amagus and in return I must give you something of what you want. Otherwise, we're all in the shit. So he tells me, that if I want to know about

Amagus, I need to see into his thoughts. And the only way I can do this is to let him..... Bond with me.'

'You are already bonded.'

'So I told him. That's the pact, he said. What I am talking about is much, much closer. We will share each other's thoughts. Be able to see through each other's eyes. Hear what the other hears. I am not liking this. Will it allow you to control me, I ask. I will be able to put thoughts in your mind, he replies. Any other Pash would obey without question. But fratten.... think differently. You will be able to know what thoughts are mine. I could promise not to control you, but you would know this is a lie. So, I will share my thoughts with you. It is the price for knowing about Amagus. I can do it no other way. If you need this knowledge, you will have to pay the price. And he's sad. Oh, he'd like to be in my head. But not this way. He wants to be in my head because I want him there, not because I want to get something out of him and it's the price. He's well unhappy about that.

'Okay, I say. Do it. He looks at me like I've really, really hurt him. Do not treat this as some sort of bargain, he says. This is part of what I am. I have offered to very few mortals to share the ophosis with them, like this. It means a great deal to me. And you see it as a means to an end only.' She fell silent.

'I felt really sorry for him then. Rina was still screwing him from beyond her grave. Let this be between you and me only, I tell him. I will listen to you, but I don't promise to do what you say. Bargains don't have to be cold blooded. And he laughs at that. Your blood is warm, he says, and mine is cold. Yet you make the colder bargains. I am fighting for my life here, I tell him. So you are, little one, so you are, he says, and strokes my arm. So let us share. A little blood, a little flesh, and the tales of Amagus.'

'And?'

'He took me to the back room, the one where we went last time. Only we get the bed. So I strip....'

'You WHAT?'

'Come on. Fee, it's no big deal. I'm a farer, remember? I'm not ashamed of my skin. And there's a light in his eyes, looking at me, standing by the bed starkers. I may not be able to control my urges, he says. You'd better, say I, or I will control them for you. Tease me, tease me. The next I know, I'm on my back, and he's on top, and he's lost the shirt. Again. And he's grinning at me. His teeth are showing. A little bite, a little blood, and the pressure of flesh against flesh, no more, he says. A little heat to warm my cold heart. I've not that much blood in me to warm you, I tell him. There's not enough blood in the whole world to do that. And he laughs, and goes for the jugular. And there's a pounding in my head, it's a while before I realize it's my heartbeat. Then, he cuts his shoulder, and that's his blood falling all down his skin. Oh well, I said to myself, I've been here before. And if I need to do this again, I will. So then, I start hearing another beat in my head. And it, like, started to match with the beat already in my head, until all I could hear was one beat, thundering on and on.'

'How much?'

'Too much, from the state of my belly. It's really roiling, Fee.'

'So. Amagus.'

'Yes. While I was…. ummmm…. yes, well….. It sort of slid into my mind. I *knew* Amagus. I could see him. Doing stuff. You wouldn't believe what I saw. I don't believe what I saw, what I know.'

'If you don't tell me, right now, I will probably strangle you.'

'Let me put it this way, Fee. How did the metae come into being?'

'The tales say a pact with the Devil.'

'You don't believe that any more than I do. Did.'

'You tell me.'

'The first meta was Amagus. And that's not the worst of it.'

'Get on with it while I'm still breathing.'

'Fee, Amagus was a *frater*. He used his wyth to try to live for ever. But it went wrong. He didn't complete the ritual. Instead of *living* forever, he got to *die* forever. It was like I was watching him do what he did, *and* listening to a voice telling the story. The two weren't always the same.

'He was trying to bargain that bit of him that isn't his to bargain with. The Ayat. The immortal bit. But it went very wrong. The wyth collapsed on him. The Tale, that's what I am calling the voice I was hearing, told it like it was a sort of revenge thing. The gods were displeased with what Amagus was doing, so they cursed him. He was turning his back on the real, everyday world, so he couldn't be part of it any more. So if the sun shone on him, it would burn him up. But he didn't want to die, so the grave wouldn't receive him either. So he was condemned to live forever. His ayat was locked inside his body. For ever. And the only thing that would nourish him was fresh human blood. If he wanted to continue existing, he would have to kill, again and again. He hated it. Hates it. But he can't leave it alone, you know? He craves it and hates it at the same time. And because of what it did to him, he can't tolerate even the slightest bit of light. So he retreated into the caves where there was no light. But he had to come out, to hunt, and it was driving him crazy. So, anyway, one night, so the voice said, he met and killed a young woman. When he saw her dead, he recognized her as his own daughter, and he went mental. He tore at his own skin trying to get rid of her blood, and some of it fell into her mouth, and she became the second vampire. Only what I saw wasn't like that, Fee. He lured her to the cave. Deliberately. He took days to kill her, to make her like him. And when he'd done it, she was so pissed off she sealed him in his lair by bringing down the roof, and this is the kicker, *THE BUGGER'S STILL DOWN THERE.*'

'So how come there are so many metae?'

'Once he was sealed in, and realized he couldn't get out, he started to call up his other victims. They rose out of the earth and came to dig him out. But Amagus' daughter made metae of her own to stop them. She could hear her father's voice in her head, she knew what he was planning. Eventually, after some minor skirmishes, the two gangs tried to slaughter each other. It was a major gorefest, guts and body parts everywhere. Valacia won. That's not her name, by the way, but it's what the voice was calling her. Since none of the metae left could hear Amagus, they assumed that they managed to destroy him. Just to be sure, Valacia persuaded one of her kin to do a weaving that prevented any of the survivors passing the legend on. The memory lives in the blood, they say, not the mouth.'

'So every meten that gets made gets this …… story? With the blood?'

'Apparently not. Some get it, some don't. Don't ask me why. But with each passing, it gets weaker, less compelling. I got that too. The first generation remember it very clearly because they were there. The second get the memory to a degree, *if* the meten that makes them chooses to reveal it. Few do. And Fee, get this. The memory was clearer from Theo than the voice. He saw it, Fee. He was there. I got this emotional content from him. It was very confused. Anger, pain, loss. Exultation in the new strength and the promise of eternal life.'

'But they don't get to live forever, do they?'

'If they don't meet a Van Helsing wannabee, they do. If they don't go mad, of course. It's like depression, only worse. Theo called it the boredom event horizon. Nothing in the world interests them any more. They just sit and brood. They won't feed, they won't do anything, and they eventually turn to dust because they aren't nourishing themselves. They starve to death. But they can recover from awful damage, Fee. It just takes time. I always thought that Hammer was trying to cash in, resurrecting Christopher Lee all those times. But that's how it goes. A damaged mete can regenerate, from their dust if needs be. All they need is a little blood.'

'So how the hell do we kill one?'

'Forget holy water, crosses and garlic. The vampire blyds were walking the earth long before Christianity got to be more than a Judaic cult. Beheading is good. Stakes are good. But if you really want to get rid of a mete? Flush them down the toilet.'

Chapter Sixteen

Fee spent a restless night. Her dreams were littered with fangs and black dancing girls spattered with blood, interspersed with headlights roaring down the motorway. And, strangely, Sophie's serene face in the middle of it. She was grateful the night was over, but the day brought new worries. What had Zoe done? Few of the Family who had dealings with the metae invited further intercourse - further anything else for that matter - and that was a very appropriate word. Theo was a lounge lizard with fangs. He relished fleshy pleasures almost as much as he did the blood he fed on.

In the kitchen, Zoe was pouring boiling water into a teapot. She still looked a bit pale, but her movements were brisk. She tended to wince a bit when the clouds parted and sunlight streamed into the room. Fee slid into a chair and accepted a cup of tea gratefully.

'How are you this morning?'

'You mean have I grown fangs yet? No. It's weird, Fee. No, that's the wrong word. There's no word for how far past weird being me at the moment is.'

'So tell me.'

'I hardly slept at all last night. I sat in the window seat looking out at the night. It was calling to me. I really wanted to go out, to walk in the night. To join it, become it……. And, I could see. Not like colours, but shades of black. Different colours, all blacks and greys. I could see every leaf on a tree, I could see the mice moving in the hedgerow. I opened the window and it smelled like nothing I've smelled before. Clean, sweet, inviting. And I could hear things. I could hear a bell tolling, far off, far away. And I heard a barn owl fly past, I swear I could hear the bats squeaking. I could feel the night, feel it coming into the room, coming into me.' She sat down and nursed a cup of tea. She inhaled the steam. 'I never really knew how nice tea smelt before. And I'm not a bit tired. I feel really alive, which is silly, considering.' Fee waited.

There was more. 'And when the sun came up….. The colours I could see! They were so bright, so pure, so alive…… I could see the sunlight streaming down, dancing over the ground. It was beautiful. I could see live things…… the life in them, like glowing prisms of colour. I sat watching a starling on the lawn for ages until it flew away. It was a glittering rainbow. I can still see it. The edges of light are rainbows. I always knew light was made of colour, and now I can see it. And when I came downstairs, I nearly flew. I'm faster, Fee, faster, stronger, more alive, more aware than I was before. I always imagined that ……….. it…. would make me slower, more tired, but it didn't.'

'And what's the downside?'

'You are worried that I'll go back for another dose.'

'You hit it. I am worried.'

'Oh, no, I've got other plans for my life than being Theo's Pash. It's all very new now, but it will wear off a bit, given time.'

'Theo told you that?'

'No, I *know* that. Comes with the blood memories, I suppose. Here's the downside. I know why metae don't like the daylight. It's way, way too bright. I can hardly see. And it's hot. When the sun hit my arm, it felt like it was burning. Sunburn. I got sunburnt through the glass on an autumn morning. Well, not really: it just felt like it would be a good idea to stay out of the sun, today at least.'

'Anything else?'

'I keep seeing this face. It ought to be familiar, but it's not. It's young man with very short, dark brown hair and a thin face. He's got an odd smile, sort of sardonic and contemptuous. He knows more than he ought to. It's not a nice smile, and he's not a nice person. I wouldn't like to get to know him better, anyway.'

'All of which hardly moves us on.'

'Give me time. I've lot of data to sift through.'

'Time, my girl, is a precious commodity around here at the moment. I don't think we've got too much to play with.'

'I feel it too. Things are moving, and we're so far off ready we might just as well have not been started.'

Fee got up and put slices of bread in the toaster.

'So what do we have? Possibly a rogue vampire or frata,

possibly not. A sword in a glass block that I will need, but might not be able to use. An ancient grandaddy vampire immolated under a pile of rock somewhere. Rina. The end of something that started ages ago and isn't finished yet. My youngest sister turning into a bloodsucker, and a list of dead relatives longer than my arm.'

She leant against the kitchen counter. Zoe was uncharacteristically silent. Finally, she spoke.

'There's something there, I can feel it. It's like a jigsaw, but I'm missing some of the pieces. Two good things you missed, Fee. He's not infallible. Dave got away, and Lucy got away. And we are all on our guard now. He'll find it more difficult to get at us.'

'Aye, we've had our eyes well and truly opened. And we'll keep them open. I think I'll go over to Jean's, see if she's noticed anything. You feel up to outside yet?'

'Only if it's cold enough to need gloves. Okay, I'll say I've caught a chill. That'll explain why I'm pale and interesting, and wearing more woollies than is normal. I might have to endure one of Margie's concoctions, but I can always pour it down the sink when I get home.'

'That's the spirit. Do you want toast?'

'No. That snack I had last night is quite enough for now, thank you. I don't think I'm ready for solids yet. I feel as if something very hard hit me in the middle, you know?'

'Funny, I feel the same. A pain, right here.' Fee touched her midsection. 'I feel really sore.'

When they went out, Zoe was swathed up to the eyeballs in hat, scarf, gloves, coat and long boots. She had even covered her eyes with outsize mirrored sunglasses which wouldn't have been out of place on Posh Spice. She looked quite exotic in the rural setting. They tramped over the Green to Station House in the fitful sunlight.

Jean met them at the door. Lines of worry creased round her eyes and she looked tired. Margie's continued illness was telling on her, obviously. They had been friends for a long, long time. She looked hard at Zoe. She was unconvinced about the 'chill', feeling Zoe's forehead and announcing it to be 'cold and clammy, not feverish.' She hadn't seen anything unusual, that is if you didn't count Fee's abrupt comings and goings. She felt, she said, unsettled. Something was definitely 'in the wind', and it wasn't good, not good at all. Fee agreed with her. There was an air of heaviness over the place. The air was hanging. Perhaps there was a storm brewing. She insisted on giving Zoe a 'tonic' which from Zoe's expression after the spoonful she couldn't very well avoid went down, tasted foul. They left as soon as they could. The atmosphere in Station House was gloomy. Jean was resigned, Margie sicker than usual. Whatever was going on, it had stopped the normal whingeing and complaining. Jean had given up. Good job her stove ran on solid fuel and not gas, or they might find her one morning cold and blue with her head in the oven. Not a nice thought.

As they made their mournful way back - half an hour with Jean in that state was enough for the most cheerful mortal to feel suicidal - Fee noticed a figure standing at the gate to Pippin Cottage. It loomed large, and was dressed in dark clothes. A pang of fear raced through her. She gripped Zoe's arm, and her sister looked up from her intent scrutiny of the grass beneath her feet. Say what she might, Zoe was uncomfortable out-of-doors today. She looked up.

'It's Sergeant Brice.'

Fee's anxiety eased slightly. Okay, it wasn't the Family stalker. But what was Sergeant Brice doing on her doorstep this morning? Did some traffic cop clock her doing a hundred and twenty down the M4 last night? Surely not, they would have stopped her right away, not left it to some village plod.

'Morning, Sergeant Brice. What brings you to our door today? Someone broken into Blue Moon again?'

Some of the local lads thought it was a hoot to break into the factory and nick stuff to impress their would-be girlfriends. It had happened before, and would again. No amount of locks, bolts and bars, nor a security system that set all the dogs in the neighbourhood to barking their socks off, and incidentally earned Fee a lambasting from the Parish Council - which she had ignored - seemed to deter them. Short of razor wire, searchlights and a machine gun emplacement on the roof, Blue Moon would have the occasional raider. If it went on, she'd a mind to tell Theo that his associates could up the body count. Well, perhaps not going quite that far.

'No, lass. As far as I know, the lads are leaving your place alone. Can I come in, like?'

As bad as that. Well. It had been a long time since anyone complained about 'goings on' at Pippin Cottage. Oh, there had been some, when incomers had seen 'lights' moving through the wood. Rumour, ranging from alien invasion, clandestine surveying for roads and even, too close to the knuckle for comfort, satanic bloodthirsty rites, started to circulate. A quick tale about badger watching, moth catching - environmental stuff - had seen that off. It was on private ground, after all. As far as the village proper knew, the meetings at Pippin Cottage were for 'nature study'. What sort of nature, they hadn't gone into. Enquirers were left to draw their own, very wrong, conclusions. It suited everyone to have themselves thought of as woolly-hatted tree-huggers. It only became awkward when enthusiastic incomers wanted to share in the fun. They, regretfully, declined. The house was small, and they couldn't really accommodate more people. Why don't you start a group of your own? We can meet occasionally and compare notes. One couple only had taken them up on it: they had joined the great back-to-the-land movement and had, surprisingly, survived. The work was harder than they thought, but they persevered and now ran a small organic vegetable business, delivering fresh produce to local hotels and pubs. In their spare time, they tramped the footpaths and made detailed notes on what they had seen and found. With Luke running interference, they hadn't been much bother.

Zoe escorted Sergeant Brice into the parlour while Fee made a pot of tea. When she brought in the tray, he was firmly ensconced in a sagging chair. He didn't look happy.

'Look, girls, what I have to say……. I mean….. Ladies…'

'Spit it out, Stan.' Fee was pouring tea. She felt a little annoyed at the intrusion. She had enough to think about without Sergeant Brice's adding his two penn'orth of woe.

'Will you sit down, Miss Harris? Please sit down.'

He accepted a mug from her, and placed it on the arm of his chair. Fee sat. He obviously wasn't going to go any further until she did. Zoe was already buried in her favourite perch. Sergeant Brice pulled out his hankie and wiped his forehead.

'I'm not cut out for this sort of thing. Orter be someone from Okehampton, but they dumped it on me. Miserable sods, they are.'

The girls waited impatiently.

'I'm sorry to have to be the one to tell you this.'

Alarm bells were ringing now. Zoe was sitting straighter. She exchanged a glance with Fee.

'There's been an accident.'

What? Where? Who? This was way, way past bad.... Fee could almost feel the blood draining into her feet. She felt light-headed. This was so, so, not happening........

'They found her on the beach....'

Found her? Found who? She could hardly hear him now. Zoe's face had gone completely white.

'Miss Sophie Harris.......'

Sophie? *Sophie*? No, no, *nooo*........

'Think she may have died of exposure........'

Whatttt!

'Sometime last night....... Caleb........ Helping with our enquiries....'

She was going to be married, and have a baby......... What's Caleb doing at a police station?

'I am so sorry. She was a lovely girl........ Watched her grow up, I did....'

Sophie? Dead? Can't be.......... Luke, Sophie..... Sophie........

'.... have to go to Truro....'

Truro.......

'.... to identify the body.'

Body? Sophie?

286

Chapter Seventeen

Zoe had risen from her chair to come over to the sofa. She was cuddling Fee, or maybe she was seeking comfort, reassurance, where there was none to be had. Fee was past reacting. She was numb. Stone. She just sat, hands in her lap. Finally, she reached out to Zoe. Funny. There were no tears. Sergeant Brice was standing now, as if sitting in the room was somehow impolite after delivering such devastating news. He was still speaking, but neither of them were hearing him. The air had been sucked out of the room. Other lungs had used it all up. Fee couldn't get her breath. There was a massive ache under her ribs. *She'd protected the wrong sister.*

Finally, she made her voice work.

'How?' It came from her mouth, but it wasn't her voice.

'I don't know all the details, Miss Harris.' Sudden formality from Stan Brice. He'd known her since she started to walk. From 'OI! you!' to 'Fiona' to 'Ffion' after she had corrected him, cheekily, for the umpteenth time. Now she was 'Miss Harris.' 'The Okehampton station is sending a car. But they thought it'd be better coming from me, like, being local. Not that it makes much difference to my mind who it is who tells them as is left that one of theirs is gone. I'm truly sorry, Miss. Is there anyone I can call for you?'

'I'd better call Lily…..'

'I'll do it,' Zoe said, taking charge. Fee was useless at the moment. 'There's no-one who can help, Sergeant Brice. They've all got troubles of their own. Uncle Tom and Ellen have got Luke in hospital. Jean's got Margie, she's sick. Claire's abroad. And I don't want to upset Lottie with the baby and all. So there's just us.' She went into the hall to call Lily. How do you tell your mother that your sister, her daughter, is dead? Snag sidled into the door and leapt onto Fee's lap. He put his paws on her chest and chirruped, butting her face with his damp nose. Absently, she stroked his soft fur. He settled in her lap, kneading her knees through her jeans, and started his rumbling purr. It vibrated through Fee's legs and into her chest, easing the ache lying in her stomach. Petrified. She knew what that felt like, now. Her insides had turned to stone, to cold, hard stone. A lead weight in her belly. The tea was going cold, forgotten. Let it go. Oh, Sophie……….

Zoe came back.

'I've told her, Fee. She's coming down. I've told Jean too,' she turned to Sergeant Brice, 'So there's no need to tell anyone else. It'll be all over the place in ten minutes.'

She bustled out. Busy-busy. Anything to avoid stillness, the awful contemplation of reality. Stan stood awkwardly, looming over Fee, blotting out the light. Zoe flipped in and out, organizing bags and coats, checking doors and windows. Fee's body clock was running late. She was ten minutes behind everyone else. In a different time zone. Zoe was pressing house keys on Brice, telling him to drop by and feed Snag, when a car drew up by the gate. Two policemen got out: more correctly, one was a policewoman.

'I am sorry for your loss.' She had removed her cap, and the light reflected off short, gold-blonde hair. She looked too young to be a police officer. Isn't that what they said, you know you are old when policemen start looking young? Fee could count her years in thousands now. 'If you could come with us, we'll take you to your sister.'

Her eyes slid from the unresponsive Fee to Zoe, standing by the door. Zoe moved to the sofa and unhooked Snag from Fee's lap, dumping him on the chair behind. There were too many people in the room. They were using up all the air.

'Come on, Fee. We've got to go.' She was wearing the outsize specs again, topped off with a cherry-red beret. She helped Fee up and draped her coat over her shoulders. 'Someone get our bags, please.' She steered Fee out, hissing in her ear. 'Pull it together, Fee. I can't do this all on my own, you know.' She led the police out, and inserted Fee in the backseat of the car. Across the green, she could see people watching. Well, they would. They'd know soon enough. News like this travels fast, especially with a talent like Jean's to help it along. A lad on a bike cycled past and skidded to a stop to gawk. Women with shopping baskets put their heads together. Sergeant Brice gruffly moved the cyclist along. 'Nothing to keep you here, lad.' He would be a very popular man once the car moved off. Everyone would want the grisly details to pass along. Villages like this ran on gossip.

Zoe slipped in next to Fee. The policeman slid behind the wheel, and the woman joined him in the front.

'Buckle up, ladies. I'm Katie Holloway, and this is Laurence Vernon.' The car moved off, bouncing a bit over the uneven roadway.

'You'd be better to turn around. This road doesn't get much better.'

'Thanks. Don't get out here much.' the driver executed a point-perfect reverse turn in a gateway. They drove back past the green where the vultures were already gathering around Sergeant Brice.

'He won't get much more done today,' Katie commented as they left the village behind. She soon realized that her fellow passengers were still in shock, and gave up on attempts to talk with them. She knew only the barest details: that the girls' sister had been found dead on Swanpool beach near Falmouth. They didn't 'suspect foul play', but were 'concerned.' Her attempts to elicit information were met with a polite 'Not now, please,' from Zoe. Fee heard a faint undertone in that voice. She would have to speak to her later. You didn't use the tone of control, the wyth, on cops. Katie gave it up, telling them it would take just over an hour to reach their destination.

Fee felt Zoe grip her hand. She was aware of the seething presence of her sister beside her. Her hand started to tingle, then grow warm. She turned to Zoe. She was going to tell her to stop, but Zoe pursed her lips and shook her head. Under the influence of her sister's wyth, Fee's mind started to clear. The whirling thoughts welled up, threatening to overwhelm her, but they slowed in their crazy dance, and started to line up for inspection. There was a cold logic there. Sophie was dead. Nothing I can do about that. I must watch, and listen, and ask questions. I must see Caleb. I must see where she was found. I must see Sophie. I must find out what the police, and the other authorities, intend. I must *not* tell them of my suspicions. That is for me and mine alone.

The weight of sorrow in her stomach became a cold intention, a deadly purpose. She squeezed hard on Zoe's hand. I'm all right now, I'm back. We will do what must be done.

Falmouth police station. The 'soft' interview room. A detective. DI Susan Malone. She also, was sorry for their loss. Zoe was fiddling with her mobile. They were offered tea. It came in actual cups, with saucers, and not from a vending machine.

'Tell me about your sister.'

'Sophie was an artist. She lived in Falmouth with her boyfriend, Caleb.'

'They were getting on all right, Sophie and Caleb?'

'He just came back from Norway. They were going to get married. Sophie was going to have his baby.' Fee's voice broke.

'I am sorry if this upsets you.'

'What are you thinking? That Caleb and Sophie fell out?'

'At the moment, I am thinking nothing in particular. Your sister was found on Swanpool beach in the early hours of this morning, by a man walking his dog. He does that every morning, very early, before he goes to work. She was found above the high tide mark. Her clothes were damp, but not wet.'

'What was she wearing?'

'A long cotton dress and light shoes. No outer clothing, or underwear.'

'She doesn't usually wear a bra. And she only wears underpants under short skirts.'

'I see. So for your sister, wearing just a long dress was normal?'

'Yes.'

'We were thinking sexual assault that went wrong, because of the lack of underwear. What you are telling me lessens that probability somewhat.' She made a note in the file. 'Can you think of anyone who might want to harm your sister?'

Just one. And you won't believe me.

'No, no-one. Sophie was….. not the type of person who made enemies. Ask anyone.'

'We are going to. Now, what about her friends?'

'There were the artists here. And she took classes at the

holiday camp. And the Galleria owner where she exhibited. Caleb could tell you better. There's family and friends at home, but we've all been too concerned with Luke……'

'Who is Luke?'

'Uncle Tom's boy. He's in hospital with concussion. Fell off a tor.'

'Which hospital?'

And so it went on. Gentle probing into Sophie's life and habits. And all the time, Fee knowing that she knew something she couldn't reveal, and that, worst of all, she had been warned about this danger and had chosen to be with the sister who didn't need protecting at the expense of the one who did. But Sophie had been surrounded by her friends here in Falmouth, Caleb by her side, and last night that the only thing she was going to do was be dragged into bed and sleep safely next to Caleb. Zoe had been more isolated and was of a mind to invite more danger by visiting a meta. What would you have done?

'So you spoke with Sophie last night? How was she?'

'She was having a party. With her friends. To celebrate her engagement. She was very happy.'

'Had she been drinking?'

'It was a party. It was at her home, and yes, she had been drinking. It was the final blowout, she said, before she was seriously pregnant.'

'Did she make a habit of drinking heavily?'

'If you knew Sophie, you wouldn't need to ask. Hangovers interfered with her painting. She never let anything come between her and her paintbrush.'

'Even Caleb?'

'He wouldn't do that. He'd go off and do his photography, and Sophie would paint. When I saw them the day before yesterday, they were so happy about the wedding, the baby, all of it. And so were we.'

'I see.'

'Can I see my sister now? Or Caleb? You've got him here, haven't you?'

'Yes, we have.'

'Surely you don't suspect that he…'

'I have an unexplained death on my hands. A healthy young woman does not usually keel over and die on a popular beach overnight. Especially when that young woman was, a few hours before, happily throwing a party for friends some miles away. And was definitely too drunk to drive.'

'Believe me, if Sophie was too drunk to drive, Caleb would have been the worse.'

'Unless they had a falling out.'

'If they had, Sophie would have called. She used to call us two, three times a day. She'd sometimes call because the sun was shining. She didn't. They didn't. I know my sister. If she and Caleb had fallen out over something, she'd have told us.'

DI Malone turned searchlight eyes on Zoe, who had so far remained silent.

'But not recently. We have her mobile.'

'You have her new mobile. Her old one got broken. She was with us up to yesterday. And she called me twice. You check. And when she wasn't phoning or texting, she was e-mailing.'

'You were a close family, then.'

'We are.'

'Yet you live in Upper Congrieve with your other family and friends. Your eldest sister splits her time between London and Congrieve. Your other sister lives in Falmouth, and your mother lives in Norfolk.'

'And not a day goes by that I don't hear from at least two of them. Some more than once. Some families live in our village, together in one house, and they don't communicate as much as I do with my sisters and my mother.'

'I see. This doesn't leave me with much.'

'Can we see Caleb now? I think he's missing Sophie as much as we are.'

'I'll see if my colleagues are finished with him.'

She left them sitting on upholstered chairs which weren't exactly comfortable. Another policewoman sidled into the room and stood by the door.

'Is it possible for you to scare us up something to eat? We haven't had anything since breakfast.'

The woman nodded at Zoe, and opened the door, speaking to

someone in the corridor outside.

Some minutes later, a tray turned up with soft drinks in cans and assorted sandwiches. Zoe popped a can of Lilt and settled down to wait. Fee half-heartedly tried a sandwich. Chicken mayo with salad. Pretty good. But swallowing it was another matter.

The clock ticked off the minutes. It had completed over a half a turn before the door opened again.

'Caleb.' Fee stood and walked over to him. 'You look awful.'

'Don't hold back, Fee. What's been going on, Caleb?'

'Don't ask me. The party stared to peter out about one-thirty, two o'clock. Most people crashed on the floor downstairs. Soph and I went to bed. She was all happy and giggly, but she was out like a light once her head hit the pillow. I wasn't much better. When I woke up, she wasn't there. It didn't worry me. You know Sophie. She wakes up, and the light looks right, she's off with her paints or her camera. I thought she might have gone down to the harbour. She's been doing a series of studies of the boats and the water which are selling quite well. So I creep out, find one of the early shops that open for the fishermen, get some coffee and pastries. I think I'll find her, and we'll sit on the harbour wall, have coffee and eat pastries.

'But she's not where I expected her to be. So I walk further round, and I can see blue lights flashing. I wished I had brought my camera then. Crass, I know. But I think, maybe she's gone to see what's happening. I walk down, and ask one of the coppers what's going on. Found a body, mate, he replies. And I look over. I couldn't miss the hair. No-one has hair like Sophie. I call out her name, and try to get closer. But they're holding me back. I try to explain that I think I know who it is. And they bring me a guy with a camera, and he shows me a shot of her face. She's pale, very pale, and bits of her hair are stuck to her face, and her lips are blue, her eyes are closed. But it's Sophie. And I lost it. They stuck me in a car and brought me here. I've been in an interview room ever since.'

'Have they charged you?'

'No.'

'Then we're leaving. Right now. Later I will have words with

293

whoever's in charge. They have no right to treat you like a criminal when you have lost the mother of your unborn baby. Come on.'

Fee walked towards the door. 'When in doubt, act as if you know you're in the right' is a good maxim and it deserved a bit of exercise. She put on her game face.

'You can tell your superior officers that we wish to leave. I want to see my sister. Now. You have no grounds to detain us, any of us.'

The woman moved away from the door. It opened to reveal DI Malone.

'We are leaving now. You can either help us by taking us to my sister, or you can let us out to find a taxi. Either is acceptable. Remaining here is not.'

'I came to tell you that the pathologist has completed his preliminary investigations, and is satisfied that your sister died from natural causes. There are some further tests he wishes to carry out before he can release the body, however. Hypothermia is not usual at this time of year, but he can find nothing else wrong with her. However, how she came to be on that beach is still a concern.'

'It is a concern to me as well. But unless you wish to prefer charges on us, any of us, we are leaving.'

'I'll get someone to take you to the…….'

'I won't faint if I hear the word morgue. I've heard it before.'

'Hospital.'

'Thank you. Oh, and Inspector Malone. I'd make sure that all your paperwork, and your colleague's paperwork, is in order. I think you could have treated Mr McIntyre better. After all, he's just lost his wife to be, *and* the mother of his baby. I will be asking for a full report, believe me.'

She would have liked to sweep out of the room, nose in the air, but discretion won. Save the theatrics for when you need them. Team Holloway and Vernon were waiting in the reception area to take them to the hospital. She hoped that they had been able to score a cup of tea at least. It was a long drive back to Devon.

They were a bit cramped in the back now there were three of them, but Fee had no intention of leaving Caleb behind. She considered offering to take him back with them, but perhaps he would prefer to stay here and be comforted by his own friends. She would let him decide. Either way, he would have no part in what was to come. Something was hardening in Fee. The nearest the killing had come to her up until now had been Luke. Oh, she liked Luke, liked him a lot. But he wasn't her sister. The chickens had come home to roost, and they had become harpies. There would be no resting place in earth or sky for whoever had taken Sophie.

Police have it easy when it comes to hospital parking. They don't have to cruise round for hours, wasting petrol, scobing for a vacant space. Neither are they subject to the exorbitant fees that hospital car parks charge. They can park where they like, and no-one is going to come round with a Denver boot or parking ticket. The only people who have it easier are the ambulance drivers.

Vernon led the way into the bowels of the hospital. He'd been here before, then. What was so strange about that? Escorting people to see the dead was part and parcel of a cop's life. He left them in the Bereavement Suite with Katie while he scared up an Igor.

The Bereavement Suite was littered with pamphlets from bereavement councillors, funeral homes and insurance companies. Vultures, every one of them, feeding off the despair of the hopeless. One caught Fee's eye. Are You Worried About Funeral Expenses? it asked solicitously. As if. When I'm dead, someone else can do the worrying. Littered was the wrong word for the neat piles of paper on the low table. The room was done in tasteful pale lilac with 'ambient lighting'- in other words, virtually dark. To make it harder to read the pamphlets? Possibly. Every little helps. Each well-upholstered chair had its own box of perfumed tissues. Why waste money here? Once you're down here, all hope is gone. The great god Medicine has failed you. So his acolytes will spend money making you feel uncomfortable, in this cozy room without windows, streets better than the ward above where there's too little money to get the floors cleaned properly so people catch bugs that eat their still-living flesh. The mood music, playing softly, grated on Fee's ears. Caleb had collapsed into one of the overstuffed chairs. The light from a table lamp glittered as a tear slid down one cheek. Katie Holloway was trying carefully not to look directly at any of them. Zoe perched on the arm of Caleb's chair and was stroking his hair absently. The tears started to flow faster.

'I loved her so much.'

'I know.'

Their wait was interrupted by a fluffy haired woman well past her use-by date. She murmured condolences and offered tea. Again with the tea. That will be the third lot today that's left to go cold. At least it will give her something to do. Tea and biscuits, on a tiny china plate with a paper doily, arrived with a balding man holding a brown paper envelope.

'Commiserations on your loss. If you have any questions, I will be pleased to answer them. Or would you like to see Sophie now? Are you all relatives?'

'Yes. And you are?'

'I'm sorry. I'm Doctor Bovis, Alan Bovis. Please come with me.'

Questions could come after, then. He led them through a corridor to a quiet, shaded room hung with dark green drapes against paler green walls and faux windows through which pale yellow light glowed. At one end of the room, two electric candles stood on a table covered with the same dark green as the drapes. A single, gentle spotlight illuminated the box standing in the centre of the room. By the walls there were wooden chairs. Sombre churchy music was playing softly. They trooped into the room and surrounded the box. Inside, draped in cream silk, was Sophie.

Her face had been washed and her hair combed. Her body was hidden in the swathe of silk. There was a tiny smile on her lips. Tears ran down Caleb's face, and Zoe took his hand and stroked it.

'I'm sorry. Could you please….'

'That is my sister. That is Sophie Harris.'

'Thank you.' Katie Holloway and Laurence Vernon left quietly. The three of them were alone. Fee reached out to caress her sister's cool cheek.

'Go softly, cariad.' She bent over, to kiss the coral lips one last time. Her nostrils caught a faint, musty scent that was quite familiar, and not at all Sophie. She knew that scent. She had been close, very close, to someone who smelled exactly like that. A cold certainty coiled round her heart. She stroked Sophie's hair. 'Thank you,' she whispered.

Zoe let go of Caleb's hand. Her attention on Sophie was more curious, more analytical. She had seen Robert in his coffin, but had been too distraught to take too much interest, and had cried simply because she couldn't hug him. So this was not her first dead body. Fee hoped she would behave. She also hoped that the tears in Caleb's eyes would blind him to the fact that Zoe was openly sniffing. She reckoned without her sister's duplicity. Zoe merely pulled out a hankie and started wiping her eyes and nose.

As Caleb cried over the body, both of them, his lover and his child, Zoe slowly walked over to Fee and stood close.

'I know. Wait.' Fee muttered.

Zoe had picked it up too. Faint but distinct. The reek of vampire.

Chapter Eighteen

Tired, cold, and numbed inside by the experience of seeing Sophie, they decided to return to her home. The loft was empty now of the friends and companions who had celebrated late into the night before. The litter of the party was strewn about, but no-one had the inclination to sort the mess out. Sophie was dead. Her home was vacant, vacant as the body they has seen in the morgue. Not even the echo of her laughter pervaded the high-ceilinged spaces. She was utterly, completely, gone. Fee sent the police away. They weren't very happy at that, but she promised they would see them back at the station. Falmouth isn't that large, and it wasn't that far to the police station.

Caleb collapsed into a chair. He started to weep, with great, gasping sobs that wracked his frame so deeply that the chairlegs chattered on the wooden floor. Fee held him, murmuring soft words and phrases of comfort. He was too deep in his own grief for her wyth to penetrate. She could do nothing to relieve his agony except be there, a presence and reminder of what was gone and would be no more. Zoe, still in her coat and hat, ferreted among the detritus of the party until she found enough clean china to attempt making tea. She brought a tray over to a table and glared at it, then swept it clean of paper plates and plastic cups and deposited the tray with a thump and rattle. Caleb looked up, the tear tracks smearing his face.

'How? Why? Why *her*? And who... who could have done such a thing..... To Sophie? My Sophie?'

Fee and Zoe exchanged a meaningful glance. But Caleb wasn't finished.

'If I ever.... *ever*... find out who did this, then... then... I'll kill them myself! I will! I swear it!' He became aware of the silence between the two sisters. He heaved himself from his perch and flung himself at Fee. Grasping her upper arms, he shook her. 'You know, don't you? You do! Tell me! Tell me now!'

'Caleb.....' Zoe laid a restraining hand on his arm. His gaze lit upon her. It was terrifying. Almost mad.

'If you don't tell me, right now, I'll ream it from you! I'm not joking! I will go into your mind and tear it from you by the roots!'

'Be sensible.'

'Sensible! She asks me to be sensible! *Demands* I be sensible! My Sophie is dead! And you know who is responsible! I have no interest in *sensible*! Tell me!'

'She was my Sophie too. And we don't know, for sure, who did it.'

'But you suspect someone. Who?'

'So you can race off and let him have you, too?'

'Who. Is. The. Bastard….. Who. Killed. Them?'

'**NO**, Caleb. No, no and no. This is for me to do.'

'Says who?'

'Says the Gya. Only Fee has a chance to stop this. Not you. Not me. Not anyone else. Only Fee.'

'To hell with the wyth and the Gya and all your cyscan cant! I *will* find him, and I *will* kill him! I won't have it any other way.'

'Okay. How?'

'How what?'

'How will you find out who their killer is? How will you find out where he is? How will you find out how to kill him?'

'I'll search the Gya, and….'

'The very same Gya you cursed just now? Feels helpful, does it?'

Caleb wilted.

'I won't let this go.'

'Neither will we. Do you want to help?'

'How?'

'Do you remember what I told you, back home? I think that, whoever it was, they got to Sophie.'

'I didn't really believe you then.'

'But you do now.'

'Yes.'

'You can start by telling us exactly what happened between the time you left us, and the time you found……'

Caleb wiped his hands over his face: took time to compose his memories. It took a while.

'Well, we drove back. Sophie was very happy. We laughed, we sang. We dumped the car over by the pier like always, and came back here. Then I said, we ought to celebrate. Have a party. She kissed me and sent me out for vittles while she called the mob...'

'Where did you go?'

'Over to the Arcade. We've got loads of friends there. I thought that Keith and Petra might cook us something, they run the wholefood emporium and café, okay? They were over the moon with the news, and I stayed there chatting.... Ran into some other pals, told them.... Then I came back.'

'Anything out of the ordinary there?'

'Not that I saw.'

'Soph was still here?'

'Yeah. She'd strung up some lights and was having a bath. I sneaked some pictures, then left her to it. Uploaded them onto the hard drive, then got changed. People started to arrive, then. After that, it's a bit of a blur.'

'You got wasted.'

'It's not every day you find out you're gonna be a father....... *were* gonna be a father...... and your girlfriend has agreed to marry you......'

'It's hard, I know. Stick with it.' Fee hugged him, gently. 'Anything else you remember?'

'I forgot. There was a letter waiting for her when we got back.'

'And?'

'I don't know any more. It was gone when I came back.'

'What did it say?'

'We didn't discuss it. Couldn't have been that important.'

'Where is it now?'

'Probably in the waste bin.' He pointed to a wicker basket over by the door. 'She slings all the old stuff in there......'

Zoe wandered over and peered into the bin.

'Nowt there. Strange.'

'How so?'

Zoe flipped an arm round, taking in the mess.

'Nothing else's been tidied up. But this bin's empty. All the others are overflowing.'

'Maybe that detective took it.'

'All of it? There were magazines, old sketches, all sorts of crap. And only that bin? Why not the others?'

'We could ask.'

'Aren't the fuzz supposed to give you a list if they've taken stuff?'

'They gave me an envelope…'

'And?'

'Where is it now?' Fee asked, with exaggerated patience.

'Stuck it in my pocket.'

Caleb fished around and handed Fee a brown A4 envelope, crumpled and creased from his pocket. She tore open the seal and extracted a wad of paper.

'Wazzit say?'

'Bugger all, really. Caleb's gotta stay in town and report to the police daily. In other words, he's out on bail. They've taken Soph's mobile and laptop, and will be investigating her finances if appropriate…'

'What's that supposed to mean?'

'They suspect a fiscal motive for her death.'

'In plain English?'

'Someone topped her for her money.'

'Ah. Who?'

'That would be me.'

'Got a wodge of insurance on her, have you?'

'As if. We were living hand to mouth. We made enough to get by, pay the bills.'

'So no massive savings squirreled away.'

'No, all she had was this.' Caleb waved an arm around.

'Worth enough to kill for, is it?'

'Get real. Anyway, she was a generous lady. She wanted us to share. She said so.'

'And the police didn't take the trash.'

'Not according to this.'

'So, who did empty that bin?'

'Search me. I suppose the fuzz cleared everyone out when they came here. I certainly didn't.'

'So, whatever it was, the letter's gone?'
'Must be.'
'What sort of letter was it?'
'Eh?'
'You know. Was it an official buff envelope about taxes and stuff, or was it private?'
'No, it wasn't a scary one. Anyway, Sophie was careful about official crap like that, bills and stuff. She kept records. As far as I can remember, it was large - like the ones you get with birthday cards. Sort of creamy, not white, you know?'
'Well, it wasn't a card. She would have kept it else. Put it on the mantel or something.'
'Tell, me, how much did Soph drink last night?'
'She had a glass or two of red. Then we toasted the baby with champagne. It was pink. I brought the ordinary kind, but I saw Sophie putting something else in it.'
'What?'
'Pomegranate juice, I think. There's the bottle, over there.'
Fee looked. It was pomegranate juice, right enough. In a little bottle that looked like a stack of three balls. Sophie was addicted to the stuff, and it was getting hard to find.
'She called you.'
'She calls everyone.'
'She sounded - well, the worse for wear.'
'No. We weren't that plastered. Couldn't have been, unless someone was slipping us Mickeys.'
'You sure? It's hard to tell when you're soused yourself.'
'Give it a rest, Fee. I've counted the bottles. It's all wine and fruit juice. Unless it was an exclusive party, no-one would have got much more than merry. And what if you did? You get drunk, you fall down, you wake up. You don't take a walk along the beach before dawn, alone.'
'Soph might have.'
'Did she take her camera?'
'No.'
'Did she wrap up? You can't take good pictures while you're shivering.'
'No.'

'Then this trip wasn't for art's sake. And if she wanted to see the sun come up, she was in the wrong place.'

'Maybe she wanted to be alone with her thoughts.'

'Then why traipse through the place? Why not just go out on the balcony? She loved the view from there.'

'I know. That's why she bought the loft in the first place.'

'I'm as flummoxed as you are.'

Zoe shared a glance with Fee. She ignored it.

'What will you do now? Stay here?'

Caleb looked around.

'I don't think I can. Too many memories. That's why I kept on moving.'

'You could come with us.'

'I don't think I can do that either. Not only do I have to stay in Falmouth and report to the police, I can hardly go and sleep in Sophie's old room, now can I? Feeling as I do.'

'Where will you stay, then?'

'Keith and Petra have a room they let out to tourists sometimes.'

'Call them, and see if they're amenable. Meanwhile, we'll tidy up a bit.'

'Can we do that? The fuzz might not like it being disturbed and all.'

'Frankly, I don't give a rat's arse about what the police may or may not want. They've had their chance. We can leave the trash in binbags so they can rummage through them to their little heart's content. I'm not leaving Soph's *cair* in this mess.'

'I'll get a mop.'

Keith and Petra were only too pleased to offer Caleb sanctuary. They would have called in any case, to offer. 'He shouldn't be alone right now,' Keith said, arriving in the middle of the cleanup and pitching in. Petra, meanwhile, was burning up the ether: Caleb's phone was ringing constantly. No sooner had he disconnected one call that someone else rang. Once the place was tidy, Keith bundled up the sheets for Petra to wash and headed out with Caleb. All he needed was in his haversack - he carried his home on his back like a snail before he settled with

Sophie, and maybe was looking to resume his wanderings. Fee and Zoe walked from the loft back to the police station: Fee wanted to clear her head and swallow her anger before encountering that detective again. Sophie was coming home for the last time as soon as it could be made possible.

This thankless task was made easier because the pathologist could find no evidence of malfeasance and was content to call it death by misadventure. Unless the police could turn up any evidence to the contrary before the inquest, and Fee was as certain as she could be about the likelihood of that (they were more likely to discover that hens were agents of some terrorist squad bent on world domination) the matter would be closed. She couldn't expect a pathologist to be able to find what she and Zoe had both concluded. A mete had been associated with Sophie's death. And police didn't believe in the metae.

Chapter Nineteen

The drive back had been uneasy. Zoe was bursting with questions that could neither be asked nor answered in present company. The funeral would be the day after tomorrow. They had been lucky there. The police saw no reason to keep the body (Body! Oh, Sophie, Sophie....) any longer. It would be described as death by misadventure. As it turned out, one of the partygoers wasn't as somnolent as the rest and had been up and about when Sophie left. Not that he had spoken to her, just seen her go out. And he knew Caleb had still been in bed, since he'd sneaked up to say 'Ta-ta' to him before going on his way. Caleb had been asleep, so the nice man had simply let himself out. Sophie would be a statistic, nothing more. Two doctors signed the certificate while they waited. The local crematorium had been available, and Family funerals were limited to immediate family otherwise the mass of cousins would be unmanageable. It had been Zoe's unparalleled skills at organization and ferocious energy that had made it possible. She had wheedled and bullied and delegated the entire afternoon until she had matters arranged to her personal satisfaction. It wasn't indecent haste anyway. In the days when corpses were routinely housed in someone's living space instead of a distant funeral home, it had become the norm to place the inconvenient if much beloved corpse in its final resting place as soon as possible. This world was for the living, not the dead. The dead have their own business to attend to and don't usually get offended by the speed with which their cast-offs are dealt with. Get it done, and dusted, and get on with the business of living. The dead are no longer your concern. Save your efforts for the living. In a small community it is generally easier to arrange a quick funeral than in a busy city. More people die in a crowded space than in a less highly populated one.

There was no resting place once they were home either. Wearied beyond endurance by the constant ringing of the phone, Fee had switched the ringer off and left the machine to take messages. That didn't stop the influx of people. She was grateful that Zoe hadn't done her usual trick of escaping upstairs to Computerland. No sooner had she disposed of one lot than another arrived. They used up all her energy. Zoe chased the last lot out, locked the door, drew the curtains, switched off the lights and retreated to the kitchen at the back of the house, refusing to answer the door any more. Fee joined her.

'I am drinking no more tea. Wine, or something stronger?'

'There's Voignier in the fridge. I put it there this morning.' Zoe rummaged for the corkscrew and filled one glass half full and another almost to the brim. 'There you go.'

'Will you say it, or will I?'

'Go on.'

'That smell on Sophie. It was mete.'

'Oh, yes.'

'But she still had all her blood. The pathologist said so. No marks, no damage. She died of hypothermia.'

'On a relatively warm night. She would have got cold, true, if she spent the night on that beach. She might well have needed medical attention after. But to die of it? No way.'

'A meten killing, but it didn't take her blood. Not enough to kill her, anyway.'

'This particular mete isn't after blood. I think he's after wraiths.'

'That's straight out of left field, Zoe. How did you come up with that?'

'It's what Amagus was doing.'

'You have a nasty habit of keeping things to yourself, Zoe. Would you care to explain so those of us who haven't opted for the meten lifestyle can comprehend?'

'Part of the ritual Amagus was working on involved the collection of wraiths.'

'That breaks down when you consider how few … beings know that much about Amagus.'

'What one person knows, another can find out.'

'Only from a mete. And, specifically, an *old* mete. Not one of your Jonnny-come-latelies, which rather restricts the list of perps firmly to the realms of the undead.'

'Back to Theo, then.'

'And gloves off this time. No, Zoe, I won't do it your way. I won't wheedle and coax my way through this one. A mete was intimately involved in my sister's death. It might even have killed her. In fact, I'm dam' sure certain. And if Sophie was killed by a mete, then Theo's foresworn.'

'What are you planning on?'

'I will bring down the wrath of the Ayen on the vampires. I will destroy every one of them. There will not be one undead standing when I am finished.'

'Nice plan. Is Theo going to stand still for this one?'

'He goes first.'

'And when will the slaughter start?'

'It's not slaughter. That's for living things. Tonight. I am going to confront Theo tonight.'

'You're tired, Fee.'

'You have no idea about how much strength I can get from the rage I'm feeling right now.'

'You realize that telling me this will mean he'll know you are coming?'

'I'm counting on it. You stay out of this, little sister. You stay out of it or I might decide to include you in my vendetta.'

'I'm not a meta, Fee.'

'Not yet. But you're on the way. And you've no idea how much that fact irritates me either.'

Zoe looked at her and saw the deadly conviction in her eyes.

'I'll get myself over to Tom's, then.' Her voice was flat, but there was no shaking Fee's resolve. Tonight is a good night to die, and I'm not about to do it myself.

Fee sat at the kitchen table, nursing her wine, listening to the sounds of Zoe's departure. She was on her own now. Time to prepare.

She rustled up an old, fat red candle, ink and heavy paper. A bowl of salt and a glass of water joined it on the kitchen table, along with a censer and a jar of incense which had been stored with the candle.

Fee took time over her personal preparations. When she returned to the kitchen, she was wearing a long black dress and heeled boots under her cloak. She had combed her hair carefully and painted her face. Bright red lipstick and heavy on the kohl and mascara. A Goth look. Tonight was going to be all about gothic horror.

She went through the motions of calling the spaca, then a triangle round the candle on the kitchen table. Incense rose from the bowl, wreathing her in tendrils. She lit the candle.

'Vassago. Vassago. Vassago.

'Master of truth and delusion, I call on you. Heed my call, and attend me.'

Wyth, Gya and cyscan. All the Fratris knew how to use the wyth, it was what set them apart. Most could call the Gya too, but only some of them extended their talents into the realms of cyscan. Rathing, weirding and calling were cyscan arts, and you needed the Skyen to use them. What Fee was doing now was pure cyscan, calling a being from another world into hers to help her. Oh, the worlds intersected, but generally carried on as if they didn't. But with wyth and Gya you could punch a hole between them and let things like this pass through. It had its cost though, and few Fratris chose to pay the price.

Carefully, she drew an oblong on the paper. In the oblong, a circle, and from that a line to two crescents. Two more crescents hung from the base of the oblong. Beneath the circle she wrote 'vassago'.

With her finger, she drew the same sign in the air above the candle flame, then lit the corner of the paper. As the flames licked up to consume the design, she spoke again.

'By earth and water, air and fire, I conjure thee.

'Great and holy Vassago. Vassago. Vassago.

'Descend from your abode. Bring your influence and presence into this place that I may behold you and enjoy your society and aid…………..

'By sun and moon and star do I conjure thee.

'Great and holy Vassago, Vassago Vassago.

'Who knows the secrets of Elanel and rides on the winds, and has the power to move between the worlds, come to this place and be present I pray you……….

'By Satandar and Ascentacer I conjure thrice three times.

'Great and holy Vassago. Vassago. Vassago.

'Descend and appear to me, speaking secrets of truth and understanding.'

She dropped the remains of the burning paper in the censer. The candle started to flare and flicker. Deep within the flame, a small figure appeared, growing larger and larger. By the time it was the size of a Barbie doll, she could make out its appearance. It was an old man in a long, dark robe. Grey hair hung round his hook-nosed face and behind his back. He had the look of a raptor about him, an eagle trying to pass for human and nearly making it. Under one arm he held a large book. You could never make out the details, but you were sure it was a book.

The figure was growing larger, but not taller. It was filling out, a full-sized, if slightly small man with a scholarly stoop, standing through the table, a ghostly form superimposed over the room.

Fee bowed her head, and scattered more of the incense on the charcoal.

'Welcome, lord Vassago, to this place. Thank you for answering my call.'

'*As if I had any choice.*' The thin voice was peevish. '*Why do you seek to interrupt my studies and summon me to this place?*' It was evident from his tone that 'this place' was not one he would choose to visit. It had undertones of the word 'slum'.

'Be nice, old man.'

'*Oh, you again, fire maiden. What is it this time? A lost slipper?*' One of Fee's first forays into Gramarie had been to summon this being to discover the exact whereabouts of a brooch. One of Lily's. One she had borrowed without permission, then lost. The old guy had come through, but had been none too pleased about it. Such minor matters were obviously below his notice, important as they were to the health of Fee's backside.

'I have need of your great talents, mighty lord.'

'*Obviously, or you would not have dragged me here. Get on with it.*'

'I require and command you accompany me, this night, and see into the mind of one I would confront on a weighty matter.'

'You do not need me for this. Your own talents see into men's minds.' He was always awkward.

'Into this mind I cannot see. He does not live.'

'Then summon him, silly child. Leave me in peace.'

'This one who does not live is not dead either.'

Now she had his interest. He was looking at her properly for the first time, and took the information right out of her head. He did that, and it was annoying.

'A vampire, Hhmm. I do not have much intercourse with those beings.'

Be grateful you don't. Oh, hey, you've got no blood to lose. Oops.

'I know what happened to your water girl. Why not ask me?' He was wheedling now. Oh, yes, he could tell her. But she had an ulterior motive. He caught that too, the bugger. *'Ah hah. So you will use me to force a vampire to do your dirty work for you? Intriguing. I find myself interested enough to indulge you. However, if your ploy backfires, do not come to me seeking the name of the one who did slay the red haired wench, for I will not tell you.'*

'Then I bind you to obey me and accompany me wheresoever I will go, and speak to me those things I would have you so speak, and not to leave my side until I dismiss you.'

'Then let us be on your way. The tides turn, the stars wheel. Much goes on which requires my attention. But your little ploy interests me, and I shall be fascinated to see if ..... you can pull it off.'

'Then come, and see.'

Fee swept past the table and out the door, leaving the candle to burn unattended. It would burn for hours and if she didn't get back within a couple of them, it wouldn't matter to her anyway if the entire cottage burnt to ashes.

Chapter Twenty

Ffion slammed the great double doors back as if they were plywood. They slammed into the walls and ricocheted back, the crash echoing a knell of doom. She marched through lamplit gloom toward the raised dais with the table and candelabra, the soft light throwing shadows over the gold and scarlet chair. Her heels tapped a staccato accompaniment to the soft rustle of her long cloak, swaying to and fro from her shoulders. There was a suppressed murmur of uncertainty among the vamps and their pashs on the divans and cushions that lined the walls on either side of the throne. She had been here before, but always as a courteous and wary visitor. This time she brought something else in her wake. Something they did not like, did not like one bit.

She stopped, clenching her fists at her sides. She let her cloak fall, hiding them, but she couldn't conceal the pure fury in her face, her eyes.

'All of you, out, now! I won't ask twice!' She did not need to raise her voice. The power, her wyth, was boiling in her blood, her body, brought to a white heat by her rage. It was riding in her wraithlight, snapping and cracking. Her eyes blazed with incandescent fury. Stray sparks ran down her hair, lifting it from her face and shoulders.

The vamps decided that they wanted no part of what she brought with her. Not now, at least. They melted out as silently as only vamps could.

'Dave! DAVE! Get out here, NOW!' She knew he was standing just behind her, slightly to the left. Silent and smooth as always.

'My name is Theo, kitten.' Such a soft, seductive voice. All velvet and rose petals. Velvet scratches when rubbed the wrong way, and roses have thorns.

'Your name, at the moment, is immaterial.' She turned, slapping her hand on his chest, on the white, white shirt that almost glowed in the subdued lighting. The slap had echoes that it shouldn't have. Theo tried to move back, but Ffion's hand held him as if she had welded it to his body. 'I will ask you once, and once only. WHICH ONE OF YOUR SCUM KILLED SOPHIE?'

'Let's bring it down to Defcon Three, kitten.'

'Don't irritate me now, Theo, I'm not in the mood for it. From where I'm standing, you are Ground Zero. At this moment, I don't care one way or the other how this ends. Answer the question.' Sparks trailed out of her hair, down her arm and hand and onto Theo's shirt. Charred dots appeared on the white, white linen. He didn't even look down. His shadowed eyes held hers in regard as the Gya flared in them.

'Once, we were almost friends.'

'We had an agreement. You left us alone, we left you alone. Mostly. Those days are *over*, Theo. THIS IS WAR. I will bury you, all of you. I will lay waste to you, for what you and yours have done to me and mine.'

Finally, he met her eyes.

'I swear to you, by any oath you care to call, that I have no knowledge of this.'

Fee looked at him, hard. Vamps, in general, you did not trust beyond the eyes of your sight. But this vamp had been a friend of her grandmother's. And that counted for something. Even now. The invoked power told her he was not lying. She could not read his aura: the dead had no aura to read. But Vassago could read the dead and he was reading this vamp cold. Truth.

He moved, ever so slightly.

'Please, Lady. You know I can't love, but a world with no Sophie is darker to me than you could imagine. I saw you both born. Please, let us talk of this. No metet of mine would harm Sophie: they, at least, still fear my wrath.'

That Theo would lapse back into archaisms, and use two pleases in the same sentence meant that he was distressed. Well, in as much distress as an undead could get, anyway. Fee racked the power down a notch.

'A vamp killed Sophie. The reek was all over her, even in the morgue. Yours are the only vamps here: you wouldn't tolerate another vamp on your hunting grounds.'

'Tell me, Ffion, how any mete could kill Sophie? When she

drew her wyth about her, none of us could touch her, not even with so much as a fingertip. She always knew when we were abroad, just as you do. You know we kill rarely these days. Your grandmother could not, would not, allow wanton killing. And there are more willing victims.' He grimaced. That there were wannabee mete who would rip open their blouses, oh yes, shirts and t-shirts, too, and invite the undead to feast on them in the vain hope that one undead might take a shine to them and convert them into the ranks of the immortals was a sad fact of life. That no vamp worth his or her immortal blood would even consider for a moment making most of them into companions of Eternity did not seem to matter. They craved the small notoriety that came with being a living lunchbox, bathing in the glamour that the vamps spread about themselves like honey on toast. No, to get to be a vamp you had to be special, as Sophie had been special. This Blyd would not have killed Sophie, they would have visited the Metargh on her. And she would have hated it. Fee knew that. All this force was not for killing: it was for cutting through the crap that vamps threw up in front of you. She killed the power.

Fee drew back her hand gently. Theo looked down at the charred pinholes on his shirt, then up at her.

'Shit. That *hurt.*'

Fee comforted her hand, trying not to wince.

'You are telling me.'

'But confrontations are such fun. I haven't felt power like that in years, not since your great-grandmother came and laid down the law to me in this very spot. She ruined more than my shirt, though.'

'I wasn't really trying.'

'I could tell. Do you think you scared them enough, or shall we play some more?'

They had been watching. Of course. Right up until the consideration of the lunchboxes, then they had gone, as Theo had commanded them. He caught on fast for a Renaissance guy.

'So which one of your kind killed Sophie?'

Theo strolled over to a small table at the foot of the dais, shucking his shirt as he walked. He gestured elegantly to Fee, pulling out a chair and smiling with his lips, so the fangs didn't show. He had barely sat down himself when Cecile appeared with a clean shirt in one hand and a teatray in the other

'Orange pekoe, I believe.' She smiled, her fangs showing. Well, she was just shy of three hundred, and slight social gaffes were acceptable in such a young immortal. She placed the tray on the table and snagged another chair. 'I'll be Mother, shall I?'

'Thank you, Cecile.'

Cecile poured three cups of tea, and offered a plate of tiny cakes round. Fee took one. Theo did not.

'Can we drop the Dave? It is so insulting. A vampire called Dave. Really.'

This was more than surreal.

'Leave it, Cecile. Ffion knows my name. Such petty concerns are irrelevant. Sophie is dead. Ffion believes a mete killed her. I believe Ffion. This is what is relevant. Relevant to the revenant.' Theo inhaled the aroma from his teacup, lifting it to his face with evident appreciation. 'I prefer this to Earl Grey. Too much borage, not enough camellia for my taste.'

'Stop it, Theo. You are making Ffion choke on her tea. If it was a mete, then they would have magical help. No mete could take a farer like Sophie, not alone. And whoever it was, they do not fear you.'

'Not so small a list as it once was. My metae will by now be spreading the word that Sophie is dead, and that Ffion has accused us. Everyone who knows us, knows that I would not leave Sophie's killer alone for long. I watched her sleep, her very first sleep, after she was born. I am bonded to this bloodline, as you all are, through me. If any mete knows anything, they will know to inform me of what they know, or I will be displeased. Between a displeased Hegarsa and an irritated farer, there will be no rest between earth and sky. Ffion need not concern herself with wasting this metet. I will do it myself.'

'Back of the queue, mongrel. This is Fratris business. You only get to kick the corpse when I've finished with it.'

'And I will not be far behind. Without Sophie, I would still be wearing a crinoline, or a bustle.'

'You are only wearing a nightgown now.'

'It's traditional. I hate black anyway. But you can keep those cantilevered bras, thank you. How you mortals can wear them I do not know.'

The nightdress was an affectation. Cecile loved vampire movies, though she had refused to watch Van Helsing all the way through. The very idea of a werewolf being superior to a vampire in any respect, she was not prepared to tolerate. Otherwise, she would have been bitten by a were, not a mete, she sniffed.

'So, are any of the Blyd missing right now?' Ffion asked, sipping her tea.

'Vincent is in Italy, visiting his Strega. She must be over ninety by now, but none-the-less he cleaves to her as if she still was that raven haired beauty he seduced these seventy years past. Andre is in Nice, at the festival, hunting for film stars. One day, he may even catch one. Reiza is with him. All the rest are, so to speak, at home.' Cecile cast a long-suffering glance at Theo, who sighed theatrically.

Metae were traditionally lone hunters. They did not share anything much willingly. A meten, discovering another immortal in his or her territory, would chase them off with a disturbing singleness of purpose. A bit like robins, really. Although robins rarely killed each other: they had enough sense to leave the field of combat to the victor when beaten by a greater show of strength. A vamp was more likely to come back and dispute the matter. One would usually die, and it would be bloody. Quite unlike robins, in fact. A Hegarsa might make a mete and keep them close by for a while but the bonds rarely endured. It would sooner or later end in the meten version of divorce. There was usually blood involved in these events somewhere, which made Cecile and Theo's association exceptional - especially so since they kept a large number of their kind with them, apparently without too much infighting. Ffion, in a typically adolescent show of curiosity, had asked why. It was apparently a very rude question. Cecile had marched off in a huff. Theo had chosen to answer.

'It was Rina's doing. Cecile had been unwilling that I had tried to seduce her. she feared that Rina would replace her in my eyes. She would have been right.' Theo was showing uncharacteristic honesty and insight. Ffion had caught him at the right moment: he was feeling nostalgic. Just provided he didn't go back to Ancient Greece and his conquests there. 'After she bested me, she could either dominate me or be rid of me. She explained that either way would have been wrong. Sending me away would just give the problem to someone else, not solve it. Had she dominated me, she would have been responsible for me, my actions, my feeding, my killing. And one day she would die, the problem would pass on to someone else: neither would this solve the problem. So she sought another way. One that would leave me responsible not only for my actions, but also of those of my kind, thus solving her problem for her. No metet had ever thought of it before. She laughed, did Rina. She said to me, you were alive before the Galilean walked the earth, and know so little of your own nature? Yes, we need blood, human blood. There is no substitute. But more than this, even more, we need to seduce our victims. We need them to love us, because we cannot feel that for each other. Yes, we killed for blood alone too, a cold kill, hunger only. But we feel a different hunger. Hunger for the chase. To cut a victim out of the herd, to slowly, over the weeks and months, gradually weaken them until they die. To seduce them until they give the blood willingly. This willingly given blood sustains us far longer than the blood of a victim killed cold. This was the key. Sustenance. The blood flowing in our living, willing victims still flows in their veins when they arise from the first sleep after the Metargh. And continues to flow. But we did not, then, seek blood from the newly arisen. Nor did we again share our blood with them after the first Changing. Rina suggested we might like to try. 'Never try, never know,' she said to me. And the look on her face then was mysterious, like love. So I shared again with Cecile, and she with me. It was a revelation. Her blood sustained me as ever it had. More so. I lost my hunger, as did she.'

'So you no longer hunt humans?' the young Ffion had asked, her eyes round.

Theo had laughed. 'No, my kitten, that is a game we cannot abandon. It is so delicious, so absorbing. To catch the glance of a bright eye in the crowd. To draw them to us. To touch, to see, to breathe the air around them, taste their aura, their essence. To taste their skin with our lips, the salt, the sweet, the hint of blood.

The pulse in the vein, the warmth of the skin......' Lily had interrupted them at that point. 'Don't you go corrupting her, Theo, at her age! She's much too young for such strong meat.' Theo had laughed again, and Ffion couldn't get another word out of him. She got the rest of the story second-hand from Sophie. She drank in every word.

'They get the biggest kick out of seduction. The harder the chase, the sweeter the fruit, Theo said. And fratten, he said, fight hardest of all: they hate to give it up. So, the metae try harder with fratten. The idea of an Immortal lifespan doesn't have the same pull on us as it does to other humans, and we live our lives harder, live more in our skin than they do, apparently. That makes us prime targets. Apparently, a mete who seduces a Fratten gets something really special out of it, that's why Theo went after granny. She was a real looker then. They always go for the special ones, Theo said, that's why the wannabees have no chance. They don't play the game. They give it up too easily. It's no fun. What did he say: 'A farer is special fruit. The consummate prey. The worthy adversary. So strong, so full of life to the ends of her fingertips. So aware of the life in them, to drain it is... wickedly arousing.''

'He said that? Wickedly arousing?'

'They are supposed to be the bad boys after all. Every girl loves a bad boy. Maybe she thinks she's going to be the one to change him. How the hell you are supposed to change a vamp I don't know. Get them to give up immortality and live on salad greens?' Sophie was on a diet for her spots. She went on to explain that Theo had instigated 'The Blood Rite' every year, on the twentieth day of January, in honour of Rina. It had been her birthday. 'I would have preferred to have it on the day she died. But she would not have it. It was an affirmation of life, she said, life in this world, not the next. She chided me for my vanity. I did not understand her then. I do now. I was wary of her in life, and now she is dead, she scares the pants off me. She invades my dreams. She would have made the consummate meta.' It was the highest accolade that Theo could offer. He did not regard that being made a mete was a tragedy. It could, however, become tedious. Some centuries were, to put it simply, boring. The first

Blood Rite had been a runaway success. The tribe Theo had called to him had been overwhelmed by the bloody eroticism that had stunned them out of a centuries-old torpor. It had given a new dimension to what it was to be meten. Now it was becoming fashionable amongst the other metae. It had its own name now: The Ophosis. Envious of his thriving, while the rest of them languished on the fringes of the busy, teeming world, this started to breed discontent. Theo had to defend his territory more than once. Rina had advised him to share the secret. Not all of it, naturally, so it left him an edge. He was regarded in some portions of the meten world as a sort of Messiah. He laughed at that. 'Just so long as they don't try to sacrifice me. That would really be boring. It has been done before. I require the novel, the new, the untried.' A word, coming from Theo, opened all sorts of doors - some of which you weren't sure ever should be opened.

'Grandma did.'

'Did what?'

'Changed a meta.'

'I will go and see if any of the other blyds have a rogue.' Cecile stood up. 'I will need clothes.' If there was one thing about Cecile which annoyed Theo, it was her attitude to clothes. Since the Sophie makeover, Cecile brought clothes, wore them a few times until she was bored with them, and then stored them in closets. He was forever buying new closets for Cecile's castoffs. When boredom set in, Cecile had no further interest in the garments. Attempts to get her to sell them - on EBay, for instance - were fruitless. It was not as if she or Theo needed the money, and Cecile did not shop at Primark. But she was not in any way attached to the clothes. Ffion's first business suit had been 'a little number from Gap' in deep midnight blue generously donated by Cecile herself. Ffion had paid for it to be cleaned, carefully omitting to tell Cecile. It wasn't that the suit was in any way soiled. To the eye, it was still as perfect as it had been when Cecile first unwrapped it. The only odour it held was a hint of Nina Ricci. But to Ffion, it had the aura of meten, faint but unmistakable. It set her teeth on edge the first time she tried it on. Thankfully, a professional clean banished the taint. Surprised and pleased, Ffion had stored this fact away for future reference. Would dry cleaning fluids harm metae? One never knew when a small fact like that could turn the tables to one's advantage in a nasty situation. The theory remained untested. One didn't ask one's friends to hold still while you poured the equivalent of acid over them in the spirit of scientific enquiry.

That gift had sown the seeds of discontent in Zoe.

'Look, Zoe, if you really like that Ozzie Clarke dress, tell Cecile. I'm sure she will let you have it.'

'Okay, But I'll need to grow a bit first. Cecile's got a bigger bust than me. Everyone's got a bigger bust than me, including Damon.'

'Very well. But kiss me first.' Theo reached out an arm to Cecile, and tilted his head back. She lowered her face to his, and their lips met. A thin trickle of blood ran from their mouths over Theo's face.

'Uh uh, kids. Cue for me to depart if you're going to get jiggy. The idea of watching you two writhing over each other is not one I care to entertain.'

'Nor one I would willingly offer.' Cecile carefully wiped the blood off her face with one finger and sucked it off, slowly and sensuously. Ffion left them like that, a pair of cats sharing the cream. Ugh.

Chapter Twenty-one

Zoe seemed neither relieved nor satisfied to learn when she returned to Pippin Cottage that Fee hadn't spent the night in a glorious orgy of slaughter, but had been getting tea and cakes instead. Oh, and incidentally getting Cecile to cater for the funeral. What's the use of having friends if you don't put them to good use when you need them? The idea of spending the day baking and shopping and chopping up lumps of bread into little triangles with tomato and ham and chicken in them, when you can get a pal to deliver said comestibles to your door is to deny the gifts god gave you in the first place. Your ability to make friends. And since the whole village would be coming - try to keep them out by saying 'Family only' would be a waste of breath - there would be a lot of sandwiches.

Zoe was punishing Fee for last night's subterfuge by not speaking to her. Fee bore the punishment bravely. The full house of curiosity beats the broken flush of pique any day of the week. It would stop anyway once Lily arrived at about eleven o'clock. Dilys wouldn't consider making Lily do the trip in one hop without an ambulance, and that was beyond even Zoe's powers of persuasion to produce at such short notice. The cortège would arrive with Sophie over by the church at about half-past one, and would stay there until two o'clock and the mourners would meet it by the lytch-gate. That would give them an hour and a half to get to the crematorium. The local vicar would give an address by the hearse. Although the Harris family did not attend the local church on any regular basis, they were a part of the parish, and the parish wished to pay their respects to one of their own. If the village wanted to give them a sendoff, well, okay. Tom and Ellen would come. Matt would go to the hospital to be with Luke. Jean would stay behind with Margie, then pop over to put the kettle on ready for the family to come back. Her and the rest, thought Fee. We will be returning to a reception committee. And no doubt Theo will put in an appearance, as will Cecile if she hasn't gone already.

After she had left the meta's enclave, Fee had gone home to put out the candle which had mercifully not totally destroyed her home. And, incidentally, to banish the hired help.

'*Most diverting,*' Vassago had commented. Fee had tried to get some hint from him as to the identity of Sophie's killer, but the old git had been adamant. He had merely taken his leave, saying only, '*He will discover you all too soon.*' Unhelpful sod.

Dilys and Lily arrived on schedule. Zoe emerged from her self-imposed exile for the orgy of hugging and a light lunch. Soul food: chicken soup and fresh bread. Dilys vanished to check that all was in order at Claire's. It was a modern bungalow, and Fee had cheerfully usurped it since Claire showed no signs of returning from France just yet. Getting Lily upstairs would have been possible, but Lily herself had vetoed the idea of staying at Pippin Cottage. 'It's only for one night. No need for domestic upheavals if there is an alternative.'

Once the kitchen was tidy again, Lily turned to Zoe.

'And now for some mother-daughter quality time. I am sure you have things that need your attention elsewhere, my girl. I will talk to you later. Run along now.' Her smile took the sting out of what was really a curt dismissal. It had taken them some time to get used to the new Lily, with her slightly stilted speech and the lack of affect. Underneath that was their mother, and she loved them as she always had.

'When are you bringing Greg to meet me? Girls usually bring their boyfriends home.'

Fee looked out of the window. She didn't want to meet Lily's eyes. They saw too much.

'He's been asking.'

'Then bring him.'

'Not yet.'

'Not sure?' Lily reached round, touching Fee's face, bringing their eyes together. 'It's there, all right. Why does my daughter not bring her lover to meet her mother? Scared I'll steal him from you?'

Lily was still beautiful, but she was teasing. Fee swallowed. It was like trying to choke down a lump you hadn't chewed properly.

'He isn't Fratten, Mum.'

'You so sure? You hide it well. Think no-one is as good as you at it?'

Fee couldn't answer. Her throat hurt, burning. Soon there would be tears. Did she really love Greg that much? Lily drew back into her wheelchair.

'He's a true Ross, you know. On his father's side.'

'What!!! How do you know?'

'Do you think I sit in this wheelchair, day after day, doing nothing? Do you think only Zoe knows how to use the Internet? That I cannot use the telephone? That I am not interested in my Family, simply because I can't walk? It's my legs that don't work, girl, not my mind. The first time you mentioned Greg, I took the time to get to know him. In ways you did not. You can be very ignorant at times. I am almost ashamed of you. You were going to fuck him, and leave him, weren't you?'

'Yes.' How that hurt.

'Because he didn't demonstrate, to someone he hardly knew, that he was wythen? Of a Fratris family? That he hid it, as you did?'

'Yes.'

'Then thank the Ayen for the Mothers Mafia, my girl. Greg's been talking about you. To his father. Who told his mother. Who is related to a Howe. Who told another Howe. Who told me.'

'What?'

'Your Greg is as wythen as you are, you silly girl. Both of you dancing around each other, careful not to slip up, not to let it out. Anyone would think that we are ashamed of what we are, the way we hide from each other. I wonder now how we ever managed to breed.' She shifted uncomfortably, and gazed out of the window at the leaves falling on the back lawn. 'Since you have been so negligent in your duty to your mother, I called his mother myself.'

'You asked him over here already? For the funeral?' Fee was indignant. Not even mothers ought to interfere between a girl and her swain.

'I did not. I suspected there was something like this. Your father and I tiptoed around each other for months before we finally admitted to each other the family secret. I suggest that you move things on with Greg before I get impatient and take matters into my own hands, which I suspect you will not like.' She started to manoeuvre the wheelchair past the table, making for the door. Fee reached to grasp the handles, but Lily waved her off. 'No, no. I can manage very well on my own. I am not yet incapable of independent locomotion.'

'Incapable' and 'Lily' were like 'military' and 'intelligence'. They just didn't go together. Didn't go together at all. Lily angled her wheelchair at the door.

'You can come down now, we've finished.'

'Mum, Zoe doesn't need to listen behind doors in here. She's got the place wired for sound.'

'And video. Never forget the video. You'll like Greg, mum.' Zoe was half way down the stairs and accelerating. 'Pity I couldn't send you a picture.'

'You mean you've.... told... been colluding with mum....' Fee stuttered.

'Oh, yes. Noticed it as soon as I saw him. But I've always been better than you at scouting talent, and you wouldn't have listened to me. So I told mum.'

'Close your mouth, girl. You look stupid, standing there gawping like a fish out of water. Now you can go upstairs and spy on your sister if you like, while I find out exactly what she's got herself into with our charismatic vampire. Oh no, my girl, don't try to wiggle out of it. I have eyes in my head, and it is very apparent that you have been sucking at the immortal fount again. I am not about to condemn you for it: I am about to advise you. Sometimes you can be too clever for your own good. What's done is done. I am sure you had your reasons. Maybe I would not have agreed with them, but it's your life after all. Away with you, Fee.'

She scooted the wheelchair back to the table and waited for them to obey her.

Whatever Lily said to Zoe would remain secret. Fee didn't share

Zoe's enthusiasm for eavesdropping. It left her feeling faintly soiled. Anyway, she had other things to chew on. Why had Greg not reacted to her tats? Everyone in the Frais had tats. Okay, so maybe other Fratten didn't go in for such elaborate skin decoration, not having a talent like Tom's around. Tom, who could see the pictures your mind's eye weaves on your flesh and seal it there, under the skin, in ink forever. Getting the Mark was part of the Ritual. All the Fratten had the ritual, so why was Greg's body unmarked? She had seen every square inch of skin with her own eyes and fingers. And other things. Unless the wily sod had the Mark under his hair? There were certainly some burning questions that needed to be asked and answered. Had he, too, been looking for a Fratten to share his life with? Did he know that she was, like him, different? If so, why had he not spoken? Was it her fault? Had she concealed her apartness so well that even in the throes of passion, she had not let anything slip? Why? Lily was right, the Fratten were too far up their own arses for their own good sometimes. So what if someone let something slip? Unless you were Fratten yourself, you'd hardly notice it. And if you did, a little chymer could gloss over the 'oops!' moment and the partner would not remember. Bugger, bugger and bugger. Greg had been as good at subterfuge as she was. Which was a good indication of his own abilities. All of a sudden, she wished that Lily had invited him down today after all.

At last, the funeral cortege had arrived, and they were ready for the off. Tom eased Lily into the car, and the village waved them off. At least the vicar had kept his eulogy to the bare minimum, and Sophie's coffin was buried in flowers. It had arrived unadorned. What use had the dead for flowers? The living knew very well how much they missed the departed, and the Fratris saw no reason to advertise that fact with art, floral or otherwise. No, the flowers were from the villagers, their tribute to Sophie's life, and that of her unborn child. How that little snippet had got out was beyond Fee. Maybe Sophie had confided in her friends? That didn't matter now.

It was a quiet drive down through the fields and moors to the crematorium. Caleb and Sophie's artist friends would meet them there, and some would come back to the cottage. The rest had other ideas, mostly including getting stinking drunk back in Falmouth. Sophie would be missed.

Caleb had chosen the music. Snow Patrol, was it? Fee's musical knowledge seemed to stutter and die in the mid-seventies for some reason. 'If I lay here... If I just la-ay here…. Would you lay with me, and just forget the world….' There were some speeches: really, it can't be avoided. If someone's determined to say something, best let them get on with it. 'Go laughing….. Go dancing…. Go flying home….' Fee tried hard for no tears. Sophie had said, 'if anyone cries at my funeral, I will come back and haunt them. And I won't be nice.' The best thing that could be said for the funeral was that it was quiet and short. They trickled out into the wan sunlight to the lilt of The La's There She Goes….

There were hugs and kisses and tears after, and promises of eternal friendship that would peter out before the week was over. Caleb had kissed Fee's cheek, shook hands with Lily and embraced Zoe, then stood back to let the wash of Sophie's friends engulf them. The family loaded themselves back into the cars for the journey home, and the procession wended a weary way back into an early darkness. Clouds were boiling over the sky, heavy and threatening. Perfect.

Home felt….. empty. Oh, there were bodies. Bodies, and noise and voices. It had been Dilys who had, finally, ushered everyone out into the gathering night. Fee was running on empty by then, and Zoe had gone upstairs to cry. That or say something she might regret later.

'Bloody seagulls, that's what they are. They sweep in from afar, make an horrendous noise, shit on everything and eat all the sandwiches,' she commented on the way up. Fee had to admit that she agreed with the sentiment. Greg had called on her mobile after the service. He had wanted to come down that night, that much was obvious. 'We've got a lot to talk about, you and me.' Had they ever. How much would she share? How much could she? All of it? Strange deaths, metae? 'Leave explanations to me,' Lily had said before getting out of the car. Perhaps that would be best.

Eventually even Lily had to admit defeat, asking Fee to take her to her bed.

'Take me to my rest. I find I am quite exhausted. You must help me to Claire's since I am to stay there. Foolish, the girl taking herself off to the Continent at a time like this. Dilys has already taken my things over. I find I need assistance with the wheelchair, if you please.' There was no 'if you please' about it. It was a royal decree. If Lily wanted to be wheeled over to Claire's, then she would be, will-they, nil-they. Fee had hardly returned when a figure appeared at the gate.

'Lemme in, will-ya.'

It was Brenda the would-be vampire.

Chapter Twenty-two

Fee might have expected Theo, or even Cecile. But not in a million years Brenda. She looked almost normal, if skin-tight black jeans and a t-shirt with a fanged skull across the tits were normal. But there was a wildness about her eyes, an erratic halt to her movements. Something was going down that was urgent and unwelcome.

'Enter, and be at peace.'

It was always wise to be serious around metae. Even if they weren't really fully fledged bloodsuckers yet. Brenda bolted into the parlour and sank into a chair. Under the brighter lights, her face looked sunken, with white lines around her mouth. She was seriously scared, and when a girl used to being around the seriously scary was troubled, then something really catastrophic was happening.

'It's Theo. He's gone doolally. Apeshit. Cracked. Loopy. Batty. He's sent everyone away. Last I saw, he was breaking the furniture.' She was crying, actually crying. 'He was screaming. All in foreign. Then he told us to get out. All of us. Lauren tried to talk to him, and he threw her into the wall. He threw her so hard the stones cracked. We ran for it then. Bevan told me to come here and ask you…..'

'Ask me what?'

'If you could, you know, do anything……..'

Yeah. Die.

'Where's Cecile?'

'She's gone. At least, she wasn't there to see Theo breaking the walls.'

Zoe chose this moment to rejoin the party. Fee was surprised by the relief she felt to see her. Neither sister was a match for a meta in a frenzy, but both together……..

'Okay, we'll go over. Now, tell me everything.'

'After you came by, you know, he got very upset……..'

'And started on the furniture?'

'Not then. No, he went all quiet like, and just sat there. Wouldn't answer anyone. Then he said, If any of you know aught about this, you will tell me now.'

'And there was a great shaking of heads, right?'

'Yeah. No-one admitted to anything. Then Lyo pipes up.........'

'Lyo?'

'Lionel. You don't know him. He came down recently from up North. Don't know where he's from, y'know? Said there had been a witch-killing in Aberdeen. Then he just shut up. Theo just, like, fixed on him, kept firing all these questions. Lyo refused to answer. Just kept stchum, y'know? Then Theo was right in front of him, yelling and shouting. Lyo just shakes his head. Then he orders us all out. Go, go, he says. This Byld is no more. I am betrayed, and my fate is sealed. Last thing I heard was Lauren hitting the wall.......It was horrible.'

'Have you any place to stay tomorrow?'

'Bevan's got a place on the coast. He was going to get transport.'

That would be polite for steal a car. Theo might have wheels, but anyone purloining them at the moment ran a real and serious risk of having their head torn off, like as not.

'Then what?'

'Before he went off on one, Theo asked me to go visit Simon Lake. Check him out, like.'

'And you'll still do that?'

'Theo hasn't told me not. And the way he is, I don't want him going off on me. Anyway, there's bugger all else for me to do.'

'Where did Bevan tell you to meet him?'

'Over by the church, in that gate thing. Look, if I give you my mobile number, can you let me know what's happening?'

'All right. But don't expect too much too soon. I'm not at all sure what we can do.' Except, perhaps, die. There it is again. Lovely thought. At least we're dressed for it.

Zoe hustled Brenda out. When she came back, Fee handed her her cloak.

'What's the plan?'

'I haven't got one. I'm hoping he'll have run out of steam by the time we get there.'

'Fat chance.'

'Beautiful. Well, if this goes wrong, it's been nice knowing you.'

'Cow. You nicked my line. How's this for a plan. I'll distract him so you can clobber him.'

'How is that supposed to help?'

'It's better than nothing. We need him, Fee.'

'Why is this all happening to me? Why right now?'

'Can you think of anyone else you'd trust with this?'

'No. And that includes you. You are far too close to that vamp for my comfort.'

'Lily's okay with it.'

'She's Lily, and I'm me. Okay, let's go and see how far up the wall Theo's got. You'd better have something really special ready to grab his attention if he's as bad as Brenda says he is.'

'On the other hand, it might send him right over.'

'In which case, feel free to say I told you so.'

It was a fairly wild night out. The wind was gusting, scudding evil bruised clouds over a glowering sky before it sank into an eerie calm. It was hotter than it ought to be, too, and it was destined to get even hotter. After a short silence, Zoe spoke again.

'It doesn't worry you, does it, that Theo's like as not killing this Lyo?'

'Not in the slightest. I'd watch with complete equanimity.'

'And scoff choccies?'

'Oh yes. I might wince occasionally.'

'Only when you bit down on a hard centre. So why are we taking the walk of doom?'

'How well you know me,' Ffion murmured. 'Since you ask, if this Lyo knows something, I want that knowledge.'

'At any price?'

'Well, no. But if I wasn't going, you'd be off on your own, right?'

'How well you know *me*. But I've got advantages you haven't.'

'You sure of that?'

Zoe pursed her lips.

'About ninety percent, yes.'

'Well, I'm the other ten percent.'

They could hear Theo wrecking his residence from outside the barn. By the screech of rending timbers and occasional thud of heavy stones, he was making a thorough job of it. Fee reconsidered her state of sanity. It was well past insane to confront any creature who was capable of wholesale destruction, and by the sound of it, Theo was being ecumenical. If it was capable of being broken, he was breaking it, including acrows and rolled steel joists. He would hardly notice two farers until it was way too late. Oh well.

The double doors were hanging off their hinges. The massive table that had squatted on the dais had been thrown clear across the room and through them. They climbed over the wreckage gingerly.

'My my. He has been a busy boy,' Zoe was looking at the trail of destruction. 'I think he's starting on the bedroom.' She winced as a particularly loud crash coincided with plaster falling off the back wall. Zoe led the way past blocks of masonry and splintered timbers. If the internet failed him, Theo could find work demolishing skyscrapers.

Theo was in the bedroom. So was the bed. The rest of the furniture was beyond redemption. He heard them enter, and wheeled to face them. Zoe backed up a step. The urbane, slightly bored facade was gone. In that place was a monster. A snarling monster with icy fangs, and he was drooling. He was crouched half over, his hands clawing by his thighs. No trace of humanity remained: what they saw was pure undead, arrested in motion before awful violence took hold. The first shift, the first faint motion, would be enough to unleash a rage that could, in all probability, be terminal.

Dark, glittering eyes, shaded by heavy lowering brows, focussed on Fee. It was enough to stop your breath, those eyes, and the insensenate rage behind them. A rage that had been leashed and collared for more than twenty centuries was making up for lost time. Some idiotic scientist in ancient times had suggested that, with a lever long enough, and a firm place on which to stand, he could move the earth itself. Even that lever would not be long enough to separate them from the meta now. Theo was in a world beyond levers and firm ground. He was wading through the morass of madness. The next breath would initiate an Armageddon of fangs and blood. All their blood. Theo wasn't in a sharing mood.

'Sherintzemath! Sie'sy t'fasti. Non benyan' mi!'

The monster that had been Theo swung round, his attention caught by the words Zoe had spoken. It was all Fee could do not to look as well, since the beat of wyth in the syllables was as subtle as a kick in the groin. She kept her attention in the danger zone.

'Sie'sy t'fasti. Non benyan' mi,' Zoe repeated. 'Non benyan' mi.'

Fee found an inkling of sense in the alien words. Turn your face to me. Do not betray me.

Theo looked up from his crouch, and began to straighten.

'Ni be Val. Ni, nie be Val.' You are not she.

'Ni, ni. Mi' ont te shanath.' no, no, I am your little one.

There was a fustle of fabric. A gleam of interest dawned in the depths of Theo's eyes. A tiny trickle of sanity. He straightened up, but the face was still the face of the monster. Where the hell ever Zoe had dredged those words from, they had reached him. But they were far, far from safe. Safe was the far away country. It was practically unreachable now.

He started to move towards Zoe. Fee turned slowly, tracking him. Zoe was standing, tall, proud and utterly naked in a puddle of cloth. That had got this attention, right enough. Fee wasn't even sure he was fully aware of her, right at this moment.

Just before he reached Zoe, Fee swung her staff in front of his throat. Where it approached his skin, it began to glow with an actinic light, making the lines and hollows of his face even more evil. He stopped, blinked, and slowly looked round at her. There was something in his eyes that she had never seen there before. The bored, amused dilettante was gone. It was the look in the eyes of a velociraptor in the heat of the hunt. No pity, no mercy. Ancient cunning and hunger and power. All illusion had been stripped from Theo, and they were seeing him as he really was, for the first time. This creature had sat on the shabby chairs in their front room and told them tales of ancient Rome, of Greeks and Gauls, Vikings and Vandals. Of Kublai Khan and ancient Cathay, the Renaissance, and the glory of Mother Russia before the communist decay.

'Now, you see me. You see me. Me.' The voice was rough, wet. He was making no apology for what he was, but there was a tiny tinge of regret in that voice. The relationship had changed, forever. Now, whenever they saw him, no matter what face he wore, they would see this behind it.

'I see you. Theo.' It was Zoe who answered. She was using wyth in her voice, probably to stop it shaking. She met his eyes. 'And, now, you will see *me*.'

Whatever Zoe was making Theo see, Fee could only guess at. All she could see was the sixteen year old Zoe. Theo was seeing something different. Zoe had said that after she had shared with Theo, things looked different. Perhaps only metae could see what she was showing him.

She reached up one hand, her palm towards him. He mirrored the gesture, their hands an inch or so apart.

'So. You do see me.'

'But she does not. Neither will she, unless she follows the path I have taken.'

What were they seeing in each other? Where was this going? That face turned to her now.

'And will you see me?'

She was missing something here. Something important. Rina had sent Zoe to Theo, and she had known very well what would come of it. So much of this was Rina's game…… How could she play, and win, if she did not take this risk? Should she take it, even? An echo of Rina's voice: 'You must become the hunter.' Did she mean this? *This?* Metae were the consummate hunters: lethal, cunning, patient and sly. She made up her mind.

'I will see you.' And how, she asked, were they to do that? Frolicking with Theo while Zoe was there was not an option. Neither was sending Zoe home alone. 'What has happened, that you should do this?' She gestured at the wreck of the room.

Theo's eyes fixed on a puddle of shadows by the wall. Fee couldn't see what was hidden in the shrouds of darkness.

'I heard something I thought never to hear. I have been betrayed by my own blood, and Rina is both the cause and result of it.' He stalked over to the wall. Reaching down, he dragged a bloody and broken form into the uncertain light. There was a faint groan from the tattered mass. 'This,' Theo said, letting the body drop to the stones with a wet thump, 'is Lyo. Tell them what you told me.' He kicked the bloody mass. 'Tell them! TELL THEM! TELL THEM WHAT YOU TOLD ME!'

A head wobbled up, retching and coughing. Blood dripped from a gaping hole where the mouth ought to be.

'I were in Aberdeen,' the voice grated, 'wiv Simon Lake. I were part of the show......' Lyo coughed up blood and clots, spat them on the floor. He was propping himself up on one arm, shaking. 'After the show, Simon offered to show me magic, real magic. It was heavy. Real heavy. He had three others......... Tole me never to breathe a word of it, never.......... We went to this liddle house, dunno where....... he stops by the gate, did some foo-fah like in the show.....I were gigglin', like I'd shared wiv a drunk, he tole me to shut the fuck up......... She comes out, this woman, all in her nightie, walking up the path to the gate, an' I thinks were gonna get a feast....... but no, we walks off and gets in the car an' drives to the coast, an' all this time this woman's sittin' there in her nightie.... It were all sheer, an' you could see her tits....' He screamed as Theo kicked him again.

'You were right to call such as he scum.'

Fee shot a look at the still naked Zoe, and bit back the retort that sprang to her lips.

'We pull up on top of the cliffs.... you can hear the waves down below. Long way down...... An' he whispers to her, din't hear it all.... About the sea, all that crap, how her lover's waitin' down there for her, he'll catch her and they'll make love in the waves....... An' she just walks off the cliff, jus' like that. I asks, what's so special about that? We can all control our food....... An' he tells me, that she were a witch, and her power's his now........ How he were a witch once, and it were took from him.... an' he's like, laughing.......'

Theo's next kick sent the broken meta spinning across the floor, leaving a streak of thick blood in his wake.

'So now you know. At Rina's behest, I created the monster that is Simon Lake. At her urging, I forged the weapon that would destroy me. Her curse hunts me now, and will claim me, for the death of my Sophie. But before the curse claims me, I will exact my revenge on the so-called Vampire Witch Simon Lake.'

A frisson of something like fear ran down Fee's spine. The freezer ants were on patrol again.....

'No, Theo. Simon is my problem. He was a Frata before he was mete, and that makes it my business, not yours.' She kept to herself the rest of the revelation.

'Listen to her, Theo. The Gya is talking to her.'

'No might of charms, not magic, nor your Gya can deter me. I gave him the blood that animates him. Without my blood he would be dead meat. With my blood he has betrayed me, and there will be vengeance.'

'There will be vengeance all right. He killed my sister.'

'He is my responsibility, not yours.'

'Listen to you both. Quarrelling over who gets to kick the shit out of Lake.' Both of them turned to Zoe, regal in her nakedness. She held up a hand. 'I say we do it together. There are things that only we can do, Theo, and things only you can do. If we co-operate, we'll have the little bugger banged to rights. If we don't, he'll have the both of you. He's good enough to see Sophie dead, which means he's a force to be reckoned with. We underestimate him at our peril. Only by doing this together can we bring the bastard down. Okay?'

'A pact, then. Until the death of Simon Lake, we will work together.'

'Agreed. But I still must go. I feel the weight of Rina's anger on me even now.'

'Theo, take me to Lily.' Zoe wasn't going to let Ffion wriggle out of it, then. She picked up her clothing, and reached an arm out. Theo scooped her up.

'Wait for me, kitten.' And they were gone.

Brilliant. Here she was, waiting in a meta's boudoir, what was left of it, with an injured meta snuffling and choking on blood by the wall, while he took the spare away back to her mother. And what would Lily have to say about that? Or Theo to her? She had gone with him, hadn't she. But had she gone back? Oh, brother. Another fine mess, and one I can't get out of now. A meten kills my sister, and I am standing here, waiting for another meten to come back. I am completely insane.

The light had died in her staff as soon as Theo had moved away from it. Yet the staff had held no warning. No alarm bells clanged in her mind. There was not even the merest whiffle of concern troubling her wyth, and in this place, that was incomprehensible. Oh, well. She might as well make herself comfortable. The chairs were history, but Theo hadn't started on the bed. She tossed one of the heavy drapes over the bloody mass by the wall and climbed inside what was left of the heavy tapestry curtains and made herself comfortable on the pillows and cushions, and settled down to wait. She was unaware of the passage of time as she waited. Hours, minutes……

A soft chuckle awoke her. Theo was standing by the foot of the bed, cuddling the bedpost, looking at her.

'Such an enticing prospect. My beloved farer, asleep on my bed.'

That annoyed her. She was becoming more and more annoyed of late. Sharp, prickly, temper as short as a hen's nose.

'Zoe is with Lily now, then?'

'Lily had some words with me. She was quite explicit. It troubles me, the damage that is in her.'

'She won't do it, Theo.'

He sighed, and moved closer.

'Still, I have you.' He made no move to join her on the bed.

She unclasped her cloak and let it fall. The shadows gathered around her neck and shoulders. He reached out one hand and gently drew his finger down her arm.

'Here I am, with what I desire put before me. But it is not by your choice, or mine. We have been manipulated into this, both of us, and I resent being manipulated. Beware of that little sister of yours. She is quite ruthless.'

'Singleminded.'

'If you will have it so. Between Rina in my dreams and that one in my waking, I fear they will leave me no space for my own free will.'

'Just be thankful that she hasn't bugged your quarters.'

'She did.'

'What?'

'When you and she came here that night, when Mavron's Blyd came a-visiting, our innocent little Zoe managed to conceal three devices in this very room.'

'Ooops.'

'It is part of the game. Naturally I found them. Now, she does not need them, since she shares my thoughts and memories. She is being gentle so far. But I suspect that if she sees fit, my mind will be plundered. She will find it not so easy. I may have to teach her better manners, sooner or later. She is young, and I am old. She will learn, as they all learn.'

'I will have words with her.'

'There is no need.'

'Oh yes, there is. I am her Mysten, and her actions are my concern as well. You are an ally. We may not entirely trust you, but there *are* rules, and my sister *will* heed them.'

He inclined his head, graciously.

'Then I will defer to your status in this as you defer to mine. But there is no escaping it: you and I will become closer.'

'If I will it.'

'Your sister wills it. She requires it. And I believe her to be correct in this case. I would not be keeping faith with Rina, should I not offer you this chance to protect yourself.'

'The sacrificial lamb role does not become you, Theo.'

'Is that how you see me? A tool, to be used by your sister and ancestor, to further their own agendas? Is this how you see yourself?'

'A wise person once said, it is foolish to resist the inevitable. The only thing we can do is be ourselves, as hard as we can.'

'So you do not simply accept this as inevitable.'

'I see the benefit in it.'

'But you will not take joy in it.'

'You get out exactly how much you put in.'

He sat down on the bed next to her, leaving a little space between them.

'Let me tell you something. We have talked often, you and I. I do not talk merely to hear the sound of my voice, or to satisfy your idle curiosity, though I have done so.' He glanced down at his hands, laying in his lap. 'Those who do not know us think that we regard blood as simply blood. Nourishment. But the blood is different, as fine wines are different each from the other. The nature of the person dictates the nature of the blood. A young victim's blood will not be so ripe, so mature, as that of an older person. It may be sweet with hope and dreams, or bitter with resentment and failure. Some of us relish the younger, more vibrant blood of young men and women. Some prefer the deeper blood of those older, rich with memories and living. The blood of a victim looking for death is very different from one who relishes their life. Every taste is different. The sparking sweetness of a youth, full of life unlived, who sees the world gleaming before them in hope and promise: a man or woman in the bloom of maturity, certain of their place in life, with lessons learned and rich with fulfilment. The old, who live in their memories and treasure their past glories sweetly. Then there are the disappointed ones. Those who live on the borders, the young who have no hopes to be anything more than they are; the men who did not achieve as they wished, the unfulfilled women, and the older ones who resent that life has passed by them, they are bitter. Some live their lives and fill them. Some waste their time. The blood always tells.

'Some of you draw us to you with your vibrancy. Some draw us with despair. And when we are attracted, we will come close. Some we will cherish. Some we will destroy. Some we will take to ourselves. But we will not ignore you as many of you do each other.

'So, my kitten, who cherishes you more? The humans you share this world with, or those of us who hunt in it?' He reached a hand out to her face, not quite touching it. 'Who studies your natures more closely? Most humans live from day to day almost carelessly of the precious few years they are given. Some live each second to the full. Some pass through their days, wishing them gone. Some realize they have too few. And I, who have seen many, many days and will see many more, greet each new day when I arise, and am in haste, yes, kitten, haste, to see what wonders it will bring. So am I less than human? Or more?'

She didn't know what to say. The monster was a philosopher after all. He was a family friend. He had always been there. Ayen take it, he had even babysat for Lily and Rob! He had comforted her in the dark, before she had known what he was. He'd even fed her milk and rusks. And now, she considered him little more than a psycho bloodsucker. What was so different, apart from the diet? Did she despise vegetarians because they didn't eat meat? The world shifted under her gaze.

'I'm sorry, Theo.' She stroked his face. 'Zoe's right, I don't really see you. But you see me.'

He looked her full in the eyes.

'And will you see me now?'

She looked at the torn and stained shirt, the shadowed face, and nodded.

'Then I will open your eyes.'

His hand slid beneath her hair, drawing her face close. Their lips touched. Her heartbeat was loud in her ears. His fingers were lazily busy with the buttons on her dress. His weight forced her gently back onto the bed. There was a moment of panic, then his hand found her breast, and the kiss became more urgent. Her fingers found their way between the fabric of his shirt to his cool flesh, feeling the skin over muscle. He ran his lips over her brows and cheeks, kissing her eyes, nuzzling her neck. No panic now, just heat, heat and wanting. She made a small sound as his weight moved away, and she opened her eyes: she watched as he pulled the ruined shirt over his head to expose a perfect torso, pale, sleek and muscled. Of course. If you are going to live for eternity, why be ugly? If you don't get out of breath, you can exercise until the cows come home, and with good diet (Hah!) the really great bod is a given. He'd only been working on it for a couple of thousand years, so why not?

He started to kiss his way down her body, freeing her from her layers of clothing, emerging her from a chrysalis of cotton and silk and wool. He traced the lines where the fading tan of summer met the modesty of white skin, fascinated by the change in hue and texture. She allowed her hands to trail over the swell of muscle, tracing the contours with palm and fingertip, lips and tongue. She gasped when first his fingers, then his mouth, found their way to the juncture of her thighs. Her hands reached for his hair: This was not part of the contract….. surely…… She made fists in his hair as slow waves of heat washed over her.

   He crawled up her body, kissing and nipping her skin, caressing and sucking her breasts. Enough of lying here! She bit his shoulder, sharply, and pushed with her legs, rolling him over so she was on top. She sat, straddling his flat stomach, and when his hands stroked up her flanks, she gripped his wrists and threw her whole weight against his arms, pinning them over his head. They stared into each other's eyes at close quarters. There was a small flicker of humour in his eyes, then, it was gone. Effortlessly, he rolled her onto her back, letting his weight pin her beneath him. Above her, the face of the monster hovered. A pang of fear washed through her body from the soles of her feet to the roots of her hair. She did not see him move as he buried his fangs in her neck and her body arched from the suddenness of it, the implosion of pain that ebbed as swiftly as it had begun. The body above her was hard as rock now. There was no inclination to fight against what was happening, and when it stopped, there was…. Disappointment.

   He sliced into his chest with his fingernail, dragging it over the skin until the blood flowed. Then he sank back down, finding her neck again. This time, he entered her as well. A sharp thrust of his hips was all, and it arched her back again, throwing her head against some scattered pillows. She felt blood on her face, and his hand beneath her head, urging her to take from him as he took from her. It was hot, salty. Metallic in her mouth. Thick, rich and warm, like cream. Before, at their first sharing, she had simply let the blood flow into her mouth. Now she started to suck at the wound, and with the blood came a thundering roar, banging like a jackhammer, drowning out the beat of her own heart. It pulsed on and on, calling to her own, fainter rhythm to catch up, join the beat….until there was only one great heart beating, slowly, lazily, in a red cocoon of warmth, blood joined to blood and body to body, and another, sharper tempo, no less insistent, lower in her body, until a flood of warmth enveloped her, sweeping through her body in a flood of electric delight as the body above her convulsed in its own throes……

She must have blacked out for a moment. When she opened her eyes, it was to a sea of enfolding darkness. It had texture. Velvet. The pale flesh on hers was limned with a soft wash of shadow on skin. She could see every aspect of the demolished room in startling clarity, black on black. The night whispered seductively in her ears: she could hear the caress of the breeze on the far off roof and the thunder in her own body of two hearts. Awareness of memories not her own in her head, a voice in her mind, more than one voice, silky, just below the level of awareness. She sank into the whispering darkness and listened to those voices. Metae. Talking to each other. And another awareness, there with her, in her mind. She looked up into the face hovering over her own. It wove its own darkness, and she could see it. It had the deadly beauty of a hunting leopard, and the eyes held a possessive glint. However it had come about, Theo possessed her now, which was what he had wished for so long. And with that knowledge came the power of knowing that this possession was a two way street. If he had her, then she also had him. It will be a truce for now, the eyes said. But when battle is joined, neither of us will give the other quarter.

She made no attempt to escape from the weight of his embrace. His skin no longer felt cool against hers, but hot, almost feverish. She lay in the bed, listening to the night, trying to feel for any changes in body and mind.

Theo slipped his body off hers, and lay on the bed, calmly regarding her.

'There will be differences, kitten. Some of them, you might even enjoy. Some, you will not.'

'Between Zoe's spying and your mind in my head, I have no privacy whatever.'

'You will find you will have more privacy than you expect. And Zoe will have less. As I see your mind, I see hers, and in your seeing, you will see her also. And she you. A determined mind can shut out all but the most insistent, unless that one is determined to see. If the one who wishes to see elects to break the mind it wishes to plunder, well, that is a different matter. And your mind is trained to behave as you wish it to. Any coming to you with such a threat....' His voice tailed off. 'It is like the opening and closing an eye, this link in the group mind,' he continued. 'Close the inner eye, and you will be alone with your thoughts. Open that eye, and you will see, and be seen.'

'And whatever thoughts that linger will also be seen.'

Theo laughed. 'You see, you know already. I hate to kiss and run, but as I have driven my blyd from here, so must I go. There is danger on the wind, for you and me both. I will not invite it by waiting here like a sitting duck until it falls on me from the skies. And there is someone waiting for you.'

He rose out of the bed, lithe and naked as she watched. He slipped past a hanging tapestry in the corner. Fee found most of her clothes. The absence of her knickers brought a memory and wash of guilt. Greg standing by the bed, her smalls hanging from his hand. The thought of leaving anything of hers here to be found by heaven knows what sent her ferreting between the bedcovers and scrabbling under the bed until she retrieved a tiny handful of silk. One look told her she would never wear these again. Oh, well. One pair of knicks was a small price to pay for the work done here this night. She was combing her hair with her fingers when Theo returned, saturnine in black jeans and a leather jacket.

'I will walk a little way with you. Do not seek me here again, for I will not return until I have seen us all safe.'

He walked with her past the church gate, then indicated she should go on alone. With her newly enhanced night vision, Fee could see a figure standing by a parked car at the cottage.

'Bugger.'

It was Greg. Of all the times for him to come calling, now was perhaps the very worst. And he had seen them. He was coming this way.

'Farewell, kitten. Although we may not meet in flesh for a while, I am but a thought away. What I find out I will share with you, you have my word on that. Go well, and go with care. I would not lose you now, since my hunger for your blood is not sated.'

He melted in the shadows of the churchyard. Fee wouldn't put it past him to sleep there. It would amuse him to do so, and Theo never let a chance like that pass him by. She turned to face her approaching lover, trying to read the clues in his blank face.

'Hello, Greg. What are you doing here?' As a lover's greeting, it rated at about 0.1 on a scale of one-to-ten. Well, how often does your lover drive over half the country, come to meet you in the dark, and you with an undead you had just finished playing the two-backed beast with? Awkward, or what?

'I could ask you the same question. Who was that?'

'No-one you know.'

'Foregone conclusion, since I know only two people in this entire county, you being one and the other is fast asleep in bed.' You reckon? I'd bet Bond Street to a china orange that the conniving bitch is watching us right now. 'So who was it?'

He was right to be suspicious. Today, I buried my sister. He comes down, on some tom-fool errand of mercy, seeking only to comfort me in my grief (especially if that comfort involves sex) only to find me walking the midnight lanes with some strange bloke. You got that right. Strange isn't the start of it.

'That was Theo. He's an old family friend.' That much, at least was true. Now, will you leave it there?

'I see.'

Too much, by the tone of it. I don't need this right now...... Fee stepped out along the path to her front door. After a second or two, Greg caught up with her. They walked in silence until they were inside. Fee didn't try to hide the scrap of silk in her hand, she just threw it into the bowl under Gene's perch. Greg eyed the unfortunate crumpled mass, and realization began to dawn in his eyes. At least, he thought he understood. He had come down here to console his lover, only to find that she had been taking solace in the arms of a local yokel.

'I can see now why you never wanted me to come down here.'

'It's not what you think, Greg.'

'So tell me.' His entire stance radiated hurt and confusion and anger.

'It's complicated.'

'So you say.'

From where he was standing, it looked very simple. The girl he professed to love was screwing someone else behind his back. Fee drew a deep breath. You want the truth? Let's see how much truth you can handle.

'My father is dead. My sister is dead. My mother is crippled and my cousin's life is hanging by a thread. All four of them are victims of a serial killer, and they are not the only ones. Everything is going to shit. I am fighting for my life here! We are being targeted because of who we are, *what* we are. If I don't find out who is behind this, they may well kill me too.'

'You're mad.'

'Damn right I'm mad! Mad because someone killed my sister and my father, damn near killed my cousin and put my Mum in a wheelchair for the rest of her life! Not because he wanted to hurt her, but because he wanted to hurt *us*. And don't say 'Police' to me. I have no evidence except my convictions, and if I tell them what I know, what I suspect, they'll lock me up in the funny farm.'

'So who was that man you were with? And don't say you haven't fucked him, because I'll know you're lying.'

Fee lost it. One hundred percent, totally, lost it.

'Okay!' she screamed in his face. 'You want the truth? The real truth? The whole truth and nothing but the truth? Theo's a vampire. And yes, I did fuck him. I need all the help I can get, and I'll take any Fate offers or throws in my way, and if that means I have to fuck a two thousand years dead corpse, then I will! And if you won't help, and you aren't, Greg Ross, then you can fuck off back to London, or Manchester, or Timbuktu, or wherever! Sod off and let me try and make sense of this buggering mess, because if I don't, I will be in the coffin next to my sister, and then I won't give a rat's arse about anything any more because I'll be dead ! Now fuck off out of my house, out of my life, piss off back to where you came from and *LEAVE ME THE FUCK ALONE!'*

He looked at her, dumfounded. Whatever unpalatable truth he had been expecting, this was not it. They stared at each other. Fee defied the tears that were burning her eyes to so much as start on her cheeks.

'I am a farer, Greg. All my family are fratten. It's because of that this…….. thing…. is stalking us and killing us. If I have to do the unthinkable to stop him, I will do exactly that. I will lie, cheat, steal, connive and fuck whatever and whoever I have to. Yes, I am mad. Now, fuck off before I kick you out.' She sounded tired, defeated, to her own ears. There was no passion in her words now.

He didn't say a word. He turned and left. She could hear his car starting up and driving away. A tear slid down one cheek. Then another. And another. She could not stop them: she did not want to. She threw back her head and screamed her anguish, her frustration, her pain, to the ceiling. The tears flowed hot and fast. Just when she needed a shoulder to cry on (again!) circumstance had interfered, and she had sent away the one living man in her life, just after she had realized that not only was he the man she really loved, but that he was from a fratris bloodline. They could have been together. Bugger didn't cover it. Fuck didn't cover it. There was no swearword invented or uninvented that could would express the frustration and loss she felt right now. She stumbled into the parlour and fell onto the couch sobbing.

Chapter Twenty-three

She awoke, cold, on the sofa in a grey predawn light. The cushion on which her head had rested was soaking wet with salty tears. The night gorilla had been at her hair: you couldn't call it a bird's nest since no self-respecting bird would have made such a bollock of a mess to raise chicks in. She yawned and stretched, and then the full horror of last night crashed into her memory. She'd fucked Theo and chucked Greg. It should have been the other way round. The tidy elves were on strike, and the place was littered with cups, mugs, stained wineglasses and paper plates, some holding curling sandwiches. This would not do. She flew upstairs, taking the steps two at a time, and halted in shock on the landing. Meten blood. Might as well put it to some use, then. She changed into sweats, bounced downstairs, found a rubbish sack in the kitchen and started on the mess. It was ridiculously easy. She picked up the sofa with one hand to check there was nothing organic underneath. What she found instead was a twenty quid note and a bracelet she had lost ages ago. Greg had given it to her, right at the start of their affair. Tears threatened at that, but she shoved the bracelet over her wrist, pocketed the twenty and carried on. Dawn wasn't even threatening by the time she had the place to rights. Time for a run, clear her head and settle down to the business of revenge. Oh, yes, it was revenge now. Sophie was dead, and someone was going to pay. There was nothing else left.

Fee locked up the house and jogged down the road, over the stile and across the fields to the moor. High above, the tors beckoned while an unseen sun painted the clouds in gold and amber. A low mist hung round the valleys, blue-grey in the shadows of the hills. A brisk breeze lifted her hair as she ran over the ground, and the early birds were singing about unfortunate worms. Fleet of foot, she leapt from one boulder to the next, heedless of risk. It was a morning made for speed, and she had that in plenty now. Ayen bless that meten blood. She swarmed up the face of the tor. Who wants to go the long way round when you have this level of speed and agility? She stood, tall and proud on the highest rock, and watched the sun inch up through the mist, changing it from dusky blue to golden. A shaft of light hit her eyes and she winced. Dragging out her running glasses, she shoved them on. Zoe wasn't kidding when she said the sunlight was too bright. A handful of rooks were wheeling in the sky, calling for the rest of the gang to join in the hunt, charcoal diamonds against the dawn light. They were beautiful in their prismatic splendour. We are all hunters today. Then she slowly became aware of a resting consciousness within her mind. Theo was hitchhiking, watching the dawn with her. Perhaps she owed him that small pleasure at least. She recalled him telling her that one of the things he missed most about his life was not being able any more to watch the sunrise. Sunsets were all very well, but 'sunrise has its own magic. A new day, unsullied and pure, ready for the taking, like a virgin trembling on her wedding bed.' He could have a poetic turn of phrase when he wanted. Provided it included sex. Most things did when Theo was saying them. It occurred to her that she was standing alone on Buzzard Rock. Where Luke had that unfortunate encounter. But there were no men dressed in black to sully this moment of pure pleasure: she had the world to herself. A new day, a new Fee. But not a better one. What had Rina said? 'You can win this confrontation if your motives are pure.' Was revenge a pure motive? Was hate? Not when you came down to cases. Yes. It had become personal. And she couldn't win a one-on-one, not now, not here. The most she could do was stop this chain of events, and that wouldn't be enough. Her opponent would slink back to his lair, regroup and visit the whole blessed mess right back on them. No, this clash had to be righteous, as the American cop novels had it. And that meant impersonal. She didn't need to go out looking for the perp: he would come to her, all too soon if Vassago was to be believed. She needed to be alert and ready to snap the trap shut when he appeared. Right.

She scampered back down the easy slope, avoiding the dark pools of water and clumps of sharp reeds, splashing through the trails of dank water when they crossed her path, skimming over the tumble of boulders and back to the scant track that went from

Letts Head to Bounds Brook and the clapper bridge over the stream. Ten miles, and it felt more like two. How long would this new vitality hold out? And if it was only temporary, would she go back for seconds? She was hardly winded as she loped up the lane back to Pippin Cottage. What slowed her was the looming presence of a man standing at her gate.

She hadn't seen him ever before. Of that she was certain. The phrase 'brick shit house' flitted through her mind. A slightly over fleshed Arnold Swartzenegger. The Governator of California had come to pay his respects? One tap from a meaty fist would throw her into next week, mete enhancement notwithstanding. This one lived in a gym with weights that bent the bars. I'm about to meet the man who put the meat in meatloaf. He had seen her, so there was nothing for it but to do it. She strode purposefully up to the gate. He watched every step.

'Good morning. Can I help you?'

'I'm lookin' for Miss Harris, Miss Ffion Harris. I'm told she lives 'ere?' He had a curiously light, high voice for so large a frame.

'You've found her. I'm Ffion Harris.'

'I 'ave message for you from my employer. 'E says you might know 'im. Mr Lake, Simon Lake. 'E's your cousin?'

Not exactly, but it'll pass.

'Yes, we are related.'

'He's sorry he couldn't come 'imself, wot wiv 'is commitments an' all. 'E's very sorry to 'ear wot your sister got took dead. Sends 'is condolences, like. 'Ere.' He thrust a large, heavy envelope into her hand. 'All in there, 'tis.'

'Thank you.'

He made no movement to shift himself off her gateway.

'Is that all?'

''E'd like a reply, like.'

Like he would.

'No, no reply.'

''E said I waz ter wait for your reply. Like.'

'There will be no reply.'

''E sez there will be, an' I'm ter wait for it.'

'Then you will wait some time. I have no wish to reply to Mr Simon Lake.'

'I gotta wait, 'e sez.'

'Then go wait elsewhere.'

'Can't do that, Miss. Gotta 'ave that reply.'

Fee tried to shift past him to the gate. He stood impassively in her way. Shoving him would be like shoving a cliff. They shoved back. She was contemplating vaulting the fence and making a run for the door - surely she would be faster than him, even without the added bonus of mete blood? Or scoot off back over the moor, and come back through the woods behind the cottage. Yes, better.

'Good morning. Miss Harris. Who is this? Another friend of yours?'

Greg? By all that's holy, what's he doing still here? I thought he'd have hightailed it back to civilized parts by now.

'No, he's just delivering condolences from a relative.'

'Very nice of him. And since I see he's delivered the said condolence, he can bugger off.' Greg was rumpled and unshaven and ragged with lack of sleep, and she'd never seen anyone look more lovely or welcome right at that moment. 'The lady told you there was no reply. So be a gentleman, and be on your way.'

'Or wot?'

'I have asked you politely twice. Third time I won't ask.'

'Gotta 'ave the reply for Mr Lake.'

'You have your reply. There is no reply. Go deliver the message like a good boy.'

Oh-oh. The gorilla showed no signs of impending departure. He started to pick his nose, then thought better of it.

'Mr Lake won't be 'appy. 'E won't be 'appy at all.'

'That's not my concern. Nor is it Miss Harris' concern. Miss Harris' concern is that you are standing between her and her home, which is not polite. And were are being polite here, are we not.'

It was starting to look like they were squaring off to each other, dogs circling each other, and she the bitch of their attentions. Lovely. Then the second welcome sound of the morning: a rough, coughing engine that could only be Tom's jeep making its way up the hill and complaining about every inch of it.

The mud-encrusted heap rolled to a stop, and Tom poked out his head.

'Mornin' lass. You're up early.' He eyed the stranger with a certain amount of distaste. 'And who might you be?'

'Jus' delivering a message, like.'

'It'll be your bloody Merc blocking my drive then. Had to go out back and through the stream. It's a right bugger, that. So come and move your wheels before I drag 'em off and leave 'em in the water. The wife's got to get to work. Get on with you, while I'm still in a good mood.'

He nodded at Fee, and rolled the window back up. The gorilla sighed, and went up the road followed by the noisy clatter of the jeep.

'Two out of three's not bad. I thought I'd sent you off with a flea in your ear.'

'So you did. I came to my senses just south of Crediton.'

'What the hell were you doing in Crediton?'

'I don't know the sticks like you do. I came without a map. Bloody stupid I know, but when Mam said your sister had died and Lily had been calling, I got the urge to see you. I remember you saying that you took the M5 from Brum, so I followed that till I got to Exeter. Asked for directions at a local garage, then hedge-hopped until I saw the signs for Upper Congrieve.'

'Then I happened along with Theo in tow.'

'Not the best moment of my life so far.'

'Ditto.'

'And we both lost it. Anyway, back to Crediton. I was that dragged out that I sat in the car, dozing and thinking. And I decided to come back.'

By this time, they were in the kitchen. Polly-put-the-kettle-on. Sunlight was slanting through the window, bright enough to make Fee wince.

'I'm glad you did. I was contemplating doing a bunk.'

'Good decision. I saw you legging it across the moor.' He paused. He wanted to say something, then thought better of it. 'I thought you might try to smack the bugger, so I waded in.'

'Thanks for that. If I'd've smacked him, I'd be decorating the hedgerow from here to wherever.'

'That'd be you all over.'

Fee winced, and it wasn't from the sunlight.

'Ouch. Another one like that, and I really will give you your marching orders.'

'The jury's still out?'

'For now.'

'I've still got a chance then. Look, let's go back to the beginning. Please. Just what the hell is going on out here in pigshit land?'

It took two pots of tea, gammon and eggs and a plate of toast before he'd got it straight.

'I'll understand if you want to slide off quietly into the sunset about now.'

'Don't think the idea isn't attractive. But I'd never hear the end of it if my Mam found out.'

'So you'll stay because you are scared of your Mam?'

'Anyone with the remotest scrap of common sense is terrified of being on the wrong side of my Mam. If I skelped back up north with my tail between my legs, she'd be on the phone to Lily before I'd shut the door. Once the besom had her end, I'd be cursed six ways to Hallows and back. Mothers.'

'Lily called it the Mothers' Mafia.'

'Thank the gods they haven't discovered guns yet, or they could give The Sopranos lessons.'

'You realize that once those two discover our guilty secret, we'll be condemned to matrimony.'

'I can think of worse fates than being married to you.'

'You haven't lived with Zoe yet.'

'Is she that bad?'

'Worse.'

'So will you?'

'Will I what?'

'Marry me.'

'Is that a proposal?'

'I rather think it is.'

'How very romantic.'

'Look, I wanted to take you somewhere exotic, like out on a

speedboat....'

'So I couldn't get away...'

'And have it break down....'

'Cliché. Go on.'

Fee was sitting opposite him, her chin resting on her fist, elbows on the table between the dirty plates, her eyes fixed on his face.

'Get you to go and radio for help, and the ring would be on the microphone. Then I'd ask you, on my knees, in the swaying boat, to be my wife and love me forever.'

'And then I'd be sick.'

She stood up and started to clear away. He joined in.

'You get seasick?'

'I don't know. I've never been in a boat. Anyway, you deserve to be covered in puke for such a corny stunt.'

'So how would you like to be proposed to?'

'I've never thought about it.'

She was up to her elbows in hot soapy water. Greg picked up the tea towel.

'So think now.'

'Let me see......Swish restaurant in London? White sandy beach in Goa? Posh hotel in the Lakes? Top of Snowdon? Skiing in Norway? Nah.'

'How about right here, right now?'

'You got a ring, then?'

'Not on me, no. Didn't think it was right to propose to a girl when she's in floods of tears mourning her sister.'

'So you have got a ring.'

'Yes.'

'Which one of your exes didn't want you?'

'You don't give an inch, do you.'

'Never.'

He sank to his knees, ignoring the puddle of dishwater by the sink. Fee wasn't the tidiest of cooks.

'Miss Ffion Harris, will you do me honour of becoming my wife?'

'Look at you! You stink of sweat, petrol and cooking oil, your hair is greasy and you've got two day's worth of very bad beard.'

'So I'll get a bath. I scrub up pretty well. Answer the question.'

'Are you very sure of what you are getting?'

'You are a short-tempered bitch with some very peculiar relatives and friends. I, on the other hand, am a handsome, well-to-do city slicker with a bulging portfolio, astounding prospects and an exceedingly good bloodline.'

'I've never heard it called a portfolio before.'

'I am champing at the bit here, woman.'

'What if a better offer comes along?'

He looked up at her, exasperated.

'Will you two daft buggers get on with it? It's freezing out here.'

Fee sighed and unlocked the back door to admit a shivering Zoe. So much for romance.

'So where's your coat? You deserve to be cold, wandering around half dressed like that. Get up, Greg. There's no need to kneel in the presence.'

Zoe made directly for the teapot.

'Didn't want to wake Lily and Dilys. Otherwise I wouldn't have escaped so easily.'

Zoe's teeth were chattering against the mug. She didn't get that coldness from the short hop from Claire's to Pippin Cottage. Especially with a dose of mete blood.

'So what's up?'

'What makes you think anything's up?'

Fee looked at her with a mixture of vexation and impatience.

'I know you. Come on, give.'

'I had a dream.'

Greg had found a coat in the hall, and was draping it over Zoe's shoulders. Every little helps.

'I saw *him* again. In my dream. It was awful. He's been hunting, Fee. I could feel it. So I came back here to check my e-mails in case he's... been at it again.'

'Greg knows.'

'And he's still here? Wonderful. If you so much as suggest something pink and frilly, I will curse your eyes out.'

'There will be nothing, pink or frilly, or otherwise, until we get past this. Serial killers first, weddings second.'

'Then I need my computer, and you need a bath. Let's go find this sucker.'

Zoe's e-mails did not fail her that day. The list was getting longer. Mack Edwards and Julie Burrows had been found dead in a caravan over by Dawlish way. It was being blamed on a faulty gas heater. Carbon monoxide poisoning. Both were Family. Greg perused the list. A sick look stole over his carefully blank face.

'Forty years. Whoever it is must be well into their sixties by now. Have you any idea who it might be? Are you sure these are not accidents?'

'Was Luke's fall an accident? Definitely not. We didn't want to believe it either, but we've got no choice now.'

'We need to know if he'll come calling again. I could weirdweave for you, if that would help.' Strange, but comforting, to hear Fratris speech in him.

'No. Higgins' Paradox.'

'Pardon?'

'Higgins' Paradox. If you know about a future event, even knowing about it can change it. Trying to prevent it can precipitate the event you're trying to avoid. And if you do avoid it, it might trigger off something worse.'

'Not knowing what might happen could be worse. If you know the shape of the future, you could have a starting point. As it is, you don't know bugger all.'

'What do you need?'

'A water mirror. I'd prefer my own, but I'll take what I can get. I'm Family too, remember. This thug might be on my case right now. If I stick my head in the sand about this, I might end up with a bad case of dead.'

'It's an incentive.'

Everyone has their talents, things that they are better at than anyone else. Usain Bolt is a fast runner. He'd won gold for it. But ask him to jump, or vault, or chuck a javelin and the chances were that he'd plough out. You played to your strengths, and called on others to play theirs. What Jean could detect, Fee could rip up. Zoe could make sense of apparently random facts and weave them into a seamless fabric. She even left holes for other, undiscovered facts to slot in. Sophie had been able to tell when you had a cold coming on..... Jean was their seer, but she insisted on putting her own interpretation on what she saw rather than giving you the bald facts. Greg was offering that, here and now. Anyway, she was curious to see how he did it. Jean would gather the wyth of the frais, then conduct her own seeing in private. Apart from the fact that she commonly looked out of sorts after she had ventured into the hinterlands of time, she was tight-lipped about what she actually did to unwind the threads.

Greg's preparations were simple. He sat at the kitchen table, a black breakfast bowl filled with water in front of him. Next to it was a spoon, a bottle of olive oil and another of malt vinegar. A candle burned on the draining board behind his back. Another bowl, a metal one, held incense. His own concoction. A heavy, musky scent filled the air until the shadows were drowsy. He slumped at the table, his wet hair combed back. A sheen of unhealthy sweat covered his face, the result of a tea he had mixed and drunk. He had been very cagey about the ingredients, and had spent some time ferreting about in the cupboard that held the less palatable seasonings kept in a Fratten household. It had looked like sludge, and smelt like rotting fruit. He was breathing deeply, almost gasping. Fee and Zoe sat facing him, waiting.

He roused enough to crush a scrap of paper onto the grains in the bowl. He lit a match and ignited the grains. Red flames licked round the paper, burning it to ash. As it burned, Greg poured a spoonful of oil into the water, then a spoonful of the malt vinegar. He dropped the spoon into the unlikely mixture and gazed at the patterns in the bowl. His eyes flickered from here to there, opening and closing slowly.

'Time and space are the streams in which we move. No event exists in isolation from all other events, and now weaves its shadows into the times to come. No action is divorced from its repercussions. A stone is thrown into the water, and the ripples show its passage.

'The stone is thrown, let the events unfold.'

He added a pinch of hot ash to the liquid in the bowl, and went back to his intent perusal.

'I see cliffs. Cliffs and the sea. I see a train, moving between the land and the sea.'

Dawlish?

'I see a caravan. One of many. I see a car. A black car. Someone is sitting in the car. The car is on the cliffs above the caravans. In a carpark on the cliffs. Above the town........'

'The car moves off…….' He trailed into silence.

'I see the car moving. There is a large building. The car stops……….

'A large space, inside. Dark. Bright things, bright things and boxes…. A small room…….

'Computers, screens. Blue light. A man sits at the screens, looking. Pictures on the screens, tiny pictures. Many pictures. Two pictures are added to the screen……..

'Staircase. Spiral metal staircase. Bare floor. On the floor is a white circle. A candle burns in the circle. A large yellow candle. Dead flowers in a metal vase…...

'There is a dresser. An Irish dresser, open underneath. A large book on the dresser. An old book. Open. Old paper, faded ink. A knife with a curved blade. The handle is inset with coloured oblongs. It looks like a lazy S…….

'A child. I see a child. No more than ten years old. She is sleeping on a bed. She is wearing jeans and a red sweatshirt. Her feet are bare….

'I see a fire……. Three figures, running. No more.'

He reached, blindly, for a glass standing on the table. He chugged down the faintly murky contents. His head sank into his hands and he sat at the table cradling his head.

Fee got up quietly. She had hoped for more, but she'd take what she could get. She drew back the curtains and opened the window. Fresh, cool air blew into the kitchen.

'Greg?'

'Gimme a minute.' His voice was slurry and heavy. 'That stuff always gives me a blinding headache.'

Zoe made to touch his hair, but Fee warded her off with a Look. She placed both hands on his head and concentrated. It was like lifting heavy air. His scalp felt listless under her fingers, but she persisted until she felt the languor lift. They both knew about the Waters of Vision. The ingredients, and their relative proportions, were a closely guarded secret. Ditto for the antidote. They were both powerful stuff. Zoe had gone for the brandy.

'Isn't it a bit early to start on the hard liquor?' Greg asked when she shoved the glass under his nose. He sipped it anyway, then set the still mostly full glass on the table.

Before they could even get a start on unraveling Greg's vision, there was a bang at the door. It swung open to reveal Lily.

'Don't just stand there, child. This contraption can't handle steps. Or will you force me to wait in the front garden until I die of old age?' Zoe ran to help. 'And at my own house, too.'

She was barely in the kitchen before she started.

'You could have waited for me,' she glowered at Zoe, who had the grace to look slightly ashamed. 'I would not leave before saying goodbye. Or hello, in your case. You must be Greg. Enchanted to meet you, finally.' She extended a limp hand. Greg took it and kissed her knuckles.

'Mum sends wishes.'

'I'm sure she does. Things are moving on, are they not. We must speak of times to come. The future. Whatever it holds for us. I see you have been busy.' She eyed the table. 'I hope you remember Mr Higgins. Smart man for a philosopher.' She steered up to the table and cocked a bright eye at Fee. 'Tell me.'

'Greg's been weirdweaving.' Lily nodded. That much was apparent from the debris on the table. Lily knew the score.

'So that is your talent,' Lily mused. 'One among many, if I read the signs aright. Now that you are being honest about yourself, anyway. And, your results?'

Zoe consulted her notes.

'Two more deaths. Which confirms the dream I had.'

'So that is why you ran out so early. You could have spoken to me about it.'

'You had a bad night.'

'So solicitous of your mother, now. Or is there something else that you have omitted to tell me?'

Zoe glanced at Fee and Greg, then blushed.

'I - ah - know about the metae,' Greg offered.

'Do you now.'

'Not all about them, obviously.'

'Quite. It is a very long story. And one I am not inclined to go into now. Suffice to say that what we do is necessary, and leave it there.'

'Oooo-*kay*.' Greg did not look satisfied. Lily stared at him until he dropped his gaze.

'There is more.'

'Yes. Horror boy's kidnapped a kid.'

'Do we know that?'

'Why else would a child be sleeping in his lair?'

'And are you sure of that? You seem to be making many assumptions on the basis of little evidence.'

'After the deaths in….'

'Dawlish.'

'Dawlish, yes…. I followed him back. He went to a warehouse. There was stuff stored there. And he had a computer. Quite a setup really. He was uploading pictures onto a screen. There were dozens of photos there - black and white, colour….. all pictures of people. And somewhere else in the building there was a ritual space, with books and dead flowers. The girl was in another room. Asleep on a bed.'

'I take it that you did not recognize this man.' Greg shook his head. Carefully. He wasn't over the Waters of Vision yet, not by a long chalk. 'A pity another cannot share your visions with you. That may reward whoever decides to look further into such matters. Did you see anyone else?'

'Not really. There was someone with him in the car. A driver.'

'But you did not see him.'

'No. But you can't drive sitting in the back.'

'You saw no other images?'

'Just those. And they weren't too far in the future, I could tell that. They were really clear.'

'So they may even have happened.'

'The deaths have.'

They sat silent, pondering.

'I am concerned about this child. Could he have taken her - it is a her?' Lily glanced at Greg, who nodded. '- at Dawlish?'

'No. Mack and Julie were alone.'

'I have heard no word of a missing child. It may be he has not taken her yet. A word to the wise is in order. I will call Dilys.'

Lily edged the wheelchair out into the hall. Fee pushed the door to.

'What's with the kid?'

'I don't know. But it felt bad.'

Fee fussed with the kettle. Zoe sat, mute, staring blindly at her laptop. Then Lily was back.

'Dilys will call me if there is any word. In any case, we must leave today. So we will look closely at this now. Ah, yes, a cup of tea would be most welcome.' Fee passed mugs around. 'I see you, also, have been visiting our old family friend.'

'Yes. He's gone. He heard something that upset him.'

'Putting it mildly.'

Lily banged her mug down on the table.

'Tell me before I decide to drag it out of you.'

'One of the vamps told Theo that he'd been with Simon in Aberdeen and witnessed him mesmerizing a frater into walk off a cliff.'

'I can see why that would upset him,' Lily murmured. 'He'll be running from Rina's vengeance now.' She sipped her tea. 'Now, this weaving. We must examine carefully what you saw, my boy.'

'And milk it for all it's worth,' Zoe put in.

'Exactly. And there is Higgins to consider. Remember, that at every nexus where a choice is to be made, all possible futures co-exist together. Once the choice is made, the future will follow the path that the choice dictates. That does not mean that the alternative future ceases to exist. It does not collapse as the probability lessens. It will continue, in another world separate from our own. Our decisions now will shape the path we walk, and if we make the right choices now, we will find ourselves travelling along the path we would choose, and not another. And since choice follows choice, a wrong turning can lead you back to the most fortunate path, if you choose wisely. Fate does not condemn us if we make one wrong choice, only if we continue to make the unfortunate ones time after time. Mistakes are recoverable. Now you have looked, you have changed the parameters of your quest. So, look at what was seen, if it can give you any clues.'

'I saw a warehouse, I'm sure of it. A big warehouse on an industrial estate.'

'Was there any detail about it that you recall, which would help us discover where it is?'

'No, most of it was in shadow. Wait. There was a map, when the car turned into the estate. And there was a flash of orange on the side of the building.' Greg sank into thought.

Meanwhile, Zoe had linked up a laptop to the video scanner in the kitchen. Lily's eyebrows lifted, but she made no comment as they watched a re-run.

'From this, I think that whatever happens, it will happen in that warehouse. We will need to locate it, and since Greg was the only one who saw it, he must do this.'

'He can't drive all over looking at every trading estate between here and…. Wherever.'

'No. he will do it by using Google Earth, Yourstreet.'

'Oh.'

'I'm remembering something. A name. Turncoat, or Turnstone. It might be the name of the estate, or the name of the company that owns or uses the warehouse. And I've a feeling that it was fairly close to a motorway, but not near a big city. And it was an old warehouse, not one of the new plastic ones. It was brick and timber. It might even be a converted barn, it had that look about it.'

'And how will you locate his next target? I am convinced that there is one. This is too well planned for him to deviate from his intent.'

'Wherever that is, it won't be near here.'

'Why so?'

'Because he never hits twice in the same place………'

'Not necessarily. I need a map. I think I'm onto something.'

Greg called up a map of Great Britain on Zoe's laptop, and started to plot the places where the strange deaths had taken place, joining them one after the other. As they watched, a complicated glyph began to appear on the screen.

'Can anyone recognize that?'

'I have a feeling I have seen it somewhere. Long ago. Or something very like it.'

'Where did the first victim die?'

'Here.' Zoe said, poking at the screen. 'Why?'

'If this is a glyph, it can't end just anywhere. The design will have to close up to be completed.'

'The first victim was Mary Hughes. Keeled over in her garden with a massive stroke. Lingered ten days, and never spoke a word again. July twenty eighth. Ashburton.'

'So I'll start my search around there. Plenty of places to choose from, near the motorway.'

'I have got it now. I know where I have seen that design. And if you have been to see Theo, you will have seen it too.'

'What?'

'That old tapestry hanging behind the table at the end of the hall. It was not so faded the first time I saw it, and the design was clearer. I asked Theo then what it meant, and he told me it was something that I would rather not know about.'

'Could it possibly have something to do with Amagus?'

'You would know more about that that I.'

Greg cocked an eyebrow at Zoe.

'Amagus was the nutjob responsible for the plague of metae. He decided he didn't deserve to die, and set out to live forever. It didn't work out quite the way he wanted.'

'Bummer.'

'He deserved what he got. I hope he's in total wretched agony, wherever he is.'

Lily was regarding the discarded envelope on the dresser with something like distaste. Fee and Greg had forgotten that incident already. Fee felt her stomach turn over with apprehension. It was not like her to forget such an unusual event so completely, so fast.

'And what, pray, is that? It has the feeling of something I do not like.'

'One of Simon Lake's gorillas dropped it off this morning.'

'Then open it, sis. Let's see what our other family meta wants to communicate.'

Fee picked up the envelope. It felt faintly greasy. Maybe the delivery boy had stopped off for a burger on the way. Why had it not felt like that when he had handed it to her? She dropped it on the table, rubbing her fingers against the fabric of her pants. Rubbing off the dirt...... Zoe reached for it. Fee caught her wrist.

'No, Zoe. I wonder why that Neanderthal was so intent that I open the thing right away? It doesn't feel right.'

'Bad wythen?'

Lily reached forward and laid one finger on the envelope.

'I would say so.'

The four of them stood around the table, all staring at the paper. It had come to them. It was in their stronghold. And Fee had carried it in. Danger, UXB.......

'What would have happened if I'd have opened that envelope?'

'You'd have vanished.'

'We have an opportunity here.' Lily subsided back into her wheelchair. 'Our enemy has sent us an envoy. And we have it in our power, beneath our hand. That is an advantage we cannot afford to squander.'

'I suppose it really did come from Simon?'

'Let us keep an open mind. None of us would be suspicious of a family member sending regrets at the death of one of our own. Simon has always kept his distance, and has always been polite in his few dealings with the Family he has met. He has been gracious and courteous. To consider that he has been systematically slaughtering us at the same time...... is hard to believe.'

'This may be the trap we have been waiting for.'

'How, Zoe?'

'The best trap is one your opponent doesn't suspect. What better than to use one of his own? Walk into the trap, willingly, ready to ignite a something nasty of our own?'

'Right. Here's what we do. Greg, you must find out about that warehouse. Zoe, I want you to saturate this place with every tripwire you can invent. Mum, you organize the Families to build me a powerhouse. I have the feeling that our opponent is a heavy hitter, and he's got something exotic up his sleeve. You don't go on a rampage like this out of pique. There is a method to this, and

I still don't know what that is.'

'And what will you be doing?'

'I'm going to call the only weapon I have. I have a feeling I will need it.'

'And I must be on my way soon. But first, we must deal with this inconvenient epistle.'

Chapter Twenty-four

Lily pulled a metal tray onto the table and lifted the envelope onto it with a handy knife off the draining board.

'Zoe, go get the green wrap from the bedroom. It's in the wardrobe, left hand drawer. Fee, fetch your blade. Greg, there is a bottle of Scotch in the cupboard there. Get it for me.'

They scattered for their errands. When they came back, Lily had found a salt shaker and instructed Greg to draw the curtains again, and fill a bowl with water which now rested on the table next to the tray.

'Weave your spaca, daughter.'

Fee did as she was told, weaving the strongest spaca she could. Lily carefully unwrapped the green cotton bundle Zoe had placed in her lap. Inside there was a knife, a black cord and a wythstick polished by years of handling. Lily placed them on the table in front of her, along with a small bag, an ink bottle and old-fashioned dip pen. There was also a dark red candle in a squat holder, which joined the rest.

Carefully, Lily lit the candle and sprinkled some grains from the bag onto a fiercely burning charcoal disc which she had told Zoe to put in a miniscule bowl on the tray. Pungent smoke rose into the air.

'Servant, heed my call, and attend me, your mistress in the Midess. Come without delay, from whatever realm you now inhabit, to my side and obey my commands.'

She spoke in a strong, assured voice. The incense smoke belled out, trailing round her, caressing her, mingling with her hair, passing through her fingers. Whatever damage the accident had done to her, it had not affected an indomitable will. Her wyth was as potent as it had ever been: they could all feel it.

Lily took up the pen, dipped it in the ink and drew a circle on the envelope. She sprinkled salt on it, then brought the knife round in a swift arc, defining the edge of the tray.

'Force born of wyth, I confine you to this spaca through which no evil wyth may pass. This is my will, and so shall it be.'

She replaced the knife and leant back, raising her hands over her head.

'Ayen which ordains all, secret of life, whose commands are absolute, I invoke you now for the health and well-being of the bodies and souls of those within this Frais. You have commanded us to rise and make our way in this, our life. Be there turned aside from us all that would seek to take our lives from us.'

The incense trails were creeping over the envelope. Feeling it? Fingers of incense, testing the paper. The salt crystals sparkled in the scant candlelight. A dull blue haze lay over the tray.

Lily dropped a pinch of salt into the bowl and dipped her fingers in it. Dripping water, she picked up the envelope and held it up to the candle.

'Servant, protect your mistress and those with her from the designs of the one who sent this. Hold fast to the weird, subject to my will.'

She took a deep breath and slit the envelope. Inside was one sheet of paper. She drew it out, tracing a sigum in the air over the black letters.

'Thing of wythen, I bind you to this paper. I command you to hold and not complete your purpose, but to remain as you are until I alone release you by my words and commands.' She read out the words.

"My dearest sister,

I feel I may call you that, since you are born of my brood and blood.

I am most desolate to hear of the death of your beloved Sophie. If there is anything I can do to help you in this dire time, you must ask. I will deny you nothing. I would lift your distress, if this is at all possible.

I will come to you, when time permits, and speak with you. Though I hold myself aloof from my family, rest assured that I hold you all in my heart in high regard, and that my thoughts are with you in your grief. My family is never far from my thoughts, and I reacquaint myself with family matters when it seems appropriate.

My dearest Ffion, be assured my deepest sympathy lies with you and your sister.

Deepest regards

Your cousin

Simon Lake."

'Beware the meta when he speaks fairly,' Lily commented wryly. She held the paper between herself and the candle.

'Do you see it? Here? And here? A sigum has been drawn on this paper. Secretly.'

'That looks familiar.'

'Greg?'

'I've seen ones like that before. In one of the old books. It was part of a weave. "To cause one to come to you and do as you will." It was a love spell. A man would draw it in sperm, a girl would use menstrual blood or... secretions.'

'We all know what happens in our lady gardens. What did this freak use?'

'Don't touch the paper. One of us is enough.'

Lily moved the paper and sniffed at it.

'Neither of those. I suspect.... Plant sap. Perhaps mandrake root extract. And other things.' Lily replaced the paper on the tray. 'Now I will interrogate the weave. This will bear watching, since you will have not seen it done before. Few of us indeed have needed this skill.' She turned back to the table, and straightened up in her wheelchair. 'Servant, you who hold this weave, reveal it to me. Reveal its purpose and creation.'

'Lilia' The voice was ghostly. *'Long it has been since you and I have held converse.'*

'I trust you have found ways to stave off boredom since last we held court.'

'The days have been weary. I crave the sound of your voice, the vision of your flesh and the joy of your commands.'

'We have done much together, you and I. But those days are

gone, Fate has other paths for me now.'

'That which I have captured for you will reveal itself now. Have conern, for it will care not for your existence.'

'Allow it to reveal its secrets. But hold fast, let it create havoc in my presence.'

Lily sat with her hands resting in her lap, a picture of perfect ease. On the tray, a grey mass began to writhe and take shape. A cross between a tiny dog and a lizard rose out of the smoke, craning upwards. Feral eyes watched them.

'Which is she to who I was sent? For her alone I am come.'

'You have been stopped in your way. You will reveal yourself to me. You cannot evade me. I will hold you in this place until you satisfy me.'

'I will speak with she to whom I am sent. No other.'

'You have no authority here. You will speak when you are commanded, and by whom you are commanded.'

The thing howled in torment. It writhed, trying to escape. Each time it tried to pass the rim of the tray, a red light flared. It raced round the tray, leaping up, falling back, but the barrier held.

'You know I can hold you for eternity, should I so wish. End your pain, and reveal to me that which I ask of you. Then you shall have peace.'

It panted, crawled round and round upon itself. It was in agony. Lily watched impassively.

'What would you know. I cannot bear this.'

'Then name yourself, that I may bind you.'

'No, No.'

'Then be cursed to eternal torment.'

Lily drew a sigum in the air between them. It lingered for a moment, and the creature writhed away, trying to hide and screaming in its thin, high voice.

'Render to me your name, your true name.'

'No...ooo.'

'You will reveal to me the name by which you are truly known. You will answer now, or face my wrath.'

The thing whimpered and shivered. Whatever Lily had done, it was causing the little thing intense anguish.

'Biehail. I am named Biehail. Cease this torment.'

'Biehail. To whom were you sent?'

'To the eldest sister. She who confronts the Master. She who stands in his way.'

'Name her.'

The thing wailed. It lashed it's tail. It was clearly suffering.

'Ffion. Ffion, daughter of Lily, daughter of Jane, daughter of Rina.'

'And what did you intend with her?'

'To bring her to the Master.'

'Where?'

'To the place where he is.'

'And where is that?'

'In this world. I know not this world. Let me return to my world.'

'What reward were you offered in return for this service?'

'That once I delivered her body to the Master, I could return to this world and play.'

'Who is your Master, the one who promised you this?'

'I was summoned by Ghalidor, the new Lord who rises from the ashes of the old.'

'He does not own you now. I own you, and your reward is denied you. I will end your existence, blot you out for ever. But I will torment you first, for you have crossed me.'

'Then let me serve you. I will be a willing servant. Torment me no more.'

'What need have I for so petty a thing? As you have betrayed your former master, so would you betray me.'

'I will not. I will serve you faithfully.'

'Then I will offer you one chance, and one chance only. Fail in this, and I will teach you the meaning of torment. Seek not to escape my rule, for I will pursue you and visit my wrath upon you for your disobedience.'

'Command me, Mistress. If it be in my power, I will do whatsoever you command.'

'You will find it in your power, for I will accept no excuses. You will go from this place, to the place where you were summoned. You will return and reveal to me the exact location of that place, and betray to me all it's secrets. Every tiny detail, you will lay open to me. You will go secretly and return swiftly. You will reveal nothing of what is between us. Should you fail me, and be trapped again, you will cease to be. Your substance will be cast on the winds, there to blow hither and yon until the end of Time. Your doom is upon you. Obey my wishes, and return, and I may find some small reward for you. Fail, and you will cease to be.'

Biehail mewed sadly, hanging its head between its front legs and lashing its tail.

'As my mistress commands, so shall I do.'

'Then go forth, my Mischief, and work my will.'

The smoke on the tray billowed out and lost cohesion. Biehail had gone. But Lily wasn't finished.

'Servant, approach.' The tiny speck of flame on the candle flickered and grew tall. A long plume of smoke lifted from the flame. If you looked hard, there was a face in that flame. 'I thank you for your service this day. You have served me well. I feel your sorrow that we no longer enjoy the diversions of youth, and ask you if you would seek service other than mine.'

'Your mind it was that created me out of the darkness and gave me purpose. That purpose was to serve you. Would you now send me away from you, your mind in which I rest?'

'I would offer you to another, one who has more need of those services for which I created you. I would not serve you badly, for you have served me well.'

'Desolate I would be to depart from she who created me.'

'Life demands changes of us, that we survive and continue. That when I am done with this my life, that you would find service with my blood would be my dearest wish for you, old companion.'

'Grant me then the benison to be in your gracious presence from time to time.'

'So will I grant, if it be acceptable to the one I command you to serve.'

'Then do as you will. As you ever have.'

Lily turned to Fee.

'Daughter of mine, this is Saiba. He has been my guardian and protector, and now he is yours.'

'Greeting, Saiba. May you serve me as you have served my mother.'

'Then for the last time. Depart, servant, with my thanks. Farewell.'

The candle flame convulsed, and the tiny face disappeared.

'Ferae fecerunt, nos domis ubis.'

Miniature sparks appeared in the paper, flickered and died. Lily clapped her hands three times.

'Nice one, Mum.'

'I still have it, then.'

'Well, that just about confirms it. Tunfen is Ghalidor, and Ghalidor is Simon Lake. But why?'

'We may find out, eventually, but that is of lesser importance. We need to know where he is and what his intentions are.'

'That's clear enough. He's going after Fee.'

'I may let him do just that.'

'That's it. You've finally lost it.'

'Why should I wear myself to a frazzle hunting him, when he's so keen to meet me? Let him do the work for a change.'

'It's your skin.'

'Yes, it is. And very tasty too.'

'When will that critter be back?'

'Soon, I hope. Be sure to call him Mischief now. And do not speak the name you have learned. He may be able to connect with you, should he hear his name mentioned.'

'He can do that?'

'Let's not take any chances.. From what he's achieved so far, I wouldn't put it past him.'

'Guard that letter carefully. It may have some other wyth concealed, so keep it safe. Once we discover where he expected to deliver you, I fear you must make that journey.'

'And I cannot express how much I am looking forward to that.'

Fee started to clear away the debris. Lily carefully wrapped her belongings back into the green cloth.

'We know more, now. We are entering the endgame.'

'Great care we must take.'

'Thank you, Yoda. Go put these back where they came from.

You are not Jedi, and this is not Star Wars. I do not look for happy endings. I look to endings only. If they are fortunate, that will be a bonus.'

'Stay in touch.'

'I will do my part. I will pour wyth into the Well of Memories for you to draw on. And do not shut Greg out, now he is part of this.'

'I'll do whatever I can.'

'I am sure you will. Ffion will need you now, she will need what only you can give her. Oh, and Ffion. Do not hold back because you imagine circumstance indicates you delay your communion. You will find no dissent in me in should you feel that need. That goes for you too, my lad. Do whatever you feel you need to do. We may bow to ancient usage and ritual, but that doesn't mean we should be slaves to it, nor die because we cling too closely to it.'

'Did she mean what I think she means?' Greg whispered to Fee as Lily inched the wheelchair back outside.

'I rather think she does,' Fee responded in a low voice, 'and the sooner the better.'

Chapter Twenty-five

It was a strangely docile Zoe who walked over to Tom's that night. Maybe Lily had spoken to her, or maybe she realized that some things require solitude. Curious and nosey though she was, she knew enough to back off. The time would come (Hopefully!) that she would also require such consideration back, and was laying up credit. Before she had gone, she had helped with the preparations. And asked endless questions. The answers to these, Fee didn't know, yet. Nor would she tell when she did know. They knew the bones of it, but to know it was to do it. Nothing else would suffice. Zoe had to be content with that. Times like this, you went with the flow. There was no right way, no wrong way, to do this. It mattered only that you did it with the right partner, and Fee's right partner was Greg. She had somehow hoped it would always be so, and now she was certain. No, Fate don't do certain. It was as good as she had the right to expect. Only they could make it perfect, and if Fee could, she would. Lily had told her little, inferences only. 'When your lover's touch flutters against your skin like a remembered dream, and not an unknown thing of mystery, then you can contemplate this. When you are hungry, you swallow food without tasting it. When you are ready to taste the fruit of this tree, you will have not hunger but delight: you will be content to wait for what happens, rather than hunger for the sensations it promises. You cannot fall on this feast and gorge. You must sample each delight delicately, relish it to the full. When Ayen and Gya combine with the delighted flesh, the aware mind, and your wyth mingles with that of the beloved, then all becomes one. So delicate, like a gossamer dream, the wrong thought can shatter it, yet so strong, so powerful, nothing can stand against it.' Yum.

 The letter waited in solitary splendour on the dresser. Just to be absolutely sure, Zoe had wrapped it in black silk, tied it with a red ribbon and sealed it with wax. She impressed the wax with an impressive sigum. Talk about belt and braces. Zoe was nothing if not compulsively single-minded about what she did, and she was leaving nothing to chance. Once they knew where they had to go, the gloves would be off: but until then, the fewest risks they ran, the better. Fee intended to survive. At least this part of the process might bring her a measure of joy. Frolicking with Theo was one thing: this was a very different encounter. Greg was alive, for a start.

Way, way back in time, she remembered. Something had happened. She did not know what, back then, nor did it matter. What mattered was what she had felt at the time. After Andrew had died and his ashes scattered among the falling apple blossom, Lily and Rob had inherited the Frais. As part of the ritual, they had made communion with each other. Oh, they'd done it before. When they married. But Fee hadn't been around then. She'd known that the Frais had met to set their seal of acceptance on Lily and Rob's rule - hard not to when your home is invaded by that many people, even for one night. She and Sophie (Sophie! How I miss you…) had sat up in Fee's bedroom, on the bed, listening to the rise and fall of voices, the cadences if not the words. Bells and chanting. Tom's deep voice, almost clear enough to hear… 'And will you rule with compassion and love, justice and truth, honouring all those you are sworn to protect….' and Rob answering 'This so will I do, as far as it be in my power…….' After a while, there had been silence, then footsteps on the stairs, a door opening and closing… murmur of voices, one, then another, then together, Lily and Rob, then silence again. The girls fell asleep, but Fee woke later in the darkness. It was warm, and close, and comforting. The night was a huge teddy bear, cuddling to her, holding her close and safe in its embrace. As it held everyone in the house, all of them, sleeping downstairs and up on beds and sofas and chairs. The darkness was alive with a throb of closeness and love. Fee had snuggled down, perfectly content, enfolded in her parent's wythen. And now, she would complete the circle. With Greg. It was a warm and fuzzy thought, and she cuddled it to her. She only hoped he wouldn't get too serious. Laughter and love ought to go together. Which was why Zoe and offered to make herself scarce. How can you throw caution to the winds and be perfectly abandoned if you know your kid sister is listening in? Zoe had even disabled the bugs. Greg had indicated that he might like a memento, but one look at Fee's face made him drop it. She was the only memento he was going to get.

The sun inched its lazy way to the horizon and the shadows lengthened. The day began (days don't start at midnight, when everyone's asleep. They begin at nightfall) in purple and gold: the Eve of Remembrance, when you thought about those you loved, who had done this before, and would be with you now. An unbroken chain reaching back through time, swirling into the present and snaking off into the shadows of the future.

She was watching the sunset through the parlour window, her face painted in scarlet and bronze. Greg came up behind her, and his arms wound round her waist. He kissed the point where her neck met her shoulder.

'Time to get started. The bath is filling. Everything is ready.' Was he trembling? Well, he'd not done this before. Had he? Neither had she. Oh, they had explored and enjoyed each other's bodies many times. The memories of his skin were etched on Fee's fingertips. Her body remembered the warmth and pressure of his flesh on hers. But *this* had about the same relationship to a casual shag as a length of the local swimming pool had to swimming the Channel. It was a matter of degree. Delight of the body was one thing. Delight of the ayat? One's a lazy housecat. Comfortable and predictable. Feed it regularly and it will, in its way, love you back. The other's a hunting leopard. One scratches in pique, the other rends you down to the bone. Force and danger go hand in hand. You do not blink in the gaze of the leopard.......

Greg took her hand and led her upstairs. In the steamy warmth of the bathroom there was the generous soft lambency of candles massed on the windowsill and round the bath. A soft, dreamy fragrance of frangipane and ylang-ylang filled the luminous air. Wisps of steam rose from hot water dotted with flower petals. In the drowsy, wet warmth, Greg helped her undress. She pulled off his sweatshirt, undid his jeans and slid them down his legs. Hairy legs. His shoes and socks were already gone. Wise boy. Men look so silly with bare legs and socks. One of her past boyfriends had insisted on keeping his socks on. All the time. He hadn't liked her touching his toes, which had led first to tussles with the socks and later to the parting of the ways. Socks, really. The pile of discarded clothes grew, over in the corner, topped off by two pairs of pants, one black and one red. Naked, they had faced each other. Greg reached past her for a bowl of salt on the windowsill, and held it between them. There was a curious expression on his face, half serious and half wondering. This is the new country, the other side of passion, where it slips into other worlds and brings bits of them back to live with you, haunt you, entice and baffle you. And sometimes, hurt you.

'Creature of water, I bless and invoke you for the health of the body and the strength of the spirit. Be you an aid to us, cleanse us.'

Fee's light tones were replaced with Greg's tenor.

'Blessed be this creature of earth. As water purifies the body, so salt laves the soul. So do I bless you, that you may aid us.'

Fee took the bowl and poured the contents into the tub.

'Three times blessed, three times invoked, all good be herein and all malevolence cast hence from. In beauty, truth, peace and love we conjure you.'

'Cleanse us and we shall be pure. Wash us and we shall be whiter than snow.'

Why do we say that? Have you looked at snow lately? Its purity is evanescent and fails so swiftly. One touch, and it's gone. But it's beautiful, that winter blanket, washed with the blues of a moonlit night, stars sparkling on the earth as well as in the covering sky, or warmed by hibernal sunshine into eye-blinding brilliance, adamantine glare. Snowblind.

From somewhere came soft music. Enya? Adeaimus? Mike Oldfield? Subtle strains of gentle melody. Zoe's parting gift for the night. Greg stepped into the water and offered a hand to help Fee over the side of the bath. By accident or design, the old tub was quite big enough for two. It even had taps in the middle. Fee cursed those taps when she had to use this as a shower instead of the better screened cubicle. The water either splashed generously onto the floor, leaving you to mop it up after you had showered, which was a bitch, or the shower curtain wrapped you in a cold, damp embrace. The hard shower screen had been on the shopping list for ages, but somehow there was always something more immediate than replacing the shower curtain, embossed as it was with mermaids and fish. Now she blessed those taps. No arguments about who gets to sit on the plughole with the hot tap burning one shoulder while the cold tap froze the other. The water lapped a scant inch from the top. It water was warm and silky and fragrant. What was it about men that most of them hated hot water? Or was it a woman thing, to sink into liquid so hot it left you looking like a boiled lobster? Gracious ripples lapped Fee's breasts and plastered her long hair in tendrils over the swelling mounds. They swirled round Greg's knees. He had nice knees. Some men have bony knees, especially if they exercised. The contrast between Fee's sleek legs and Greg's muscular, hairy limbs was slightly comic. Wasn't it always? A sponge, generously lathered, was coming her way. He felt for one arm under the water, lifted it clear and washed it gently. Then the other. He sat up, pulled her towards him and washed her breasts and neck. Cradling her head against his shoulder, he squeezed the suds over her back, then leant back and started on her legs. Each ankle, foot and toe, lazily, thoroughly. So gently the lapping water didn't slop over the bath. Fee claimed the sponge and knelt between his legs. She stroked the loaded sponge over the swell of his chest, his arms and armpits, lifting his leg onto her shoulder and kissing the ankle while she caressed the sponge down the length, oh so slowly. She leant forward to kiss him, a bare touch of lips, then behind him to let the lather flow over his back. He cupped water and bubbles in both hands, pouring it over her belly and thighs, slipping his hands round to the mounds of her bottom, sliding over them, slippy with soap and water. His lips touched the flesh of her breast, a mere tickle, then he lay back, gathering her against him in a watery embrace. She lay on him, head on his shoulder, her wringing hair covering them both and floating between the petals on the water, hiding in the piles of foam that drifted on the surface. He stroked the length of her thigh, then poured water from his hand onto her hair. He worked up a lather in her hair, massaging her scalp and neck and back, then attended to his own head, a much quicker affair. There were no words.

There was no need. Just the sound of water lapping and the faint strains of the music. Fee slid beneath the water to rinse the shampoo out of her hair. She slid back up his body, wet and sleek as a seal, and lay against him as he smoothed on conditioner. He lay back, resting one hand on her bosom, stroking down to her belly under the water. Again she immersed herself. He was not the immersion type, and rinsed his hair with the shower head. Now the bath was really full. The slightest movement would cascade the water out all over the floor. Rob had given up with carpets after his daughters had ruined the third one, and had rubber flooring put down instead. It wouldn't matter. They lay there, entwined in the hot water, watching the steam rise in the candlelight. Greg turned her face to his and kissed her on the lips, gentle pressure. Hands moved over her flanks, her back. She let hers wander over his chest and thighs. There was time enough, more than enough, to enjoy the slow delight of a caressing hand before those hands became more urgent and personal. Why rush when you don't have to? What else is there to do but enjoy each other? There is no hurry, no haste to get on with it, complete the act. Why not relish the movement of skin on skin, the slide of a leg against yours, the touch of lips on your ear and forehead and eyebrow, your fingers falling over his torso, over the muscles of his belly and sides. Relax and enjoy.

The water was cooler now, though far from cold. Fee's skin was pink and vibrant with caresses. The mat of hair on Greg's chest sparkled with droplets of scented water. Fee stood up in the lazily curling steam, Venus rising from the foam of her pelagic birth, fresh and unsullied. Well, almost. Major sullying would come later. Oh, yes, it would. She extended a hand to her Triton, who folded his legs beneath the water and rose with her dripping foam and water and petals. Two soft towels waited to embrace them, to dry their skin, return them from water to land. Life emerges from the water and takes the land into its embrace and fills it with life, hopping, crawling, walking and eventually flying to populate the airs above. Water is the womb of life, from which all things come and to which they all return. The land holds them, will take them into its arms in death, but finally the water reclaims her own again. Bathing was a sacrament, a return to the solace of the mother, every sodden emergence a rebirth. Fee sat on the side of the bath, swathed in the towel, combing the tangles out of her hair tress by tress. Greg sat by her, one leg touching hers under the weight of fluffy terry. He had pushed his hair back with his fingers: one lock fell over his eyes. Fee lifted it, planted a kiss on his lips.

She stood, the towel falling to the floor in a damp heap, discarded. Mother-naked, she led the way into the master bedroom.

Here also, the soft effulgence of candles vied with shadows. They highlighted her skin in pagan tones, soft flesh against dark holy shadows. The mystery of the feminine, her power to give and receive, secrets concealed in the dark and revealed to the fortunate and worthy, the ones who had passed the test and won the prize. She turned to Greg, standing by the door. Pliant female, powerful male. But it is she who leads him to the consummation: it is hers to give, not his to take. He who thinks to take it by force will gain something, but not the ultimate gift. That is given freely, or not at all. He looked at her, gazing back over one shoulder, candlelight delineating the curves and hollows of her body.

He shut the door. What ought to have been a mute click as the latch caught was more……. the room felt sealed. It was. The closing of the door had sealed the spaca with them inside.

The master bedroom was a huge size for a cottage. Flanking the massive bed, draped in pale linen, two side tables stood, each graced with a small tealight in a cut glass holder glinting through the panes of the glass, refracted into rainbows. A small window faced the bed, cream curtains falling to the floor. Over where Fee stood was a golden wood coffer carved with linenfold panels. A white vase with Madonna lilies stood there, flanked by glowing lights. Greg padded over to her, barefoot. The room was warm enough even for the approaching autumn nights, and they were still heated from their bath. He took her face between his hands and kissed her soundly, thoroughly. Her response was as warm, yet her hands stayed away from his body. He stroked a finger down her cheek. Was that a tear glittering there?

'Let us bring forth the great Ayet of true worship,' he began.

'Which in times past, all revered.' She responded. They were losing themselves in each other's eyes. There were the words, which uttered, flowed around them while the sweet smoke of incense drifted up among the lilies.

'So is it made and placed, and the holiest pace is the centre.'
'And therefore we adore it.'
'That which we adore we also invoke.'
'The starry circle has existed since before Creation.'
'The great mystery of time and space……..'

The words flowed one to the other and back as the candles twinkled and the incense rose in the air. The atmosphere was charged with an aura of wythen, making it hard to breathe…..

'Reaching past the gates of time.'

They stood, silent now, lost in each other. Nothing else existed. Wayward metae, hunting murderers, interfering sisters, all had drifted away. Greg kissed her again, holding her close. There was a heat in her, and she took him into her arms and returned the kiss with more passion than it had been given.

She disengaged from him, and climbed onto the bed. From the table, she picked up a glass and held it out to him. He joined her as she knelt on the linen, her weight indenting the surface. The wine was sweet and heady. He lay on the bed as she trailed kisses across his body, here and there, the ancient siga that woke the wyth in him. As she reached back up to kiss his lips, he rolled her onto her back and traced those same kisses on her body. Her eyes were part closed and her lips soft and open. He sat on the bed, cross-legged, his back to the pillows and cushions by the headboard, and waited for her to rise and join him. She sat facing him. They looked at each other. To Fee, Greg had never looked so male and powerful. What he was seeing, she couldn't guess. The shadows hid his features. He reached out his hands to her, pulling her towards him. She inched up until she was sitting in his lap, her legs behind his back and her hands draped over his shoulders. The feelings in their closely held bodies began to build, slowly. Fee used her hands on his shoulders to lift herself up as he held her waist and guided her back down. Their bodies joined, they gazed into each other's eyes. There was nothing else in the world but themselves, on that bed, in that room. Nothing.

Fee breathed deeply, warding off the tension of awakening desire. Hell, it had been awakened long before. Greg's breathing was matching hers. Far away, the music rolled on. Fee's breathing became faster, and her cheeks mantled. Sweat was creeping down her spine, but still she kept motionless. Oh, this art was not taught openly. No-one had sat her down and told her how to do this. She just knew. But if you will sit in a man's lap, and admit him into your most intimate inner spaces, things will happen. Your body will respond. You can delay the final denouement, but you can't deny it forever, not if you carry on doing what you were doing. And if you invite his wyth, and his ayat as well….

    Greg's breathing was becoming slightly ragged now. He was losing the smooth rhythm in the upwelling sensations. He sought her mouth, and his breath was hot on her cheek. That small movement nearly tipped him over the edge. Tantra is a difficult discipline, more so if you crave to indulge your gross senses. But they were reaching for the perfect moment. It lies on the brink of orgasm, and is fleeting. Writhing bodies and gasping mouths can't catch it. The bodies unite, and part, but the souls never achieve symphysis. The passion that normally shows itself in the kiss and the caress was internal, not external. To achieve the very heights of bliss, to experience the perfect moment needs a measure of control over gross passion. To share each other fully, body and mind and ayat as one, to slip between the interstices of each other's body and psyche would require an act of passionless passion. Patience is not usually a virtue in bed, but here it is of the very essence. This, to put it mildly, was no thoughtless shag but a stately act of worship, one of the other, which would pass beyond either into the realms beyond the Midess, the world we inhabit.

    Fee kept her body relaxed, feeling the waves of passion mounting in her body. The wyth would move up her spine, a glowing presence in a transparent vessel, to meet with Greg's in an overwhelming explosion when it met the Gya. In the crucible of her belly, the fires were building higher and higher. Her head wanted to throw itself back and allow a scream of sheer ecstasy to escape. It was almost like pain. Incandescence coiled, seeking the way up through her body. To keep breathing now was simply impossible. Still she pulled in her breath, forcing the laving sensations to build up even higher. Their eyes were locked on each other, exchanging wyth, urging the other to hold on, hold on. Everything was gone now, even the bed beneath them. They were afloat in a sea of sensation and nothing, nothing would stop the final flow.

Then it came. Welling up from the profoundest depths, up, up, out of the red-blood drenched body darkness and into the light, carrying consciousness with it, flooding into a place beyond sound, beyond light, beyond feeling, on and on and on.

They fell back into their bodies with the gentleness of falling snowflakes. Hearts thundering, breath rasping, returning to a room transformed. Silk textured darkness, warm golden light, and everything alight and alive with…. Love? Wythen? Life? All of these? The atmosphere was alive, vibrant, warm. Even the most prosaic of objects held a mystery in its heart. They were still joined: well, they would be until Fee recovered enough to hoist herself off Greg's lap, or he rolled onto his side, or something. But it was peaceful to sit there, looking at normal things which now had the added glamour of wythen. Looking at them with enhanced sight. Colours were brighter, more alive….

Greg shifted beneath her. How long they had been sitting together? Not important. She allowed him to lift her, and slid to lay down next to him, pillowed by cushions. Slowly he unwound long legs and cuddled up beside her.

'Well.'

What else was there to say? They fell asleep, entwined on top of the covers while the candles burned out, leaving the room in swathes of shadows. Occasionally, a flicker of pale fire trailed over the bed, the curtains, the sleeping bodies, but they were oblivious to the relics of their wythen.

Chapter Twenty-six

They awoke to the smell of fresh ground coffee and bacon. Zoe was back, and busy in the kitchen by all accounts.

'Trouble at t'mill. The night shift didn't show up. Not surprising, really. Tom ran me over. He and Colin Maybrick loaded the hoppers after I finished off. We'll have to make alternative arrangements until Theo comes back.'

'If he does…. Thanks, anyway. I'll call Colin and see if any of the others want a bit of overtime to tide us over.'

'Problems?'

Greg entered the kitchen, wearing an old bathrobe of Rob's. It was a little large, and bunched round the waist where he had tied it tight. Modesty? Hah.

'You could say that. Theo's just eviscerated my night shift. They were only doing it as a favour to me, anyway. I'll get Colin to scare up alternative staff, there's always people round here that are on the lookout for extra cash. Perhaps I can get Jean to pop in, at least until Lottie's available. I'm sure she'd be grateful for some extra income for the baby, and it's only a few hours after all.'

'You seem to be on the ball.'

Zoe was serving bacon butties. Greg fell on them like a starving man, and Zoe watched him in wonder.

'I think I'll need more bacon. That boy of yours surely has an appetite.'

'I wonder why.'

'Let's not go there.'

'Reticence? From you? I'm surprised, Zoe.'

'Spare me the details. Please. Remember my tender years.'

'So what now?' Greg asked, swallowing a mouthful of bread and bacon. 'Topnotch.'

'You're easy to please. You are finding that warehouse. Fee is hunting weapons. Big weapons. Lily is providing ammunition. I am providing information.'

'I am truly sorry to have to cut and run, but I still have a job to do today. One I can't put off. It will, however, put me close to someone I think can help me. A bloke called Jordan. He owes me a favour, and I'm about to cash it in.'

'Do tell.'

'He's a finder. You know when film companies, advertising agencies and the like, need a location? And they can be very specific about what they want. Jordan finds those places for them, and he's the best. I helped him when he was starting out. Dropped his name, arranged some work for him. He didn't let me down. Came up with the goods every time. If I tell him I want to find this warehouse, it's as good as found.'

'How does he do it?'

'He won't tell me. I think it's a combination of Google Earth and a fast motorbike. And a wasted youth traipsing over the country with a camera. Whatever. If that warehouse is findable, he'll find it. And who owns it, and if they are willing to make a few bob renting it out to a film crew. Worth his weight in gold, that boy.'

'Won't that alert someone? We don't need that.'

'I'll tell him I want it as a backdrop only. If we film on the streets, we only have to deal with the cops. And if it's on a trading estate, which we think it is, then it will be easy…. What am I thinking? We only need to find the place, not arrange a shoot.'

'Then get your kecks on, man, and get going. Time's ticking away here.'

'I wish I knew when he's planning to hit us next.'

'Don't we all. Are you any nearer to knowing how you get your hands on that sword yet, Fee?'

'I have a feeling about it. But I have to find it here first, I think. And it's not the sort of thing you can practice with. When the time comes, I think I'll either have it or I won't.'

'Don't you just hate that. We charge in, yell 'Hands up, sucker!' then find we're up shit creek. Not a comforting thought.'

'Sometimes you've just got to wing it.'

Zoe growled, pouring hot water into the dirty pan. Greg vanished upstairs to make himself decent. He hugged Zoe briefly, and Fee walked him to the door.

'I really hate to go. I feel I'm leaving you in the lurch. Right when I've got you where I want you, I have to run off. Not what I want at all.'

'Come back as soon as you can.'

'Count on it. I'll call if I get anything.'

'You do that. I'll be here.'

She seized his sweatshirt and pulled him close. A through kiss followed. He waved as he sped to his car, gunned the engine and left in a cloud of exhaust and sprayed gravel. Fee hugged her housecoat close against her body and watched until the car was out of sight. Out of the kitchen a voice floated.

'My, my, girlfriend, you *are* a piece of work. One shag from you and they run away like rabbits.' Fee snorted and thumped upstairs to make herself decent.

Zoe sat at the table in the kitchen, nursing a mug of coffee. Fee joined her and sank her head into her hands.

'We're getting closer, Fee.'

'And it's not an easy place to be. I feel like my ass is naked in the wind. Dem ole black clouds o' doom is hanging over me.' She fingered the mojo bag she had picked up from the hall table.

'Well, anyway. Here is the news. The body count is now at one hundred and sixty six. If I don't miss my guess, then there will be three more victims. Then the cycle will be complete. One hundred and sixty nine. Thirteen times thirteen. Over forty years. Do you see, Fee?'

'But the first death was in April. It's August now.'

'The first death needn't mark the start of the cycle. The inaugural ritual does that.'

'Where are you getting this from?'

'The tales of Amagus. First comes the pact. The agreement between Amagus and the sponsor about the terms of the pact. If I give you this, then you will give me that, sort of thing. Then the party of the first part goes forth and satisfies the terms of the contract, whereupon the party of the second part delivers his end.'

'But Amagus' pact went wrong.'

'So it did. But that doesn't mean that another sleazeball could succeed where Amagus failed.'

'So Simon is seeking true immortality.'

'And he's not doing it by the traditional means. Sitting in front of an alembic for years making the Elixir of Life.'

'He's trading the wraiths of sacrificed fratten in exchange for eternal life?'

'Looks like it.'

'But why? We all accept the idea of rebirth. Opting out from that…. It's not a Fratris thing.'

'He disagrees.'

'I wonder who else might be involved? Surely he can't be working alone.'

'And why would Simon want eternal life? He's got it already, as good as.'

'Hum. There have always been a few true immortals wandering about. And not vampires, either.'

'He wants to join the club.'

'Best of luck to him, then. But not if it involves interfering with *our* cycle of eternal life. He's taken all those people from the Family. Out of the mystery. We'll never see them again. That can't be allowed.'

So Simon had interrupted the life-cycle of the Fratris. They moved from the Midess to the Asha and back, weaving a golden chain of love given and received and renewed again. A lover, a child, a parent, expected to live and love and die, then meet those they had connection to again when life in the Midess renewed, or they returned to the Asha. The Ayen gave them this, gave them the wyth in their blood and the ability to unite with the Gya. Reverenced as The Karna, the Lord of Asha and his Lady, The Arda, this was their gift to the Fratris. And it ought to be defended. In the Midess at least.

'And it's been landed in our lap. Thank you. Thank you ever so much.'

'No, Zoe. Remember what Rina said. I can win if my motives are pure. Yesterday, I wanted to stop it because Sophie had been taken from me. I wanted revenge. A selfish revenge. Now, I want to stop it because it's an abuse of the wyth. It can't be allowed to continue. I have to stop it. It's my duty, almost. It *is* my duty.

That means I have a pure motive. I am one step closer to winning.'

Zoe looked at her oddly, but instead of making a comment, flipped open her laptop.

'I've got an e-mail from Theo. He's gone to ground in Romney Marsh, of all places. Apparently there's a blyd there, in Appledore, and three of the blyd work for Simon. Cecile's gone up north. He says no-one is aware of anything going on. But get this: we're not the only ones who've lost relatives. Metae have been vanishing too. There's always been some traffic between the blyds, but since they don't keep tabs on each other, a vamp can drop out of sight for years before resurfacing. It's no big thing. But every blyd they've contacted has lost at least one member. It hasn't worried them, and it still doesn't. They believe that the missing vamps will come back, sooner or later. But Theo's not so sure. He says to do nothing until he comes back.'

'When?'

'He doesn't say. Only that he will return. In the meantime, Brenda is in London with a wodge of cash getting tickets for Simon Lake.'

'Bugger could have sent me a ticket, or two. Cheapskate.'

'Hold that thought. Tickets for a Simon Lake extravaganza are gold dust, you know that.'

'Brenda will find a way.' Ffion mused a moment. 'While we're waiting, I must see to the nightshift. Be a dear and check when Lily's back. I can't do squat without some serious wyth on hand. I probably won't have time to gather it myself.'

'You whack a serious punch anyway.'

'So did Sophie.'

With that, Fee raced upstairs to tidy up. So much to do, so little time. And she still had to find that sword, and she had no idea where to start......

It was refreshing in a way to deal with smaller worries. No-one at Blue Moon was actually trying to kill anyone else, for one thing. It was ticking over nicely. There was sufficient stock to fill the orders that were coming in, and ample orders to keep everyone busy enough. The place didn't work anything like full time, and the only reason Fee had a night shift was to hide the fact that every batch of gloop they packaged contained a weave. Her natural paranoia that someone would find out the secret was easing. Maybe it was time to be a little more open. Get the afternoon shift to fill the hoppers before they left, or get a early morning crew in……. One less problem.

A few things needed her personal attention. She donned a white coat, hairnet and overshoes and sallied forth onto the filling lines. Jars and tubes were debouching onto the line, being filled and capped in good order. The white clad machine minders looked happy enough, and voices raised over the clatter of machinery. The other line was down: a timing chain had broken. That was no big deal, but the machinery on this line was old. Breakdowns were becoming an issue, and new fillers were expensive. She collared Dave, the supervisor, and told him to see what machines might be available to replace the ailing filler.

'Poor old gal. She's given us her best. I'll miss her. But it's way past her retirement date, really.'

'Aye, time to let her rust in peace. Doesn't do to be sentimental over these things.' Dave grinned at his own pun. 'Should be able to find a second hand filler somewhere. Factories are always retooling. We might have to rethink the packaging, though.'

'That is the least of my worries. See what you can find. You know where to reach me.'

'Oh, by the way, I told Pauline to shove off. I was getting tired of her excuses. She was slightly annoyed.'

'I'll bet she was. Well, she had it coming. Leave it a while, and maybe she'll see reason. She was a good worker, when she was here.'

'She was muttering on about unfair dismissal when she left.'

'Everyone's on temporary contracts, Dave. Work comes, work goes. We always hit a quiet spell about now. Once we've got the stock in for Christmas, we'll be letting more go. We can re-hire them next season, they all know that.'

'Think of it as their Christmas break, they do. Been asking if there'll be a bonus this year, they have.'

'I'll do the sums and get back to you. Privately, it's been a good year. There'll be a nice fat present for everyone. But keep it under your hat for now.'

She smiled and waved. It had been a pleasant couple of hours, a respite from the grim reality. Surely it ought to be the other way around? Work was the grim reality, leisure the respite, and here was her work acting as an anodyne for bleak leisure. Perhaps she ought to start to worry.

Zoe had developed a dose of the 'larraping mardies' as Sophie would have said. When Fee arrived back, much improved in humour, she found the girl was acting like a hyperactive ant. No sooner had she sat down than she would jump up again, prowl restlessly, grab a book, then throw it away: sort through CD's, put one on then change her mind and switch the player off. It was distracting. Zoe could sit straight hours staring at her computer, and now she was a mega fidget. ADD on uppers. She was filling the entire cottage with restless energy.

When the call came, it was the landline. Zoe went for it, a greyhound released from the trap.

'It's Mum. She wants to know if we've seen her Mischief yet.'

'So that's why you're acting like a lemming on speed. Tell her he's probably here, but he hasn't checked in yet.'

A soft chime came from the antique bell that hung by the door, and a chuckle came over the phone. Zoe listened for a moment and replaced the receiver. She marched back into the parlour and flung herself into her favourite chair.

'Mischief, reveal yourself to me this instant.'

There was a scuffle and a faint chitter. The dog-lizard swarmed up the side of the chair and sat on the wingback, tail swishing. He was mewling with... pleasure.

'Mischief, go sit on the table.'

Zoe was not anxious to have a semitamed gwhylli that close to her jugular. Bigger things had been there, and perhaps she didn't want to repeat the experience. At least not with Biehail. His kind had a weird sense of humour.

It made an elastic leap, skidding slightly on the polished surface. Snag had the same problem. Speaking of the cat (figuratively) Snag had woken up from his nap on the windowsill and was eyeing the visitor with a little too much interest. Fee caught him in a double armed hug, and he squirmed round to keep the object of his attention in plain sight.

'Well, Mischief. Where is the place you were to take the oldest sister? Have you found it?'

'Indeed I have. Mistress.' He looked as badly dubbed as an old Kung Fu movie. The lips worked, but the voice was off by about half a second. It wasn't pleasant to watch. It made your ears want to water.

'Then where is it?'

Biehail mewed sadly, and shook his head. Fee could understand. Gwhyllen went from *here* to *there,* but they didn't go in between. Since Biehail had been instructed to find the location, he must know where it was: it was a matter of getting the information from him.

'If I show you a map, can you show me where you have been?'

'What is it, map?'

'A picture. One that shows our world, where the things in it are.'

'Let Biehail look at mapthing. Maybe.'

Fee left at a glance from Zoe, who was watching the imp as intently as Snag. She took the cat with her: she didn't trust him. She returned with an AA atlas, and minus the cat, whose complaints could be heard from the kitchen. Biehail's tail was twitching eagerly, and he was making little leaps of impatience on the table.

She opened the map book and put it on the table. He crawled onto it, muttering and mewling. He was quite cute, really. He sniffed at the map, and ran blunted fingers over the paper. His claws scratched at the colours, and he was confused when the lines stayed on the paper. He looked at his claws, then went back to sniffing and scratching. Fee began to fear for the integrity of the book as the page crinkled.

'Here. Biehail is here.'

He stabbed one claw at the map. He was pretty close, but then it was a big map. His claw covered the whole of Lower Congrieve, or would have, if the place had been big enough to merit any indication of its existence on that scale.

Biehail put his nose back to the paper. He started to scrabble at the edge of the page.

'It not here. It there.' He pointed to a place some few inches away.

'Get off the book, Mischief.'

He scrambled off, and watched curiously as Fee turned the page. He grunted, sidled back up to the book and turned a few pages himself. Then he leapt back onto the sheet and resumed scrabbling. He examined the lines, their colours, tracing them with a claw until they left the page, then turned the pages until he found them again. If he'd never seen a map book before, he was intent on an accelerated learning curve. His antics were slightly comic: Fee had to suppress a grin when, losing a line, the imp had (most probably) sworn in his own dialect. Sounds like chewing wet eggshells with a mouth full of sticky toffee, she thought. Expressive.

'Biehail was here! Thisplace.'

His claw rested on a page somewhat northeast of Newton Abbot.

'If I find you a bigger map, can you find the exact place?'

Biehail cocked his head and mewled again. He didn't understand. Fee grabbed the local OS map and unfolded it on the table. She pushed the book aside and returned it to the first page they had shown Biehail. It was difficult because the creature had creased the pages in his excitement and they didn't lay flat anymore.

'We are here, this place. We are also here. This is a bigger map, and it shows more detail. More of where we are.' It was like communicating with a three year old. The creature looked at her as if she were daft. They could only be in one place, not two. Not even the great lords could do that. 'It is two pictures of the same place.'

Biehail grabbed at the map. Good job it was laminated, or he'd have torn it to shreds. He bounced back to the book. Book, map. Map, book. He was moving very fast, a miniature dervish frantically whirling from place to place. Finally, he settled on the large map, and stabbed his claw directly into the miniscule dab that was, to Ordinance Survey, their house.

'Biehail see! Biehail here, and here. Now show Biehail big map of thisplace.'

He scrabbled back through the map book to the Newton Abbot page. Badgers could have been using it for bedding by the look of it.

'We don't have an OS map that shows Newton Abbot. We'll have to use the computer.'

Biehail swore again, and sunk his head into his front paws. This was more than he bargained for. Thisworld was not a simple a place as he had expected it to be. Snatched from his comfortable nest into this distressing, bewildering place, crammed into a bit of paper only to find at the other end of an excruciatingly boring and smelly journey in a roaring metal monster, that he was caught and captured and tortured, then sent back under sentence of death right where he came from: to return mostly unscathed, to the second location, only to have a lesson in mapreading from two horribly ugly large beings with only two legs and no (Horror!) tail.

'Stop sulking and come over here.'

The smaller of the two beings had opened what looked very like another bookthing. Biehail touched it, and jumped back, swearing. Galvanic liquid! They might have warned him. That hurt! Tentatively, he peered round the upstanding side of the book, cheeping curiously. On the luminous page he could see the same lines as from the mapthing. He skittered back, looked at the picture of the placeNewtonabbot then at the same Newtonabbotplace that was moving on the lightpagething. The smaller being was holding a curved creature captive in the lower part of the new book, and was stroking it to make the lines on the page move. She must have great power. Biehail decided in his ferrety mind to be very wary of this one.

'You see that little black square? No, don't touch the screen. Tell me 'up' or 'down' or 'right' or 'left' until that square is right on the place where you were.'

Zoe guided the pointer to increasingly excited gibber and chatter, increasing the resolution each time to raptured coos from the tiny gwhylli as each changed compiled on the screen. Finally the little critter started to jump up and down in excitement.

'Biehail here! Thisplace!'

Zoe sent the computer through more convolutions.

'Lower Ashcombe Farm Park. KoziToes Footwear. Looks like a brick and timber building, all right. Barn conversion, probably. Only a small site, a bit like Blue Moon.'

'Face it, Blue Moon would be almost a ringer. We'll have to wait until Greg gets back to be sure.'

Zoe saved the information and decided it was time for a snack. She went into the kitchen to hunt down whatever goodies the fridge had to offer, accompanied by the now closely attentive Biehail.

She eventually decided on chicken sandwiches, and brought back a tray for them both. Biehail eyed it hungrily, making small attacking manoeuvres towards the tray. Did gwhyllen get the munchies? Zoe offered him a slice of chicken. He seized it avidly and began chewing it with evident relish, smearing the mayo over the table.

'Messy boy.'

Zoe wiped up the mayo with a paper napkin. Biehail took advantage of her distraction to steal a crisp from her plate.

'Hey! You thieving bugger!'

Biehail crooned anxiously, and offered her the remaining shards of potato.

'No, you have them now. But don't go stealing stuff. Ask.'

The gwhylli approved of chicken and crisps. Tomato was beyond the pale and lettuce useful for bedding and not much else. The jury was out on bread. He fell asleep in the remains of Zoe's lunch.

'What the hell are we going to do with him? He's barely housetrained.'

'That will be up to you, I suspect. He seems to have adopted you. Snag's no fan, for sure.'

The only other news they received that day was a brief text from Greg.

"Jordan onside. Is smarmy git. CU 2mro. Lv G."

They pottered through a pearly evening, grateful to get to bed and end it.

Chapter Twenty-seven

The night was too warm to be comfortable. Their new houseguest kept them awake with his scrabbling until Zoe corralled him in the bathroom sink with a couple of face flannels for company. He settled down, alternating mewling and stroking the towelling fabric with chewing it. They wouldn't make good dusters by morning. Downstairs, Snag howled, deprived of what he saw as his rightful quarry. He did not approve at all. He would share a portion of his digestive tract with the new guest, but that was all. Fee threw him out, hoping that a nocturnal hunt would occupy him. She tossed and turned under her one sheet, drifting from wakefulness and dream. Towards morning, she found herself dreaming of Greg. For some obscure reason, they had gone fishing for prawns. In a pond, if you will. She turned over and sank back into a fitful doze. Memory began to overlay plans for the day ahead. She was standing by the garden gate, talking to Lily. Lily was wearing her cloak, and she had walking boots on her feet. With her fellstick, she pointed over the trees. Looking where she pointed, Fee saw a church spire. It couldn't have been the village church, it was too tall. Lily was telling her a legend, some mishmash of Arthur and Bedivere, which ended with 'then it stuck in the mud, but before he could wade out, a bird took it and flew away.' Fee said something about Caliburn, and Lily answered 'Of course not. It wasn't a sword.' She awoke hearing church bells and more refreshed than she had any right to be. Zoe, on the other hand, had given up on sleep and spent the night in the window embrasure, watching the night. As soon as the first sickly fingers of dawn had crept over the horizon, she had gone downstairs and made a pot of tea, which she carried up to her sister's room. They sat companionably on the bed, sipping the hot brew.

'What's on the agenda for today? Besides continuing breathing, of course?'

'Apart from finding that sword? We wait. There's very little we can do. Hunting can be like that. Tedious.'

'Especially when you're the bait.'

'Tell me about it. We could ask Mischief about KoziToes. Lily told him that she wanted to know everything about the place. All we've done so far is find out where he thinks it is.'

Questioning Biehail, it turned out, was a non-starter. Zoe had let the cat in, and with typical single-mindedness he had sneaked upstairs and breakfasted on gwhylli. They found him sitting in the bathroom licking his chops.

'So what now?'

'Buggered if I know, sis. We can only hope he chewed his food well.'

'You're thinking of that scene in Alien with John Hurt.'

'Yup.'

'Can't we do anything?'

'Like what? Take him to the vet and say 'Excuse me, I think my cat's swallowed a demon?'

'Put like that, no. Stupid bugger. You think he'd know not to eat just anything, he's lived here long enough.'

'*You* would. He'll eat anything. Remember that rat?'

It was another family legend. Snag, then little more than a kitlin, had gone out hunting and scored a rat, which he had brought back and stowed under the sofa to mature. In the sofa, actually. The stench had driven the family wild, but despite extensive searching they had been unable to locate the source of the stink and had to live with it. Until Snag had deemed the titbit ripe enough and retrieved it while the family were watching QI on the telly. He had dragged it under the coffee table and proceeded to masticate with much relish and crunching. Abandoning Stephen Fry and Alun Davies (no relation) to their amusements, they had chased Snag out. Clamping his prize between locked jaws, the cat had fled to the garden to resume his interrupted feast. QI had been a washout.

Snag proceeded to clean his whiskers, blissfully unaware of the gruesome fate that might await him in consequence of his unfortunate breakfast. Fee sat in her favourite chair, trying to make sense of the senseless muddle of memory and dream from last night. She sighed.

'No closer, then?'

Fee shook her head.

'It's gotta have echoes. A thing like that'd leave traces.'

'Then it's not round here. Otherwise, we'd have noticed it before.'

'Unless it was keeping stchum until it was needed.'

'Well, I bloody need it now.'

'Then you'll have to find it. You're the only one who can, Fee.'

'Here, swordy, swordy, swordy,' Fee intoned listlessly.

'You won't get it like that,' Zoe admonished crisply.

Fee, needled, leapt to her feet and flung her arms wide. Theatrically, she gestured to the air.

'O thou Great Sword of Destiny, I summon thee to my hand! Come thee, from whatsoever place thou rest, and deliver thyself into my keeping! Come thou swiftly and without delay, I command thee!' She turned to her sister. 'There, satisfied now?'

There was a second of absolute silence. The moment between one second and the next, stretched impossibly into the now. Faintly and far off, a bell tolled, dolefully, once.

'BLOODY HELL.'

The bell tolled again. Then once more. The two sisters locked a glance.

'What is this that is calling me?' they exclaimed in unison. There was a mad scrabble for boots, and two figures erupted out of the back door.

'It came from over there,' Zoe said, pointing down the valley. The sound was gone, but it left afterechoes in the air. Clear as clear.

'What's down here?' Fee asked. Zoe's knowledge of the surrounding countryside was superior to hers.

'Belton Hollows. Pile of old ruins. Was a hamlet once. Horribly muddy. No-one goes there much. Too soggy,' Zoe shot back.

'Hollowmarsh.' Something clicked in Fee's memory. 'Isn't there some legend, something to do with a soldier and a sanctuary?'

'You'd know better'n me.'

The details of the old ghost story welled up. Fee related the tale as they walked.

'It's a very old myth. Celtic, they say. Some old woman was busy dying one foul winter's night, and she's upset that she'll go before she finds out what's happened to her grandson, her only surviving relative, who's away fighting some petty war somewhere. Anyway, the old dame who's tending her has to go home to get some medicine or other, and leaves her alone. Well, she hears a knock at the door, and a voice says, 'Will ye no let me in?' But she's too sick to get out of her bed, so she quavers 'Who calls?' and whoever it is knocks again, and repeats, 'Will ye no let me in'. 'Be off wi'ee,' the old girl says. The knock is repeated, only faintly now, and the voice whispers for the last time, 'will ye no let me in', then fades into the noise of the rain and wind.

'Anyway, the other old girl returns, and the dying one asks her to leave the door open, so when her grandson comes back, he can come in. No, says the other, for it is too stormy without, and shuts the door fast.

'So she falls asleep, and again the old girl hears the knock and the voice. 'Will ye no let me in', but she can't get to the door nor rouse her companion. Eventually, she manages to wake the old gel, and tells her again to open the door for her grandson. Well, she won't. A third time the knocking comes, and the two are too scared to open the door until the voice says, 'I cry thee sanctuary, for the Lord's sake.' And the old girl pipes up 'Who do you own as Lord?' 'Him I prayed to at my mother's breast', comes the reply, so, quaking and quailing, the old gel opens the door. Of course, there's no-one there. But the other one calls out 'Bonny boy! I knew you'd come to me afore I died!' and breathes her last. The old girl shuts the door and spends the night in the hovel with the corpse, and in the morning, amongst a wreck of branches and stuff thrown up by the wind, she finds and old sword driven into the ground by the door.'

'So the grandson had come back?'

'The implication is that his ghost did. In any case, they took the sword and buried it with the grandmother. Another version says they kept it in the church. Still another says it's where the ghost left it.'

'Anyone ever look?'

'Not to my knowledge.'

The tale had woven time away, as they scrambled over stiles and wove through clumps and tangles of bracken and gorse. And the ground was getting soggier by the minute underfoot.

'Well, this is it. Belton Hollows.'

'Not much, is it?' Fee's eyes ranged over scrubby hillocks nestled in a soggy dell. You could see why ghost stories were told about the place. It had that sort of air to it. Otherness. A dead tree, bone-white now, sagged into the soaking moss. The hills around kept the wind away: there was a curious breathlessness about the hillocks. Sour disappointment clogged Fee's throat. Maybe it was too much to ask, to be summoned by bells and find a magic sword sticking out of the moss just like that. 'Here, swordy, swordy, swordy,' she muttered. She spared a glance over the surrounding hills. Steep and unwelcoming. The only way in was the one that they had taken, unless they wanted to wade knee-deep through soggy peat. Her eyes narrowed: was there a shadow on that hill? In the grass? No, it wasn't clouds. A vague shape… standing stone, maybe? The place was littered with them.

'Hey, Zoe. Up there.' Her sister squelched over, shading her eyes with her hand. 'Standing stone?'

'Could be. It's a fair way up, though.'

'Let's go look.' The stone had excited her interest. Maybe….

Struggling up the nearly vertical hillside left them breathless and wet to the ankles. There had been a watercourse down in the moss, and it had taken them unawares. Zoe flung herself down under the stone, where the slope slackened a bit - if you were on drugs and were very generous with the geography. It might have been a standing stone, or it could equally have been a worn protrusion of rock, a baby torlet. The surface was pitted and dotted with lichens, as unremarkable as any other vagrant rock. Fee collapsed belly-down on the stone, and wiggled out, heedless of the edges that poked at her through her jeans. Resting her chin on her folded forearms, she gazed down into the valley. Up on the rock, standing stone, whatever it was, she was poised over the valley like a bird in flight. Warmth from the stone, stored sunlight, seeped into her skin. She let go of her disappointment, and let the solitude blossom in its place. She stared around, and saw.....

'There's a really great view of our village from up here.'

'Take your word for it.'

'I can see the sun shining on the church steeple.'

'Well, hallelujah.'

'You can even see the three lancet windows from here.' Zoe grunted a response. Church steeples were not her primary interest in life. 'You need to see this, Zoe. Quick, before the sun's gone.'

'I can afford to wait a bit, then. Several billennia from now, I've got.' Despite her words, Zoe heaved herself up and crawled to join her sister. 'Otch up, then.' Fee wriggled sideways, and Zoe flopped down next to her. 'Very nice. I can see......'

The breath caught in her throat.

'Never noticed that before.'

'Me neither. Perhaps you can only see it from here.'

'I could reach out and touch it.....' Fee extended her arm. She meant it as a joke, but the tingle in her fingers warned her that any levity was wasted. She could feel a weight in her palm, and if she closed her eyes, her fingers could.... could... grasp a firm weight, and lift it off...... Something hot and liquid ran down her arm, from wrist to elbow to shoulder, singing through flesh and into bone, lacing through her spine like fire. There was a moment of disorientation, as if she was spinning, spinning, and the world was turning.... A firm, warm arm snaked round her waist, and Zoe's voice was in her ear.

'Stone ground me, water bear me up, air embrace me and fire cherish me for ever....'

Then she was back, gasping, sweating, her free arm clutching onto the monolith, her fingers scrabbling.

'It's gone, now?'

'Not gone. It's in me....'

With Zoe helping, Fee slid on her bum back down the slope. By the time her toes met the runnel of water, she had regained her balance, though the world seemed different, somehow. They returned the way they had come, making a slight detour to take in the church. Zoe insisted on buying ice lollies at the Post Office, and they sat on the bench in the churchyard, letting the sun warm them. In the church wall, the lancet windows gazed serenely down, innocent of any embellishment.

'You know, now I think of it, There's some gobbledegook in Dad's Diaries that mentions something about the church. About there being more to it than met the eye close to.'

'You read Dad's Diaries?'

'After Lily scarpered to Norfolk.'

Rob, the chemist, had kept careful notes of all the work he had done in service to the Government. Maybe there were mentions there of the dreaded death ray, hints of strange and exotic devices of destruction. Or not. Rob the cyscan had kept equally detailed notes of his experiences. Day by day. Everything he had done, all noted and annotated, hotly defended against the incursions of his daughters. After he died, Lily had kept them. It might have been an oversight: she had been seriously ill for a long time after he left her alone in the world. Then again, it might have been deliberate. It was the custom to destroy all traces of someone's cys once they passed into the Asha. Dad's Diaries had survived, most probably because Jean hadn't known about them. Certainly they would have been consigned to the flames had she been aware of their existence. Fee had found them, carefully concealed in a hidden niche in Rob's nightstand. He had built it himself, so the hiding place was both secret and secure from prying eyes and fingers. Perhaps he had intended them to survive him. Sadly, Fee could only understand a small portion of what she read in them.

'You ought to study them, Mouse.'

'Maybe. One day.'

'I think he'd want you to.'

'So,' Zoe ventured after a few moments. 'Just what was going on back there?'

'Congruence.'

'Now I'm much wiser.'

'Two times coming together. Like ink spots on a piece of paper. When it's flat, the spots are separate. If you fold the paper, they can come together, occupy the same place in spacetime.'

'Wow. So sometime else, someone stood on that rock, and

threw that sword onto the church steeple. Why?'

'To hide it until it was needed again? And it was probably chymed there, not thrown. It's not altogether real, you know.'

'So you say. And it's in you, now?'

'Occupying my space with me, I think. For now.'

'Then you'll have to put it back?'

'When I've finished with it. Yes. Definitely.'

'And you can, like, pull it out when you need it?'

'I suppose so. It's not something I'm about to experiment with. I'll know when the time comes, I expect.'

'Hope.'

'Expect. Something to do with my state of mind when I called it to me. It's like that with the things of Gya.'

They trailed back home. Fee, still somewhat light-headed, found her attention wandering. She stopped trying to cook when she found she had put sliced cucumber in the kettle. Zoe found a cache of teabags later in the butter dish, and wondered out loud what had happened to the garlic that had been on the windowsill. (Days later, she discovered the missing cloves in the washing machine, fortunately before she used it.)

Greg arrived shortly after lunchtime with a suitcase, which prompted Zoe to ask if he was planning to move in permanently.

'With just one case? Do me a favour.'

'She's just testing you.'

'Just as well that I've sisters, then. I felt the same way when they started to bring boyfriends home. It was a trial not to be rude to some of them.'

'You have sisters? Fancy that.'

'I hope you'll like them.' He unslung his laptop into the sofa. 'Jordan found three possible locations for our warehouse. I told you he was slick. There's one out by Cullompton and one near Ottery St Mary. The other is near Newton Abbot.'

'We found the one up past Newton Abbot.' He raised an eyebrow at her. 'Mischief came back.'

'Is he still here?'

'Yes and no.' The eyebrow went up even further. 'The cat ate him.' Greg started to laugh. 'It's not funny.'

'No, it's not,' he agreed as soon as he could talk again. 'Have you done anything about it?'

'Such as? I don't think this is covered in "Everyday Household Remedies."'

'You could try cod liver oil.'

'Will that do any good?'

'Well, Mam always used to dose our moggies with cod liver oil when they got hairballs and stuff. Hawked them up a treat after. It's worth a try.'

Zoe turned up with coffee and they sat down to discuss options. They were arguing about this and that when the phone rang.

'Ffion? Ffion, are you there?'

'Claire?'

'Thought she was in France….' Zoe started, only to be cut off as Fee engaged the speakerphone.

'Ffion, Josie's gone missing.' There was a thin thread of panic in Claire's voice. 'We were coming back to tell you that Mel and I were going to New Zealand in the New Year, and that I was going to sell the house and move over there with him. We drove up, Josie and I, and came over on the ferry. We'd got to Ilminster and stopped for a break, stretch our legs. Josie wandered off, and the next thing I knew I couldn't find her. I've got the security here looking for her, and they're calling in the police…….. I'm frightened….. *He's* got her.'

Fee knew who *He* was.

'Hang on a minute.' She hit the privacy button. 'Zoe, have we got a photo of Josie? Can you show it to Greg and ask him if it's the kid he saw?' She turned back to the phone and the distraught Claire. 'What do you want me to do?'

'Find her….. I don't know. Look, I've got to go. The police are here.'

'Keep calm, Claire. We'll find her.' But Claire had disconnected the line. 'Bugger.'

Zoe was scrabbling in a cupboard. She sorted through a handful of photographs and handed one to Greg. 'Here.'

'Yes, that's her. Long fairish hair, slim, small face. Yes, I'm sure.'

'Then we need to find her, and quickly. Greg, you've seen the warehouse. What's your best guess?'

'We don't even know if He's got her. And he might not have taken her back to his lair yet.'

'His first ploy failed. He must know that by now. What better way of flushing us out than to use Josie?'

Greg pinched his nose. Whatever choice he made, it would limit their options. Newton, Cullompton or Ottery St Mary? He made a decision, based more on geography than instinct.

'We go and collect Claire, taking Ottery St Mary on the way. Then we can split our forces. Two of us can go to Cullompton, two to Newton. Then no-one's alone, as Claire is right now.'

'How long until dark?'

'Why, Zoe?'

'Because if it's dark, we can call on Theo and Cecile. Theo said not to move until we heard from him.'

'He didn't know about this.'

'Okay, yes. So I tell him. He can meet us.'

'He's in Romney, dammit.'

'Your point being? He can travel real fast.'

'Not fast enough, I suspect.'

'I'm going to tell him anyway. He can pick it up when he wakes. If he's asleep. Maybe he found somewhere he can avoid daylight. He does that, you know.'

'Okay. We'll check out the Ottery St Mary site, as it's on the way. Then we can consider splitting up and scope the other two.'

'I'm not comfortable with the splitting up thing.'

'Can't say I'm all that happy either. If you've got a better idea, now's the time to air it.'

There were no other suggestions, better or otherwise. They piled into Greg's car and shot off to Ilminster, leaving Snag, well dosed up with cod liver oil, which he had taken to with evident relish, shut up in the annex with the washing machine. Just in case of... accidents.

The Ottery St Mary site turned out to be an old brick warehouse lit with blazing arc lights, busy with lorries coming and going. Such a hive of activity would not be the place they were looking for, surely. Zoe wandered up to the gatehouse and back.

'It's a warehouse all right. Distribution. I told them we were looking for Turnstone, or maybe something similar. He said, not round here. Then he said there was a place called Turnpike over by the M5 that they delivered to. They've been here forever.'

Scratch one place then. Next stop, Ilminster.

It took quite a time to find Claire. There were no motorway services, so it was left to Fee to call her back and ask where she was. It was an uncomfortable reunion. Claire was understandably upset, and the police had little to offer. They had gone by the time Fee found Claire. No-one admitted to seeing Josie: all the police could suggest was to go home and wait. No chance. They found a small café and sat down to hold a war council.

They argued it round until it was getting dark. Claire was sceptical that a random tour of warehouses would bring her any closer to finding her lost daughter, and said so vehemently. Zoe talked her down, explaining Greg's weirding. 'He thinks the kid he saw was Josie, don't you see?' Eventually, the bereaved mother capitulated. Or at least shut up.

They had to split up. Claire's car was full of luggage and she wouldn't hear of leaving it behind, so Fee went with her, leaving Greg with Zoe, much against her better judgement. Putting Zoe with Claire was not an option. Zoe had annoyed Claire, and Claire wasn't speaking to Zoe: so it was as it was. They would go back home, and check out the Cullompton site on the way.

Greg and Zoe would return via Newton, and they would meet up back at Pippin Cottage. No heroics. Snap and go. Regroup, plan and execute. Just shows how wrong you can be.

Fee drove. Claire opened the window and spent the time chainsmoking, a habit she had kicked years ago. Fee tried to be sympathetic, but Claire was sunk in her own personal hell and was beyond registering. They drove in frigid silence, the slipstream whipping Claire's short hair about and completely failing to clear the tobacco fumes from the car. Fee pulled in at an all-night garage, ostensibly to get coffee, but really to breathe some cleaner air. The car was starting to stink. At least Claire stopped smoking while she drank the coffee. Small mercies, thank God.

The warehouse at Cullompton was small, old and deserted. Grass was growing on the hard standing in front, and the chain link fence was garlanded by bindweed and thistles. Fee grabbed the camera and got out, intending to just take a few photos, but Claire had other ideas. She found a gap in the fence and wiggled through.

'Come on, Fee. Let's take a closer look. If someone's been here recently, there ought to be some signs.' She trotted off before Fee could open her mouth. Sighing with resignation, she followed Claire.

She caught her up at the corner of the building. Weeds were making a spirited attempt to colonise what had once been a lawn surrounding a willow tree. They were winning. The wall was innocent of any opening except a second floor hoist complete with rusted lifting gear which was swaying in the wind and creaking a mournful dirge to itself.

Round the back was the marshalling yard, inhabited with the rusting hulk of an ancient flatbed truck: industrial archaeology at its most dire. The roll-up doors were jammed shut. They had been used for target practice: dented and scorched black in places, with debris and broken bottles scattered around. A short flight of steps led up to a door flanked by broken windows. Fee shone her torch through the dirty glass. Inside was once an office. An old Imperial typewriter sat mouldering on a desk, and windrows of dust were collecting in the corners.

'There's no way in here. The windows are too small.' Fee shook the door handle half-heartedly. 'And the door's locked.'

'Wait a minute.' Claire scampered off on kitten heels to the rusty pile in the yard. She came back with a metal bar. 'You've dragged me all the way out here, and I'm dammed if I'll leave before I've at least taken a look inside.'

Fee stood back as Claire attacked the door. The rending and tearing of rotten wood filled the yard as the door gave way before the determined onslaught. Claire yanked the door open and vanished inside.

'Great, now we get done for breaking and entering.'

She followed the sound of Claire's tapping footfalls in the darkness. The pitch of the sound changed as she went from the office into a larger space. This was more Zoe than Claire…….

Meanwhile, that young lady was instructing Greg in music appreciation. They were bowling down the road arguing the relative merits of Nick Drake and Leonard Cohen, with a side order of Syd Barret. Someone ought to have been paying more attention, but there you are. You get what you get…..

Fee passed through the open door and into a vast space. The beams of her torch picked out cobwebby walls, the whitewash crumbling off to leave patches of the red brick showing like some obscure and possibly terminal rash. The concrete floor was littered with rope and broken pallets, and her footfalls echoed. She could not hear Claire's footsteps, so she called out.

'Claire, where are you?'

'Over here,' came the reply. Claire was over by the far wall, feeling the scabby surface for doors. 'Bring that torch over here.'

The beam stuttered and flared over the walls as Fee picked her way through the debris of long-departed manufacture. Claire had found a set of double doors leading out of the vast space into a more confined corridor.

'Left or right?'

'Right. There are some more doors there.'

Fee shone the beam on a second set of doors. They led to an entryway with a door, another corridor straight ahead and stairs to the left. Claire wrestled with the handle, but it was locked.

'Upstairs.'

Fee watched her, regretting every step that took them further inside. From the state of the stairs, no-one had been here for ages. Past generations of workers might well be under their feet: from dust we are born and to dust we return. There was more than enough for a full shift here.

'Claire, come back! No-one's been up there. Let's go back and look downstairs.'

Silence answered her. She sighed and started up. The stairs turned a dog-leg and led to another long corridor stretching to right and left. There was no sign of Claire, but the dust was a pristine grey woolly layer to the right and there were traces of footsteps in the left.

Fee stopped. Inside, parts of her mind was clamouring for attention. Wrong! Wrong! they were shouting. If Claire wanted to waste time clattering about on kitten heels in ankle deep dust that was her affair. She had run off and left Fee alone despite the repeated warnings. She debated the relative merits of returning to the car, driving off and leaving Claire. The heroine in the scary movie always gets caught by the monster when she's alone. That meant either Fee herself or Claire was a target right now. Claire was acting like a complete airhead, and if Fee joined her in Cotton Candy Land, they would both get it. She couldn't hide, not here. The dust would show quite clearly where she had been. She cursed under her breath. Whatever else, she was Mysten here, which meant Claire was under her protection. She couldn't leave her to whatever fate might be waiting in the grimy halls. Neither did it mean that Fee had to be stupid. She drew a deep, shuddering breath and started a weaving. The torchlight started to waver, and the beam warped, dimmed and grew brighter. In the umbra where the beam met the wall, a shadow started to form.

'Icastis, servant of light, answer to me.'

The shadow flickered.

'Go thou forth and seek she who came to this place with me.'

'I hear and obey', the shadows whispered back. The torchlight flickered again, and the umbra brightened back to a clear circle.

Fee's fingers moved, touching and crossing in a complex dance.

'Spaca of life and light, protect and guard me from that which seeks to end my life. Wrap me in shadows, and let me pass.'

The words echoed down the hallways. It was as much as she could do right now. She would sense if there was any other being close by, but it would not protect her from physical force. But that small warning might be enough. If she couldn't find Claire soon, she would cut and run. She would protect Claire, but there was a limit. If the woman continued to do stupid as well as she was doing now, then on her own head be it.

She switched off her torch and waited in the darkness. Slowly her eyes began to adjust. Meten sight kicked in. Grey light was seeping from somewhere off to her right: she could see a short flight of stairs leading away past double doors. To her left the passage stretched endlessly. Well, about twenty yards really, but the darkness merited a bit of hyperbole.

A rushing sound came to her ears, soughing through the double doors and stirring the dust on the steps into tiny windrows. The doors opened slightly, then swung to.

'Up here,' a thin voice floated on the dying breath.

Looking closely, Fee could see slight depressions on the dust on the stairs. Why had Claire trodden so carefully that the dust was scarcely disturbed? What about the footsteps to the left? They ended after five prints, and were slightly smudged, as if the walker had stepped back carefully in her own prints. Definitely a female shoe: perhaps a size five, and men didn't wear heels like that. Only her enhanced vision gave the game away. Alarm bells were clanging loudly now. This was wrong. Only scary movie girl might tentatively mount the stairs, chirruping 'Claire?' in a quavering treble. Fee had two choices: turn and go back down the stairs, or do the completely unexpected. She half turned, as if to descend, then with a sudden burst of speed took the low staircase three at a time and burst through the doors at a dead run and kept right on going. She ignored the half-seen shapes looming in the dusk and pounded through the open space. It would have worked, too, if there hadn't been someone hiding behind a partition who clouted her legs as she raced past. Sprawling, she fell onto the grainy concrete and saw the shadowy figure standing over her with an iron bar in its hand before utter darkness crashed down and the lights went out.

In a car happily bowling down the motorway many miles distant, a female voice screamed loudly enough to drown out Freddy Mercury explaining that he was 'Mr Farenheight, burning at the speed of light, they're gonna make a supersonic woman of you.......'

Ignoring Mr Mercury's exhortation not to, Greg did an abrupt emergency stop and skidded onto the hard shoulder. Thankfully there was only light traffic, since the car performed a four-wheel drift and power slide worthy of Jeremy Clarkson before juddering to a halt. Following cars screamed past, blaring horns at the stupid fuck on the side of the road with clouds of smoke erupting from the rear wheels. Thank ayen for active suspension and antilock brakes. As the headlights flickered past, he turned to the white face in the passenger seat.

'What?' he demanded tersely. He refrained from complaining that Zoe had come within a whisker of getting them both killed.

'Gimme a minute.' Zoe closed her eyes, and Greg watched the taut white face shake. It wasn't a visual effect from the strobe of racing lights inches away. Zoe was trembling all over.

'Something's gone horribly wrong. Take me home, Greg. Right now.'

'Shouldn't we go to Cullompton and see what's up? If Fee's in danger....'

'What use will we be to her if we walk right into the same trap? No, I'm going to do what we should have done right at the start. What we do best. Wythen. And I can do that best at home. Take me there now, Greg, please.'

For answer, he thumped the wheel double-handed. Then he ran both hands through his hair.

'If you don't take me home right now, I will get out of this car and stop someone. I will do it, Greg.'

'You won't get far hitch-hiking at this time of night.'

'Who mentioned hitch-hiking? I'm not about to *ask* for a lift, Greg. I'm going to *command* one. I *will* stop a car, and I *will* force that driver, whoever they are and whatever they are driving, to take me right to my front door. Now, you can help me, or you can just get the hell out of my way. Which is it to be? Quickly now, I'm losing time sitting here. I can't afford that right now.'

'Your way or the highway?'

'I don't have time to be nice. I may not have any time at all.'

Greg sighed. His potential sister-in-law was way ahead of his sisters in the pain-in-the-ass stakes.

'Okay. I'll take you home. Then I'm going to Cullompton. No arguments.'

'Then harness the horses, James. Pile on the automotive power. I'll ride shotgun. No-one's going to catch us.' She flipped open her mobile and started texting as the car rejoined the stream of lights hastening into the bleak night, laying down twenty yard of steaming rubber in the process.

Chapter Twenty-eight

Fee floated back to consciousness and immediately became aware of intense discomfort. There was no part of her that didn't ache, from skinned knees and hands to a pounding headache. Her shins ached. The bruises would be spectacular. Whoever it had been, they had copped her a right wallop. There had been venom in it, and it stung. Returning awareness wasn't cutting her any slack either. Her hands were straining over her head and her feet barely touched the floor. She blinked, clearing blood, sweat and grime from her eyes. Shafts of light knifed through her retinas leaving behind a wash of sheer agony. From the feel of it, someone had copped her a right wallop over the ear as well. Her neck felt sticky. Squinting, she could see a mass of candles on the floor, and she was betting that there were more were behind her. She was hanging suspended surrounded by candles. What's not to like about that? Apart from practically everything. Beyond the light a figure moved. Detaching itself from the pitch black, it approached.

'Claire?' Fee choked on her voice, coughed and tried again. Her throat was scratchy and sore: her mouth was full of gritty cotton wool.

'So. You're finally awake. I suppose you want to know what's going on?'

'I know what's going on. Why interests me more.'

Claire stalked round the candles, tapping the iron bar on the floor, on her hand, against her leg. She was nervous. And angry. Fee tried to jump-start her brain: it was just not co-operating right now.

'He'll be coming for you soon.'

'He won't give you Josie back, you know.'

'What?'

'He'll cheat you, Claire. Let me down, and we'll get Josie back, I promise.'

Claire shoved her face right up to Fee's. She had to glare up at her. Fee was shocked at the rage in her friend's eyes.

'You aren't getting the picture, *Mysten*.' She spat the last word. 'This isn't an exchange, fool. This is a gift. Yes, Josie's with him. *I* left her there. She's quite safe, I assure you. No, there's something else I want, something *he* can give me. And you're the price.'

'Whatever it is, you won't get it. His type doesn't share.'

'Oh, he'll share, all right. Sharing makes him more powerful.'

'Provided all he shares with are yes-men, toadies and arse-lickers.'

Claire laughed, a horrible, bitter laugh that echoed with spite.

'Do you know where I've been, these past days? Think I've been in France, do you? That was a lie. It's all been lies, lies, lies. Want to know why? Because of you. Everywhere I look, all I see is you, you, you. You think you've got it all, don't you? Mysten of the Frais, high mistress of wythen, successful businesswoman, consort of metae..... there's nothing left for anyone else round you. We dance attendance on your whims, and you dole us out bits and pieces, enough to keep us quiet, but you don't *share*. You've never taken me rathing. Yet your sister, that petty scrap of a girl, you take her.......'

'I wouldn't expose you to danger. You know I can't do that.'

'Petty weaves, that's all I'm good for, isn't it? Little wyths. A love potion here, a glim there, a bit of weirding..... You never helped me with the Gya. You never taught me to ride the winds, release my wraith, create servants, amass wyth. I was never good enough for that.'

'Neither's Lottie, but I don't see her here. If you don't have the talent, or you can't be bothered to practise, then I can't make you into what you want.'

'The same old story. Well, he can give me those things.'

'Sez he.'

Claire didn't bother to respond. She walked back into the darkness. Fee tried to watch, but the brightness of the candle ring was foxing the meten sight. She tried to move her wrists, but the bindings, whatever they were, were tight enough to cut off circulation. At this rate, she would be handless by the time Claire got to the handover point. Handless, but not harmless.......

Bodily escape was as close to impossible as it could be. Oh, Fee might try to swing her legs up, try to take weight off the bindings, but she was betting that such gyrations would bring swift retribution by way of a discouraging clout with that handy iron bar. But her mind was free. She started whispering under her breath, closing her eyes. So she didn't see Claire's return. She only felt the sharp tug as her jeans were pulled down to her hips, exposing her flat belly. Her coat and boots were already gone, and Claire pushed her jumper up over her bra, exposing more flesh. She ran her hands over Fee's belly, tracing the swells and hollows, frighteningly lascivious.

'I always preferred women, did you know that? When I took all those girls from Alex, it was the best time of my life. They were *mine*, I owned them. I knew then that I could never go back to being a wife. I had Josie, and I could find new lovers. Better lovers. You never saw that in me, did you?'

'I can't say I did.'

'Well, I'm not your butch lesbian. I prefer women because they give more pleasure. Alex only wanted to hump away. He never had enough time for pleasure. I tried to get him to appreciate Tantric sex, but he wouldn't bite.' She pressed her lips to Fee's skin. 'Neither would you. All that oiling of bodies by the pool, all those compliments, all wasted. I could have given you such pleasure......' She looked up at Fee, who stared down, unblinking. Her wyth flowed into her eyes, striking at Claire, but she saw it coming and looked away. 'Stop that. If you had been nice to me, I would have simply handed you over. I'm not a bad person, not really. But I want what I want, and I *will* have it. So, now, before I hand you over, I'm going to have some fun. *He* wants you alive, but he'll accept slightly damaged goods, I'm sure. *He* doesn't want you for that. And this offering will give me more power, more to bargain with. I'm dicing with the Devil, and I want all the chips I can get. And your body can give me that.'

Hello, Darth Vader. She's been seduced by the Dark Side. One problem with that. To be a white farer, really be a white farer, you not only needed to be aware of the dark, but have embraced it and all it had to offer. Otherwise, your choice was meaningless. How can you fully reject something you don't properly appreciate? You can mouth platitudes, resist temptation by never inviting it. Never try, never know. Fee, as Fee, hadn't embraced the Dark. But she could remember when she had, and what had come of it. The other side of white is black, and white lives in the heart of darkness just as darkness is at the core of light. Wythen wasn't good or bad. It was amoral. If you want to cure someone who's dying of cancer, then you need to kill the cancer cells. No-one ever considers what the cancer cells think about that. Just like everything else, Fee had two sides, and she knew them both. She started to summon the dark.......

Claire drew a triangle in the dust, round Fee's feet. At each apex of the triangle she placed a bunch of dried twigs, and sprinkled them with a thick liquid that glittered redly in the candlelight. A faint unpleasant scent wafted up. Blood and semen. Oh, joy. Let's not even speculate how *that* came about.

There was a fierce tug on her hair. The sudden involuntary movement made Fee cry out.

'Open your eyes, bitch. I want you to see what's coming for you. I want to watch your eyes when you see. I want to drink your fear, your horror. And I will.' She stepped back.

'Ayen of darkness and chaos, accept this my offering I pray you......' Claire dipped a brush into the bowl she held, and started painting a complex sigum on Fee's flesh. Fee concentrated on the brushstrokes, trying to see the glyph in her mind's eye: but it escaped her. Claire finished painting Fee's stomach, and walked around her, flicking the muck on her skin, her clothes and finally her face. Fee hung immobile, eyes closed. The outside might be compliant, but inside she was seething. Ah......

'I summon you, prince of fire. Athebas, come you here, and receive my homage....'

What the hell had the girl been reading? It was not on the Jean-approved Frais booklist for sure. Or had someone been whispering in her ear? When?

Crackling, and a sharp acid aroma. Claire had lit the piles of dry tinder. Small flames hid below plumes of dense smoke, rising straight in the still air. Fee hoped that the floor, underneath the dust, was concrete and not planks. Claire continued her incantation, her voice rising and falling. The girl had talent. Pity.

She moved away, and scratched herself a second circle in the dust outside the candle ring. She lit more candles, sticking them to the floor with their own hot wax, until she was surrounded: an evil gnome on the most outrageous birthday cake imaginable. Secure in her defence, she continued her invocation, arms out and head flung back. The incantation poured from her lips, seamless, endless, repetitive.

The dark round the candlelight oozed with menace. Things were moving in there, wicked, joyless things. Cold and silent. If Claire was aware that her efforts were attracting attention, then she wasn't showing it. That was her blind spot. She didn't grasp that beings like this didn't politely wait until you'd finished summoning them before they put in an appearance. The buggers often tried to confuse those who summoned them by appearing early, appearing invisibly or not appearing at all. Claire was intent on her invocations, rapt by her own voice. She wouldn't even look for the presence she was calling until too late. Fee's eyes, a mete's eyes, pierced the darkness. She thought to the creeping presences, called them to her. Then she started on the circle of candles. One by one, she took them into her consciousness, enfolded them, made them hers. Spaca thief.

A larger, darker presence started to form out of the shadows. Surely Claire would be aware of that? But Claire's eyes were all for Fee, waiting to see the first stirrings of panic. Sorry, sister. More sorry than you could possibly know. But there it is. You did it to yourself. You underestimated me. Or, more likely, you couldn't conceive what I can do. What I am capable of in the face of betrayal. I might not like it, but I will do it…….

Oh, she's noticed. But not all of it.

'Athebas, I welcome you. Receive the gift I have prepared for you, and when you have enjoyed it, render to me those gifts I desire.'

Yellow eyes sparked in the gloom. A wide mouth yawned, showing fangs any vamp would be proud of, a whole mouthful of them, white and sharp and ready. A long tongue snaked out of the mouth and curled lazily round the fangs.

'*Sweet, I hear your summons. I come to you, hungry for the gifts you bring.*' Ancient whispers, old and evil. Contemptuous of the monkey bag of dirty water pretending power over something more ancient than sin.

'I offer you this flesh for your pleasure and enjoyment. I set no limit on your frolic, but that you leave this gift alive at the end of your play. Offer it pain, offer it pleasure, as you will. Only leave the life within a spark.'

'*As you will, so shall it be.*'

The presence glided to the outer limit of the light. Still welded to the darkness, it stood there, immobile. Claire turned her face to Fee. She was glowing with accomplishment, a grudge held and nursed and delivered.

'Anything to say before I leave you to him?'

'Not staying to witness your handiwork?'

'I wouldn't miss it for the world. But I've a long way to go before daylight. And you'll be safe here. Well, relatively safe. Until tomorrow night anyway.'

Claire beckoned to the presence standing outside the circle.

Chapter Twenty-nine

There's speeding and there's *speeding*. Do a hundred down the M5 and the boys in blue will flash their blues-and-twos at you and haul you before the beak, raid your wallet and stick little black dots on your license. Do a hundred and ninety and they'll ignore you. Few production cars can match that speed and keep it up. But this car wasn't exactly a car. It was an illusion, a chymer, a trick of the light. Looking back at their records, the cops might puzzle over why so many speed cameras were sparking off in sequence and only showing sedate lorries and other law-abiding (more or less) fauna of the tarmac, not something travelling at lift-off speed. But there was one: and everything got out of its way. No, that's not right. Nothing was *in* the way of that travelling one-ton missile hurtling down the highway. Zoe was riding intention, not technology, and it's much faster.

The car settled outside Pippin Cottage and the cold fingers of dawn were not even stirring under the cosy duvet of darkness. She rolled over for extra *zzzzs* and left the night for the farer.

Zoe made a beeline for the Roundhouse. While she was not in Fee's class, she was no slouch when it came down to instant spacas. She had been practising for years. She didn't *exactly* cut corners. Circles don't have corners; they're famous for it, it's their particular quintessence. Zoe could go from ground zero to light speed in a blink when she wanted, and she wanted. Sod Abracadabra. Sod robes and all such flummeries. It was the mind that did the work, and Zoe's mind was in overdrive and doing overtime.

'Okay, what now?'

'Seeing comes first. Then knowing, then doing. I thought you were off to Cullompton?'

'Are you dismissing me?'

'Not if you want to stay. If you are determined to walk into a trap, feel free. But you might like to see what you're intending to walk in on, hhmmm?'

Greg grimaced. Zoe was right. He would do Fee no favours if they both had to be rescued. He wanted to play the part of a rescuer, not a rescuee. Call it male pride, call it what you will. Heroes can't afford to be stupid. Not if they want to do it twice. His coat and shoes joined Zoe's on the floor.

Zoe was hovering over a bowl of water, whispering to it. The surface shivered and clouded.

'Ikos, be my eyes. Let me *see*.'

The surface of the water shivered again and went silver. It was like looking through a fish-eye lens. They could see a tree, a willow tree, shaggy silver fronds stirring in the moonlight, brooding over a rough pasture.

'Willow tree, willow tree,
Show me truly, what do you see?'

It was an old cantrip. Old weaves work as well as brand new ones. The scene panned round, showing a wall, a deserted parking lot innocent of anything except weeds: a broken chain-link fence and a badly parked car. Two figures walked past the tree, hugging the wall. Overhead, a rusty hoist swung in an errant wind.

'That's Fee and Claire. What are they doing?'

'Did, did. My talents don't extend beyond the past. Wrong, is my guess.'

They watched as the two figures broke into the back of the warehouse.

'Is that the place you saw in your vision?'

'No. Definitely not. It's too low, and has a flat roof in front. Mine was more like a traditional three-bay barn.'

'We're pruning down the options. Looks like it was Newton after all.'

Events unfolded in the water. Claire running off, Fee standing at the top of the stairs. Then her rush through the doors.

'The bitch! She hit her! Claire hit Fee!'

In the bowl, Claire struggled with Fee's limp form, stripping off her coat and shoes, binding her hands and hauling her up on a chain hoist.

'I'll kill that bitch…'

'Can you fast forward this?'

'Yes, because it's already happened. If we were watching real time, then we'd be bollixed.'

'Try it.'

'Even if it's happening now, I don't think you can't get there fast enough to stop it.'

Zoe flicked her fingers over the water. It shivered again. Fee was awake now, and Claire was…..

'The stupid bitch! Stupid, stupid bitch. What the hell is Athebas?'

'One of the Lords of Chaos. He likes to experience the joys of the flesh.'

'Oh.'

'Those who consort with him give mixed reports. One lot say he gives exquisite pleasure and reveals hidden secrets and makes his consorts powerful. The others say he deals in pain. Not torture, pain….. Don't you know your grammarion?'

'Lily never let me at that bit. It was a temptation, see, and no-one who couldn't master the cyscan of summoning, all of it, got their itchy fingers on the grammarion.'

'Hang on, what's she doing?'

In the water, they watched as Claire beckoned to a shadowy figure outside the circle. Since her full attention was on the lord of chaos, she didn't notice the windrows that were stirring at her feet, blowing dust over the scratched lines of her protective circle. Behind Claire, candles guttered and went out, sending up thick wisps of smoke into the darkness above. Fee, even bound and marked as she was, never gave up. Having already summoned help, it was closer to hand than her adversary had the right to imagine. And she had not checked. First rule of summoning: Is the entity you summoned the one you called, or is it something else? Has it brought anything with it? Or is there some - interference - with your summoning? Claire was a relative newcomer to the delights of gramarie. This might have been her very first attempt. If it was, then the girl had a fearsome talent. She, however, was approaching it very naively, and the things she was summoning were far from simple. A corkscrew mind, one that could see round corners, was an essential part of a cyscan's toolkit. You had to be sly and devious, or at least understand slyness and deviosity. Fee was experienced and devious. Behind Claire, another of the candles guttered in an errant breeze and died in a swirl of grey smoke. Everything shifted…... An arm reached out of the darkness, and drew Claire into its embrace. Her face was screaming, the mouth wide, wide open. In the light, Fee's eyes were round, and she was looking into the black. Tendrils of smoke curled up round her. She winced.

'I wonder what she's hearing.'

'Be thankful you can't. It would give you nightmares. What happened?'

'If I know Fee, she nicked the spaca. Made it hers and not Claire's. So she was protected and Claire wasn't.'

'So when the candles went out, the spaca…'

'Was breached. Claire expected the Chaos Lord to step in and take Fee. Only it wasn't her spaca then: it was Fee's.'

'And no request goes unanswered. Claire offered the demon a body, meaning Fee……..'

'But Fee made herself unavailable, so Athebas took Claire.' Zoe completed the line for him.

'So now we go unhook your sister and bring her back here. Athebas won't bother us, he only bothers those who call him. He's got no interest in anyone who won't play.'

'He plays too rough for me.'

'Exquisite pleasure, don't forget.'

Greg was collecting his discarded clothes when a sound from the doorway stopped him in mid-motion. Snag, who had wandered in after them and had been quietly attending to his oversize feet, was retching, a total body convulsion starting at the base of his tail and travelling through his spine into his drooling maw.

'That's not hairballs.' Greg commented, walking over to the heaving mass of fur.

Drooling and gurgitating, the cat continued his attempts to turn himself inside out. Zoe bent for a closer look.

'Is that a paw?'

'I think you're right. I'd say, all things considered, that your cat is mouth-birthing a gwhylli.'

Biehail finally slid onto the mat, covered in slime and

unmentionable things from the cat's stomach. Snag sneezed, regarded the puddle with supercilious disdain and stalked away.

'*Mistress must not go! She must not go! It is wrong place! Biehail show right place!*'

Zoe recoiled as the dripping form launched itself onto her chest and grabbed a double handful of breast and wool. It was trying to shake her, but only succeeded in shaking himself against her jumper, smearing the cloth with slime and other, worse, body fluids.

'*Mistress watch telling bowl! She see! She must see!*'

It leapt off her and raced back to the bowl. Zoe and Greg exchanged glances.

Fee tried not to listen to the sounds emanating from the darkness. Screams had given way to panting, gurgles and worse. They finally drifted off into silence as Claire's body gave up. Her wraith, on the other hand, was most probably sampling Athebas' hospitality in some other place. Fee's imagination was running riot. Unlike her sister, Fee knew her grammarion, and knew what Athebas could do. And he was showing his talents for agony, not ecstasy. Her feelings about Claire were mixed. On one hand, a friend (or someone she had thought of as a friend) for many years was experiencing pain beyond comprehension. On the other hand, the bitch had intended the painful experience to be Fee's. It was Josie that was foremost in Fee's thoughts. She was trying to get a handhold on the bindings round her wrists when a voice came out of the shadows.

'What do we have here, then?'

It was a male voice, and one she didn't know. Amused, rich and unctuous, each syllable carefully rounded. A trained voice. Very probably not a night watchman, then. Fee was trying to find a good response when a clatter of footsteps distracted her.

'Thank goodness we've found you! We've been *soo* worried. Zoe texted Theo, and we've been looking for you, all of us. We were lucky to be close by. Are you all right? No, of course you're not. Let's get you down from there.'

Brenda of the purple lipstick and artless hair. She scattered candles as she walked up to Fee and lifted her legs, taking the weight off her hands. Blood started to flow back into the abused flesh, and Fee almost screamed. Hands worked at the bindings as relief flooded through her body.

'Thanks for the rescue.'

'Oh no, my dear. This isn't rescue.' Fee looked up at the owner of the smooth voice. He looked faintly familiar. 'This is reclamation of what was promised to me.' Relief, short-lived, died. She turned to look at Brenda's smiling face.

'Meet Simon Lake.'

That slightly familiar face smiled down on her. There was nothing nice in that smile.

'Miss Harris. We meet at the last. I regret that my akelyte attempted to harm you. This was not my intention. I have other plans for you.'

Between the two smiles there was no escape. Brenda's baby fangs showed at the corners of her mouth. Out of the frying pan into the blast furnace. For the second time that night, the dense fog rose up and claimed her.

Chapter Thirty

Zoe had indulged herself in an orgy of swearing which sent Biehail cowering into the ferns that crowded the walls of the Roundhouse. Once she had screamed herself to a stop, she started in deadly earnest. Disregarding the lateness, or earliness of the hour, depending on whether you had been to sleep or not, she phoned and texted furiously. Greg was sent out to an all-night garage to refuel the car - more, he suspected, to get him out of the way than anything else. Zoe in full flow was a force that could not be reasoned with, only avoided or endured. Compliance was the sole route through to sanity: she was taking no prisoners. Only one message, winging its way through hyperspace to her laptop, brought any response and that was a tight, satisfied smile. The day had dawned, cold, overcast and windy. It howled around the corners of Pippin Cottage and was a perfect counterpoint to the atmosphere inside. Greg felt surplus to requirements, a bit like a fighter pilot in WW2 waiting for the bell and the call to 'Scramble!' - knowing that the enemy was out there, somewhere, and up to no good, but to start a flap too early would be to give him the war on a plate. 'Not for nothing did my Dad give me a copy of Sun Tzu's Art Of War,' was all Zoe would say. If all the cards had been dealt, then this was the last hand, win or lose: and Zoe was the last man standing on one side. At least, she was acting that way.

In a country far to the west of surprise, Greg heard Zoe call 'Lunch!' When had that happened? Had he fallen asleep? In the kitchen he found that she had produced a ham pie from somewhere. Biehail was already scouting the table, attracted to the intense aroma coming from the golden heap of pastry. It came with a thick, creamy sauce, mashed potatoes and braised red cabbage. Under the table, Snag was determined filling his belly before Biehail could lay claim to anything in the bowl but fresh air. Perhaps he always ate like that, since Zoe was taking no notice of a cat chasing another bellyache. She served Greg generously, and even doled out small portions of everything to Biehail, who immediately sat on the plate, in the cabbage, and started to chomp vigorously.

Greg couldn't find it in himself to be hungry despite the wonderful aromas. Zoe ate stolidly, hardly tasting the food, shovelling it in like stoking a furnace.

'Get it down you. You need the energy,' she informed him between mouthfuls.

'What are we going to do?' he asked eventually. Zoe swallowed.

'You are going to sit in the spaca and hold the wyth. I am going to see this bastard broken, and Fee's going to need the wyth you'll be feeding her to do that.'

'You can't do it?'

'Be sensible. You two have been together, you're lovers. The bond is closer between you two now than it is between me and her. And you're a man: the wyth flows better between a man and a woman than it does between two men or women.'

'I don't see why you can't feed the wyth to me, and I'll go get Fee and finish this?'

'You are thinking with your balls, not your head.' Zoe had obviously given upon tact. 'Rina said that only Fee has the chance to finish this. And I'm going to see that she has that chance.'

'And what will you be doing?'

'I'm going to meet Theo and Cecile. We can't face down vampires on our own, and Theo's got a duty to protect Fee and me.'

'He had a duty to protect Sophie as well.'

'Then he failed. Rina will be mucho disappointed in him. This is his chance to make it right with her, and us.'

'Then why don't you stay in the spaca with me?'

'Because the vamps can't do it alone. I have to go. Someone on the other side has wyth, and cys, so a fratten has to confront them. And it can't be you. Do you really want to go with a couple of metae and help them? Can you move with meten speed? Can you see as a vampire does? If you can't, like I can, then you will be a liability. And they've got no call to be protecting you, so they won't bother. If I let you go, I might just as well kill you here and now. Me they will protect, you they will throw to the wolves. If you go with them you'll die. And what will Fee say to me after? If she deigns to speak to me at all? No chance, mate.' This juggernaut of logic was incontestable. Greg tried. He was opening his mouth to put a counter-argument on the table when something oozed up his leg between flesh and trouser. He froze as a muffled pronouncement from his groin informed him that the gwhylli was offering violence to his most cherished boy bits.

'If manthing not submit, Biehail bite. Biehail teeth sharp. Manthing agree, stay, do as told.'

The notion of having a set of fangs in his scrotum decided the issue. Biehail had the last word.

It was late morning when Fee returned to her abused body. The scrapes and bruises were aching, and there was a little guy in her head with a jackhammer mining behind her ear. She felt sick and dizzy. Some bastard had confined her in a box; they must have thought that a great joke. Metae locking a living farer in a wooden coffin, kept on ice, so to speak, until nightfall when the monsters came out to play. They had padded the box too, since any attempt to move met soft resistance. Surely they hadn't put her in an *actual* coffin? That would be too much. There must be some airholes where she couldn't see them, because the air was not stale at least. She was aware that she was far from clean. To be quite frank, she was stinking. Dried blood matted her hair and had run down her cheek and neck into her cleavage. Well, maybe to a mete that was alluring. To Fee, it was just uncomfortable.

She was on the move. She could hear the distant rumble of a diesel engine, and a vibration through her back. There was an aroma of fuel that brought a gorge to her throat. On the thin edge of panic, she fought the urge to vomit. The gag in her mouth would……

Her hands were confined with the plastic ties used by cops as handcuffs, and they were biting into her skin. By the feel of it, her captors had pinioned her ankles as well. Her mouth was dry, aching with the need for liquid. There was, however, plenty lower down. Some huntress….

Funny, she felt no edge of panic once the nausea had eased. Light was seeping faintly round the lid of the box, so Simon and Brenda were unavailable. Probably. The thought that their boxes might be cheek by jowl with hers was an uncomfortable and uncanny notion. Shouting for help would be little use, since the nearest living things would be the sods driving the truck, lorry, whatever. They would most likely be akelytes of Simon's, and she could expect no help from that quarter. Why waste her reserves of strength? She schooled her mind, and *reached*.......

Zoe was busy at the sink when the landline shrilled. Greg launched himself at it, only just beating the imp who leapt onto the hall table and started to do his four-paw bounce dance.

'It's Lily. Fee's alive, and shut in a box...'

Zoe emerged from the kitchen, wiping her hands on a tea towel. Biehail crooned at the handset, enraptured by the sound of Lily's voice, remote and tinny as it was.

'Where is she? The vision conked out after Brenda lifted her down.'

'She doesn't know. She got the impression that Fee was in a lorry, and it was driving somewhere.'

'*Biehail knows! He knows! He can tell!*' The little thing was reaching for the handset, his tail lashing to and fro in excitement, scattering keys and loose change onto the floor.

'Lily says to mind Mischief. And not to name anything after night falls.' Greg replaced the handset, which was immediately claimed by the gwhylli, who wound himself round it, stroking it and crooning to it lovingly.

'So, we're all set. Help me with the preparations.'

'I'm still not comfortable with this.'

'Who is? We didn't ask for this, Greg, none of us. But it's happening to us, and we'll just have to cope with it as best we can. I know you're worried for Fee, but you've never seen that side of her at all. I have. I hate to say this about my own sister, but she's a better practical Cyscan than anyone since Rina.'

'Better than you?' Greg cocked an eyebrow at her, attempting an amusing aside.

'Give me a chance. I've only been at it sixteen years, and five of those were pre-verbal. I'm an Intelligencer. Fee's the warrior, the fighter, the wielder of force. What are you? I've never asked.'

'Really don't know. No-one ever defined themselves other than as fratten. Mam and the others said that their wyth was always stronger when I was around, so I suppose I'm a sort of catalyst.' His tone said clearly that he didn't like it.

'Get away. For what I want, you're bloody perfect. Still don't want to hold the spaca for us?'

'Put like that……. Well, I always saw myself as…. Well, I wanted to be a hero.' He had the grace to look a little shame-faced about it. Boys and their gonads.

'Don't we all. I wanted to be a female James Bond, but I ended up as Q.'

'And where would Bond be without his gadgets?'

'Touché. If I can stomach being Q, you can stick being a catalyst. Intelligence, resourcefulness and strength. How can we lose?'

Too bloody easily. But he didn't say it.

Chapter Thirty-one

The overcast day crept towards evening and segued into night without fuss. It just got a little darker as the Earth rolled away from the sun towards the kingdom of night, and the denizens of the midnight hours stole a march on the day. A lone figure appeared at the gate of Pippin Cottage shortly before sunset, and was not invited inside. Zoe, dressed from head to toe in olive drab commando pants and shirt, her long cloak billowing behind her, locked the door. Cecile had gone classic, for a female mete at least, in a pale dress which swirled round her calves.

She had acquired a car from somewhere, a low slung chromium yellow Lotus Elise. Zoe wondered where it had come from, and who was missing it - or if, indeed, they were still capable of missing anything. An old friend, Cecile had said, a very old friend: and she scattered gravel as the car roared away into the gathering night. Cecile insisted on the top being down. It was going to be a cold journey, and Zoe half-wished that she could go back for a hat. But tonight there was no going back. Cecile had got the bit between her fangs and wouldn't hear of it.

Fee watched the light fade through the cracks in the lid of her prison. She had dozed intermittently during the day, but the heavy ache in her bladder was becoming increasingly hard to ignore. The children of the night would come out to play soon. She only hoped some of them might be on her side. The noise and vibration had stopped. Had they reached their destination, or were they parked in some lay-by or motorway service station? Something bumped the box, and she froze as prey freezes when it is small and weak, in the hope the fangs and claws would pass them by. No such luck. The box creaked and jolted as it moved, heavy footfalls echoing in the space outside. The box lurched and Fee, unable to brace her abused legs, slid down a few inches inside the padding. The bumping and jolting became more pronounced. The buggers were moving her on a sackbarrow or something. A final jolt and a bang, and she was back to being flat out. She had arrived. The lid of the box creaked open and Fee squinted in the indirect light of a hurricane lamp somewhere on the floor beside her: she could hear it hissing, smell the paraffin, the burning wick. She could also smell a touch of BO masked by Davidoff..... Whoever was letting her out was alive at least. If they were letting her out, of course. It wasn't a given.

An upside down face floated into her vision, and hands heaved her up until she was sitting in the box. Oh, a packing case. Cushions cascaded onto the floor as the movement dislodged them. She was in the middle of a storeroom. Shelves filled with archive boxes crowded nearly all the space that wasn't taken up with her personal... coffin? Box? The gag was removed, and some skin went with it from her parched lips. A bottle was shoved against her mouth. She swallowed the water gratefully. Whoever it was helping her was being careful: one hand behind her back and the other tipping the water slowly into her mouth.

'Thank you,' she said when the bottle was taken away. You lose no points for showing gratitude when it's due. They could have left her thirsty.

'Should've been here earlier, but there was an acciden' on the…….. There was an accident on the way.' He was going to tell her something about where they were, only he'd thought better of it. Damn, an intelligent henchman. This one isn't going to respond to requests to loosen the too-tight bindings on her wrists, though they were genuinely too tight. Her hands were mottled blue. We could try the toilet ploy, because that is genuine too……

'I'll take you to the john. Sorry an' all that, but I'll have t'go with you. Nothin' personal, y'unnerstan'.'

He heaved her up over his shoulder. The most she could see was his lower back, buttocks and the floor. They were nice buttocks, considering. He barged through some doors and sat her on a toilet.

''Scuse me.' He undid her belt and jeans, then heaved her off the seat and pushed the material down to her knees. Fee felt her face flame with anger and embarrassment, but the sheer relief of not needing to lay in wet underpants and denim, which she had been preparing to do, was heaven. It comes in small doses sometimes.

If she was humiliated, this man's embarrassment matched hers. He had given her water. He had given her the opportunity to relive herself like a human being, not an animal in captivity. Maybe he just didn't want to heave a box dripping wee about, but anyway, it was welcome. If humiliating. He re-arranged her attire and lifted her over his shoulder again, man-handled her back to sit in her box.

'You hungry?'

Fee nodded, and he produced a bag of sandwiches. Ham and tomato, home-made. He held one for her. She chewed and swallowed.

'I'll be leaving you soon. When *they* come.' *They* would be the metae, obviously. He seemed torn between two opposing values: he wanted to be kind, as to a fellow human, but wouldn't allow himself to be too kind in case it upset his paymasters. And they could do nasty things to you when they were irritated, and just about anything could irritate a mete. They couldn't be predicted. One day they would want their captives treated well, fed, watered, attended to, but another they would choose to have them ignored. And they rarely communicated these desires to their akelytes. Maybe it was some sort of obscure test.

Trying to lure this new acquaintance into conversation was a dead duck. Apart from offering her more water and a damp cloth to wipe away some of the blood and muck that was still stuck to her skin, he just wasn't going to interact with her at all. He sat on a discarded packing case, eating his sandwiches and watching her silently. As a companion, he was no trouble at all. Fee closed her eyes and concentrated. At this, he came over and gave her a sharp poke. When that didn't deter her, he slapped her face. Hard.

'None o' your witchy tricks, now.' He returned to his seat and continued to watch. Intelligent and careful. Why oh why can't I get a stupid one, once in a while? They're so much easier to manage.

She fixed her eyes on the middle distance and concentrated. She could feel Zoe's energy, moving. And Greg's, pulsing presence, a dark heart beating warmly. She felt him react to her thought, and it was a wrench not to reach out to him. She could feel the wyth he was holding, a blue-white light in his hands. He was holding them out, offering the wyth to her. She tamped the link deep in her mind, storing it like she would store a mobile number on speed-dial, ready to activate at a touch. Her mind moved, touching this and that. Little things, but it only takes one too many snowflakes to bring down an avalanche.

Her stillness was making her companion edgy and nervous. He suspected that she was up to something, but he didn't know what. He decided the only way to stop her was to distract her.

'What d'yuh do then?'

'Pardon?'

'What do you do. For a livin', like.'

'I'm a prostitute. I specialize in pain and domination. I do a good rate for friends.'

'I bet yuh charge a few bob.'

'Five hundred a night. That's for the usual. If you want more, the cost goes up.'

'How far do yuh go, then?'

'How dead do you want to be?'

'Yuh don't screw, then.'

'You don't screw slaves.'

'So how come yu'r'ere, then?'

'Special services, mate.'

He knew she was lying. He didn't care what she said, just that she was paying him attention. And therefore, presumably, not doing something 'witchy'. She didn't disturb the level of his ignorance. When you've lived with two sisters, you learn to multitask. That or go completely nuts.

'So what's your line?'

'I move stuff.'

'What sort of stuff?'

'Anyfing wot wants movin'.'

'No questions asked, eh?' He nodded. 'You do live stuff, dead stuff, drugs, what?'

'Anyfing wot wants movin',' he repeated. 'Live, dead, inbetween, don't matter to me s'long as I'm paid.'

Not an akelyte then. Possibly.

'I could pay you to let me go.'

'And then they'll kill me. No fanks.' Scratch that.

'Not thinking of moving into the ranks, are you?'

'What ranks?'

'The undead.'

'Not me, sister. Can't be havin' with that crap.'

'You might not get the choice.' He didn't deserve to feel secure.

'Nah, been workin' wiv this crew some time now. Pretty fair, they are. Reg'lar haulin' too. Always useful.'

I bet it is.

Then, they were there. Soundless as always. Of course. They're dead.

Chapter Thirty-two

There was a gang of around half-a-dozen, flitting and zipping from place to place so swiftly it bewildered the eyes and made counting the exact number difficult. One vampire is trouble enough. They were dressed in the best going-out-on-the-town-for-the-night fashion, all glitz and glitter. There was a party mood in the air. They were all looking forward to something that they were really going to enjoy being part of, which boded no good at all for their unfortunate captive.

One girl detached herself from the crowd and sashayed over to Fee's box. She had cream-in-your-coffee skin with an iridescent dress that clung to her curves in a plum so dark it was nearly black.

'My word, girl, you look a sight.' She lifted Fee's hair, grey with dust. 'Can't see what *he* wants with things like you, really.'

'Come away from that, Denice. You might catch something.'

'Like life, you mean?'

They all laughed, and Denice went back to the throng, her hips swaying seductively. Doesn't take much to amuse a vamp. Or to annoy one.

'Let's get it ready. We haven't got all night.'

'You're late.'

'So we are, so we are, boy. Don't let a little thing like that worry you.'

'I ain't worried.' Liar.

Someone, or something, grabbed at her legs and pulled her back to lie supine in the box. Her head crashed onto the base, making her see stars.

'Careful. You don't want it to die. Yet.'

They started piling cushions into the box, pushing some under her, along the sides, by her head, under her legs, until she couldn't move. That was nearly okay. It was the touch of the cold hands that made her cringe. Almost. They were plucking at her, long cold fingers prying and pinching, razor nails against her exposed flesh. Chiming laughter and bitter smiles. If the haulier had any sense, he'd haul his ass out now while they were distracted. Useful or not, if one of them got the notion to play with him, they all would and no mistake. One of them was hovering over her face, smiling that smile, the one that like as not preceded the sinking in of fangs, when………

Exactly what happened, she couldn't see. She could hear things. Scuffles, and damp thuds. The white, smiling faces vanished. All at once. One moment there, shiny happy vampire faces, the next - gone. Just like that. Then another face appeared, one she knew. This shiny vampire face was definitely not happy. He gripped her arms and pulled her bodily from the box, holding her close, too close to his body.

'Pleased to see me?'

'Yes, yes. Now get these things off me and let's get out of here.' She lifted her hands, blue and white and purple now. It hurt.

He produced a knife from somewhere, and laid it against her cheek.

'There's no real hurry, kitten. You are not in any true danger. Yet.'

'Stop mucking about, Theo. There's only so much night left, and I've got a really bad feeling that it's the last one left. Let's not waste it with playing.'

'You are no fun at all.' Still, he did cut the plastic ties, and it was agony. Her hands felt twice as large as they ought to be, and throbbed abominably. Her legs were stiff, but the thick socks had protected her feet. Her boots had gone with her coat, courtesy of Claire. She could walk out of here in her socks. Provided she could walk. Her shins still ached bone-deep. She hoped that Claire hadn't cracked the bones.

Theo took her arm, and they started to walk towards the doors. In Fee's case, it was more of a painful hobble than a walk, but she was dammed if she was going to let Theo have the satisfaction of carrying her out. The damsel might have been in distress, but she was streets away from helpless.

'Okay, where have all the vampires gone?'

'Long time passing… Where have all the vampires gone, Long

time ago. Where have all the vampires gone: gone to flowers, every one…….' he sang. Trust Theo to make a production out of something. For such a long-lived being, he had an unfortunate knack of inappropriate levity. Theo, take something seriously? Then there's something really, really wrong with the Universe.
'Hell, I don't know what happens when we die. Do you?'
'Sorry.'
'Don't be. I suspect I shall find out one day.'
She passed a crumpled figure. Ah, The Transporter.
'You didn't kill him?'
'No. Should I? He seemed to be treating you… kindly.'
'How long have you been here?'
'Long enough. I hoped to discover what they intended with you, but they were being wise, for such young creatures. I decided that evening the odds was the more productive option. We are at KoziToes after all.'
'The shoe factory?'
'*Was* a shoe factory. *Was*. Now, it is where a certain stage magician keeps his…… tricks? Props?'
She was about to ask where the hell he had found that little nugget, when the doors slammed open. Framed in the doorway were three figures. Two, she knew. One, she didn't. Simon and Brenda, the Gruesome Twosome. The third was much, much older. There was a weight of years that the young face, framed with longish blonde hair just shouldn't have. And an air of malice. Palpable. Bloody hell, you could *taste* it.
'Well, well. Riff-Raff and Magenta, we meet again. And who is this? Frankenfurter?' Fee was sometimes her own worst enemy. The flippant words were out before she had time to consider their impact. Oh, please, please, engage brain before opening gob……
'It has been a long time…….. Theo.'
'Vassily. So long, I forget *how* long. You look….. well.'
'So nice to meet old…. We weren't really friends, were we? What were we now?'
'Enemies, Vassily. That is the term. We were enemies.'
'And are we still, enemies?'
Theo chose not to reply to that one.

'Simon. You have been a busy boy since last we met. Morgana, too. I see you have made your Metargh. And where is Bevan?'

Simon touched Brenda's arm just as she opened her mouth to reply.

'Morgana is no longer with Bevan. She is with me.'

'How nice for you both.'

Fee was waiting for the ruck. It would start once the initial posturing was done with. So polite, vamps. First they catch up with business, shoot the breeze, exchange *very* small talk, then they rip off each other's heads. How civilized. Personally, she would just as soon ripped off their heads on sight. Maybe she was the uncivilized one. Somewhere between her ears and brain, she felt an imperative command. Once violence erupted, and it would, Theo wanted her to run. One against three was acceptable odds. Bloody hell, hadn't he just seen off more than twice that number without breaking into a sweat? But they had been young. This Vassily was a different kettle of cod altogether. He could strip you down to bone with a glance. She might be able to take Brenda. Right. When it starts, straight through Brenda. The usual impulse, when running, is to run *away*. Running *toward* might put them off their stride long enough. Good plan.

There wasn't so much as a twitch. Metae don't really have a tell. You have to have nerves, and glands, to evince a tell. They might have nerves and glands, but they didn't use them much. Fee bolted. Brenda, between Simon and Vassily, gaped as Fee, ducking to evade a grasp from Simon, powered her hand up under Brenda's chin and slammed the pearly whites together with an audible snap. She hoped she had made Brenda break a fang, or at least bite through her lip or tongue. Simon, blindsided, crashed into Vassily, making him miss his first feint at Theo, who punished the mistake by kicking Vassily in the mouth. Something wet and warm splattered on Fee's back, but she was through and past Brenda and accelerating down the passage. A shriek of pure rage followed her. Don't look back. She vaulted over a stair rail, not caring where they went and trusting her vampire strength to cushion the fall. But she didn't have the sheer grace, and landed with feet on different steps, and stumbled. She rolled out of the fall, was up and running again. Something swooshed past her, stopped and turned. She crashed headlong into Vassily, who clamped his hands on her upper arms and held her easily.

'Fast, but not fast enough, little one. But well done. You have spirit. It is a pity that Simon will use you to complete the ritual: you would make an excellent mete. Such spirit. I admire you. Now, come.'

Blood was running unheeded down his face as he hustled her back up the stairs, past a snarling Brenda who had indeed lost at least one fang. Diddums.

Back in the storeroom, Simon was standing, arms extended, in front of Theo. He was snarling, held immobile by a weave. Fee could hardly comprehend the scene. A meta? Using wyth? How could that be?

'Morgana, my dear. Would you like to deal this this minor inconvenience?'

Fee looked hard at Simon. No matter what he had said, or how casually he said it, he was finding it hard to contain Theo. Pinkish sweat was collecting in droplets on his face. Ah ha, not so proficient as we claim to be. Proficient or not, he still had the upper hand. Fee let her face gape as her mind worked furiously. Let them think I'm stunned by this virtuoso performance, and perhaps, just perhaps, I can break Simon's hold on Theo. It must take all of his concentration to maintain that weave. Distraction, where can I find a distraction?

Brenda picked up the knife that Theo had dropped after releasing Fee from the restraints. She swayed over to him, blood dripping off her chin. She had lost the faint heaviness that had marked her as a human when Fee had met her before. Now, her body language was vastly different. Assured, graceful, languid. She was going to draw this out. Good. Time, I need more time......

There was a sudden clattering up on the ceiling. Two pairs of eyes swivelled upwards as a dark mass of fluttering shadows descended, filling the spaces between the shelves with their hissing, rustling flight. Crows, obsidian wings and grey claws, gor-crows, carrion crows, fit for carrion...... They fell on Vassily and Brenda. Pecking, clawing, beating with their wings. They had bloodlust here. Brenda flinched.

'Do it! Do it *now!*' Vassily's mind strained out towards the cringing Brenda, even as his hands convulsed crushingly on Fee's arms. The avian onslaught faltered as Fee gasped with the pain of it. Woodenly, Brenda moved behind Theo and grabbed at his hair, pulling his head back. The knife moved towards his throat, exposed and tautened from his bent-back head. Fee steeled herself against the pain and drove the crows directly at Simon's face. He ducked. A slight, involuntary movement, but it was enough to break his concentration and free Theo from the weave which had held him immobile. He started to turn, but Vassily, his mind riding Brenda's body, was just that millisecond quicker. The knife flashed, and a gout of dark blood flowed down over Theo's chest. Brenda hacked again, and Theo's headless body fell to the floor, leaving his head to stare at Fee from Brenda's hand.

Fee, still held in that vicelike grip, screamed. Her voice had overtones that shook dust from the ceiling and rattled the boxes on the shelves. They started to fall, first the boxes and then entire shelves, crashing into each other, a giant's domino rally. The birds converged on Brenda, a wave of feather and talon and bloody beaks, hit her, and went through her, scattering vital organs and blood and skin. Her face convulsed in a ricktus of horror as her head exploded, scattering blood and hair and brains over everyone. She collapsed in a broken heap over Theo's corpse, her blood spreading, mingling with his in a hideous pool. Papers from the scattered boxes landed in the gorefest, and the echoes of the scream died. Simon turned to her. She glared at him.

'Congratulations. Enjoy your small victory, for it is all you will have. Tonight, I will pass beyond the need for such petty tricks. And you will be the means to that end. Sadly, you will not share it with me, but you will be privileged to witness, and be part of, an act of cys that has not been seen these several thousand years. You should be proud to be a part, a small part, of such a momentous event. I understand that you might not see it that way, but your opinions are irrelevant.'

Fee could feel the lapping of the blackness. Oh no, not again. She flung her mind away from her body, ripping its moorings as the blackness washed over her consciousness. Carefully, she laid her wraith body closely against her mortal one, sagging in the grip of the ancient undead.

'Looks like she got away,' Vassily growled.

'No, I have her. She tried to release her wraith, but failed. I can see it lingering in her flesh. We are close, Vassily, very close. Tonight we shall see the culmination of our Great Work.'

Why, oh why, does such an *intelligent* man want to sound like the bad guy in an Austin Powers movie? Tonight, the farer: tomorrow, the world! Ah Ha! Ah ha!… Give me strength…….

Vassily threw her limp body over one shoulder, a life-size rag doll. As he moved off, Fee tried to regain control of her physical body, but each time she started to sink into it, the darkness rose like tide and tried to claim her. Instead she spent some time mourning a dead guy who was really dead now……..

Chapter Thirty-three

Zoe had problems of her own. Cecile had suddenly blanked out. Arms locked on the steering wheel, foot slammed to the floor, the Elise was roaring along heedless of the traffic. To add to her plate of woe, there was a blue light strobing in the rear-view mirror and approaching fast.

She knew what had happened. She had felt the dark wash of disbelief, a winking out, a wrenching behind her eyes. A fellow consciousness torn out by the roots, a gaping hole where an alternative awareness ought to be. She pulled back, seizing the fading throes with all her strength.

'Bugger it, Theo, don't do this to me now!'

The hole in her mind started to fill up. She shied away from the rage and hunger in that returning awareness before it submerged her. By her side, Cecile appeared to be recovering from the rigid catatonia, and the Elise was slowing down.

'Heads up, Cecile. We've got company.'

'How tiresome. I thought you were taking care of this?'

'I was distracted, okay?'

Cecile turned to Zoe and stared at her, hard. There was venom in that stare. Cecile was fiercely protective of her status as Theo's consort. If she thought that Zoe might be a threat, she was not beyond eliminating her as a rival, Rina or no Rina.

'Can we deal with this later? After we've got rid of the fuzz?'

Slowly, Cecile's gaze cooled. She did not look away from Zoe's eyes until there was a tap on the window. A slightly useless gesture since the top was down, but protocol is apparently protocol. She turned, slowly, graciously, as the window lowered.

'Yes, Officer?' Her voice was a honeyed purr.

'You were going a teensy bit fast there, Miss.'

'I am so sorry. But my friend here, something hit her face. She screamed, and it scared me. I was worried that she might be hurt.'

'Can you get out of the car, please, Miss.'

Cecile slid out of the driver's seat, elegant as a snake.

'Are you all right, Miss?'

He was shining a torch on Zoe's face. She assumed a look of confusion, fear and puzzlement.

'Something hit me.' She raised a hand to her forehead. It trembled as it passed her lips, hiding them as she mouthed a glim. She took her hand away. 'I'm bleeding.'

There was a lot of blood. She wanted it to look impressive, and scalp wounds bled a lot. From the look on his face, she had overcooked it. Badly.

'Ron! Get over here with the first aid kit!'

'Is it serious?' Cecile crooned from behind him, faking deep concern with remarkable accuracy for a dead girl. She craned over his back, one hand creeping up on his shoulder…..

A second cop materialized. He had a small green zip-up case in his hand. He took one look at Zoe and started to rummage in the case. Cecile flexed her hand on the first cop's shoulder, and leant in to look. Her face was right by his neck, her lips close to his ear. Zoe hoped she was faking breathing. As if Cop One would notice, riveted as he was by the appearance of blood flowing freely down Zoe's face…. But you never knew, with cops.

'Keep still, Miss.' Cop Two now had his shaking hands in a pair of latex gloves and was trying to stem the gory flood with a large wad of bandage. Zoe faked quaking with shock as she watched the interest drain from Cop One's features.

'My companion will be fine. She is a little shaken up. When we complete our journey, we will seek medical advice. This incident is not worthy of your attention. We thank you for your care. We will go now.'

Cop Two's eyes swivelled up, only to be caught by a kilowatt stare. His mouth fell open.

'It is merely a scratch. It is of no importance. You have warned me of the dangers of driving with the roof down. I have accepted your suggestion. I am a silly girl. You can go now.'

Woodenly, Cop Two collected his zip-up first aid kit and walked back to his car, followed by Cop One.

'Pity. I could have done with a snack about now.'

'You can call them back if you want.'

'Get rid of that illusion. It is childish and it is distracting me. There they go.'

The panda car drew smoothly away. Cecile slipped back into the bucket seat with the same sinuous grace as she had left it.

'Are you ready?'

'Willing and able.'

'Then let us go, or we will miss all the fun.'

Zoe sighed. Vamps had such a peculiar slant on life. Or death.

'He survived, then.' Zoe commented as the car drew back into the streaming mass of traffic.

'Yes. You called him back. But he awoke hungry, as we all do. Someone will die, soon.'

'Oh dear.'

'It is the way of things.' Cecile settled the Elise in the outside lane. 'Pay attention, now. I want no more distractions.'

Chapter Thirty-four

Fee had company. Unwilling to stray far from her body, and alert Simon to the fact that his weave had failed, she was enduring a walk sprawled over Vassily's back. Occasionally, Simon would peer at her. Other than that, they proceeded silently. She became aware of a presence hovering nearby. She engaged her other vision, the one that saw alternate levels of being. Floating in the air, between Vassily and Simon, was a white-haired woman in a long pale dress. She was surrounded by a hazy blue tinged mist that obscured the details. She smiled, and her hair, free - flowing, curled round her face. She moved like she was floating in a sea of light that moved her hair and skirts in a gentle ebb-and-flow. The old-not-old face was luminous, kind but determined, sad and gracious. Knowing but concerned………

'Rina.'

'*My child. The nexus approaches. Soon you will find out if you are worthy to end this battle of wills and designs.*' The voice echoed, far off, remote. The emotion was far from remote, though. '*I grieve that this trouble has come to you. I pray that you will be able to end this sorry chain of events, and restore peace to your heart.*'

'What must I do?'

'*Be ready for the confluence of wythen. Only then can you discharge the obligation that has fallen to you. Only then can the sword come to your aid. Events speed to their designated destinations, and carry us with them. Only through understanding can we alter what happens then. Aid will come to those who deserve it.*'

'To those who love without desire shall wythen be granted in the darkest hour.'

'*Pray it be so. My prayers go with you, my child.*'

Fee felt a soft touch on her brow, a butterfly kiss, and felt the warmth of her ancestor's wraith. The ghostly blue glow faded slowly, and Fee was alone again. No, not alone. She could still feel the tenuous link to Greg, see the tiny lights winking. And on the ayet, a frosted jar containing a yellow glow that flickered and eddied with a life of its own.... ('What the hell's *that*?' 'It's a pharsee. We've all got 'em. Helps us to link up. We've had them for years. Fee caught the first one with me, and they're all sort-of sisters. It'll be her link back here. She's called Ayah. That's Hindi for nurse, by the way....') Fee could see, and hear the past in overlay of the present. She felt for the pharsee, wound her consciousness around it until the link was well-nigh unbreakable. Wraith vision could see the eddies of wyth and Gya in the circle. The boy had a lot to contend with, all on his lonesome. Not the least of which were his own tumbled emotions. He had wanted so much to rescue her. He had wanted to drive like a demon, chase down the lorry, truck, van, whatever, that had been carrying her through the day, Zoe had vetoed that.

'Rescue her? *Rescue her?* Haven't you been listening to a word we've said?'

Fee's heart warmed at the thought. He was confused, like anyone who's misplaced a loved one. They want the beloved back in the place where they ought to be, and were the means available to them, they would execute that with all dispatch. Instead the poor lamb was being made to stay home, alone but for an incorporeal being who had scampered up his pants leg and threatened to bite his balls. Nice.

She touched the seething mass of Zoe's energy. Bless the rage. Zoe would not give up, not if there was a nanometre of wiggle room.

Vassily stopped in front of a set of sliding doors while Simon rapped on them. The noise echoed, and she heard soft footsteps on concrete. That must have been something to do with what she had gained from Theo, since when the door opened it was another undead who stood there. Vassily dumped her unceremoniously onto the cold, hard floor into a limp, gangling heap. Sharp grit dimpled the flesh of her abused hands and dug into other places.

'Bring her.'

She was heaved onto another shoulder. Annoyance at being treated like a sack of grain rose and was tamped down. Now was not the time. Later. She would let them have it later. Each and every indignity, let them fuel the rage. But keep it cold, stone cold. From the feeling and smell, it was definitely another meta. The flesh of the hand that held her had a peculiar resistance, cool, like putty. A faint waft of something fusty, way past rotten. Mouldering dust.

The quality of the air changed as they passed the doors. Fee risked a peep, floating away from the cortege. It was a brick - and - timber building, two stories high. A barn. On the side was a discreet copper plaque: Touchstone Magic PLC. They had entered by a small door set into huge double barn doors. The air inside was still and stale. It felt like a large space.

She was tumbled onto a concrete floor, and rolled onto a carpet, boneless. Well, she wasn't in her body, not really. Just slightly attached. She could see, but not feel. The grit that was embedded in her hands would be painful later, as would the collection of bruises she was unconsciously amassing. For now, this could all be ignored. She added it to the charge sheet. Each personal injury, pinprick, scratch and abrasion would be returned with interest. She feared that damage to come would be more deadly, more serious and far more painful. There would be no redemption: no coin could ransom her from these killers. On the other hand, no coin would redeem them from her. She looked round. Shadows everywhere, and hiding in them, fantastic things. A glint of tarnished gilt here, a brilliant colours there, sombre and garish: very yang. It was a circus graveyard. Vassily was sitting at his ease on a shabby leather couch, watching Simon light a hurricane lamp. Stage setting: someone's living room. Someone with too much money and too little taste. Or who shopped out of skips and reject bins, and had all the taste and discernment of a magpie. Old and new rubbed shoulders: a grandfather clock, its pendulum still, grimy glass obscuring a face that showed moon phases and a corpulent jolly sun. An occasional table made in imitation of a travelling trunk with leather corners and brass handles. A Tiffany lamp, unlighted. A chest made of myriads of tiny drawers, and a fivefold screen with peacocks and geishas, the colours faded where it had caught the light. There was even a throne, its gilding tarnished and the plush faded to an unhealthy pink, even pale yellow in places. And lurking like a spare corpse at a funeral, an enormous plasma screen, ashamed to be seen in such otherwise tawdry company.

'Where are the rest of your blyd? They should be here by now.'

'They are entertaining themselves. Ah, to be young.'

'The night wears on. The time will be upon us soon.'

'Ach, you worry too much. So many years you have been crafting this, your revenge. But what is time to a mete?'

'I have told you before. All things have a proper time, when they can be accomplished. The nexus of Gya approaches, I can feel it. Ahhh! To feel the wyth again. I did not know what it meant, to be frata, until it was ripped from me. Now, I know. And I will have it back, Vassily, you can be sure of that.'

Simon was turning the pages of an enormous book. Carefully, reverently. He found the page he wanted, and smoothed both hands on the open pages.

'Take her upstairs, Vassily, please. And make sure she is secure. Then you can round up the errant members of your blyd.'

'Do not fear, Simon. You will have an audience for your show.'

Vassily glided over to Fee's body, and slung it over one shoulder. Again.

'You are becoming flippant, Vassily. This is no mere show. Once I have completed my side of the bargain, I will obtain my desires.'

'And mine. This project of yours has been wasteful of our resources. You have lost your pet human, and your new akelyte. I have lost six of my blyd to your scheming.'

'Claire was no mere human, remember that. She was blood of my blood, and the wyth flowed in her. As such, she had her uses. Theo I did not expect. When he ran from his nets and went to ground, I thought never to encounter him again. To have him interfere so blatantly was somewhat of a surprise. Never fear. You will have them back, Vassily. And the entertaining Morgana. Remember, you stole them all in the first place, did you not? Claire, I presume, is lost to us. Her mind is in turmoil, and I can establish no link with her. Still, it was her own foolish desires which led her into fatal error.'

'You should not have instructed her, maybe.'

'Perhaps. Now go, and prepare our final offering. I will join you at the proper time.'

Vassily moved easily through the room, Fee's weight nothing to his strength. Her wraith floated after. She caught a fleeting glance at the book Simon was studying. She did not recognize the language, or any of the siga on the page. Oops.

The meta carried her up a spiral staircase to the upper levels, his feet silent on the metal treads. It was as black as the inside of a cat in a coal cellar up there, but to Fee's wraith vision it was darkly luminous. Heavy doors barred the way, swinging silently open at a touch. Wythen had been used in this room. The residual effects were palpable. Fee could distinguish stray sparks of wyth winking lazily on the walls. Vassily poured her onto a bare wooden floor by a fat pillar, and unhooked a rope from it. He pulled the rope down. Attached to the end were leather cuffs. He then wandered off into the dark recesses.

They were in an atelier of sorts. One of the lofts so beloved of the modernistic architects, all open space and wood and iron and brick. Several fat pillars rose up to a corbelled ceiling, huge trees of rafters on old brick pillars which pierced this floor from the floor below. Over to the right was a solid block of stone. Behind it, a heavy cloth masked whatever lay beyond. It was moving slightly, so there was at least a room behind there, and possibly an exit. On the stone block, two candelabras stood, each with nine fat candles. Between them sat a squat bowl on a stubby base. Other things lay beside the bowl - among them a peculiar knife, its double curve making an elongated s-shape, the handle inlaid with oblongs of coloured stone. A large jar was on the floor in front of the stone block. To one side was an old Irish dresser, the carvings lost in the darkness of the wood. Books stood on the shelves, old books. Fee would bet her last ten pence that they had never been seen in any library. Vassily returned, carrying a very prosaic yellow plastic bowl and a white dress over one arm. He knelt by her body and started to remove her dirty clothes, putting them in a cardboard box. Fee watched with some misgivings as her underclothes joined the rest, leaving her naked body open to Vassily's gaze. He ran his palms over her midriff, her thighs, then seemed to think better of it: he left her alone. He then gave her a through sponge bath, cleansing away the grit and grime and blood that had collected on her skin in the past hours. Fee was betting the water had been cold: she had seen no welcome steam arising from the bowl. She would be freezing when she awoke. The least of her worries, really.

Once she was sufficiently clean, to Vassily, anyway - Fee would have taken at least two hours soaking in a hot tub before she would deem herself fit for polite society after the day she'd had - he pulled the white dress over her head and inserted her arms into the long, close sleeves. Since he hadn't taken the trouble to dry her skin first, he was having some problems. He was very proficient at removing garments, but lacking practise in replacing them properly. And he was putting her into a lace dress. The long, tight sleeves met a fitting bodice with an indecently low cut neckline. He rolled her over. How old was that dress? It had buttons up the back. And laces. Who had worn it before her? She watched as Vassily manipulated the laces until the bodice fitted perfectly over her torso. How nice of him to ensure that she would look perfect for her final curtain. Well, perfect to a meta's taste, in virginal white lace with her tits hanging half out. Fee had not worn white, or lace, since she had had any say in the matter. And probably before that too, since Lily's tastes didn't run to white lace either. Zoe would have a fit. Fee would never hear the last of it.

Satisfied that she now looked her best - or at least as good as she was going to look, given the scrapes and bruises - Vassily dragged her over to the pillar and attached the leather bracelets on her wrists. Then he turned and started to haul her up the pillar. Hung up by the hands twice in twenty-four hours - whatever have I done to deserve this? I must really have pissed at least one ayen off at some time. That or I am in arrears with my Karma, and the Bank of God is calling in the loan. Once she was upright, he tied one rope around her waist and a second around her ankles. He had to fuss with the lace skirt. The previous inhabitant had been somewhat taller than Fee. Then he released her wrists from the rope overhead and tied them behind the pillar. Her head hung forwards, her long hair tangling down. He took advantage of this to carefully brush her hair smooth out of the bird's nest of rattails that it had morphed onto. Static sparks lit the darkness as he brushed and brushed again. His actions had the taste of an obsessive-compulsive disorder. Brush, brush, brush. Did he have a thing for long brown hair? He lifted her chin and parted her hair, arranging it in two wings on either side of her face. He inspected her closely, holding her head up and stroking her neck. If Fee had been awake, she would have felt a frisson of panic when he nuzzled his face in her neck and shoulder, feeling her skin with his lips and teeth, inhaling her fragrance. But then he stepped back and admired his handiwork. Perfect.

Alone again, Fee began a minute examination of her prison from ceiling to floor. Apart from the stone block, and the dresser, the place was bare. But behind the faded hanging was another chamber, and this contained enough to confirm that Simon had been using wyth. Coloured robes were hanging limply in an alcove: shelves held jars and bottles, all carefully labelled in a fine free copperplate hand. A bookshelf held several volumes, some printed editions, but more than half handwritten. And the titles weren't comfortable. If you were going to have the vapours over books called The Dark Arts and Demonology, these would give you the screaming habdabs. Forget the Necronomicon and the Grimoire of Honorius. Ignore the Key of Solomon and the Magic of Abramelin. Sob into your hankie, Aleister Crowley, this guy's got you beat up the street and down. Fee could 'read' the books. Or, more properly, the memories they had. A record of an esoteric journey, made by one man - using the term very loosely indeed - who had no limits either of decency or morality in pursuit of his goal. Nothing would hinder him nor get in his way. He was doing whatever it took, whatever the cost in horror or degradation, and worse still, enjoying it. Every bit of it. Especially the nasty bits. Simon was seriously bent out of shape. Could have been the trauma of accepting eternal life from Theo's hand (teeth) or maybe the seeds had been sown before. Germinated, even.

Fee left the library feeling soiled. Killing was one thing. A death is simple and uncomplicated. One moment alive, the next dead. Okay. But this piece of offal went beyond that. The deaths were a means to an end. The deaths of the fratten were to gain wyth. The vanishing metae were to gain the assistance of…….. Something else. Fratten he had been killing for himself. The undead he had been acquiring for another. Maybe that's why he had joined forces with Vassily? The sod had known that Theo would try to rescue her despite his protestations, and he had sent those metae in deliberately. Fee wondered if Vassily knew that. Or if he would care. He seemed to be put out by the loss. Simon had used his blyd, not Simon's own, in that debacle. Maybe she could use that to drive a wedge between them, given the chance…….

She continued her slow investigation of her prison. There was no escaping until Simon lifted the darkness that dwelt her body now. She drifted over to the far wall, and found it to be a partition. More stairs led back down to the lower level, into a short corridor. Behind one door was a bedroom. On the bed was a bright knitted coverlet, and under the coverlet was a child. One Fee recognized. Josie. She was tucked up with her favourite toy, a blue rabbit. She was fast asleep, her thumb in her mouth. Natural sleep, or enchanted oblivion? Not much she could do about it now. Even if she roused the sleeping child, getting her out would be the mother of all problems. Best to leave her alone until Fee had her flesh back. By the bed was a nightstand with a child's book. Harry Potter. How… apt. *We both have Dark Lords out after us. But it's going to take more than Expelliarmus to get me out of this hole. No Basilisk, no phoenix, no Dumbledore inhabited this nightmare place. Not even a Macgonagall.* A nightlight, battery powered, now dark, sat by the book. Helpless to alter even one tiny factor in this sorry state of affairs, Fee drifted back into the main arena to wait for what would happen.

Chapter Thirty-five

Zoe was freezing. She hadn't been able to feel her ears for hours. Her face felt flayed by the wind. Cecile was dismissive of her discomfort. They left the car part hidden behind an abandoned unit well away from their ultimate destination. Cecile had locked it, and Zoe glimmed it. Anyone looking at it would see a rusty heap and be disinclined to investigate further.

'The walk will warm your blood. We should not leave the car too near. It will excite too much interest. Then I will investigate. You are not as able as I.'

When Zoe found out that Cecile intended a large part of the sortie to be on the roof of a two storey barn, she agreed. She settled down behind an inviting wall. Time to phone a friend.

By the time Cecile rejoined her, Zoe had the schematics of the barn on her laptop. Jerry had done her proud. When the barn had been converted into a shoe factory, the developers had to comply with building regulations when running in power and water lines. Especially interesting were the arrangements for the disposal of liquid waste. Shoe manufacture apparently used a lot of water, and needed it delivered fast. Which meant that intake and outflow pipes were unusually large. Large enough to crawl through, and hopefully, empty by now. Well, *mostly* empty. The other schematics showed a suite of offices and a large empty space. There was an upper floor, but it only stretched over part of the internal. Very few alterations had been done - officially, that is - since its new incarnation as a vampire's lair.

Cecile had other ideas, mostly involving a rickety skylight. She was really not the sort for crawling through sewer pipes, or air vents. She would have been useless on the Starship Enterprise.

'I can get you to the roof.'

'And how far is the drop on the other side?'

'Twenty feet. It's nothing.'

Zoe bit back a retort that would have sent Cecile into the granddaddy of all snits had she delivered it. 'And we get out how? Levitate?'

'First, we get in. Then, we get out.'

Zoe lowered her face into her hands. 'What about security?'

'A simple system. It is disabled, now.'

'You ripped out the power cables, didn't you?'

'No. I removed the fuse.'

'When?'

'When I came out. It is by the front door.'

'Then why can't we use the door?'

'I thought the skylight would be more - dramatic.'

'Only if there's someone there to see. And if there is, it defeats the object of getting in *secretly*.'

Cecile pursed her lips. 'The front door is now open. If they expect us to be inventive, they will not expect us to access the building that way.'

'You're good at this.'

'I have had practise. Now, come. Before we are discovered.'

One glance at the schematic was all Cecile needed. Zoe knew her memory was phenomenal. The dead lass could quote whole pages of recipes at the drop of a hat. Useful when you're a caterer. She had a good visual memory herself - it came from years of memorizing siga and cys and demonstrating them back to Lily. She had been helped by her father. Rob was valued not only for his extensive knowledge of his speciality, organic chemistry, but an almost perfect recall. 'Benzadiene? On yes, we did some work on that back..... when was it now? Ah. Look in the diary, page one hundred and forty...... six.' And there it was! Every year, Rob started a new workbook, noting down not only what he did, but what he had thought at the time in a personal shorthand. He had let Zoe examine these ledgers, filled with diagrams and pointed cursive script as difficult as any doctor's to read. Well, he was a Ph.D. and merited the title of Doctor Harris, one he claimed, like Jubal Harcourt in Stranger In A Strange Land, he was 'too stinking proud' to use. 'Once they start handing out doctorates for comparative folk dancing and extreme embroidery, it's not worth the parchment it's written on.'

'What are these, dad?' Zoe asked, peering at the strange squiggles and designs that wandered over a full double page.

'Mind maps, pet. They remind me of what I was thinking back then. I look at them and they remind me of the thoughts I had then.'

'Why don't you do lists?' Lily was a devil for lists, they littered her workspaces and clogged up the family cork-board at home.

'It's easier to remember pictures than lists. Memory is far more visual, usually.'

Led by her father, Zoe began to compile memory maps.

'Think of the house, Zoe,' he suggested once when they were playing Kim's Game. 'You know the house very well. Now you come to the gate. The stapler is running staples up the gatepost. See it. The plate is balanced on the gate and it falls off when you open it. The pencil is writing 'hello' on the path, and......'

'The stuffed cat is sitting by the door, the ring is hanging on the doorknocker.....'

Later it was 'What do I do when I run out of rooms?'

'Use them again. Like overlays. The rooms aren't the same every day, are they? They're different in the morning and evening. Use your imagination.'

Zoe was smug in the knowledge that her personal memory palace was at least as extensive and complex as the one attributed to Hannibal Lecter. To compare your mind with that of a serial killer is perhaps not the best recommendation in the world, even if he were a fantasy dreamed up by Thomas Harris. But then Zoe was cast from a different mould.

Since she had shared with Theo, her memory had also become eidetic. She could recall anything. It had taken longer to evolve, longer than being faster, or seeing differently. But it was there. Mind you, it could be a tad embarrassing. There were some memories that floated up to the surface that could make her run hot and cold together. Shame, humiliation and other emotions she really didn't want to own up to. Many of these recollections she wished she could bury again forever. Some were shining jewels she could treasure. Not those involving nappies and toilet training, however. They could sink without trace as soon as they wished.

She and Cecile were starting to move when headlights shone

over the wall. Three sets, in convoy. They ducked automatically.

'Shit. That will be the stormtroops. Fifteen at most.'

'Less, I think. We do not like to be crowded. Twelve.'

'I think,' Zoe said, sitting back down, 'that I had better find out first. Simon won't want any more than twelve others sitting in the ritual with him. That could leave up to five of the buggers lurking, waiting for us.'

'He will want the leader with him. The rest will be younger. He is confident that any meten, no matter how untried they are in their natures, can subdue a fratten. Especially one so young.'

'So your plan is to shove me in first as bait?'

'Distraction. They will not see you as threat, but as entertainment. They will not take you seriously, and will want to play.'

'Then let's go educate a few bloodsuckers in good manners.'

'Please. That term is offensive.'

'But accurate. Present company excepted, of course.'

'Then I will enter by the roof, which will please me. You will enter by the door, which will please you. Give me five minutes, then make your entrance. And make it worthy of attention, but not too much attention.'

'Let's synchronise watches.'

'What watch? I know what five minutes feels like. And I will know when you enter.'

Cecile was gone. Zoe sighed, and looked at the time ticking down on her laptop. Carefully, she let her mind's eye range. Funny, she could swear she could smell blood. Faintly, but clearly. Then, the knowledge came to her. 'I always know where my blood is.' Theo's voice, from way back in time, long rambling conversations by the fireside in Pippin Cottage. Of course she could scent blood: it was part of the 'protection' that Theo had endowed her. As she concentrated, she could identify Cecile, and feel her walking confidently upright on the roof tiles, see the skylight through her eyes. An internal gaze, laced with irritation, made her back off. She was much more careful as she traced the other signatures. Some were fainter than others: further away, or more remote in a familial sense? Blood brothers and not blood brothers, perhaps. It was something she could sort out later. At least three were more easily discernable. So, three guards to prevent inconvenient interruptions. Three dead guys - no, one was definitely female - to bamboozle. Okay. Here we go.

She stood up. Leaving the laptop safely hidden in its weatherproof satchel under some brambles that had been digging into her back, she squared her shoulders and sidled up to the front door. Four cars and a white panel truck sat in the forecourt. Crouching low behind a bumper, she whispered a weave. A spark of brilliant red light appeared. She repeated the spell until five of the dense sparks were slowly gyrating in the dirt. For all the brilliant colour, they shed very little light. Well, they were hungry: at least she hoped they were. She whispered to them, gesturing towards the cars. With a final gesture and a whispered 'Go feed, my pets,' she sent them off, each to a separate vehicle, where they vanished beneath the bonnets. A few crackles and a surge of blue actinic light later, all five batteries were as dead as dodos. Hah. And they say electricity is inimical to wyth? What do they know? All life depends on electricity, and those five sprites would be very grateful little sods now. She spread her cloak and called them back, hiding them in the inner folds of thick wool. They were bigger and brighter now, so a faint red glow cast upwards onto her face. Uplit faces always look weird and demonic and up to nothing good. Her face creased into a phony smile, a tight, evil grin. Now she looked the part she was ready to enter Spooky Towers. Beware, all you ghosties and ghoulies and long-legged beasties, I'm coming to get you! Then she remembered she was supposed to be the fluffy-bunny victim. To hell with it. The grin broadened. I'm coming to get you anyway. She stood up and walked slowly towards the door. Behind the frosted glass panels it was black as pitch, but to meten sight, eerily radiant. She could see a curved desk in front of a plain door, and another door, panelled and important, to the left. She whispered again, a glim for silence and concealment. It might work well enough for her to surprise the three guards. They were further within the building. They wanted to lure her deeper before… doing whatever they had been told to do, or chose to do. The thought was not a comfortable one. Still, what threat is one sixteen year old farer to a seasoned meten of - a couple of months? Years? Decades, even? Praying for overconfidence in her adversaries, Zoe opened the door.

The door opened silently. *Good* door. *Nice* door. All senses operating on overdrive, she slipped inside. She felt the vamps come to attention. Well, not exactly attention. Bored interest, maybe. Pretending a search for her sister, Zoe investigated the important panelled door. Inside was a large table, once shiny with loving (or at least attentive) polishing, now covered with a fine grey layer of grime. Opulent comfy chairs stood round the table. Management meeting room, then. A dead computer lay forlorn and unused on one end. Zoe poked it experimentally. Dead as the cars outside. The other door lead to a restroom done tastefully (not) in beige tile. Expensive tissues, their scent wasted by neglect, lay by a hand basin big enough to launder a medium sized dog. Well, metae don't visit bathrooms often. Ever. Back behind the desk was an intercom telephone system, a fire warning board and another computer, all dead. Looking to the far wall, Zoe could see a passage stretching behind double glass doors, with other doors, some open, leading off. Offices, probably. Still, she ought to search them, even though her senses told her they were deserted, except for the thin dust that shrouded everything. The doors were propped open. She slipped through the gap, alert for any slight movement that might indicate the presence of the non-living being spooky. She ought to be ready to be spooked. Metae could come upon you without warning when they wanted. Theo had scared the living daylights out of her more than once when playing hide-and-seek. Stupid game to play with a meta, but there it was. She would find a cosy nook, and hunker down, only to find minutes later, that she was sitting next to, or even on top of, Theo, who was meant to be It. 'Found you,' would come the low, shivery whisper, and she would scream and run pell-mell for light and safety. Delicious fear when you are safe in your own house: gut-freezing ghastly terror when you are wandering round a deserted, darkened warehouse peopled (if that's the word) by undead monsters.

She crept through a series of rooms, all deserted. Whatever Simon was using this place for, he hadn't engaged staff, certainly not cleaning staff. Papers lay untidily on tables, chairs lay on the floor, upturned and unwanted. Silent computers dotted the desks next to redundant telephones. Cubicle world gave way to individual offices as she found the management suite at the end of the corridor. A dead ficus had dropped its leaves in the corner onto a royal blue carpet. Most of the offices were still locked, the dust on the floor undisturbed. No prisoners in there awaiting blessed release, then. One showed signs of recent use: some letters dated five, ten, even twenty years ago lay on the blotter, mostly to do with schedules for shows. Simon's tours, arrangements for moving equipment and the like. Nothing remotely personal, only a mighty lump of quartz doing duty as a paperweight.

The loitering metae hadn't stirred. They were waiting, like spiders in a web, for her to blunder in. Time to spring the trap: she could feel Cecile's impatience, and something else, which she shied away from. It was too feral, too bloodthirsty to be scrutinised closely, for there was a gleeful eroticism in that expectation. Cecile would enjoy hurting these beings, and would take great pleasure from their pain. As she herself had said more than once, she was not a *nice* person.

A wide passage led off from the offices, deeper into the monster's lair. The carpets ran out, and she was walking on bare concrete now. She passed a lift, obviously meant for moving large items from this floor to another, but no stairs. Anyway, the vamps were down here, not up there. As she drew closer, she could discern other presences. Among them was the one she had come for. Ffion, still alive, but far from conscious. Her presence was not open. For whatever reason, she was avoiding contact with Zoe. Since she hadn't exactly come to rescue her sister, no matter what she had told Cecile, it didn't matter. She hadn't been totally honest with Greg either. 'Fetch' did not equate to 'Rescue'. If he assumed that it did, it really wasn't Zoe's fault that he thought so. Fee was surfing the disaster curve, riding the event horizon, where the slightest miscalculation would cause her to wipe out. Zoe had to trust that Fee knew what she was about and was capable of doing same. Had she known the truth – Fee was trapped in a weave, helpless – she might have been more concerned. She didn't: she wasn't. Blissfully ignorant of her sister's straights, she continued in her mission oblivious to the potential for disaster she was ambling into.

She passed into a vaster space. To her left, heavy sliding doors masked whatever was in the room beyond: but since she could feel no thoughts behind that, she carried on, following the spoor of the metae who were waiting for her. So far, so good. They could sense her, but not Cecile, who had the art of concealment down pat. She was better at it than Theo. 'Tighter than a duck's arse, that one,' Lily had once said. Zoe could feel Lily's watchfulness. It was like being on stage, the lights in your eyes hiding the audience. You knew they were there, you could feel their presence: you could not see them but they could see you. I am in a play: Girl And Ghoul. So where the feck is the ghoul?

She reached the corner. Oh, Theo, blessed be thy blood by which I see. Over by the far wall, three metae were taking their ease: a stage set it was, chairs and a sofa, an oversize block of wood performing the services of an occasional table between them, with an unlit standard lamp rescued by its looks from a skip: a tatty carpet, probably from the same source, a bureau and tallboy, all framed with a folding screen. Posing in an empty space that could house several pantechnicons with ease. You would have thought that an immortal would have better taste, but there you are. All it wanted was a trio of flying ducks on the wall. They were watching her, as she pretended groping in the dark.

Suddenly, silently, one of them was by her side. It was all Zoe could do not to flinch, and continue a hesitating progress further into the emptiness, away from the grinning duo, who were enjoying her antics. Watch the show, suckers.

'Can I help you, pretty lady?' The voice came over her shoulder. Oh, he was enjoying scaring the little virgin heroine who had come to investigate the scary monster behind the creaking door in the haunted mansion. Shame to disappoint him, really. Zoe let out her best knicker-wetting scream and bolted into the darkness, followed by a low, evil chuckle. Then he was right in front of her. Enough of this crap. Fingers rigid, she drove at his face, using her momentum behind the blow. Bone crunched, and he went down. Concealed in her hand was a very special blade - silver over cold iron, forged long ago by Uncle Tom, just in case some metae got frisky. The heel of her hand had driven it clean through his skull.

Seeing their comrade fall, the other two scrambled up, only to be met by a cold fury: Cecile, not to be outdone, grabbed one in each hand and slammed them together with bone-shattering force. Alive they might still be, but broken. Hang on, vamps aren't alive, are they? Anyway, Cecile had reduced them from the equation.

'Where is he? You can tell me now, or later, but you *will* tell me.' She had one of them by the shirtfront, her face a scant half-inch from his. The other one was lying on the floor, her fingers the only things that could move. Surprisingly for Cecile, there was little blood. Maybe she was saving it for later. One look at her face, and the most hardened hard man would have given up on the instant. It promised an eternity of pain, and she was looking forward to giving that pain. Come on, punk, make my decade. Make my *century*. Let me do this to you. Give me the excuse. No, sod it, I'll do it anyway.

'Let me. He may not want to tell you, but he can't avoid telling me.'

'As you wish.' She let him fall, a boneless heap on the floor and wandered off, disinterested now in her games.

Zoe stood over the two.

'Not so much fun now, is it? Now, you can tell me, and I'll take her away. If you make me take it from you, and I can, I'll just go away and she'll still be here. What's it to be? Quickly now, I don't have all night.'

'We will heal, *witch*. And then we will come after you.' That was rude. She must be hurting to forget her manners like that.

'No you won't. By the time we're finished, there won't be as much as a smear left for you to resurrect from. I will delete you. I will destroy you utterly. That I will do, now or later. You can spend the rest of your immortal life, short as it will be, in such agony that only a Hegarsen can deliver to you. Your choice, Take it or leave it. Whichever way, I don't care. Last chance, I'm running out of patience here.'

'Go to hell, witch.' OOooo. Perverse, even.

'Not on your nellie. I don't do requests.' Zoe raised her hands.

Between them a white light grew. 'Vassago, master of truth and delusion, come to me, here, now, as I command. Do my will. Vassago, Vassago, Vassago, appear to me, speaking secrets of truth and understanding.'

The light grew in intensity, and in it there appeared a face. No matter which way you looked at it, it was looking right back at you.

'What is it you wish of me? I tire of these unseemly interruptions.' A voice, cold and ancient, echoed in the space and whispered back. It was enough to make the fine hairs on your body stand to attention.

'Look at these two before me. Tell me what I need to know of my eldest sister, where she is, and who is with her, their intent towards her.'

'You are wise, youngling. What I know of these matters will be of more use to you than what these pathetic remnants have to offer.'

'I want them to know that they have betrayed their Hegarsa. And there is nothing they can do about it whatsoever.'

'Your venom does you credit. You play the game well. But do you play it well enough?'

'Reveal to the Intelligencer what she needs to know.'

'Very well. The ones you want are above. The stairway to them is behind the screen. There you will find twelve others. One is ancient, and you must beware him. He has great pride, and has survived through craft and guile. Him you must defeat first if you are to succeed. The Mysta is next. You must not confront him. Another must deal with that entity. The others are not important.'

'And is that all? Reveal it in it's entirety, I command you.'

'Naturally,' the being sighed as if wronged. Of course he had more to tell. He always did. *'Ten others there are who do not live as others live in this world of yours. Should you block them from their power, they will give way to you, as they will to all who demonstrate a more profound force. Look to the head: all power comes from the head. Remove the head, and they will succumb to your force.'*

'Give me more.'

'If you name him Ogan, he will succumb. Name him other, and

he will prevail.'

At this, Cecile whirled round. Zoe caught the motion.

'Cecile, be still.' By the rage in her face, Zoe would pay dearly for that insult later. There were more immediate things to be dealt with right now. 'Master of truth, I thank you. Be there any further words from you to me?'

'All endings are the birth of beginnings, youngling. Your feet are set on a path that will lead you far, and your journey has but begun. There is wisdom in this: those who gather dust will be rewarded.'

Bloody mystic twaddle. But the face in the light still looked at her. A strange thought entered her head, and it wasn't hers. **'How fast can you run?'** The face started to melt. Vassago had said all he was going to say, and it was up to her now.

She started to whisper. The light between her hands snaked out and coiled around the two recumbent vamps until they were surrounded. Above them reared the head of a gigantic snake, fangs dripping with venom. One drop fell on an undead hand, and the vamp screamed. Zoe gestured, and the scream died to a gurgle.

'.... that you can neither move, nor see, nor hear, nor make utterance unless I myself will it.' Zoe regarded the two with an evil eye. 'So you'd better pray to whatever ayen it is that vamps pray to, that I don't get myself good and dead up there, or you'll be stuck like that forever.' She stepped back from the glowing pile.

'What have you done?' Cecile regarded the scene with a mixture of interest and apprehension.

'Tied them up in my dream. I imagined what I wanted to do to them, and made it real. They saw it because I saw it, and then it *was* real. For them.'

Cecile nodded with approval, her earlier pique evaporating in the face of Zoe's feat. She had regarded Theo's obsession with the fratris with some exasperation: she hadn't seen the need to propitiate any mortals, no matter what their talents. Now she was beginning to understand what sort of duress Theo was under. She could feel the fear, the very real torment of the stricken metae in the toils of a farer, and a sixteen year old one at that.

'What was that back there? When I told you to shut up? Sorry, by the way. Forgot you wouldn't know not to interrupt a weaving.'

'I will remember that. I did not know that such.... power existed. I am impressed.'

'We don't have the excuse to be so dramatic very often. Other kids get Janet and John, or See Spot Run when they're learning to read. I got cys books. Never mind Where The Wild Things Are: I read *What* The Wild Things Are. Lily sang me to sleep with glims. Fee and Sophie were always chyming or weaving something or another. I got very jealous. Sulking was no good, so I got good instead. You won't *believe* what I've been reading these past ten years.'

'I heard what your sprite said. It is not possible, Zoe. *That* one is dead.'

Zoe took the hint not to repeat the name. 'Not dead enough, to my mind. Let's go correct that.'

Cecile seized her arm in a crushing grip. There would be bruises later. She could feel the waves of.... fear? roiling off Cecile. 'You misunderstand me, Zoe. *I saw him destroyed.* He was judged too dangerous to exist. *She* condemned him. I saw it done. We all did. The Ancient instructed us not to pass his history on, so he would be dead indeed. And we have obeyed. Few know that name now, and fewer still the history behind it.'

'He's here now.'

'He cannot be. He cannot!'

'So he must be from the time of...... I won't say the name. But I saw it all, when Theo....'

'Shared with you.'

'The ophosis, yes. Well, he's back now, and we've just got to deal with it.'

'But how?'

'I've got an idea. But this time, you can be the bait.'

Chapter Thirty-six

Upstairs, the scene was being set. Vassily was ordering his stolen blyd around. Fee watched as they strung hangings between pillars, creating the illusion of a grand hall. The subjects of those hangings were, to put it mildly, exotic. Someone must have been either deranged or on some serious acid to have created those. Heraldic beasts out of a psychotic nightmare pranced amid metae sporting and playing with the peasantry. You could easily tell which were the metae: they had fangs that would make a sabre-toothed tiger think twice. Her mind briefly skated back to some of the more salacious wall paintings from Pompeii - the ones associated with the houses of pleasure. That sort of exaggeration. Red was the dominant colour. The peasants weren't having much fun, but then peasants never do. She was betting that she was pegged for a part as a peasant.

Someone somewhere had lit a censer. Clouds of scented smoke started to fill the air. It was the smell of overripe fruit and overblown flowers: too sweet, with a touch of rot. More than a touch. It would climb in through your nostrils and clog your throat, then go hunting for the neurons in your brain. What it would do to your head was anyone's guess. Nothing pleasant was odds-on. Flaming torches had been set on the pillars, and the smoke coiled in low tendrils. A blood-red cloth had been thrown over the stone table. Of course: what else?

Every bloody vamp in the room wandered over to pay their respects to the guest of honour. Vassily had already copped a feel of her flesh, and now the hangers-on were getting theirs. Cold hands touched her face, lips and teeth snaffled at her neck, but none of them dared to break the skin. At least two had a good lick, though. One slimy sod slid his hand up her leg, lifting the too-long lace skirt while his girl (or was it ghoul?) friend kissed her on the lips. They were laughing at their own joke. So funny to play with the captive human and do things to her while she was supposedly unconscious. Ha ha. Wraiths don't have feelings like that. They could touch her flesh, but they weren't touching *her*. It might get personal later. She was hoping it would. She had some serious scores to settle.

The main event hadn't started. It couldn't start without the star performer, and he was not here yet. Or was he behind that hanging, watching the fun? She thought not. He was not the fun type. When he emerged, she could expect things to get more humourless, and possibly more sanguine. Blood would flow. Of course, it would be hers.

Then, he was there. Standing in front of the table. Like the table in the hounfort in London, this was now covered with bottles. Gin, rum, whisky. Red wine. Or was it? Dead flowers, wreaths collected from the local graveyard most likely, edged for space between idols of the more salacious kind. At least one portrayed a meta crouching low over a recumbent, dishabille human who was very definitely female. One was a prancing gwhylli sporting a massive erection highlighted in garish pink, as if it needed anything further to draw attention to it. The whole thing was a celebration of execrable taste, or a sense of humour bent too far out of true to be in any way amusing. What were those vamps drinking? They were giggling a lot, all except Vassily who stood impassive, his arms folded over his chest.

'Get on with it.'

Simon snarled at this breach of cysan etiquette. He turned on his heel, the burgundy velvet robes swirling around his calves, light catching the gold embroidery at neck and wrist. He stood facing the table for a few heartbeats, mastering his pique at being ordered about in front of the younger metae. He probably didn't approve of the giggling either. Vassily was darting dark looks at his metae as a wave of understanding washed over him. He had not realized that Simon would stoop to drugging his blyd. Something leapt in Fee's mind. Perhaps she had an ally there. He is beginning to think he's been used. And if Theo's anything to go by, he'll be annoyed. No, not annoyed. I don't think there's a word for what a Hegarsa feels when someone's put one over on him. He'll be wary of Simon now. He'll distrust him. How essential is he to tonight's shenanigans?

Simon snatched up the curved knife and began making passes

in the air over the table, muttering. More smoke billowed from the censer, far too much smoke. If breathing was optional, a body might survive in that level of atmospheric pollution. Simon seemed unaffected by the gouts of smoke that were massing round his body. Had Fee been standing there, she would have been coughing her lungs up by now and trying to see out of streaming eyes. Once she had her flesh back, it would be hard to see. Sod that, breathing might well pose a bigger problem. She fixed the important details of the room in her mind. If she had to run through it blind, then she could. Meten-sight only went so far. Wraith vision was much better, but it was hard to hold wraith vision when you're fleeing for your life from a mob of enraged undead. She could feel the tickle of wythen starting. She tried to snag the wyth, but it slipped through her fingers like grease. It had an alien quality. Bite into an icecream and there are some flavours you expect. Vanilla, strawberry, chocolate. But if it tastes like fish or cheese, you won't see it as icecream. The wyth was like that. Fishy icecream. Then, she snagged a thread she recognized. And another. They seemed to recognize her, too, and floated round her, trying to make contact, but sliding off. It must be the weave. She concentrated: she needed this weave to be gone now. Quietly. She slipped further away from her body, turned and looked at it, hard. Wraith vision saw dark, greasy strands winding round her head, much like a crown, writhing and intertwining. There was one place that seemed.... different. It didn't twine like the rest. Carefully, she started to pull it apart, holding it so it wouldn't snap back and alert anyone to the fact that the bound and helpless victim was not so helpless after all. They were all intent on Simon and his mutterings, and he was totally involved in what he was doing. Still, no time to be careless. The wisp parted, leaving the ragged end dangling in her hand. She wiped it off on the face of a passing vamp, and it stuck. Idly, she wiped her cheek, but the strand stayed where it was. The crown started to fade.

The room was full of wraiths. Each one was standing in his or her own space, not seeing anything else. Some were mere patches, nothing more than stalagmites, uneven, lumpy pillars. Others were more, or less, recognizable as human. The less human ones looked indistinct, melted, wax dummies who had been drenched in boiling water. If these were human wraiths, *Fratten* wraiths even, whatever had happened to them to deprive them of their humanity? Then she saw. Their substance was being leeched from them by the red-robed Simon. Wisps of what they were were being pulled out by the roots. To feed him, feed his wyth. From the tortured expressions on the wraith's faces, it was hurting. Fee bit down on her rising anger. The bugger was trying to feed off her as well! Faint tendrils started to emerge from her fingertips and snake towards the red back. Bugger that! She pulled back on the errant strands, binding them to her, calling them back. You're me, not him. It was akin to how your legs feel after a long arduous run, and you making them run further. Pushing up that last rep in the gym. Doing the final ab crunch. Only all over, and all at once. There was no place that didn't hurt. Doggedly, she closed her mind, folding it on itself. Hanging on to the last rung of the ladder with Titan cavern below your feet and no safety rope, a quarter of a mile of darkness below, and under that, rocks. Your broken corpse will lie there forever forgotten, the icy water running over it until you turn into stone. No way.

When the pull stopped, Fee didn't feel it. She was too tightly clenched in. Virgin thighs braced against prying male fingers. Figuratively speaking. She'd had Theo to practise on. He'd always congratulated her on her ability to block him out. She'd suspected that he hadn't really been trying: but then, he'd been trying to get in, not leech her out.

Simon was facing his audience now. The girl vamp was sweeping her face with her hand, again and again, and pushing her fingers through her hair, trying to dislodge something she vaguely felt and didn't like much, but the weave stuck fast. He gestured grandly towards Fee's body, still hanging in its ropes over by the pillar, and a path opened up between them. He marched over to her. Did he expect her to be awake and aware? Or would he need to release the weave before she could be conscious? Would he know she had fiddled with his bindings?

He smacked her face. The way her head rocked, it had been a hard slap. A couple of the vamps giggled again, and were rewarded with a hard stare from Vassily.

'Wake up, Ffion. It does not do the guest of honour to fall asleep during her party.'

He smacked her again. Enough, already. She sank into her body. The rolling darkness had gone. She blinked her eyes open. Even this far away from the smoking censer, her eyes stung. Simon was bending over, looking up into her face from inches away. Her cheeks burned: the urge to spit in his face was very strong.

'Ah, Sleeping Beauty awakes. Very good. Let me instruct you in your part in this drama. I am sure you will appreciate the breadth of the work that has gone into creating my opus. I would like for you to understand me, my dear.' He turned to Vassily. 'I think she is too weak to stand up. It would be a pity if she could not fully appreciate the trouble I have been to, to create this actuality. Especially as she is it's crowning glory.'

Hands, cold hands, felt for her wrists. She did not struggle: what was the point? Soon, her hands were fastened together and hoisted over her head. Again. Pulling her upright, but no more. She could at least take her weight on her feet. She rested one cheek against her arm, and watched through her lashes.

'Tired, my dear? Too tired to take an interest in your own death? So sad. Have we not been kind to you? Have we hurt you? No, we have not. The hurt came from your own kind. I would have saved you that. You have my apologies for my oversight. But I said that already, didn't I? Hhhmm.'

'This is not one of your extravaganzas, Simon.'

'Is it not? I rather thought it was my best illusion ever. The Death of a Witch. After all, she will not die, will she? Not as such.'

Said with such frigid venom that it made Fee's blood run cold. Colder. Now she knew how a meta, no more than an animated corpse, could be fratten. He was using the wraiths. Death interrupted. Killing the body but trapping the wraith between life and death, using the pseudo-living essence to power his wyth. Raping the dead for their wyth. I will see you dead for this if you weren't dead already. There is no punishment to fit this obscenity, not yet. But there will be.

'The dead are here. The unliving are here. The farer is here. And the world turns on. Soon, the time appointed will come. The tasks are completed, or they will be when her blood flows. One part for my Master, one part for me, and one for you, Vassily. Sadly, there will be none left for my dearest Ffion. It is time for you to know the truth, my dear. Unpalatable, but the truth nonetheless. You are interested in the truth, are you not? It would be churlish of me not to satisfy your curiosity before you leave us. To know why you, and your relatives, have been my concern, my close concern, for so long. Hhmm?' He turned away, walking to and fro between her and the red-draped table with its assortment of bad taste icons. 'Years ago, when I lived in the sun, there was a girl. Oh, she was the vision of beauty with her pale hair and swimming eyes. And so young. So... pretty. Porcelain skin, amber hair, teasing fingers. But there you are,' his voice hardened, 'things did not go as I had planned. I believe she would have come to love me, given time. But that time was not mine to give. Rocks are hard and unforgiving things, but we are all immortal, are we not, when we are young? When I saw her again, I was... changed. Inside, I was still the same, but she rejected me. Again and again, I pleaded my cause. But then her mother took a hand. My metarger forbade me to tryst with the girl, to see her again. My pale beauty, gone from me.......'

His voice trailed into silence, musing on what he had lost. Or never had in the first place.

'I disobeyed my metarger. I took the girl anyway. Oh no, not as a changeling takes a girl, but as a man takes a woman. I drew veils over her eyes. I followed her when she left with her mortal swain. I haunted her nights, but she never saw me. Never realized, as her belly started to swell, that the seed growing inside her body was mine. I was a young changeling then, and still able to...... do as men do. When she realized that her lover was not, could not be, the baby's father, she returned home, and I thought, to me. But she did not. She would have none of me. Her name was Jane. My Jana, my Juno, my Queen of the skies.' He turned to look directly at Ffion. 'Your grandmother.'

If he expected Ffion to react to this, he was badly mistaken. So her grandfather was meta? So what? Some girls have to live with the fact that one of their parents was a murderer. Both, even. However you got born, it was up to you to make the best of the life you had been given. Lily had inherited closer blood ties with Simon, but had never shown any inclination to bite you on the neck. Except their father, of course, and he bit back. Neither had Ffion, and she wasn't about to start now. Not unless she could develop the gape and teeth of a leopard seal: then she might attempt to rip out a throat or two. Right here, right now. Oh, he's off again.

'She was the first, the very first, of my pash. But I killed her carelessly and without profit.' Cold bastard. 'Then I discovered Vassily. I was travelling then, making contacts, searching for a purpose to while away the empty years, mourning the death of my wyth, so newly in my hands and so callously ripped away from me. I found him and revived him. He was on a quest also, and very soon it became apparent that our separate quests ran aligned. He had a purpose, and I saw that should I choose to assist him, I could regain my lost abilities. I instructed him in what I would require, and he found those things for me. No-one suspected. With the information supplied by Vassily, I made my pact with the dark Ayen. Soon I was able to make my first proper offering. It was not easy, that first sacrifice, but I accomplished it. I cannot tell you how wondrous it felt to have the wyth flowing in my body again after so long. The sacrifices became easier. I was guided, Ffion, guided. It was my destiny. With each kill I became stronger, more able to kill again, until I became able to kill at a distance. I could be miles away, but my chosen victim would succumb. But that was nothing to being on the spot, feeling the death. I wanted to watch them die, relish the pain that my actions caused. Seeing the horror of the wraiths when I imprisoned them, cut them off from the life force that had been their bedrock. Feeling their anguish when I fed. It was glorious, glorious!'

And you call yourself a frata. Shame, shame and triple shame on you.

'But now my revenge is almost complete. When you die, I will eat you. Thus, I can free my ayat. Then I shall seek out the one who caused me all this anguish, and I shall visit my revenge on her.'

Good luck with Rina. She may look like a frail old lady, but she's as tough as old boots. And there's Zoe to consider, and Cecile. She's not going to stand still for this one. You've ended Theo's immortal existence, and she's going to be royally pissed about that. And me? I'm not going to go quietly. All the others had no idea what was going on. I do. They had few defences against you. I have prepared. You have got me where I want you. In my eye and under my hand. You think you've got me subdued. You have no idea what I am capable of……

Apparently Simon had finished with his monologue. Perhaps her lack of response had disappointed him. Ffion hoped so. She was getting mightily irked by being the victim in a bondage spree. He stalked back to his ayet. Picking up the curved knife, he wheeled round to face his audience, the red, red robes swirling about his ankles.

'Children of darkness, the hour has come! Prepare to welcome the mighty lord and receive his gifts! You are the chosen of the chosen. Abase yourselves before the might of the First, the Ancient, the great lord whose vast intellect conquered Death itself! Prepare to receive the eternal gifts and release your powers into this world, which shall be yours now and forever! From this time forward, you will rule this world and all that is within it. Night shall reclaim her proper place in the order of things, and Day shall be subservient to her power. Children of night, the hour is come!'

'It is come! It is come!' They had stopped giggling now, and were kneeling, actually kneeling. All except Vassily, who was still standing, arms akimbo, looking ominously on the gathering. Pale faces raised, they were wrapt by the aura of wyth exuded by Simon. He was lapping it up. He knew how to give the marks what they wanted. He was famous for it.

Ffion could feel the wyth in the room moving. It came to her that she was not the first to be held here, tied and apparently helpless to await whatever fate the metae were about to unleash on her. These buggers had done this before. It was a parody of Theo's Ophosis. She had heard snippets: no living things were privy to Theo's rituals. He would call his blyd to him. He would embrace them, and invite them to feed on him. All of them. At once. As many as could find a vein, he would feed them all. And then, they would offer the blood back. The danger in that was a celebrant refusing to return the gift: Theo, clever boy, had a backup. Cecile would always share. No, she would share back forcibly. She had enjoyed the first experience so much she was avidly seeking more. Anytime. Once Theo had shared with the blyd, and they had shared back with him, they would fall on each other. It was supposed to be a blindingly erotic, immensely satisfying experience. So would this be, for the metae at least. They would drain her, down to the last drop and share it between them again and again, but there would be no offering back for her. She would just die here and become one of Simon's battery hens. No release for her ayat into the streams of Eternity. Not even an undead future to look forward to. She would wither and fade into a pillar of stone, her wyth exhausted and her lights put out. For ever.

The wyth started to coalesce beside Simon. He gestured to Vassily. Join me. Your place is here, not grovelling with the lesser immortals. Vassily glided over and stood on Simon's right. I wonder if he knows Simon has assigned him the more dominant place? Simon would assume that the mysten was less dominant than the mysta. He wouldn't accept second place himself. Actually, the two are complimentary: queens usually sit to the left of their kings. It has to do with the sword hand. You don't want to accidentally behead your queen when you unsheathe your sword. Probably. You'd want her to know that it was personal, and not an oversight. There was a distinct gap between the two vamps. Whatever Simon was summoning, it was going to appear between the two of them, isolating them from each other. Good. That means I won't have to deal with the both of them at once.

Shadows and the pervasive smoke from the incense began to coagulate. A form started to emerge from the murk, separating itself, creating itself. It should have been tall and commanding, not dwarfed by the figures beside it, but it was. It was barely five feet tall. The head and shoulders appeared first. The body was indistinct. Vassily was looking at it with a degree of puzzlement: You are so small! The figure wavered, and shimmered, and began to grow. In response to the disparaging thought, perhaps. Maybe three thousand years ago, five feet was an impressive height. Now it was ridiculous. The cloudy figure increased in height until it was towering over the two who flanked it. Features began to emerge. Dark eyes sparked in the face over an impressive beaked nose. Below that, fleshy lips protruded from a bushy dark beard. Thick lips. Moist lips. Nasty lips. Ever seen a picture of Rasputin? Like that.

Long dark hair fell over the shoulders. The body was swathed in a loose cloak. It might have been grey. On one shoulder a brooch gleamed gold and red: a massive red stone (a ruby? O gosh, that alone must be worth tens of thousands, it's huge!) sat in a gold circle at least six inches across. Zoe would have recognized him.

Chapter Thirty-seven

She did. Discretion being the better part of valour, Zoe had persuaded Cecile that a more covert operation than slamming through the doors and demanding the surrender of all within was in order. She needed, she said, to assess the risks before committing her troops to action. Since she was the totality of those troops, Cecile had agreed. It wasn't that she was reluctant to confront Vassily without Theo, oh no. It was Theo's right and privilege to do that, and she would not usurp his rights in the matter. Not unless Fee was in clear and present danger: Theo would let her have that excuse, she felt. So they were currently sitting on a mucky and rat-haunted internal roof, peering through a grimy window at the scene below. If Zoe had expected Cecile to demur at crawling through the rat shit, she was disappointed. She had slept in worse, Cecile told her, and mourned the fact that she had chosen to wear a pale dress. But this garment did not come in camouflage drab, and she, Cecile, was not to be caught dead in 'slacks' 'So unladylike.'

Zoe had listened in tight-lipped silence until the revelation that Simon was the father of Jane's child.

'Sod me! It all fits now!' she muttered under her breath.

'So, you are part meten, then? I had heard such beings existed, but I had never thought to encounter one.'

Cecile had been so still by Zoe's side, as still as ever a mete can be whose heart does not beat and whose breath does not flow, and she so intent on listening to the scene below that Cecile's soft words made her start. She swore her knees left the floor, and she very nearly smacked her head on the low canting roof above. She swore.

'Hush.'

'They won't hear me. They're too interested in what they're doing. And those three lumps of meat downstairs were supposed to take care of us. Well, me at least.'

'One small witch is no match for three metae.'

'Not.'

'Not.' Cecile grinned a tight, feral smile. 'I would venture that they have revised their opinion.'

'A sharp learning curve, all right.'

'What is that?' Cecile asked, pointing at the thing taking shape between Vassily and Simon.

'Not *what*, who. It's *Him*. The father of your people.' Zoe had passed on Lily's warning about naming. Vassago didn't count: metae, by and large, don't hear gwhyllen. Cecile just nodded.

'I have never seen him in the flesh, so to speak. But my Hegarsa shared the memory with me just before we parted, I needed to know him, he said. It is one memory I wish I did not have: he is a monster. But then, so is the one who stands at his right hand.'

'And on his left, don't forget.'

'Oh, no. As the Ancient decreed immolation on the one, so would she decree the same to the other. I would not waste my tears of blood on either of them, as I would for my Hegarsa.'

'You love him, then?'

'Love is an alien concept to a meta.'

Zoe smiled a tiny, knowing smile. Whatever she might say, Cecile loved Theo.

'Stop smirking.' Cecile returned her full attention to the scene below. 'We must stop this before it goes too far.'

'It hasn't gone far enough yet for us to stop it. You can't destroy smoke and mirrors. When the illusion becomes real, it becomes subject to the laws of the Midess. Once it does that, and if I know my boy, and I think I do, he won't stop until it does. Then we can act. Not before. Ripeness is all.'

'You and your nexus. I grow weary of this waiting.'

'Some attitude for a woman who's been on the planet for several hundred years.'

Cecile subsided into an irritated silence. Below, the grisly drama unfolded.

Chapter Thirty-eight

Ffion watched the shade fuse into something resembling a human form. Whatever intelligence was behind it had no sense of proportion. The arms were too short, and the legs too long and spindly. A short man standing on a box wearing a long cloak, was the best simile she could come up with. The faint ridicule of the disproportioned figure paled to insignificance beside the menacing air which surrounded it. This had been a man to fear, even before he became meta. Then he became a complete abomination. She could see he was a meten. He was grinning, displaying his fangs. From Theo, she knew that his was a crude display of aggression. A meten pissing contest. No-one took him on. Cowed by reputation, obviously. Or was she being wilfully dense? This short-arse had something the rest wanted, and wanted badly. They would not risk pissing him off if it meant they would miss out on their objective. World domination would be a good guess, given what Simon had been saying before. Oh joy. Not for the first time, Fee wished she had a flame thrower stashed up her pants. Stop thinking with your muscles, girl. Start thinking with your brain. It's convoluted and sneaky and as greasy as a ferret up a pole, which is exactly what you need right now.

'Prepare the sacrifice.'

That would be me, then. My part begins. And I'm going to ad-lib. The lesser metae gathered about her, stroking her body with cold fingers, smiling lasciviously at her. Tongues wet lips and glided over fangs. A couple were even drooling. They started to undo the tiny pearl buttons that held the sleeves close to her arms. One by one, the buttons opened the sleeves until her arms were bare and the sleeves hanging loose by her sides. Cold fingers stroked her arms, fangs scratched her skin. Teasing, the buggers were teasing her. Enough, already.

'You are making a mistake, Simon.'

He put his head on one sided and viewed her quizzically through her beauty chorus.

'It speaks, at last. What has it got to say? What portentous excuse will the farer give, to try to save her life, her ayat, her very existence?'

'You said I was the one hundred and sixty ninth sacrifice. But you're out by one.'

Vassily shot a glare first at her and then at Simon.

'How so?'

'Luke isn't dead.'

'Irrelevant. He lives only by courtesy of your technology. I know that death very well. And I have his wraith. I have consumed it. My tally is complete. The presence here of my Master confirms it.'

The ghoul in the middle grinned, showing the fangs to good effect. The rank and file shied away.

'You name him Master. Do you think for one second that he will share power with you? Either of you?'

Vassily hesitated, uncertain. He glanced quickly at the shade by his side, then away. Doubts, he was having doubts. Simon wanted to rule and control the fratris and their wythen. Vassily wanted the metae for himself. He would rule the undead and leave the living to Simon. Now it was beginning to dawn on him that there was a fly in his ointment. And it was hovering at his elbow. The vibe coming from the shade said plainly You are *all* food. I will have it all. You will serve me. What is not food will be eliminated. Exterminated. Vassily might never have heard about Daleks or Cybermen, but he was standing right next to their first cousin. Their *Granddaddy*. And the present representative of Doctor Who was currently being held captive, helpless. Perils of Pauline helpless. For what *that* was worth. He'd probably never heard of Doctor Who either. Big mistake, to ignore human mythology.

Simon was more sure of his reward. That or so far gone in insanity that he plain straight didn't care. Down the throat of the black hole, falling forever. And cackling, probably. Though that might be optional in his case. Fee turned all her attention to Vassily.

'Having second thoughts, are we?'

He looked back at her, puzzled.

'I am mete too, if what Simon said is correct.'

He looked back at Simon, who nodded. They locked stares. Short-arse had eyes only for Fee: or, rather, the pulse that beat at her throat. Vassily looked away first, subdued.

'Let us complete the communion. Then, we can gain our reward.'

'Or at least, *you* will, Simon.' There was no mistaking the bite in Fee's tone. She was excluding Vassily from the picnic.

Impatient, the shade in the centre started to float towards Fee. Simon caught up in two steps. Vassily almost tripped when he started to follow. A threatening, murderous fury built in his face. The seeds of dissention had been well and truly sown. The trinity of power was, if not broken, severely damaged.

Still they came forward. Simon grinned in her face. One hand seized her hair, balling into a fist. He yanked her head sideways. The tendons on her neck stood out. He placed the flat of the blade against her cheek.

'What is it like to lose, witch?' he spat. The blade twitched and went for the crook of her elbow. The point dug into the tender flesh, and Fee winced. A bright drop of blood flowed down the blade of the knife. Slowly he drew the blade up, and the blood flowed faster. He turned his attention to the other arm, and repeated the process. Gore was freely running down her arms now, soaking into the lacy dress. From somewhere, Vassily produced three bowls. Golden bowls. He held one against her arm, and the blood started to collect in the bowl. Hungry eyes watched the red flood filling the bowls. Simon had butchered her arms, opening the veins down their length, and it stung. The evoked shade watched avidly as the bowls filled, one in Simon's hands and one in each of Vassily's.

Leaving her to bleed out under the covetous gaze of the lesser vamps, Simon, Vassily and the spook each took one bowl. They stood facing each other, one impatient, one excited and one suspicious.

'Let them feed. But do not kill her, yet.'

Vassily nodded at the urgent throng. They washed over her, a wave of cold flesh and seizing fingers, avid and ready for the blood which still flowed unchecked down her arms. She was becoming light-headed from blood loss, holding on to a thread of consciousness by willpower alone. She could hear the sounds of hasty, sucking mouths. She caught a glimpse, through the dead flesh that crowded round her impatient for their turn, of the spectre. A trickle of blood was running down his face as he slurped noisily at the bowl. Was his hand ruddier? More solid? He lowered the bowl, smacking his lips with relish. Yes. He looked more…. Human? Physical? Yes, more physical. His cheeks, once pale and cadaverous, had filled out and become more flushed. Flushed with her good, red blood. Ichor flowed in those dead veins now. There was an ancient cast to his countenance, and a ravenous look in his eyes. He wanted more of the blood. He waded into the metae clinging on Fee, and threw them bodily away. He stood in front of her, and she saw the rage in his face when he realized that, at a bare five foot, he was unable to reach the wounds on her arms. Being solid has its disadvantages when you are a serious shortarse. He could change his phantom's appearance, but he could do bugger all about a pair of physical legs.

One mete barked out a laugh. It was the last sound she would ever utter. He whirled on her and had his fangs in her neck before she could blink. He fed at her throat, chewing and swallowing flesh and blood with equal relish. A new emotion flashed over meten faces. *They were afraid.* For the first time in their undead existence, they felt fear. Serve them right too, Fee thought woozily. Oops. It was horrible. Ten times worse than listening to Snag snarf down that crunchy rat. He rose from his meal, but the frenzied look on his face spoke amply. He was not sated by his feast. More, More! His body language was shouting. Vassily moved: to restrain him? Pick him up and sicc him on Fee's arms, rather than his blyd? Either would be a lethal error. Simon placed a hand on his arm, restraining him. If he realized that his evoked Master was out of control, he was oblivious. Maybe he had intended this all along. Vassily snarled at him in fury as the ancient meta leapt on the back of another victim. They were panicking, now, trying to get away: but the door was locked. Simon reached into his robe, and from the pocket of his waistcoat, he drew a key, and waved it in Vassily's face. His expression was pure evil. The dawn of realization turned Vassily's face puce. Roaring, he launched himself at Simon. He was older, stronger, faster. From ally to enemy in one fell swoop. He buried his fangs in Simon's throat, to rip, to tear, to kill. But Simon had another ally, one who needed him still. A spook, no matter how fleshy, is bound to the spaca of his evocation unless the cyscan releases him, or he himself kills the cyscan. If Vassily killed Simon, the shade would be forever bound to the spaca with no possible escape. He might kill Simon later, but he could not permit him to be killed by another. With astonishing speed and strength, he leapt from his current victim onto Vassily's back and wrenched his head away from Simon. Unfortunately for Vassily's prey, part of his throat came away too. Simon reeled back, blood gouting from his ravaged throat, gasping. One hand tried to stem the flow as he reeled backwards. Vassily roared his rage at being denied his revenge, and threw his assailant off his back. They squared up, raging at each other, fangs bared. Whatever was going to happen now, it would be terrible.

Then, another Presence was in the room. It seized a choking hold on the space, the wyth. Gya boiled in the air. Anarchy poured over the place, unchecked. Up was down. Left was right. Back was forwards. The air thickened. Menace lurked in every corner, every shadow, every speck of light. Something howled, hissed, cawed, croaked. A weighted cloak of riffling fear fell. The fear of the blank darkness, not of night, but of non-existence. The door of Chaos opened, and nightmares flooded out. Ball-lightning swept the room. As a chymer, it was…… stupendous.

From above came a crash, and two figures fell into the maelstrom, accompanied by shards of broken glass and shattered window frame. One dark and one light. From the dark figure came balls and streaks of fire: and a voice roared. '**Ogan!**' The roar was not human. **'Bow before me, Ogan, let me see the back of thy neck!'** it continued, **'for I am thy doom, thy true death, and I will see thee destroyed forever!'**

Something tickled the back of Fee's mind. Those words had a slight familiarity about them.

Vassily swung round, seeking the source of the bellowing. But he was looking for a giant figure, not the small, slim slip of a girl who appeared before him, eyes blazing. She threw back her cloak, and out of the folds blasted a welter of fat, cracking sparks. There was a moment of shock as the fat sparks hit Vassily, then he was wreathed in a thrashing net of electricity which ate over his clothes, his skin, his hair, sizzling and burning: blue, lurid and flameless, dissolving his substance down to the bone within. He shrieked inhumanly in shock and horror as the electric charge earthed itself in him, and leapt from him to the nearest meta in the room. She burst into flame and died, wailing. The pale avenger was not being left out. Wet meaty rendings surrounded her. Using her bare hands, she was ripping the vamps apart with every sign of a visceral enjoyment. She was intent on getting her fair share in before the electricity claimed too many victims to make her contribution not worth the effort of coming along for the ride. She could have made a fortune selling the dress as a Jackson Pollack painting, provided you liked red on greyish-white. She paused for a moment in the mayhem to lick blood off her hand: a curious, kittenish gesture. Cute, if you didn't count the bloody corpses littering the floor around her.

One of the metae took advantage of the apparent distraction and ran at her, howling, brandishing a torch. Dervish like, she whirled on him with lazy grace and threw him clear across the room. The impact rocked the wall, and he slid down to the floor, smearing blood and brains behind him. He might have survived, but the torch fell from a broken and bloody hand into his lap. He screamed like a girl, wavering, as the flames fed up his body and turned his face to a melted mess.

One vamp, lucky enough to have evaded both the deaths-du-jour on offer, took a step forward. Cecile cocked her head to one side and smiled at him coquettishly. One hand lifted, and she wagged an admonishing, bloody finger. He sank back down onto the floor in the hope that she might let the gaffe slide. Some hope. But she had more immediate concerns.

Fee's head was swimming. She kept a death-grip on the one wisp of consciousness left. Through the haze a neuron fired off and roused another. Connection. The words that puzzled her were from a Star Trek book. It was enough to anchor her. In a dream, she saw Cecile drift through the mayhem, a nightmare woman with strings of blood splashed over her skirts. As she watched, Cecile lifted one wrist to her mouth and bit down. She reached up and ran her tongue over Fee's arms: first one, then the other. She raised her wrist to Fee's mouth.

'Drink, Ffion.' The words echoed hollowly. Fee was on the verge of passing out through exsanguination. Blood soaked her dress to the hem. In the fashion stakes, she was in no better case than Cecile. Unless they were going to a corpse party. Then they might make the grade.

'Thanks all the same, but I'd rather have a transfusion.' She slurred the words and grinned inanely.

'They would not reach you in time. I have fed well. Drink, Ffion. If I allow you to succumb after all this, Theo would truly kill me for it. And you would become as I am now. Do you wish to become metae? If not, drink.'

Silly. Ffion was seeing the scene in Terminator Two, when Arnie reaches a hand down to the female lead and says in that gravelly foreign voice, 'Come with me if you wish to live.' Only it wasn't a shotgun her rescuer was holding, it was a bleeding wrist. Cecile pushed her arm against Fee's mouth, and she tasted the metallic note of blood. Her tongue touched her lips, then she was lapping the blood, sucking the wound, as Cecile wrapped her other arm around Fee's waist and held her close. She ventured a glance upward. Cecile's eyes were closed in rapture, her face blank. Slowly, her mouth opened, revealing her fangs, and her face began to fall towards Fee's neck. Before she could complete the move, someone yanked her back.

'Enough of the vampire shit. Both of you.'

Zoe was casting wary eyes round the room. One meta was watching suspiciously. Another was sitting in a pool of blood - someone else's by the look of him - knees drawn up and face resting on them. Utterly dejected. Beaten. Not so the other.

Slowly, Cecile regained control of herself. She shot a glare at the watching vamp. He looked away quickly, not wanting to excite her attention. She continued to glare.

'Well? Where is he?'

'Who?'

Instantly she was standing over him, pulling him upright to her face. Less than an inch separated their noses. He would need exceedingly good vision to see her expression. He probably didn't want to. He sagged in her grip. The defiance was all front. He was beaten and he knew it. He gestured towards the hangings behind the table.

Cecile loosed her hold and he fell to the floor. What else could he do? One move she didn't like and he was dogmeat. Cecile swept past the table, but before she could reach the hanging curtain, a snarl stopped her. Simon might have vacated the premises, but his Master was trapped in the circle.

'Amagus!'

Even a Hegarsen can be surprised. That millisecond of immobility was all he needed. The ancient bloodsucker flew through the air, mouth gaping wide, and went for her neck. It would have worked had he been bigger and more solid, more meaty. She met his charge with her hands and fended him off, tossing him away towards the wall. At the same moment, Zoe threw a blast of wyth and Gya which coruscated around the flying figure, adding to the impetus of Cecile's throw. The added force was enough to carry the body over the painted edge of the circle on the floor.

There was a vast concussion, a blinding flare of light. The dying wail of the spectral master meta was lost in the shimmering sound of a huge bell being struck. While you were inside it. Deafened, blinded, blasted by the concussion, both Zoe and Cecile were flung backwards. It was only the bindings that saved Fee from following them onto the floor. As it was, the blast threw her cruelly onto the ropes and wrist cuffs. She knew she screamed, but she couldn't hear herself.

Chapter Thirty-nine

Silence descended like snowflakes over the room. Cecile was nowhere to be seen. Zoe was a puddle of dark cloth over by the far wall. Amagus was gone completely, not even a mote of dust remained. The remaining two metae were sprawled on the floor, either dead or insensible. Fee didn't really care which, provided that stayed that way.

'Zoe? Zoe, can you hear me?' She could only hear the voice in her head. The blast had deafened her, and she had been further away from it that the others. Zoe lay still on the floor. The first wave of panic started in Fee's stomach.

Seconds passed. Fee threw her weight against the wrist cuffs, but the leather held firm against her struggles, At least she wasn't bleeding now: the wounds inflicted on her arms by Simon had vanished. Only an echo of the pain remained to remind her of them. She swore under her breath. Amagus had gone (probably, she wasn't taking anything on trust now) and Vassily, or Ogan, whoever he had been, had been burned to a crisp by Zoe's sprites. She must remember to ask her overly clever sister how she had done that. Provided they got out of here. Preferably in one piece.

The curtains twitched, freezing her in the midst of her attempts to release herself from the ropes and cuffs that still confined her. But she was regaining strength with every heartbeat. Cecile could rend those cuffs easily. Maybe she had gained enough from her to do the same.

From behind the curtain emerged Simon. Meten that he was, the gaping wound in his throat was closing already. He surveyed the wreckage with a cool eye.

'Well done. Very well done, in fact.' She could just hear him through the buzzing in her ears. 'But I would expect nothing less. I thought you were going to succumb without a fight and that would have surprised me. I expected better of you. I am gratified to see that my estimation of you was correct. You are indeed formidable opponents. You have rid me of a serious inconvenience, and I thank you. Vassily had his uses, but he was going to die anyway. There would have been no place for him in my new world order. It is an insignificant setback. I am still here. You are still here. And here also is your sister. I can summon my Master again, and offer him your blood and your sister's blood both.'

He waded through the wreck of the room and lifted Zoe from the floor and placed her on the table. He straightened the cloth and replaced the candles. Her face looked pale in the soft light.

'How angelic she appears. You will be gratified to learn that her efforts have not caused her death. She will be a valuable addition to my wythen hoard. If she survives the attentions of my Master, who will no doubt prefer her over you. Especially as she is now... more accessible to him. But do not be afraid. You will not be passed over. Once his full strength is restored, I am sure he will discover a means to feast on your succulent neck.'

Clarity suddenly flooded through Fee's brain. The nexus that Rina had spoken of was so close now. Inside she mourned that she might lose Zoe to it as well as Sophie. But this bastard was going down. She felt a weight of presence at her back. She knew that sense of someone. There were three sisters in the room now. Sophie was there. She could not see her smile, her face, but she knew that she was there. She could feel others, too, known and unknown. Their substance was flowing into hers, augmenting it. This was not the thievery that Simon had practiced, but an act of generosity. The wraiths were giving of their vital essence to her, sharing, and she almost wept with the joy of it. Something of Simon's power had been shattered by Zoe's commando tactics. Maybe it hadn't been a rescue attempt, but something far more subtle. She could almost feel ghostly hands on her shoulders, hear whispered words of strength and encouragement.

Simon was arranging Zoe on the table, making passes over her body with his hands and muttering intently. He had got the brazier going again, and blue smoke was wreathing them. But the room felt dead. Deader than it had been when it was full of metae. Fee hoped that the wyth had not earthed itself through Zoe. The kid was too inexperienced to take that kind of force without harm. She packed a wallop, that much was evident. But could she take one?

She stared into Zoe's face. Simon had turned her head so she was facing Fee. The eyes opened. No fluttering eyelashes, just those pale, ice-blue eyes. And right behind them was Zoe, going from full stop to Mach four in the blink of an eye. As babies do. One moment they are fast asleep, then they are wide awake, without that in-between hesitation that most adults experience.

Fee mouthed 'Knife!' to her. Simon, hovering over the supine body, was brandishing that wickedly sharp curved blade, before he plunged it into the living flesh lying on the table. Without so much as a twitch, Zoe reared up, one hand going for the knife and the other clawing at his eyes. Zoe was taking no prisoners today. She knelt, she stood on the table, her grip on the knife unwavering. Let go, or I will pull you up bodily. I can. I will. Both hands, one bloody-nailed from raking his face, gripped the knife below the hilt, trying to wrest it from him. He swung his arms round wildly. The strength of a young man usually outmatches that of a younger girl, and the knife plunged towards Zoe's thigh. Simon threw his weight behind the blade, and it sank deeply into her leg. She screamed and loosened her hold enough for him to rip the blade upwards, slicing through the muscle. Blood poured out of the ragged gash as Zoe fell, the leg giving way under her. She launched herself sideways off the table, a one-legged heave, and fell to the floor. She crabbed away as fast as her injured limb would allow, leaving a streak of bright arterial blood over the floor behind her.

He turned, following her, brandishing the bloody knife in his fist. She rolled over onto her back to watch him come, and he was fast. He was on her in less than a second. Panting more from anger than exertion, he towered over her.

'You will die now. Your blood will be the vehicle that summons my Master, again. He will feast on your flesh while you still live. I would have been merciful, and let him feed on your unconscious body. You would have felt no pain. But now you will suffer the agonies of his feeding. I will enjoy it.'

Oh, how he needed an audience. No wonder he was so good at illusions. A good man will strike you down in a second, but bad men always feel the need to gloat. Terry Pratchett was dead right there. Simon wanted to draw out the apprehension, the fear. He fed on it. Zoe was doing a good imitation of weeing her pants at his feet...

Someone rose up like an avenging angel behind the 'Vampire Witch Simon Lake'. It was Cecile, looking like the wrath of God. She raised both arms high and smacked him across the back of his head with both fists, and he slumped. One handed, she threw him across the chamber and stalked over to Zoe, her long white dress swishing against her ankles.

'You are injured.' It was not a question. Cecile could smell blood three streets away, and tell whose it was. But in this bloodfest it was no mean feat. Zoe was holding tightly to her ripped leg with both hands, blood pooling under her. She was trying to stem the flood with a wadded handkerchief. 'Let me. Otherwise you will bleed to death here on this floor. You will heal cleanly, no scar.' She lowered her head to Zoe's thigh and licked over the gash from top to bottom. 'It will not infect you. Come, quickly, before he recovers.' She pulled Zoe to her feet and she ran across the chamber to Fee and started to untie the cords

'Use his knife, Zoe.'

She snatched it up, and the keen edge parted the cords with one swipe, cutting Fee's wrist into the bargain. Zoe was shaking.

'Sorry.'

'Don't mention it. I've had worse.' Fee hugged her sister. 'Let's amscray out of here.'

They started to move, but it was too late. Simon was hurtling across the floor, roaring his rage at being thwarted again, a blur of speed too swift for the eye to follow. Cecile pushed the sisters out of the way, and her figure blurred as she raced to intercept him. They met with a mighty crash, and Simon was flung back. Cecile was older, stronger. She had centuries in which to perfect her meten talents: Simon had a few decades.

'Run! Now! I will keep him here. You must find Theo, he is close by. He will find you safe to home,' Cecile shouted. When they didn't move, she turned to them and snarled like a wildcat. This was not the Cecile they knew, who baked cakes and showed young boys where bats roosted. She was a monster, her face contorted in rage, fangs on display, all veneer of civilization obliterated. 'I tell you, RUN!' she screamed. Bits of plaster fell from the ceiling. They started like scared rabbits towards the doors, scrabbling at them.

'He's locked us in.' Ffion drew a deep breath. There would be no escape. Simon had the key in his pocket. They had both seen him place the key in his waistcoat fob. He was a magician. That meant the key could be anywhere. He had trapped them. But some prey had teeth. She drew herself up. She opened her mind, ignoring the sounds of bodies hitting the walls, the floor, and possibly even the ceiling from the other side of the room. This was it. Make or break. Are you a farer, or are you not? Does your wyth speak to the Gya, does it flow in you? Will you stand here, and let this happen? Up until now, she had been almost passive. Zoe had made all the running, and this was meant to be Fee's party. In her mind's eye, she saw the spaca which had been so carefully traced all those hours ago. Saw the candles burning, felt their heat. Smelt the incense smoke rising from the censer. Saw the light in her lover's hands. Felt the warm rush of wyth, heated by the Gya. She embraced it, focussed it. There, floating in the spaca, in her mind's eye, was a sword, black and silver. A bastard sword with upswept hilts like a new moon.

'It will not come unless you need it. You will not grasp it unless you deserve it. And you cannot keep it. Do you have the power to wield it? You will not know until you try, and then it will be too late.' Rina's voice echoed inside her head. Ffion was StaffWode, but that was not enough. Was she Wode enough for the sword? She was faintly aware of Zoe shaking her arm, yelling 'Fee! Do something!'

Cecile swung her head round. Seeing that they were trapped, she heaved Simon into the far wall and started to run for the door. She intended to crash into it, break it down, allow them to escape. Zoe dived for cover. Mesmerised, Fee reached out a hand. She was in another place, beyond thought, beyond fear, beyond any action but that of a slowly reaching hand. Cecile passed her in a blur of blue white speed, crashed into the doors and out the other side. She turned back to grasp Zoe's arm faster than a striking snake, and threw her bodily out of the shattered portal. She turned to face Fee, reaching. But Simon was close behind her. He screamed, mouth wide, fangs gaping in the blackness of his mouth, impossibly wide.

'Die, bitch!' he screamed as he rammed a broken spar into her back. Mad or not, injured or not, young or not, he found his target. Her heart. Two things can kill a mete. Silver can slow them down, running water is a bit of a problem, but there are only two ways to kill them. Sever their heads from their necks, or pierce their hearts with a wooden stake. Cecile's body trembled, the bloody end of the jagged wood protruding from her torso. Blood trickled from her widely open mouth, stained her gaping fangs and ran down over her chin onto her dress. Her eyes were round with shock, her features rigid. Lifted up onto her toes, she pirouetted, snarling, trying to reach Simon. The spar was too long. She couldn't reach him. She froze. Ffion had a last vision of her face, a mask of sheer fury, before she disintegrated into a blast of grey ash, covering Simon, Ffion and Zoe in a coat of fine crumbling dust. Zoe screamed 'Cecile!' in horror. Simon yanked back the spar like a samurai completing a kata. He was grinning, a feral face alight with a fierce joy. He straightened up, slowly, savouring his victory, relishing the bloodbath to come. Zoe was scrabbling on the floor - trying to get further away from this mad creature? Ffion's hand was still reaching. She was still in the place of peace, her mind clear, her eyes serene as she gazed at Cecile's assassin. Her fingers closed round leather and steel. Her arm felt a weight that had not been there before. She brought her arm round, and between them, gleaming, was the sword. It formed out of the very air, flowing, creating itself out of legend. They met eyes around it. Slowly, the tip began to lower, pointing at Simon. In the calm place, out of the peace, Fee found a voice.

'Why, Simon?'

'You have what should have been mine. I decided to take it back.'

Still in the grip of that unnatural calm, Fee spoke.

'What have I that should be yours?'

'The frais, you little fool. The wythen. Catrina made me a meta, and I lost all my wythen. Oh, yes, Theo gave me eternal life and youth. He gave me strength, speed, and hunger. Blood hunger. But now I hunger for a different fruit. Catrina took away more than Theo ever gave me. And I want it back.'

'You cannot be both fratten and metae. You can be either, or neither, but not both.' The words came from Ffion's mouth, but not from her mind. Someone else was talking through her.

'Why not? I am Simon Lake, the vampire witch. I can be anything I choose to be.' He reared up, throwing out his chest and arms in a wide, threatening gesture, the broken spar still dripping with Cecile's lifeblood. 'I *can* be both, I WILL be both!'

'You cannot. The wyth of a farer is welded to her life. You are not alive. The wyth cannot flow in you. Your body is dead, nourished by the cys that created the blyds. Amagus chose death over life, and created the metargic nature. He traded his wythen for Eternity, exalted his life over his death, and so died. But he could not rest. He became the first meta.'

'I can remedy that. I have found the cys, the weaves that Amagus created. You are of my blood. I can steal your ayat, weld it to mine. And steal your wythen. I have the wyth. I have created an army of slaves who nourish me. You will be the last, the final sacrifice, the one hundred and sixty ninth victim of my campaign. Thirteen frais.' He paused, for effect. Even now, forever the showman. 'With you, the last, the direct descendant, to seal the pact and give me, finally, what I deserve.'

'Your count is off. Luke is still alive.'

'His body lives. But his wraith is mine. Even though you broke my hold, he is still my sacrifice. And when you die, your weave will vanish and he will be mine again. You have played your hand and failed. Your own sister has shed your blood in this place, and the pact is complete.'

Wythen was building in the room. Wind it was, circling round the chamber, raising Fee's hair, hissing past her skin, faster and faster, until it was like standing in a hurricane. Grating in their teeth, humming in their ears, pouring round them like treacle. Simon put his head to one side, like a bird.

'Give it up and I will make it easy on you. I will even spare your sister, your one remaining sister. Yes, she will be Mysten in my new frais of metae. I will create a new race. She will be Queen over all of them. Oppose me now, and I will make your dying hard, and her life a torment.'

'Easy for you to say. I have the sword.' Ffion had got her own voice back.

'What does that matter to me? A sword cannot kill me.' If he had been mad before, he was completely insane now.

'You think you have won, don't you? Think you know it all. Well, here's a gem for you to chew on. Your count is still wrong. SOPHIE WAS PREGNANT. That means the spilling of Zoe's blood invalidates your sacrifices. Even more so, since it was blood willingly given for the release of the wraiths you hold. If you spill more of my blood, the blood of your own daughter, then the fate of Amagus will be *your* fate. Face it, Simon, your dream of eternal life is **toast**.'

'No sword can end my life.' He was too far gone to be reached. There was no coming back for him, ever. Especially now he had killed Cecile. Theo, wherever he was, would hunt him down now.

'This one can.' Fee was absolutely sure of that. Sure in a way that came from beyond knowing. This was THE sword. From a dream of this came the flaming sword at the gates of Eden. Michael's sword that defeated the dragons. Arthur's sword Caliburn that united Britain. The Sword From The Stone. It had existed from a time before metae. They were ephemeral, this sword was real. Really, really, real. And neither did it exist. How's that for a conundrum? It was not a sword, but the *idea* of a sword. It was the *meaning* of a sword. It was the wyth of a sword, the ayat of a sword, the swordness of all swords that had ever been forged and used in anger, or war, or combat. It was the ancestor of every weapon ever devised by Man. It was a killing thing, and it would kill this mad thing. 'Suck it and see.' (I knows the likes of you, you bugger. I'll skelp your arse, see if I don't.)

Then, again, a figure rose up behind Simon like the wrath of angels. A tsunami of force with ivory fangs, roaring. Fingers crept round Simon's face. A look of sheer horror washed over his features. The hands tightened, and Theo ripped off the head of the vampire witch Simon Lake.

The body collapsed into a heap. Theo stood, holding his gory trophy, staining his white ruffled shirt.

'Suck it and see? *Suck it and see?'*

Ffion lowered the sword. She started to giggle. It was probably hysteria. Zoe appeared from nowhere, hugging her, as she subsided to the floor, next to the headless corpse unheeding the blood that flowed from the ruined neck round her legs. The giggles became laughs, great belly laughs, and then sobs. Zoe held her while she cried, sitting in a pool of blood at the feet of a centuries old meta holding a severed head. Suck that and see.

Theo dropped Simon's head on the floor, and kicked it away from his body. Slowly, he walked over to the place where Simon had stabbed Cecile. The tornado of wythen had scattered her ashes too widely. Theo could not collect them and revive her now. He knelt by the rags of her bloody dress, lifting one corner. From one eye, a line of blood began to inch down his cheek.

'Cecile....'

He was crying, really crying. Zoe eyed the headless corpse with distaste.

'Why hasn't he disintegrated too?'

'Not old enough, I guess. Look, his hand's all mottled with age spots.' Fee glanced at the severed head, lying in a corner. 'And he's gone grey, too.'

'That would surely piss him off. So full of himself, the late, great Simon Lake.'

'If he is late. Metae can come back, you know.'

'Not after I've finished with him, he won't.' Zoe heaved herself up, her movements older than her years. This night had added to her age in ways she would find it hard to recover from, even with the resilience of youth. She came back with a guttering candle, a mass of red fabric and a bottle of Glenmorangie from the stone table. Carefully, she wiped the blood back towards the corpse, dropped the redder fabric on the body and poured the whisky over the lot. 'I need more than this. What a waste of good drinking likker, as Tom would say.' Gin, rum and vodka joined the cocktail, the bottles rolling around the floor. She added several candles and then poured a jug of scented oil over the heap. A sweet, cloying aroma wafted up, redolent of mint, rotting flowers and other things Fee didn't want to consider.

'There you go. Vampire Sling. Like Singapore Sling, only different.'

'We must get Theo out before you light that. There's no sense in him at the moment. He might just decide to join Cecile.'

'I've got it covered. Don't worry.' Zoe kicked the candle over, and the flame fell into a puddle of mixed alcohol. 'Let's go.'

'Delighted.'

They each took one of Theo's arms. Dumbly, he stood between them. There was a slight whoomph, and flames started to lick up over the pyre of the late, great Vampire Witch Simon Lake.

'Come *on*, Theo. I've got Cecile. We have to go, *now*!' Theo turned to Zoe. In her hand she held a wrap of cloth. 'I collected her in my hankie before she blew away. Come *on*!'

They hustled the stunned Theo out of the doors. When Zoe started a fire, she didn't muck about. It was already climbing the walls. Theo was rapidly returning to his unnatural self. Without so much as a by-your-leave, he collected a girl under each arm and took the stairs three at a time. When you are meta, you don't get out of breath. You don't even breathe. He just accelerated until they left the warehouse. Then he really let rip. The walls of the industrial estate flew past, gateways, car parks all blurred into a chiaroscuro of light and shade...... a fire siren started to wail in the distance. Theo slowed to a stop. The three looked back, then at each other.

'We look like an accident in an abattoir. If the cops see us like this, we will never hear the end of it.'

Zoe ignored her. She was looking back to where flames were already lighting up the sky.

'I did wonder for a minute when I heard the siren if Simon had sprinklers fitted in that fun palace of his. I thought, Damn, now we're going to have to do the whole lot all over again. Looks like he forgot. There's never a fire inspector handy when you need one.'

'Josie!' Fee's bloody hands reached up to her mouth. 'We left Josie in there!'

She started back, pulled up short by Theo's grip on her arm.

'I have taken care of Josie. The rescue services will find her. It is better this way, that she remember nothing.'

'Claire?'

'Lily has dealt with Claire.' Theo grimaced. 'When I left her, she was still trying to scream. She is quite mad. I fear it will be permanent. Lily had one of your kind call the police about a possible break-in. They will find the car, and Claire. The unfortunate man who fed you and gave you water, they will not find.' Fee looked at him. 'Vassily's will and Morgana's hand ended my life. Her blood revived me. But then I needed to feed. We are mad when we return, and I fed. He will not come back.' Best to let the matter drop, his tone said.

In the distance, they could make out the rhythmic flash of a blue light. The emergency services were on their way.

'Time to make ourselves scarce.'

'Time to make ourselves *absent*. Where's the car?'

Theo gestured elegantly.

'You have got to be kidding. You have a stretch limo?'

'Hey, Theo, cool wheels. How fast can this thing go?'

'Fast enough.'

'And it has.... tinted windows?'

'How else am I going to travel from place to place?'

There was a polite, crisp cheep, and the indicator lights flashed. Theo held the pale grey back door open. Zoe scrambled in.

'Well cool.' She settled into the soft seat, smearing blood all over the pale cream leather. 'Oops.'

'I don't think it's the first time this seat's seen blood, Zoe.' Ffion followed her inside as her sister retrieved two bottles of water from a floor cooler.

'All mod cons.' Theo smiled as he slid into the front seat. 'I believe it would be the meten equivalent of a 'pussy wagon'.'

'Wash your mouth out, Theo, and whip up the horses before the cops come looking for witnesses. And I don't think they will believe us if we said we saw bugger all tonight.'

The car moved off in a stately manner, painted by red flames and blue light. Mission accomplished. Zoe, however, looked worried.

'I hope she doesn't blame me.'
'Who?'
'Cecile.'
'Why?'
'My hankie wasn't exactly clean.'

Aftermath

Theo dropped them off at home, promising to send someone to retrieve the Elise and Zoe's laptop. Okay, the laptop would be no great loss. Five hundred quid was nothing to a merchant prince with some thousands in the bank and part ownership of a soon-to-be national corporation. Global, even. But the owner of the Elise would be a mite pissed off to lose the car. He would be more pissed off not to see Cecile again. From Theo's tone, it appeared the guy was human. And sweet on Cecile. Very sweet.

'Do not seek for me here. I must take Cecile away. She will be too interested in you both now. Until she recovers, she must be apart from you. Her first act on her rebirth will be to seek you out, to feed on you. I must prevent this. You are both mine, you understand.'

He had told them, during the journey home, of the rage and hunger that accompanied a meten's regeneration. 'We must feed. On the first thing, the nearest thing. To its extinction. Having escaped the claws of death, we must return a victim, in exchange for our own life, perhaps.' he was not inclined to philosophise further, though it was clear he had mused on it. 'I regret that the young man had to die. He was gentle to you. But there it goes.' It had been his first kill in several decades. Then, he explained, the newly risen would actively seek out those they had tasted in life. Those they had connection to.

'She will be mad. Insensenate. Until she is herself again, many miles must separate you. Then and only then, can we return. We have been happy here. I hope to return. But things change, as things are wont to do. I will stay in touch.'

He closed the car door and drew away quietly. Early dawn was silvering the eastern skies as Zoe unlocked the door.

'Stand down, Greg, it's us.'

They made straight for the Roundhouse. Greg was standing in the pale light. The last few candles were still defying the shadows and the spaca felt sleepy. Greg looked tired from his night watch, the long dark robe he wore was crumpled over his bare feet. Unshaven, eyes sunken from sleeplessness and worry, he was still a glorious sight. He said nothing, but spread his arms and embraced them both. Snag wound round their feet, complaining that it was surely breakfast time by now, and why was no-one paying attention to his needs? Biehail sat forlornly on the ayet. After all, he was a servant of their enemy. Despite their feeding of him, and consideration of his needs, he was still part of the enemy, and fully expected to be tossed back into whatever hell dimension he had been summoned from. He had come to quite like this crazy place, with its puzzling maps and ugly, frightful beings. But they were ignoring him. Rightly so. Ears hanging, he mewled piteously.

Zoe snaked an arm out of the human comfort ball.

'Biehail.' It was the first time she had called him by name. He raised a besotted gaze to her. She was a creature of rare power. She controlled galvanic liquid. She could weave the fabric of time and space. She would be a fine master to serve. 'Thank you.'

He leapt to her arm in a transport of joy and clung to it. He had never been thanked before. Ordered around, cursed, kicked, ignored, but never, ever, thanked. He would do anything for her now, whether she asked him to or not. He would never leave her. She would have to destroy him to get rid of him. He chittered at her, nuzzled her face. Mewled in anxiety at the scrapes and bruises, and stroked them with gentle fingers, growling low in anger that she had been hurt.

'Please, please, don't ever pull a stunt like that again.'

'Not if I can help it.'

Whoever said the words, they all meant them.

They spent a lazy day, bathing away the grime and bad memories, sleeping, and raiding the stores for titbits. They talked, putting it all together. In the afternoon, the phone rang.

'Hello, Uncle Tom.'

'It's Luke! He's awake.'

'How is he?'

'A bit confused. Very confused, actually. He can't remember a thing. We haven't told him about Sophie yet.'

'Don't, Tom. Let him recover first. Then he can mourn her when we all do, when we lay her to rest.'

'That bash on the head damaged something inside. He can't speak properly, not yet. But the neuros are quietly confident that he'll make a good recovery. Matt's with him now. Crying on him. Some of the nurses are looking a bit sour about that: I'll get them chucked off his case.'

'We can weave for him now. One way or another, I'm not losing anyone else.'

Tom chuckled, a rich, happy sound. 'Too late, m'gel. Ellen's already been there. Still, a little extra wouldn't go amiss. By the way, tell that Zoe to drop in on me. I've summat for her.'

Remembering how effective Zoe's tricks had been up until now, Fee wondered what else her sister could get up to once she was a properly 'thated farer. Ohmigod.....

'So what exactly was that you dumped on the vamps last night?'

They were sitting at the kitchen table, around the wreck of a late meal, sipping wine. Mellow, ready to talk, to share. Biehail was hunting crumbs. Zoe regarded him with exasperation tinged with fondness. Despite all attempts to separate them, the little gwhylli had stuck to her side with dogged tenacity. He had even found a way through closed doors to observe the ritual of the bath, and finally falling asleep on her bed. Waking to find him there, unexpected, Zoe had shrieked, which had brought Fee and Greg at a run from whatever they had been doing. Whatever it had been, it didn't involve many clothes. No clothes at all, in fact. In panic, Biehail had climbed the curtain, screaming. Everyone had screamed. At everyone else. Finally, peace had been restored, but Biehail, shut out, had whimpered so piteously that Zoe had relented and let him back in.

'I remembered two things. One was what Theo said, that night we played Dungeons and Dragons.......'

'Something about metae being Chaotic?'

'That's the bunny. He said that he realized that metae were creatures of Chaos, not good, not bad, just......'

'Unclassifiable.'

'Thereabouts. He also said that although they were Chaotic,

they hated chaos. They craved order, not mayhem. Then, there was the Seahorse….'

That had been a day to remember. Fee was surprised that Zoe even recalled the incident. One summer, Rob had treated the family to a surf safari. Lily had loved surfing, and had been pretty good at it. But not good enough, that day. They had found a beach, not one of the emmet ones, and hauled their kit down to it. Cozzies, towels, windbreak, a tiny tent to shade little Zoe from the sun: a picnic, two surfboards and all of themselves, a gargantuan task. Impressive rolling breakers crashed onto the beach, the sun shone, and a brisk breeze blew the spray off the whitetops. They pitched themselves near to the base of the cliff on the dry sand. Sophie had perched on a rock and immersed herself in her watercolours, Zoe had babbled, collected shells and waterworn pebbles and dug holes with a tiny pink spade. Rob pretended to read a book. Fee sunbathed, surreptitiously removing most of her swimsuit. She needn't have bothered being coy: there were several other locals stripped down to the buff. One man they watched had come down the cliff in a business suit, ducked behind the rocks and emerged, naked, to run into the surf.

Anyway, Lily had taken her surfboard out into the breakers and was having a wet and wild time. The beach was known for a certain wave - called The Seahorse by the surfers - which periodically lifted itself from the far-off ocean floor and ran a mighty crashing course to the beach. Normally, Lily would never have tried to catch so massive a wave, but on this occasion, it picked her up, and she rode it. Nearly. She lost her balance as the wave crashed down, rolling her under into a vast green tumult. Her initial panic had slammed into all of them. Rob had thrown away his book and ran to the boiling surf, standing thigh-deep, trying to make out where Lily was. Fee was left to deal with a screaming, crying sister while Sophie, her eyes locked on the sea in disbelief, ignored everyone. Finally, she had espied the surfboard bobbing up and down, screamed 'There! There!' and pointed. Rob dived into the surf, escorted by now by others, and swam out. He dived beneath the surface twice before he came up with a barely conscious Lily. Helped back to the beach by willing hands, he stretched Lily on the sand and forced the seawater out of her, then used mouth-to-mouth resuscitation before Lily coughed up more salt water. Anxious faces broke out in smiles as he carried Lily back to her crying daughter.

'I'm all right, I'm all right. Stop crying now.'

But the damage had been done. Someone had called the coastguard. You gotta bless those mobile phones, and before they knew it, an ambulance was on the cliff top and paramedics were descending grimly. A lifeboat hove into view, bouncing on the water.

'All this fuss.'

Lily, swathed in towels, was checked over while she was given oxygen. A police car appeared next to the ambulance. It was all very exciting. Despite her protestations, Lily was carted off to the ambulance. The lions of the Serengeti, sorry, paramedics of Cornwall, would not return to their lair empty-handed once having caught sight of their prey. Eager hands help lift Lily, her family and all their worldly goods back up the cliff. Everyone wanted to be part of the gallant rescue. They might get their pictures in the paper! Their five minutes of fame. Even the saturnine businessman retrieved his pants and helped Zoe over the rocks.

The one thing everyone remembered was Lily's projected feeling of being turned, helpless, in the boiling water. Confused, disorientated......

'I dumped that on them, only *worse*.'

No wonder they had been distracted.

'Then Cecile grabbed me. I didn't intend to go through the window, honestly. It was all I could do to hold her back until Amagus......' Least said about that, the better.

'Well, it's over now.'

'You think? Vassago had other ideas.'

'Sufficient unto the day, sister mine. When the next big thing comes, we'll deal with it. Until then, we'll do the best we can to be happy.'

Extracts from Google news (Complied by Zoe Harris)

Woman Found Unconscious In Deserted Warehouse

Police were alerted last night over a possible break-in at a local trading estate. A local resident alerted police that an abandoned car had been left near a disused warehouse on the S*******ner Trading Estate.

Upon investigation they found the unconscious body of a woman whom they suspect may have been the victim of an horrific attack.

The woman, who is yet to be named, is now being cared for at St Anne's Hospital, Cullompton. Doctors say she is being kept under sedation.

'This was a premeditated and vicious attack. The woman had been held captive and tortured for several hours,' a police spokesperson told this reporter. 'In all my years in the force, I have never seen anything so chilling as this. We are determined to catch and charge whoever is responsible as quickly as possible. To our mind, whoever they are, they are a danger to the public.'

Women in the area have been warned not to go out alone after dark.

Police have appealed for witnesses.

Tragedy Strikes Famous Illusionist.

The emergency services were called to a warehouse near Newton Abbot in the early hours of the morning.

The warehouse, belonging to Touchstone Productions PLC, is owned by the famous illusionist, Mr Simon Lake.

The building was well alight by the time the fire service reached the scene.

One casualty was taken to Exeter General Hospital. No details have been released.

It is feared that Mr Lake may have been in the building when it caught fire.

Sources close to Mr Lake report that, following his sell-out Dark Desires tour, Mr Lake had returned to the warehouse to work on a new show with some of his assistants.

Police report that no further casualties have been found.

Death Of A Legend.

Police released the news today that in all probability, Mr Simon Lake, the famous illusionist, has died in the fire which consumed his warehouse last night.

Mr Lake, billed as 'The Vampire Witch' was well-known in magic circles as an accomplished illusionist and magician. A spokesperson for the Magic Circle described the loss as 'A tragedy. Mr Lake was unique. It is a great loss to the magical community.'

It is feared that a number of his co-workers may have been with him at the time.

A police spokesman said that they were treating the tragedy as misadventure.

'We think we was practising an illusion using naked flames, and it got out of hand. We are not looking for anyone else in connection with this incident.'

The survivor of the fire, a Miss Josaphine Thoms, is being cared for by her family.

Simon Lake Tragedy- Further Details Emerge.

In a public statement by family today, we were told that the survivor of the fire which destroyed Mr Lake's warehouse was in fact the daughter of Mrs Claire Thoms, the woman found unconscious in a Cullompton warehouse after being set upon by unknown assailants.

It is believed that, after leaving her daughter in the care of Simon Lake, the famous illusionist, (an old friend and distant relative) Mrs Thoms had gone to Cullompton to view some properties there, with a view to moving house with her daughter in the near future.

'She had spoken several times about moving away. She felt that the rural location was too limiting on Josaphine,' family said today.

The reason for her being at the Cullompton warehouse is a mystery. 'We suppose that she misunderstood the directions to Touchstone PLC, and went there to collect Josie,' a relative informed us. 'She was always useless with directions, couldn't tell her right from her left, actually.'

Through her father, Josie told us: 'It was meant to be a treat. We'd been all over, looking at houses, and it was really boring. So Mum arranged that I could visit with Simon Lake that afternoon, and she would pick me up before she went home.' Josie told police that she can remember nothing before the fire. 'Simon took me to his museum, showed me all the tricks he'd made. I was very tired. There was a camp bed at the warehouse, and I went to sleep.' She was found in the parking lot, and cannot remember escaping the fire.

Her father, Alec Thoms, requested that the press leave Josie alone to recover from her ordeal.

Simon Lake Leaves Fortune To Unknown Relative

Simon Lake, the late illusionist, left an estate worth over five million pounds, we heard today.

In his will, Mr Lake left the entire fortune to a Mrs Lily Harris, a resident of H********w in Norfolk.

Mrs Harris, who is mostly confined to a wheelchair following an accident several years ago which killed her husband, is currently mourning the death of her daughter Sophie Harris, a painter of some note, from Falmouth in Cornwall.

A family friend told us, 'Lily is devastated by the news.' She went on to request the Press to respect the family's privacy as they mourn this double tragedy. It is understood that her two remaining daughters are comforting their mother in her hour of grief. Our hearts and prayers go out to this tragic family at this sad time.

Glossary

Vampire language

Akelyte - a vampire's human servant
Blyd - a vampire clan
Hegarsa / Hegaren - clan leader, master, mistress
Meta/Mete /Meten/ Metae - male / female vampire. Vampires
Metarger -a vampire who makes / has made others
Mete / Metis - a newly arisen vampire , male / female
Pash - a feeder, referred to as snacks or lunchbox: a vampire's pet human
The Metargh - change that makes a human a vampire
The Ophosis - The Blood Rite, a ritualistic sharing of blood between vampires

Witch language

Aya - presence, power of a god
Ayen - spirits, usually non-human
Ayat - immortal soul
Asha - the spirit realms
Ayet - place where a spirit lives: altar
Cast, casting, throw a cast - a spell, to cast a spell
Chymer - an illusion
Courting -learning the knowledge before becoming wyted
Cys - magical ability, knowledge of spells
Cyscan - magician, magic
Dom - female elder, most respected
Dath - will, intention
Eldren - older Fratten, advisors
Fath - familiar spirits
Frais - coven
Frata / Farer / Fratten - male / female witch, witches
Glym / glim - enchantment

Gya - power, lines of power like ley lines.
Lanta / Lente /Lenten - men / women preparing for the wyte
Loksey - scrying, overlooking
Magistra - great leader, one who controls several frais
Midess - physical world
Mysta - male leader of a frais: the dominant male in the group
Mysten - female leader of a frais: the dominant female
Rathing - astral travel
Reach - use telepathy
Sigum, siga - magical glyphs
Skyen - morals, ethics, obligation to the wyth and the Gya
Spaca - holy space, magic circle
'thated, 'arthated - having possession of the Blade and the Wythstaff / stick
The Fratris - the Families, the magical community
Weird - the future, look into the future of a person
Wichen - non- Family witch, one not brought up in the wyth
Wish - early attempts at casting, very minor casts
Wraith - ghost, spirit, the vehicle of rathing
Wyte, wyted, wyten - the ritual that opens a fratten's wyth to the Gya: to have had the ritual, to be able to use the Gya: use of the Gya.
Wyth - power used in spells, natural ability of the fratten
Wythen - magic
Wythstaff, wythstick - magic wand

Other terms:

Emmet - Cornish term for tourist: meaning, ant
Assoun - magical rattle used in Voodoo
Veve - magical glyph used in Voodoo
Hounfort - Voodoo temple
Mamaloa, Papaloa - Voodoo priestess and priest
Mojo, ouanga - voodoo magic
Loas - voodoo spirits: Ayen, gods